TRIUMPH IN THE TORN KINGDOMS

JUMPSTART DUCHY
BOOK 6

STEFON MEARS

Also by Stefon Mears

The Rise of Magic Series
Magician's Choice
Sleight of Mind
Lunar Alchemy
Three Fae Monte
The Sphinx Principle
Double Backed Magic
Mercury Fold (coming soon)

Cavan Oltblood Series
Half a Wizard
The Ice Dagger
Spells of Undeath

Power City Tales
Not Quite Bulletproof
No Money in Heroism

Standalones
Between the Cracks
Sects and the City
Prince of a Thousand Worlds
Devil's Night
Portal-Land, Oregon
Stealing from Pirates
Fade to Gold
With a Broken Sword
Twice Against the Dragon
The House on Cedar Street
Sudden Death
On the Edge of Faerie

Short Story Collections
Spell Slingers
Twisted Timelines
Longhairs and Short Tales: A Collection of Cat Stories
Confronting Legends (Spells & Swords Vol. 1)
The Patreon Collection, Vol. 1-8 (Vol. 9, coming soon)

Nonfiction
The 30-Day Novel and Beyond!

Spells for Hire Series
Devil's Shoestring
Zombie Powder
Spirit Trap
Dragon's Blood

The Telepath Trilogy
Surviving Telepathy
Immoral Telepathy
Targeting Telepathy

Edge of Humanity Series
Caught Between Monsters
Hunting Monsters

Jumpstart Duchy Series
Into the Torn Kingdoms
The Dragon's Gold
The Gift Castle
The Deadly Feast
The King's Test
Triumph in the Torn Kingdoms

Published by Thousand Faces Publishing, Portland, Oregon

http://1kfaces.com

Hardback ISBN: 978-1-948490-48-1

Paperback ISBN: 978-1-948490-41-2

TRIUMPH IN THE TORN KINGDOMS

FOREWORD

The man known as Aefric Brightstaff was not born on Qorunn. He was born on the distant world of Earth, where he went by the name Keifer McShane.

On Earth, he knew the world of Qorunn only through *The Torn Kingdoms*, the setting of his favorite roleplaying game. His primary source of joy and solace, following the untimely death of his beloved wife, Andi.

When a Jumpstart crowdfunding campaign for the next edition of *The Torn Kingdoms* offered him the chance to become a duke in the world he loved, Keifer pounced on it. Imagined they would send him a patent of nobility. Ask his opinion about the non-player character who'd bear his name and title. Perhaps even allow him to include Andi as his duchess, when the books went to print.

He couldn't wait to become a part of the world he loved so well.

But he mistook it all for make-believe.

Keifer didn't expect the great Mage of Marrisford himself, the one and only Kainemorton, to show up on his doorstep.

Keifer didn't expect to be transported to Qorunn, where he would start life anew as an orphan boy on the streets of the fabled city of Sartis. That shining beacon on the southern sea.

Now known as Aefric, he grew into a powerful adventurer. Widely believed to be a wizard, he is in fact the first of the dweomerblood. It is said that magic itself flows through his very veins.

As Aefric, he mastered the fabled Brightstaff. He fought in the Godswalk Wars, and saved countless lives at the Battle of Deepwater, in the kingdom of Armyr.

In gratitude, King Colm of Armyr named Aefric Duke of Deepwater. And no sooner had Aefric taken possession of his duchy than he prevented an invasion by Armyr's southern neighbor, Malimfar.

Since then, he has worked to unite his vassals. To heal his lands and his peoples — including not only humans, kindaren, eldrani and derekek, but even the borogs — from damage done by the Godswalk Wars. He has dealt with intrigues both foreign and domestic, and the threat of coming war. Battled assassins, slavers, smugglers, and even the influence of the great pirate queen, Nelazzi.

All while being pressured to marry, and sire an heir who will one day inherit his duchy...

Keifer McShane. Aefric Brightstaff.

One man who has lived two lives.

This is the conclusion of his story...

PROLOGUE

Aefric Brightstaff rarely used his ducal temple, in the Castle at Water's End.

For anything public, such as the high days of the various major gods, he celebrated at the castle's main temple, along with his court, any visiting nobles, and most of the prominent citizens.

Water's End, the castle, was so large that its public temple — under part of the massive, stained glass dome covering a portion of the first floor of the main keep — could accommodate more than three hundred without feeling crowded.

For anything private — such as his own regular offerings to Kalinda, goddess of magic — he tended to use the small altar in the corner of his bedroom.

Still, on the first floor of the ducal apartments — what he thought of as his "public floor" — his rooms included a small temple. Round, maybe a dozen strides across. Cedar for the floorboards, because it was sacred to Halstaffur the Green Lord.

Deepwater gray paint over the plaster on the walls and ceiling. Tapestries on those walls featured a dozen important gods.

In the center of the room, a raised, granite dais, with a round altar fashioned from burnished red calinwood.

Just the right size for private rites, services and celebrations.

Aefric entered that temple though ornately carved double doors, whispering the word that would trigger the spells of his predecessors and light the room with a soft, white glow.

In his right hand, he carried his signature weapon. The Brightstaff. A heavily enchanted six-foot length of white thunderwood — only a handful of inches shorter than he was himself — wrapped at just the right gripping spot with a soft piece of light brown leather, and embedded in the top with a yellow diamond about the size of the last part of his thumb.

Slung over his left shoulder, his old leather backpack. The one he'd borne for most of his adventuring career, and which still carried a number of things he hadn't told anyone about. Including a certain sack, deep in the backpack.

He closed the doors for privacy. He needed no priest or priestess for what he had in mind.

He set the Brightstaff to stand on its own, just inside the doors. He set the backpack down at his feet.

He unbuckled his dark brown leather belt, where he carried his pouch, his noble's dagger, and his sheath for the wand, Garram. He hung the belt on a peg intended for cloaks.

He stripped off the pale blue silk tunic that his valets loved, because it brought out his eyes. He draped the tunic over the same peg.

His dark brown shoes came next. They were a remarkably good fit — considering he'd never met the cobbler — and made from soft calfskin. He set them on the floor below the peg.

Finally, his black hose and undergarments, which joined the tunic and belt on the cloak peg.

He mused for a moment over the differences he saw in himself.

When he had still been Keifer McShane and living in Portland, Oregon, on the planet Earth, his body had been softer. Less muscled. And certainly less scarred.

But then, when the great mage Kainemorton brought Keifer here to

Qorunn, he didn't bring across a twenty-five-year-old man. Whether it was through the magics involved in crossing the planes, some other spell of that great wizard's, or even the intervention of one god or another — when Keifer McShane arrived in Qorunn, he was a small child.

A small child named Aefric with no memory of Keifer and Earth. A small child turned loose as an orphan on the streets of that magnificent city, Sartis. The gem on the Southern Sea.

Keifer had never grown up to be an adventurer, the way Aefric did. And so Keifer had never taken a spear wound here, an arrow wound there, a sword slash here, a trap's spike there...

If he was being honest with himself, Keifer had never been as ruggedly handsome as Aefric grew to be either. And Keifer had kept his hair short, while Aefric's sandy blonde locks fell to about his shoulders.

But right now, Aefric needed to feel his connection to Keifer, to Oregon, to Earth.

So he dug into the main pocket of his backpack, and into a certain magic sack down at the bottom.

From within that sack, he pulled clothing that no one from Qorunn would have recognized.

Well. Except for Kainemorton.

Elbar's Blood, Aefric himself wouldn't have recognized the clothing before that day at Kainemorton's tower this past spring, when the memories of his two lives came crashing together.

A pair of machine-made dark blue underwear came first. Purchased at PriceCo, the kind of massive store that Qorunn couldn't even imagine.

They were a little loose on him. As were the denim jeans that followed. Fastened with a button, yes, but also a zipper. A fastening that hadn't been developed on Qorunn yet.

Gray socks, but not the soft tone of Deepwater gray. Darker. Less interesting. Fit well, though, clinging to his calf muscles.

Next came the tee-shirt. Old and a little worn, but a favorite. With the pinwheel logo of the Portland Trail Blazers. A little tight through the chest and shoulders, a little loose through the stomach. No shock in either case.

Finally, the shoes. Not handmade calfskin. Machine made leather and rubber. Tied with cotton laces.

Gods, the sneakers felt weird on his feet now. Their soles so thick and springy. How had he worn these things without bouncing with every step?

This was the only outfit of clothing he still had from Earth. The only set he'd packed into the one chest of personal belongings that Kainemorton had allowed Keifer to bring to Qorunn. And the agreement about these clothes had been that no one else got to see them.

Just as well. Aefric had never felt the need to wear them before anyway. He donned them now only for one very good reason.

Andi knew these clothes.

Andrea McShane. Keifer's wife, and the love of his life. Stolen from him far too soon. Accidentally murdered by a drunk driver, while she walked out of a downtown coffee shop. On the sidewalk. In middle of the afternoon.

Her death had sent Keifer into a spiral. Odd that it took becoming Aefric to pull him out of it.

The part of him that was Keifer still loved her. Always would. But it was finally time to move on. Not just because of the pressure Aefric was getting to marry and produce an heir. But because it was time. And because Andi wouldn't want him to live the rest of his life alone.

Which was why he was dressed in these old clothes now. Why he was alone, here, in one of the few places that he could spend as long as he wanted without getting interrupted by urgent advisers and well-meaning servants.

He had his magic laboratory, of course. But trying to contact Andi there, that would have felt like summoning her. Like necromancy.

He didn't want to do that. To compel her into appearance. To demand answers from her. For all he knew, she was at peace. In the afterlife. Happy. Possibly even reborn somewhere on Earth.

But if she were willing to answer him now, he needed to hear what she'd say.

Finally, he donned the most important item. The small crystal pendant she'd given him, on its gold chain. A gift for their first anniversary.

Finally ready, he knelt before the dais. Hands on his knees. Closed his eyes.

"Andi? Love? I don't know if you can hear me. But if you can, I could use your advice.

"If you're watching... Well, you're probably as amazed as I was to find out that the Torn Kingdoms aren't just a figment of Del Baker's imagination, but a real world full of real magic, real monsters, and real people.

"It's not the magic or the monsters I need your help with. I'm a pretty good hand with the magic, and if you've been watching, you've seen me take down my share of the monsters.

"The people, though. Oh, love. I don't know that I'm any better with people here than I was there.

"I'm a duke now. Well, technically, I'm also a baron and a knight, but the point is, I'm part of the nobility. And, well, that means I'm expected to get married. To have kids. Heirs, to continue after me.

"We never got to have kids. Seems wrong to me, sometimes. The idea that I should have kids with some woman who isn't you."

He snorted. "I can just hear your answer to that one. 'I'm dead, Keif. I'm no longer an option.' How many times did you use those words? 'No longer an option.' Couple of hundred, at least."

He shook his head sadly.

"Wish you were here to share this with me. You'd love this place. Well, you wouldn't love how often I end up in the firing line, but this castle...

"I have *five* castles now. Can you believe it? I always used to say that if we won the lottery, I'd buy a castle." He shook his head. "After that settlement came in, I had the money to do it. But without you ... didn't seem right.

"Here though, I've got *five*. And this one, it's the crown jewel. You'd *adore* it. The clothing, too.

"But that's not what I need to talk to you about. Everyone wants me to get married. And I think ... maybe ... I'm ready. Even had a dream where you said goodbye. Told me to move on."

He shook his head. "But if you can believe this, I've got too many women to choose from."

"There's Princess Maev. Beautiful. Clever. Remember how you always loved to play the forester class? She's a forester. Good one, too. I think she might be my favorite, but she may not be an option. She's down in Varondam, negotiating an alliance for her father. An alliance she likely has to seal with marriage.

"There's Byrhta Ol'Caran. Remember that friend of yours? Candice? The one you always said was too good looking for her own good? Byrhta's kind of like that. Models and movie stars *dream* of looking as good as this woman. She looks like she inspired some of Larry Elmore's works. And because of all that beauty, almost no one spots how smart she is. How sensitive.

"If Maev isn't my favorite, then Byrhta is. All the servants here love her — which says good things about her — but some of my advisers harp on the fact that the Ol'Caran family doesn't bring enough to the table for a man of my station.

"A man of my station. Still weird to think about. I mean, you knew the McShane family. Not exactly blue-bloods. And even here, half a year ago, I was just an itinerant adventurer. I'd be the one advisers would complain wasn't good enough to marry *any* of these women.

"But I'm getting off track.

"Next, I guess, is Zoleen Fyrenn. She's rich and well-born enough to suit *anybody*. She's got one sister who's a duchess, and another who married the widowed king. Her family is one of the oldest in this part of the world.

"I don't know, though. Zoleen and I, we get along well, for the most part. But with that family of hers comes *a lot* of baggage. Political baggage. I like *her* well enough, and I get along with her sister Ashling, but I don't know if I want to marry into that family.

"Which brings me to Sighild Ol'Masarkor. I like her even better than Zoleen, though, honestly, not as much as I like Maev or Byrhta. But Sighild is a cousin to the Fyrenns, and the Ol'Masarkors are another old Armyrian family in their own right. She doesn't have Fyrenn money or prestige, but she might be the best compromise choice.

"From there, love, it gets complicated. There are at least four princesses coming to visit me soon. All four potential marriage candidates. There are a number of others, too. All nobles, who've made clear they'd like consideration.

"My chief adviser, Beornric, is talking about inviting those minor nobles for a visit before the princesses get here. Thinks one of them might win my heart and make my choice easy. I'm not sure I need more choices, though."

Aefric snorted a small laugh. "You'd like Beornric. I give him leeway, so he calls me on my shit." He shook his head. "I can't get off track, though, love. I was hoping maybe you could give me some guidance. You know me better than anyone. Maybe better than I know myself. What do you think I should do?"

Aefric knelt there for quite a while, hoping to hear some kind of answer. Even if only a small tug at his heart, or an unexpected thought burbling up in his head. Something with the character of Andi to it.

But no answer came.

1

———

A princess was coming.

Aefric had gotten a rika that morning from Mayor Vagran Ol'Talas of Ajenmjoor, Aefric's port city on the coast of the Risen Sea. They'd sighted a royal ship passing through port around dawn, heading up the Searun River.

Of course, a royal ship *could* have meant a king or queen. In theory. But no kings or queens were expected at Water's End anytime soon.

Princesses, though, were another matter. Aefric was expecting princesses from three different kingdoms to arrive sometime this aett or the next. Raedrun Al'Trener of Hatay. Jodis Ol'Nariss of Shachan. And from Rethneryl — Armyr's oldest and staunchest ally — *two* princesses: Brigit and Adsaluta Haltallan.

Unfortunately, if Mayor Vagran was right, the ship arriving today wasn't carrying any of them.

If Mayor Vagran was right.

He could have been mistaken, though. Not a lot of light around dawn. Not a lot of wind that morning, either. Easy to mistake a flag half-seen. Get the colors wrong. Maybe even the device.

And then there was the question of escort ships. Reportedly, two large warships had escorted the royal vessel to Ajenmoor, but didn't enter the harbor, where their presence might've been taken as a threat.

Instead, once the royal ship entered the harbor, the warships turned further out into the Risen Sea. Likely to stay within spyglass range.

All reasonable actions that any foreign power might take.

And yet, rather than approach the mayor for an Armyrian escort of river patrol ships — as was customary — the incoming royal vessel sailed straight through the harbor and up the Searun, accompanied by two smaller, armed caravels as escort.

That was strange. And swift. Which meant that early reports about flags and devices could not be checked and verified.

Yes. The mayor's information could be wrong.

Aefric *wanted* it to be wrong.

At least the day was beautiful.

Autumn was almost four aetts old, and yet the skies above were clear and blue. The midday sun smiled with a memory of its summertime warmth. Even the breezes down on the docks at Water's End were gentle, and carried the good clean smells of massive Lake Deepwater. A lake vast enough that its far shore could barely be seen from the higher places in Water's End. Might look like an ocean, if not for the Threepeaks Mountains to the northeast.

A lake so deep that it was said to be bottomless, emerging as its own twin somewhere on the other side of Qorunn.

Aefric hardly needed the soft, gray felt cloak he wore over his dark red silk shirt and black hose. And he never really felt comfortable wearing his ducal coronet.

Always seemed excessive to him. Hammered gold, with a large sapphire in a central triangle, and smaller rubies and emeralds alternating around the rim.

He wore the coronet now because — whatever princess was arriving — he was expected to wear his coronet whenever he greeted royalty. Especially foreign royalty.

He stood at the foot of the pier reserved for visiting nobility. Like the rest of the docks here at Water's End, this pier was magicked from smoothed coral. Its colors dark, muted shades of green and red.

The coral look was part of the lake theme of the castle itself. Which stood well over a hundred feet tall even before the many towers began, and without including the Seven Great Spires of Water's End.

The Great Spires extended hundreds of feet into the air. Six of them in a loose arc toward the lake side of the castle, and connected by many high arching bridges.

The seventh — The Spike — towered high above them all from the center of the keep itself.

And so far as Aefric had been able to tell — and he'd spot-checked while flying sometimes — every inch of that massive castle exterior, including the walls surrounding its courtyard, looked like shimmering, dark navy blue water from the center of the lake.

A castle beyond anything Aefric had ever dreamed of being able to call his own. Of course, in truth, it was the property of the Duke of Deepwater. It went with the title. Like the responsibility of greeting even uninvited royalty...

Gulls gossiped in the skies above the docks as they circled, looking for food. At most of the other piers, the sounds of workers moving cargo on and off ships. Shouting to one another as they worked...

Then again, most of them shouted whether they were working or not. At least some of what Aefric could hear were jests and good-natured insults, hurled back and forth by those who made their way into the city to find lunch.

Out in the harbor, dozens of merchant vessels waited their turns to be guided by local pilots through the reef to their designated slips.

All of them had to wait, because a royal ship was arriving.

Aefric could see it now, coming around the line of merchant vessels. A two-masted schooner. Fast-looking ship. Sleek. But armed all the same. He could see a ballista up on the foredeck, and a cata-pult aft.

No escort vessels surrounding it, which meant they must've

broken off just before the royal ship entered the harbor. Hard to spot them among the rest of the harbor traffic, so Aefric turned his attention to the royal vessel.

On the mainmast, the ship's flag snapped out wide in a burst of wind.

Nerves crashed in Aefric's stomach like cargo dropped through a wooden deck. He tightened his grip on the Brightstaff without thinking.

Mayor Vagran was right.

That ship flew the red narwhal, facing to the dexter, on a background of pale blue. The flag of Malimfar. Armyr's southern neighbor and recent enemy.

Aefric didn't need to see the device on the next flag down now. He knew what ship it had to be. The *Hippocamp*. The personal ship of Astrid Eadredsdottir, Crown Princess of Malimfar.

"Steady, your grace," Beornric whispered from Aefric's right hand.

Good, reliable Ser Beornric Ol'Sandallas. Aefric's chief adviser, and captain of his Knights of the Lake. He'd seen at least fifteen summers more than Aefric, with most of his years spent in service to his majesty, King Colm Stronghand.

Beornric was a big man, with rough features, more than his share of scars, and a growing amount of gray in his short black hair and bushy mustaches.

But he still wore his polished, full plate armor with comfortable ease, and handled his longsword with swift, deadly efficiency.

"If it weren't her," Beornric continued, "this greeting party would be woefully underattended."

He was right, of course. Aefric stood there without his court, nor even most of his advisers. Accompanied only by Beornric, the six Knights of the Lake, and—

"Well, if she had to come, better she gets here first," Yrsa said, from Aefric's left. "Better we get this over with before the more important guests arrive."

Ser Yrsa Azenai, Aefric's general, stood even taller than he did, and looked the very definition of "menacing." Her blonde hair had red highlights so dark, it was rumored that to have been dyed in the blood of enemies that never quite washed away.

Given how good she was with those two massive, ridged maces that she wore at her belt, the rumor was believable. Aefric had seen her fight. She made those maces look as light and well-balanced as any rapier.

The strength in her hands and wrists was unbelievable.

Yrsa had one prominent scar, on the left side of her face, where a sword tip had cut a groove from her forehead to her chin, right through the eye.

Healers had saved the eye, or at least its functioning. But it was now pale red. A sharp contrast to the dark gray of her other eye.

"I'd really rather not insult a crown princess," Aefric said.

"You don't get much choice about it," Beornric said.

Yrsa scoffed. "Malimfar has to be expecting this anyway. They even brought their own river escort."

"Well, if they are, Princess Astrid won't admit it," Beornric said.

"Doesn't matter if she doesn't or does," Yrsa said. "And don't worry, your grace. I've recalled both the *Lake Monster* and the *Calming Influence*. They'll make sure those Malimfari ships behave themselves."

The *Lake Monster* and the *Calming Influence*. Two warships so large and heavily armed they couldn't leave Lake Deepwater.

"Neither one of you is helping my nerves," Aefric said. "I don't want to be the one who starts a war."

Both Beornric and Yrsa opened their mouths to respond to that, but stilled when Aefric raised a halting hand. Probably because he rarely did so. He encouraged them to speak their minds.

But right now, he focused on watching the *Hippocamp* approach the docks.

Instead of docking right at the base of the pier, it tied off at the far end. Easily two hundred feet away.

"As I said," Beornric said softly. "You don't have much choice about this."

HUNDREDS OF FEET OF SMOOTHED, DARK CORAL PIER STOOD BETWEEN Aefric and the newly arrived *Hippocamp*, with its royal passenger.

Why did they dock at the far end? Did they expect Aefric to come down the pier to meet them? That would be against protocol.

Then again, nothing about this followed protocol. No court surrounding Aefric under the midday sun. No red carpet. No musicians.

Of course, Princess Astrid hadn't exactly followed protocol herself. She'd come without invitation, or even advance notice of her arrival...

Sailors aboard the *Hippocamp* lowered a gangplank. The local pilot departed quickly for a rowboat to take him to his next ship.

For a moment, there was only the jeering of gulls and the shouts of working sailors from up and down the docks.

From the *Hippocamp*, nothing.

Nothing.

Something.

At last, a lone woman descended the gangplank. Pale as a noble, she wore a tomato red dress, slashed at the sleeves and skirts with dark orange. Her hair was the same light blonde as Princess Astrid's, and done in ringlets the way the princess usually wore hers, but this was not the princess. Princess Astrid was tall and slender. This woman was shorter, and fuller of figure.

Alone, and holding her skirts, she walked down the pier. Shoulders back and head held high. As she came closer, Aefric could see that she wore a necklace of amber, and two gold bracelets on each arm.

She was older than the princess. Princess Astrid was about Aefric's own age, but this woman was closer to Yrsa's age. About five years older than Aefric.

She stopped a dozen paces away and bowed low to him.

"Forgive me for introducing myself, your grace," she said, "but I do not choose the circumstances. My name is Ingdis Bodvarsdottir, lady to her highness, Crown Princess Astrid Eadredsdottir of Malimfar. And, of course, I know that I am addressing his grace, Ser Aefric Brightstaff, Duke of Deepwater."

"There is nothing to forgive, Ingdis Bodvarsdottir," Aefric said. "Though I confess to some surprise to see the *Hippocamp* arriving at my docks today. We received no advance word of a royal visit."

"Then I must apologize for that as well, your grace," she said with a smooth bow. "For a rika was sent to allow ample time for preparations."

"It must have gone astray," Beornric said, his tone neutral enough to provide *just a hint* of disbelief. The rika bird was a very strong flier. And though they did not *always* reach their destination, they did far more often than they didn't.

"It must have," Ingdis agreed easily. "Her highness has come to pay court to your grace, and to present him personally what she promised him this past summer."

"She has completed her research then?" Aefric asked. "Into who at her father's court authorized sowing dissent and fomenting rebellion in my lands?"

"As to the findings of her highness' research, it is not my place to say," Ingdis said with another bow. "Her highness wishes to present her findings to your grace personally."

Ingdis made a show of looking at the armed and armored knights around Aefric.

"Her highness, however," Ingdis continued, "has a justifiable concern that she will be greeted not as the royal guest she is, but as an enemy to be taken captive."

"Here it is I who must apologize," Aefric said. "For while I, myself, have kept an open mind regarding Malimfar and its royal family — as I promised her highness I would — my king's mind is not so open. My orders regarding her highness are quite clear."

"She is to be captured, is she?" Ingdis asked haughtily. "A *crown princess*?"

"Not in the least," Aefric said. "However. I am not to host her, nor even *receive* her, without *prior* royal permission. As I received no word of her coming, this prior permission was impossible to obtain."

"She is here now," Ingdis said reasonably. "Certainly she should be offered proper hospitality, as befits her station, while this misunderstanding is cleared up. Should it help, I myself would be willing to write the explanation for his majesty about the rika."

"Would that I could," Aefric said, grimacing. "But my instructions from his majesty are quite clear. I am only to receive or host Malimfari royalty or nobility if they arrive carrying a letter of invitation from my king, or if I receive a writ of royal permission *before* the Malimfari arrival. Not after."

"I don't suppose you have a letter of invitation from our king," Beornric said softly.

Ingdis ignored him.

"This is most irregular, your grace," she said.

"I agree," Aefric said. "But certainly you recognize that specific orders from his majesty must override even the usual conventions regarding hospitality. My hands in this matter are tied."

"Princess Astrid was very much looking forward to renewing her acquaintance with your grace."

"As was I," Aefric lied. "But my first loyalty must be to my liege."

"Why did your grace allow us to dock at all?" Ingdis asked, looking at Aefric as though she could see through him. "Why not send a ship out to meet us and turn us back?"

"Because I wished to present the situation myself," Aefric said. "So that her highness would know that these actions are my duty, not my choice."

"Must we leave at once?" Ingdis asked. "Or may I consult with her highness, to bring her this news?"

"Most certainly," Aefric said. "In fact, you may wait and leave with the evening tide, should you choose. But duty requires me to ask that you and yours remain with your ship."

"Of course," Ingdis said, and bowed. "Though I would ask that I continue to be allowed to act as messenger, should her highness require it of me."

Beornric gave an almost imperceptible nod.

"You may, good Ingdis," Aefric said. "In fact, I shall tarry here for a time, in case her highness has a reply at the ready."

"Your grace is most kind," Ingdis said, then bowed again and made her way back down the pier.

"You shouldn't have offered to wait," Yrsa said. "Looks weak."

"I disagree," Beornric said. "It shows goodwill to a member of foreign royalty who is being refused the sort of hospitality that custom demands."

"How much hospitality should an uninvited guest really expect?" Yrsa asked.

The two of them went back and forth about this for a time, while Aefric thought about the cost of his refusal to host Princess Astrid.

She'd seemed sincere this past summer, when she offered to root out the source of the intrigues played against him in the spring. To punish the guilty, and bring him a full report.

He might never see that report now...

"She's coming back," Beornric said, triumphantly enough to get Aefric's attention.

And indeed, Ingdis *was* once more strolling down the pier as though she had all day to make the journey.

When she did finally reach Aefric, she stopped a dozen paces away again and bowed.

"Her highness, Princess Astrid, suggests that if your grace cannot host her, she should host him for lunch aboard her ship. Which would give her the opportunity to keep her promise to him."

Yrsa got about halfway through her no before Aefric said, "I accept."

INGDIS WAS GOOD ENOUGH TO BRING WORD BACK TO PRINCESS ASTRID while Aefric calmed his advisers.

Yrsa's prominent scar had already darkened three shades, a clear sign that her anger was a storm, preparing to break.

Beornric had both hands up as though ready to restrain Aefric from proceeding down the coral dock at once.

"Before either of you say anything," Aefric said. "We've all read the report of the king's justiciar about the problems Ser Grud and his agents were causing among my vassals this past spring."

Yrsa narrowed her eyes suspiciously, but was listening. Beornric lowered his hands, frowning in thought.

Aefric lowered his voice as he continued.

"We know a good deal about what was happening, why, and how it came to pass," Aefric said. "But right now, I have a chance to get an official report about it from Malimfar's viewpoint."

"Lies, you mean," Yrsa said.

"Yes," Aefric said. "I'm sure there will be plenty of lies. But they will also try to work in whatever truths they think we already know."

"Yes, but ... ah," Beornric said. "You think they may slip up and reveal a truth we didn't know about."

"Or you think we'll officially catch them in a lie," Yrsa said.

"I think we may do both," Aefric said. "Either way that report will make a good present for the king. Don't you think?"

Yrsa frowned as she considered that. Beornric gave a wolfish smile. Clapped Aefric on the back, but it was Yrsa he spoke to then.

"I told you," he said. "Our dear Aefric has been thinking more and more like a duke."

Yrsa managed a twisted half-smile and shook her head. "All right, your grace, the politics of this lunch have value. I'll concede that. But will you concede that if you board her ship *you're placing yourself in the hands of our enemies?*"

"I must confess," Beornric said, "given your refusal to see Princess Astrid *here*—"

"And the fact that they have capturing nobles on their minds," Yrsa interrupted.

"—we must acknowledge the possibility that they're only inviting you aboard to take captive a peer of the realm."

Aefric's turn to frown at them.

"Here at my own dock?" Aefric shook his head in disbelief. "With the *Lake Monster* and the *Calming Influence* between them and any escape? Or don't you think those two massive warships pose enough threat? Not to mention our own defenses here at Water's End?"

"If they hold you captive with a blade at your throat," Yrsa said, "just how likely are we to risk attacking them?"

"Especially with your court wizard still away from Water's End," Beornric said.

"You could close the lake," Aefric said. "Raise the chains at the mouths of the rivers." He shook his head. "Anyway, I'm only a duke, while she's their crown princess. How likely are they to risk *her* life just to capture *me*?"

"And if they have a magical means of transportation aboard the ship?" Beornric asked. "Ready to spirit you *and* her away to Svar-turvigi?"

All right. Aefric hadn't considered that. Still...

"You *do* remember that I'm carrying the Brightstaff, the wand Garram, and wearing my blade-turning bracer?" Aefric tapped his left arm, where the bracer lay under his shirt. "Not to mention the toys in my belt pouch, and, oh, yes, that I might know a spell or two myself?"

"By the same turn I would ask *you* to remember," Yrsa said, "that wizards can be captured, same as anyone else. It only requires more preparation."

"And," Beornric chimed in, "we don't know what her plans truly were in coming here. She might always have planned to get you aboard her ship and capture you."

"Which means," Yrsa continued — speaking once more as though the two of them had rehearsed a message for Aefric — "you might well be walking into a trap."

"After all," Beornric said. "They've had ample time to research your reputation and powers. That would allow them to prepare just the right trap for you..."

"Huh," Aefric said, quirking a smile. "Irony tastes a little like oranges."

Yrsa and Beornric both gave him disgruntled looks.

"Or," Aefric continued thoughtfully, "perhaps orange is simply the last taste my tongue recalls from breakfast. And now I'm building the association."

Yrsa opened her mouth to say something but Beornric, in resigned tones, said, "No, don't bother. He'll get to his point."

"I should have thought the point was obvious," Aefric said. "For two seasons you've both been pushing me to think like a noble, not an adventurer. And here you are, looking for traps like an adventurer, while I'm trying to play politics like a noble."

Beornric looked at Yrsa. "Do you want this one? Or should I take it?"

"I will," Yrsa said, then turned to Aefric. "You have it backwards. A noble would know the likely political outcomes of boarding that ship, including the possibility of capture. Only an adventurer is arrogant enough to assume his power will see him through."

"Look," Aefric said. "You want me to play politics, I'm playing politics. The king may have ordered me not to receive Princess Astrid, but if I refuse to board her ship and have lunch with her, that insult is from *me*, not the king."

While they turned that point over — likely looking for flaws — he continued.

"The latest word I have from Ashling is that Malimfar is at least two or three years away from being ready for war again. If they try anything with me, here and now, they invite King Colm to invade. They risk losing their half of the Indecisive River Valley, and possibly more."

"Especially since," Beornric muttered, tugging on his mustache, "they must know by now that Princess Maev is down in Varondam, negotiating an alliance for us."

"Exactly," Aefric said. "They feel surrounded by enemies. I think they're more likely looking for a friend."

"Or a husband," Yrsa warned. "There's more than one way to capture a noble, and that way is far more dangerous."

Aefric chuckled. "They can't force me into marriage."

Yrsa and Beornric glanced at each other, then turned dark looks on Aefric.

"Can they?" he asked.

"There ... is precedence," Beornric said. "Marriages involving royalty have always been upheld. Even when ... there is a question of duress."

"As long as they've been *consummated*," Yrsa said firmly. "Which is probably what she's after."

"It does sound likely," Beornric said, nodding slowly. "Malimfar doesn't openly practice the noble privilege—"

"Hypocrites," Yrsa scoffed.

"—but they know *we* do. They might assume that the princess need only utter a few reassurances while stripping off her gown to get more from you than the bliss moment."

"We should send for some nysta tea," Yrsa said. "Just to be safe. Eliminate the possibility of your getting her pregnant."

"We could do that," Aefric said patiently. "*Or* I could just not have sex with her. I mean, you two have been encouraging me to sleep with damn near every noblewoman who offers, but that doesn't mean I *have* to."

"True," Beornric said. "But the princess *is* beautiful—"

"*Everyone here is beautiful!*" Keifer's exasperated words coming out of Aefric's mouth. It was true though. Men and women both.

Some stood out more than others — especially those with eldrani blood — and now and again he saw someone specifically unattractive, but compared to what Keifer had known on Earth, it was as though this world were populated only by top models and movie stars.

And these people just rolled out of bed in the morning looking like this. No special regimens. No professional makeup artists.

Sometimes, when Aefric lay sleepless at night, he wondered — were the people here so attractive because decades of fantasy art depicted mostly beauty? Or were decades of fantasy artists inspired by dreams of Qorunn?

"My point is," Aefric said, "as far as I'm concerned, Princess Astrid is no more beautiful than half the ladies of my court. Let alone women like Zoleen, Sighild, *Maev*. And obviously she doesn't begin to compare to Byrhta."

"*That's* certainly true," Yrsa said.

"Very well," Beornric said. "But if you're going to insist on this lunch, keep your wits about you for *any* kind of trap."

"And bring bodyguards," Yrsa said. "Just in case."

"Of course, bodyguards," Beornric said, as though he thought Aefric might debate the point.

"All right," Aefric said, frowning as he pondered what insult he might give by bringing bodyguards. "Who's on duty?"

"All six are going," Beornric said.

"I concur," Yrsa said.

Aefric looked from one to the other, but neither looked willing to budge. He sighed. "All six."

He turned to the Knights of the Lake. Three men and three women. All highly skilled combatants, and all of them sworn not only to his service, but to his defense.

Leppina. Tanned and muscled, with her brown hair in a thick braid that hung to her waist.

Temat Ol'Lazenac. Dark and lean, with that wicked scar across his neck giving him a roguish look. His head shaved as polished as his armor.

Vria Aldellac. Short and pale, with fine-featured beauty, golden eyes, and a natural orange tint to her hair that spoke of her eldrani heritage.

Micham Ol'Talas. Ruggedly weathered and missing half an ear, but with his brown hair and beard always trimmed to the latest fashion.

Arras. Aristocratic in bearing and beauty, but her black hair cut short, and a challenge always in her hazel eyes. The only Knight of the Lake to fight with a sword in each hand.

Wardius. Wiry, lean, and still handsome, despite being the most scarred of the lot. His cheeks were jagged, and he was missing the tip of his nose and the smallfinger of his left hand. In his eyes, the look of a man at peace with himself.

These were the Knights of the Lake. Identifiable by the image of Lake Deepwater etched on the breastplates of their gleaming full plate armor.

"This may be a trap," Aefric said to them. "But it's not likely the kind of trap we'll need to fight our way out of. All the same. Keep your eyes and ears sharp, and your wits about you."

"Yes, your grace," they said in imperfect sync.

"Let's go," he said.

The walk down the smoothed, dark green and red coral to the end of the pier to where the *Hippocamp* sat at dock might only have been a couple of hundred feet, but it felt much farther.

Aefric could feel eyes on him. From the *Hippocamp*, he was watched by soldiers and sailors. From the docks, some of the locals and sailors both had stopped to see what their duke and his knights were doing.

Of course, it likely helped that anyone who either lived here at Water's End or sailed here regularly knew that this pier was only used by nobility and royalty. So even if they didn't recognize the narwhal flag of Malimfar, they knew that whoever owned this ship was important. And yet, was not being made formally welcome.

Crowds. One aspect of being duke that Aefric was still adjusting to. When he'd been a traveling adventurer, he never had to worry about throngs of people watching while he went about his business.

They might cheer him after a victory, or they might glare at him with suspicion as he rode into town a stranger on a rainy day. But while he was delving into lost tombs, battling bizarre monsters, or doing some other thing that normal people wouldn't dream of doing, he never had to cope with crowds of onlookers.

Being duke, though, meant always being on display…

An unproductive line of thought. So Aefric turned his attentions to the clear, beautiful sky. The welcoming heat of the midday sun. The gentle breeze with its lake smells. All of these things much happier than the notion of committing some colossal blunder in front of a crowd.

When he reached the foot of the *Hippocamp's* gangplank, Temat and Leppina closed ranks in front of him.

Aefric looked up at the rail. Archers, a dozen of them. All with arrows nocked, though not yet aimed. The sailors had withdrawn from the rail. Aefric couldn't even spot them on the rigging or minding the wheel.

Instead, there were only the archers in their leathers, plus a dozen pike-wielding soldiers in chainmail and half-helms. Overseeing them, two people. Ingdis — frowning — and a bent, wrinkled man whose white hair and beard weren't much paler than his skin.

He wore robes of brown and gray, and leaned on a staff. But he was no magic-user.

The old man called down in a surprisingly strong, clear voice.

"Who approaches the ship of her highness, Princess Astrid Eadredsdottir?"

At Aefric's nod, Arras answered.

"His grace, Ser Aefric Brightstaff, Duke of Deepwater, Baron of Netar, and Hero of the Battles of Deepwater and Frozen Ridge, approaches at the invitation of her highness."

"Does his grace believe the invitation to include a battle with lunch?" the old man asked.

"Does her highness always menace her invited guests with archers?"

"Only when an invited guest makes the mistake of arriving armed for battle."

"Were his grace to arrive armed for battle," Arras said, "there would be no question of mistake."

"Enough," Ingdis called loudly, then whispered harshly into the ear of the old man.

The old man shook his head several times as she spoke. They held a harsh, whispered argument.

Ingdis won. At her gesture, the archers put away their arrows.

She stepped forward, bowed, smiled, and said, "Her highness extends her greeting to his grace, and to the knights who safeguard his grace's life. Please, come aboard and be made welcome."

Temat and Leppina preceded Aefric up the gangplank. Arras and Micham flanked him. Vria and Wardius followed.

As Aefric stepped onto the smoothed, dark wood of the *Hippocamp's* deck, the old man cocked an eyebrow at him.

"First your grace denies our crown princess the welcome and hospitality that are her due," the old man said. "Now your grace refuses to so much as attend her luncheon without a passel of armed knights. Her highness might choose to overlook your grace's rudeness today, but I assure him that Malimfar will not forget it."

The man turned about and went aft.

"I pray your grace," Ingdis said with a troubled expression, "pay little heed to the words of Arl Halldor. He may have the king's ear, but he does not speak with the king's tongue."

"I understand," Aefric said with a forced smile. "And I know that I … am not a popular man in Malimfar."

"Oh, then your grace misunderstands our people," Ingdis said. "True, there are many who grieve their losses, and may hate your grace for them. But even they know the value of so fierce a warrior as your grace. And Malimfar values warriors highly."

"Then why does Arl Halldor hate me so?"

Ingdis sighed and gave Aefric an exasperated smile. "Politics."

Ah, of course. The catch-all answer when refusing to give an answer.

"Will your grace consent to dine privately with her highness?" Ingdis asked. "By which I mean in the presence of only her chaperon?"

"Of course," Aefric said, thinking quickly, "although my advisers bid me bring a chaperon of my own."

"Oh," Ingdis made a show of looking around for Aefric's chaperon. "Is this person hiding behind your knights?"

"No," Aefric said. "In the interest of not keeping her highness waiting, I have chosen not to send for a noble to act as chaperon. Instead, I designate Ser Arras for the duty."

"Your grace wishes a chaperon in full arms and armor?" Ingdis said with a slightly deprecating smile. "To dine with Princess Astrid?"

"Of course Arras would surrender her swords," Aefric said. "But it would take as long to send for her clothes as it would to send for an alternative chaperon. If her highness prefers to wait…"

"Her highness is most eager to see your grace."

"Then I trust that a noble knight, reared and trained right here at Water's End, suffices for a chaperon."

"In Malimfar it is not customary for a man to require a chaperon."

"I understand," Aefric said. "But this is Armyr."

"I was not under the impression that it was the practice in Armyr, either."

Aefric smiled and sighed. "Politics."

"Ah," Ingdis said. "Very well then. Allow me a moment to inform her highness about the … necessary adjustment to the lunch arrangements, and then I will see your grace to her presence."

"Thank you," Aefric said.

Well, whatever else happened at lunch, now at least he'd have a witness of his own.

FOR SOMEONE SO EAGER TO SPEAK WITH AEFRIC, PRINCESS ASTRID didn't seem to mind keeping him waiting.

On the deck of her ship. In the midday sun. With her soldiers and sailors all just standing around watching him suspiciously. As though they thought he might order an attack or something.

Exactly what had Arl Halldor been saying about him? Or was the arl only part of the problem?

Aefric wasn't the only one who didn't care for the situation. He noticed that his Knights of the Lake surreptitiously arranged themselves around him.

Not in anything so obvious as a tight circle, but so that no one could approach him from any direction without meeting one of them first. And they didn't take their places in a quick, military fashion, but casually. Almost as though they simply happened to wander to their current positions while looking over details of the *Hippocamp*.

Certainly they had time to make it look casual. If he'd known how long he'd be kept waiting, Aefric could have sent for a change of clothes for Arras. A change of clothes she would have had time to don.

There was one advantage to the delay, though. Aefric had ample time to study the local magic. Accuracy enchantments on the ship's ballista and catapult. Strength enchantments woven into the hull.

But no blind spots. No illusions. No confinements waiting to trap him. And perhaps most important, no magic-users hiding belowdecks.

Still. How much longer would they keep him waiting?

By the time Aefric finished thoroughly checking out the magic in his surroundings, he could have sent for any noble in Water's End to stand as chaperon for him.

Much longer, and he might have been able to send to *Behal* for a chaperon before he finally sat down to eat.

Aefric was about to remark on that fact when Ingdis emerged, smiling, from a cabin door.

She approached Aefric, but stopped several paces away, frowning, when she noticed the way his knights adjusted their attention as though she might present a threat.

She bowed. "Your grace. I must apologize for the delay. It is entirely my fault, and your grace should hold no blame for her highness."

"May I ask what the delay was?" Aefric asked.

"Logistics," Ingdis said. "Nothing more. A ship's cabin is not the ideal setting for a luncheon such as this one. But I have done the best I can, under circumstances not of my choosing."

Aefric almost reassured her, but he was pretty sure that last part carried an implied insult to Armyr. "I understand."

"Your grace is most kind," she said with another bow. "If his knight will be so good as to surrender her blades, I will now escort your grace to the royal presence."

Arras removed her sword belt and handed it to Micham.

"What about his staff?" Arl Halldor yelled down from the after-decks. "And his wand. I think we're all too aware of the havoc he can wreak with those."

Ingdis raised her eyebrows at Aefric.

"If her highness insists," Aefric said slowly, "I will leave my wand with my knights. But the Brightstaff goes everywhere with me. I have carried it in her presence before, and see no reason I should not now."

"I believe her highness would make no objection to your grace's signature instrument. His affectation for carrying it everywhere is well known. But I think she might take it amiss for your grace to carry the wand Garram into her presence. Given how your grace made use of its powers this past spring."

Fair enough. It was the wand Garram Aefric had used to hammer Malimfar's armies with a heavy, unseasonable blizzard.

Aefric pulled the wand from its sheath — trying to ignore the way all the archers in his line of sight reached for their quivers — and handed it to Vria. He suspected she could produce at least a little power from it, given a reason. She had no formal magical training, but she had eldrani blood. And the eldrani seemed to have some affinity for enchanted weapons...

"Your grace is most accommodating," Ingdis said. "And now I believe we are ready."

Ingdis led the way. Arras was willing to go second, but Aefric chose to. He'd rather have Arras in a position to clear their way out, if needed.

The wood of the cramped hallway had an orange tint under the light of the oil lamps at either end. Aefric found himself crouching, so he didn't bump his head, even though it wouldn't be a long walk.

The hallway's smell of tallow and sweat was overlaid by an unusual vanilla scent from the burning lamp oil...

Ingdis knocked twice on the door at the end of the hall, then opened it and led the way inside.

The moment the door was opened, the vanilla smell got stronger. Eight lamps in here, two hanging in each corner of the room.

The fragrance was a bit cloying now, but at least the room was comfortably lit.

More low ceilings though. Joy.

Aefric wasn't sure what this cabin was usually used for, but his guess was meetings. It was square in shape, maybe five strides across, and too crowded for its space.

Two guards just inside the door. Both big men. Both in recently oiled chainmail, with half-helms, short swords and bucklers. Two servants on the opposite side of the room. Both of them short and slight enough to be children or kindaren.

Along the right-hand side of the room, a small table set for two. In the center of the room, a larger, round table, also set for two.

In the chair facing him from the center table, Princess Astrid looked properly regal in a taffeta gown of royal blue, slashed at the sleeves with purple. Her pale blonde hair was done in ringlets, and crowned by a golden diadem that featured a single large ruby, surrounded by smaller diamonds.

Gold and amber at her wrists and on her fingers, but more importantly, at the delicate skin of her throat, a golden torc.

The torc was enchanted. Felt like defensive magic. And on her fingers, one of her rings was also enchanted. He recognized it at once. The poison-detector she'd worn this summer.

Princess Astrid didn't rise from her seat as he entered. A statement.

Properly speaking, she was his peer, not his superior. She should either bow to him first — because she was visiting his duchy — or bow to him in return, claiming the position of hostess on the flimsy basis of their meeting aboard her ship.

Either way, she had no right to expect him to bow without offering a bow in return. She might've been crown princess, but she wasn't queen yet.

She did neither, though, but remained seated. Smiling, to emphasize her high cheekbones.

"Your grace," she said. "Here I sailed all this way to fulfill a promise. And yet, because of a single stray bird, I find I've not only put your grace in an uncomfortable position, but come perilously close to causing an incident between our kingdoms. I trust he will forgive me for this?"

"How could I do otherwise?" Aefric asked. "Especially when I must ask your highness' forgiveness for her reception."

Ingdis made a small sound of objection when it became clear that Aefric didn't intend to bow, but Princess Astrid didn't bat an eye.

"Think nothing of it," she said with a dismissive wave. "I understand how the ways of kings only make life more difficult for the rest of us."

She gestured to the chair across from her. "Please. Join me."

As Aefric took his seat — standing the Brightstaff beside his chair and leaving his back to those guards, which caused an itch between his shoulder blades — Arras and Ingdis took seats at the other, smaller table to his right.

"I'm sure your grace is as eager to learn about my findings as I am to share them," Princess Astrid said with a coy smile. "But I trust he will remain patient while we share a meal, first? We needn't be so barbaric as the Caiperans or Varondami."

Aefric chuckled, but noted the slight against Varondam included in her expected insult to Caiperas, Malimfar's traditional enemy.

"Of course I am eager for the report," Aefric said. "But how could I be less eager to share your highness' company?"

An obvious compliment, but still effective. Princess Astrid looked visibly pleased as she called her servants forward — clearly kindaren now, one male, one female. Kindaren looked much like humans, though proportionately smaller. These two wouldn't have been tall enough to reach his sternum, had Aefric been standing.

"We're ready to begin," Princess Astrid said, then turned to Aefric. "I fear I have none of your Armyrian palate wine."

"None is required," Aefric said, dismissing the faux pas.

"Your grace is most kind," she said, turning back to the servants. "Then we will begin with the chowder."

A clam chowder as it turned out, and quite good. Better than the rest of lunch, to be honest.

The ocean salmon was clearly fresh-caught overnight, and grilled well, but too heavily peppered for Aefric to enjoy it. Masked the subtler flavors his cooks usually brought out in ocean salmon.

The tossed salad served with the fish with wasn't nearly fresh enough. As though they'd stored the three types of lettuce and variety of root vegetables ready-cut, instead of whole.

Perhaps that was why they added so much pepper to the salmon. To help mask the limpness of the salad. A dressing would have helped.

At least the white wine that accompanied the meal was light enough to help dilute the pepper.

And Princess Astrid did make for a good meal companion.

After listening to Yrsa and Beornric's urgent warnings, Aefric half expected her to try to seduce him. Instead, she treated the lunch as might any charming, vivacious hostess.

She told stories of riding and hunting and sailing. Of this ball and that one. Of amusing things she'd seen at court over the years, and places she'd visited where Malimfar had trade. She asked questions about Aefric's life, but never of anything deep or intense. Places he'd been. Foods he'd tried in his travels. Wonders he'd seen.

Before Aefric knew it, the meal was finished, and the servants were clearing away the dishes.

"Now," Princess Astrid said with a smile as she handed her napkin to a servant. "I am ready to send for your report."

WHILE AEFRIC AND PRINCESS ASTRID WAITED FOR THE KINDAREN servants to return with her report, Aefric tried three times to get her to start telling him her findings.

Each time, she only smiled mischievously and answered, "All

things their time, your grace." Followed by changing the subject. First to sailing, then to the gentle autumn weather so far, and finally to the sad increase in piracy on the eastern shores of the Risen Sea, which surely affected both Malimfar and Armyr.

It was the closest she'd come to discussing politics so far, which made Aefric curious. Especially since, if anything, the pirate queen Nelazzi had been *less* active on his shores since the start of autumn. Which he didn't trust at all...

At last though, the kindraren returned. One carried a large leather scroll case while the other struggled with a simple wooden chest — well varnished — that was larger than his entire torso.

"Mmmm," Princess Astrid said, as though considering the relative merits of the contents of each, even though she clearly knew which one she wanted first. "The chest first, I should think."

As Aefric realized the rough size of that chest, he felt a sinking sensation in his stomach. She'd made noises this past summer about bringing him the head of the person most responsible for the espionage committed against Aefric...

The kindaren managed to heft the chest onto the table, but looked relieved to be free of his burden. Something weighty then? Kindaren weren't all that weak, physically, unless these two were still young...

Princess Astrid herself slid the chest to the table's center.

"Your highness," Aefric said slowly, "is that—"

"Please, your grace," she said, smiling. "Open it and see."

Aefric stood for a better look. He removed the chest's lid and was immediately hit by the odor of pine resin, the base of an important alchemical preservative.

Sure enough, inside that chest sat a severed human head, without so much as a pillow to rest on. The dead man had seen close to three score summers, before his steel gray hair and beard had been roughly hacked short and his head parted from his shoulders.

Clean cut at least.

The preserving solution had done its work well. The dead man looked as though he'd lost his head sometime while Aefric and Princess Astrid had been eating lunch.

Aefric had seen many dead bodies over the years. Far too many during the Godswalk Wars. But this kind of display always struck him as unseemly.

"Am I supposed to recognize this man?" Aefric asked, looking closer.

"There was always a chance, your grace. Does he look familiar?"

"No," Aefric said honestly, deliberately keeping his tone light.

"Too much to hope that he would, I suppose," Princess Astrid said, sounding somewhat disappointed.

Aefric wondered though. Did she actually expect him to recognize the head? Or was she disappointed that he hadn't given her a stronger reaction?

"That is all that remains of Arl Reynar," she continued. "Once a trusted adviser to my father. Now, not fit to feed fish."

Aefric took his seat again. He knew what he was supposed to assume from this. But he wasn't going to ask leading questions if he could help it.

"I take it he didn't die by natural causes?" he asked.

"No," Princess Astrid said, chuckling. "Not unless your grace considers the headsman's axe a natural cause."

"Execution then?"

"Your grace is being quite cautious today," Princess Astrid said with a smile. "Yes, your grace. Execution. Arl Reynar's head was taken for usurping the king's authority. It was he and his who were ultimately responsible for the actions taken by Ser Grud Ol'Garan and his agents. As well as a great deal more, as your grace will see."

"Oh?" Aefric said. "And why would this Arl Reynar do such a thing?"

"Well," Princess Astrid said with another coy smile. "I don't suppose there's any point in pretending that Father wasn't after Armyr's half of the Indecisive River Valley this past spring. It used to ours, after all, and he felt it was past time to reclaim it."

"I trust your highness will understand if I point out that Armyr disputes that claim," Aefric said. "After all, my understanding is that the Indecisive River Valley was split when the principality of Fyr fell, and that the northern part has belonged to Armyr ... more or less ever since. Certainly since Armyr was founded."

"Yes," Princess Astrid said easily. "But my family are the true heirs of Fyr, descended directly from the last prince."

"I believe the Fyrenn family would dispute that," Aefric said. "Though I suspect I would enjoy watching your highness debate the issue with Duchess Ashling."

"There is nothing to debate," Princess Astrid said without her smile wavering in the least. "We have the documentation to prove the truth of our claim over hers."

"And if she provides documentation to prove her claim is superior?" After all, Aefric had heard that the library at Ashling's Fyrcloch Castle was vast...

"I'm not here to accuse your neighbor of anything," Princess Astrid said. "Rather instead to explain why Father was prepared to retake the river valley."

"King Eadred amassed quite the army if all he wanted was the river valley," Aefric said. "Well more than twenty thousand strong, I believe, including the mercenaries."

"Ah, but that's part of my point," Princess Astrid said, sitting forward a little now. "Father would not need such a force to do nothing more than retake the river valley. Especially with surprise on his side. Which is why he *did not send* such a force to the river valley."

"I beg to differ," Aefric said. "I myself flew above your ridge that day. I myself saw the size of the armies Malimfar amassed for invasion."

"And what exactly did your grace see?" Princess Astrid asked patiently.

"Well more than twenty thousand troops, including battle wizards and a great deal of siege equipment."

"And could your grace tell if all of these troops were Malimfari?"

Aefric frowned at her. "I saw the banners of several mercenary companies. Large ones. If that's what your highness is asking."

"It is," she confirmed. "Because you see, your grace, Father did not hire any mercenaries. Nor did he commission more than a small amount of siege equipment." She patted the large leather scroll case. "As your grace will read in these documents."

"The mercenaries sprang forth out of thin air, I suppose?"

Princess Astrid's laugh was a surprisingly pleasant sound.

"Your grace is most droll," she said, smiling. "No, of course not. They were commissioned by the arls, believing they were acting on Father's orders."

"And your highness suggests that they were not?"

"I more than suggest it," she said. "I officially confirm so on behalf of King Eadred of Malimfar. Only Malimfari troops were to be involved in the planned conflict, and of *them*, no more than half the number your grace estimated that day."

"Quite a misunderstanding then."

"Oh," Princess Astrid said with another small laugh. "There was no misunderstanding, your grace. There was greed, on behalf of Arl Reynar."

"Ah. I wondered when we'd be getting to his part of this."

"It all goes back to him, I fear," she said. "He really was quite clever. You see, Father knew by the end of the Godswalk Wars that, to survive what the wars had done to our lands, we would need to reclaim my family's old holdings in the river valley. A plan he shared with his most trusted advisers that they might see to the necessary preparations."

"What I saw certainly looked well-prepared," Aefric said, affecting as neutral a tone as possible.

"Your grace must be patient, to hear the whole of the tale."

"Very well. Please do continue, your highness."

"Arl Reynar, one of those trusted advisers, decided, entirely on his own, that Father was thinking too small. That so long as we were crossing Armyr's border, we should retake *all* of the old Fyr lands."

"That would take you all the way to the Kingsroad and include half my duchy."

"It would," Princess Astrid confirmed. "But Father would never have approved it. Too much land to try to take and hold, with the forces we had available. Our line would be stretched too thin."

"Thus, mercenaries."

"Your grace is getting ahead of me."

"Excuse me. Please do continue."

"It seems that Arl Reynar believed we could do it. *If* groundwork were first laid by sowing dissension and discontent in the outlying areas. In other words, in your grace's duchy. Which is why he hired Ser Grud Ol'Garan — who until then had been nothing more than a hanger-on at our court. We didn't even notice when he left.

"While Ser Grud began his work in your grace's duchy, Arl Reynar met privately with some of the lesser arls, and persuaded them to join his scheme. Together they raised not only every fighting man and woman they could from their own lands, but commissioned a great deal of siege equipment, and hired as many mercenaries as they could afford. And some they could not."

"Intending to pay them in spoils?"

"Father would not have approved spoils," Princess Astrid said quickly. Then, hesitantly, she added, "Although it seems that Arl Reynar thought otherwise."

"Arl Reynar seems to have presumed a great deal," Aefric said. "Did he believe his king would simply fail to notice the way his army had swelled, unbidden?"

"He believed exactly that," Princess Astrid said. "And he had reason to. You see, your grace, Father suffered a severe leg wound during the Godswalk Wars, at a time when no healer was available. His leg has been saved, but he can only walk with a cane. And he can no longer take to the field of battle."

"And what general did he designate in his stead for the invasion?"

"I believe your grace could guess."

"Perhaps I'd rather hear it from your highness' lips."

"Very well, then. Arl Reynar had the command, as he knew he would from the time Father first spoke of reclaiming the valley. Of course, field command would also give Arl Reynar control of the flow of information from the front lines."

"Does your highness suggest that Arl Reynar could have conquered all the way to the Kingsroad without his king even learning he'd gone beyond the valley?"

"Of course not," Princess Astrid said easily. "Nor, I think, did Arl Reynar expect to keep his secret so long. However, there are many in this world who believe that forgiveness is often easier to obtain than permission. The arl was one of them."

"And doubtless he thought that forgiveness would be easier to come by, if his apology included success in battle and quite a bit of land."

"Precisely," Princess Astrid said. "According to one letter," — she patted the scroll case — "he expected to be *rewarded* with most of that land. In Father's name, of course."

"Enough power and money to make him second only to the king, in importance?"

"Just so. As I said, his plan was quite clever. Or would have been, had he not failed to account for the powers of Armyr's new duke."

She inclined her head to Aefric. He ignored the compliment.

"I note that your highness said nothing of any of this when I saw her this past summer."

"Of course not," she said, as though the reasons were too obvious for words. "Your grace must remember that the arl's plans were laid in secret. And after your grace's blizzard devastated the arl's forces — and the lands beneath it, by the way — accurate information was difficult to come by for quite some time.

"Then word began to trickle in. Kivash, taken by Armyr. Our forces dead or routed by magic. Mercenaries plundering our farms and towns."

"Mercenaries you say you didn't know your arls had hired."

"Just so. We thought your grace had sent them after us."

———

For a moment, the only sound Aefric heard was the creaking of the ship and the beating of his own heart.

Mercenaries? Malimfar had believed that *Aefric* had hired mercenaries to plunder their lands?

Clearly his distaste must've shown, because Princess Astrid called for more wine. Something red, and a little too sweet. Aefric's first sip tasted more like sugared blackberries than wine. A taste that wasn't helped by the strong vanilla scent given off by the oil lamps.

If this was a lie on her part, it was a good one. She'd thrown him, and there was no way she didn't know it.

Aefric could feel the chaperons studying him from his right. Arras, likely to make sure he was all right. Ingdis, possibly deducing something from his reaction.

That itch between his shoulders made him want to look back at the guards. See if they'd gone for their short swords...

That was paranoia. Arras could see those guards and didn't look concerned.

Aefric steadied himself through a deep breath, then shook his head.

"No," he said, finally. "That's ridiculous. Why would anyone believe that *I* hired mercenaries? Let alone that I sent them into Malimfar to plunder?"

Princess Astrid smoothly shrugged one shoulder. "As I said. Your grace's blizzard was followed by a great deal of death and confusion. And we at Svarturvigi had no idea that Arl Reynar had ... *usurped* Father's authority and brought more than twice as many troops as he'd been commanded to lead."

"Still," Aefric said, shaking his head and forcing down another swig of that too-sweet wine. "It makes no sense that they would pin the blame on me. Ashling, I might've believed. Armyr's half of the Indecisive River Valley is in her duchy. But my lands must be seventy miles away from that valley. If information was so hard to come by, how did you even know I caused the blizzard?"

"Ah," Princess Astrid said with a small smile. "But your grace was recognized by one of our few surviving battle wizards. Seen flying up above, and raining down icy death. While Duchess Ashling's armies had not yet taken the field."

Aefric frowned, wanting to dispute that, but unable to.

"So first, reports from the front told us that Armyr's new duke *himself* had destroyed our armies with his magic. The next report was of Duchess Ashling's troops — and your royal armies, I should add — capturing Kivash. While your grace had not been seen since the blizzard. So who else would we blame for those ravaging mercenaries?"

"Wait," Aefric said. "Where was Arl Reynar during all this? Did he survive the ridge?"

"No, he wasn't there." Princess Astrid said with a sigh. "He was riding from Svarturvigi to the front when your grace attacked. So he had ample time to figure out how to apportion blame and leave himself looking innocent. Which he did. All through the summer. He even persuaded some at court that he could have stopped your grace's blizzard and mercenaries. Had he been there. If only he had left a day earlier."

"So your highness suggests that Arl Reynar blamed me for the mercenaries?"

"Not immediately," she said. "Reynar was at least arl enough to speed to the remains of the ridge, and do what he could to take command and save what lives could be saved. Blame had already fallen on your grace before Arl Reynar returned to Svarturvigi. Though he was quick enough to augment the cries, and ensure that no blame for the catastrophe landed on him."

Aefric considered that. He almost took another sip of the wine, but put down his goblet instead.

"What of those lesser arls who'd rallied to Reynar's cause? And the troops they'd gathered from their own lands. Surely no one tried to blame *me* for that too."

"As I said, your grace. Sorting through it all took time." She shook her head, with a slight furrowing to her brow as though puzzled. "And one element always seemed to be missing."

She pointed at Aefric. "Then your grace told me of the intrigues committed against him. And your grace spoke of them with such certainty and confidence that I knew your grace had to at least *believe* they'd taken place. Even though I knew well that Father would never have countenanced such base activities."

"And you recognized the name of Ser Grud."

"Yes," she said. "As I admitted at the time. And it was through your grace's suggestion that Ser Grud had been acting on Malimfar's orders that provided the missing piece. The rest" — she patted the scroll case — "followed from there."

"And the contents of this scroll case will substantiate what your highness has told me?"

"All of it," she said confidently. "Including the list of conspirators who have been ... punished appropriately for their roles in Arl Reynar's treason. I can assure your grace that the lesson of Arl Reynar will not be forgotten."

Aefric wanted to ask what lesson Malimfar took from this. Was it to not exceed the king's authority? Was it to not underestimate enemies? To plan better?

Assuming this story was true in the first place...

"What of the people of Malimfar? Have they been told the truth about who was behind the mercenaries that plundered their lands?"

"They have," Princess Astrid said. "Your grace's name has been cleared of everything save the events of the Battle of Frozen Ridge itself. Which, of course, is proper."

"Well, yes, but—"

"Please, your grace," Princess Astrid said, holding up a forestalling hand. "There is no need to excuse a justifiable act of war. We of Malimfar respect warriors and warfare. My anger on the topic this past summer was ... excessive and unjustified. Though I did not know that at the time. I hope your grace will excuse me."

"I find holding grudges a bad policy," Aefric said carefully.

Princess Astrid beamed at him. "Thank you, your grace."

"Well," Aefric said, looking at the scroll case. "I look forward to reading your highness' formal report."

"Oh, but I have not yet finished, your grace. I've saved perhaps the most important point for last."

"Oh?"

"Given what I said about the damage sustained by our lands and peoples during the Godswalk Wars, did your grace not wonder how Arl Reynar managed to find the funds to support so many troops? Let alone hiring mercenaries?"

"He offered them spoils, I believe your highness said."

"I did," she said, nodding. She quirked a small smile. "Ah. Your grace truly never has hired mercenaries. They will accept spoils as partial payment and bonuses, but not as full payment. Spoils can be of varying quality, after all, and they might have to compete with others for the best selections."

"So how did he and his conspirators pay them?"

"They had the support of a patron. Caiperas."

Caiperas. Which had tried to assassinate Armyr's entire royal family not so many aett's ago…

Aefric shook his head. Not something to reveal here and now.

"Why would Caiperas support Malimfar — their traditional enemy — in a conflict with Armyr?"

"Simple," she said. "Of our three kingdoms, Caiperas was harmed least by the Godswalk Wars. If they were able to set us at war with one another, they could let us kill each other then sweep in and conquer what remains."

"No," Aefric said. "Even if Armyr and Malimfar fought a long, drawn-out war full of casualties, Caiperas wouldn't be able to take us both."

"Alone, no. They would rely for support on their traditional ally. Varondam. Who would invade Malimfar while Caiperas invaded Armyr."

Varondam. Yes, they shared part of a border with Caiperas. But their entire northern border was Malimfar's southern border.

Were Varondam and Caiperas traditional allies? Aefric didn't know. All he knew for certain was that Maev was down in Varondam negotiating an alliance…

"That's right," Princess Astrid said sadly. "I don't believe King Dalius of Varondam is at all interested in alliance with Armyr or even marriage to Princess Maev. She's far too strongwilled for him. No, I believe he's stringing her along merely to have a hostage, once their part of this spring's events comes to light."

The thought of Maev being held hostage twisted Aefric's guts. "How certain are you of that?"

"Oh, dear," she said with a smile. "I'm afraid I'm as certain as your grace looks upset. I take it your grace has feelings for her?"

Aefric didn't answer that, but apparently he didn't need to.

"Don't worry, your grace," Princess Astrid said reassuringly. "Royal hostages are always treated well. They'll likely let her do anything but leave. And even that they'll let her do eventually."

"I need to get word of this to my king."

She sighed.

"Here I'd hoped to pay court to your grace, and I find him ready to go to war over another princess." She shook her head. "Just as well, I suppose. Even if I won your heart, King Colm would never approve a marriage between us. Not in light of recent events."

"No," Aefric said gently. "I believe he wouldn't."

"Then I have but one more present to give your grace, before our lunch is over. Well. A present ... and a request."

"There's no need for your highness to give me a present," Aefric said quickly. "I'm not even sure I'd be allowed to accept it."

"That won't be an issue, I'm sure," Princess Astrid said, gesturing for one of the kindaren to fetch this other present, whatever it was. "Ask your chaperon, if you wish."

Aefric looked over at Arras.

"Gift-giving among nobility plays an important part in politics," Arras said softly. "It should be fine."

"See?" Princess Astrid said with a smile.

The kindaren came back into the room, carrying another scroll case. A smaller one, and of black leather.

This one carried the royal seal of Malimfar.

Princess Astrid accepted the scroll case from the servant, then turned to Aefric and held it out for him to take.

Aefric couldn't sense any magic from it.

"Your grace," she said, "on behalf of my Father, King Eadred of

Malimfar, I confer on you, Aefric Brightstaff, the lands seized from the traitor Arl Reynar, along with all due moneys and incomes, and the title of Arl of Storbakki."

A Malimfari title?

For Aefric?

Of all the...

But how could...

He was...

A Malimfari title?

It didn't make sense. Not at all. Not from any angle.

The chain of events was pretty simple, if a bit extreme.

Malimfar had decided to invade Armyr and take land. Their reasoning, and exactly *how much land*, might've been points of contention. But that first point was absolutely clear.

This past spring, Malimfar tried to invade Armyr.

Which led to the second point.

Aefric stopped them.

Single-handedly. By using every once of magic he could bring to bear — plus the considerable ice powers of the wand Garram — he battered Malimfar's forces beyond anything they could have borne.

True, doing so had nearly killed him. He'd only survived — as he understood it — through the direct intervention of Kalinda, goddess of magic.

Without even the slightest clue as to why She did it...

No. Not the time to think about that.

What mattered was that, apparently, Malimfar didn't know those little details. About Aefric nearly dying and his salvation.

Malimfar knew only that Aefric alone had battered them with truly legendary amounts of lethal ice magic. Not only stopping their invasion, but likely also setting back their ability to defend their own borders for *years*.

Not to mention leaving their countryside open to pillaging by mercenaries.

And for doing all this, Malimfar ... wanted to ... *reward* him? To give him *land* and *money* and a *title*?

Nope. Didn't make any sense at all.

Was this one of those things that being born into nobility would have prepared him for? That he simply didn't know about because he'd grown up a street rat and then an adventurer, rather than being raised as a duke?

No. No. It couldn't have been that, either.

He'd talked to Ashling many times since Frozen Ridge. He'd spoken with the king and queen as well. And his advisers — including Kentigern Ol'Klimath, who was something like the sixth or seventh consecutive Ol'Klimath to serve as seneschal at Water's End.

Certainly *one of them* would have mentioned this possibility. If this was just a noble thing.

And his life on Earth as Keifer McShane offered no answers. In Earth's history were plenty of wars for land, but never had he heard of an invader getting beaten back, *then freely offering their would-be victims land for their trouble.*

He certainly couldn't remember any mention of such a practice showing up in Keifer's old *Torn Kingdoms* sourcebooks and adventures. Not even *C12: Under the Ruins of Knuivigi*, which was set in southern Malimfar.

How was such a gift even supposed to work?

If the lands and title had been couched as post-war reparations, Aefric might've believed it. But as he understood the situation, King Colm was getting reparations directly from King Eadred. Or was supposed to be.

Aefric couldn't imagine those reparations would amount to much. After all, Malimfar never actually got to invade. They'd done no damage to Armyrian lands or people.

Still, King Colm had insisted that King Eadred would have to pay the cost of mobilizing Armyr's armies...

Which Aefric was supposed to get a part of...

But *this*.

Nothing like *this*.

Well ... maybe if...

No.

No. Aefric simply couldn't make sense of this offer. He had to have heard wrong. And he needed to find out what Princess Astrid had *actually* said as soon as possible.

But his mouth wouldn't move. And he was pretty sure he wasn't breathing. Elbar's Blood, he couldn't even feel his heartbeat at the moment.

All he could do was stare slack-jawed at that scroll case in Princess Astrid's hand.

It took her delighted laughter to snap him out of it. And to close his mouth.

"Oh, your grace," Princess Astrid said, sounding immensely pleased, "I take it this gift comes as a surprise?"

Aefric had to sip a little of that too-sweet red wine to get enough saliva back to let him talk. His mouth had gone completely dry. For some reason.

"I ... can't imagine that I can accept this," Aefric said.

"I must insist," Princess Astrid said, gently but firmly. "If your grace were to refuse this gift, he would not only be insulting me. He would be insulting the crown, all the nobility of Malimfar, and, indeed, our very history."

"I ... don't understand," Aefric said, as carefully neutral as he could.

"Obviously," Princess Astrid said with a smile that took the sting from her wry tone. "It is well known that your grace is not only new to nobility, but new to this region of Qorunn."

"I *did* travel rather extensively in my adventuring days."

"Of course, your grace," Princess Astrid said, still smiling. "I meant no insult by my words. Surely your grace must know that visiting a kingdom, even if one spends a good deal of time there, is not the same as having lived there all one's life."

"Of course."

"And while I do not doubt your grace has been learning a great deal about the history of Armyr since taking up the duchy of Deepwater, he has had little reason to learn the details of the history of Armyr's southern neighbor."

She arched her pale blonde eyebrows at him. "Or am I mistaken in this?"

"Your highness is not mistaken," Aefric said. He still felt numb from surprise.

"Naturally. Though, to be fair, even were your grace to have learned recent history, he might not have encountered this important point."

Princess Astrid set the black leather scroll case down in front of him. Patted it. Sat back a little farther in her seat.

"Before my ancestors asserted kingship in Malimfar, it was a collection of arldoms. They frequently warred over land rights, water rights, other resources. As many are wont to do, when they lack strong leadership."

She paused for a sip of her wine. If she found it too sweet, she gave no indication.

"Eventually, of course, the larger, stronger arldoms began simply conquering their smaller neighbors. Until there were no more than ... a score or two in all.

"They reached a sort of uneasy balance. The remaining arldoms were all closer to the same size and power. No longer could they simply wipe each other out. Not without weakening themselves in the process and risking becoming prey for other arls."

"Peace through fear of mutual destruction."

"Essentially," Princess Astrid said breezily. "But they still had their disagreements. And inevitably, wars would break out."

"And they started giving each other land?"

Princess Astrid laughed. "Your grace can be most impatient at times."

"Please excuse me," he said. "Do continue."

"It is true, of course, that any given war always has one winner and one loser. But it is also true that both sides take their losses. And any war would put both arldoms at risk."

"More for the losing side than the winning side," Aefric said.

"Very good, your grace," Princess Astrid said. "And so, after one of the early such wars, Arl Glodis negotiated a marriage into the terms of her surrender. Her daughter would wed the son of Arl Drifa, binding their families."

"Which was why your highness came to pay court to me," Aefric said slowly. "Prince Killian is already promised. Princess Maev might be promised by now to King Dalius of Varondam."

"I consider that highly unlikely, personally," Princess Astrid said. "But her presence in Varondam did remove her from possibility. Duchess Ashling already has a bastard, which removes her from consideration by any of our better nobles, let alone our royal family. And Duke Wylyn, of course, has been married for a great many years."

"I don't understand, though, where the land and title come into it."

"The *fact* of a war did not guarantee that both sides would have children available to marry when it ended. And yet, the loser needed to see the winner invested in the loser's continuance."

"With a gift of land," Aefric said breathlessly.

"Just so," Princess Astrid said. "A different kind of marriage. The land was not given to the winning arl, of course, who would then rightly consider the gift now part of his or her arldom. No, the gift would be given to one of the winning arl's important lords. Who would then become a lord in the losing arldom as well, and invested in not seeing it fall."

Understanding made Aefric chuckle. "So your highness was sent to marry me if possible and, if not, to see me invested in making sure Malimfar..."

Aefric gave Princess Astrid a curious look. "These lands. I take it they border either Caiperas or Varondam?"

"Oh no, your grace," Princess Astrid said with a smile. "They're in the Indecisive River Valley. Father wishes to make sure that neither

King Colm nor Duchess Ashling get any ideas about taking the whole of the river valley while we're weak."

Aefric nodded slowly. That would also mean that Aefric could visit these lands without traveling deep into Malimfar. Possibly seeing things he wasn't supposed to see, or being seen by people who might hold Frozen Ridge against him...

In a careful voice he said, "I should still check with my king before taking possession of these lands and their title."

"May I have your acceptance contingent on that permission?"

Out of the corner of his eye, Aefric saw Arras nod rapidly.

"Your chaperon seems to agree that it is a good idea," Princess Astrid said, sounding amused.

Aefric drew a deep, vanilla-tasting breath. Nodded.

"Very well. I accept this gift, with the understanding that I must seek royal permission to keep it. Though even if the gift must be refused, allow me to thank your highness for the spirit in which it was given."

Aefric picked up the scroll case.

"Excellent," Princess Astrid said with a smile. "And if I may be so candid, your grace, I am glad that we will not be betrothed. Not that your grace isn't comely and powerful, but I would prefer a husband who fights with a sword, not a wand."

Of course, Aefric fought quite well with a sword. But he didn't think this was the time to point that out.

"Your highness also said something about a request?"

"Yes, a small one. Your grace has been so kind as to allow four of my knights to remain in Water's End since my last visit. I would like three of them to leave with my ship, and the fourth, Tohr Duisson, to remain behind as an official ambassador from Malimfar."

"To remain here?" Aefric asked.

"No. He would ride for Armityr," Princess Astrid said. "But under the ... current climate, doing so might not be safe for him. My request is that your grace provide him an escort, as a gesture of goodwill."

"Certainly," Aefric said. "I'll send word to your highness' knights as soon as I leave her presence, and see Ser Tohr well escorted to the capital as soon as possible."

"Your grace is most kind." She reached her hand back to one of the servants, who passed her a parchment scroll, sealed in blue wax.

Princess Astrid set the scroll on the table beside the two scroll cases and the box with the head.

No magic in the scroll...

"This is Tohr's commission as ambassador from Malimfar, as well as his first instructions. Your grace is, of course, welcome to read either if he wishes."

"I'll see that he gets it," Aefric said, standing — which drew a frown from Ingdis. "And now, I must ask that your highness excuse me. I've a great many duties waiting for me, and" — Aefric patted the scroll cases — "important matters to discuss with my advisers."

"Of course, your grace," Princess Astrid said. "I've enjoyed this lunch a great deal, and hope we may enjoy another soon."

"I do as well," Aefric said, surprised to realize he meant it.

He picked up the scroll cases and scroll and turned to Arras.

"Your grace," Princess Astrid said, and when he turned back to face her she added, "The chest as well. Arl Reynar's head is also your present."

2

Normally, Aefric's preferred room for meeting with his advisers felt comfortably small, if a bit close when tempers rose.

The walls were paneled in black oak, like the floorboards. And the blackwood table in the center — currently covered in the contents of those scroll cases from Malimfar — was large enough that the two long walls were only just out of touching range for those in the closest of the ornately carved blackwood chairs.

The short walls were farther away, but not *that much* farther, because one was full of cabinets and overstuffed shelves, and the other had buffet tables, which often provided breakfast during the morning meetings.

The meeting room felt positively *spacious* today, though. Especially the high ceiling. Aefric must've felt more confined in that ship's cabin than he'd thought.

And here the soft, comfortable light was provided by the spells of past dukes and duchesses. So the air carried none of that cloying vanilla odor.

It was in his clothes, though. He'd need to change before...

"...and so I must say that Princess Astrid was right about the

Malimfari exchange of lands and titles after war. Though I dispute that it began with the conflict between Arls Drifa and Glodis..."

Elkari Ol'Nuval, Aefric's ducal historian, was the one speaking. She sat directly across from him today, behind a stack of books and scrolls. Her dusky skin was ink-stained, as usual, but she'd branched out a bit in the colors of her clothing. A dark red tunic today, to go with her usual dark brown breeches. She'd cut her hair short again, hardly much more right now than a thatch of dark brown fuzz.

She was an absolutely brilliant historian. She might've known more about the history of Armyr and its surrounding kingdoms than Aefric knew about magic. Impressive, considering she only had maybe five summers on him.

"Thank you, Elkari," Aefric said, cutting her off. "Exactly when and how the practice began is less immediately important than that it has precedence."

"Respectfully," she said — finally learning to forgo Aefric's courtesy during a meeting like this one — "I disagree. The Drifa-Glodis War was significant not because it was the first to include a marriage with its terms of surrender, but because its end was almost simultaneous with the first outside threat that Malimfar had faced in nearly a hundred years. A threat that forced the arls to band together for the first time, and paved the way — over the following decades — for the rise of Malimfar's first king, Tyr I, ancestor to their throne's current occupant, King Eadred."

"I take it," Yrsa said from Aefric's left hand, her expression dour, "that threat came from Caiperas?"

Like Beornric, who sat at Aefric's right hand, Yrsa was still in her full plate armor.

"It did," Elkari confirmed. "Violating several treaties signed with the arls who bordered her lands. Treaties that were no more than a few years old at the time, and now are widely speculated to have been signed only to put the Malimfari arls at their ease while Caiperas began readying for war."

"Speculated by Malimfari historians, certainly. I suspect the Caiperans view it differently."

That last was from Ser Garnotin Artaretek, castellan of Water's End, who today sat at Beornric's right, with an empty chair between himself and Elkari.

A dark-skinned man who would have been tall in any room that didn't include Aefric and Yrsa, Garnotin was of middle years, but still looked as though he could wield his warhammer with deadly efficiency.

He wore that warhammer strapped to the back of his bright yellow tunic.

"It isn't just Malimfar saying it," Elkari answered quickly. "The great sage Ceolgifu Ol'Rettek wrote about that war extensively in her treatise on the rise of Malimfar as a kingdom. I could have it sent to your office, if you'd like."

"You said 'speculated,'" Aefric said. "And you tend to be precise with your phrasing, Elkari. Do you consider that speculation unconfirmed?"

"I believe that most theories I have read on the subject are too quick to attribute motivation to what might very well have simply been opportunity. That the arls fell to quarreling only a few years after the treaties were signed does *not* imply that those treaties were signed to *cause* those arls to fall to quarreling. The evidence presented in—"

"If I may raise a point," Beornric said, holding up a hand. Elkari nodded patiently. "What matters more here is that Princess Astrid raised the Drifa-Glodis War because she was confident we would see the Caiperas connection."

"That sounds likely to me," Elkari agreed, to general assent.

"Which, I'm sorry, makes its importance suspect," Garnotin said. "By now, Malimfar must have heard of the attempts on the lives of the royal family. As they were not behind those attempts, they would want to cast blame on Caiperas without looking like they're doing it."

"Caiperas *was* behind those attempts," Aefric said. "King Colm himself told me it was confirmed."

"But Malimfar doesn't know we know that," Garnotin insisted.

"His majesty has held this information close, the better to surprise Caiperas with vengeance come springtime."

"So," Beornric said, "you think they gave our duke land and a title as an excuse to make us worry about Caiperas? Seems pretty thin."

"No," Garnotin said. "I think they're worried about invasion from the north. I think that they heard about the assassination attempts while they were busy manufacturing all this."

He waved his hand dismissively at the evidence provided about Arl Reynar's conspiracy.

"They know they're the obvious target for retribution," Garnotin continued. "And they're trying to do everything they can think of to make us look elsewhere."

And Princess Astrid *did* mention Aefric's known enemy, Nelazzi, even though the pirate queen had been quiet of late. Ever since...

"Do you think Malimfar knows about the attempt on my life at Asarchai?"

"Did Princess Astrid mention it?" Garnotin asked.

"No."

"Likely not then."

"I agree," Beornric said. "She was obviously trying to get on your good side. If she knew about the attempt, she wouldn't have missed a chance to express her happiness that you survived."

The others all knocked the table in agreement.

Aefric considered all this through a sip of water.

"So you think Arl Reynar is just a scapegoat?" Aefric asked Garnotin. "That King Eadred knew exactly what was going on the entire time?"

"I do."

"And I agree," Yrsa said. "Raising and mobilizing armies of that size takes time, money and *land*. No way they weren't witnessed. And if the arls managed a conspiracy of this magnitude without their king finding out, then he has internal problems *far worse* than the threat of any invasion."

"Though they do have reason to worry about invasion," Beornric said. "After all, Duchess Ashling's preparing for war come spring, same as we are. And Malimfar's scouts have probably spotted that."

"What's more, officially, his majesty has been grumbling loudly about Malimfar."

That was from Aefric's seneschal, Kentigern, who sat at Elkari's right.

Hardly much older than Aefric, Kentigern was one of the rare Armyrian nobles with tanned skin. He wore a quilted, dark yellow tunic today, and brushed one hand down his long, thick, dark brown beard as he continued.

"Our king has been giving King Eadred good reason to worry."

"Thus," Aefric said, "gifts and an ambassador."

"And *this*," Yrsa said, waving one hand over the reputed evidence.

Most of the evidence, anyway. Somewhere down in the castle, Arl Reynar's head waited to be sent to Armityr along with the contents of that scroll case.

"Yes," Elkari said, practically drooling as she looked over those papers. "I trust I'll be allowed to study these papers in more detail?"

"Study *and* copy," Aefric said. "We'll send the originals to Armityr, but I want a copy in our archive."

"Thank you," Elkari said, bowing her head slightly. "I look forward to both."

"In the meantime," Aefric said, gesturing at the reputed evidence. "Surely some of this must be true. So the question is, how much of it can we trust?"

Elkari looked up, surprised. "Well, *none of it* of course."

That actually silenced the rest of the table for a moment.

"How, exactly, do you mean that?" Kentigern asked.

Yrsa scoffed, as though the answer was obvious.

"Well, these are reports written by an official enemy of Armyr," Elkari said, as though she couldn't believe she had to explain this to everyone but Yrsa and maybe Beornric. "Obviously we can trust only what we can verify. And as of now, I have had no opportunity to verify any of it. We must begin with the assumption that everything written here is mere propaganda, until such time as corroborating evidence proves that *any* of it is true."

"It doesn't matter anyway," Garnotin said.

"How do you figure?" Aefric asked.

"Doesn't matter *to us* if it's all a pack of lies," Garnotin said. "Any more than it matters if it's Taesark's own truth. What matters *to us* is what *his majesty* declares about it."

"And his majesty won't tip his hand about Caiperas," Beornric said, shaking his head. "Not anytime soon."

"I still need to know," Aefric said. "Regardless of his majesty's official stance. I'm one of their nobles now and—"

He grimaced and shook his head. "Gods, that's a strange thing to say. Does this mean Malimfar will expect oaths of vassalage? Are they expecting—"

"If I may," Kentigern said, before Elkari could get the words out. At Aefric's nod, Kentigern continued. "Your..." He cleared his throat. "You have the option of being involved in the running of the arldom, of course. But they do not expect you to do so."

"How do you know that?"

"Precedent. His majesty holds several minor titles in Rethneryl, and King Talesin of Rethneryl similarly holds multiple small titles in Armyr. They derive incomes, of course, from those lands. But they leave the rule to their castellans. Malimfar would expect you to do the same."

"This case is unusual though," Elkari said, clearly unable to hold back her words any further. "Such arrangements are typical only between staunch allies. Which phrase *might* have been stretched to include Malimfar once, but after Frozen Ridge..."

They were interrupted by a knock on the door.

"Didn't I say we weren't to be disturbed?" Aefric asked, honestly not sure he'd remembered to do so. He got a quick round of quiet agreement.

That meant the knock had to be important.

Aefric craned his neck to face the door behind him. "Come!"

Ser Leppina stepped in and bowed. "Your grace. We have received word that another royal ship has been spotted at Ajenmoor. Based on timing and speed, it's likely in the lake by now."

"Hatay, I expect," Kentigern said. "They always like to be first to arrive."

"Wait," Yrsa said, turning to Leppina. "You said 'been spotted.' But if the ship followed protocol..."

"General, it did not," Leppina said. "It sailed unescorted through the harbor and straight up the Searun. River patrol was dispatched to keep an eye on it at a discreet distance."

"Not Hatay then," Yrsa said, turning to Aefric. "Visits from Hatay have always followed protocol and gotten a proper escort."

Aefric nodded. Turned to Leppina. "What else did the message have to say?"

"The ship itself was said to be ... distinctive," Leppina said, frowning at the imprecision. "And the device on the flag it flew was the circle of nine white skulls, affrontant, on a black background. In this case, surrounding a crown, indicating royalty."

A chill washed down Aefric's spine. All around him, his advisers' eyes widened. The circle of nine skulls. That could only mean—

"The ship can only have come from Kefthal," Leppina concluded.

<hr>

THE SHIP FROM KEFTHAL WAS A HUGE, THREE-MASTED THING THAT looked large enough to transport a small army.

Its sails were black. Its hull was black. Its decks, its masts — all of them a flat, matte black shade that seemed to try to blend in with the rising dusk.

And yet, it could be seen clearly enough because it was limned in a faint, flickering purple glow. Likely related to how it moved so smoothly against the evening tides.

Magic. A lot of magic on that ship. Aefric — standing once more at the foot of the pier reserved for royalty — hardly needed to try to sense that magic lay thick about that vessel.

Made him feel a little better to have the Brightstaff in his hand. To have the area about him lit comfortably by a soft glow from the large yellow diamond embedded in its top.

"Heavily armed," Yrsa muttered about the ship, standing again at Aefric's left.

"With more than those ballistae and catapults, I'll wager," Beornric said, from Aefric's right.

The Knights of the Lake stood arrayed behind Aefric, but he'd refused to have more guards or soldiers than that. Despite protestations from both Yrsa and Beornric.

He didn't want to look as though he expected trouble.

Nevertheless, he'd ordered the harbor cleared, requiring all waiting ships to sail deeper into the lake for the night.

No point in unnecessary risks.

The oncoming evening had brought a chill with it. Or maybe that was just the thought of Kefthal coming for a visit. Certainly a prospect that tightened many of his muscles and sat uneasily in his stomach. No reason it couldn't chill the air, while in the area.

"They'll have no reason to use those weapons," Aefric said pointedly. "We're not at war."

"They're ruled by necromancers," Yrsa said. "And they openly practice not only necromancy, but necrophilia, cannibalism, slavery. They'll even tan the hides of anyone stupid enough to stand still long enough. Human, eldrani, whatever."

"I'm not contesting their reputation for evil," Aefric said. "But this is politics. I spoke to Princess Sorcha before the Feast of Dereth Sehk, after all. I can't refuse to speak with her now. Not unless you *want* me to start a war…"

"None of us want that," Beornric said. "But I do hope you won't be boarding this ship?"

"No reason I should have to," Aefric said.

"I don't like the precedent here," Yrsa said, frowning hard. Her main scar was a deep, angry red. "They're not a kingdom. They're not ruled by a monarch. I don't even know what you'd *call* the Nine Beyond Death. A council?"

"A loose political affiliation," Beornric suggested, but Yrsa pushed on.

"I don't like even *acknowledging* a princess—"

"Too late for that," Aefric said. "All I can do now is try to keep the situation from getting worse."

"And if this Princess Sorcha has come to visit? With hopes of marriage?" Yrsa demanded, turning to face Aefric. "You'll insult our allies if you allow it, and you'll insult Kefthal if you don't. Might as well insult them up front and have done with it."

"What if I can get through this without insulting anyone?"

Yrsa scoffed.

"At least Princess Astrid's already gone," Beornric said.

"I wish she wasn't," Yrsa said. "She and hers had to have seen these evil bastards coming in. If she were here, at least we could explain—"

"She'd get no explanation from me," Aefric said firmly, surprising both his flanking knights. "This isn't Malimfar business."

"So you'd let another kingdom think we're dealing with Kefthal?"

"What am I supposed to do?" Aefric asked. "Open fire on a ship flying a royal flag? Start a shooting war with a magic-thick country *just* to avoid a conversation?"

"You could turn them back," Yrsa said. "Refuse to see them. It's not too late."

"They've entered the harbor," Beornric said.

It was true, even now a pilot was guiding them through the reef. Aefric would have to see to it that this pilot was paid extra for his or her services today...

There was an eeriness to the air. As though the incoming ship oppressed noise into something like silence.

It wasn't true silence, though. Aefric could hear the breeze. Could hear the sounds of some late cargo getting offloaded hurriedly about five piers down. The sound of his own heart, beating a little harder now than it needed to. They way it used to sometimes, just before entering someplace he knew was dangerous.

And yet, all of these sounds *felt* muffled.

The ship pulled smoothly into the slip at the base of the dock, only a few dozen paces from where Aefric stood. With it came a whisper of cold power that carried the taint of necromancy.

Just enough to set the hairs on the back of Aefric's neck to standing.

The deck hands looked human enough, seen from a distance. But there was something off about them as they settled the ship. A strange precision to their movements, perhaps. Or maybe it was just that they worked in complete silence. As though they had another means of communication available to them.

Or as though they were guided by a single mind...

The gangplank was lowered, and hardly in place before the very human pilot came running down. Wild-eyed and slack-jawed, he ran straight past Aefric's little welcoming committee. Likely heading directly for the nearest beer.

The ship would need another pilot to take them back out. That one would need a bonus, too.

The sailors retreated from sight. Two knights emerged. Both clad in full plate armor of black steel, and wearing bat-winged helmets with the visors down. They took up flanking guard positions on the deck, at the top of the gangplank.

In a single movement, they drew greatswords from scabbards on their backs. All around him, Aefric heard swords loosened in scabbards.

"Steady," Aefric said softly.

Up on the ship, looking straight ahead into the distance the entire time, the two black knights lowered their naked blades until they held them point down, in both gauntleted hands.

Not offering any threat. But ready.

A man stepped forth between them. Bald of any hair at all. Not even eyebrows on his chalky, bone-white skin. He wore robes of bloodred, embroidered in gold. He carried an ebon staff in fingers that looked a little too long, and two wands in sheaths at his belt.

A powerful wizard, once more holding his power in check. As he had been when Aefric met him at Asarchai, where he'd carried a greenwood staff, and acted as herald for Princess Sorcha.

For Aefric recognized the feel of this man's power, as much as he recognized his look and his bloodred robes.

His name was Quintabis.

Quintabis descended the gangplank with unhurried steps. Once he reached the pier, he continued until he stood only a handful of paces from Aefric. Closer than form usually required, and Aefric felt a wave of uneasiness pass through his knights.

Quintabis bowed so low his forehead almost touched the smooth, dark red coral at his feet. When he came back up he smiled with an uncomfortably large number of teeth.

"Your grace," Quintabis said, in a voice so oily his words seemed to ooze. "We of Kefthal are pleased to see that the Duke of Deepwater has survived the attempt on his life, and indeed appears to be thriving."

Aefric managed not to ask how they knew about the attempt. But something of his surprise must've shown on his face, because somehow Quintabis' smile got even wider.

"We of Kefthal possess ... a great deal of experience at the art of haruspication. Foretelling an attempt on the life of a man so important as your grace was only too easy. More concerning was that our chief haruspex could not determine the outcome."

So Kefthal divined the future by reading entrails. Not very surprising, though Aefric chose not to ask what sort of entrails they used.

"So you claim you knew the attempt would happen at Asarchai?" Yrsa asked.

Quintabis bowed his head, and even that movement felt unctuous.

"And you chose not to warn us?"

"Are we allies then?" Quintabis asked. "For of course we would share such information with an ally, and would be wrong to withhold it." He tightened his focus on Aefric. "Were we wrong to withhold it?"

"No current alliance between Kefthal and Armyr exists to the best of my knowledge, Quintabis," Aefric said carefully. "I would have to consult my historian to learn if one existed in the past. As to the future, well, I claim no great skill at prognostication by any method."

"As is only fair," Quintabis said. "For your grace is known to have powerful gifts for many other kinds of magic. And as for the results of our own meager prognostications, those must be withheld to ourselves and our allies, by order of the Nine."

"Is it those prognostications that bring you here today?" Aefric asked.

"A clever question, your grace," Quintabis said with another smile that seemed to increase the number of teeth in his mouth. "For if I answer in either the affirmative or the negative, I provide information that I have just said we keep to ourselves, do I not?"

"Saying no doesn't tell us anything," Beornric said, frowning. "Unless you're trying *not* to say no."

"Ah, but I have already admitted that we of Kefthal have interest in the future of your grace," Quintabis said, turning that wide, wide smile back to Aefric. "Thus, even a denial of the question suggests something of the future, does it not?"

"Let me ask differently then," Aefric said. "What is it that brings the princess to my pier today?"

"Ah," Quintabis said, bowing, "and let me thank your grace for the kindness he shows in rephrasing his question. But alas, Princess Sorcha Diadiniu is not here. She is about an important diplomatic mission ... elsewhere. After all, what better ambassador to represent the Nine than their only princess?"

"If she's not here," Yrsa said, "why are you flying the royal flag?"

"Because I am about royal business at the bidding of my princess, of course," Quintabis said. "When your grace was good enough to speak with her only a few aetts ago, he was also kind enough to grant her permission to send a gift. I come bearing that gift on her behalf, along with her regrets that she could not present the gift herself."

Great. Aefric had forgotten that part of their conversation, but apparently Princess Sorcha hadn't. Well, as long as she wasn't giving him land and a castle. The last thing he needed was land in an evil place like *Kefthal*.

"Very well," Aefric said, with only a trace of hesitation.

"The gift is in two parts," Quintabis said. "Here is the first." He turned back to his ship and raised his ebon staff. A flicker of surprisingly warm power followed.

The spell was quick, silent, and inoffensive, but still, it felt familiar.

A type of message spell?

A moment later, a sailor emerged on deck, carrying a small chest in both arms.

A small chest? A gift of gold, maybe? Or a small work of art? Or...

No. It couldn't be.

Aefric muttered a quick prayer to Nilasah the Merciful that he wasn't being given two severed heads in one day.

DUSK WAS RISING. THE CHILL ON THE AUTUMN AIR WAS CORRUPTED BY A whisper of necromancy. The likely necromancer — Quintabis — stood right in front of Aefric at the foot of the royal pier at Water's End. Smiling that disturbing smile of his.

And a likely product of necromancy — a sailor — approached carrying a chest in both arms. The sailor wore rough clothes in dark shades. His hair and beard — both on the dark side of blonde — were unkempt.

He was also undead. There was no decay to his tanned, weathered flesh. No foul odor surrounding him. Nothing obvious to mark him as no longer among the living.

Still. The closer he came, the clearer Aefric could feel the cold necromancy animating the sailor's limbs. Putting something behind those eyes that wasn't life, but a mockery of it.

The sailor stopped beside Quintabis. Bowed to the smiling necromancer. Bowed to Aefric. Each movement unnaturally precise. Then, the sailor simply stood there, as though he would do exactly that until the end of the world.

"Would your grace care to open the chest and view his gift?" Quintabis asked. "I can provide complete assurance as to his safety."

Before Aefric could answer, Beornric said, "Wardius."

Ser Wardius stepped forward. Moved to take the chest from the sailor, but paused and looked to Quintabis for permission.

Quintabis spoke to Aefric. "Of course your grace is free to accept the gift through his knight. But I would ask that your grace open the chest in my presence. There are points about it that I must clarify, once he has seen what lies inside."

The sailor made no move to resist or assist when Wardius took the chest. As Wardius brought it to Aefric, the sailor turned and walked silently back towards the ship.

The chest's lid was hinged, but not locked. Aefric opened it.

Inside, another human head. This one on a pillow of red satin.

Unbelievable.

Aefric had somehow managed to go about twenty-five summers without anyone ever giving him a severed human head. And yet now it had happened twice in one day.

Was there something wrong with the way he was living?

Perfectly preserved without even a *hint* of pine resin odor, this head, Aefric recognized. Said the name without thinking.

"Calder."

Calder Ol'Ulith. Formerly Ser Calder, and formerly castellan of Water's End. Where he'd served faithfully for years — reputedly — before he began not only embezzling, but also informing for the pirate queen, Nelazzi.

He gave her shipping information. He kept her informed about private conversations with the ducal advisers. And he'd been doing these things since before Aefric was made duke. Years, at the least.

A traitor. Calder even freed the wizard Gwawl — an important confederate of Nelazzi's — from Aefric's prisons so the two of them could make good their escape. Literally hours before his treachery was discovered.

"That's right, your grace," Quintabis said. "The head of Ser Calder Ol'Ulith was not the present that Princess Sorcha had in mind, when she offered. However, Ser Calder—"

"Just Calder," Aefric said. "He betrayed his knighthood when he betrayed his oaths and his duties. He was no knight when he died."

"Of course, your grace," Quintabis said with a bow, and enough oil in his voice to make the entire Kerrik Forest a fire trap. "Calder Ol'Ulith came to our lands two aetts ago to negotiate on behalf of Captain Nelazzi."

"Won't your new ally take it amiss that her emissary didn't return?" Yrsa asked.

"We of Kefthal do not ally ourselves with pirates," Quintabis said, and for the first time his voice sounded firm, not unctuous. "We are scholars and artists. Dreamers and visionaries."

"Slavers and necromancers," Yrsa said.

Quintabis smiled his too-wide smile, but condescension filled his eyes. It vanished as he turned back to Aefric, his voice oily once more.

"What we do *within* our own borders is our own concern. But we of Kefthal do not invite trouble to our shores. Nor do we harass the sovereignty of other kingdoms. Nelazzi does both, and casts a wide net for enemies in the process."

Quintabis indicated Aefric with a bow of his head.

"Your grace is known to be opposed to Captain Nelazzi, and we of Kefthal consider it likely that he will seek to destroy her. Undoubtedly, those who harbor her will suffer in the process. Thus, we wish to assure your grace that she will not be found hiding on our shores. Nor will any of her confederates."

"Did your haruspex tell you this?" Aefric asked.

"We of Kefthal have many sources of information, your grace," Quintabis said with his widest smile yet.

"Well, thank you," Aefric said. "You've saved me the trouble of hunting this one down."

"I am prepared to do more than that on your grace's behalf," Quintabis said. "Should your grace wish to question Calder Ol'Ulith, I have been instructed to conjure his shade and bind it to this head.

Your grace could then question the traitor at his leisure, confident that the dead lips of Calder Ol'Ulith would be compelled to answer all questions with unvarnished truth."

Eww. Keep a dead man's head around? Ask it questions? The mere thought was enough to turn Aefric's stomach.

And yet...

And yet he had to admit that this could be a *significant* resource. The shade would possess fairly current information about Nelazzi's whereabouts and activities. Information that could help to hunt her down, stop her raids, save countless lives and livelihoods...

Aefric forced out a breath.

No. He could not do this.

It was true that there were many kinds of necromancy. It was even said by some that the healing powers of the clerics of Nilasah were a form of necromancy.

But this. This was disgusting. And wrong on every level.

Not to mention explicitly illegal in Armyr...

"No," Aefric said, disturbed to hear a touch of regret in his voice. "I appreciate the offer. But necromancy is illegal in Armyr, and I ... have qualms about the practice myself."

"As do many, your grace," Quintabis said, his voice practically dripping with reassurance. "But the offer stands, should your grace change his mind. In the meantime..."

Quintabis raised his ebon staff and loosed another likely message spell.

"May I present the second half of the gift from her highness."

Noise. Up on the deck. The eerie silence of that black ship was broken by the sounds of people. Living people. Lots of them...

Oh, gods. Surely this didn't mean...

Aefric could see them now. Mere shadows in the rising dusk, outside the radiance cast by the Brightstaff.

Two sets of shadows. One set with precise movements. Silent movements. Likely undead sailors guiding the living.

The other shadows, the guided. Life visible in their movements, even though they weren't much more than shadows yet.

He saw them clearer as they began filing down the gangplank, two abreast.

Aefric felt a cold twist in his guts.

Slaves. He was looking at slaves. Clad in roughspun. Wrists and ankles manacled, with just enough play for movement. Humans. Eldrani. Even a few kindaren. All of them young — though admittedly, it was tough to tell with eldrani — and likely still shy of the age of majority by a handful of years.

"When you say gift..." Aefric began, but let his sentence trail off when Quintabis moved his free hand to cover where his heart should have been, as though disturbed at the very idea behind Aefric's words.

"Oh, your grace must understand," Quinabis said quickly. "We of Kefthal know well his distaste for slavers and slavery. It was not the intention of her highness to make a gift of the slaves themselves."

"I'm afraid," Aefric said carefully, not quite trusting his voice past the anger burning its way up his spine, "that I'll need more of an explanation than that."

"Please do forgive me, your grace," Quintabis said with a bow. "I did not mean to obfuscate. When Calder Ol'Ulith came to our shores to negotiate on behalf of Captain Nelazzi, he brought with him a gift of one hundred eight slaves. Twelve for each of the Nine."

Quintabis waved his staff to indicate the slaves now forming ranks on the pier.

"Sorcha Diadiniu, daughter of the Nine Beyond Death and Crown Princess of Kefthal, presents those slaves to your grace that he might have the honor and pleasure of freeing them."

"Now *that* is a gift I can accept," Aefric said.

"Excellent," Quintabis said, smiling so wide his skull must've held three times as many teeth as a normal person's. "And in the interest of clarity, may I hope that these gifts today establish two things. The first, that Kefthal wishes no enmity with Armyr in general, nor with your grace in particular. The second, that we of Kefthal hold out hope that a lack of enmity today may lead to a friendship tomorrow. And perhaps, one day, to an alliance."

"I can make no such promises," Aefric said quickly. "Not for Armyr, certainly, nor even definitively for myself, here and now."

"Nor do I expect any, your grace," Quintabis said with a bow. "We of Kefthal, however, have the patience of eternity on our side."

The patience of eternity...

Quintabis bowed deeply then. "I have now accomplished the tasks set before me, and stand ready to sail at your grace's pleasure. I would not place your grace in an uncomfortable position by asking hospitality of him."

"That's kind of you," Aefric said. "Might I ask two questions before you leave?"

"Your grace may ask whatever he desires. I request only that he recognize that my position may require that some questions go unanswered."

"Of course," Aefric said. "But they relate to politics, and I think Kefthal will likely want to make some public statement about them."

Quintabis bowed, his expression curious as he straightened.

"Since it has no monarch, how is it that Kefthal has a princess at all? And which of the Nine could claim her as a daughter?"

"Ah," Quintabis said with a too-wide smile. "The Nine Beyond Death rule with the authority of any monarch, and thus have the right to designate their own inheritor. Which title, by tradition, is prince or princess, as appropriate."

"So she isn't really the child of any of the Nine?"

Quintabis chuckled, a sound that sent a shiver down Aefric's spine.

"Why, your grace. Princess Sorcha is the child of *all* of the Nine."

"But how..." Aefric didn't bother finishing the question. He could tell by the look on Quintabis' face that an answer would not be forthcoming.

He shook his head. "I suppose that's an internal matter to Kefthal, and none of my business."

"More direct that I would have said, your grace, but a statement accurate in its essentials."

"Are you one of the Nine?"

Quintabis laughed again, this time with actual amusement in his voice. "Oh, no, your grace. I am but a messenger. My magic compares to that of the Nine as a chill summer breeze compares to the icy heart of Nerrazz itself."

Nerrazz. The sixth and coldest of the Thirteen Hells. It was said that a small handful of ice from the heart of Nerrazz could turn all the scalding deserts of the Southern Wastes into frozen tundra so cold that even ice dragons could not live there.

Given what Aefric could sense of Quintabis' magic, if there was even a spark of truth to the comparison, the Nine had power beyond anything except perhaps Kainemorton himself. Possibly two or three of the Silver Arrows, the champions of Kalinda and arguably the mightiest mortals walking the face of Qorunn.

Power enough to obliterate Aefric, even with both the Brightstaff and the wand Garram in his hands.

So why was Kefthal so eager to make friends?

***

The Kefthali ship was only just departing dock when Aefric turned to his knights.

"Micham," he said, "bring me..."

Aefric's words trailed off as he spotted Garnotin approaching rapidly from the castle, with a squad of twenty soldiers armed with bows, spears, and in a few cases, lanterns against the risen dusk.

"Your grace?" Micham asked.

"A moment," Aefric said, but before he could say anything further, Garnotin called down as he approached.

"Your grace. What is happening? Why is that ship leaving? Do we need to close the harbor?"

"No," Aefric said. "Why would..." He realized the archers were fanning out and starting to nock arrows. "Stand down! Now! All of you!" He turned to Yrsa. "Take charge of your soldiers." He turned back to Garnotin. "What is the meaning of this?"

Yrsa strode forward, barking orders. Garnotin passed her,

approaching Aefric, and gestured at the assembled group of bound people as he closed.

"Those are clearly slaves, your grace, which means that the Kefthali ship is trafficking slaves in Armyrian waters. Royalty or no, we have to arrest them."

"They didn't come here to traffic slaves," Aefric said, struggling to keep his voice calm, but Garnotin cut in before he could continue.

"But with a ship that size, they could be carrying three or four hundred *more*." He frowned at the hundred eight people wearing manacles on their wrists and ankles. "Wait, how did—"

"*Stop*," Aefric said sharply. "And *listen*."

Garnotin suddenly seemed to remember whom he was speaking with.

"Of course, your grace," he said carefully. He bowed, but he looked suspicious. As though actually wondering if Aefric had just bought a bunch of slaves.

"According to the Kefthali messenger, these poor people were enslaved by the pirate queen Nelazzi. Nelazzi sent Calder Ol'Ulith to negotiate with Kefthal, and offered these poor souls to the Nine Beyond Death as a gift."

Garnotin's eyes widened.

"Kefthal refused Nelazzi, and apparently they wanted to prove that to me. So they sent me Calder's head" — he nodded to the chest still in Wardius' hands — "and the slaves he brought them."

"That's obvious enough," Beornric said. "They know you're going to go after Nelazzi. Don't want you poking around in their business."

"They gave you *slaves*?" Garnotin asked, and Aefric couldn't blame him for the disgust in his voice.

"Not quite," Aefric said. "Specifically, their Princess Sorcha wanted to give me 'the honor and pleasure' of freeing them. And there's certainly nothing illegal about freeing slaves."

"No," Garnotin said, frowning, as though still trying to find cause to arrest the Kefthali ship. "But considering that Kefthal is known to practice slavery, it *is* puzzling."

"I agree," Aefric said.

"Frozen Ridge," Beornric said. "We all know that Kefthal is evil. But they're a very practical kind of evil. And they've admitted they've been reading omens about you. Odds are they know your life was saved at Frozen Ridge by the direct intervention of Kalinda. And since they owe their lives to magic…"

"They'd want to make friends with someone touched by the goddess of magic," Aefric said. He nodded. "There's logic there."

"That Quintabis even admitted they play a very long game. If you could be a threat to them one day in any significant way, that could be enough reason to maintain a friendly stance, confident that you would die before the Nine will."

"But his grace is a *wizard*," Garnotin said. "He'll likely live for hundreds of years."

"Kefthal's rulers are known as the Nine Beyond Death for a reason," Beornric said. "Ask Elkari how long they've been around."

"The point is," Aefric said to Garnotin, "I appreciate your diligence. But I refuse to start a war by arresting a Kefthali vessel about royal business. Especially when I have no evidence that they've committed any crimes here in Armyr."

"So we're letting them leave?"

"We have more important things to deal with." Aefric called over to Yrsa. "Send one of those soldiers to fetch my seneschal and physician."

"Here, your grace," Bebara said, stepping out from behind the squad of soldiers and approaching quickly while Yrsa sent a runner for Kentigern.

A vibrant, older woman with long, steely gray hair, Bebara wore the yellow robes of her clerical order, complete with the hand-shaped symbol of Nilasah in the center of her chest.

"I took the liberty of bringing her along," Garnotin said. "Just in case she was needed."

"Well done then," Aefric said, then turned to Bebara. "These are one hundred eight people pressed into slavery. I want them checked over thoroughly before Kentigern gets their shackles off and finds them rooms and clothes. I want them as healthy as possible before they start their lives as free people."

Somewhere in there, Beornric must have walked over to the slaves. Because he called back, "These shackles. They're not locked."

"Good," Aefric said. "We won't need a smith then."

"Not good, your grace," Bebara said, shaking her head. Aefric followed her over to join Beornric beside the closest of the former slaves. A tanned young woman, human, who looked as though she'd lost all hope in life.

Garnotin joined them, while Bebara examined the shackles on the young woman's wrists, and then those on her ankles. Neither set were locked, and the flesh beneath showed no signs of struggle.

She looked into the young woman's eyes, then shook her head and clucked her tongue.

"I've seen this before," Bebara said softly. "The shackles are left unlocked to prove how completely a slave has been broken. Physically, any one of these people could free themselves anytime they want. But they no longer have the will to do it. They have no will to do anything but follow orders."

"What good is living like that?" Garnotin said. "It might be kinder to kill them."

"Kinder still to heal their minds. Make them whole again." Aefric stepped in close to Bebara, who was still looking into the young woman's eyes. He hoped she saw more life there than he did. "Can it be done?"

"It can," Bebara said slowly. "If done slowly and with great care."

"When can you start?"

"Oh, your grace," Bebara said, turning an astonished look on Aefric. "I could not begin to treat them all here at Water's End."

"Obviously I'll pay the cost of any rites needed, if that's the issue."

"Your grace is most generous, but the matter is not so simple," Bebara said patiently. "Great harm has been done to these people's minds, and the mind is a great deal more complex than the body. These people need peace. Quiet. Time. Care. With enough of these things — and the appropriate blessings of the Merciful One — they might again develop a sense of themselves as individuals, with their *own* thoughts, feelings and desires. Learn to understand again that they are more than just chattle to be used."

She gestured vaguely over her shoulder. "And they need all these things away from a bustling city and castle like Water's End. Which is just the sort of place these poor souls expect to be sent, to perform whatever duties would be required of them."

"Where then?" Aefric asked, not hiding his frustration. "Where *can* we get these people help?"

"My order has a large temple outside Lachedran, your grace," Bebara said. "The setting is bucolic. The pace much slower. And all the clerics, priests, novices, and dedicants of the temple will be able to contribute to their care."

She nodded firmly. "That temple is the best place for these people. And their best shot at recovering from what has been done to them."

"Good then," Aefric said, and turned to Garnotin, but Bebara interrupted with a tug on his sleeve.

"I'll have to be the one to take them there," she said firmly.

"Why?" Aefric asked. "Are you saying they'd be turned away without a cleric vouching for them?"

Bebara frowned. Huffed out a breath.

"No, your grace. But I still want to be the one to take them there. Slavery is a great sin in the eyes of Nilasah the Merciful, and I wish to personally escort these poor souls to where they can get the help they need. To consult with the high priest myself, and ensure that all will be done properly."

Bebara did something then that she rarely did outside of the most formal of circumstances. She bowed to Aefric.

"Please, your grace," she said. "Allow me this."

"Of course," Aefric said, understanding. He was tempted to go himself, but he couldn't. Not with more princesses inbound sometime in the next aett or so.

He turned to Garnotin.

"Oversee this in my name. Take the *Swift Wave*." Aefric jerked a thumb at the soldiers Garnotin had brought down with him from the castle. "Bring them along as escorts, if you like. But set out at once, and let no one impede you. Am I understood?"

"You are understood, your grace," Garnotin said with a satisfied smile and a deep bow. "And this will be my pleasure."

EVEN AFTER THE *SWIFT WAVE* SET SAIL FOR LACHEDRAN, ON THE NORTH shore of Lake Deepwater, Aefric's evening hardly felt less busy.

First, there was dinner with his court. Which inevitably led to a great many questions about the two royal vessels that had docked and left again, without any visiting royalty receiving hospitality, or even a proper reception.

Not to mention all the gossip and speculation about why this Princess Sorcha was giving their duke gifts. What she might want in return...

It didn't help that Aefric couldn't give his court a good answer about why Kefthal — arguably most evil country in all of Qorunn — wanted to make friends with him.

On the other hand, at least the lively conversation about Kefthal distracted the nobles from talk about the visit that wasn't a visit from the crown princess of Malimfar. And none of them seemed to have heard yet that he'd been given land and a title in the kingdom of their recent enemy.

They'd hear soon enough, though. They always did.

But long as dinner *seemed* to take, it didn't *actually* stretch into the late hours of the night. When dinner was over, there was still a good deal of work to do.

Kentigern and Yrsa could handle the arrangements for Ser Tohr's escort to Armityr — which would leave in the morning — but Aefric himself wanted to write the king about his visits from Malimfar and Kefthal. About the possibility that Maev was a hostage down in Varondam, even if they treated her as the visiting royalty that she was.

And Aefric wanted to explain about the arldom he'd been offered.

To go over the reasons his advisers had given for accepting it, as well as his own concerns about what it could mean for him to have a tie to lands in Malimfar. He made sure to include all speculations he could think of about why King Eadred was making this offer in the first place.

Of course, Aefric also tried to make quite clear that he accepted this gift only on the condition of being given royal permission to keep it. Further, that he was in no way assuming such permission would be forthcoming.

And as for Kefthal, Aefric wanted to make sure to play up Calder and the Nelazzi connection. She'd been denied a hideaway in one of the most dangerous places for Aefric to look. Surely that would help convince his majesty that Aefric should be given permission to hunt her down and end her threat before winter descended on the Risen Sea and made such a venture too dangerous.

Aefric even reminded his majesty that he possessed a bronze pendant that would guide him and the ship he sailed safely through Nelazzi's wards. But that the longer he waited to use it, the greater the chances that she would change her wards and render the pendant useless...

The letter took a long time to write. And multiple attempts.

It had to be finished that night, though, because it — along with the documents from Malimfar — had to leave in the morning with Ser Rondohal, who would commanding Ser Tohr's escort.

Aefric had several offices scattered throughout the Castle at Water's End. But he wrote that letter in the office on second floor of his apartments, up high in the main body of the keep.

It was a small, simple office, but private. And well furnished. A desk of expensive, red calinwood, burnished to show off its deep tones, but otherwise of simple design. Allowing the elegant wood to speak for itself.

The chair Aefric sat in matched the desk, but had been enchanted for comfort. He'd been told that past dukes and duchesses of Deepwater had conducted their most important private meetings in this office. Apparently they refused to face discomfort while making key decisions.

Logic he couldn't fault.

The floorboards in here were white oak. The walls and ceiling plastered and painted soft, Deepwater gray. No bookshelves. One cabinet — also red calinwood — containing various liquors and the goblets and cups that went with them.

The tapestries on the walls did not bear images. Instead they bore geometric designs in dark, comfortable colors.

The desk itself faced a large window with an excellent view of the night sky, and the huge lake down below. A view that included, when the sun was shining, the towering Threepeaks Mountains in the distance.

Like all of the rooms of the ducal apartments, this one was lit with the soft, gentle glow of old magic. There were no flowers in the room, but Aefric could faintly smell zinnias. How his servants managed that, he didn't know. He thought sometimes that servants had a kind of magic all their own.

Aefric was staring at the night sky and contemplating his fifth draft of that letter — all four pages of it — when someone knocked on his door.

A short, orderly knock, only just loud enough to be heard without demanding attention. Which meant the knocker could be only one person.

"Come in, Dajen," Aefric said.

Dajen, Aefric's chief evening valet, opened the door and entered. He stood tall and straight in his Deepwater livery. In fact, only his halo of snow white hair and the few wrinkles on his face admitted he was approaching his sixtieth year.

He bowed.

"Your grace asked me to remind him when Mistress Ettarma Al'Qarruq would be due to arrive."

"Is she here now?" Aefric asked, alarmed.

"No, your grace. But I have received word from the staff that she has drunk her nysta tea. As this means she should arrive shortly, I felt it best to warn your grace now."

Nysta tea. Aefric had already drunk a cup himself, could still taste a bit of its bitter tang on his tongue. But he was glad to hear she had drunk some as well.

Strictly speaking, only one of them *had* to drink it to prevent conception. But he always felt safer when both did.

The news made Aefric relax through a breath. He still had a few minutes yet.

Ettarma was visiting court from her family's lands near Ajenmoor. In theory, she was here negotiating trade deals with local artisans for her family's shipping company. But she was a bright, vivacious woman who fit in well at court. Very pretty, too, with her dusky skin, her long, dark brown hair, and her flashing hazel eyes.

She'd been here three days, but was already quite popular.

Dajen looked pointedly at Aefric's white silk shirt and black hose, his leather belt with its wand sheath.

"Will your grace be changing into more appropriate garb to meet his assignation?"

"I suppose," Aefric said with a frown, looking back down at the letter. "If there's time. I'm not sure this letter is ready for his majesty."

"If I may," Dajen said gently. "Your grace has had something of a day, even by his rather extraordinary standards. I think his majesty will understand if your grace's letter contains the occasional imprecise phrase or ill-chosen word."

Aefric sighed out a chuckle. "I suppose you're right."

He leaned down and signed the letter, then impressed it with his seal. He enclosed it in an envelope, which he then sealed formally with wax. He handed the letter to Dajen.

"Please see to it that this letter leaves in the morning with Ser Rondohol."

"Of course, your grace. Shall we now see about appropriate clothing?"

"Not yet," Aefric said. "There's one more matter I want to deal with first."

Dajen gave Aefric a patient, but curious look.

"A private matter," Aefric said.

"Of course, your grace," Dajen said with a bow. "Please do forgive me."

"Nothing to forgive, good Dajen, but do close the door as you leave."

"At once, your grace," Dajen said, doing just that.

Aefric cleared his thoughts through a quick breath, while staring out at the lake. One more breath, slower and deeper this time, and he turned to face south.

Didn't matter which direction he faced while he did this. But he liked the thought of looking towards Maev as he cast the spell that would carry his words to her, and hers back to him.

He didn't use it often, but he needed to cast it now, shifting his focus into the flow of Qorunn's magic, and whispering the key words of power.

The air about him shimmered slightly, waiting for him to speak.

"My sweet Maev. Malimfar accuses Varondam of conspiring with Caiperas against us. Claims they hold you hostage. Please be careful. I miss you terribly."

A rush of power as the words left, but the shimmer lingered in the air, waiting to bring Maev's answer to him. Perhaps twenty-five words spoken by her own lips. No more than that.

"Dearest Aefric. Naturally I'm a hostage. But don't fret. I know tricks they can't imagine. You guard yourself against foreign princesses. Our hunt isn't over."

Aefric smiled despite himself. "Our hunt." Her phrase for their mutual pursuit, couching them each as both hunter and prey at the same time.

In fact, the whole message was typical of Maev. Her droll tone, as though more concerned that some foreign princess would win Aefric's heart than she was about being held in Varondam against her will.

Of course, he wouldn't be surprised if she *could* simply leave, no matter how Varondam tried to keep her there.

She was an experienced forester, and she'd learned secrets from eldrani and kindaren foresters that no other human had been taught. At least, not that Aefric had ever heard.

Hells, not that Keifer had heard of, either. She even knew the Cat's Eyes. And according to the rules of all five editions of *The Torn Kingdoms*, that power was *exclusive* to eldrani foresters. Not something that seemed likely to change with the new, sixth edition.

Well, he'd warned her, and there wasn't much more he could do. Not unless he went to Varondam himself...

No. King Colm would be furious.

Maev could handle herself. And she had her great, spotted forest lynx, Sylkanis, with her. Between them, Varondam might not know what they were in for, if they tried to hurt her.

Oh, if they tried to hurt her...

Dajen knocked on Aefric's door.

"Yes?" Aefric asked.

Dajen opened the door enough to lean in. "I do apologize for disturbing your grace, but Mistress Ettarma has arrived."

"Well," Aefric said, shunting aside personal concerns through a deep, fast breath. It was time to play the duke again. "I guess I don't have time to change then. Please, Dajen, invite her up."

In many of the places Aefric had traveled during his adventuring days, a late night assignation would be an entirely private matter. No one else would need to know it was happening, and talking about it publicly could be considered bad form.

And if one of the parties involved were married, that could invite a whole *host* of problems.

None of this was true in Armyr.

Sometime back, Armyrian nobles had decided that jealousy and frustrated desire led to more political problems than land, gold and trade rights combined.

So they instituted what they called the "noble privilege." In brief, it meant that all Armyrian nobles — from the royal family itself to the least cousins of the most minor ler — were free to pursue the bliss moment together. Regardless of rank. Regardless of marital status.

So long as they weren't related by blood within three or four generations, they just had to noble, Armyrian, and willing.

That last part was important. There had to be mutual desire. Pressure was not allowed. No gifts could be offered or accepted. But where there was mutual desire, there was freedom to pursue mutual satisfaction.

Undoubtedly the advent of nysta tea had been a factor here.

The practice had even spread to the common folk. In most Armyrian cities and large towns, commoners had become as free with their sexuality as their nobles.

The dividing line, however, was kept clear. Nobles pursued the bliss moment with other nobles, and commoners with other commoners.

There was only one exception to this. The ancient custom of *leaba*, which referred to the pleasures of a bed mate, offered freely by a commoner only to a visiting member of the ranking nobility.

It had to be volunteered, not assigned or ordered. Gifts afterwards from the receiving noble were permitted, but not expected, and nothing that could be construed as payment was allowed. No coinage, for example.

The custom had fallen out of practice during the rise of the noble privilege, but had made a recent comeback.

So that Ettarma came to Aefric's rooms that night was not unusual. It was even expected. The whole court likely knew it was happening, and he was pretty sure that the moment she'd arrived, Yrsa and Beornric had placed bets about how long it would take her to find her way to Aefric's bed.

But what *was* unusual was that she didn't stay, afterwards.

Most women who joined Aefric for the noble privilege stayed the night. They wanted to pursue the bliss moment multiple times, bend the duke's ear about one matter or another — technically discussing business at such times was considered gauche, but it still happened — and, if his schedule allowed, to join him for a private breakfast the next morning.

Not Ettarma.

Once she'd had her bliss moment — fortunately a shared moment with Aefric — she'd slipped back into her dressing gown and cloak, kissed him goodbye, and returned to her own rooms.

It was all rather abrupt, really. One moment they were both naked and sweaty and smiling together, the next she was dressed and closing the door behind her as she left.

But after the day Aefric had had, falling asleep alone might not be so bad. He could stretch out in his own, comfortable, immense bed and nod off to sleep...

...only to be jerked awake by a rapid knock.

He woke so suddenly he called the Brightstaff to his hand without thinking, sitting up naked in the sheets.

Dajen entered, carrying a lit taper and an urgent expression.

"Your grace," he said. "I apologize for the disturbance, but we've had a rika. The *Laughter* has come up the Haven and passed Behal. It looks to be backed by unnatural winds, and should be arriving here shortly."

"The *Laughter*?" Aefric said, his mind trying to catch up with the adrenaline that had kicked his body awake. "But that's Ashling's personal ship. What's she doing here?"

"A question I have no doubt she will answer in short order," Dajen said, then spoke the word to light the room and extinguished his taper while turning towards Aefric's closets. "Awake in there! Your duke needs garb fit to receive a duchess."

Aefric used the butt of the Brightstaff to help untangle himself from the sheets, found his way to the edge of the bed, and got to his feet. The white maple floorboards were cold underfoot, even with a small fire going in the large gray stone hearth.

Focusing for a moment on the smell of hickory from the fire helped wake him up, though.

"Shall I awaken the court, your grace?" Dajen asked. "Offer her grace a formal welcome?"

"No," Aefric said. "She's arriving unannounced and... How late is it?"

"One bell past midnight, your grace."

"She doesn't want a crowd, then," Aefric said. "She wants to talk to me. Have Beornric and Yrsa meet me at the foot of the docks. And have Kentigern prepare her rooms, and see if any of the night staff would like to offer her grace *leaba*."

"I'm sure she'll have many volunteers, your grace."

"She always does. Kentigern may make the selection from among them."

"I'll see to it as soon as your grace is dressed."

"See to it now," Aefric said. "The other valets can get my clothes together."

"Of course, your grace," Dajen said, but he left through the closets, undoubtedly to issue quick orders to the other valets about what Aefric should wear to meet Ashling at this hour.

Aefric took a moment to cast a quick spell he'd cast many times over the years. As an apprentice, it had been an important time-saver. As an adventurer, it had been a public service. But as a duke, it was always a testament to hurry.

A cleanliness spell. Cast with little more than a gesture and a moment's concentration, it swept away all dirt and grime, as well as any traces of his earlier activities, leaving him clean and fresh head to toe.

Then he was ready to see what clothes his valets had selected for him.

The outfit was a good ensemble. A midnight blue silk tunic, embroidered in silver thread, worn under a black, velvet doublet. Black woolen breeches with silver-threaded stripes up the sides. Calf-high boots of thick black leather that matched his belt. And to top it all off, a midnight blue bycocket hat, with silver threading in the upturned brim.

Positively dashing.

Aefric took the hat in hand as he strode out onto his small, private floor balcony and took to the air. His apartments were high up in the main keep, and if Ashling was docking, he didn't want to waste time walking down flight after flight after flight of stairs.

He preferred a different kind of flight. The kind that allowed him to descend swiftly and smoothly, and land gently at the foot of the same pier where he'd spent so much time that day.

Ashling's ship had not yet reached dock, but Aefric could see it out in the harbor. A two-masted sloop. Swift and as elegant as its owner.

The harbor itself was otherwise empty. As ordered, all the other waiting ships were out in the lake for the night. Aefric could see their lights.

Along the docks, all was quiet. The ships more or less settled, and the only noise from them the occasional all-clear call of whoever watched them by night.

Beornric was catching his breath as he and Yrsa joined Aefric at the pier. He was wearing a rust brown tunic over dark brown hose. She wore dark orange over dark yellow.

"Honestly," Beornric said. "She couldn't wait for morning?"

"This is a bad sign," Yrsa said. "Anytime she comes this late. It's never good."

Aefric had only seen Ashling arrive late at night once before. At Behal, this past spring, when she'd heard that he'd captured Ser Grud Ol'Garan. She'd wanted to take him back to Fyrcloch for trial and punishment for his crimes against her duchy.

It was only the second time he'd met Ashling — the first had been brief, at the ceremony where King Colm had created him Duke of Deepwater — and their meeting that night had been rather tense.

Surely this one wouldn't be so bad?

AEFRIC WATCHED THE *LAUGHTER* DOCK BY MOONLIGHT AT THE FOOT OF his pier reserved for nobles and royalty. Ashling hadn't needed a pilot for this, of course. She'd been traveling to and from Water's End since long before he became duke, and her own pilots knew well the reef.

After that Kefthali ship earlier, though, there was something comforting about the noisy bustle of human and derekek sailors going about their work by warm, yellow lamplight.

No sooner had sailors lowered the gangplank than Ashling started down, flanked by Sirondfar and Ser Limic.

Ashling wore a fox fur cloak over a complex gown of dark reds and bright yellows. Her raven black hair was bound in a thick braid, likely against the unnatural winds supplied by Sirondfar, her ducal wizard. He was a *ventavis*, a specialist in the magic of birds and weather.

Sirondfar wore his usual robes in various shades of gray and carried a staff of gnarled oak. His long white beard had been braided, which was unusual for him, and his bald pate had been covered ...

...by a dark gray bycocket hat. Well. It seemed that Dajen and Ocheda had been right. If Aefric stared wearing hats, he would bring them back into fashion.

Ser Limic didn't seem to care about fashion trends. Even though her scalp had only a few gray hairs remaining, she wore them as proudly as she wore her slightly dented, well-polished full plate armor.

"Is it your doing?" Ashling called out in an angry voice as she stepped onto the smoothed, dark reds and greens of the coral pier.

"Is—" Aefric started, but Ashling continued talking even as her boots clicked a quick stride that brought her almost nose-to-nose with him. Her sapphire eyes dark with anger.

"Tell me truly, Aefric. Did you make this happen?"

"Did I make *what* happen, Ashling?"

Ashling leaned in closer still. Her eyes bore into his.

"Zoleen cried when she heard the news. Cried as I haven't heard her cry in *years*."

"Why would—"

"Yes, it's a magnificent opportunity. But the subtext came through *loud and clear.* So I need to know. Are you behind it?"

"Ashling," Aefric said, his own anger starting to rise now, "I don't know what you're talking about. Now tell me what made Zoleen cry."

"Your grace," Beornric said gently, addressing Ashling, "we've heard no recent news of your sister here at Water's End."

"You really don't know?" Ashling said, and she *was* nose-to-nose with Aefric now. Or as close as she could get, given the height disparity between them. But she was more or less chest-to-chest with him.

"Ashling," Aefric said, fighting to keep his tone even, "I swear I am at a complete loss about what could be upsetting you and Zoleen. But if I'm not told soon, you won't be the only angry person in this conversation."

Ashling frowned. Tilted her head and narrowed her eyes.

"I'm inclined to believe him," Ashling said, backing off a half-step. "Am I alone in this?"

"His puzzlement looks sincere to me, your grace," Sirondfar said simply.

"He *could* be a good liar," Limic said, her expression sour. "But I don't think he's *that* good a liar. He's likely telling the truth."

Yrsa scoffed. "If he were a good enough liar to fool *you*, Ash, those two would never spot him. You know he's telling the truth."

Yrsa? Speaking so familiarly with Ashling? Did those two have some history he didn't know about? If so, why did Yrsa always warn him not to trust the Fyrenns?

Or was *their* history that reason...

Ashling snorted softly, and quirked a familiar smile at Yrsa.

"You're right, Yrs, as usual," she said through a sigh. "Aefric, I'm sorry. It didn't seem like your kind of intrigue, but I could have been mistaken—"

"*What?*" Aefric snapped at her. "*What's* happened? *What* has you yelling *accusations* at me in the *middle* of the night on my own *docks*?"

Ashling raised her hands as though in surrender.

"I plead a sister's protective anger," she said. "Can we go inside and—"

"We're not going *anywhere.* Not until you tell me what's going on."

Ashling nodded slowly. "All right. I deserved that. We just received word today that Zoleen was named ambassador to Becheadam. With orders for her to leave at once."

Aefric frowned. "I don't even know where that is."

"North of Rethneryl and east of Shachan," Yrsa said. "They don't share a border with us."

"Good sheep country," Beornric said. "Decent mines for copper, tin and salt."

"And excellent musicians," Ashling said. "But all of that is beside the point. She's being shipped off, well away from *you*, Aefric. By order of the king himself."

Ashling shook her head. "She knew it too. Soon as she read the missive, she was inconsolable. Colm even specified that she leave 'at once,' precluding her stopping here to say goodbye. Went so far as to send a ship for her, kept waiting while she packed."

Understanding washed over Aefric and settled down, cold, in his guts.

"It's an important enough post that the queen can't complain—"

"Not in front of the court, no," Ashling said. "But Eppi's giving Colm an earful behind closed doors. I guarantee it. No way this is intended to do anything but remove our sister from contention to be your bride."

"Wait," Aefric said. "Why would you think *I* had anything to do with it? Zoleen and I have been getting along great lately."

"When last she saw you, yes," Ashling agreed. "But that was more than an aett ago. For all we knew down in Merrek, Byrhta Ol'Caran has been in your bed since you got back. And a woman like her could talk someone into almost anything."

By the small smile suddenly playing about her lips, it seemed that once more the topic of Byrhta Ol'Caran had distracted Ashling.

"I haven't seen Byrhta since I got back from Netar," Aefric said quickly. "She's been busy helping Vercy prepare Riverbreak for its harvest festival."

"She's not coming here for the festival?" Ashling asked. "I was sure she'd use it as an excuse to come visit you."

"Byrhta is coming," Aefric said. "But Vercy's staying there and overseeing Riverbreak's festival herself."

Ashling nodded approval, then gave Aefric a considering look. "Byrhta Ol'Caran is doing quite well for you as baroness regent, isn't she? She'll have Vercy Ol'Karmak ready to become a strong vassal for you. Won't she?"

"She's doing an excellent job," Aefric said, not hiding the admiration in his voice. "Even found good conditions for growing nysta tea. From what she says, their crop will rival Motte's in a few years. Should be a real boon for Riverbreak's economy."

Ashling laughed.

"Ah, well," she said, clapping Aefric on the shoulder. "Perhaps it's just as well that Colm is sending Zolly away. I don't think any woman but Maev could win you over Byrhta Ol'Caran. Can't blame you, either. I'd love to tumble her myself."

"All right," Aefric said, cutting off Ashling before she started waxing poetic about Byrhta's beauty again. "Let's get you and yours inside and situated for the night."

The distraction didn't work. Ashling went on about Byrhta's beauty the entire walk.

SLEEP. IT'S SUCH A LOVELY LITTLE WORD.

Back when Aefric was an adventurer, sleep was often risky. Done out in the open, or among whatever cover he could find.

At least, in the early days. Later, he learned spells to see about his safety. From weather. From being spotted by predators, both natural and otherwise.

Even so. Sleep back then wasn't truly safe. His magic only did so much to abate the risk level. Too many creatures and other threats had senses he couldn't account for or overcome. Or they had counter-magic that could sniff out the spells he used to keep himself and his fellows hidden.

Even with his magic, every night in the wild meant a turn in the watch rotation. And what sleep he got was often fitful, because he knew in the back of his mind that he might need to snap awake and fight for his life at a moment's notice.

Not quite a *regular* occurrence, but not all that infrequent, either.

Even on those occasional nights at inns, along roadsides and passing through towns. When he got to enjoy an actual bed, instead of a bedroll on hard ground. Even then he couldn't risk sleeping *too* deeply. There were often thieves about who loved to prey on "rich" adventurers.

Not to mention that some of his old traveling companions — especially Lauszen, that great oaf — had a knack for finding fights at the *worst* hours of the night...

Aefric's adventuring days were behind him now. As duke, he had a better bed every night — even while traveling — than he ever got to enjoy as an adventurer. Not to mention regular company in that bed, and more than enough protection to make sure he felt safe and could sleep deeply.

And yet, there were times like this one.

When he found himself awake, in the small hours of a chilly autumn night. When the breeze smelled like rain to come. Brightstaff in hand, as usual. Clad in nothing but a thin, white linen dressing gown, soft leather sandals, and a soft, gray, woolen cloak. Pacing the wide expanse of his public floor balcony.

He took a break from pacing to stand at the rail. Stared up at the stars while they played hide and sneak behind wisps of speeding clouds.

He *should* be sleeping. But he couldn't. Not now that he was awake again. Not while his mind was trying to puzzle through the strangeness of his day.

Zoleen. Sent off to play ambassador. A woman not a full year into her majority. Were she not from a family so old and steeped in politics, the mere *assignment* of her to a post like this would be scandalous. Possibly even insulting to Becheadam.

But she was a Fyrenn. So the assignment was nothing more than a compliment from the king to her savvy, despite her youth. And a message to Becheadam that they rated an ambassador from an important family.

In that sense, it was an astute move on his majesty's part. The sort that should have pleased Queen Eppida ... Ashling ... really, the whole of the Fyrenn family.

Except that Ashling was right. His majesty was clearly trying to make sure that Aefric didn't marry Zoleen. Without taking so blatant a step as forbidding it.

The question was *why?* Was this part of the power game their majesties were playing? Because they *were* playing one. That had become clear recently when Aefric officially claimed his secondary post as Baron of Netar.

The way Aefric had handled the problem of borogs in Netar's mines had been a victory for the king and a loss for the queen. That much was clear. Even if Aefric didn't understand how or why it was true.

From what he could figure out, the king had gained because Aefric hadn't killed the borogs. Instead he'd won their leadership through trial by combat — without killing his opponent, Lo'kroll — and escorted them back to Deepwater, to join his clan, mining gold in the Dragonscar.

And how strange was it that Aefric was *chieftain of a borog clan* these days? Clan Thunder Stick. Not exactly something he could have seen coming, when the king named him Duke of Deepwater.

So through Aefric's actions, the king had gained a victory at court, and the queen had lost. And apparently, his majesty was flexing some of ... whatever kind of capital he'd gained ... by sending Zoleen away. Undoubtedly over the queen's objections.

Was he removing Zoleen as a potential distraction, before the coming princesses reached Water's End? Trying to ensure that Aefric's inevitable marriage would strengthen an Armyrian alliance?

A thought to make him sigh. Princesses. Two coming from Rethneryl. One from Hatay. One from Shachan. And Maev, down in Varondam.

How safe was she really? And—

"Your grace?" Dajen's voice, from the balcony door. Somehow he knew exactly how loudly to pitch his voice so that his words would be audible, but not intrusive.

Even with the slight breeze. A good dozen paces away, on the other side of the greenwood patio furniture that Aefric was coming to love.

Dajen's words were *just* loud enough to get his attention, without a sense of intrusion.

"Yes, Dajen?" Aefric asked, turning.

"Duchess Ashling is at the door, seeking admittance."

Of course she was.

"Fine," Aefric said with a sigh. "Show her into the sitting room, offer her refreshment, and ask her to wait while I don something more appropriate."

"If I might ... your grace's current attire is a suitable match for that worn by her grace."

"She came here in a dressing gown and a cloak?"

"She did, your grace."

"Did she say what she wanted?"

"Your grace ... given her choice of garments, she certainly appears to have come for the obvious reason."

Aefric frowned. "Ashling prefers women."

"She does, your grace," Dajen said with a nod. "And yet, in all my years as valet, I have only ever seen a man or woman come to these rooms clad in such a fashion when exercising the noble privilege."

"Still..." Aefric said, then sighed again. "No. I think she's dressed like that to tease me. I guess I wasn't good enough sport earlier when she was going on about Byrhta."

"Shall I refuse her admittance, your grace? Tell her that your grace is about his meditations?"

"Thank you for the offer," Aefric said with a grin, "but no. She's leaving in the morning. If she's here, there's something on her mind. And I doubt it's the bliss moment."

"I shall admit her as your grace instructed then," Dajen said with a bow.

"No," Aefric said, smiling. "I have a better idea."

ONCE DAJEN HAD GONE BACK INSIDE, AEFRIC TOOK FLIGHT. A QUICK
trip through the brisk night air up to his private floor balcony. A fine
little balcony in its own right. Perhaps even more elegant, with the
engravings on the greenwood furniture even finer than those on this
balcony's larger cousin downstairs.

Too small, though, for proper pacing as he'd been doing earlier.

In quickly through the glass doors, across the sitting room and
into his bedroom. A bedroom larger than the common rooms in most
inns he'd stayed at, back during his adventuring days. With furnishings that cost enough to purchase a small town.

The fire still crackled merrily in the hearth, lending the slight
scent of hickory to the air.

His bed had been made, of course. Even though it had probably
taken a team of three to make a bed that big. Could easily have slept
five, with some room to spare. But the vast comforter, a dark red with
gold trim, looked so smooth Aefric might never have been to bed
tonight.

At the bed's foot, Aefric had a magically locked chest, given to him
by Kainemorton, that stored those few things he'd brought with him
from Keifer's life on Earth.

He stood the Brightstaff beside that chest, and mentally
commanded it to remain there until called.

The staff had a habit of following him sometimes, when he wasn't
carrying it. In fact, more than once it had followed him while his
unconscious body was being moved.

He smiled at the sight of it there.

He messed up the bed. Yanked down the comforter and silk
sheets. Beat the pillows and moved a couple of them about as though
he'd tossed them in his sleep.

Aefric looked over the carnage with a critical eye. Adjusted a
couple of details.

He never expected Ashling to see the bed, of course. No. Pretending to come for the noble privilege, that was just a game on her part. Possibly even less about Aefric himself, than about getting his court talking about the two peers of the realm, chasing the bliss moment together.

Just the sort of thing she'd do. And definitely the sort of gossip his court would *feast* on.

The noble privilege between a duke and various ladies of his court? That was so commonplace as to scarcely rate much conversation, unless something about the event made it remarkable. If the woman was someone considered to be a bridal candidate, for example.

But for a visiting duchess to go to the duke for the noble privilege? Well. That hadn't been seen in Deepwater since...

For that matter, Aefric didn't know if it had *ever* happened in Deepwater.

Certainly the old duchess, Arinda Soulfist, hadn't particularly gotten along with Ashling.

So Ashling's whole point of coming to his apartments, clad in nothing more than a dressing gown and cloak, that *had* to be to get the court talking about them. Possibly to have them *still* talking about it when the princesses began to arrive...

Either way, the private sitting room was only a door away. If he left the door open, she might see the state of his bed. Might even believe she'd roused him from sleep. Should help the deception.

He crossed next into his bath room. Even that room was larger than any *two* of the old rooms he used to rent in inns, back in the day. And the bath room was all gold-veined white marble, including a tub so large Aefric sometimes thought it could fit half the court at the same time.

He'd already cleaned himself magically. But there was one advantage to washing his face with warm water from the silver basin. That he could then dry his face roughly. Or as roughly as he could, given the soft, Deepwater gray towel that hung nearby.

With any luck, he'd look sleep-warmed.

Into the immense clothes closet next, with its many, many racks and cabinets and drawers full of outfits and accessories.

When Aefric spoke the word to light the room, he startled awake the two young valets on duty — Tattur, a gangly young man, and Kitturea, whose hands always lingered when she dressed him. Both had clearly thought they were done for the night and gotten comfortable on their stools.

"Alas," Aefric said, affecting a sleepy tone. "If I have to wake up for the duchess, so do you."

"At once, your grace," Tattur said, jumping to his feet and almost missing.

"Ready, your grace," Kitturea said, also jumping to her feet, though with a little more grace.

"Take care of this for me, will you?" Aefric asked, tossing Tattur his cloak.

Tattur frowned. Likely wondering why his duke had been sleeping in a cloak. Or perhaps he was just sleepy. Either way, he nodded and did as he was asked.

"I need you to comb out my hair," Aefric said to Kitturea. "Get the knots and kinks out of it, but leave it slightly mussed."

"For a good, bedroom look," Kitturea said with a wink. "I understand, your grace."

While Kitturea fussed with his hair, Aefric kicked off his sandals, which got another frown from Tattur, who then shook his head.

Apparently he'd decided that whatever his duke was up to was not his problem to puzzle over.

Once Kitturea finished his hair, Aefric stood and examined himself in the mirror. Face still slightly flushed. Hair just a little messy. He nodded. Turned to Kitturea.

"What do you think?"

"Were your grace a visitor to Water's End, I'd be first in line to offer him *leaba*."

Tattur winced as though Kitturea had crossed a line. And it was true that Aefric had never heard any of his own servants reference *leaba* that way.

"You're too kind," Aefric said, nodding, but not meeting her eye. Just in case.

Kitturea made a sound as though she were about to say something more, but Tattur coughed and cleared his throat.

Aefric made a show of looking himself over in the mirror one more time to give them whatever moment they needed.

He nodded.

"Good enough," he said. "Wish me luck."

He gave them a quick smile then, and went to meet Ashling.

Aefric's private sitting room, here on the second floor of his Water's End apartments, was lavish.

Not just white maple floorboards, but jewel-toned carpets on those floorboards. Carpets so soft and plush that his bare toes sank into them. Just walking on them relaxed muscles he'd forget were tensed.

Two couches and a single chair, all facing the large hearth — currently blazing, and filling the air with the homey smell of cherry wood — with the couches angled to make the chair their vertex. All three were padded enough to sink into, and upholstered in dark, hunter green. The couches were even long enough to sleep on, which Aefric had done once after a late-night meeting with his advisers.

Ashling sat on the couch that faced him as he entered the room. Her bare feet were curled underneath her, showing off the impressive body barely concealed by the thin, pale blue linen of her dressing gown. She'd doffed her cloak, and left it folded over the back of the chair.

Her sapphire eyes sparkled in the firelight as she smiled at Aefric across a crystal goblet full of emerald green sharabi. A variety of wine whose taste varied with a number of factors. Aefric knew already that the taste of this vintage would be mint, but not too sweet. Exactly what he'd told Dajen to provide.

The bottle, and Aefric's own ready goblet, waited for him on the triangular table of red calinwood that sat between the couches.

Aefric noted that his goblet was positioned for him to sit *beside* Ashling, not across from her.

"Aefric," she said softly, raising her goblet to him. "A pleasure, as always."

She seemed to realize then that he wasn't carrying the Brightstaff. Her eyes widened the barest bit.

Aefric picked up his goblet as he sat beside her. Raised his in toast. "To pleasures yet to come."

Ashling's eyebrows went up a fraction, but her smile didn't waver as she raised her drink to confirm the toast. She drank with him.

"You remembered my favorite vintage," she said.

"Of course."

"And you meet me without your fifth limb in hand."

"I don't carry it for everything," he said, letting his voice get low and intimate.

"I could blush," Ashling said softly.

"Now *that* I would count an accomplishment." He leaned a little closer.

"And what would you do to see me blush?" she asked, her own voice getting more intimate now.

"What would it take?"

"Telling you would be cheating." She shook a finger at him gently.

"I guess I'll just have to experiment until I find what works," he said, letting his voice get breathy now. Leaning closer still.

"I look forward to it," she said, and closed her eyes as their lips got closer.

At perhaps a fingerbreadth apart, Aefric stopped moving. Was she just going to let him kiss her? Had she *actually* come here for the noble privilege?

Wait. When had she opened her eyes again?

Then Ashling was laughing and backing away.

"Oh, Aefric, teasing you is no challenge at all."

"You were going to let me kiss you," he accused.

"Of course," she said, shrugging one shoulder through a curtain of raven hair. "Why shouldn't I be curious? Zoleen certainly seems to enjoy it." She frowned. "Not that she'll get to again. Not anytime soon. Damn Colm anyway."

"So you're telling me you *did* come here for the noble privilege?"

She laughed again. "I should say yes. I really should."

"And if I took you up on it?"

"Then I'd find out if Zoleen was telling the truth about you," she said shrugging again. "Personally, I suspect her feelings for you colored her experience." She quickly lifted a forestalling hand. "Not that I doubt you're a perfectly competent lover. For a man."

Aefric refused to rise to the bait that time. Sipped his sharabi instead while giving her an irritated look.

Ashling had the gall to laugh again.

"Honestly, Aefric," she said. "Simply too easy. And you should have *known* I didn't come here for the noble privilege, even dressed like this."

She gestured to her dressing gown, and Aefric declined to look as she did so. He could already see all too well how enticing the view was. He didn't need a close-up.

Then he realized what she meant.

"You came alone," he said.

"Very good," she said, nodding approval. "I told you that when I came to you for the noble privilege, I'd bring a woman for us to share. Although seeing you like that" — she nodded to him — "any woman would be tempted. Your shining hair organized but still tousled. Your skin warmed by sleep. Your lean muscles teasing me from behind that thin curtain of fabric..."

She made a show of looking him over with enough heat in her eyes that he needed to concentrate not to rise to the occasion.

She snapped her fingers. "I actually thought that would work. I should have remembered that you magic-users all need wills of iron."

"Maybe I just don't find you that appealing."

She gave him a droll look.

Aefric held a straight face.

Held it.

Held it.

They both burst out laughing.

"Come, come," she said, still laughing. "Let's not play *that* game. You are certainly one of the most handsome men in all Armyr. And I, I am the most stunningly beautiful woman this side of Byrhta Ol'Caran."

"If I agreed with that," Aefric said, "Zoleen would never forgive me."

"No," Ashling said simply. "She wouldn't. And as poor Zolly is having a hard enough time right now, I won't ask you to confirm what we both know is true."

"Ash," he said, "since you haven't come here for the noble privilege, why *have* you come?"

"Because I can't sleep. Obviously. And I knew that if you were the man I believe you to be, you wouldn't be able to sleep either. Not after what I'd told you."

"So you refused your *leaba*?" Aefric said. "You *are* upset."

"Of course I didn't," Ashling said. "She's enjoying a bath in that marvelous tub in my rooms. I must say, I had my troubles with the Soulfists over the years, but Deepwater hospitality has always been exemplary."

Ashling smiled a very different — and far more sincere — kind of interested smile. "Oh, how her soft skin will taste of lavender and hyacinth."

"Are you sure you don't want to get back to her?"

"Let her enjoy her bath while I enjoy the anticipation," Ashling said, regaining her focus. "I wanted to ask, though. Did Colm say anything to you when you last saw him? About marriage, perhaps? Anything that makes sense now that you know what he's done to Zoleen?"

The king did promise him a gift of thanks. Nothing too overt. Could it be this?

No. The only time Aefric had ever discussed Zoleen with the king, neither one of them had said anything that could have led to her being sent away...

Aefric shook his head and sipped his sharabi.

"Honestly, no," he said. "I know he and the queen were enmeshed in some kind of power game, and he won when I brought Netar's borogs to join my others in the Dragonscar, rather than killing them."

"Netar's borogs," Ashling said, frowning for a moment before realization set in. "Wait. The problem in Netar's mines was *borogs*?"

"*You* knew?" he said. "Did everyone else know Netar's mines were having problems? *I* didn't find out until I got there."

"Colm's childish idea of a surprise, no doubt," Ashling said with a grimace. "If I'd known you were kept in the dark about it, I'd've told you. Once he named you baron, you had every right to know."

Of course, that didn't answer the question of how *she'd* known. But he probably wouldn't get that answer out of her anyway.

Instead he settled for answering her question.

"It was borogs, all right. Not many of them, either. About two score. Refugees from a number of different clans, all broken by the Godswalk Wars and united as Clan Blood Stone under a leader named Lo'kroll. They'd gotten into Netar's mines following the scent of a gold vein."

Ashling raised a skeptical eyebrow. "They can *smell* gold?"

"I've witnessed it," Aefric said with a nod. "From about as far away as I could smell frying bacon."

"And one vein of gold was enough for them to dig in and fight over?"

"Borogs consider gold divine. Their word for it translates as 'god metal.'"

"Borogs," Ashling said, shaking her head. She scoffed. "I can't believe she bet against *you* about *borogs*. Honestly."

"Did I miss something here?" Aefric asked.

"Do you have siblings, Aefric?"

"No," he said, then crinkled his brow, thinking back to his youth. "Well, not really. I was orphaned on the streets of Sartis. So, no blood siblings that I know of. But in a way, all the other orphans were my siblings."

"Are you still in regular contact with any of them?" she asked, positively radiating irritation. "Would you stand by them, even when they act the *complete* fool?"

Aefric gave Ashling a moment to compose herself, before answering her question. He enjoyed a little more of the sharabi's cool, mint taste. Crisp, this bottle. Quite refreshing, considering the late hour.

Then he answered.

"Haven't seen any of them since Karbin first took me on as apprentice."

"Then they don't count," Ashling said. "And you're just as well off. They never listen. Oh, they'll *ask* your advice. But then they'll just do whatever the hells they want anyway."

Aefric thought about interjecting here.

"If they'd only *listen* to me. Zoleen might be your bride by now. And Eppida's position at court would be…"

She frowned. Shook her head. Sipped some more sharabi.

"I'm sorry, Aefric," she said. "You don't need to listen to me rant."

"What are friends for?" he asked.

Ashling startled a moment, then smiled at him.

"To be honest, I don't know. I'm not sure I've ever really had one before you. Allies, yes. Toadies, certainly. Enemies, I'd rather not number them. But friends, those have always been in short supply. I'm not sure what the protocols are."

"Well," Aefric said, refilling their goblets, "I think you can guess most of it. But in case you aren't certain, friendship does involve listening to each other's problems, even if only to provide a friendly ear."

She snorted a soft laugh. "I was raised to believe that anyone you tell your problems to will use them against you."

"That's a sad, sorry way to live," Aefric said.

"Yes," Ashling said, then shook her head. "But it's safer. And there's value to that, when you're a noble."

"Then stop worrying about being a noble for a little while," Aefric said. "Just sit and drink and talk with your friend."

"All right," she said. "I'll try."

Aefric and Ashling stayed up far too late that night, but it couldn't be helped.

Now that she had license to discuss her problems without fear, Ashling went on at some length about issues among her vassals. Who was holding back troops or taxes or niggling over details in trade agreements. And even worse, which ones were already jockeying for position when it came to gains in the coming war with Caiperas.

A war that wasn't likely to happen for half a year, with uncertain results. And yet, they were assuming victory and that Ashling would be given disbursement of some of the lands and titles Armyr might gain.

"And with all of this going on," she added, "I have to drop everything and leave tomorrow for Caiperas."

"Ooh, yes," Aefric said, wincing. "That part I did know about. It was actually my idea for Armyr to send a peer to treat with Caiperas about planning our supposed mutual invasion of Malimfar."

"It's *your* fault, is it?" Ashling said, reaching out and poking him with a bare toe.

She'd gotten quite comfortable on the big, deep couch. Between the hearth warming the room and supplying the pleasant scent of cherry, and the sharabi providing light, cool, minty refreshment, she seemed more at ease than Aefric had ever seen her before.

Perhaps talking about her problems had been good for her.

"I'd suggested sending Wylyn, so that he could sell that you were busy preparing your end of the invasion."

"Wylyn's good for this sort of thing, but I'm better," Ashling said simply. "Let me guess. Eppi pushed for me and Colm readily agreed."

"He did. He said the plan would benefit from your touch."

"He knows how to play the game," Ashling said in an admiring tone. "I'll give him that."

"Didn't realize you had to leave so soon," Aefric said. "I mean, I know your ship leaves *here* in the morning, but—"

"Afraid you'll miss me, Aefric?" Ashling said, teasing her toes on his thigh. "I was supposed to leave today. But I couldn't. Not without ... well, I think deep down I knew you weren't behind it..."

"It's all right," Aefric said. "I'd rather hear the news from you than some other traveler. Even if you were a bit heated when you told me."

"Zoleen should've gotten to tell you *herself*," Ashling said bitterly. "She should've gotten to come see you. At least gotten to tumble you one more time before being exiled to that land of mountains and sheep."

"It *is* a good post, though, isn't it?"

"Yes, yes," Ashling said with a sigh. "It's a tremendous compliment to her and to the Fyrenn family. And it'll help her build her own name and reputation and influence. And damn Colm for thinking of it."

She poked Aefric with her toes again. "I'd much rather see Zolly make you part of the family than run off and play ambassador."

Aefric wasn't sure how to answer that, but she poked him with her toes again while sipping sharabi. "You *would* have, wouldn't you?"

"Would've what?" he asked carefully.

If Ashling noticed the caution in his voice, she didn't show it.

"Bedded her one more time. If she'd been the one delivering the news, not me."

"Yes," Aefric said sincerely. "Absolutely."

"Damn you, Colm," she whispered, then shook her head. "Let's have a change of subject. What problems do *you* need to grouse about?"

Aefric told her about his day. About Malimfar and his new arldom and their accusations about Varondam and Caiperas. About Kefthal and Calder and Nelazzi.

The news about Kefthal didn't disturb Ashling nearly as much as it had Aefric.

"It's a common tactic," Ashling said, pillowing her head on the padded arm of the couch now. A pose that made her long throat entirely too inviting.

Aefric shook away the thought.

"When a conflict between two powers is coming," she continued, looking at the ceiling, "those with the wit to foresee it either pick an ally — if it will profit them — or remove themselves from the field. Where they can watch from safety, and take advantage of the results."

"So you disagree with my advisers that this means Kefthal is concerned about me?" he asked.

"You're the type who makes friends as well as allies," she said with a shrug. "That makes you dangerous. Because when something happens to a man like you, others will come to investigate. Far less trouble to keep away from you."

They discussed that possibility for a while. Even tipsy on sharabi, Ashling displayed an intellect that could have made her a mighty wizard. If she'd ever chosen to go that path. Of course, in her own way, she was a wizard of politics...

The Malimfar situation she found more concerning, but not for the reasons Aefric expected.

"Of course they're worried about invasion," she said dismissively. "That just means Colm's plan is working. He's complained about them at length, in public, and their scouts see my armies gathering and training, as they're meant to."

She shook her head. "No, that's to be expected. Even giving you some land is just setting a small, controlled fire in a forest, hoping to prevent a wildfire claiming it all." She frowned. "But what they're saying about Caiperas. *That's* disturbing."

"Not Varondam? Even though they're holding Maev?"

"Aefric," she said, drawing out his name and rolling her eyes. "Right now Maev is their hostage the same way I'm *your* hostage."

"But—"

"I'm important enough to worry about, and I'm here. If you decided to keep me here — say, pending Merrek ceding something to you — I'd be hard pressed to refuse you."

"But—"

"Of *course* you won't do that. It's not done. And Varondam won't do it either. Because if they did, no matter what concession King Dalius *thought* he could get from us, he'd be making us his enemy. More importantly, he'd be *murdering* his marital prospects. No other princess worth marrying would visit Varondam for *generations*. He'd either have to humiliate himself by marrying down, or his line would end with *him*."

She patted Aefric's thigh with her foot. "I'd say King Dalius is more concerned about his legacy than some small, immediate gain."

Aefric's turn to frown. "Then why did Maev confirm to me that she's a hostage?"

"She..." Ashling chuckled. "Ohhhhh. You keep in touch with her by spell, don't you?"

"Only now and again."

"Clever boy, keeping yourself in her thoughts." Ashling patted his shoulder with her foot, exposing entirely too much leg in the process for him not to notice. "And clever girl, keeping herself in yours. After all, King Dalius might not be much competition for *you* — apart from his title, of course — but Byrhta Ol'Caran—"

"Ash?" Aefric said. "You were saying why Maev confirmed she's a hostage?"

Ashling chuckled.

"Because it's understood that she could become one at any time. If something were to happen between Varondam and Armyr. She's been taught that since she was a little girl. Same as Killian's been taught it. And *he's* even more valuable, because he's the *crown* prince."

"So you don't think she's in danger?"

Ashling chuckled again. "I thought you knew Maev, Aefric. Tell me. If things get tense between Maev and Dalius, who's in more danger?"

"Dalius," he said without hesitation.

Ashling nodded.

"If you hope to ever become more to Maev than an occasional bedwarmer," she said, poking him in the chest with her toes again, "you'd do well to remember just who she is and what she's capable of."

Bedwarmer? The closest he'd come to sharing the noble privilege with Maev had been interrupted by the queen herself. And they'd both been fully dressed at the time...

"I was just worried about her," he said. "I haven't seen her in so long."

"I know," Ashling said, and patted him on the shoulder with her foot.

Her dressing gown rode even higher up her thigh this time. She left her smooth, shapely leg outstretched and bare when she brought it down.

She gave Aefric an amused look. As though entertained, or perhaps pleased, that Aefric found her leg distracting.

And honestly, his gaze wouldn't normally have lingered. If he weren't tired. A little stressed from the day. And still a little wound up from Ettarma, who left so abruptly...

"I'm more worried about what Malimfar is up to," Ashling continued. "If they approach any other kingdoms about what they say Caiperas is doing, King Makarios might get nervous and start bolstering his defenses, instead of preparing to invade Malimfar. And *that* we don't need."

"I guess it's a good thing you'll be going there yourself," Aefric said. "Give you a chance to calm King Makarios, and get Caiperas thinking the way Armyr wants them to think."

"You give me a great deal of credit," Ashling said.

"If anyone can do it, I'm looking at her."

Ashling smiled, then her smile quirked and became pensive. She played her finger along the rim of her goblet.

"You know," she finally said. "I'm at risk of breaking my word to you."

"How so?"

"I promised you that the next night we spent under the same roof, I'd come to you for the noble privilege."

"This was hardly a night either of us planned for," Aefric said. "And you did sail with the expectation that I might've been guilty. Not exactly the right frame of mind."

"I don't think I really believed it," she said, waving away the thought. "I just needed to hear the truth from your lips."

"Even so. It's not as though you had the mindset or opportunity to find us a suitable third."

"True," she said, frowning. "Nevertheless. You may be the first real friend I've ever had. And I don't relish the prospect of breaking my word to you. Even unintentionally."

"As your friend," Aefric said seriously, "it's in my power to commute your promise. Or even release you from it."

"No," she said. "That power, my good Aefric, you do not possess. My word is my word. It has meaning or it doesn't."

She sat up.

"It's the sharabi talking," he said.

"It's not." She moved closer.

"You're teasing me," Aefric said carefully.

"Am I?" Ashling took his sharabi and set both crystal goblets on the table without taking her eyes off him.

"Jokes are jokes, Ash, but as you put it once, I'm too masculine for your usual tastes."

"My *usual* tastes, yes." She moved closer still. Her hair fell forward over her shoulders. He could feel the heat of her body now. Smell the sharabi on her breath. "I also recall telling you that you wouldn't be the first man inside me."

She put her hands on his chest. Could probably feel the way his heart had started racing. Tell that his breaths were coming quicker now. Shallower.

"You have a bastard son, I know," Aefric said, keeping his own hands to his sides and working to calm himself.

"I also told you I experimented with men quite a bit around my majority."

"But—"

"Hush," she said softly. "Tell me truly, Aefric. Do you want this? To share a night of pleasure with me?"

"Not if you're doing it out of obligation," he said. "When you made that promise, you said you wanted to share a woman with me.

And maybe, in that context, bring me the bliss moment yourself. This is—"

"*And normally* that's how I'd prefer it," she said, leaning closer still. The lines of their bodies almost touching. "But maybe I've been teasing myself as much as I've been teasing you."

Her lips drew slowly closer to his.

"Maybe it's been long enough that I want to remember what it's like to have a man again. Maybe I want you to remind me."

Her lips, closer still.

"And maybe, just maybe, I want to see what it would be like ... if I married you myself."

Ashling wet her lips. Less than a fingerwidth separated her lips from his.

"If you want to tell me no, Aefric, you'd better tell me now."

Was that ... was that a touch of uncertainty in her eyes?

Oh, that was just too much. That a woman as breathtakingly beautiful and supremely confident as Ashling Fyrenn could *possibly* be uncertain in a moment like this.

Aefric kissed her.

———

IT WAS WONDERFUL AND SURREAL ALL AT ONCE.

Ashling Fyrenn. She'd gone from likely rival to probable enemy to uncertain ally to friend and now...

Now Aefric was holding her in his arms. So warm. So right. Only two thin, nearly transparent layers of linen between their feverish bodies.

Her hands, on his face and in his hair. His, on her back and waist.

And the kiss. Her lips, so soft and slippery. And hungry, the urgent way they moved against his. Her tongue, aggressive. As though she were fighting him for dominance but not sure she wanted to win. A wild contrast to the taste they shared of that cool, mint sharabi.

He slid one hand up behind her back so his fingers could play in her hair as he cupped the back of her neck, and she showed her approval by sliding one of her own hands down until it hit the collar of his dressing gown.

She made a frustrated sound. Pulled back from the kiss. Both of them a little breathless.

"Nysta tea," she said between heavy breaths that pressed her breasts against him. "I want nysta tea and I want to tear that dressing gown off you."

"I drank some already," he said.

Ashling's eyebrows shot up and her smile was incredulous.

"Are you telling me you saw this coming?" She ran her hands over his chest admiringly. "Because I didn't."

"Drank it before I heard you were coming," he said, but before he could say anything else, she cut in.

"Oh?" Her voice got teasing again. "Here you pointed out that I hadn't found us a third, but you've got a woman waiting for you in bed?"

"No," he said, shaking his head. "Ettarma Al'Qarruq came to me tonight, but she didn't stay past the first bliss moment."

"Well," Ashling said, eyebrows coming together in disapproval. "Sounds abrupt."

"It was."

"Still..." she said, sounding intrigued.

She ran one hand down his dressing gown, past his waist, and took hold of his ready manhood with an assessing kind of grip.

"With Sirondfar speeding my ship..." She leaned down to nip at his neck while stroking him slowly and smoothly through the linen. "...I didn't give you time to ... freshen up. Did I?"

"Quick spell..." — oh, that felt good — "took care of that."

"So what you're saying is" — she sat up again and gave him a squeeze down there — "if I were to *taste* this, the flavor would be all you? Not stale sex?"

Aefric could only nod. What she was doing felt good, and he was afraid of letting it feel too good.

"Tell me about this Ettarma," Ashling said. "Is she pretty?"

"Very. But nothing on you, of course."

She gave a throaty chuckle.

"Good answer." She gave her wrist a quick flourish, then tilted her head thoughtfully. "If she only stayed for one bliss moment, she didn't really take time to *explore* you. Did she?"

Aefric shook his head.

"Then that settles it." She leaned in and licked his ear while her hand continued its slow, steady movement. "Looks like I'll be having a snack before we go to your bedroom."

Aefric gave a sound of approval that made her smile wickedly. He couldn't see that smile, but he could *feel* it against his throat.

"Like that idea, do you?" she purred softly.

"Yes," Aefric whispered.

"You like the idea of me, getting down on my knees for you? Pleasing you?"

Aefric leaned down and nipped at the spot where her neck met her shoulder, making her shiver.

"Of course," he said softly. "Just as I expect that you like the idea of me getting on my knees for you afterwards and pleasing *you*. Which I fully intend to do."

"Just what I wanted to hear," she said, sitting up again and looking him over as though she had a thousand things she wanted to do, and couldn't decide which should be first.

She shook her head hard enough to whip her raven black hair.

"Nysta tea first," she said. "I know you had some earlier, but I'd rather we both had some. It's safer."

"I agree," Aefric said, then called out, "Dajen!"

Dajen stepped into the room, carrying a silver tray, with a silver tea set and two matching cups, along with an assortment of short-bread cookies on a small silver plate.

"Given her grace's choice of raiment," Dajen said, managing to sound respectful and avert his eyes without looking like he was doing so, "I had some nysta tea prepared in case it was needed, and some cookies to abate the aftertaste. Was there anything more your graces require? Another bottle of sharabi, perhaps?"

"Thank you, Dajen," Aefric said. "Nothing else."

Dajen poured two cups of tea, then left the room.

Ashling, all but straddling Aefric, reached over for the cups while Aefric ran his hands over her back and hips. He couldn't wait to feel both without her dressing gown in the way.

They both tossed down the hot, bitter brew. Ashling put the cups back, and picked up a cookie. Put it half into her mouth and turned to Aefric with one eyebrow raised.

He leaned in and bit off his half of the cookie.

She snickered through her nose as they chewed. The shortbread was sweet, but not too sweet. A good antidote for the bitterness of the tea.

"Now," Ashling said, looking him over pensively. "Where was I? Oh. Yes."

She reached up and ripped open his dressing gown, straight down the middle.

Aefric scoffed in disbelief. "You're stronger than I thought."

"In every sense," she said absently while looking over his naked body. "Oh, yes. Much better." She ran his hands over his chest again. "Good muscles. Well-formed chest hair. *Marvelous* scars."

She met his eye for a moment.

"Exactly what I hoped for," she said. She wiggled her eyebrows. "This will be fun."

Before Aefric could say anything else, she leaned in and began nibbling his neck.

He gave up worrying about words then and just enjoyed the way her lips and tongue and teeth danced across his skin. The way her hands roved over his muscles. Stroking. Squeezing. Searching out his scars.

While she did these things, he stroked her hair and shoulders, but she was still wearing her dressing gown.

He growled irritation.

Ashling looked up from nibbling his collarbone on the way to a scar on his left shoulder.

"Something wrong?" she asked, with a look in her eye that said she already knew the answer.

"Lose the dressing gown," Aefric said. "I want my hands on your skin."

"Mmmm," she said, fluttering her lashes. "So do I. But not yet."

He made a small, frustrated sound, but she laughed teasingly and started sucking on the arrow scar on his shoulder.

He contended himself with watching her and stroking her hair and neck, and what little he could reach of her back and shoulders under the collar of that damned dressing gown.

She worked slowly down his chest that way. Kissing and licking everywhere, but paying special attention to his several scars.

By the time she reached his waist, her hands were on his legs. One of them found an old stab scar on his thigh and the even older trap scar on his calf. So she skipped over the place he most wanted her mouth and worked her way down first one leg, then the other.

She clearly enjoyed his skin and his muscles, but took special pleasure in his scars.

Finally, though, she brought her attentions to her ultimate target.

She met his eyes then, with a smile. "Ready?"

He nodded, sure he was.

But he wasn't.

He'd expected her to be a little awkward here. Or maybe a little ... simplistic about her approach.

But Ashling Fyrenn knew exactly what she was doing. She knew just when to use her tongue, her lips, her hands, her cheeks even. And more. So much more. And she did it all so very well that when she finally — after *three* deliberately false starts on her part — brought him to his culmination, he was pretty sure he shouted out her name.

Hard to remember for certain. The bliss moment she gave him hit harder than a mountain troll.

And then she was kissing her way back up his body until she could share another deep, passionate kiss with him before cuddling in and pillowing her head on his chest.

"Well," she said, sounding pleased with herself. "I admit, I worried I'd forgotten how to do that right. But really, it's like riding a horse. Once you're in the saddle, most of it comes right back to you. And the rest, of course, the horse will tell you."

"I'd be mad ... about you comparing me to a horse..." Aefric said, "but I don't think ... I'm capable ... of being mad at you ... right now."

Ashling chuckled. "You wouldn't be mad at me anyway. You know I'm only teasing."

"I also know," Aefric said, getting his air back, "that if you don't strip off that dressing gown, I'll do it for you."

"Oh?" Ashling said, lifting her head to smile at him with her eyes. "Would you rip it in half with your magic? Or simply disrobe me with a spell?"

Her specificity gave him pause. Ripping off a dressing gown with magic, that was what Eppida liked him to do. And the first time he'd taken Zoleen to bed, he'd used a derivation of a knot-untying spell to get her out of her complicated dress quickly without damaging it.

"Which would you prefer?" he asked.

Ashling pushed off of his chest and stood.

She crossed her arms around her hips and took hold of her gown. In a single, swift movement she swept it up and off, tossing it over her cloak on the chair beside them.

Ashling Fyrenn. Naked and beautiful and smiling in the firelight. Her raven tresses tumbling loose over her smooth, pale shoulders. Her full breasts, her tapering waist, the perfection of her hips and legs.

She was glorious. And she knew it.

Aefric could only shake his head in admiration and drink in the sight of her.

"Flatterer," she teased.

"Not a bit," he said. "Your beauty is astounding. I look forward to investigating every inch of you."

"I know you've been with Byrhta Ol'Caran," Ashling said simply. "So you can't pretend I'm the most beautiful woman you've ever seen. Even if I might take second place."

Aefric laughed softly, which made Ashling lift her eyebrows at him.

"I had to tell your sister this too," he said, standing up. "Beauty is not meant to be compared. It is only meant to be admired."

He slipped his arms around her, thrilling to the touch of her skin under his fingers.

"And enjoyed," he said, and scooped her up in his arms.

Ashling actually gave a small yip of surprise, so unexpected that he laughed.

"I ... can't believe you just picked me up like this."

"No one's done it before?" he asked.

She shook her head.

"Do you like it?"

"I like it right now."

"Good enough," he said.

"I thought you were going to kneel for me before taking me to bed," she said. Not accusing. Just wanting an explanation.

"I'd rather have my silk sheets against your skin while you enjoy what I do for you."

"Good counter-argument." She nodded approval.

And with that, he carried her to bed.

It still seemed unbelievable to Aefric. So many ways this day could have ended, but this was an ending that he could never have foreseen.

Ashling Fyrenn, gloriously naked and slithering about in his silk sheets while he went slowly over her entire body. Kissing and licking and nibbling and fondling every smooth, soft, firm inch of her. Savoring the slight taste of rose petals on her skin.

He paid special attention to anyplace that got more reaction out of her. And Ashling wasn't shy about letting him know what she liked. Encouraging him with her hands, her moans, her movements.

Especially when he reached his own ultimate target. There, well, he couldn't pretend to compete with the quality of lovers he was sure she'd had over the years. So he tried to make up the difference with enthusiasm, endurance, and careful attention to her reactions.

His attentions did culminate in bliss for her. Or at least, they seemed to. She might've been humoring him. But if so, she was a good actress.

Either way, when she settled down again, panting for breath, she grabbed him by the hair and ears and tugged for him to come up and kiss her.

Aefric kissed his way up her body then. Licking away some of her salty perspiration, and lingering a moment over her breasts before giving her that kiss and settling in beside her.

They lay together in contented silence for a moment.

"Damn Colm anyway," Ashling said.

"Excuse me?"

She laughed. Kissed him and kept laughing.

Finally she managed to say, "Oh, no. I wasn't thinking about him while you were pleasing me. Believe me, I knew exactly who was where and doing what."

"Then..."

"I was just thinking. Poor Zolly. Off to Becheadam without even a chance for one more go at what I just got. Not to mention what I'm going to get next."

She swung around to straddle Aefric.

"She really should have had a chance to win your love. A chance to maybe become your bride. And if none of those things, she should have *at least* gotten a chance to ride you one more time."

Aefric wasn't sure what he could say to that. But he never got a chance, anyway.

"Oh, well," Ashling said with a wicked smile. "More for me."

And then the night began in earnest.

They never did go to sleep. Not really. A fitful doze at one point, maybe. But from the moment she straddled him until the servants knocked with the news that it was time for the day to begin, they never really stopped.

They would chase the bliss moment together, in one position or another, until their fulfillment. Then, while resting, they would chat about little nothings and start exploring each other again, which would begin the cycle once more.

At one point, after they finished together, Aefric looked down into Ashling's eyes and startled.

"Oops," he said.

She didn't even ask. Just arched one of her sculpted, black eyebrows.

"I was just thinking," he said, moving to lie down beside her among the rumpled, silken sheets. "That poor servant girl. Waiting for you in your rooms, ready to give you *leaba*."

"Well," Ashling said with a sigh. "Obviously that's not going to happen." She ran her fingers through his hair. "Pity she couldn't join us, but that would cross a line."

"I'd understand if you wanted to go back to her," Aefric said.

Ashling shoved him flat on his back. Pinned him down by his wrists.

"I'm not done with you yet," she said, and started after his scars again.

Later, while they rested in between times, she started laughing.

"What?" he asked.

"Oh, just thinking," she said, then turned and traced circles in his chest hair as she spoke. "I let myself be seen coming here in my dressing gown and cloak. Figured I'd have fun letting your court speculate about us."

"Well," Aefric said. "Now they'll *really* speculate."

"Yes," she said, pleased. "They will. Be good for both of us, I expect."

"It'll also start the rumor that you're a bridal candidate."

"Maybe I should be," she said thoughtfully. "We're obviously good as friends. And while I'd want our regular nights together to include some sweet, young noblewoman, I think I wouldn't mind doing this once in a while, just the two of us. At *least* to make sure we have children."

"You've acknowledged your bastard," he reminded her. "If you want serious consideration here, you'd have to set him aside. I'd have to know that my children with you would be heirs to Merrek, just as yours with me would be heirs to Deepwater."

She sighed. "True. And I won't do that. I love little Dives. And I have every intention of seeing him become duke one day."

"Then it's not fair to ask me to accept that, while expecting your own children to inherit here in Deepwater."

"But what if you had a bastard of your own?" she asked, sitting up. "Hear me out. Bed Byrhta Ol'Caran without nysta tea. Do it more than once, just to make sure. Hardly a hardship there. Keep at it until you get her with child."

She gestured vaguely to the room. "Everyone here at Water's End already loves her, so they'll be on your side when you acknowledge the bastard. The child will be next in line for Deepwater. Dives will be next in line for Merrek. And any other children we had would follow, as appropriate. If we married."

This was the second time someone had mentioned the possibility of him having a bastard. The other had been one of his knights — that amazing dweomerblade Deirdre Ol'Miri — who had openly offered to have his bastard...

No. That wouldn't be fair to Deirdre. And as for Byrhta...

"You know Byrhta wants to marry me."

"Of course she does," Ashling said. "In her position, I would too."

"So you'd expect me to ask a *bridal candidate* to *have my bastard* so I could marry *you*."

"Come, Aefric," Ashling said, leaning down and nuzzling his chest. "However clever a baroness regent she might be, she *must* know that all she brings to a marriage is herself. No great family name. No riches. No land that isn't already yours. This would be a good option for her."

"I'm sorry, Ash," Aefric said, stroking her hair. "I couldn't do that to her. And before you ask, I couldn't do it to Sighild either, or anyone else."

"Oh?" She picked her head up to give him a sharp look. "Feel a moral objection to having and acknowledging a bastard, do you?"

"It's not the same situation. You were worried about dying heirless during the Godswalk Wars. In my case it would be a deliberate political move. One that makes me uncomfortable."

Ashling quirked a lopsided smile. "Worth a shot." She sighed and put her head back down on his chest. "Colm would never willingly let us marry each other anyway."

"Why not?"

"Aefric," she chided. "Think a moment. Between us, we control more than half of Armyr. Add to that your popularity and my savvy, and Colm would worry we'd usurp him."

"But we wouldn't."

"Oh, not today, no," she said, shrugging one shoulder. "Probably not tomorrow, either. But suppose he created some law we objected to. Suppose our relationship with him soured. Separate, he could try to play us against each other. United, we'd present a real threat."

She shook her head, without lifting it from his chest. "No. He'd avoid that risk by refusing us marriage. Pity, too. We'd make an *unbeatable* couple."

Rise up against his majesty? That just seemed ... impossible to contemplate.

Ashling licked an old spear wound. "Tell me how you got this scar."

She played her tongue over it while he told the story. From there, she went over his body again, this time getting the story of each scar as she gave it special attention.

And then they were busy with other things again, until finally...

That knock on the door.

Terrible timing. They were wrapped around each other and breathless, frantically seeking one last bliss moment.

"Your grace?" The voice of Ocheda, Aefric's chief daytime valet.

How late had it gotten?

"In ... a minute!" Aefric shouted.

"Make it five!" Ashling shouted, then looked him in the eye. "Don't you dare quit on me, Aefric Brightstaff."

A challenge he was most happy to meet, leaving them both a

sweaty, exhausted — but satisfied — mess among the tatters of his sheets when Ocheda finally came in.

The word *severe* might have been invented for Ocheda. It applied to everything about her. Her build — she was almost as tall as Aefric, but quite thin. Her eyes were sharp and her temper sharper, with any servants who dared slack in their work.

She was only about a decade older than Aefric, but she gave an impression of great age. As though she'd been around since the castle was built, and knew it — and the needs of nobility — better than anyone else ever could.

"Will her grace be joining his grace for a morning bath?" she asked.

"I think not," Ashling said, groaning slightly as she got out of bed. "If I do, we'll only delay more." She winked at him. "And I *must* get back to Fyrcloch, then it's off to Caiperas. For that matter, don't bother seeing me to my ship. A formal goodbye will just make us both later than we already are."

Ocheda clapped her hands and a serving girl rushed in with Ashling's dressing gown, cloak, and slippers while Ocheda strode past to go see about Aefric's bath.

Aefric, still naked, got out of bed.

"Not at all what I expected when you arrived last night," he said with a lopsided smile. "But I'm glad things went this way."

"As am I," Ashling said, matching his smile. "But I still want to share a woman with you sometime."

"I'll look forward to it."

She stepped in close. Kissed him on both cheeks, which was a formal declaration of friendship from one noble to another. Aefric returned the gesture.

"Have a good trip," he said. "And good luck in Caiperas."

"Thank you," she said. "And good luck to you with ... well ... everything."

Before Aefric could ask what she meant by that, Ashling had whisked out the door and was gone.

3

———————

AEFRIC'S USUAL ROUTINE INVOLVED HIS MORNING MEETING WITH HIS advisers, which took place shortly after dawn.

But that morning had already dawned when the servants came to rouse him. So by the time he finished his morning ablutions, and donned something presentable to wear for the day — a pale green silk shirt over black hose, with a black leather belt and soft leather shoes that had been dyed to match the shirt — he half-expected that Garnotin had run the meeting in his absence.

Well, no, he realized. Garnotin couldn't have run the meeting. He'd left last night aboard the *Swift Wave*, along with Bebara and those newly freed slaves from Kefthal.

Wow. Ashling had put that right out of his mind.

"No hat today, your grace?" Ocheda asked. She'd been waiting for him just outside his closets, likely to ask about where he wanted his breakfast.

"I'm not expecting to leave the castle," Aefric said, glancing out the glass doors that led to his balcony. In the sky beyond, the sun was fully risen. "Was my morning meeting canceled?"

"No, your grace," Ocheda said with a precise bow. "Breakfast and your grace's advisers await him even now, in his meeting room."

Aefric grimaced. "How long have I kept them waiting?"

"They only just arrived. When your grace ... accepted Duchess Ashling's company last night, Dajen sent word that the morning meeting would likely be delayed. I sent for the ducal advisers once your grace was in his bath."

Aefric gave Ocheda a lopsided smile that she didn't seem to notice. "You and Dajen truly are treasures. I don't know what I'd do without you."

"Likely commit some grievous breach of etiquette," Ocheda said in a matter-of-fact tone. But he thought he saw a sparkle in her eye.

Brightstaff in hand then, he chuckled and went to join his advisers in the smallish room so full of black oak.

As he entered, they all rose from their ornately carved chairs at the round, blackwood table.

Yrsa, in shades of brown that Aefric hardly noticed when he realized that her major scar was a dark, angry red, and her expression just this side of murderous. Her hair was pulled back in a tight braid, as though anticipating combat.

Beornric wore dark orange over dark red, and a concerned look on his face as he tugged his bushy black mustache.

Elkari wore dark browns, and even as she stood there, she continued scratching notes on parchment, frowning in that way that meant she was considering about a dozen different angles on a problem.

Kentigern wore a troubled expression with midnight black velvet, embroidered in silk thread, with his black velvet cap over his thick brown hair.

The black velvet cap. Always a harbinger of bad news, when Kentigern wore it. The same reason Yrsa was angry?

Their greetings were tense, except for Elkari's, which was distracted.

He considered asking what was wrong. But then his empty stomach complained, so he figured whatever it was could wait a moment. He gave a quick good morning, stood the Brightstaff beside his chair, and turned to the spread on the buffet.

The standard Armyrian breakfast waited for him there. Sliced meats — turkey, ham, and roast beef. Sliced melons and fruits — a broad assortment of these, but he selected mostly apple, casaba melon — a treat not available all year long — cantaloupe and a handful each of blackberries and blueberries. Two rolls of honeyed oat bread and a silver goblet of fresh, cool water completed the meal.

He'd only just turned toward the table when Yrsa finally snapped at him.

"Have you lost your mind?"

"Well," Aefric said carefully — he didn't like the way her fingers twitched, as though they itched to draw her maces — "as I am standing here and speaking, it *seems* to be behaving normally..."

"She's talking about Duchess Ashling," Beornric said. He sounded as cautious as Aefric, but his hands were loose and ready. As though he thought he might need to tackle Yrsa.

"Of course I'm talking about Ashling!" Yrsa barked. "You *bedded* her! *Gods*, tell me you're not *stupid* enough to be *smitten* with her."

Yrsa's anger was a powerful thing. Aefric could practically *feel* it radiating from her. Like heat. Survival instincts begged him to either hide, fight, or give her whatever she wanted.

If he were still just an adventurer, he'd probably cast a spell, putting an invisible wall between them. Just to remind her that he wasn't someone to take lightly.

But he was duke now. And he refused to be browbeaten by an adviser. Even so trusted and important an adviser as Yrsa, whose anger was likely more on his behalf, than at him.

So he kept entirely aware of exactly where she stood and exactly what she was doing. And he took his seat. Right in the chair beside her.

Yrsa growled, sounding far too much like a wolf for Aefric's comfort.

"That's enough."

Wait. That didn't come from Beornric. It came from Kentigern. And he didn't even sound frightened as he continued, although he was talking to a woman who could pick him up and snap him in half.

"General, you are addressing your *liege*," Kentigern said. "Kindly take a respectful tone. If you cannot, perhaps you should leave this meeting until you can."

"He's right," Beornric said firmly. "His grace affords us considerable leeway. But there are limits."

"Precedent does not support you here, General," Elkari said absently, still writing. "We are answerable to his grace. Not he to us."

Yrsa turned away. Punched one of her hands with a sharp smack. Whipped in a long, fast, noisy breath through her nose.

Aefric took a bite of turkey. Tried to focus on the sweet, moist taste. Honey roasted?

Yes, that was right. Definitely honey roasted.

All right. Enough delay.

He lowered the slice and turned to Yrsa, who faced him now.

"I need to know," she said in a low voice. "How badly did she get to you, Aefric? Are you smitten or not?"

Aefric took a sip of water.

"As I understand the practice," he said, "the noble privilege is supposed to *avert* political problems. Not cause them."

"Supposed to, yes," Yrsa said, voice still low and angry, but controlled. "But it doesn't always work that way. And a woman like Ashling Fyrenn—"

"*Duchess* Ashling Fyrenn," Kentigern corrected.

"I've earned the right to call her by name," Yrsa snapped at him. "A right confirmed by Ashling herself."

She turned back to Aefric. Looming.

"If she gets in your head, she's *dangerous*," Yrsa said. "Believe me, Aefric. I *know*."

Aefric nodded slowly.

"I understand," he said, gesturing for everyone to sit. Surprisingly, they did. Even Yrsa. "And one reason I'm not upset at you for that tirade is that we have an agreement, you and I. You would watch for threats, and I would make friendships and alliances. Your anger is only an extension of that arrangement."

"I need to know." Her words were soft, but compelling. As though she could *will* an answer out of him.

"I'm not smitten with her," Aefric said. "She didn't even intend to come to me last night for the noble privilege."

"Well she can hardly of gotten the wrong room," Beornric said dryly, then groaned. "She was trying to start a rumor, wasn't she?"

"She was," Aefric said. "Hence, she made sure she was seen coming to my rooms in nothing but a dressing gown and cloak."

"Her plan worked," Elkari said, most of her attention still on whatever she was writing.

"She's right," Kentigern said. "Word has already spread through the court. Some are saying her grace wants to marry you."

"She doesn't," Aefric said. "Well, actually, she said she does. But I won't. You all know why. And anyway, she said King Colm would never allow it."

"No," Elkari said, still writing. "The Stronghand family has never approved a marriage between the peers. They won't even like hearing what was rumored to happen last night."

"And you're saying it *is* just a rumor?" Yrsa asked suspiciously.

"No," Beornric said. "He said she didn't *intend* the noble privilege." He turned narrowed eyes on Aefric. "That's not that same as saying it's just a rumor."

"And the servants are all chattering about it," Kentigern said. "Saying things that ... well ... don't sound like all you did was talk."

"I never said all we did was talk," Aefric said. "Only that she didn't arrive with that intention."

Yrsa scoffed. "Tripped and landed on you exactly the wrong way, did she?"

"What *matters*," he said, "is that Ashling and I are *friends*. I'm not smitten with her. I'm not going to marry her. In fact, Zoleen is officially off the list of candidates now, too, so it's safe to say I won't be marrying a Fyrenn."

"Thank the gods for that much," Yrsa muttered.

"Already struck Zoleen's name from the list," Beornric said. "Just wasn't sure if I should be adding Ashling's."

"Remember what I told you in Kivash," Yrsa said. "Ashling Fyrenn has no concept of friendship. To her, people are only pieces on a game board. Right now, she finds you useful. But as soon as that usefulness ends, everything she's ever learned about you becomes a weapon or a tool, depending on her needs."

"I'd like to think that's not true," Aefric said, then clapped her on the shoulder. "But just in case, I need your watchful eye."

Yrsa nodded, still unhappy, but mollified. At least for the moment.

"Now," Aefric said, turning to the others. "Shall we start the meeting? I'm starving."

WHEN AEFRIC HAD FIRST TAKEN UP HIS DUCHY, ACTUALLY MAKING decisions that affected hundreds and thousands of lives had caused him more than a little stress.

Yes, he had good, experienced advisers. But at the end of the day, the responsibility for all these people was his. And he'd never had anything close to that kind of responsibility before.

As Keifer, he'd never been in management. Not really. Highest he'd ever risen was senior editor in the reseller contracts division of a major shoe company. And a couple of junior editors answering to him just didn't compare to all this.

As Aefric, he'd only ever really been responsible for himself. Even if he saved a town from a sand giant — as he'd done for Kal'ikan, down in the Southern Wastes — he never had to worry about what happened to those people after he left.

Of course, part of what had made Aefric a good adventurer was that he didn't shy away from challenges. If anything, when he wasn't sure he could do something, he dug in and worked twice as hard.

That didn't mean the minutia of running a duchy was *fun*, per se. But it was an important part of being duke. And so, whenever he could, Aefric liked to hear about everything from disputes between vassals or guilds to details about the expected coming harvest and preparations for winter.

He couldn't take time to rule on everything himself. There was simply too much. Deepwater was a vast duchy, and even the lands he held himself were considerable, to say nothing of those he held through his many vassals. Three counties, four baronies, and more lers and landed knights than he wanted to count.

But he did what he could to establish a pattern of rulings that erred on the side of the safety and well-being of his people, whenever possible.

Not that he always had that choice.

The last thing his people needed right then was another war. But his majesty had been quite clear about Aefric not only providing his standing army for the coming conflict, but raising at least a thousand more troops besides.

He could only hope that, with surprise on Armyr's side, the war would be quick and relatively painless.

But what war was ever quick *or* painless?

Of the rulings Aefric did make, few were made entirely by himself. After all, he had those good, experienced advisers. Sought their opinions freely, and weighed their judgment against his own.

Elkari was always ready to tell him how similar cases had been handled in the past. She could cite precedents for almost anything that came up — especially important when there were border disputes between lers. She not only covered the most recent trends in rulings, but would make clear when those trends had started, how rulings had gone before then, and often even why there were changes.

Kentigern kept abreast of the ebb and flow of opinions and politics, not only here at Water's End, but all throughout Deepwater. And beyond. He frequently knew what was happening at Armityr, Fyrcloch, and Stormsent even before travelers and rikas brought the latest news.

Yrsa, of course, kept one eye on Deepwater's defenses, military capabilities, and logistics. As well as adding her good, practical — if a bit conservative — opinion to other matters.

Garnotin might have been absent that morning, but overall had been settling in well as castellan and contributing to every meeting. He'd gotten to know not only the nobility, but met often with the merchants and guilds. Learning their structures, their major players, and their issues. Averting problems before they escalated, when he could, and when he could not he often had solid advice about how to resolve matters equitably.

Beornric had no specific role beyond his position of captain of Aefric's personal guard. But he'd been raised part of an old noble family, and had served the king in his court at Armityr before the Godswalk Wars. So he knew at least a little about a lot, especially how the games of politics were played.

They were a good set of advisers.

In the end, though, each decision, like the responsibility itself, was Aefric's. And the more such decisions he made, the better his advisers would understand how he wanted things done when he was *not* in residence.

That was particularly important for Garnotin, the newest member of his advisory council. As castellan, a lot of the rulings would fall to him in Aefric's absence. And Aefric wanted to make clear how such rulings should go.

Pity he missed this meeting. But at least Elkari would make sure he received a good summary of what was covered and how Aefric had ruled.

So while Aefric agreed with Yrsa that, for example, the lers could not be allowed to withhold troops from the coming campaign, he gave exemptions for those whose lands were hit hardest by the Godswalk Wars.

And he took steps to make sure that those areas still recovering had help that would see them through the coming winter.

Elkari was notably quiet through most of the minutia. Apart from offering a distracted opinion or precedent here and there, she continued busily writing away.

Not just her usual note-taking, either. Though she did have a sheaf of notes going beside whatever else she was working on.

Doing two things at once was very much like Elkari. But writing two different things at once *during a meeting* was odd.

In fact, Aefric nearly stopped six times to ask what she was working on. Because she simply *didn't do* things like this. While she always brought a pile of books and scrolls to the morning meeting — indeed, he rarely saw her without such a collection at hand — this was the first time she'd brought work and *continued working* once the meeting began.

Which, in Elkari's case, meant that whatever she was doing had to be important. The woman didn't seem to have an ounce of pretense in her body. So Aefric suppressed that need to ask, each time it surfaced. And reminded himself again and again that she would tell him what she was doing when it was complete.

Kentigern had just finished reviewing Garnotin's latest list of requests for aid from the rebuilding towns along the coast — which were coming along better than expected, overall — when Elkari set down her quill pen and said, "There!"

The word came out so sudden and sharp that Kentigern stopped mid-sentence.

Everyone turned to stare expectantly at Elkari.

For a moment, all was quiet at the round, blackwood table in Aefric's meeting room. Aefric had even paused with a bite of casaba melon halfway to his mouth.

Elkari startled when she realized that everyone was looking at her. Flushed behind the fresh ink stains on her dusky forehead, the surest sign of thinking while she worked.

"Excuse me, y—" She checked herself from adding his courtesy. Cleared her throat. "I hope you'll pardon me for finishing this here, but I'd hoped to complete it before the meeting began. But then I realized I had to look up the precedents surrounding potential marriage among the peerage."

She flushed even harder. "Well, that is, when I had been told—"

"It's all right, Elkari," Aefric said, lowering the melon slice. "I appreciate your having those precedents ready, in case I needed them. Your ability to anticipate my needs is almost as impressive as your knowledge of Armyr's history."

"Thank you, your grace," she said, clearly without thinking.

Kentigern — who often had trouble leaving off Aefric's courtesy during these meetings as well — smiled fondly at her.

"But now that you *have* completed whatever that is..." Aefric said, trailing off hopefully.

"Oh, of course," she said at once. "Do excuse me. After yesterday's meeting, of course, I wanted to begin work on determining whether or not any elements of the report from Malimfar could be confirmed."

"And that's what you have there?" Beornric asked, amazed. "A report of what is and isn't accurate? Already?"

"Oh, no," she said, looking affronted. "That will take a good deal more time, I'm afraid. There are the slants of their views to take into account after all, which could lead them — intentionally or unintentionally — into phrasing or entire modes of presentation which, while accurate in their essence, would prove *in*accurate if read uncritically—"

"Elkari," Aefric said, as patiently as he could manage.

"Y... yes?"

"I look forward to that report when it's complete."

"Thank you. I'll finish it as soon as I can."

"I know you will. But what I *don't* know, is what report is *that*?"

Aefric pointed to the parchment in her hands.

"Oh, of course," she said. "Excuse me."

"No excuse necessary," Aefric said, fighting now to keep patience in his voice. "But..."

"But I should get on with telling you," she said, chagrined.

Aefric smiled.

"At yesterday's meeting, I explained the precedents for Malimfari arls giving land to a trusted noble of the leader who defeated them in war. But it occurred to me last night that I hadn't spoken of the precedents in Armyr for a noble being *given* land in another kingdom."

She shook her head and frowned. "Even worse, I realized I didn't *know* them." A tremor ran through her as though the thought of not knowing something disturbed her. "So I spent a good deal of last night researching land grants from foreign kingdoms."

"Have there been many?" Aefric asked.

"Over the last seven hundred years, there have been eight. Well, one of those — Rethneryl — I'm only *counting* as one, even though more than one parcel of land was given, and on more than one occasion. But the giver and givee were the same in each case — the monarch of Rethneryl to the monarch of Armyr — so they were essentially the same gift, so far as precedence was concerned."

She frowned. "Well, no, now that I say it out loud, that's not *quite* accurate. Technically, the repetition itself acts to strengthen the precedent established by the first such gift, so that gifts of this sort—"

"Elkari," Aefric said.

"Your grace?"

"While that detail is important, I am more immediately concerned about gifts from foreign monarchs given to Armyrian nobles who were *not* monarchs."

"Of course," she said. "Apart from the Rethneryl exception and two other gifts to past monarchs, over the last seven hundred years there have been five. That is to say, five gifts of land from a foreign monarch to a member of the Armyrian nobility who was *not* Armyr's monarch."

"*Five*," Yrsa said. "I'm not sure if I should be surprised there were so few or so many."

"Two of these," Elkari continued, "were to members of the Armyrian royal family. Each was permitted to keep the gift — which is to say to hold the land and title, and receive all accompanying monies — unto death. But they were not allowed to pass those titles down to their descendants. In each case, when the receiving noble died, the gift lands and titles were claimed by the crown."

"An attempt to avoid creating division in the royal family?" Kentigern asked.

"Apparently," Elkari said, which was as close to agreement as she'd likely get. "That agrees with the official statement at the time of the first, which was when King—"

"Elkari," Aefric said, and when he had her attention, continued. "As I am not a member of the Armyrian royal family, are the details of these two gifts relevant?"

"They might become relevant," Elkari said, "if your grace were to marry Princess Maev."

"Well," he said with a sigh, "as that doesn't seem likely, let's move on to the other gifts for now."

"Of course," she said. "Of the other three, one gift was given to a knight. Ser Nerri Ol'Philan. Given by Hatay as a gift of thanks for her heroism in stopping an incursion of taroks on the Hatay side of the Endless Mountains. She had been a landless knight of Armyr at the time, and the gift represented more wealth than she had ever possessed before."

"She was allowed to keep it?" Aefric asked.

"More than that," Elkari said. "In the interests of good relations with Hatay, King Dakon — King Colm's four times great grandfather — permitted Ser Nerri to shift her allegiance to Hatay, where her descendants continue to hold that land, and are now called Ol'Nerri."

"Hardly a comparable situation," Beornric said.

"No," Elkari said, "but important for the sake of both completeness and clarity in points of precedence. Knights are noble. A noble received a gift of land and title, and was allowed to keep both and pass them down to inheritors."

"What about the other two?" Yrsa said.

"Those two are likely the most relevant, as they were gifts to peers of the realm. One to the Duke of Merrek, and the other to the Duke of Deepwater."

Aefric struggled not to ask immediately about Deepwater. Elkari always had a reason for presenting information in an order.

"The Merrek gift was from a small kingdom called Delbar."

"Delbar?" Yrsa asked, before anyone else could. "What's Delbar?"

"At the time, it was a small kingdom between Malimfar and Varondam," Elkari said. "As my phrasing might indicate, it no longer exists. Malimfar conquered and subsumed it, subsequently rescinding the Merrek gift."

"So it's worthless as precedent then," Yrsa said.

"Not in the least," Elkari said, temper flaring. "It was a gift of land and title to a peer of the realm from a foreign monarch. Even though the gift was later rescinded, the *facts* of the gift demonstrate *clearly* what past kings and queens of Armyr have permitted. That is all but the very *definition* of precedence."

"Elkari," Aefric said, raising a calming hand, "I do not believe that Yrsa meant to give offense. *Did you, Ser Yrsa?*"

"Your grace, I did not," Yrsa said, bowing her head to Aefric. She turned to Elkari. "I do apologize. I meant no offense. I am a warrior, not a scholar. If a former ally breaks a treaty, I must see that ally now as an enemy. I cannot afford to consider the ways in which their alliance once aided us."

"I'd say the value of the precedent is obvious," Beornric said. "Malimfar rescinded a gift of land and title. Which means they may do so again."

"Oh, no," Elkari said. "That's the wrong lesson here. Malimfar was quite explicit in a letter delivered to both Armityr and Fyrcloch. In conquering Delbar, Malimfar claimed ownership of *all* Delbari lands and titles, and the right to redistribute them as their monarch saw fit. Any land gifts stemming from the past monarchs of Delbar were now considered null and void."

"I suppose that's fair," Aefric said. "If Merrek didn't defend the land, Malimfar didn't have to uphold their claim to it."

"Just so," Elkari said, as though pleased someone was finally making sense. "But there's more to the gift's importance as precedent. That gift had value for the dukes tand duchesses of Merrek for close to a *hundred years* before Malimfar conquered Delbar. And what matters most here is this. At no time did any monarch of Armyr issue any objection to Merrek enjoying those lands, title, and monies, nor to Merrek passing them to the next duke or duchess through the usual inheritance laws."

"They passed down with the title?" Aefric asked.

"They did."

"So the gift was given to *Merrek*, and not to an individual who happened to be duke at the time."

"Explicitly," Elkari said with a nod.

"I see your point. This is the most pertinent precedent so far." Aefric grimaced. "Why do I have a feeling that the Deepwater case is different?"

"Because it is," Elkari said simply. "Some two hundred years ago, Shachan gave a gift of land and title to the Duke of Deepwater. Matters were ... uncertain between Armyr and Shachan at the time. So Queen Celia Stronghand, the young daughter of an old king and who arguably inherited too young, declared it inappropriate for a peer to have ties to another kingdom, as that might weaken their loyalty to the crown. She claimed the land and title, and Shachan rescinded the gift."

"Now *that* sounds comparable," Yrsa said. "'Uncertain' is a kind way to describe our current relationship with Malimfar."

"Quite so," Elkari agreed. "But it's also the older case of the two. The Merrek gift came during the reign of Queen Celia's son, King Iounn. And so I could make an argument that the Merrek gift should be the controlling precedent."

"What matters more, I suspect," Aefric said, "is that King Colm can rule either way and claim to be in the right, as far as precedence is concerned."

"Unfortunately, I believe so," Elkari said.

"Well, if he really wants it, he's welcome to it," Aefric said, exasperated. "Anything else pressing this morning?"

"Pressing?" Kentigern asked. "Not really." He checked over some of his papers and shook his head. "Only one more matter requiring your grace's attention."

"And that is?"

"A royal messenger was spotted boarding a ship at Behal this morning. Likely to arrive ... sometime before midday, if the wind is southerly today."

"That settles it then," Beornric said with a wolfish smile. "His majesty has already heard about Malimfar's gift and sent someone to collect it."

Aefric joined in the laughter of the others, but couldn't help wondering.

A royal messenger. What could his majesty want?

IF THE GODS WERE WITH AEFRIC THAT MORNING, THE WIND WOULD have been strong and southerly, and he would have received that royal messenger by the time the morning meeting was finished, no more than an hour before midday.

The gods, alas, had other things to do that day.

Which meant that, as midday approached, the prospect of lunch with his court was hanging over Aefric's head.

Now, it wasn't as though his court was filled with vipers and sycophants. Part of what had been so disturbing about Quintabis' manner was that very few people tried so obviously to suck up to Aefric.

In fact, his court could be downright pleasant sometimes.

Sure, the nobles were often jockeying for favor and position, but rarely very openly. And since Aefric had made clear early in his tenure that he enjoyed hearing others talk about themselves and their lands — especially when they could talk about things they were doing for their people — he often could pass entire meals without feeling too much in the spotlight.

But he was dreading his next meal with the court.

In just the last day...

Malimfar's princess had docked and been denied a proper reception. Even more gossip-worthy, word had spread by now that Aefric had joined Princess Astrid for lunch, and that he'd been offered land and a title. In the country Armyr had recently defeated in war.

Kefthal had docked a royal ship. Oh, they'd been denied a formal welcome, but that was to be expected. But they were allowed to leave without threats or violence.

More than that, they too had given the duke gifts. And knowing his court, the freed slaves wouldn't generate a lot of gossip. After all, he'd rescued a good many refugees from slavers just this past summer, and the court hardly spent much time on the topic.

But word had to have spread by now that Kefthal had given him the head of Calder Ol'Ulith.

Almost everyone in the court had known Calder much longer than they'd known Aefric. When Calder's treachery had been revealed, the scandal had wounded many who had once called him friend. Or at least considered him the trustworthy and honorable knight he'd pretended to be.

The scandal still echoed through Water's End. Word of Kefthal's gift would amplify those echoes once more.

And finally, there was Ashling. Arriving late at night, under cover of darkness, with no advance notice. Exchanging fierce words with Aefric on the pier, only to come to his rooms for the noble privilege.

Yes, it would likely be some days before Aefric could get his knights, lers and nobles to talk about themselves again. And he simply could not bring himself to face the rumor mill that day.

So as midday approached, Aefric skipped his public lunch, and took to the training ground with his knights. Not his personal training yard, up high in the keep, but the main castle training grounds, where he'd be easier to reach when the royal messenger arrived.

The northern wind carried a chill, and hinted that rains were coming. But that was no bother. Aefric had fought in ragged downpours and once even a snowstorm. A little chilly wind was hardly worth noticing.

The training yard was a cleared stretch on the north side of the castle, inside the shimmering, navy blue walls. Toward the back of the main keep, but not *too* near the docks.

Large as the keep was, that left a lot of space. The training yard was more than large enough to host two training jousts at the same time, while still leaving space for melee training at either end, as well as at least one archery range.

Even so, midday was the best time of day to make use of that space, because there was direct sun. Between the castle and the walls, direct sun was a blessing. All too often, the area was shadowed.

Of course, even direct sun today wasn't worth too much. Not with the first clouds incoming like scouts before the army of rain.

Aefric wasn't the only one taking advantage of what direct sun there was. Archers worked targets at the far end. Local soldiers and castle guards trained at melee towards the middle. And from the sounds of clashing steel and criticism, at least two dozen of them were well into today's training.

Good. If Aefric had wanted an audience, he'd be at lunch.

He wore simple linens for this. A blousy white shirt, and brown breeches tucked into good, calf-high brown boots. No wand on his belt right now, but a longsword whose edge had been blunted. The Brightstaff not in his hand, but standing on its own over by the rooms along the outer wall, where training weapons, armor, and other equipment were stored.

One guard stood watch over the Brightstaff, to prevent accidents. Touching it wasn't safe for anyone who wasn't Aefric. Not without Aefric actively permitting the touch.

Beornric, who oversaw Aefric's weapons training, frowned at the linens.

"Your grace really ought to wear your leathers for this," he said. "Keeping in practice with the blade is good, but do you really want your muscles to forget the feel of armor?"

Aefric nodded to the Knights of the Lake, who stood in a wide circle, giving him space and making sure that no one intruded.

"They don't care for me carrying or using a sword anyway," Aefric said. "So this is more about keeping in practice than being practical."

"Really," Beornric said, as though springing a trap. "And if his majesty wants your grace on the front lines of the coming war? Do you think your knights will object to your sword then? Or your armor?"

As one, the Knights of the Lake clapped their hilts in accord.

"Fine then," Aefric said. "Next time. But today—"

"Today your grace's healer is in Lachedran. Is the chance of a training accident greater or lesser when your grace has armor protecting him?"

Aefric dropped his shoulders and sighed. "Shall I put on the bracer too? *Ensure* my safety?"

"Of course not. Training with the bracer would give you bad habits," Beornric said, not giving a fraction. "But if your grace goes into battle, I'd prefer him wearing both his bracer *and* his leathers."

Aefric made the mistake of hesitating. Into the bare moment of silence came the clap of his knights on their hilts.

"Fine," Aefric said. "I'll put on my leathers."

***

AEFRIC USED TO WEAR HIS LEATHERS ALL THE TIME. BACK ... OH, ABOUT ten years ago. When he was still training as a dweomerblade with the Iron Wands, before they threw him out for getting distracted too often with spellwork that had nothing to do with dweomerblade training.

Wasn't his fault he was more magically flexible than they were. But then, how much flexibility should he have expected from an order that called itself the Iron Wands?

Even after he stopped wearing leathers every day, he'd made sure he always had a set handy. His most recent were some he'd bought late in the Godswalk Wars.

They were a good set. Dark blue. Supple. Practically molded themselves to his body and almost as comfortable as those linens he'd put on earlier.

Wonderful armor. Why did they have to be all the way up in his apartments when he needed them?

He could have sent a page for them, but that would have taken time. He could have flown up himself, but Beornric would have given him a hard time for not having the right equipment on hand when he needed it.

So he'd settled for these.

They were good brown leather, at least, and thick enough. And whoever had cleaned them last did a good job, because they smelled like leather oil, not sweat or anything worse.

But they were stiff. And they didn't fit right. And they weren't quite long enough.

Worse, Beornric knew all this before he'd ever raised the question. Must've checked them while Aefric was picking out a training sword. Because by the wolfish grin only just hiding under that bushy black mustache, he was *hoping* Aefric would utter even a small complaint. Likely so he could make that comment about the duke coming to his own training yard unprepared.

So Aefric just wedged a smile onto his face that he *knew* didn't look sincere, stretched a little as he drew his blunted longsword, and called out, "Ready!"

Micham came at him first, with blunted longsword and round shield.

Aefric had a few inches of reach on Micham, which could be negated by the shield, if Aefric wasn't careful.

He immediately spun to Micham's shield side. Not even to set up a blow yet. Just to gauge how the knight responded.

Micham shifted his footing, shield guarding and sword lying high alongside it. Ready to stab, yes, but limiting how he could swing.

Aefric feinted high, shield side, then swept a low cut that should have been out of parrying range for Micham's sword.

Micham read the feint. Stepped into the low strike, parrying it with the bottom edge of his shield. Cut a high sweep over its top.

Aefric ducked the cut. Gave Micham a thrusting kick that drove him back a step.

Micham recovered too fast. Had his shield in line to parry and his blade coming around to counter.

One thing about the Iron Wands, though. Rigid they might've been, but their training had been demanding and effective. And most of what Aefric'd learned from them had been acrobatic. So it was a bit of dweomerblade combat magic he did then by instinct.

A burst of inner power flowed down into his legs as he leapt right over Micham. Tumbling through the air and striking as he passed. Micham, impressively, managed to get his shield in the way. Aefric landed behind Micham ready to strike.

Micham leapt forward — away from Aefric's swing — before whirling back around. Shield high and sword ready—

"Your grace!" Beornric's voice. "The royal messenger arrives!"

Micham immediately lowered and crossed his sword and shield, bowing his head in surrender to end the fight.

"Hardly a surrender," Aefric said, sheathing his sword. "We were just getting started. I'm not even sweating yet."

"But, your grace," Micham began, but Aefric waved him to silence.

"Oh, I know," he said, quirking a smile. "Means we have to stop. Doesn't mean you should offer a surrender, and I won't accept yours now."

The training duels didn't mean anything, of course. But still, there were always small competitions going among the Knights of the Lake. Little bets they placed among themselves.

Micham grinned when Aefric refused his surrender, likely escaping the loss of a few coins and a measure of pride. Aefric winked at him, and turned to approach Beornric and the messenger.

Royal messengers were, by tradition, always nobles. Usually they were chosen from pages who had trained at Armityr before coming of age, but were not next in line to inherit, and had no pressing need to return to their family lands.

Certainly fit the look of the young blonde man in royal livery right now. He had fashionably pale skin, coiffed short brown hair, and as his gaze swept over Aefric's ill-fitting leathers, a slight twist of disdain entered his eyes and the set of his mouth.

Not that he could have had a lot of room to judge. Given the stiff, ill-used scabbard holding the rapier at his side, if he'd ever drawn a weapon, it had only been on a training ground.

But then, his disdain might've been about more than Aefric's armor. It seemed to increase as he looked about.

That was strange. Water's End was even larger than the royal palace, and between the Great Spires and the shimmering dark blue walls, hard to believe he wasn't impressed...

Then Aefric recognized the attitude. He'd seen it often in the great cities like Goldenmoon and Sartis. Where the citizens believed themselves at the center of the cultural universe, and everyplace else a foolish backwater...

"Do I have the honor of addressing his grace, Aefric Brightstaff?" he asked, and made it sound like a sincere question.

"You," Beornric growled, "have the honor of addressing his grace, *Ser* Aefric Brightstaff, Duke of Deepwater and Baron of Netar."

"Of course," the royal messenger said blandly. "Do please excuse me, your grace. I meant no offense."

"Funny way of showing it," Arras said, stepping closer. "From your tone to that dung-smelling look on your face to the fact that you *have yet to bow before the duke.*"

"Again," the royal messenger said, sounding bored by the conversation, "I must crave your grace's pardon. I meant no offense. I only wished to ensure that I addressed the correct individual. Given ... your grace's adornments and the lack of his ... most famous accompaniment—"

With a gesture Aefric brought the Brightstaff speeding to his hand.

That widened the royal messenger's eyes and got something closer to a respectful tone as he said, "Understood, your grace."

His bow was still a bit shallow, all things considered, but Aefric didn't see any reason to press the point.

"I have for your grace a missive from his royal majesty, Colm Stronghand, King of Armyr, to be delivered only into your grace's own hands."

Aefric extended his empty hand and raised an eyebrow.

The messenger reached to his belt for the black leather scabbard of his noble's dagger. Suddenly a scroll appeared, tied to the dagger.

A neat little bit of magic, that. By tradition, every Armyrian noble carried a dagger at all times. So common and accepted a practice that most eyes would glaze right over it. Perfect place for a small spell to hide a scroll.

The royal messenger raised the scroll to show that the wax seal was still intact — the golden oak tree on a field of forest green — then placed it in Aefric's outstretched hand. His gaze lingered a moment on the scroll...

Oh, of course. That tiny pulse of magic in the seal. Likely a spell that would destroy the scroll if tampered with by anyone but Aefric. And the royal wizard — Nayoria — certainly knew him well enough to key such a spell to him.

Aefric stood the Brightstaff beside him, broke the wax seal, and unwound the scroll.

"I believe his majesty intended it to be read in private," the royal messenger said.

Irritation flared through Aefric then. This youth was pushing his luck.

Apparently something in Aefric's expression triggered the royal messenger's survival instincts, because his eyes widened and his mouth clapped shut.

"Pray," Aefric said, "did his majesty instruct you to tell me that?"

"No, your grace," the royal messenger said, quickly now. "But—"

"Because if his majesty told you to tell me that, and you waited until I broke the seal to say anything..."

"I swear, your grace," the royal messenger said, hands coming up as though trying to show how harmless he was. As though Aefric didn't know already. "It's merely custom at the royal palace—"

"The royal palace has eyes everywhere," Aefric said. "This is my castle, these my training grounds, and surrounding you are my knights. Which of them, in your great depth of experience, are you suggesting I should not trust?"

If Aefric had thought the royal messenger was pale before, now he looked as though he'd been drained by a vampire for three straight days. His pallor now could have given Quintabis a run for his money.

"Your grace! I didn't mean! I—"

Aefric raised a hand for silence. Spoke a little more gently now.

"I know you didn't. And more importantly, my knights know you didn't." He shook his head. "I know you consider Deepwater the far end of civilization, boy, and therefore all of us ignorant bumpkins."

"Your grace, I—"

"*But you would do well* to remember that everyone around you right now has seen a great deal more of life and this world than you have. *You* are the one with the small mind and the small experience. I suggest, in the future, you offer courtesy and respect until given a reason to do otherwise. It'll save you some *harsh* learning experiences."

"Yes, your grace," the royal messenger said, bowing deeper this time. "Thank you, your grace."

"Good," Aefric said. "On your way with you."

"Your grace ... is so certain he will not wish to send a reply with me?"

"Did his majesty tell you to await a reply?"

"Your grace, he did not."

"Then likely he doesn't expect one. And if I need to send one, I'll send my own messenger. You know, we do have them, even all the way out here."

"Your grace, I—"

"Save it," Aefric said, waving away whatever the royal messenger was going to say. "You're welcome to guest here for the day and leave with the morning tide, if you like, or start your way back now if you prefer. Either way, you are dismissed."

"Yes, your grace," the royal messenger said, bowing again. "Thank you, your grace."

He turned and left quickly.

"Some of these royal messengers," Beornric said, shaking his head. "Bad enough that most of them think the sun rises and sets on Armityr and that they're gracing us with their presence. But they also know they're untouchable to almost everyone. Good of you to remind this one that their untouchability does not extend to the peers."

Aefric chuckled. "I didn't know if it did or didn't. I just didn't like his attitude."

All around Aefric, his knights clapped their hilts in agreement.

Aefric opened the scroll and began to read.

My Dear Duke of Deepwater,

I trust this letter finds you well, Aefric. My spies in Malimfar suggest that their princess may be coming to visit you. Try not to offend her too deeply when you send her away, but my orders stand. Do not receive her, and certainly do not host her.

Ah, but you don't need me to remind you of that. You know well what's going on, and I have more important princesses to write you about.

I know you're expecting four. More than enough to keep even your hands full, I should think. And yet, I've just given permission for Varondam to send a fifth princess to court you as well.

I'll be blunt here, Aefric. I know you appreciate directness.

I'm not happy that I felt the need to say yes to Dalius in this matter. If you were of an old Armyrian family, I could have refused him, despite the delicacy of our current situation.

Then again, were you of an old Armyrian family, I doubt Dalius would even consider sending you this particular princess.

You see, Princess Kiala is what they call in Varondam an "unspoken" bastard. Meaning she's a by-blow of Dalius' father, Dalius II, granted a kind of half-acknowledged status. The sort of sad station in life that most civilized kingdoms wouldn't permit.

"Unspoken" means that her parentage has not been denied, but that she is not permitted equal status with his trueborn children.

Thus, she may call herself a princess. She is entitled to attending maids, an allowance, even a dowry, and should she never marry, she would live in comfort as part of the royal court to the end of her days.

But because she has not been fully acknowledged, she cannot call herself a Swiftblade, nor will any of her offspring be acknowledged as members of the royal family. She cannot sit regent nor hold titles in Varondam. She cannot represent Varondam in negotiations. And neither she nor any of her offspring shall ever be given the right of inheritance. Not even to the least of King Dalius' titles or properties.

Effectively, she is a sort of quasi-noble. Most courts would not consider her a member of the Varondam royal family at all, nor would they consider a marriage between her and any of their important relatives. Much less would any marriage be considered to indicate an alliance.

In fact, as you are a duke and peer of the crown, this request could be taken as something of an insult, should you choose to view it that way. And I would not blame you if you do. But I do not believe it is meant as an insult.

You see, I believe she requested this of Dalius because Maev has been telling stories of you down in their court, and done too good a job of it. I suspect this Princess Kiala has become taken with the image Maev paints with her words.

I believe Dalius agreed to ask me for permission to send her to you because he is fond of his unspoken sister, and because he considers you little more than a jumped-up adventurer. And therefore, a good match for her.

I, of course, know you are a good deal more than a jumped-up adventurer. And I only granted permission to show pliability to Dalius, as Maev brings him closer and closer to agreeing to the alliance I desire.

I'm not worried that you will be disrespectful to Princess Kiala. I know you better than that. But I do worry that when the other princesses realize who she is — and more importantly who she isn't — they'll take insult at her presence.

Especially if you treat her as well as you treat them, which I suspect you will.

This puts you in a tight spot, Aefric. And I do apologize for that. You will not face it alone, however. I am sending Killian to you, to help. Between your nature and my son's charm, I trust you'll be able to handle even this.

Of course, there's always the possibility that you'll fall in love with this Kiala. Maev has mentioned her in letters. She considers Kiala "a dear,"

which suggests that she has a good heart, though she might be a bit shel-
tered for your tastes.

If you do fall in love with her, fine. Killian will help you smooth things
over with her rivals. If you don't, if you prefer another princess, or perhaps
Byrhta Ol'Caran or Sighild Ol'Masarkor, that's fine too.

Either way, do choose your wife soon, Aefric. I want you married with
an heir on the way before the coming spring, for reasons you know well.

Do not require me to choose one for you, which — although I invoke it
as rarely as I am able — I trust your advisers have warned you is within
my rights.

I realize you do not care for such pressure. But I did warn you on the
day I created you Duke of Deepwater. Duchess Arinda died without heir. I
will not have you doing the same.

To take away some of the sting you may be feeling right now, let me tell
you that Killian also brings with him the present I spoke of when last we
talked. I trust you will enjoy it, and put it to good use.

And do enjoy courting the princesses. Such an event comes only once in
a man's life, if it comes at all. Do see it as a blessing and a pleasure, not a
responsibility.

Though not too much of a pleasure, I hope. Rethneryl practices the
noble privilege as we do, but you should know that Hatay and Shachan do
not. And you know already that Varondam does not either.

There. I've given you more than enough to think about.

And in case you think I've grown irritated with you, let me reassure you
that I still consider you a trusted and invaluable vassal.

Be well, Aefric.
By the hand of his majesty,
Colm Stronghand
King of Armyr

GIVEN HIS WAY, BEORNRIC WOULD PROBABLY HAVE CALLED TOGETHER
all of Aefric's advisers to discuss the king's letter, what it meant, and
how Water's End needed to prepare.

And deep down, Aefric knew that each of his advisers would likely have something useful to contribute on the topic. And certainly Kentigern and Garnotin needed to be informed before the end of the day.

Well, Kentigern needed to be informed before the day's end. Garnotin could wait until he got back from Lachedran.

Either way, it meant at least one more meeting, and long discussions of preparations and priorities.

All of that could wait.

When Aefric finished reading the king's letter, he handed it to Beornric, turned back to Micham and said, "Where were we?"

By the time Aefric left the training grounds, the sun had passed into the rain clouds, the wind had shifted easterly, bringing in good lake smells, and — though he had not won a single bout against his Knights of the Lake — Aefric felt better than he had in days.

Tired, sweaty, a little bruised and likely sore later, but good. He even fought down the urge to simply fly up to his apartments, and made his legs carry him up those long, long flights of stairs, all the while listening to Beornric go over what Aefric had done right on the training grounds, and what he had done wrong.

Of course, in a sense, Beornric was not the best person to do this. The best person would have been Deirdre, who was not only another dweomerblade — and therefore able to critique aspects of Aefric's fighting style that Beornric could not — but possibly the best individual fighter Aefric had ever seen.

Certainly if he'd seen anyone better, he couldn't think of who.

But Deirdre, of course, was off on a mission for him. And Beornric was a seasoned veteran who had probably forgotten more about melee combat than a magic-user like Aefric had ever known.

So Aefric listened to the critiques of his timing, his vision, his use of range and mobility. All of which were topics where Beornric found room for improvement in Aefric's efforts.

But on reaching his apartments, he was ready for a break, so he promised a *small* meeting over late lunch, and went to bathe.

Ahhhh.

Was there anything better for tired muscles than a steaming hot bath scented with lemon blossoms?

Aefric all but lost himself in that giant, white marble tub with its gold and silver veins while wet heat soaked him. Eased sweet relief and loosened many knots and tight places.

Oh, how often this simple pleasure had been little more than a dream, while he'd been struggling and battling through his adventures. And now that he could enjoy it, he refused to rush.

He lazily took in the view over busy Lake Deepwater. Idly wondered if any of the ships he saw might have been carrying one or more of the inbound princesses. And if so, what they would be like. What they would think of him.

Would they be pleased to have been sent to court an Armyrian duke? The "hero" of the battles of Deepwater and Frozen Ridge?

Or would they be doing nothing more than their duty as princesses, seeking to build or strengthen an Armyrian alliance through marriage? Even if it meant their husband might be nothing more than a "jumped-up adventurer?"

Would he see the disdain of that royal messenger in their eyes, even while they laughed at his jokes and pretended to find him charming?

Maybe he should have just married Byrhta or Sighild and had done with it. But he knew deep down why he hadn't married either of them yet — he held out hope that he might still marry Maev.

But in truth, that was a fool's hope.

Maev would end up married to King Dalius. Not just for the alliance, but because he would make a better marriage for her than one of Armyr's own dukes.

Her children, her bloodline, forever tied to the throne of Varondam.

She preferred Aefric. She'd made that quite clear. But what did that really matter? She was a princess. Her preferences made no more difference than Killian's had, back before he was promised to Princess...

Gitta? Was that the woman's name? Aefric wasn't sure.

Well, Killian was promised to a princess of Rethneryl. Aefric knew that much.

The point was, in the end, King Colm would decide whom Maev would marry. Just as he might decide for Aefric, if he took too long…

A depressing line of thought, and a sure sign that Aefric was done with his bath.

He dried himself off. Dressed in the clothes provided by his valets without really thinking about what he was wearing. A fine, pale blue silk tunic over rust red hose, and leather shoes that had been dyed the same shade as the tunic.

Brightstaff in hand and the wand Garram at his belt, Aefric walked downstairs and out onto his public floor balcony, where he expected Beornric to be waiting with Kentigern and lunch.

He was two-thirds right. Beornric was there. Lunch was there — looked to be trenchers of spiced roast beef with melted cheddar, served with silver tankards of good, crisp day beer — but Kentigern was not.

Yrsa, however, was.

His knight-advisers stood from their fine greenwood chairs as Aefric stepped out onto the balcony. The wind had picked up, and smelled even more of rain. The clouds would open by evening, at the latest.

"Your grace," they said, and though they said the greeting together, they said it differently. Beornric, with a hint of concern in his voice. Yrsa, with more than a hint.

Aefric nodded to them as he sat, allowing them to sit too.

"Why do I have a feeling we've gotten worse news while I cleaned myself up?"

"Long as you were in that tub, you're lucky the war hasn't started," Yrsa said dryly.

"You look as though it has."

And she did. She had that set to her jaw, and that wary look to her eyes. No darkening to her major scar, but if anything, that was just a clearer indicator that she was ready to deal with trouble, not feeling restrained from action.

"Nelazzi's activities have picked up all along the coast."

"Has she hit us?" Aefric asked, thinking of his towns.

"She's been leaving our ships and towns alone so far," Yrsa said.

"Why?"

"Word is, she's hunting for something. Which means it's something she knows we don't have here."

"A weapon?" Beornric asked.

"My first thought," Yrsa said, "but if so it's something smallish. Or at least, smaller than a ship's armaments."

"Stickyfire?" Aefric asked.

Stickyfire was an alchemical brew that had been outlawed across most of Qorunn. Few knew how to make it, though Aefric was among the few. Karbin had taught him, because while it was considered a war crime to use stickyfire in any kind of conflict — and death to use it against people or property in nearly any kingdom — where adventurers delved, laws were few, and stickyfire, a tool that had its uses.

Stickyfire could burn through a great many seals and locks, without requiring an adventurer to stand nearby, in case such an opening might trigger a deadly trap.

Not to mention that in some places, deep beneath the surface of Qorunn, dwelled *things* that might only fall to a weapon as persistent and dangerous as stickyfire...

"Let us hope not," Beornric said. "Even the Godswalk Wars saw little of that hellish stuff."

He whispered a prayer.

"I've heard nothing of what it is she's seeking," Yrsa said, "only that she strikes with ruthless speed any ship she believes might be carrying it."

"And nothing about the ships she's struck suggests a pattern?" Beornric asked.

"Had there been one, would you need to ask?" Yrsa said, then scoffed. "A mind like Nelazzi's is too tricky for that. She'll hit some ships just to cloud the question, knowing in advance they *don't* have what she wants."

"I assume she's still robbing them of what they *do* have?" Aefric asked.

"Is she still a pirate? Of course."

"Nelazzi is tomorrow's problem," Beornric said, laying out the king's letter and tapping it. "This is today's. I've informed Kentigern of its contents, but we need to talk about it."

"I suppose," Aefric said, taking a bite of his trencher. Oh. Not as hot as it likely was a short time ago, but still warm and wonderful. The blend of spices was exciting on the tongue, but the melted cheddar kept them from becoming overpowering. And the bread of the trencher had been toasted to perfection.

"...I'll have to repeat all that, won't I?" asked Beornric, who apparently had continued talking while Aefric...

Had he already eaten the whole thing? Huh. Must've been hungrier than he thought. He smiled sheepishly at Beornric, while taking a sip of day beer.

Day beer was what Keifer would have called India Pale Ale. A little weaker than most of the varieties Keifer had enjoyed around Portland, but a popular drink with lunches and snacks, of an afternoon in Armyr.

"I was *saying*," Beornric said, "that Kentigern tells me King Dalius is known to be quite fond of his unspoken sister, Princess Kiala. Which, I think, implies he's getting serious about marrying Maev and wants you ... removed as a matrimonial prospect from his bride's mind."

"Does suggest he doesn't see Maev as a potential hostage," Aefric said. "Not if he's sending a beloved sister to me."

"I disagree," Yrsa said. "Maev has value as a hostage. Kiala does not."

"If Dalius loves her—"

"King Dalius might love her dearly," Yrsa said. "But don't think for a moment he wouldn't sacrifice her on the altar of political gain. She's *unspoken*. I know this is a new concept to you, but I assure you it means he has been raised to think of her as a tool or a burden, but *nothing more*."

"I'm inclined to agree," Beornric said. "Though I think *favored pet* is a better term for how he likely thinks of her than tool or burden."

Aefric frowned. "Then how does her coming here suggest—"

"He may consider you just a jumped-up adventurer," Beornric said. "But you're rich and powerful. She couldn't possibly dream of a better match. If you marry her, King Dalius believes he will gain some influence with the upstart duke. And if not, he loses nothing. While she's here, she might even charm someone from a powerful merchant family. So even in losing, he gains."

"At the cost of nothing more than a sister who has no place in his family anyway," Yrsa finished.

Aefric thought about that through a sip of day beer.

"Can King Colm really—"

"Yes," Beornric and Yrsa said together. It was Yrsa who finished the thought. "In fact, some of us were expecting him to mention it before now."

"Pick someone, your grace," Beornric said. "Just pick someone and have done with it."

———

THE NEXT SEVERAL DAYS PUSHED AEFRIC'S PATIENCE TO ITS LIMITS.

None of the princesses had arrived.

Prince Killian had not arrived.

Deirdre and Karbin were still off with their investigation.

Water's End buzzed with preparations for the incoming royalty. Kentigern was in his element — having rooms cleaned, checking the cellar stores, arranging for gifts and food and clothing and more — but beyond the usual business, there was little for Aefric to do. Except bear yet more lectures about the proper way to greet royalty. When to bow and how deep. How to address them and how not to address them.

And everyone seemed to think he'd forget who practiced the noble privilege and who didn't. Despite the fact that it was those same people — especially Kentigern, Beornric and Yrsa — who always pushed for him to sleep with as many noblewomen of his court as he could.

He'd already decided, though, that he wouldn't be chasing the bliss moment with *any* of the inbound princesses. Just seemed the safer political bet.

Meanwhile, his court ran wild with speculations. Not just about the incoming royalty — what they knew and didn't about each princess and each kingdom, who Prince Killian might share the bliss moment with, and the like — but about how it all related to the aftermath of their duke's spurning of Princess Astrid, the strange appearance and gifts from notorious Kefthal, that "mysterious" night with Ashling…

Rumors and innuendo swirled and surrounded him, agitated to a frothing peak by the constant activity.

And *nothing* Aefric could really do but *wait*.

Oh, he had his usual meetings and reports, the usual daily business of being a duke. But such things didn't serve as much of a distraction. He'd been growing too used to them.

So what he really felt over those several days was the anxious anticipation of waiting. Of wanting them to get here. To get the initial meeting over with. The formalities. To find out something of these women himself. Not to mention talking with Prince Killian again. Perhaps working up a strategy with him about how to juggle the four trueborn princesses with the one "unspoken" bastard.

And he couldn't do *any* of it until at least *one* of them got here.

It was terrible.

Aefric used to think he had patience. That he knew what waiting was. He was beginning to learn now that he'd had *no idea*.

When he was an adventurer, waiting involved holding back from acting for what might *feel* like forever — perhaps while someone more skilled at sneaking about scouted out threats — but what was actually little more than a few tense minutes. An hour or two at most.

During the wars, it was much the same. Minutes here, minutes there. Perhaps a few hours or a sleepless night. Always with that desperate feeling of tension, tightening muscles and shortening breaths.

Even as Keifer, back on Earth. Waiting a few days for grades in college or a job offer afterwards was about as bad as it got. Never anything that made him feel as though his life were on the line.

His future, perhaps. But even then, he'd had Andi by his side. Helping him maintain perspective.

But this time, everyone else was as anxious as Aefric. Perhaps even more anxious in Kentigern's case, which wasn't helping...

It was waiting on a whole new scale for Aefric. Days. Aetts, maybe. With no true break in the tension to settle his stomach.

Even seeking relief in the arms of a courtier wasn't much good, because between bliss moments, they all wanted to talk about the princesses. What Aefric knew about them, if he was already leaning one direction or another. If he favored Hatay or Shachan or Rethneryl. If Ashling had snuck in and stolen his heart when no one was looking. And where Byrhta Ol'Caran and Sighild Ol'Masarkor stood through it all.

On the second night, Ler Karmilla Ol'Ealan even brought up Maev, which proved to be all Aefric could take. As of the next morning, he took to sleeping alone for the time being.

Frustrated his court, but gave him something like respite.

Worse, the decision to sleep alone while waiting for the princesses was just more grist for the court's speculations. Which were already ramping up beyond anything he'd seen before.

Why had none of these royal guests arrived yet? Had they been slowed by the size of their entourages? Did their lateness suggest that each of them — Killian included, according to some gossips — was coming for an extended visit?

Had something happened to them on the road? Or at sea? Bandits? Marauders? The Pirate Queen Nelazzi?

Was Nelazzi seeking vengeance for the beheading of Calder Ol'Ulith? Some idiot even began spreading rumors that Calder had been her lover, so her wrath would be swift and terrible...

As the days passed, Nelazzi's name got bandied about more and more, heightening Aefric's agitation. But not about his incoming royal visitors. About Deirdre and Karbin.

What could be taking them so long? When Aefric had sent them — just about at summer's end — he and his advisers had been all but certain that Nelazzi had ordered the attempt on his life at Asarchai.

The trail had been hot. Everyone had been convinced that proof would be easily found, and the two investigators would return within the aett.

Now the harvest festival was perhaps two aetts away, and there'd been no word.

What could be delaying them?

Were they in trouble? Were they dead?

Or was it just that that the proof they'd found had led them to discover some bigger problem? Something that they needed to check without delay?

Where were they?

One message spell, and Aefric might've gotten an answer. He knew both Deirdre and Karbin — especially Karbin — more than well enough to cast such a spell successfully.

But a message spell inevitably caused at least a momentary distraction in the recipient. And while they were out in the field like this — delving into dangerous places, sleeping at odd hours — a distraction at the wrong time could prove fatal.

Not a risk he was willing to take. Much as he yearned for some word...

Waiting. All this waiting. It was driving him mad.

He had a momentary reprieve when Garnotin and Bebara returned from Lachedran in good spirits.

"Oh, your grace," Bebara gushed on Aefric's public floor balcony one bright afternoon, enthusiasm stealing years from her face and lightening her step. "Thank you for allowing me to see those unfortunates to aid. Redellea — she's the senior priestess at Lachedran — has a kind and gentle soul, but not the eye for detail that is needed when it comes to setting those people on the right path."

From the way Bebara went on, it sounded to Aefric as though

Redellea had had things well in hand, and that Bebara had been doing little more than criticizing the trim on a tapestry. But it was healer's business, and Bebara was happy, so he smiled and let her gush.

And most important there, Bebara seemed pleased the with the arrangements, and sounded hopeful for a full recovery of the self for most, if not all, of those abused people.

Garnotin seemed buoyed by helping the freed slaves as well. Whenever Bebara paused in her gushing, he added a detail or two of his own.

Garnotin even brought back unexpected good news. While in Lachedran he'd met with the mayor's wife, Karaleca Ol'Nara.

"She reports that your lost lers project is coming along quite well," Garnotin said, standing beside Bebara who clearly wanted to go on more about the recovery of those freed slaves. "She's found almost thirty children ready to be placed and trained as pages, once their identities are confirmed by Kentigern."

The Godswalk Wars had devastated many families, and the lower nobility were no exception. The wars had displaced many children whose noble parents had been killed or lost during the wars, and who were in danger of losing stewardship of their lands.

"That's fine," Aefric said, "but she *does* remember she's supposed to find *every* child displaced by the wars, yes? Not just the nobles?"

"She does," Garnotin assured him. "She's found seventy-two such children of common stock."

"What's she doing with them?" Aefric asked.

"Oh," Garnotin said, clearly less concerned about the common children than the nobles, "she said something about her husband starting a commission to find them all placement in Lachedran."

"Ridiculous," Aefric said. "Lachedran *might* be able to handle what she's found so far, but if she does her job right, she'll find a lot more. And Lachedran won't be big enough to find homes for all of them, let alone work when they're old enough. Not considering the *other* local children who'll need apprenticeships and work when the time comes. The lost children will have to be spread out here, at

Behal, maybe Ajenmoor and a few of the rebuilt towns along the coast."

"She said something about coming to visit, to give your grace a formal report herself and see the noble children to Kentigern for confirmation of their identities," Garnotin said. "If your grace prefers, I can take that meeting and ensure she takes your grace's concerns into account."

"That'll depend," Aefric said with a sigh, "on when all these princesses get here."

And then he was back to waiting. Until one morning, perhaps the sixth day after that royal messenger's arrival, he simply could wait no more.

AEFRIC'S ADVISERS WERE ASSEMBLED AND WAITING WHEN AEFRIC entered the smallish black oak meeting room that morning. The moment they stood, Aefric spoke.

"Any word from Karbin or Deirdre?"

"None, your grace," Beornric said, eyes narrowing suspiciously as he took in Aefric's thick woolen doublet — navy blue over a Deepwater gray silk tunic — and leather riding pants. "If I might ask—"

"In a moment," Aefric said. "Any word on the princesses or Prince Killian?"

"Not as yet," Kentigern said, frowning too now, as he realized Aefric wasn't dressed for his usual day in the castle.

"Any dire emergencies at all?"

"Only one I can think of," Yrsa said, frowning.

Aefric looked the question at her.

"Our duke appears to have lost his mind."

"He hasn't," Aefric said, but before he could continue, Beornric cut in.

"But I trust you remember that we can't even afford to let you go hunting right now? What we talked about regarding the importance of your being here when royalty arrives?"

"You don't want a repeat of the summer incident," Yrsa said quickly. "When you kept both Princesses Astrid and Xenia waiting for more than a day while you sailed off to Ajenmoor to deal—"

"To deal with something more pressing than social niceties," Aefric said. "And I'd do it again, if there was need. But I'm not going to sail for Ajenmoor, and I'm not going hunting."

"Then where are you going, if I might ask?" Garnotin asked. He looked the least troubled by Aefric's apparel.

Even Elkari was frowning as though checking his clothing against some kind of precedent involving waiting for royal arrivals.

"I'm going to the Dragonscar. I want to check in personally with Ge'rek and Po'rek. See how Clan Thunder Stick is faring, and find out if they'll be ready to march to war this coming spring."

"That's at least a two-day trip," Kentigern objected. "And that's assuming your grace sails to Lachedran to save time."

"More like three days," Elkari said, "if he doesn't push the horses." She shook her head. "No. Two days is *likely* right, taking into account the new roads. If he leaves at once."

"You can't be gone two days," Kentigern objected. "What if a princess arrives by nightfall?"

"Has there been a rika from Behal or Ajenmoor suggesting that a royal ship has been sighted?" Aefric asked calmly.

"Well, no," Kentigern said, "but—"

"Have any of my vassals along the Kingsroad sent word of a royal party passing through?"

"Well, no," Kentigern said, sounding flustered now. "But—"

"Then the chances of a royal arrival by dark tonight are slim."

"Slim," Elkari agreed, "but certainly the possibility remains. If they sail a fast ship, they could pass either Ajenmoor or Behal as late as one bell past midday and still arrive here in time for dinner."

"And *certainly* within *two days*," Kentigern said, throwing up his hands.

"You're going to fly, aren't you?" Beornric said.

Yrsa didn't even let him answer before saying, "Do I need to ask?"

"Please, calm down, all of you," Aefric said. "Yes, I intend to fly.

No, I don't intend to go alone. But neither am I traveling with a full entourage."

Beornric snapped his fingers. "That chariot thing of yours."

"My *magari*," Aefric said, smiling. "Yes. Which means I can take three with me. Whichever two of my knights are on duty to guard me, as well as..."

Aefric raised his eyebrows at both Beornric and Yrsa, who both stood immediately.

They looked at each other.

"You go," Yrsa said. "He's more likely to listen to you, and I still have plenty to do to prepare for spring."

Beornric clapped her on the shoulder in a comradely fashion, but unless Aefric was mistaken, there was affection in the look they gave each other.

"I'll want armor," Beornric said, gesturing to his dark orange tunic over dark red hose. "I don't project the right sense of strength in this."

"You'll want armor anyway," Yrsa said. "Wouldn't want to be wearing nothing more than a tunic if his nibs gets you into a fight with some nameless and dreadful underground beastie."

"Hey," Aefric objected.

"Oh?" Beornric said, smiling wolfishly. "Does your grace mean to imply that he has never fought some sort of nameless and dreadful underground beastie?"

"You know I have," Aefric said with a sigh.

"And would your grace not agree that anything *less* than some nameless and dreadful underground beastie would be dealt with by the borogs themselves?"

"Most likely, yes."

"Then he must agree that I should be kitted out for battle. Just in case."

Of course, Aefric had never suggested otherwise. But he had the feeling that pointing as much out would only lead to more teasing.

"Fine," Aefric said. "I'll grab some breakfast then, and meet you and my knights on my public floor balcony as soon as you're ready. Garnotin, the morning meeting is yours."

A short time later, Aefric was joined on his public floor balcony by Vria, Arras, and Beornric. All three of them in their shining full plate armor.

Three knights in full armor. Perhaps it was a good thing the *magari* didn't have a weight limit to what it could carry.

Aefric reached into the magical pouch at his belt — a gift from Jenbarjen, his court wizard in Netar — and called to his fingertips a squared-off, oblong crystal of pure white.

He'd never learned the secret of summoning a *magari* himself — though he'd seen some research notes in a Soulfist grimoire that might help him figure out the formula — but he had taken this crystal and a few others beside it from Duke Wylyn's former court wizard after ... some problems this past summer.

And with this crystal, he needed only a moment of mental focus and the thought of the right keyword and...

A flaming chariot sprang into being in a cleared spot of the balcony, drawn by two *magaunts* — phantasmal horses — of flame red, from snout to mane to hooves.

Aefric boarded the chariot and took up the reins. His knights boarded behind him. Vria and Arras looking excited for the trip. Beornric, a touch green under the collar. He'd ridden in the *magari* a few times now, and while he no longer had to clutch the sides with *white-knuckled* grip, he still had yet to develop anything more than a bare tolerance for flying.

Couldn't be helped, though. This was the only means Aefric had for getting himself and three others to Dragonscar and back before dinner.

Aefric snapped the reins and the *magari* took to the air.

The *magari* soared through the air. Aefric felt the wind in his hair again. Laughed at a light morning rainfall, not even enough to make him raise the hood of his soft, gray woolen traveling cloak.

Short, slender Vria with her bright orange hair — had her hair been growing more and more orange? Aefric would have sworn that when he'd met her this past spring, the orange in her hair had been little more than highlights. Now, it dominated. Perhaps she was growing into the eldrani side of her heritage?

Either way, she joined in his laughter. She turned her face turned to the wind and rain, while she sang an uplifting eldrani song in praise of storms.

Beornric wanted nothing to do with the rain or the wind. He had the hood of his own dark green traveling cloak pulled down low, and stood at the back of the fiery chariot, keeping his gaze from straying to the countryside below. His hands held the sides, but his grip looked more like self-assurance than fear.

Arras watched the landscape beneath them as it soared past. First great Lake Deepwater itself, then bustling Lachedran and then the rolling hills and farms north, as they followed the new road past the scout outposts on their way to the Dragonscar.

Just to be out flying felt *so* much better. Getting out of the castle — wonderful as it was — with all its waiting and its gossip and more.

Made him miss adventuring, although he knew that was the nostalgia talking, and not any true desire. His life was better now, and he could do more good for more people as a duke than he'd ever managed as an adventurer.

They left the clouds and rain behind somewhere over the road past the second scout station. Aefric mused that the trip might've been faster had he flown directly over the Threepeaks Mountains, rather than following established travel routes.

But he had an easier time gauging his direction with precision when he had known landmarks to follow.

Besides. He wasn't sure how well Beornric would've handled flying high enough to clear the mountains. Flying was hard enough on the man as it was.

The sun was not quite high overhead when Aefric began their descent toward the Dragonscar.

Calling the Dragonscar a chasm didn't quite do it justice. Nearly two hundred miles long, it was, and roughly ten miles wide in places.

The Dragonscar was said to have been created back when the Risen Sea was just a valley, and one of the tremendous dragons of legend died while flying. The story went that the dragon had been so big, and that it had flown so fast, it tore through the rocky terrain in its death throes.

For nearly two hundred miles.

The evidence for the tale, such as it was, lay in the massive dragon skeleton all the way at the eastern end of the chasm.

Aefric had his doubts, though. The dragon skeleton faced outward, not inward. And he noticed that, immense as it was, the shape of the Dragonscar *might've* suggested that the dragon had caused it with one mighty, deadly breath.

Either way, truly a legendary feat. And one that Kainemorton had suggested carried world-saving implications. Though Kainemorton, as he did all too often, provided no more details than a simple suggestion.

Vria and Arras called to the scouts up on the ridge as Aefric angled the *magari* to land down on the brown and gray rocks of the Dragonscar floor.

The wind never seemed to stop blowing in the Dragonscar. And even here, well over a hundred miles from the coast, it carried with it a suggestion of the sea.

Aefric dismissed his *magari* and took a moment to look about, while Beornric pulled himself together after the stresses of the flight.

The chasm floor looked much the same as it had the last time he saw it. Nothing much grew down here, apart from patches of moss and lichen, which seemed to be reviving a bit under the recent rains.

Otherwise, it was mostly rocks and dust. Not even much dirt really, down here. Far more bare rock. Cracked and fissured in places, but for the most part coherent enough and reasonably level.

What had once been a vague suggestion of a descent from the southern ridge above had been worked by masons and engineers into a true pass, with switchbacks, broad enough for two carts to pass each other.

Aefric noticed, though, that a knotted rope dangled down from the scout camp as well, which made him smirk. Apparently not all the scouts had patience for going up and down the slow way.

"All right," Aefric said, tapping the butt of the Brightstaff on the rocks. "Everyone ready?"

"Ready," Vria called, checking her sword in its scabbard and glancing about for threats.

"Ready," Arras agreed, doing much the same with her twin swords, and covering the area that Vria wasn't facing.

"Ready enough," Beornric said, throwing back his hood and nodding. "Shall we see about your grace's borogs?"

Aefric had to bite back a denial there. After all, he didn't consider the borogs a possession. They were individuals and citizens of Deepwater, with their own rights and responsibilities.

But the truth was, they were still *his* borogs. He was their duke, and more than that, their chieftain. They would have described *themselves* as his borogs. Or at least his clan.

The word "his" still felt too possessive though.

"Let's go," Aefric said, leading the way. He'd been here enough times now that he'd set the *magari* down close to the caves where Clan Thunder Stick would be found.

There were three caves on the south side with excellent gold veins — one even richer than the other two — and one on the north side, which he shared with Duke Wylyn of Silvelake, after the first hundred feet of cave.

He didn't go into any of the caves, though. He approached the south side caves within about a hundred feet and stopped.

Although his command of Borog had grown by leaps and bounds over the last season or so, and he was developing a deeper understanding of the borogs' culture and ways, the means by which they organized their mines was another matter entirely.

He'd tried once to go into their mines. Even with a guide, he'd managed to get lost. It seemed that humans took a somewhat ... linear approach to mining. They would dig in straight lines — more or less — to find veins, then follow those veins.

Borogs, on the other hand, followed a kind of logic that he could not quite grasp. It might've been because he lacked the proper sense of smell. He knew for a fact that they could smell gold. It stood to reason that they could smell other metals — and possibly other things — in the dirt and rock.

Or maybe the way their organized their mines was just an idiosyncratic illustration of the borog thought process.

Either way, it made no sense to Aefric.

That one trip into the mines had been enough. After that, he stayed out in the chasm, and alerted them to his presence.

So when he stopped walking, he thumped the rocky ground with the butt of the Brightstaff, letting out an echoing thunderclap.

Exactly one, which would let the borogs know he was there and that he wanted to talk to Ge'rek and Po'rek, although others were welcome to come out and see their chief.

"Thunder Stick!" came the cry of several voices, from inside the nearer three caves on the south side. The cry was in Borog, of course. Few of them spoke much of the common tongue.

Borogs began emerging from the caves before him.

The average borog stood more than a head taller than the average human. Aefric was tall for a human, but he still would have been short for a borog.

To say nothing of how skinny they found him. Borogs were thick built, through the limbs as well as the torso, and even to their hides. Thick and strong enough — and usually shaded in the right colors — to remind him of the rhinos Keifer had seen back on Earth.

Aefric had never seen a rhinoceros here in Qorunn. Perhaps the borogs were as close as they came? Borogs certainly had the snouts, complete with twin horns.

For clothing, they wore armor of beaten stone, fashioned by a technique Aefric could not even pretend to understand.

He snorted greeting to the borogs he saw, and stomped acknowledgment every time one of the growing crowd cried out, *"Chief!"* and stomped and snorted.

Aefric's pulse quickened through this. He hoped he was hitting the snort right. Snorting really was a kind of sublanguage of its own for borogs. And without using the translation spell he'd gotten from a Soulfist grimoire, he couldn't be *certain* he was getting it right.

But that spell was a crutch. He'd only really understand the borogs when he understood their language. So he'd been forcing himself to go without it more and more.

At last, Ge'rek and Po'rek emerged to stomp and snort greetings of their own. Taller Ge'rek, with his darker hide. Shorter Po'rek, with his narrower horns.

Ge'rek served as Aefric's chief hand, and spoke for him in his absence. Po'rek was the clan's godspeaker, a position separate from, but equal to, Ge'rek's.

Ge'rek snorted displeasure. Likely because he and Po'rek came before their chief empty handed. Usually they liked to present him with at least some of the most recent haul of gold.

But on the flight down, Aefric had seen carts heading up the switchbacks, each pulled by at least four good horses. Not to mention guarded by soldiers.

So the latest gold shipment had just left.

Aefric tried to snort dismissively, to say the lack of gold on hand was not a problem. But from the way Po'rek scuffed his feet, Aefric had gotten something wrong.

"Mighty carts," Aefric said, swinging his nose to point toward the switchbacks, the way a borog would point with his horn. *"Clan Thunder Stick dig much god metal."*

"God metal for chief!" Ge'rek shouted, stomping.

"God metal for chief!" the rest of the two score or so of borogs who'd emerged from the caves echoed, all stomping their feet.

Aefric snorted satisfaction. Stomped for emphasis.

That snort he'd gotten right, because Po'rek gave him a slight nod.

"How fares me and me?" Aefric said. The Borog language minimized its pronouns. Their word *ul* translated as "I," "me," "my," "mine," and "myself," and when it became the plural *ulalu*, it translated more truly as "me and me" than as "we" or "us" or "our" and so on.

"Me and me..." Ge'rek frowned, then snorted, then scuffed one foot.

Finally he admitted what was clearly bothering him. *"Me and me open wrong passage. Crawler."*

Crawler. The Borog word was *urech*, but it translated about the same. A crawler was a kind of giant insect that haunted mines in places. In theory, it was a scavenger that preyed mostly on the dead. In practice, it had no trouble killing its food.

"Three twenties dead," Ge'rek said, but in the borog way, his voice was matter-of-fact. There was no hushed reverence, no sadness. To borogs, life and death were one, in many ways. *"Must be stopped or no more digging god metal."*

In the common tongue, Aefric told his knights, "There's a crawler down there that's killed about sixty borogs."

"Your grace," Beornric said in a warning tone.

"Don't bother finishing your sentence, Beornric," Aefric said. "We're going in." Switching to Borog, he finished, *"Chief will kill crawler!"*

The borogs began stomping their feet and snorting their form of cheering. Which did nothing to stop Beornric from saying, "If this gets you killed, Yrsa might just chase down your soul to kill you again, you know."

"They're my people," Aefric said simply. "And they need me."

And that, Beornric couldn't argue with.

* * *

ORGANIZING FOR THE VENTURE TOOK A LITTLE TIME. FIRST, GE'REK AND Po'rek called for their weapons — an iron longsword for Ge'rek, and an iron battle axe for Po'rek.

Interestingly, Ge'rek's blade and hilt were both iron, but while Po'rek's axe head was iron, its haft was stone.

Once they had their weapons, Ge'rek called together the clan's primary warriors, who numbered more than a hundred.

"We're not bringing this many after the crawler," Aefric said to Po'rek in the common tongue.

"No," Po'rek agreed, also in the common tongue. "But you say how many, and you choose."

"Me take six," Aefric called out to the assembled warriors, who all stomped their approval.

Aefric stepped in front of Beornric. Stomped. Beornric was given a snorting, stomping cheer from the assemblage. A cheer that was repeated when Aefric then stomped in front of Arras and Vria.

The cheer was even more vigorous when Aefric stomped in front of Ge'rek and Po'rek. He hadn't been sure it was appropriate to bring the clan's godspeaker, but he'd fought alongside both of them before.

And anyway, Po'rek wouldn't have called for his weapon if he didn't want to fight.

"One more," Aefric called out to the assemblage, which brought more stomping as he looked them over. He snorted approval of what he saw. Turned to Ge'rek. *"Who is best among them?"*

"Ku'sark," Ge'rek called out. *"Chief calls."*

"KU'SARK!" the crowd cried, then stomped and snorted their support as a borog stepped forward who made Ge'rek look small as Aefric.

Ku'sark stood more than two heads taller than Aefric, and so broad that he'd likely have had to turn sideways to pass through some of the doorways at Water's End. He carried a maul made entirely of iron, both head and shaft.

Aefric recognized that maul. It had once belonged to Lo'kroll.

Aefric snorted approval. Stomped to officially designate him as a party member, setting off one more round of borog cheering.

When it died down, a few orders were passed from Aefric to Ge'rek to a handful of other borogs, and word passed down into the mines to clear the areas nearest the crawler's stalking grounds.

With that done, into the mines went Aefric and his party.

Ge'rek and Po'rek led the way, followed by Aefric and Beornric, then Vria and Arras, and Ku'Sark watching the rear. All of them with weapons in hand. Of course, while carrying the Brightstaff, Aefric always had a weapon in hand.

The borogs would need no light in the tunnels, but Aefric and his knights would, so before they left the chasm he caused the Bright-staff's yellow diamond to emit a glow bright enough to give them good visibility, once they passed the reach of sunlight.

Ge'rek led them into the third cave, which at first was wide enough that they could have fought three abreast in perfect comfort, and more than tall enough to accommodate even overhand swings from Ku'Sark.

Beornric hunched his shoulders all the same, as though already feeling a bit hemmed in.

For Aefric, though, this was something of a homecoming. He was going underground once more to face death, surrounded by comrades-in-arms. Warriors who knew their business. All of them united in their hunt for a threat that was taking innocent lives.

Gave him a good touch of early adrenaline. Just enough to get his heart going a bit more. Get his muscles loose, and maybe just a little bit ready for action again.

Oh, it was true that Aefric would not trade being a duke to take up the adventuring life again. But it was also true that part of him missed it. And that part of him was already enjoying this particular venture. Even though it was just getting started.

Stepping inside the cave confirmed something Aefric had noticed before. Borogs moved soundlessly underground. Even just inside a cave. The moment they passed from the chasm into the cave mouth, Ge'rek's and Po'rek's tough feet did not so much as scuff the rocky ground.

Even massive Ku'sark, who all but stomped with every step out in the chasm, now moved so quietly Aefric had to glance back to confirm he was still there.

He wasn't alone in stealing that glance. Arras and Vria both frowned as they checked behind themselves. As though they could feel his presence well enough, but couldn't hear so much as a whisper from him.

Colder inside the cave it was, even without the wind. And Aefric smelled moisture on the air.

Yes. There. Off to the right, A groove had been — dug? Cut? He wasn't sure exactly. Either way, it opened up to a trickling stream of water.

The cave narrowed a bit, and they passed the first of the gold veins. To his amazement, it looked untouched.

Aefric frowned. *"God metal undug?"*

"Shallow vein," Po'rek said. *"Keep for smell. Dig when others dry up."*

Aefric nodded, and nodded again to himself as they passed three more places where gold was visible even to his eye on the cave walls.

Each time, all three borogs sniffed long and deeply of a scent that Aefric couldn't hope to share. But it seemed to give them a lift.

"Four faces, one vein," Po'rek said, perhaps clarifying why none of the gold so far had been dug.

The cave twisted a bit, before it finally narrowed to a sharp, natural ending, but smaller tunnels had been dug going four directions.

Ge'rek pointed to each of those tunnels, from left to right, naming them in turn.

"Sleeping. Digging. Eating. Connecting."

Ge'rek snorted to ask if Aefric understood.

Aefric tried to snort that he did, and stomped his foot.

He hadn't gotten the snort quite right. He could tell by the hesitation from Ge'rek and Po'rek but the stomp seemed to clarify things.

"Digging way?" Aefric asked.

"Kre," Ge'rek said, which didn't entirely translate as "yes," but was definitely agreement.

They took the second tunnel from the left.

The tunnel was narrower than the cave had been, but not much. If the crawler emerged suddenly, both Ge'rek and Po'rek would be able to fight it, without getting in each other's way.

But if it came from behind, Aefric doubted Ku'sark could swing that maul without impeding Arras' twin-sword style. Though Vria might've been able to fight around him, with her smaller size and her single blade.

The tunnel itself was hexagonal in shape. And while a human mine would have been buttressed with wooden supports, the borog mine was not. Perhaps the shape was enough to keep the roof from collapsing. Certainly the floor, walls and ceiling were all surprisingly smooth and level.

Aefric snorted approval. *"Good tunnel."*

"And the dark swallows all," Ge'rek said casually, which was the borog way of saying something was too obvious to need saying.

Down into the tunnels they went.

EVERY BRANCH OF THE MINE LOOKED THE SAME. SAME COMFORTABLE height. Same hexagonal shape. The rock face itself shifted shades of gray and brown, but the tunnels themselves remained functionally identical.

And the branches didn't come at regular intervals, but became a warren, perhaps following the paths of gold veins? If so, they were dug out in such a way as to make what remained look exactly the same as every other branch, all the way back as far as the cave.

Where was that exactly? Aefric had no idea. Without Ge'rek and Po'rek, he would have needed to map these mines the way he — or someone else in his party — used to map all his underground expeditions.

He did know this much. They'd gone down at least a few hundred feet. He knew they'd continued farther into the cliffs and beyond by … well, it *might* have been miles, but there'd been so many curves, twists and branches that he just couldn't be sure.

How so hexagonal a shape could curve or descend — or possible ascend in places — while remaining just as smooth as the rock face itself, Aefric didn't know.

But Ge'rek and Po'rek seemed to know exactly where they were. Even without any markings on the walls, floor, or ceiling that Aefric could spot...

Wait. They were sniffing the air at every branch.

That discovery made him sigh with relief. He'd started thinking

— well, not *thinking*, really, but at least wondering a little — if they were just guessing confidently.

But no. They were either following the smell of gold or the smell of the crawler. Either way was fine with Aefric.

He did regret not having eaten anything before starting down. His breakfast had been hours ago, and the last tastes of honeyed oat bread, fresh sliced ham and wonderful blackberries lingering in his mouth did little more than make his stomach rumble.

Finally, though, after what certainly *felt* like hours of walking in place, Ge'rek stopped. Glanced at Po'rek, who gave the barest stomp. Glanced back at Ku'sark, who did the same.

"Crawler near," Ge'rek said softly, and Aefric translated in whispers. *"Be ready. Attacks like sudden fissure opening."*

"Meaning..." Beornric said quietly, after Aefic translated.

"It's their way of saying like lightning, I think."

"Kre," Po'rek whispered.

They spread out a bit then. The right flank — Po'rek, Aefric and Vria — moving to one side, and the left flank — Ge'rek, Beornric and Arras — moving to the other. Only Ku'sark stayed in the center.

Their ranks spread a little more too. Ge'rek and Po'rek moving four paces in front of Aefric and Beornric, with each of the two ranks behind him spreading likewise.

Excitement bubbled through Aefric's system, irritating his empty stomach, but otherwise giving him that good, slightly tense, ready-for-action feeling.

When Ge'rek glanced over at him to check, Aefric gave a small stomp.

They continued on.

A scuttling sound echoed from somewhere up ahead. Sounded distant, but heavy and fast, though that might've been a trick of the tunnels. Or even Aefric's imagination.

He took the Brightstaff in both hands.

"Left," Ge'rek said, pointing with his horn to indicate the left-hand branch of the tunnel ahead.

"Spread out near branch mouth," Aefric said, and was repeating that in the common tongue when Ku'sark spoke.

"Me beg first hit."

Aefric hesitated, but Po'rek spoke in the common tongue.

"You never see…" A short pause while he sought the right word. Couldn't find it. "…*ik* fight. Wants to prove."

Ik was the word borogs used for anything in the third person. Male, female, neuter, other, all of them translated as *ik*.

Aefric fought down a sigh. He didn't want any of the others to take the first shot. They would have to come within melee range of the crawler. And he was hoping one good blast of lightning would end the creature.

But this was the borog way.

He turned to Ku'sark. Snorted approval and stomped softly.

Ku'sark snorted … pleasure, if Aefric understood it right.

Ku'sark moved to stand at the mouth of the tunnel. The others all formed a loose ring, watching that tunnel.

The huge borog smacked the head of his maul against the rocky ground. Chips of stone flew and echoes rang out from the blow.

The distant scuttling stopped.

Aefric threw white light down the tunnel, where it clung to the sides and shone out, about a hundred feet down. Might call the crawler. And even if it didn't, it would give him visible warning so he could…

Nothing. He gnashed his teeth. He'd just given permission for Ku'sark to take the first shot, while blocking the tunnel mouth.

"Strike and fall back," Aefric said told the huge borog warrior.

"And the dark swallows all," Ku'sark replied.

The scuttling began again. Faster this time. Heavier-sounding, too.

And coming this way.

Closer.

Ku'sark adjusted his grip. White lightning began to play along the Brightstaff's length.

Closer.

The knights and Ge'rek raised their swords. Po'rek, his axe. Ku'sark smacked the ground again and kept the maul head low, but now his grip looked ready to swing upward.

Closer...

It came through into the light so fast Aefric's eyes had trouble fastening onto it.

It was huge. Bulbous. Chitinous. With four claws clacking out front, and ... something dangling from a tunnel-shaped mouth full of teeth. Tentacles, maybe.

All four claws grabbed Ku'sark before he could act. He screamed as they crushed and pulled him towards its mouth.

Aefric raised the Brightstaff, but suddenly Po'rek was beside him, making an awkward human gesture for Aefric to wait.

How long could he wait? The crawler almost had Ku'sark in its—

Even clutched by four crushing claws, Ku'sark swung that maul into the crawler's face. A snapping sound followed, and a chittering that sounded pained. Or maybe offended.

But he'd had his first strike.

Aefric blasted lightning at that bulbous ... likely thorax ... right under where it held Ku'sark.

The lightning bounced right off the chitin and into the rocky ground beneath it.

Rocks exploded out from there, and likely *they* did more damage than the lightning did.

Ku'sark was done. Dropped his maul. But the others — knights and borogs alike — were right there, hacking at claws, chitin, tentacles, anything they could reach.

How much damage they were doing, Aefric couldn't tell. Which meant it couldn't have been much. But he didn't have time to worry about that.

Lightning from the Brightstaff had done him no good. Fire would spread to the others quickly. He had spells that might help, but the ones that wouldn't hurt his allies in the process of hurting the crawler weren't likely to do enough damage, fast enough, to stop that thing from eating Ku'sark.

He pulled the wand Garram from his belt. However big it was, it was an insect. Perhaps he could freeze it.

Before he even had the wand in his hand, though, the crawler took its revenge on the small things hitting it. With three of its claws — the fourth still clutching Ku'sark — it swiped outward. Smashing knights and borogs alike backwards and rolling.

And it wasn't staying to fight. It reversed direction and tried to scuttle away.

Aefric coated the tunnel behind it with slippery ice.

It's dozens and dozens of small — relatively, at least — legs all slipped out from under it at once. It hit the floor hard, but still not hard enough.

It tried to eat Ku'sark right then. Opened that tunnel mouth of its wide enough for Aefric to see all too many rows of needle-shaped teeth between the waving tentacles, some of which were not grasping Ku'sark.

It was enough opening. It had to be.

Maybe lightning couldn't hurt its carapace, but its belly had to be another matter entirely.

Aefric called forth a lightning blast with all the power he could muster. Not only the power of the staff itself — which was considerable — but his own spellpower backing it, and the very magic he carried inside him as the first of the dweomerblood.

A bright blue bolt of lightning burst forth from the Brightstaff's yellow diamond. Thunder made Aefric wince and stole his hearing as the blast shot straight down the crawler's gullet.

The creature exploded outward in a mess of green guts and goo. The roasting smell that followed was foul enough to make his empty stomach try to empty itself further.

Sweat drenched Aefric, and he leaned panting on the Brightstaff while Ge'rek and Po'rek ran forward to check on Ku'sark, and his knights ran to check on their duke.

Lightheaded, and only just able to hear past the ringing in his ears, he wasn't ready for their questions. Their words all seemed to blur together, before Beornric shouted for quiet.

Hey. Aefric *heard* that shout. His ears were recovering faster than he expected.

"Say something, your grace," Beornric said, loud enough that he was likely having his own trouble hearing.

Still, the knight-adviser's idea was a good one. Drawing on the power of his blood was always exhausting for Aefric, and the first few times he'd done it — well, the first few times after it didn't leave him passing out — he'd been unable to speak coherently for ... some time.

But he'd been practicing. And this time, he knew he hadn't come close to overextending himself.

"How ... is ... Ku'sark?" he said loudly, and Beornric nodded.

"He'll be fine," Beornric shouted, but he wasn't answering the question. He was reassuring Vria and Arras. "Keep an eye on him while I find the answer to his question."

"Here, your grace," Arras said — so loudly she had to have been having trouble hearing too — as she pushed a handful of cashews on Aefric. "Eat something."

"And I have your wand, your grace," Vria said, just as loudly. "When you're ready for it."

His wand? When had he dropped his wand?

THE CASHEWS HELPED. HIS EARS SETTLING BACK TO SOMETHING CLOSE to their normal hearing helped more. And reassurances from Vria and Arras helped most of all.

From their recounting, they, Beornric, Ge'rek and Po'rek were all more or less fine. Bruised and a bit battered by those claws, but nothing that wouldn't heal on its own.

Then Beornric returned with uncertain news.

"Ku'sark is breathing, but he looks bad. And those two won't let me near enough to check his wounds. Haven't seen them do it yet either."

He shook his head, his expression bitter. "Us three had good steel armor protecting us, and I'm still going to feel those claws for an aett or two. Can't imagine getting caught in those pincers. Much less with nothing more than beaten stone to protect me. Even with that thick hide of his, don't think it's likely he'll live through this..."

Beornric went on a little more, but Aefric wasn't listening. He leaned on his Brightstaff, recovering his breath and some of his strength, and quietly held vigil for the brave borog.

Ku'sark lay there on the gray, now-uneven rocky ground. His breaths shallow and quick. His coloring oddly reddish. His beaten stone armor nothing more than a mass of spiderweb cracks and gravel.

Aefric had seen death many times, especially during the Godswalk Wars. And he felt certain he was looking at death now.

What even Aefric hadn't counted on, though, was Po'rek.

Po'rek proved then why he'd been named the clan's godspeaker.

He didn't pray, exactly. Or at least, not the way a cleric of Nilasah would have. But instead what he did was crouch beside Ku'sark and — appearing to speak to the ground — addressed Keduk, the borog god of war and the afterlife.

"You want this one, Keduk," Po'rek said, *"but you cannot have Ku'sark yet..."*

As he continued on, he began a litany of Ku'sark's accomplishments that was pretty impressive. Ku'sark had fought in the Godswalk Wars — admittedly, he'd been under the vile influence of Xazik the Flayer at the time, but still his feats were many.

And after the wars, he'd fought to keep the remains of his old clan alive, even against tarok, humans and eldrani, kindaren and derekek. He'd fought them all. For clan.

He was the one who'd brought his band of refugees to the Dragonscar. Who'd gone through all the formal steps of joining his old clan — Clan Dry Rock — with Clan Thunder Stick.

Clan. That was the key. Nothing Po'rek spoke of was a *personal* victory of Ku'sark's, the way a human might think of personal achievements. Instead, everything Po'rek praised Ku'sark for was an action that benefited his clan.

When he'd been called to war, it was his chief who'd been called. He'd followed and fought for the good of the clan. When the wars were over, he'd taken leadership from a weak chieftain, because that chieftain would have failed the clan.

He'd fought enemies not to fight them, but only when the clan was threatened, or would benefit.

"All for clan," was the refrain Po'rek kept coming back to. And as he spoke, Ku'sark's expression grew less pained. His breathing less labored. His coloring slowly fading to its normal brownish gray.

Po'rek continued the litany of Ku'sark's achievements all the way through this battle, where he stepped up against the monster that was killing his clan. How he'd given the first blow for clan, received the first strike to protect his chief, and how his distraction allowed the chief to kill the monster.

"Ku'sark lives for clan," Po'rek said finally. *"Fights for clan. All for clan. And one day, Keduk, Ku'sark will die for clan. One day. But not today. Me say not today, Keduk. Ku'sark will run beside you, fight beside you. But not today, Keduk. Clan Thunder Stick needs Ku'sark. Me say so."*

Po'rek stomped his foot so hard it *smacked*. Which, for a borog underground, was unprecedented in Aefric's experience.

But Po'rek wasn't quite done.

"Now stand, Ku'sark," Po'rek said. *"Clan Thunder Stick needs you."*

Ku'sark grimaced and started to move, but fell back to the stone.

Po'rek snorted displeasure. Turned to Aefric. *"Chief! Call warrior."*

"Ku'sark!" Aefric bellowed in Borog. *"Chief calls. Stand! Stand for clan!"*

Ku'sark winced and grunted with pain. His breaths came hard and fast. But he grabbed his heavy maul, and used it to help him make his way to his unsteady feet.

"For ... CLAN!" He bellowed, thrusting the maul head high in an unsteady grip.

"For clan!" Aefric, Po'rek and Ge'rek echoed.

There'd been healing in there, somewhere. Aefric had no doubt of it. No way could Ku'sark have stood without it. He'd looked ready to die.

But he looked better now. Stronger. Not fully healed by any stretch though...

"*Is borog way,*" Ge'rek said softly, seeing Aefric's confusion. "*Keduk give Ku'sark some life, but the rest Ku'sark must seize or die.*"

Aefric nodded. "*And the dark swallows all.*"

Po'rek snorted approval.

Well. That explained why they didn't trust the healing of Nilasah's clerics, which Aefric had wondered about. It was too thorough and complete. They wouldn't see it as restorative, so much as weakening.

"*Me and me go?*" Ku'sark asked.

"What if there's another?" Aefric asked, reflexively using the common tongue.

Po'rek snorted disagreement and gave a quick translation.

Ge'rek echoed that disagreement and said, "*Crawler was female. Four claws. Males have two claws.*"

"*No mate?*" Aefric asked, snorting uncertainty.

All three borogs snorted in the negative.

"*Crawlers eat mates,*" Ge'rek said.

"*Eggs?*" Aefric asked.

"*Me and me send cooks. Crawler eggs good food.*"

Aefric chuckled. He would have had one of his knights on rear guard for the trip back up, but apparently that would have insulted Ku'sark. It would have been saying that he couldn't fight.

So Aefric allowed the injured borog to guard his rear, and in the same formation they proceeded back up through the tunnels.

The way back was faster. And more direct. Aefric was sure of it. Though how that could have been, he couldn't guess.

He might be learning more about the language and culture of the borogs, but apparently their mining secrets and methods, those would take some time yet.

For example, he had yet to see anything like a pick or hammer down here. Or any other kind of tool, for that matter. So how they were mining in the first place was still a question he had no idea how to answer.

He considered asking, but he wasn't sure it was a good question to ask. Digging out gold was a kind of holy purpose for them, which meant that their mining methods might well have been sacred, as well as secret. And the last thing Aefric wanted to do was insult them.

He did, however, note to remind himself to ask Yrsa — who spoke perfect Borog, and might know — and Elkari, who often seemed to know everything, so long as it wasn't about magic.

When they emerged once more in the afternoon sunlight — with the sun still comfortably above the western horizon — they were met with the cheers of the entire clan...

...which numbered well over two hundred. Even though sixty had been killed by the crawler.

Once the cheers died down, and Ku'sark was telling the story of their battle, Aefric took Ge'rek and Po'rek aside.

"How many now, Clan Thunder Stick?" he asked

"Fifteen twenties, after crawler," Ge'rek said proudly.

"Word travels," Po'rek said. *"All clanless wish to come join Thunder Stick. Dig god metal for chief."*

"God metal for chief!" Ge'rek said, which interrupted Ku'sark's tale as all the borogs around them echoed the cry.

"I don't know the word for spring," Aefric said to Po'rek, who didn't seem to know the reference. "The season between winter and summer."

It took a little more back and forth before Po'rek understood and translated.

The Borog word for spring was *tehrah*, which translated as "waking sun." Summer was *kalrah*, which meant "strong sun." Fall was *xehrah*, or "dying sun," and *xarah*, or "dead sun," meant winter.

"Will Clan Thunder Stick be ready to march to war come spring?" Aefric asked.

In the same instant, Ge'rek's and Po'rek's faces lit up as though Aefric had just found them a new vein of gold to dig.

"War comes in spring!" Ge'rek shouted over the buzz of excited talk among the two-hundred-plus borogs around them.

Silence spread across the chasm.

Then they all started to chant, stomping the ground with both feet and snorting for joy.

"Fight for chief! Fight for clan! Fight for chief! Fight for clan!" they chanted.

Over and over and over.

"I take it that's a yes," Beornric said.

THE FLIGHT BACK TO WATER'S END WAS WET, BUT THAT DIDN'T BOTHER Aefric. He felt accomplished for the first time in ... aetts, at least.

He'd *done* something. Not just made a ruling, or plans, or anything else along the lines of how he'd been keeping busy while waiting for his royal guests to arrive.

He'd taken action. Fought a monster. Saved innocent lives.

Yes, overall, he did more good as a duke than he ever had as an adventurer. But this kind of helping — the adventurer's way — was certainly more viscerally satisfying.

Perked up his knights, too. Vria and Arras — apparently no more bothered about the rain than Aefric was — excitedly went over and over the fight for the entire flight back.

Their enthusiasm even managed to draw out Beornric, who — as usual — had been huddling in silence at the back of the *magari's* chariot, more disturbed by their height than the chariot's heatless flames.

He added his own take on the battle, including what they'd done right — their general formation and approach — as well as what they'd done wrong.

In his opinion, once they knew where it would be coming from, they should have had Aefric slick the passage with ice. Then the crawler's speed would have worked against it. It would have sailed through the opening and smashed into the opposing wall. Allowing all seven of them to attack with impunity. Perhaps removing legs or damaging claws until they could crack through the carapace and destroy the thing without any of them getting hurt.

While Arras and Vria agreed that this would have been prefer-able, the older knight's criticisms did nothing to dampen their enthu-siasm as they discussed the feel of striking the crawler. Their speculations about which weapons had done how much damage. And on and on.

Though, to be fair, they also freely discussed the wonders of their duke's magic, and how amazed they were at the fatal blue bolt of lightning.

Aefric had to admit, he'd been a little taken aback himself, by exactly how that blast had come out. He'd been expecting white lightning, the kind he almost always got from the Brightstaff, unless he specifically called red.

Even the fires he could call with the Brightstaff were as white as its thunderwood itself.

But the blue color of the lightning had been unmistakable. Was that the result of channeling dweomerblood power? And if so, why had there been no blue tinge to any previous spells and effects he'd supplemented with the power in his blood? Even that amplified sleep spell he'd used against the bounty hunters a few aetts back had been a normal yellow fog.

Was it that he'd channeled his blood power through both spell *and* staff at the same time?

Had he ever done that before? He didn't think so. At least, during the flight home he couldn't remember having done so.

What was more, as Aefric, he'd never heard of any kind of blue lightning before. Magical or otherwise.

As Keifer, though, there'd been the old gaming joke. A "blue bolt" was supposed to be an arbitrarily fatal strike to a player character. One magazine even described the effect in game terms, calling for the game master to roll every die within a ten-foot radius.

Given some dice-obsessed gamers Keifer had known, that would have meant a *lot* of dice. Hundreds. Thousands, maybe.

But obviously Aefric's spell hadn't been that kind of a blue bolt. So where had the blue tinge come from?

Something to research, perhaps. Once he had time in his lab...

...which meant after the coming royal visits.

And that was all it took to put the topic back in his head. And tired and hungry as he felt, he just couldn't shift that topic away. Every effort inevitably brought it screaming right back.

Six royal visits. Four trueborn princesses. One trueborn prince. One "unspoken bastard" of a princess. All looming over his head. Perhaps ready to crash down.

Perhaps even crashing down while he flew back from the Dragonscar...

And suddenly the rain on the flight home felt colder and wetter than it had before. The speeding *magari* seemed slow as a muddy slog. The periodic strikes of lightning in the distance mocked his ignorance about his own magic, even after all these years.

Thus Aefric's mood was darker even than the storm clouds when he set the *magari* down at last on the same cleared space on his public floor balcony from which he'd left that morning.

"Shall I see if dinner's been held for you?" Beornric called over the rain.

"Don't bother," Aefric said back, shouting more than a little himself. "I'm pretty sure we're late enough that it's already passed. I'll have Dajen send for some food while I take a nice, hot bath, then go to bed."

For some reason, that made Beornric smile as he turned away to go in out of the rain.

Then Aefric realized that Arras and Vria were both smiling at him too. A very different kind of smile.

"Your grace must not've heard us over the storm," Arras said loudly. "But we were saying that, if your grace would have our company, we'd very much like to join him for his dinner..."

"...and his bath..." Vria added.

"...and his bed," Arras finished.

Aefric looked at them, smiling that smile despite the pouring rain. And he knew without having to ask that neither one of them would want to ask about princesses or princes or marriage or any of those topics Aefric had grown quite sick of.

What was more, he had a very strong feeling that when they *did* want to talk, they would want to relive the fight against the crawler. The way adventurers did...

"I can honestly say that nothing would make me happier right now," Aefric said, over a roar of thunder in the background.

And the three of them went inside together.

4

———————

Two more days passed with no royal arrivals. Tensions among the court at Water's End grew strained. Tempers shortened. Three duels broke out among the lers. Whispers seemed to echo off of every wall in the castle. And that castle had a lot of walls.

Something had gone wrong. That much was clear. But what?

"Nelazzi," Yrsa suggested again at the morning meeting on the third day. "It has to be Nelazzi. We know she's been hunting for something, and what better prey could she have than princesses?"

"I still don't see why rumors would say she's after a weapon then," Aefric said.

"In her hands, those princesses would be a *deadly* weapon," Yrsa said darkly.

"Even *Nelazzi* isn't brazen enough to attack *four* royal ships and their escorts," Garnotin argued counterpoint. "Everyone is overreacting. We've seen storms here at Water's End already this fall. How much worse might those storms be out over the Risen Sea? Or on the northern side of the Endless Mountains? I'm sure it's just bad weather slowing their progress. The princesses will arrive any day now."

"Enough," Aefric said, slapping the table. "We've had some variation on this same conversation every morning since I got back from the Dragonscar. If no one has anything new to say—"

Someone knocked on the door. Sharp, strong, and four beats. Wardius must've been on duty.

"Come!" Aefric called, and as the door opened and Wardius poked his scarred head in, Aefric continued, "I hope you bring news of a royal ship arriving at Ajenmoor."

"With apologies, your grace, I do not," Wardius said, and even his voice sounded a little scarred. "But I do bring royal news, if that helps."

"It helps if you tell me what it is." Aefric winced and added, "Sorry. You didn't deserve that. I'm just anxious."

"You grace cannot apologize for offense that isn't taken," Wardius said smoothly. "And to answer his implied question, my news is that we've had a rika from Behal. His royal highness, Crown Prince Killian Stronghand, sails a fast ship up the Deepwater. Fast enough that, with the winds supporting it this morning, he won't arrive much later than the rika."

The advisers all started talking at once. Aefric had to slap his hand on the table for attention.

"I'm sure you have all important things to say," Aefric said. "But our prince will be here shortly. Meeting dismissed. Kentigern, do what you do while I get ready to greet our royal guest."

Aefric got to his feet and left the meeting room before anyone could stop him.

"There's no time to assemble the court," Kentigern said quickly, catching up to Aefric as he strode across his broad, public floor sitting room, bound for his personal stairs. "No time for a formal greeting. We'll have to make it up tonight."

"Prince Killian has to know he's not giving us time for much," Aefric said. "I'm sure whatever you can put together will be more than good enough to please his highness."

"Thank you, your grace," Kentigern said, bowing and hustling out of Aefric's apartments.

It *was* odd, though, that there'd been no earlier warning. No rikas from mayors and vassals along the Kingsroad, while Prince Killian rode past.

Could he have sailed the whole way? Taken the Maiden's Blood to the Indecisive River and come through Merrek? Up the Tainfyr and the Haven into the Deepwater?

But that would've been slower. Wouldn't it?

Aefric had no time to puzzle through the details of such travel. He had to let Ocheda and her buzz of valets get him properly accoutered to greet the prince.

A navy blue silk shirt, trimmed with silver thread, and with that same silver thread embroidering the Deepwater sigil over his heart. Deepwater gray hose. Black leather shoes and belt, both trimmed in silver. The wand Garram in its place on his belt, beside his noble's dagger and pouch. His ducal coronet on his head. On his right hand, the ring given him by Queen Eppida: a large emerald inset into a weave of sixteen different shades of gold.

"I still think a brooch would work well," Ocheda said, running a critical eye over the ensemble and straightening here and there. "Perhaps something with rubies or sapphires. Would your grace consent to wear the lovely one given him by Duchess Ashling?"

"The ring and coronet are more than sufficient," Aefric said. "Especially with the silver embroidery."

"The brooch would provide an excellent counterpoint to the embroidered Deepwater device and an anchor for the outfit."

"It would also fuel the gossip that Ashling has stolen my heart, which is already more than prevalent, thank you."

"Your grace cannot stop court gossip," Ocheda said. "Why let it concern him?"

"It's not that it concerns me," Aefric said. "Irritates, yes, but not concerns. It's more that I don't feel the need to *feed* it. And I don't need to wear that brooch today. Or any other. What I have on will be sufficient."

Ocheda made a small sound of disapproval, but said, "Of course, your grace."

Aefric flew down to the docks, where he was met by both

Beornric and Yrsa as well as his Knights of the Lake, and all of them in their full plate armor.

Garnotin arrived last, the only knight among them who'd opted against wearing armor. He wore a bright purple tunic over tomato red hose, a gold ring on each hand and a thick gold chain around his neck. A look that worked very well with his dark complexion. He did, though, wear his warhammer strapped to his back.

"Kentigern sends his regrets," Garnotin said as he took his place at Aefric's left hand, opposite Beornric and Yrsa. "He simply has too much to do for tonight."

Aefric merely nodded. His stomach danced to an irregular rhythm as he looked out into the harbor. Watching for a ship bearing a royal standard. Watching for—

There. A sleek, two-masted schooner flying both the golden oak tree of Armyr, and the prince's personal device: crossed swords, points up, on a field of forest green.

The schooner was just making its way into the harbor…

…and evidently not waiting for a pilot to see it safely through the reef.

The ship didn't even slow.

THE LATE MORNING SUN SHONE DOWN, TOO BRIGHT AND CHEERFUL FOR what Aefric was seeing. The whipping wind carried good lake smells entirely at odds with what it was doing.

That wind was too strong. And it filled the sails of Prince Killian's two-masted schooner.

The ship tilted hard to port as it whipped into the harbor. Hardly slowing from the speed that had carried it so quickly up from Behal.

Far too fast to be safe.

"The reef," Garnotin said softly. "He'll wreck. Our prince has come here to die."

But Yrsa snorted. "Hardly."

She turned to Aefric.

"The prince himself must be at the helm," she said. "When he sat regent here before your grace was created duke, his highness spent a *lot* of time sailing the Deepwater. And he worked with our pilots day and night until he learned all the secrets of our reef."

"Sounds like Prince Killian all right," Beornric said, chuckling.

Well, if that was the case, Aefric hoped the prince remembered his lessons well. Because he was coming through the reef faster than even the local pilots liked to go. And he was heading...

Aefric scoffed, caught between amusement and disbelief. "He's heading for *my* pier."

"Habit, I suppose," Beornric said.

Sure enough, the prince's schooner sailed swiftly and smoothly through the reef, hardly killing its speed until it neared the ducal pier. But the rowers were as good as the riggers, and the sloop shed speed at an impressive rate on the final approach.

It nestled into a slip between the *Duke's Hand* and the *Swift Wave* with nary a hard bump.

The ship was still tying off when Prince Killian came down the gangplank, to the apparent consternation of a pack of armored knights still organizing themselves up on deck, and to the amusement of a silk-clad man who followed the prince down to the reddish, greenish coral pier.

Several of Aefric's knights sighed at the sight of handsome Prince Killian, striding towards them in the late morning sun.

The prince was a slim, yet vibrant man, with his father's rugged good looks. Under a vermilion bycocket hat, his hair was every bit as jet black as his sister's, though shorter and straighter than her long waves. His broad smile was framed by a fashionably trimmed mustache and beard that same shade, a stark contrast to his pale skin.

His tunic was velvet vermilion, worn over thick woolen breeches of a mustardy orange-yellow. His boots looked to be calf-skin, dyed as black as his hair and beard, as was the belt that carried his rapier. A chain of thick gold at his neck, and a gold ring anchored by a large carnelian on the middle finger of his right hand.

That was the finger where Armyrians wore a wedding ring. But the prince wasn't married yet, so that had to be a promissory ring.

The man who followed looked to be about the same age as Aefric and Prince Killian, though shorter, stockier, and having a little trouble keeping up with the prince's stride.

That man wore silk robes of forest green. Grew his pale blonde hair down to his shoulders, and his beard thick enough to hide what was likely at least a second chin. A gold ring was tied into the end of the beard. His belt wasn't leather, but wide cloth-of-gold, and he looked to have a pair of wands tucked into it.

Though he was clearly a magic-user of some stripe, the wands he carried felt as though they had more power than the man himself. And the wands weren't all that impressive.

"Your grace!" Prince Killian called, smiling even wider. "So good to see you again!"

"And you, your highness," Aefric said, and started to bow.

Prince Killian rushed forward and stopped him.

"No, no," he chided gently, waving an admonishing finger. "Two things I don't like there."

He extended his hand for Aefric to shake, as though they were equals in rank. Which, admittedly, they *might* have been. Aefric hadn't thought to ask Elkari.

Prince Killian must've seen the hesitation in Aefric's eyes. Laughed with honest, open pleasure.

"Damn the customs," he said. "*I* say you're my peer, so you're my peer. Now. Shake my hand before you insult me. And I'll have you calling me Killian, thank you very much. Gods know Maev's let you call *her* by name for half the year."

Aefric laughed as he shook Killian's hand, remembering the last time he'd done so. When Killian formally surrendered his regency and rule of Deepwater to Aefric, on the Kingsroad this past spring.

"Good to see you, Killian," he said, smiling. "And of course you must call me Aefric."

"Much better," Killian said, shaking Aefric's hand a little longer as he looked over the Knights of the Lake as they bowed to the prince.

"My gods. These are the knights of your new order, aren't they? The Knights of the Lake? Your personal guards?"

"Yes," Aefric said hesitantly.

"Father gives me nothing but grizzled old men who henpeck me like nursemaids and try to stop me from doing anything fun. And here *you* get a pack of young knights that look ready to cut their way through a horde of enemies, drink their way through an entire cellar of ale, and fuck their way to daylight."

He turned to Aefric. "I'm jealous. I admit it."

Aefric laughed. "I'm sure they'll be more than happy to let you try them with steel, ale, or the bliss moment, as you like."

Vria started to raise her hand to volunteer, but stopped when Yrsa cleared her throat.

"And this one," Killian said, turning his attention to Deepwater's general. "Ser Yrsa Azenai. As deadly running a battle as she is with those maces." He shook his head admiringly. "I've said it before and I'll say it again. Bed or battlefield, you'd break me in half, wouldn't you?"

"Yes, your highness," Yrsa said calmly as she bowed to the prince. "But in bed at least you'd enjoy your death."

Killian's laugh was so infectious that they all got caught up in it.

"And you, Beornric, you old reprobate," Killian said. "Still breaking heads and hearts?"

"Not as many of either these days, your highness," Beornric said with a smile as he bowed to the prince. "Too busy being a grizzled old man who henpecks his grace."

Killian laughed again. "Well, I imagine *someone* must do it." He laughed harder. "And *Father* sent you to Aefric, didn't he?"

"He did," Beornric said, smiling despite himself and apparently not taking any offense from Killian's descriptors.

"Perfect," Killian said, clapping Beornric on the shoulder. "Beornric Ol'Sandallas. Where other knights need the support of a pack" — he nodded his head at the group of older knights only just making their way down the gangplank — "Beornric holds the line alone."

Killian gave Beornric the salute of a noble to a knight. He made a fist with his right hand, and grabbed the wrist behind it with his left. Beornric answered with a bow.

"And you," Killian said, frowning as he turned to Garnotin. "No, no, don't tell me. Ser … Garnotin Artaretek, yes?"

"That's right, your highness," Garnotin said, smiling and visibly pleased as he bowed to the prince. "Newly installed castellan here at Water's End."

"And a fine choice you are," Killian said. "I remember talking to you that night about … was it trade with Merrek?"

"That's right, your highness," Garnotin said, sounding impressed that the prince remembered.

"You had some excellent thoughts there as I recall. And your ideas for dealing with the guilds were downright inspired. I've no doubt that, as castellan, you'll do great things for Water's End."

He turned to Aefric. "You're in excellent hands here, my friend."

But before Aefric could answer, Killian affected a sigh.

"Ah, but where are my manners." He jerked his thumb at the magic-user, who'd been growing visibly anxious at the frank way the prince was talking. "This one's the apprentice of your Netari court wizard, so I consented to give him a lift. Apparently he has some kind of important message for you."

"The prince speaks truly, your lordship," the nervous magic-user said with a bow and a serious tone, using Aefric's Netar courtesy because whatever message he carried was sent to Netar's baron, not Deepwater's duke.

"Of course I do," Killian said, rolling his eyes. "Honestly, Aefric, he's been like that the *entire trip*. If he wasn't bringing you a message, I might've thrown him overboard."

The magic-user managed to frown with his entire face, while still looking nervous. But he bowed to Aefric again.

"I am Batsuen Ol'Riel, your lordship. Apprentice to Jenbarjen, who bids me bring word personally to our baron about her latest developments."

"Very good," Aefric said. "But not here. I'll meet with you privately later. For now, Garnotin?"

"Your grace?"

"See to Batsuen here and the prince's knights. The prince and I have a great deal to discuss, and princesses to plan for."

"Ah, Aefric," Killian said, smiling and putting one arm around his shoulder. "You can't *plan* for princesses. I'd've thought Maev would've taught you that. But we can certainly strategize a bit."

And still talking, Killian led the way back into the castle.

* * *

THE PRINCE MIGHT'VE ARRIVED FULL OF ENTHUSIASM, BUT EVEN HIS endurance wasn't boundless. After ascending the many, many flights of stairs to Aefric's apartments even the vigorous prince was ready for a break.

He stopped in the middle of the wide hall, with its thick, navy blue carpeting running down the center, right beside a large painting of a smiling and beautiful Duchess Arinda Soulfist and no more than a dozen steps from the ducal apartments.

"Forgive me, Aefric," Killian said, fighting back a yawn. "All those stairs. I'd forgotten. Been at the helm since before dawn, you know. Wanted to see if I remembered the route and winds as well as I thought. Guess I remembered the lake better than the castle."

"You should have said something down below," Aefric said, smiling. "I could have carried you up by magic."

"Ooh, no thank you," Killian said with a shiver. "I trust you like a brother, but I don't like that levitation business. Nayoria lifted me once that way. Didn't sit right with me." He shook his head. "Maybe I should've installed a winch and pulley system, when I was regent."

"You'd trust a winch and pulleys more than my magic?" Aefric asked, more curious than anything else.

"It's not that I don't trust *you*," Killian said. "Or even your magic, per se. It's just that, well, I prefer to trust in things I understand. A winch and pulleys, that I understand. A grappling hook and rope too.

But magic? Don't know how it works. Just some mysterious, invisible force, hoisting me in the air..."

He shuddered again. "Not for me."

"All right, I'll keep that in mind," Aefric said, with a slightly exasperated smile. "Good you didn't install a winch and pulleys, though. I'd've just had them removed."

"Yes, I suppose you would." He clapped Aefric on the shoulder. "Let me go refresh myself a bit, and I'll meet you for lunch. Privately, mind. Your big balcony should be perfect."

"My court will be disappointed."

"They'll live," Killian said. "But Kentigern might not if I meet with your court before he's had time to make his arrangements."

Aefric chuckled. "True enough."

"Besides. There's Father's present to give you, which shouldn't be done in public. And we should discuss the princesses without eager ears to overhear us."

"It's a plan then," Aefric said. "Let me call a page for you."

"No need," Killian said, waving away the idea with a smile. "I remember well where the royal apartments are. You don't think I stayed in the ducal apartments when I was regent, do you?"

"Well, as regent—"

"I know, I know. I had the *right*, but not the *reason*. Not the way I saw it. I wasn't moving in, after all. Just keeping the chair warm for, well, *you*, as it turned out."

With one more smile, Killian wandered down the hall toward the royal apartments.

"His father is right to set him a pack of responsible knights," Beornric said suddenly, from right behind Aefric.

Aefric whirled around, fighting down the spell that came quickly to his fingers. Closed his fist to banish the reddish glow that had started around his hand.

"My apologies, your grace," Beornric said, smiling in a way that said he wasn't sorry at all. "Didn't mean to sneak up on you. But us grizzled old men have to be subtle about our henpecking sometimes."

"You know I don't see you that way, right?" Aefric said.

"Killian doesn't either," Beornric said, looking down the hall at the retreating prince. "Oh, he'll grouse and groan publicly — especially to someone like you — but that's just him having fun. He's self-aware enough to know he'd get into all kinds of trouble without someone more responsible reining in his ... enthusiasm, when necessary."

The older knight cocked a bushy eyebrow at Aefric. "And in his case, one knight isn't enough. Even the ones he has might not be enough. I'm half surprised the king didn't assign him a full dozen."

"You think he'll cause me problems while he's here?"

Beornric tugged his mustache while he considered that. "He wouldn't mean to, but I wouldn't put it past him."

"Well, at least he can afford to pay for anything he breaks." Aefric shook his head. "Send for that apprentice, would you? Might as well hear what Jenbarjen has to say."

Ah, Jenbarjen. Netar's baronial wizard. At least, for the moment. When Aefric formally took up that barony a few aetts back, he almost fired her on the spot when he learned that, for the past several years, she'd been privately contracting her enchanting work out to Netar's more prominent families.

Not only was she doing so without baronial permission, but she'd neglected her actual court duties for her side work.

In the end, he'd opted to give her a chance to both make up for what she'd done and prove her value to her new baron.

Making up for what she'd done, well, that was largely a matter of hard work and fees and damages paid to the baronial treasury. As Aefric understood it, she'd already worked out a payment plan with his castellan and seneschal and was underway toward setting things right on that front.

But proving herself, that was another matter entirely...

A FEW MINUTES AFTER KILLIAN HEADED OFF TO THE ROYAL APARTMENTS at Water's End, Aefric sat again in his black oak meeting room. This time with only Beornric beside him, and Batsuen Ol'Riel sitting nervously on the other side of the round, blackwood table.

The stocky apprentice played nervously with a leather scroll case while Aefric sipped from a silver goblet of water.

"Before we start," Aefric said. "I'm curious. Is this your first time leaving Netar?"

"Your lordship, it is," Batsuen said with a nod that might've been a small bow. "Have I offended the prince? I've been trying so hard not to, but he's..."

Batsuen seemed to realize he'd been on the verge of directly insulting the crown prince of Armyr. His eyes widened larger than the setting sun and he paled so fast he might pass out.

"Breathe," Aefric said gently. "Breathe as though you're about to prove competence in a new spell to your master."

Batsuen closed his eyes and followed a breathing pattern that was different from the one Aefric was taught. Looked as though Batsuen inhaled for a four count, held for a four count, exhaled for a four count, and held empty for a four count, then repeated.

After four such breaths he opened his eyes. Nodded thanks at Aefric.

"You haven't offended the prince," Beornric said. "He doesn't offend easily. But you did bore him, and people who bore him lose his attention and patience rapidly."

Batsuen's face twisted up, looking caught between relief that he hadn't offended Killian and terror that he'd bored a member of the royal family.

He closed his eyes. Did another set of four-count breaths.

Aefric nodded to himself. His earlier guess about Batsuen's age — close to his own — had been off on the high side. Misled by the beard, most likely. But listening to the boy talk, it was clear that if he'd reached the age of majority, it couldn't have been very long ago.

"Ol'Riel," Aefric said, when Batsuen opened his eyes. "Any relation to Guimond Ol'Riel?"

"My cousin, your lordship."

"Did you even have to ask?" Beornric muttered, and Aefric snorted softly.

Guimond was an excellent court historian. Might've rivaled Elkari, at least where Netar's history was concerned. But the man was … on the grasping side. Doubtless the moment Jenbarjen had expressed interest in taking on an apprentice, Guimond had produced a family member out of thin air.

"Well, Batsuen, what report do you bring from my baronial wizard?"

"Your lordship must know that he's set my mistress a very difficult task," Batsuen began.

Aefric cut him off. "So the message is that she isn't up to it?"

"No, your lordship!" Batsuen said quickly, eyes widening too much again and hands coming up so quickly he dropped his scroll case. "That's not what I meant!"

"She is required to provide me a means of fast travel between Netarritan and Water's End. Not just for *myself*, but for my *full, formal entourage*. Did I set her too great a task? Is her reputation only smoke and mirrors?"

"No, your lordship," Bastsuen said, practically whining now, which made Beornric grimace in distaste. "Her reputation—"

"Get hold of yourself, man," Beornric said, as though watching something unseemly.

Trembling, Batsuen needed sixteen repetitions of his breathing pattern to recover himself.

Clearly he was not nearly ready to graduate his apprenticeship. Or, for that matter, act as a proper messenger.

Batsuen frowned, as though unsure what to say next. So Aefric prompted him.

"As I have proven that I recall well the task I set your master," he said, "you have no reason to recount the inherent difficulties of the task itself. So, if you would, get to the meat of your master's message."

"Yes, your lordship," Batsuen said, picking up the scroll case again. "My mistress still believes that a flying ship is the best, most reliable means of providing your lordship with what he desires."

That statement alone was proof that Aefric was demanding an almost legendary feat from his Netari court wizard. If a flying ship could be built easily, someone would have worked out the secret centuries ago. Instead, none had ever been developed that Aefric had heard of in all his travels.

But given the way she'd abused her post in the past, he felt not the least bit guilty for demanding so much.

"My mistress has broken a barrier to large scale enchantments that no one before her has ever managed," Batsuen said. "Or if anyone has, they have kept that knowledge to themselves, and taken it to the grave."

"A mighty claim," Beornric said.

"But a just claim," Batsuen said, sounding more confident again. "The great Jenbarjen has discovered the secret of binding smaller enchantments together *without* the need for their materials to come from common stock."

"*What?*" Aefric said, leaning forward. "Did you say *without*? As in, she could take a board, enchant it, and bind that enchantment to another on a board that not only came from a different tree or different root system, but *an entirely different forest altogether*?"

"Your lordship," Batsuen said, smiling and proud, "that is exactly what my mistress has done."

"Why is this a big deal?" Beornric asked.

"True items of enchantment," Aefric said, "and I mean the kinds of enchantments that last years, centuries, or even longer, they tend to be limited in terms of size and mobility, because they've always required a structure made from common stock. Stone from the same quarry. Silver from the same vein." He nodded to the Brightstaff. "Thunderwood from the same tree."

"So no one's made a flying ship before because they couldn't find a tree big enough?" Beornric asked.

"If they used a conifer, then a contiguous root system would probably provide sufficient connection, as I understand the theory. Which suggests that a flying ship has other problems to overcome, or someone would have made one by now."

"Your lordship is most astute," Batsuen said.

"Then why is this such a breakthrough?" Beornric asked.

"It's like this," Aefric said, trying to figure out how to explain without getting technical...

He patted the blackwood table.

"Suppose this table were built entirely from one tree's wood. If I tried to enchant it and failed, I would need a new table to try again. This one would be ... ruined, for my purposes."

"Like a sword forged with a bad grain structure?"

"Not quite," Aefric said. "The sword could be reforged, unless something were to corrupt the steel itself."

"Ah!" Beornric said, understanding. "More like repairing armor. Once a plate has a hole, no amount of hammering will fix that plate."

"Something like that," Aefric said. "The enchanting process requires the magic-user to first build a magical structure within the physical item. This structure will hold together any other spells and powers associated with that item."

"Like the foundation of a castle," Beornric said.

"Essentially," Aefric said. "And the magic-user must have already worked out all the spells, powers and effects that the ... foundation will support. Because the foundation can't be changed later."

"Ah," Beornric said. "So if she tried to enchant a ship to fly and failed, she'd need a whole new ship to try again." He frowned. "But it would still be useful as a regular ship, would it not?"

"Most likely," Aefric said. "But since, under normal circumstances, she would have to keep drawing wood from common root structures each time, repeated failures start causing serious forestry problems."

"But if she can instead take wood from anywhere she wants..."

"Then the costs to both her purse and the local forests are significantly reduced." Aefric nodded. "Impressive, if true. Though as I said, there are still likely other significant difficulties to overcome."

"Do you think she'll be able to pull this off?" Beornric asked.

He was asking Aefric, but Batsuen answered. "Ser knight, I believe it with the whole of my heart."

"Spoken like a true and loyal apprentice," Aefric said with a smile.

"Ah," Batsuen said, holding up the scroll case, "but I also bring a detailed explanation for your grace of what my mistress has accomplished so far, with copies of all relevant notes. Because my mistress knows your grace will understand and appreciate what he reads."

Batsuen focused visibly and floated the scroll case to Aefric.

"Thank you, Batsuen," Aefric said, smiling, as he took the scroll case in hand. "You're welcome to remain here at Water's End until you're ready to travel back to the Iron Keep."

"My thanks, your lordship. But I wish to return to my mistress as soon as I may. Has your lordship any message for her?"

Aefric tapped the scroll case against his palm as he considered that.

"Tell her that I'm pleased with what I've heard so far, and look forward to her next report."

"Nothing more, your lordship?" Batsuen asked, looking disappointed.

Aefric gave him a lopsided smile.

"I sincerely doubt she's expecting more," he said. "She knows well that notes and words are one thing. Proof is another."

"Yes, your lordship."

"Safe travels, Batsuen Ol'Riel. And greet your cousin for me, when next you see him."

"Nothing would please me more, your lordship," Batsuen said as he accepted his dismissal and left.

"Well," Aefric said, tapping the scroll case against his palm as he turned to Beornric. "At least I have something to read while waiting for Killian."

But as Batsuen left the meeting room, Kentigern came in, carrying a sheaf of parchment and a harried look.

"Your grace, we must discuss the arrangements for tonight."

Aefric sighed.

Beornric took the scroll case. "I'll just have Ocheda leave this in your study, shall I?"

"Please," Aefric said, turning to Kentigern, who was already sitting.

"First," Kentigern said, "there is the matter of seating arrangements. Now, I've already handled the invitations and the entertainments, but seating for an event such as this one is really a matter of showing favor and displeasure, which cannot properly be done without your grace..."

Aefric fought down a sigh, and prepared to face one of the costs of being duke.

Lunch on Aefric's public floor balcony. He wasn't sure how many more days he would get to enjoy it this year. If everything he'd been hearing about the winters was true, then once the autumn storms came with a vengeance, he might not get to dine out of doors until the next spring.

So while lunch was still being prepared, Aefric took a leisurely stroll along the rail of his large balcony and tried to put that meeting with Kentigern out of his mind.

Kentigern was a terrific seneschal. But when it came to planning dinners like this one, he could be every bit as intense as Yrsa preparing for war.

Aefric had left that meeting feeling as though he'd been making life and death decisions about which knights and lers belonged closer to where he ate and which knights and lers needed to be moved out towards the hinterlands of his dining room.

Definitely an experience to shake off as soon as he could.

The wind was stiff today, which helped. The way it buffeted his face and tossed his hair felt cleansing. Although he might need a touch of magic to keep that stiff wind from ruining lunch.

But for now, focusing on the feel of it against his skin was good. Like flying. And the wind carried fresh lake smells from the south.

Down below, that same wind — or its sibling — turned the lake choppy, and made the pilots work for their money among the many ships out about their business.

Not just traders and merchants down there. It looked as though fishing vessels were still out hunting the day's catch. Aefric would have thought that rougher waters like these would be bad for fishing. But then, he'd never been a fisherman.

Good to see the lake traffic so active, though. Boded well for the recovering economy.

In the distance to the northeast, the majestic Threepeaks mountain range. Towering and ancient...

In the old days, Aefric would have looked at a range like that and wondered what wonders lay in its depths, waiting for him to discover them.

These days, Aefric wondered more about how the mines were producing, how well the newer miners were getting along with their work and their co-workers.

So many changes in so many lives since the wars...

"Ah, portrait of the duke, surveying his domain."

Killian's smiling voice, coming from the sitting room doorway.

"More like worrying about his people," Aefric said, turning around.

"It's the same thing, my friend," Killian said, gesturing for Aefric to come away from the rail. "Father always said that the day a king forgets that his land and his people are one is the day he risks becoming a tyrant. I imagine it's true for dukes as well."

Aefric noticed the Killian was carrying a small, red leather satchel now.

The last time Aefric had seen someone carrying a gift for him in a leather satchel, it had been Zoleen bringing him the gift of a castle in Kivash.

If the present from his majesty was another castle, Aefric might start laughing right there at the table.

He took a moment for a quick spell to shield the balcony from the stiffness of the wind.

"I notice you didn't let Ocheda announce you," Aefric said, approaching the large, round, finely carved greenwood table and taking a seat in one of its matching chairs, gesturing for Killian to join him.

Odd, the little games of formality he had to play even now. Even with a prince who acted as though he'd rather forgo them entirely.

"I swear, that woman could shatter stone with her frowns," Killian said, shaking his head in wonder as he took the chair beside Aefric, giving them both a view of the mountains. "I just knew that letting her announce me would make me feel underdressed."

Aefric chuckled. He knew the feeling.

"Your grace, your highness," Ocheda said from the doorway. "May I have lunch presented?"

"Please do," Aefric said, "and thank you, Ocheda."

Moments later, excited servants brought out silver plates covered with freshly grilled lake trout, served with an assortment of roasted vegetables and honeyed oat bread, along with chased silver tankards of day beer, and a ewer with more.

But first, the palate wine. Two small crystal goblets of a white wine so dry it seemed to evaporate on the tongue, leaving the mouth cleared of any other tastes while its own faded away.

"Did you know," Killian said, helping the servants by handing both empty palate goblets to the nearest one, "that Rethneryl has taken up our practice of palate wine?"

"No," Aefric said. "I hadn't heard."

"It's true," Killian said. "Although they haven't figured out the secret behind growing the grapes properly, so they're having to import it from us. Should be good for your Netar's economy."

"Their vineyards are small," Aefric said, "and not all that numerous."

"You're too used to the size and scope of Deepwater," Killian said, sounding serious for the first time. "I suspect that if you check with your Netari seneschal, you'll find that Netar's wines currently account for about ten percent of their exports. As orders come in from Rethneryl, that'll improve, because their demand will require more than any closer royal vineyards could produce."

"And Netar is right on their border," Aefric said.

"Exactly."

They started into their lunch then, and Aefric's cooks had outdone themselves. The lake trout was light and flaky, yet full of flavor so robust that even the roasted vegetables benefited. The oat bread was still oven hot and sweet, adding a touch of honey that seemed to work with everything else.

The crispness of the day beer helped to tie it all together.

"Ah," Killian said, about halfway through his plate, "I'm going to slow down a bit to savor this. Forgot how your cooks spoiled me the last time I was here."

"I think they work harder to impress you," Aefric said, chuckling.

"Many do," Killian said, shrugging one shoulder. "Comes with being the future king. But speaking of kings..."

He lifted the satchel, wiggled his eyebrows at Aefric, and set it on the table.

"Sure you don't want to finish eating first?" Aefric asked.

Killian cocked his head and narrowed his eyes. "I'm holding a *gift* and you think of food?"

"The gift will be just as good in a few minutes. The food, however, will grow cold."

Killian laughed. "I've dined with many nobles, Aefric, and you're the only one so practical. Let us eat then, and you'll just have to wait for your present."

As they ate, Killian regaled Aefric with tales from his trip, which had, indeed, been entirely by ship. Mainly, he told of the twists and turns of the Indecisive River, and the progress he'd seen in recovery among the towns along that river and the others he'd sailed on his way up.

He did, though, have some amusing stories about sailors and their bawdy songs, and how they needed only an hour or two in port to get so drunk they had to be carried back to the ship.

"And this is on *my* ship," Killian said. Then amended, "Well, it's not *mine* the way the *Duke's Hand* is yours, but it was carrying me nonetheless."

But then, the food was finished, the beer drunk, and the plates cleared. And Killian smiled as he turned his eyes to the satchel.

"Ready?"

"Unless it explodes, I'm ready," Aefric said.

Killian laughed. "Nothing fatal, I promise. Or at least, not to you. Father went into the vaults for this one."

"Wait," Aefric said. "Your trip. One thing you didn't mention was *why* you sailed instead of coming up the Kingsroad."

Killian gave Aefric a sly smile. "Maev's right. You're clever. This present is to *you* from *my father*. Do you take my meaning?"

Aefric nodded. This was a gift to Aefric Brightstaff from Colm Stronghand. Not a gift to the Duke of Deepwater from the King of Armyr.

"Good," Killian said. "I thought you would. Knowing that now, do you understand why I came by ship?"

Aefric considered that. His eyes widened. Coming by the Kingsroad would have meant too many eyes.

He nodded.

Killian nodded again.

"Now," Killian said, seriously. "This is a gift from the family vault. Not the royal vault." He waved a dismissive hand. "I know, I know, they sound the same, but they aren't. And there's no letter from Father, and certainly nothing with the royal seal."

He pulled out a small box made from ... teak? Yes. It looked like teak. Ornately carved, and hinged in the back. Just large enough to fill Killian's hand.

Aefric could feel some kind of contained magic to that box. Something strong, yet strangely subtle and slippery. Like swirling fog. Difficult to get a fix on.

Aefric reached for the box. Killian covered it with his hand.

"Don't open it," he said. "Not here. Not in the sun. And preferably never in the presence of another. Not even a servant."

"All ... right," Aefric said slowly.

"I don't know that you'll be able to use this," Killian said, frowning. "Father seems to think you could, but even great et cetera grandfather Iounn couldn't. And if *he* couldn't, I'm not sure *anyone* can."

He frowned. "Well, Kainemorton, I suppose."

"What is it?" Aefric asked.

"I'm not entirely certain," Killian said, still frowning. "And neither is Father. There's a kind of magical power bound inside this box. But it's bound there with a sort of puzzle lock to it. To release the power and gain command of it, you'll have to figure out the puzzle."

"What is the power?"

"I'm sorry, but I'm not sure. Nobody likes to talk about it much. I know that this box was brought back from a series of skirmishes with the dybbungstad that went well underground. It was supposedly found there by one of my ancestors."

Killian shrugged. "Apparently the dybbungstad and their demon twins couldn't solve the riddle of the box either."

"And you're sure it's a good thing?" Aefric asked.

"Study the carvings," Killian said. "They'll tell you as much as I can."

He handed over the box.

WHEN AEFRIC TOOK THE ORNATE TEAK BOX IN HAND, THE SUNLIGHT dimmed on the wide balcony. He actually found himself looking up to see if a fresh wave of clouds had been carried down by the stiff wind outside his spellwork, but no.

The sun was there. Still fairly warm, considering that this was fall and not summer.

"I know," Killian said, sipping a little more day beer. "Rather creepy, if you ask me. The way just holding the box seems to dim the sun."

He shivered. "To be honest, I'm half-glad Father gave it to you, and half-worried for you."

"Why worried?" Aefric asked, looking up from his start at

studying the carvings. They were many, and small, and done with a very fine hand. "Is there something you should warn me about?"

"Just a feeling," Killian said, shrugging one shoulder, and sipping a little more day beer. "I mean, it was recovered from a dybbungstad lair. Not what I would call a place dedicated to the forces of good. And the family lore says that the dybbungstad couldn't puzzle out its secrets, but what if they're the ones who made it?"

"Made it and didn't use its power when under attack?" Aefric asked. "Sounds unlikely."

"That's just what Nayoria said when I suggested the idea to her." Killian shook his head. "Oh, she wanted to have a go at that box. Father wouldn't let her though."

"Why not?"

"Represents an unknown power," Killian said, voice serious again as he set his tankard of beer down on the greenwood table. "Father always said that *unknown* powers are the most dangerous. Nayoria is an excellent wizard. Never let any believe I think otherwise. But she was born to a noble family, and has moved from keep to keep her whole life."

Aefric nodded slowly. "Your father believes that, as a former adventurer—"

"You have a great deal more experience with unknown magics than she does. You're more likely to take the right precautions and, if you succeed with the puzzle, handle the power without it going to your head." He nodded at the Brightstaff, standing beside Aefric's chair. "You have both *that* and the wand Garram, and you hardly throw power at every little problem, do you?"

"Of course not," Aefric said, but he understood the point.

"Thus," Killian said, "the box becomes a present Father could feel comfortable giving you to thank you for how you handled those Netari borogs."

"If I may ask," Aefric said, lowering his voice, "why was that so important?"

Killian leaned forward, smiling. "King is just a title. True royal power is like an avalanche of cascading decisions. And the person who gets to start the avalanches — who makes those keystone decisions — *that's* the true authority. And it doesn't have to be the king."

"The way I've been trying to make sure my advisers understand how *I* want decisions made in my absence."

"Just so," Killian said, rapping his knuckles on the table the way the knights did sometimes to show agreement. "When Arinda was duchess, she left a lot of the ruling of Deepwater to Calder. But every time people started thinking of him as the true authority, she did something to assert herself, and ensure that everyone knew *she* ruled Deepwater. He was only acting in her name to the extent that she allowed. And he was just her castellan. Not her duke consort."

"So the queen was trying to do something to prove that she was the true authority in Armityr?" Aefric asked, so shocked he almost dropped the teak box. He tightened his grip on it. "She tried to become the true ruler of Armyr?"

"Well, I don't know if she was trying to go *that* far," Killian said with a chuckle. "But she was definitely trying to carve out a fairly broad niche for herself."

"And by not killing the borogs," Aefric said, "by taking charge of them instead, I somehow tipped the balance against her?"

"Oh, Eppida was *furious*," Killian said, smiling broadly. "She'd been rallying supporters around the idea that she understood the peers better than Father could. They were ready to believe her about Ashling, uncertain about Wylyn, the ex-adventurer..."

Aefric huffed out a breath of disbelief. "And so, if she proved she understood me better than the king did, that would add weight to the idea that she understood Wylyn better too."

"And instead, you proved Father right," Killian said, sitting back and looking pleased. "Around the same time that Father handed Ashling a crucial diplomatic mission, both showing his understanding of her skills and demonstrating his trust in her loyalty."

"So why didn't the king give me some kind of warning?" Aefric asked. "He didn't even tell me there *was* a problem in Netar."

"Of course not," Killian said, shaking his head. "It would have proved nothing if Father had tipped the scales that way. He needed you to discover the problem when you got to Netar, and solve it your own way without interference."

"But how would..." Aefric frowned. "Did he swear to a justiciar about this?"

"No," Killian said, drawing out the word. "But he offered to, if anyone expressed any doubts or questions. And the offer was enough, because if anyone tried to call him on it and *lost, they'd* lose standing, for questioning the king's honesty unfairly."

"And he thought someone might," Aefric said.

"Eppida had rallied a *number* of supporters," Killian said, picking up his beer again. "I think she expected one of them to be willing to try."

"No wonder she's furious," Aefric said.

"With herself and her so-called supporters," Killian said, raising a finger to make his point. "Not with you. She's too savvy for that. She won't risk alienating you when she knows the mistake was hers." He nodded to the teak box. "Which is why Father's thank-you had to be given subtly and unofficially."

Killian grimaced. "Eppida's like a wounded sea monster right now. Taunting her would be risky, even for Father."

"Is this what you expect your own marriage to be like?" Aefric asked.

"Not at all," Killian said easily, sipping his beer. "Eppida, after all, is Father's *second* wife. I expect my relationship with my queen, Gitta, will be much like the one Father had with Mother. He consulted with her about nearly everything, and gave her direct control in areas where she outshone him. Ultimately the rule was his, but they worked as a good team."

"Sounds like what I hope for with my own wife."

"Have you chosen one then?"

"Not yet."

"Care to discuss the candidates?"

"What," Aefric said, smiling, "and let a strange source of magic go unexplored?"

Killian laughed loudly while Aefric turned his attention back to the teak box.

The carvings. Some of them looked like letters. Possibly Ancient Hwalish, but he'd need a better look. Somewhere with more light...

Oh. Yes. The way the box was dimming the sun. That might make lighting tricky. And under the letters were the carvings of two men. What was it they were doing?

"Your grace?" Ocheda's voice, sounding far away.

Killian's hand on Aefric's wrist. "Aefric," he said. "Your valet has called three times now."

Aefric set down the box.

The sky brightened once more. And he realized he could hear the wind whistling past his balcony, and the cries of gulls around the docks...

"Until that puzzle's solved," Aefric said, "that box is dangerous."

"Probably be just as dangerous afterwards too," Killian said, pondering. "Though hopefully more controlled."

"Your grace," Ocheda said, sounding a little worried now.

"Please forgive me, Ocheda," Aefric said, looking up at her. Her normally severe face showed real concern. "I was more than a little distracted."

"Yes," she said, lending the word about five different meanings. "But I wish to inform your grace that" — her mouth turned down in distaste — "one of his knights has returned and claims something important to report."

"Deirdre?" Aefric asked quickly.

"Yes, your grace," Ocheda said, sounding as though she were telling him that a massive pile of dung was waiting for him in the sitting room. "Ser Deirdre Ol'Miri."

Deirdre Ol'Miri. Aefric's ducal champion, and perhaps his most valued investigator. Returning at last after several aetts away from Water's End.

She had found answers for him. She must have.

"Excellent. I want her and all my advisers in my meeting room at once." Aefric stood. "And send for food and drink in case she needs any."

"Deirdre Ol'Miri," Killian said, smiling. "Isn't she that gorgeous redheaded dweomerblade? The one who's a bit..."

"Audacious?" Ocheda suggested. "Disrespectful?"

"I would have said rakish," Killian said, smiling wider now.

"Either way, that's her, your highness. The one with the mouth of a tinker and the manners of—"

"That's enough," Aefric said to Ocheda. "I believe I issued instructions."

"At once, your grace," Ocheda said with a crisp bow.

"Doesn't like her, does she?" Killian said, standing.

"There's no freer spirit than Deirdre, and no soul more devoted to order than Ocheda. They're bound to collide."

"You seem awfully excited about her report."

Killian was fishing. He wasn't even trying to hide it.

"Someone tried to kill me at Asarchai during the Feast of Dereth Sehk," Aefric said. "The crown may have decided that Caiperas was behind the attempt, but I'm entitled—"

"You are," Killian said, waving his hands as though to stop Aefric's line of thought. "Unquestionably. I won't even tell Father about any of this, if you like. I just have one request."

Aefric tilted his head. "You want to meet Deirdre?"

"Well, *two* requests then," Killian said with a grin. "Because I want to attend this meeting."

Aefric hesitated.

"I swear to Taesark that I will keep secret anything I learn in this meeting," Killian said quickly. "I just want to watch you with your advisers." He grinned. "And maybe hear what this Deirdre has to report."

Aefric still wasn't sure this was a good idea. But then, Killian *was* his future king, and maintaining a good relationship wasn't the worst idea...

"All right," Aefric said. "But I'll hold you to your promise about anything you hear in the meeting."

"I'll take what I hear in that meeting to the grave," Killian said, "and beyond, if Taesark wills it."

Killian's enthusiasm and intentions were obviously good enough. Aefric could only hope his will and his honesty were just as good.

Aefric personally deposited the teak box behind the locked doors and wards of his magic laboratory on the third floor of his ducal apartments — setting Jenbarjen's scroll case next to it on his spell research desk, for good measure — before going back down the stairs to his black oak meeting room.

He was beginning to understand why the Soulfists took so many important meetings in the ducal offices instead. That little room could feel a bit claustrophobic at times. All that dark wood, without any natural light.

Magical light was all well and good, but there was something ... uplifting about natural light. Something he'd never consciously thought about during his adventuring days, but had always been there in the background.

Probably the reason he took so many meals out on his balconies.

Perhaps he should use his public floor solarium for some meetings...

No. He could redecorate for it, but there wouldn't be enough privacy. And right now, as he so often did, he needed the seating and the privacy of that meeting room.

Ocheda, clearly taking into account that her duke and prince had just eaten, hadn't sent for the most impressive array of food. Some rolls of honeyed oat bread. A small wheel of cheese — likely cheddar — and some sliced roast beef. Two silver ewers, one of water and one of day beer, along with enough silver goblets for everyone at the round, blackwood table.

Kentigern had begged permission to skip this meeting, so he could focus on the dinner. Aefric had granted it without hesitation.

Kentigern wouldn't likely be directly affected by anything Deirdre had to say, and Elkari could catch him up on the particulars later.

Yrsa and Beornric were both still in their full plate armor. Aefric might never understand how they could seem so comfortable in all that metal.

Garnotin was still in his bright purple over tomato red, and Elkari, a stack of scrolls beside her, wore a dark brown tunic over dark brown leggings, just as she might wear any other day.

Apparently the presence of the prince wasn't enough to get her to change her routine. She even had her usual ink stains. Today they were mostly on her hands, but she had one along the left side of her chin that seemed to amuse Killian.

Beornric ceded to the prince his chair at Aefric's right hand, and took Kentigern's, over to Elkari's right.

Any moment now, Deirdre would enter. Where Ocheda could have stashed her while waiting for the advisers to arrive, Aefric didn't know. He certainly hadn't seen her in the public floor sitting area.

But Ocheda had promised to retrieve Deirdre at once, from wherever she waited.

"Deirdre is back, but Karbin is not, yes?" Yrsa asked.

"So far as I've been told," Aefric said, fighting down the worry roiling in his guts.

"Karbin knows his business well," Beornric said. "I'm sure he's fine."

Aefric wasn't sure, but there wasn't much he could do about it.

At last, a knock on the door.

"Come," Aefric called.

Deirdre sauntered in, wearing her usual leathers of deep maroon red. Hardly much darker than her hair, which she wore in a long braid down her back. At her sides, her rapier and dueling dagger practically thrummed with the magic of her calling.

A dweomerblade. A magic-user whose power worked through weapons and combat. In her case, less brute force and more speed and agility.

Watching her in battle was like watching a dancer, leaping and twirling to music no one else could hear, while her many slow, awkward partners fell by the wayside in red pools of failure.

Deirdre's jade eyes sparkled as she caught Aefric's gaze. Her smile was small, as though sharing a secret with him.

Then, as she often did, she went to one knee before Aefric. Treating him as a king and not a mere duke.

Killian scoffed, plainly amused.

Yrsa sighed and grumbled something. Beornric and Garnotin both shook their heads.

Elkari mumbled, as though trying to remember any precedents about a knight kneeling to a duke for reasons other than being knighted or swearing fealty.

Aefric kept his focus on Deirdre, and she seemed to see the worries in his eyes.

"I spoke with Karbin at dawn, your grace," she said softly. "He is safe. He simply wishes to confirm one more thing before returning. He didn't tell me what."

Something like sixty-five different muscle groups relaxed in Aefric as he let out a breath he hadn't realized he was holding.

"Thank you," he said. "And know that I am very glad to see you returning to me alive and well."

"I could not do otherwise," she said with a sincerity so deep Aefric had to fight not to look away. What he saw in her eyes, it was too private for this setting.

Killian cleared his throat.

The moment passed.

"Deirdre," Aefric said, "I'm not sure you've met our crown prince, Killian Stronghand."

Deirdre rose smoothly to her feet and bowed to the prince. "Your highness."

"You kneel to him and bow to me," Killian said, sounding more curious than offended.

"I do," she answered simply. "He has more than earned it, your highness."

Killian looked at her differently now. Caught somewhere between admiring the beauty he'd apparently heard about before, and wondering at her clear devotion to Aefric.

"You're welcome to food and drink, of course, Deirdre," Aefric said. "And you may take the empty seat between Elkari and Garnotin. The other is Karbin's if he makes it in time."

"I doubt he will," Deirdre said, taking a slice of roast beef and chewing it thoroughly, then filling a goblet with water before perching at the edge of the offered seat.

She took a long drink from her goblet.

"Well?" Garnotin said impatiently. "We all know you love being the center of attention, Deirdre, but we need answers. Was it Nelazzi behind the attempt on his grace's life at Asarchai?"

Deirdre slowly raised an eyebrow at Garnotin. "The new title suits you, Garn. But you always were a better politician than you were a knight."

"All right," Aefric said, before Garnotin could answer. "Let's leave the personal affronts aside, if you'd please. Deirdre, I *would* like to know what you learned while you were away."

"Naturally, your grace. And my adventures during this investigation are a tale best told — well, *almost* best told — with beer in hand and a roaring fire nearby."

She sighed theatrically. "But, as I am likely to be denied the *best* setting for such a tale..."

"What would be the best setting?" Killian asked before Aefric could stop him.

Deirdre smiled at Aefric. "Why, between silk sheets, of course. While naked, sweaty and recovering from a *wonderful* bliss moment."

"You *had* to ask," Yrsa said, then grumbled something about throwing Deirdre in the lake.

But Killian's attention was still on Deirdre. "I wouldn't deny you such a setting."

"Your highness is most generous," Deirdre said playfully. "But alas, this information is too important to my duke to make him wait for even the *second* best setting, let alone the *very* best. Thus, I must make do."

"Today, if you would," Yrsa said.

"Of course," Deirdre said with a smile, which she held as she turned back to Aefric. "At another time, your grace, I would love to share all the details of the dark places and desperate fights. The chases and the escapes. The near misses, the frustrating losses, and the pointed victories."

"I look forward to hearing about them," Aefric said, smiling despite himself, which brought a sparkle to her eye.

"Doubtless the tale shall delight the ears of a former adventurer such as yourself," she said with a wink.

"While naked and between the sheets?" Killian asked.

"Your highness," Yrsa said, "I'm quite sure Deirdre would be more than happy to accommodate your obvious interest at a later time. But for the moment, could we please focus on the information she has for us?"

"Of course," Killian said, turning to Aefric. "Excuse me."

Deirdre answered as though she'd spoken to him.

"No excuse necessary, your highness. Flattery is always welcome."

Before Killian could give some kind of flirty reply, Garnotin cut in.

"Your findings, Deirdre?" Garnotin rolled his wrist. "You know. The reason we're all gathered here?"

Deirdre got as far as opening her mouth to respond when Aefric cut her off.

"Please, Deirdre."

"Anything, your grace," she said, turning back to Aefric and growing about as serious as she ever got. She looked around the table. "To remind you all, I was not working alone in this. Karbin and I kept in touch twice daily through his spells, and met in person every few days. We shared findings and eliminated false leads whenever we could as we attacked the question from different directions."

She set down her goblet.

"The question, of course, was who dared to send assassins after our beloved duke. His majesty chose to slant the royal investigation to the likely false conclusion that Caiperas was the culprit. And while neither Karbin nor I believed that to be the case, we didn't exclude the possibility until we uncovered *proof* that it was not Caiperas."

"*Thank* you." Elkari's eyes widened as soon as the words were out of her mouth. "Excuse me."

"Nothing to excuse, good Elkari," Deirdre said. "I believe we all know that some investigators would have eliminated Caiperas once it was determined that the assassins hadn't been of the Order of the Severed Dream."

The Order of the Severed Dream. A guild of assassins based out of the Malimfari town of Dyrhellir and noted for their use of reddish, flame-shaped daggers. All of the attempts on the royal family had been made by assassins of that order, and hired by Caiperas. That much had been proven conclusively.

"I'll spare some of my less patient colleagues the details of how Karbin and I proved that Caiperas wasn't behind the attempt at Asarchai—"

"Could I have those details later?" Elkari asked. "I'll be happy to take notes, if you'd rather recite the story than write it down. There could be beer and a fire, if it would help."

"Beer and a fire *always* help," Deirdre said, smiling broadly. "I'll tell you the whole story later, and continue to settle for summation now."

"*This* is summation?" Garnotin said in disbelief.

"You have no soul for poetry, Garn." Deirdre didn't even look his way as she shook her head, then smiled at Aefric. "May I continue, your grace?"

"Please."

"Thank you. Suffice to say that Karbin and I traced the assassins by their movements. How they got to Asarchai in the first place, from across the Risen Sea."

Aefric's eyebrows shot up. "Across the Risen Sea? You don't mean they were Shadow Blades."

Deirdre sat a little straighter. Gave Aefric an impressed nod.

"I hadn't realized your grace was familiar with the Order of the Shadowed Blade."

"Had a run-in with them around the start of the Godswalk Wars." He shook his head. "I was lucky to survive that fight."

"I'm sure your grace is being modest," Deirdre said.

Aefric didn't think so. He mostly remembered it as a mad scramble, as an assassin melted out of the stonework of that ruined castle, right behind Lauszen.

Poor Lauszen. Unintentionally leaving a trail of enemies in his wake, one of whom must've been pushed too far.

The assassin killed Lauszen before Aefric could even raise a hand. He quickly dispatched that one with lightning, but he hadn't known there was a backup in the room. A backup ready to deal with an angry magic-user...

"Will they be sending more assassins after his grace?" Beornric asked. "We haven't seen any signs, but a group called the Order of the Shadowed Blade—"

"Not the way they work," Deirdre said. "Their assassins take jobs, not the Order itself. So if those assassins still lived, *they* might try again. But they're dead, so that ends it. Unless more are hired."

"You seem to know a lot about assassins," Garnotin said, raising an eyebrow.

"And if you got out more, Garn, you might too," Deirdre said, before turning back to Aefric. "While the order itself, of course, we couldn't get information from, we discovered that they rely on a network of brokers who do not handle pressure quite so well as the assassins themselves."

"And they gave up who hired someone to kill his grace?" Garnotin asked.

Deirdre gave an exasperated sigh. "I've said it before and I'll say it again. You're no fun at all, Garn."

"Fun or not," Beornric said quickly, "his question is an important one."

Deirdre frowned, but nodded, and turned back to Aefric.

"It wasn't as simple as asking the first such broker we came to," Deirdre said, "but in the end, yes. We were able to get enough answers to trace back a series of intermediaries to find that the assassins were ultimately hired by two men. A wizard who dressed all in green—"

"Gwawl," Beornric said quickly, referring to the wizard they'd captured along with a pack of slavers in the Dragonscar this past summer.

A wizard who was a known confederate of the pirate queen, Nelazzi.

"Our first thought as well," Deirdre said. "Though we did not jump to conclusions. And the other was an older man who carried himself like a knight. Slicked back gray hair, scarred hands, and a broadsword at his side."

"Calder," Yrsa growled.

"Again, Karbin and I thought he seemed the most likely candidate. But we didn't stop at presumption."

"Thank you," Elkari said, softer this time, but still audible.

"You're welcome," Deirdre said brightly. "Karbin and I chased down more leads to first, confirm the identities of the older man and wizard — who did indeed prove to be Calder and Gwawl — and second, track what we could of their movements to ensure that they were still working for Nelazzi."

She nodded firmly. "They were and are. And we removed all doubt that they hired the assassins. Absent questioning Calder and Gwawl directly, we must assume that they did so on the orders of Nelazzi herself."

"Reasonable conclusion," Elkari said, frowning. "But there is the possibility that they were acting independently."

"No," Yrsa said, shaking her head. "The assassins struck at the end of summer. Calder approached Kefthal for Nelazzi after that."

"You already know that?" Deirdre said, sounding disappointed. "I'd been hoping to surprise you with it."

"Wait," Aefric said. "Kefthal came here directly to tell me they'd turned Nelazzi down."

"Really?" Deirdre said, frowning. "All the *rumors* said they'd refused Nelazzi, but we had trouble proving it. I suspect that's what Karbin is off doing."

"The point stands," Yrsa said. "If Nelazzi didn't sanction the assassins, she'd've killed Calder for sending them."

"Maybe she did," Beornric said. "Maybe that was why he got the job of approaching Kefthal for her. Figured if they said no, they might save her the trouble of killing him herself."

"You're forgetting something," Garnotin said. "So far as we know, Gwawl is alive." He grimaced and turned to Deirdre. "Unless you know differently?"

"Gwawl is alive to the best of my knowledge. But I hadn't heard about Calder's death either."

"Exactly," Garnotin said. "And if Nelazzi had him killed, she wouldn't have done it quietly. She would have made an example of both of them. Hells, she might even have sent their heads to us herself, to make sure we knew she wasn't behind the assassinations."

"She might not care what we think on that front," Beornric said. "There's no way Calder didn't tell her that our duke wants to put an end to her."

"Well," Deirdre said, sounding disappointed that she'd lost momentum in her presentation, "there is one more thing we learned. Nelazzi is planning something big, soon, and close to Armyr."

She shook her head. "I had to choose between trying to chase that lead down for more information and coming back to report on what I'd already learned."

"You couldn't give the lead to Karbin?" Garnotin asked.

Deirdre sighed expressively. "I know you've never been much of an investigator, Garn. But when you're working with a wizard, you don't see much of each other. Mostly you keep in touch with spells at pre-arranged intervals. Very limited communication."

She leaned a little closer to Garnotin, speaking as though to a child. "The lead was cooling when I found it, and heading out to sea. My next chance to talk to Karbin wouldn't be until the following morning. That's what we investigators call *too late*—"

"You made the right call," Aefric said, before Garnotin could express the anger clearly building inside him. "We've been preparing for Nelazzi anyway, so it almost doesn't matter what she tries."

As soon as the words were out of his mouth, Aefric wished he could take them back. One of the things he'd learned over his years of adventuring was not to dare the fates.

Saying that a mountain pass was known to be safe before crossing it all but ensured that reaching the other side would be a fight.

Suggesting that an enemy's power was broken was asking for a resurgence.

And saying something like he'd just said, well, that almost guaranteed that Nelazzi would hit him from an angle he could never see coming.

As the meeting devolved into details and points that Aefric knew would bore the prince, he called the halt.

"All right," he said, standing up and taking the Brightstaff in hand. "This has given us all a good deal to think about. Deirdre, why don't you go over more of the details with Elkari while they're fresh in your mind. Then we can meet again later—"

"The dinner," Beornric said.

Aefric sighed. "We can discuss the details and make more plans at tomorrow's morning meeting. Deirdre, you're officially invited to that, in case there are questions."

"I'll look forward to it, your grace," Deirdre said with a smile.

"For now, this meeting is dismissed. We all have a lot to do." He turned to Killian, but Deirdre cut in, while the others were all standing from their chairs.

"Your grace!" she said. "Might I crave a private word?"

"Of course," Aefric said, while the others — except for Killian — began filing out of the meeting room.

"I was rather hoping for a private word with you myself, Deirdre," Killian said with a smile that made Elkari blush and drop one of her scrolls. She actually took two more steps before realizing it was gone and retrieving it.

"I would be pleased to hear whatever your highness wishes to tell me," Deirdre said with a bow. "But I would ask that he do so at a later time. There is a very important matter I must discuss with his grace. And I fear time may be at issue."

That was easily the most formal thing Aefric had ever heard from Deirdre. He was so surprised that his eyebrows practically tripped over each other, bunching together on his forehead.

"Of course, Deirdre," Killian said, giving her the salute of a noble to a knight. "Business before pleasure, after all."

Aefric gave Deirdre a curious look as Killian left the two alone in the meeting room, closing the door behind him.

The smile she gave Aefric explained everything.

"Especially when the business at hand *is* pleasure," she said, sauntering around the table toward Aefric and running her gaze over him as though trying to memorize every detail.

"Oh?" he said, which felt woefully inadequate, but it was all he could think of. Deirdre just ... had this way of keeping him off balance.

"Your grace made me a promise before I left," she said softly. "If I returned to him intact, he would finally take me to his bed."

Aefric nodded, remembering the conversation.

"I believe I said I'd invite you to my rooms that night. And night does not traditionally take place while the sun is in the sky."

"Night is whenever we say it is," she said, voice still soft as she stepped closer yet, but clearly taking her time. "Do the borogs in their tunnels care when the sun is down or up? Do the derekek on their ships?"

"No," Aefric said. "But—"

In a swift movement that made his heart skip a beat, she closed the distance between them and brought two fingers to his lips.

"Your grace," she whispered, "anything may happen between now and nighttime. Assassins. Pirates. Princesses. War. *Now* is all we truly have."

She moved her fingers from his lips to stroke his chin, but her gaze stayed locked with his.

"Your grace made me a promise," she said. "I ask only that he keep it while he may."

"Are you sure?" Aefric asked, his voice coming out low and a little rough. "You could be with Killian right now. The promise could wait."

"Killian," she said with a soft snort. "He's pretty enough, I suppose. And gods know he's had enough playmates to achieve some competence in the bedroom. Maybe I'll play with him sometime if I get bored."

She let her fingers play gently down Aefric's neck, while her other hand pressed against his chest.

"But if the choice is mine, I choose the man, not the boy. The one with scars to show he's *lived*. The one who *understands* how I see the world."

She swallowed. Her next words came out careful. "I choose you, your grace. If you'll have me. As you promised you would."

"As Duke of Deepwater," Aefric said slowly, "I must hold to the details of my promises. So I must not fulfill that promise right now."

Deirdre drew breath to reply. Aefric covered her lips with two fingers.

"But as a man, and something of an adventurer myself," Aefric said with a smile, "I'd have to be a *damned fool* to refuse so magnificent a woman as you, Deirdre Ol'Miri."

Her eyes lit up. The Brightstaff clattered to the floor as Aefric pulled her into a kiss. Deirdre entwined both arms and legs about him. One hand clutched his head and the other his shoulders.

Her kiss was wildfire. Blazing. Urgent. Overwhelming. He had to fight not to tip over.

No good. He got lost in the torrent of that kiss. Fell backwards to land hard on the black oak floorboards.

The kiss broke. His wind gasped out. He would've banged his head, except her hand got in the way.

No cry of pain from her though. She smiled as though catching her hand between his head and the floor was an expected part of the process.

While Aefric fought for his breath, she started undoing his

clothes. She had his shirt and belt open in moments, and before he could breathe again she was biting and kissing his chest.

Finally. Air. He could breathe and talk again.

"We can't do all the things together we want to," he said. "There isn't time."

"I know," she said between kisses. "The rest can wait." She looked up. Shook a finger at him. "But understand, your grace, I fully expect that next time, we'll explore each other properly."

"Consider it part of the promise," Aefric said with a smile. "And at a time like this, you *must* call me Aefric."

She looked up again, surprised, then smiled a different smile. Not lustful at all, but simply ... happy.

"Nothing would please me more. Aefric."

"What about taking off your armor?" he said, smiling now too. "Would that please you?"

"Well maybe you should do something about it," she teased. "I hear you're a magic-user, after all."

"Oh, you *hear* that do you?" Aefric asked.

She shrugged one shoulder with an impish grin and went back to kissing and nibbling along his collarbone while her hands played with his muscles and scars.

The spell Aefric cast then was a fairly simple one. A derivative of a spell he used to untie knots and undo locks, and he knew from experience — a single prior use, but experience nonetheless — that this derivative would work for his intended purpose.

Every bit of clothing and armor Deirdre was wearing fell off her body, leaving her naked, straddling him, and grinning down, impressed.

"Oh, even better than I expected." She preened a bit to display herself for him.

She had the slender, muscled build of an acrobat, but with enough curves to make clear she was a woman, not a girl. Made all the more beautiful by her scars, which were many. Along her thighs, arms, torso, even what looked to be a recent puncture scar on her left breast.

Whatever she started to say was lost to shaky breaths as he toyed with that scar, licking and sucking at it, while his hands began exploring her naked flesh.

No fancy scents or tastes to her. Just good clean skin, and a little extra something that was all her.

Deirdre didn't speak while Aefric played with her latest scar. Just cradled his head and made little sounds of pleasure.

When he allowed himself to start licking and kissing beyond the scar, she spoke in a breathy voice.

"Next time," she said. "All our scars. Each story."

"Every one of them," Aefric said, pulling back to look her in the eye.

"Is that part of the promise?" she teased.

"I'd do it anyway, but yes."

"Aefric," she said, sounding oddly serious for a moment, "if you don't get those hose off, I'm going to tear them off."

"You'll have to move."

"If I *must*," she said, sliding off him, and he pulled off his own clothes with a quick movement of magic.

Then they were both naked, and a dangerous thought occurred to him.

"Nysta tea," he said. "We must have nysta tea. I know you said—"

"Shh, shh," she said quickly moving in close and whispering in his ear. "What do you think I was doing while waiting for your advisers, Aefric? I made Ocheda fetch me nysta tea."

Aefric chuckled. "I'll bet she was thrilled."

"Especially since I implied I was going to have the prince with or without it."

"You are awful in the best ways," Aefric said, leaning in to nuzzle her neck.

"You say the sweetest things," she said, laying back down onto the floor and urging him on top of her.

"I figured you'd want to be on top the first time," Aefric said.

"What I *want*, is to have you every way I possibly *can*," she said.

"Every position. Every act. Everything we can think of." She shook her head. "But right now, this first time, I want you just like this."

She kept talking as Aefric positioned himself.

"I want to look up at you. To see your hair dangling down. To feel the urgency in your muscles. To—"

Aefric kissed her hard.

He was still kissing her when he slipped inside her.

Then they were moving together. Both of them trying to stay slow. To avoid urgency.

No good. Neither could hold back. All too soon they were bucking together. Moaning out a mingle of both pleasure and need. Until the bliss moment began building.

Building.

Building.

Deirdre grabbed his chin and gazed deeply into his eyes as bliss overwhelmed them.

Gazes locked together, they did their best to stretch that moment out as long as they could. Their bodies still moving together. Their sounds quieting, but still meaningful.

Finally, the moment passed. They lay together side-by-side on the hardwood floor. A light sheen of perspiration on them both, and neither of them quite breathless.

Vigorous as their pursuit of bliss had been, they were simply in too good shape to lose their breath so easily.

"Now that," Deirdre said, leaning in to nuzzle Aefric's throat, "was what I call a good start."

He chuckled. "Agreed. Unfortunately, I think anything more will have to wait for later."

"I know," she said with a sigh. Flicked one of his scars. "Tease me with a taste, then make me wait for the full meal. Mean."

"Not by choice," Aefric said with an exasperated smile. "If I could afford the time, I'd carry you up the stairs and—"

Someone knocked hard on the door. Too hard for Ocheda. Beornric?

"And what?" Deirdre asked, giving Aefric a little shake.

A muffled voice through the door. "Your grace!"

Definitely Beornric's voice. Aefric sighed.

"And *what*, Aefric?" Deirdre asked, putting both hands on his chest now. "Just *what* would you do after you carried me upstairs?"

But he didn't get a chance to answer that question, because Beornric opened the door.

Beornric, to his credit, didn't change his expression in the least when he saw Aefric and Deirdre, naked together on the floor.

"Get dressed, your grace," he said. "Karbin is back, and his news is dire."

Beornric closed the door to the black oak meeting room, while Aefric and Deirdre composed themselves.

The two dressed quickly. Aefric cleaned himself up with a quick spell, but when he offered to do the same for Deirdre, she shook her head.

"No one cares if *I* smell like sex," she said quirking a smile as she adjusted her sword belt. "Besides. I'm not ready to give up the scent of you just yet."

She winked and stepped past him, heading for the door. He reached out and tugged on her long braid.

She gave him a curious look.

He smiled. "One more kiss before we—"

Suddenly she was in his arms again, kissing him with the same urgency as that first kiss. As though she were a drowning woman frantically seeking air.

It was all Aefric could do to hold on and try to match her passion.

They were interrupted by an impatient knock.

"Deirdre," Beornric said through the door, "I think you've distracted our duke enough for one afternoon."

She laughed softly as she pulled back from the kiss. "Guess I have." She sighed as she looked him over one more time. "Once more you must be your grace. But now I can look forward to the next time I get to call you Aefric."

"I look forward to it too," he said sincerely.

A look entered Deirdre's eyes, as though she wanted to say something more. She gave her head a little shake and left the room. And unless Aefric was mistaken, her walk gained a little extra swagger as she passed through the doorway.

Aefric called the Brightstaff to his hand and left the room as well.

Beornric paused him in the doorway. Spoke softly.

"Really? Yrsa and I have been encouraging you to bed Deirdre for some time now, and you choose to wait until *the crown prince* propositioned her?"

Aefric cocked an eyebrow at Beornric. "You just lost a bet to Yrsa, didn't you?"

"I was sure you'd make Deirdre wait for nighttime," the older knight answered with some chagrin. "Yrsa was just as sure that Deirdre wouldn't wait that long to get you out of your clothes."

Aefric clapped him on the shoulder, and looked over to the public floor sitting room in his apartments, where a series of couches, tables and chairs could comfortably accommodate at least two dozen.

No one sat waiting among them.

"Where's Karbin?" he asked.

"He arrived by air on your larger balcony," Beornric said. "Yrsa is with him now."

Aefric and Beornric emerged through the glass doors onto that larger balcony, where Karbin and Yrsa sat together at a large greenwood table. Karbin devouring a trencher of hot meat and melted cheese, when he wasn't answering some question of Yrsa's.

Another trencher sat on a silver plate before him, beside Karbin's obsidian rod. Enough silver tankards for four sat on the table, along with a ewer of day beer, though only Karbin had taken any so far.

He looked good. Bags under his eyes, but otherwise his blue-black skin healthy and he had no visible injuries. He dressed in robes the colors he most favored, dusk and sand. Two wands tucked in his belt today.

No hat on his bald head. Not for Karbin. He had to be at least three times his apparent age — which was thirtyish — but so far as Aefric knew, he'd never worn a hat.

The smile he gave Aefric was tired, but sincere.

"You look worried, old friend," Karbin said as Aefric closed the distance between them. Softly, Karbin added, "I don't think dukes are supposed to hug their court wizards."

"If convention would keep me from hugging an old friend, then convention has to change."

Karbin smiled broadly as he stood and gave Aefric his hug.

"You smell too clean for a man's who's likely been up since dawn," Karbin said, while they took their seats, Aefric with the Brightstaff standing beside him. "Dare I ask what you've been doing?"

"Deirdre, and it's about damned time," Yrsa answered for him.

Karbin grinned approval.

"Can we discuss your news?" Aefric asked, then turned to Beornric. "Or were you only calling it dire to put an end to things in there?"

"It's dire enough," Karbin said, growing serious. "Nelazzi has been capturing princesses. Hatay, Shachan, even Varondam, if you can believe it."

"Believe it," Yrsa said, turning to Aefric. "What did I say? No normal delay."

"But you had no proof," Aefric said before turning back to Karbin. "What do you have?"

"Well I didn't witness it and I can't prove it," he answered. "But let me tell you. Deirdre and I had discovered that Nelazzi was planning something big, close to Armyr."

"We'd heard she was hunting some kind of weapon."

"Which princesses *are*, in her hands," Yrsa said.

"Enough, Yrsa," Aefric said. "Your guess was right. And what action do you think his majesty would have agreed to on the strength of your *guess*?"

Yrsa frowned and poured herself a tankard of day beer.

"Exactly," Aefric said.

"Not sure I can give you anything you can take to his majesty either," Karbin said. "But the buzz in all the ports was that Nelazzi has been on the hunt, and not just for treasure. I tracked rumors through dive bars, port offices, traders, anything I could think of, trying to find out what she was after."

He shook his head. "Dead end after dead end. Until, down in Wulfport, I met a warehouser and trader who'd just made the move there from Drake's Landing."

"Drake's Landing," Aefric said. "That's in Kefthal."

"It is," Karbin said. "She'd had to pack and move her operation quickly, and recently."

"Kefthal refused Nelazzi," Aefric said.

"You know that already?"

Aefric explained about his visit from Kefthal.

"We'd heard about the refusal," Karbin said with a nod, "but couldn't prove it until I discovered that Kefthal has been rounding up and killing anyone on their shores known to have worked with Nelazzi. Even one job was enough for a death mark."

"Killing them?" Beornric asked. "Not banishing?"

"Kefthal's official approach to cleaning house," Karbin said. "The Nine don't do such things gently."

"Public burnings?" Yrsa asked.

"Too wasteful. Kefthal's evil, but very precise."

"Oh," Aefric said, with sickening realization. "However they kill them, they're raising the corpses. Aren't they?"

"They like their living slaves," Karbin said, "but they like their dead slaves better."

"Back to the trader and warehouser," Aefric said. "What did you learn?"

"From her? Not much," Karbin said. "She clammed up tight when I tried. Wouldn't talk at all. But her assistants, they were angry about the move and a lot of lost income. A little charm, a little alcohol, and words flowed quickly."

Aefric knew just the charm involved, too. A spell that would relax someone and make that person view the caster as a good friend of many years.

Totally unethical under most circumstances, of course. But adventurers always did find a way to use such things in reasonable ways. And Karbin had been adventuring long before Aefric was born.

Perhaps not before Keifer was born, but that was a question of more philosophical than practical importance.

"Before they fled Drake's Landing," Karbin continued, "their boss was trying to find a way to hide kidnapped royalty, short term."

"Short term as in they'd be moved again or killed?" Aefric asked.

"Unknown," Karbin said. "All the assistants knew was that the needs were short-term storage for royalty."

"I'm surprised they knew it involved royalty."

"Kidnapping royalty is hardly without precedent," Yrsa said.

"And it requires stricter security and more privacy than even most illicit storage needs," Karbin added.

"Still," Beornric said. "This isn't much to go on."

"There's more," Karbin said. "I already knew from another port that that Nelazzi had been hiring derekek ship thieves."

"That are good enough to steal a *royal* ship?" Yrsa balked. "With all its escorts? Not likely."

"Wasn't the plan," Karbin said. "According to the assistants, the last Nelazzi ship they'd seen had a few sailors bragging that they'd snatch their prize before it even reached the sea."

"Ship thieves hitting on a river?" Aefric asked. "Never been done. There's nowhere to go."

"Exactly," Karbin said. "But think about it. No one is better on the water than the derekek. And guards relax on rivers, because they'll spot any enemy ships *long* before they could become a threat."

"Not to mention the ports and defenses between a river town and the sea," Yrsa said.

Karbin nodded. "Add that to what I learned up in Hatay."

"Which was..." Aefric prompted.

"Sorry," Karbin said. Nodded to Yrsa. "Told that part once."

"You told me that a royal ship, with escort, had been sighted on the Kalkerrik River in Hatay," Yrsa said.

"That's right," Karbin said. "And that it turned back for the capital without ever reaching the mouth of the river."

"Right there in their own lands," Beornric said softly. "No wonder Hatay is keeping this quiet."

"But Shachan is landlocked," Aefric said. "Wouldn't they ride instead of sailing?"

"Across the Endless Mountains?" Yrsa said. "This time of year?"

"They might've come by river route," Beornric said. "Except that this time, Hatay agreed to give Shachan's princess a lift and escort, as a show of goodwill between neighbors."

Aefric frowned at Beornric.

"I was discussing princesses with the prince while you were ... indisposed. Remember, foreign monarchs tell Armityr their plans long before they ever get around to telling us."

"So Nelazzi had derekek ship thieves hit a royal ship on the river and make off with two princesses?" Aefric said in disbelief. "Without getting caught?"

"Close as I can tell," Karbin said.

"And Hatay isn't admitting it happened," Yrsa said. "Which means they're trying to keep this quiet while they mount their own rescue attempt."

"Who's their wizard?" Aefric asked.

"Royal court wizard?" Beornric asked, and at Aefric's nod said, "Fiacre ... something."

"Alterran?" Karbin asked.

"Yes, that's it. Fiacre Alterran."

"Know him?" Aefric asked.

"Only by reputation," Karbin said. "Better politician than wizard. Type who doesn't like leaving his comfortable castle."

"Fits what I've heard," Beornric said.

"I heard he threw some pretty big blasts during the wars," Yrsa said.

"Big battle magic is one thing," Aefric said. "Any major court wizard will expected to know some. Hells, the Soulfists had an entire grimoire devoted to battle magic. But the little spells you learn adventuring, that's something else. Castle types rarely learn how to do things like track by magic. Consider it beneath them."

"Hatay has good foresters though," Yrsa said.

"A good forester can track as well as a wizard," Karbin said. "Maybe better, in some cases. But we're faster. And more certain across a stretch of water."

"Both of which matter in this case." Aefric shook his head. "How certain of all this are you?"

"Certain as I can be," Karbin said. "I checked word around several ports on the Kalkerrik River. Found witnesses in each who saw the royal ship pass both directions. Their talk of the time frame was consistent."

"So Nelazzi may have two princesses who were on their way here."

"Three," Karbin said, then frowned. "Or two-and-a-half, maybe. Depending on how you feel about Varondam bastardy."

"I don't know. It's complicated." Aefric sighed. "But what does any of this have to do with Varondam?"

"An unspoken bastard princess doesn't rate a royal ship or escort, does she?" Beornric said.

"She had an escort all right," Karbin said with a frown. "One ship. Wasn't even a proper warship."

"Easy pickings for Nelazzi," Yrsa said.

"Very easy." Karbin turned to Aefric. "That news is just hitting the ports today. Likely you'll have a rika about it by nightfall."

"Three princesses…" Aefric said.

"Your grace," Beornric said in a warning tone. "You've been told not to go after Nelazzi."

"I don't *know* that Nelazzi is behind any derekek ship thieves," Aefric said. "All I have is a rumor."

"Just like all you have is a rumor that the princesses have been taken," Beornric said firmly.

"Karbin?" Aefric asked.

"They were taken. I can't prove it, but I'm sure of it."

"Good enough for me," Aefric said.

"Get permission from the king," Beornric advised.

"He won't grant it," Yrsa said. "Not without a formal request from Hatay."

"Which won't come," Beornric said.

Aefric drew a breath as he considered.

"All three have one thing in common." Aefric tapped the table. "They were coming here."

"You can't do this," Beornric said softly.

"One of these women might be my bride," Aefric said. "Think they'll want a man who waits for permission? Or a man who rescues them?"

"What about a man who gets himself killed doing something stupid?" Beornric asked. "Think that's a popular option among princesses?"

"Don't worry," Aefric said with a smile. "I have a plan."

5

AEFRIC SPENT THE REST OF HIS AFTERNOON OUT ON THAT BALCONY.
Arguing with Yrsa and Beornric mostly, but slowly refining his plans
— aided here and there by Karbin, until finally the sun began to set
and breeze that had been slowly wearing through his spell grew chill.

Which was around the time that Ocheda called, "Your grace, the
call to dinner has come."

"Very good," Aefric said, standing and taking the Brightstaff in
hand. As Ocheda withdrew he added, "We'd gone as far with this as
we could anyway."

"I still say it's all foolishness," Beornric said, standing along with
Yrsa. "You're charging off like an adventurer when you should be
staying here like a duke."

"He's not," Karbin said as he stood, drawing surprise from both
Yrsa and Beornric.

"He's running off to rescue captured princesses," Beornric said.
"How is that not the act of an adventurer?"

"I'm—" Aefric started, but Karbin stilled him with a raised hand,
as though he were still the master and Aefric the apprentice.

"If you think that's what he's doing, then you weren't listening,"
Karbin said patiently as he picked up his obsidian rod and tucked it

into its customary place at his belt. "Our duke here is worried about his people. His ports. The havoc wrought by Nelazzi, and the worse havoc she'll wreak on his coastline next spring, while he's off at war. He's worried about those princesses too, and about one more thing he hasn't mentioned, but I can tell is bothering him."

Karbin gave Aefric a frank look. "Tell them. Because I think you're right, and they need to hear it."

Aefric chuckled under his breath. "Never could keep secrets from you, could I?"

"Tell us what?" Yrsa said, but Beornric put it together.

"You think Hatay will blame *us*. Say the sea route to Armyr wasn't kept safe by the Duke of Deepwater, and that it's our fault the princesses were captured."

Aefric nodded. "I think that's the other reason they're keeping the kidnapping a secret. If no one knows when and where it happened, they can claim it happened at sea and who's going to gainsay them?"

"They'd just need to send a ship flying royal flags visibly out to sea," Yrsa said, thinking it through. "Then they could come back and tell whatever story they wanted."

"Exactly," Aefric said. "And if blaming me hadn't occurred to them before, it surely will when they learn that Princess Kiala was taken. Which they will within the next day or so."

"Time presses," Karbin said.

"Why didn't you mention this earlier?" Yrsa asked.

"Didn't matter," Aefric said. "It's a blame that might not come. And it wouldn't affect the fact that the king would never approve of what I'm going to do. Assuming I was foolish enough to tell him the what and the why of it."

"It does matter though," Beornric said. "I don't think Yrsa and I would've fought you so hard on this."

"Hey," Aefric said with a smile. "My plan's better for all the holes you poked."

Yrsa scoffed. "And you think I wouldn't have poked those holes anyway? As a general, you're a terrific wizard."

Ocheda didn't speak as she stepped out onto the balcony again. Her severe presence alone was enough to draw attention.

"I must remind your grace," she said patiently, "that his crown prince awaits his presence. Along with his court. And, if I might add, if he spends much more time out here, I shall be forced to explain to Dajen *why* his grace remains on this balcony instead of down at dinner."

She raised a steep eyebrow. "Unless his grace intends to keep me on duty straight through to tomorrow night?"

"Not at all," Aefric said. "We're coming now."

She cast a critical eye over his clothes as he approached.

"I see your grace will be wearing the same outfit for dinner as he has worn all day. Is he trying to set a fashion trend?"

"Do I have time to change?"

"Only if your grace wishes to insult his highness," she said, dusting and straightening his navy blue silk shirt, and arranging the way the silver trim sat.

"Then this will have to do."

The humming sound she made then *technically* counted as agreement, but if felt more as though she were saying, *I suppose. If your grace wishes to continue to comport himself without the proper dignity expected from one of his station. But he continues to insist on doing business now that could wait for later, because his priorities are still not quite in alignment with what they should be as a peer of the realm.*

To say that Ocheda's monosyllabic sound had been expressive wasn't giving it its proper due.

Before he, Yrsa and Beornric left the balcony, Aefric turned back to Karbin. "Do you need anything else before you go?"

"No," Karbin said through a deep breath, then drew the obsidian rod from his belt again. He nodded. "I'm ready."

"Then I'll reach out to you at the appointed time." He gave Karbin a tight smile. "Happy hunting."

"To you as well," Karbin said, and flew off into the air.

"So," Ocheda said softly, "your ducal wizard will *not* be joining the court for dinner?"

"No," Aefric said. "He has business to see to." He turned to Aefric and Beornric. "Shall we?"

OH, KENTIGERN HAD OUTDONE HIMSELF THIS TIME. HOW HE HAD arranged all this on such short notice, Aefric couldn't begin to guess.

The dining hall he'd chosen was not the largest in Water's End, but the ... third largest. It was still on the ground floor of the keep, positioned under a side segment of the great stained glass dome.

The magic light for the hall was not the usual Soulfist work — apparently sourceless and a comfortable yellow-white. Instead, it was on the other side of the stained glass, shining down in imitation of midday.

This section of the stained glass dome featured primarily designs done in different colors, but anchored around the sigils of every major family in Armyr, to include counts and countesses, dukes and duchesses, all surrounding the great golden oak tree on a field of forest green. The great seal of Armyr.

With a good imitation of sunlight shining down, it made for beautiful lighting, not too bright or too soft.

The tables for the dinner had been arranged to follow the pattern of the oak tree. Their tablecloths were all cloth-of-gold, and they spread from a central dais where Aefric's table sat — the trunk — out through tables for his vassals and other guests, which were roots and branches.

And on each table, a miniature oak for a centerpiece that looked to be a living tree.

The flooring had been covered in rugs woven from rushes and sweet herbs, and dyed forest green.

At one end of the hall, musicians. A dozen string players, half as many woodwinds and soft horns, and half again as many players on the bodhrán, keeping the beat.

Two kindaren singers, a husband-and-wife pair. Known as the Reeds, they were easily the most popular singers in the city of Water's

End. How Kentigern had managed to book them on such short notice...

...well, likely involved an amount of money Aefric didn't want to think about.

At the other end of the hall, on a platform, jugglers and acrobats prepared to perform to the music.

When Aefric, Beornric and Yrsa entered the hall, it looked as though they were the last to arrive. Every table was filled, and servants moved among them — not bringing food yet, of course, but drinks before dinner — the only sight of navy blue and Deepwater gray among all the green and gold.

The musicians played the ducal fanfare as Aefric entered — Yrsa and Beornric dropped back a pace and flanked him — and at every table guests rose, bowing to Aefric as he passed.

He recognized many. Lers and knights, guild leaders and prominent merchants, but there were still faces among the crowd he didn't know.

All the same, he nodded to and greeted those he knew as he passed.

One question Aefric had about the arrangements was his own table. Most often, it would be wide and narrow, accommodating a dozen or more. At more ... significant meals, his table would be smaller. Likely only seating six or eight.

He hadn't been sure which way Kentigern was going to go tonight. Whether he would want more guests to have a chance to dine with the prince, or whether he would want to keep that privilege more exclusive.

He'd keep pressing Aefric to name the most important vassals in Water's End, and finally gotten for an answer, "I don't know. All right? I don't know who is important enough to sit with the prince. Maybe you should ask Garnotin."

It turned out, almost no one made the cut. The nearest tables to the dais included seats for Yrsa and Beornric, Garnotin and Kentigern, as well as most of the knights and lers Aefric saw most often.

His own Knights of the Lake shared a table with what looked to be the "pack of grizzled old men who henpecked" Killian. The eldest of them were much older than Beornric, but all of them looked to be ready for action at the first sign of trouble. They were all men, though, which Aefric thought was strange.

And on the dais, a triangular table, set only for Aefric, Killian — who still wore the same clothes from earlier, which was a relief — and...

...Deirdre?

Even now, for a meal like this one, Deirdre wore her maroon leathers. She preened as she looked about, as though this whole party were in her honor.

But as Aefric ascended the stairs to the dais, she left her chair and dropped to one knee before him.

A rage of whispers tore through the hall. Aefric realized then that most of his court had not seen her do this.

Killian laughed delightedly.

"Hope you don't mind, Aefric," he said. "Your seneschal intended for us to sit up here all on our own, but I simply *had* to ask this enchanting creature to join us."

"Where else would anyone expect to find Deirdre," Aefric said, smiling at her, "but in the middle of everything?"

"It's where I'm happiest, your grace," she said, rising only when Aefric gestured for her to do so. "His highness has been entertaining me with tales of his trip up the Indecisive River."

Her words were polite. Her tone ... *almost* polite. But Aefric knew her too well. She was taunting Killian that the most exciting recent stories he had to share were about a fairly uneventful boat trip.

Killian made a show of extending his hand for Aefric to shake, which set off another torrent of hushed conversation through the hall.

"Sailors," Aefric said, taking his seat and causing a second noisy ripple through the room as everyone else sat. "As entertaining as jugglers, in their own way."

"I *was* hoping," Killian said to Deirdre, "that a formal dinner might be enough to get you into a dress."

Aefric girded himself for a comment from Deirdre about how the prince would rather get her *out* of a dress. But she surprised him. Again.

"I am ducal champion for his grace, your highness," she said, gesturing to her badge of office — the Deepwater sigil done in gold and worn at her left shoulder. "I feel I must be ready at all times to safeguard him from threats."

"Is *that* what that is?" Killian teased. "I thought perhaps you were his official consort."

"*Is* there such a position, your grace?" Deirdre asked eagerly.

Killian laughed as servants began handing out small crystal goblets of palate wine.

Aefric hoped that a break for the cleansing palate wine would give him a chance to shift the conversation. But Deirdre was not to be distracted.

"What would being ducal consort involve anyway?" she asked. "Beyond the obvious, I mean. Would I be expected to hang up my sword? Or could I maintain my position as champion as well?"

"I was only teasing," Killian said, frowning. "I don't think an official consort position has existed anywhere in Armyr since the advent of the noble privilege."

"Just as well," Aefric said, smiling and taking a normal-sized crystal goblet of white wine from a passing servant. "I can't even imagine asking you to hang up your sword."

Deirdre's smile practically glowed.

"I've never seen you fight," Killian said thoughtfully. "As ducal champion, I imagine you're impressive. Would you care to try one of my knights tomorrow?"

"Only one?" Deirdre asked, looking over the salad that servants were now placing before the diners. A collection of mixed greens with sliced cucumbers, tomatoes, and three kinds of peppers, along with diced jicama and radish. "One could hardly present much challenge."

Killian laughed again, clearly impressed with her bravado, if not yet with her sword work.

"Best Ser Oudin," he said, "and we'll see."

"Oudin... Oudin..." Deirdre frowned and tilted her head slightly. "Oudin Ol'Maquill?"

"That's him."

She snorted. "Strong enough, and reasonably clever, but too slow. Far too slow. Shouldn't take me three movements."

"Care to make a wager on that?"

Aefric missed Deirdre's response. The conversation buzzing about the room had fallen silent behind him to his left, then came back twice as urgent.

A page approached. And not just any page. Meliflua Ol'Agranai, the senior page. On the cusp of her majority, Meliflua was tall and graceful, with long dark hair. In her bearing Aefric could see the impressive woman she would become. The one who would one day stand as ler over lands near the mouth of the Searun River.

She stopped at the foot of the dais. Bowed to Aefric. "Your grace." Bowed to Killian. "Your highness." Bowed to Deirdre. "Ser knight." Returning her attention to Aefric she held up two pieces of parchment. "We've had rikas from Ajenmoor and Kivash with urgent news."

Aefric gestured for her to approach. She mounted the steps while her last words made their way through many mouths out toward the edges of the hall.

Aefric took the messages.

The first was from Mayor Vagran in Ajenmoor, and said nothing Aefric didn't already know. He handed it to Killian.

"Varondam princess captured?" Killian said, puzzled. "Does that mean their ... what do they call it ... unspoken bastard?"

"It does. Princess Kiala." Aefric turned his attention to the message from Kivash. It was sent by Raedwaru, castellan of his castle there.

It read: *Rethneryl princesses captured on the river. Kidnappers fled into Malimfar.*

AEFRIC WAS SO STUNNED BY THE MESSAGE ON THAT SMALL PIECE OF parchment that he hardly noticed when Killian snatched it from his hand. And by the time he realized what the prince had done, Killian was already spreading the news.

"Rethneryl princesses kidnapped?" he said far too loudly. "On the Indecisive River?"

The hall boiled over with voices as Killian's words spread.

Deirdre actually offered — wordlessly — to strike the prince for that slip-up. Tempted as he might have felt himself, Aefric declined.

"Your grace," Meliflua said, shooting a hesitant glance at the prince. "There's one more."

Aefric took a breath to gird himself. "Go ahead."

"We've also had an official rika from Armityr. I held it for last, because it was not marked with the urgent symbol."

"Three in all? And they arrived together?" Aefric asked, surprised, as he took the message.

"Not quite, your grace, but this message was still being decoded while word arrived from Kivash and Ajenmoor."

Oh. Of course. He'd forgotten that messages sent by rika to and from the capital had be done in a code known only to the code smiths. After all, since he'd mastered the Soulfist linguistic spell, codes hardly presented much challenge for him.

Few, however, knew such a spell.

He sighed and read the words of the code smith, while Killian read over his shoulder.

Rethneryl princesses captured. Kidnappers last seen heading east through Malimfar. War moved up. Be ready to march one aett after Harvest Day by order of the king.

One aett after Harvest Day? But, that was hardly more than two aetts from now...

"The kidnappers were clearly heading for Caiperas," Killian said, with enough presence of mind to keep his voice down this time. Of course, he'd've had to shout to be heard over the tumult of speculation now rampaging through the hall.

"Officially, of course," he continued, "we must blame Malimfar. At least for the moment. But obviously this is the coin that burst the merchant's pack."

Killian shook his head. "No doubt Father already regrets letting Eppida talk him into waiting for spring. Think you'll be ready to march in time?"

Beornric and Yrsa were already mounting the steps up to the dais. Clearly they'd deduced the message from Armityr from what they'd heard the prince announce.

"We must cancel the dinner," Yrsa said. "There's too much to do for everyone here."

"She's right," Beornric said. "Even without thinking of the war."

"What does he mean?" Killian asked. "What could be more important than the war?"

"Kentigern," Aefric called down, but his seneschal seemed to already know what would be asked of him. He gave Aefric a grim nod and began the loud announcements that the dinner was canceled.

Killian grabbed Aefric's shoulder. "What does Beornric mean, Aefric?"

Aefric huffed out a breath. Deirdre was suddenly beside him. Whispered in his ear, "Shall I escort his highness elsewhere?"

Aefric considered that, but shook his head.

Using the noise of the announcements and ensuing social chaos for cover, he spoke quietly with the prince.

"It's not just Rethneryl and Varondam," Aefric said. "The princesses coming here from Hatay and Shachan have been kidnapped as well, from a ship on the Kalkerrik River."

"If this is true, why are you only telling me now?"

"Because I don't officially know it," Aefric said. "Hatay is keeping it secret. Karbin learned of the kidnappings in the course of his investigation."

"But he was investigating that attempt on your life, I thought,"

Killian said, not yet seeing the conclusion that felt so obvious to Aefric.

"The attempt hired by Nelazzi," he said.

Killian's eyes widened. "Nelazzi? Working with Caiperas?"

Aefric fought down the urge to strike himself in the forehead. Killian seemed so clever in so many ways, but...

"What would Nelazzi want with Caiperas?" Aefric said. "It's entirely landlocked. Nothing but river access."

"Ah," Killian said, with a touch of understanding finally entering his tone. "You don't think Caiperas is behind the kidnappings. You think it's Nelazzi."

"I'm sure of it," Aefric said. "I can't prove it, though."

"But Father blames Caiperas, and so does Rethneryl. And preparations for war have begun. He won't change course without proof." Killian frowned. "Might not anyway. Caiperas *did* try to assassinate us after all."

"And King Makarios needs to pay for that," Aefric said. "I agree. But it won't help those princesses."

"Nelazzi won't kill them," Killian said. "She's a businesswoman. Live, well-treated princesses are worth ransom. Abused or dead princesses bring a blood hunt."

"You spoke of the coin that broke the merchant's pack?" Aefric said. "Well Nelazzi must be stopped."

"You don't mean to go after her. Not the pirate queen. Not now."

Aefric just looked at him. Killian's eyes widened, but his voice firmed.

"Not for this. You're a duke of Armyr, man. Not *one* of these princesses is your responsibility."

Aefric only looked at him.

"You're *supposed* to be preparing for *war*," Killian all but shouted.

"If I take the bulk of my fighting forces off to war in Caiperas, I expose my entire coastline to Nelazzi."

"She may even be counting on that," Yrsa added.

"I have at least a dozen towns rebuilding on that coastline," Aefric said, staring straight into Killian's eyes, so like his father's. "Thousands of people trying to put their lives and livelihoods back together, along with their homes. And that's not even counting the towns of my vassals in Haven and Fyretti. I refuse to abandon them all to a pirate's depredations."

"Especially a pirate that's branching out into slaving," Beornric added grimly.

"You're going to do this," Killian said, voice full of wonder. "No matter what I say."

"*Officially*," Aefric said, "I'm going to go survey my coastline and its defenses while my general prepares my forces for war. Unofficially, I'm going to rescue the princesses and put an end to Nelazzi once and for all."

"And I'm coming with you," Killian said firmly.

"You're not," Aefric said, having expected that reaction. "You are the crown prince and the future ruler of Armyr. There is no way I am going to put your life at risk. Your father would—"

"My father is no fool. If you fail, he will be furious that you went hunting pirates when you're supposed to be preparing for war. If you succeed, he will pretend to have privately approved it all along, and parlay your deeds into some kind of political gain."

"Which is—"

"*What's more*," Killian said, "if I go along, I have a chance to get some of the battle seasoning I sorely need. I'm probably not going to Caiperas, and Father made me sit out the Godswalk Wars. Maev got to go play scout, but I had to remain behind. Safe. Someday I will need to lead my own troops into battle. Why would they follow me, if even the greenest recruit has as much experience as I do?"

"I wouldn't follow you," Deirdre said, shrugging.

"Exactly," Killian said. "I've done nothing to prove myself. I *must* do this, Aefric."

"And if you get killed?" Aefric asked.

"Then Maev becomes the heir," Killian said with a shrug. "She would no longer be expected to marry Dalius. She could come back here and marry you. You come out ahead either way."

"If I got his heir killed, you think King Colm would want me marrying his daughter?" Aefric said. "No. He'd have me executed."

"No he wouldn't, your grace," Deirdre said simply. "I'd spirit you away to safety across the Risen Sea. I know places that would take us in." She considered that a moment, then nodded. "I think the prince should come."

"Deirdre," Beornric growled, but Killian was still rolling.

"You're forgetting the other side of this, Aefric. What am I supposed to do if I *don't* go?"

Aefric closed his eyes and sighed.

"Why, with the war coming, doubtless Father will want me returning to Armityr at once. And I might *have* to tell him what his favorite vassal is off doing..."

"Fine," Aefric grumbled.

"I beg your pardon, Aefric? I don't believe I heard you."

"I said 'fine,'" Aefric said loudly. "You can come. But understand this. You follow my orders, and those of anyone I designate in my stead."

Aefric raised a hand to forestall the obvious objection.

"No, this does not mean sending you belowdecks and keeping you out of the way whenever anything *interesting* happens. You'll get your chance to fight, and to learn how to do something like this. But damn it all, I need to know that if I or Beornric or Deirdre give you an order under fire, you'll *follow it*. Because not doing so may get us *all* killed."

Killian sobered, seeming to finally understand that Aefric wasn't being playful or overprotective or even henpecking him.

He nodded. "You are in charge of this, Aefric. You and anyone you name. And after we pull this off, I will never forget who gave me my first true trial by fire."

"May we all survive it," Aefric said.

For Aefric, the worst part about being a noble had to be the delays.

He knew what he needed to do. And if he'd still been an adventurer, he would have left right from that dining hall.

Well. Not quite from the dining hall. He'd needed to return to his apartments for a few things, but from there — had it been an option — he would have flown straight down to his ship and set sail.

Alas, that was not an option. Not for the Duke of Deepwater. There were too many official things he needed to do, after that stop at his apartments.

For his armies — and not just his standing armies — recruitment of reserves had to be accelerated. Which meant swinging by Yrsa's office to review and approve (or deny, in a couple of cases) her methods, as well as which vassals she could draw from, and making clear which she could not.

None of those things could wait for his return.

Nor could plans for the borogs. Clan Thunder Stick knew to regard Yrsa as a chief's hand if she came to the Dragonscar without Aefric. But he still needed to discuss the time frames with her. When to bring Thunder Stick down to join with his main forces, not to mention going over the logistics of having a few hundred borogs march alongside his armies.

Or at least, *near* his armies.

Then there was another stop for the many, many needs of Garnotin and Kentigern before Aefric could leave. So many questions. So very many decisions. And all of them coming so quickly that Aefric felt as though days and aetts — perhaps even seasons — were passing by, while he remained in Garnotin's office.

Trapped, at that mahogany desk with his seneschal and castellan. Answering questions from three different angles about this crop or that product, this castle need or that city need, how to handle this guild or that one, what the demands of the merchants would become once word of war spread, and how to stave off the inevitable price hikes brought on by fear of coming scarcity.

And more. So much more. With no end in sight.

There had been a time when Aefric had believed that being a noble was a fairly cushy gig. And it was true that the benefits were considerable. But ye gods above, below and in-between, he'd had no idea just how much *work* was involved in ruling.

Finally, though, Beornric pounded on the door and Aefric pulled his head out of the sea of niggling problems to gasp for air and realize again where it was he stood, and what was around him.

Garnotin's office on the … no. Aefric didn't know where he was in his own castle at the moment. Main keep, yes. Somewhere on the docks side, certainly. What floor, though, he couldn't have guessed.

Decent enough size, the office, all of it furnished in mahogany. Cabinets and chests and drawers around the edges, but leaving room for a large tapestry of the Deepwater sigil, along with two doors besides the one leading into the hall.

He, Garnotin and Kentigern were gathered around a desk so covered in parchments and scrolls Aefric would have believed it Elkari's, if he didn't know better.

"Come," Garnotin called, and Beornric entered.

"The *Swift Wave* stands ready to sail, your grace," Beornric said. "We await only your presence."

"Good," Aefric said, while Kentigern sighed and Garnotin frowned. "Gentlemen, I trust you can handle the rest until I get back."

"I dislike lying about where you're going," Kentigern said. "If asked, I mean."

"What did I tell you?" Aefric asked.

"Your grace told me that he is going to see to the defenses of his coastline, to ensure that they'll be ready for the coming war."

"Garnotin?"

"Your grace told me the same."

"Have either of you heard me say differently?"

They shook their heads, neither of them convinced.

"Then what's the problem?" Aefric asked. "Because I assure you both, what I said is true."

"And I'm supposed to pretend I don't know how many supplies have been taken aboard the *Swift Wave*?" Kentigern asked. "Too many for a duke reviewing a double-handful of ports and defenses."

"And I'm supposed to believe it's reasonable that you're

talking all of the Knights of the Lake, as well as your champion?" Garnotin asked. "To say nothing of the two dozen soldiers of your personal guard? Seems to me like your grace expects trouble."

"As I said," Aefric said patiently. "I guarantee what I told you is true. As for your own conclusions, well, they're just that. Your own conclusions. Are you in the habit of sharing your speculations outside of my circle of advisers?"

Kentigern and Garnotin both frowned, but they shook their heads.

"Then there's no need for concern," Aefric said with a smile. "Cheer up. Both of you. I'm doing only what I have to, for the good of Deepwater and Armyr, with one eye on the coming war."

Garnotin drew breath and squared his shoulders. "Yes, your grace."

Kentigern frowned, but nodded. "Of course, your grace."

"Then let's have no more talk of lying," Aefric said. "If you believe I am withholding any secrets, at least give me the credit in your thoughts that I might have good reason for doing so. Fare you both well."

"Fare well, your grace," Garnotin said.

"And return soon," Kentigern added. "And safe."

Beornric led the way down three halls to a secret staircase that would take them swiftly down to the main floor.

Only a dozen flights of stairs. Not nearly as high as Aefric's main offices then.

Along the way Beornric said, "You'll need to do something special for those two, when you return. They know they're out of the loop on this, and they'll worry that you don't trust them. Even if they don't admit it."

"If I tell them now," Aefric said, "and a royal emissary comes to check on our war progress, they'll have to lie. I don't want them in that position."

"A justiciar would still see straight through the phrasing you gave them."

"If his majesty sends a justiciar," Aefric said, "at least they'll be provably innocent of anything his majesty decides is a crime."

"You think you're going to lose your duchy for this," Beornric said, wonder in his voice. "Even if you succeed."

"I'm going directly against his majesty's orders, and risking my readiness for his majesty's coming war. The queen will see this as a chance to get me ousted and replaced with someone more tractable. The king might need to make an example of me, to ensure that Merrek and Silverlake toe the line. Especially Merrek."

"The people support you. Your vassals support you. Both your peers actually *like* you. Removing you might not be so easy."

"Each of our monarchs is at least as good at politics as I am at magic. You think I'd survive here long if I unite them against me?"

Beornric stopped Aefric just short of opening the door to the main floor.

"Don't go," he said. "Recall the prince, but send the rest of us. We can claim we were just checking the defenses as we discussed, when Nelazzi attacked. On our own we decided pursuit was necessary and the rest just followed. Believable enough that if we fail, no blame will fall on you. And if we succeed, no one will bother *questioning* our story, let alone testing it under Taesark's three-edged sword."

Aefric clapped Beornric on his armored shoulder.

"I appreciate what you're trying to do," he said quietly. "But duke or adventurer, I'm going to do what I know is right. Even when I'm not supposed to."

Beornric snorted. "No wonder Deirdre's so fond of you. You're both thick-headed the same way."

"Come on," Aefric said with a smile. "The midnight tides wait for no one."

THE *DUKE'S HAND* WAS DEFINITELY A MORE COMFORTABLE SHIP THAN the *Swift Wave*. But then, the *Duke's Hand* was always intended as a pleasure craft as much as anything else.

The *Swift Wave*, on the other hand, had been a smugglers' ship before Aefric seized it. A three-masted carrack, and a big beastie at that. Were it even a ton heavier it would likely have had too much drag to handle the Searun River. Instead, it was just the right size.

Enough berths for the fifty or so knights and soldiers he was bringing along, while still managing separate cabins for both Aefric and Killian without displacing the captain or officers.

Also, the *Swift Wave* was armed. Two catapults, one fore and one aft. Not much, but better than nothing.

Of course, if this came to a sea battle, Aefric would be in deep trouble. Not to mention heavily outnumbered by Nelazzi's fleet. Still. A single ship could go places a fleet could not. And a couple of catapults might well come in handy before all was said and done.

Still, the *Duke's Hand would've* been more comfortable.

Roomier, for example. With proper furnishings, instead of relying on Aefric's luggage to do double duty. Fortunately, his luggage comprised a couple of chests for clothes and goods, and a couple more for the sorts of special food and drink he'd be expected to have available for himself and the prince, even at sea.

Plenty of flat surfaces for sitting or dining. And when he was in his cabin, how much more did he need?

Admittedly, Aefric could have taken the larger available cabin — the one usually designated as his, on the rare occasions he sailed this ship — which had an actual table bolted to the wall, with two bench seats.

But better to leave that for Killian, who'd probably never had it so rough. Whereas Aefric had sailed in much worse conditions, when he was younger.

Sleeping in a hammock again would be interesting. Hadn't done it in ages. Wasn't sure he missed it, either. Comfortable enough, in its way, but, well, he'd gotten used to a very large and very comfortable bed.

It would suffice though, for sleep was what he needed. The hour was late, and he wasn't due to contact Karbin before dawn. There was, though, one person he needed to contact before sleeping.

Sitting on a crate he cast the spell, hoping he faced Varondam and Maev. And the words he sent her were these: "My sweet Maev. Princesses from Hatay, Shachan, Rethneryl and Varondam all kidnapped by Nelazzi. Hatay and Shachan not public knowledge. Don't be next. Be careful."

Her answer came back even faster than expected.

"My dearest Aefric. You're off to the rescue, I just know it. Another adventure without me, while my greatest enemy is boredom. I miss you."

Boredom? He was worried that Varondam would make her a prisoner, and she was worried about being bored?

Well, nothing he could do about that. Might not matter anyway. No reason to think she'd be one of Nelazzi's targets. Not while staying at Varondam's royal court.

Still, there was no way Aefric could have refrained from warning her.

But now that was done and he needed sleep.

So he stretched out as best he could on the rough, tight ropes of the hammock, and let it rock him to sleep with the movement of the ship.

The smells of wood and varnish, and creosote from the sealant, never let him forget where he was. Even as he drifted off...

It was a spell that awakened him. And not his own. That familiar ringing sensation through his bones that told him of a message spell incoming.

Karbin's voice followed quickly: "We were right. The kidnappers stole a ship at Weasbech and sailed northwest. But handed off princesses first. Trail continues, but cold. Sail south."

Weasbech. That was the port city at the mouth of the Kalkerrik River. They sailed northwest to leave a false trail. Or, maybe, were just done with one job and doing another. No way to know, but they didn't really matter. Their part was finished.

That the ship thieves had handed off the princesses to someone going south. *That* mattered.

Aefric nodded, as he waited for the shift in sensations. That tight tingle that meant the spell was waiting to carry his own words back to Karbin.

When it came, he said, "War timeline moved up. Ship thieves stole Rethneryl princesses on the Indecisive. Rethneryl not hiding it. Officially blaming Malimfar. Possibly hotter trail. Trust your judgment."

Aefric thought that would be it for communications, but the ringing sensation started up again before he was out of the hammock.

"Rethneryl princesses likely bound for Wulfport first. Strong presence, Nelazzi allies. Could even be gathering all princesses there before final destination. Suggest sailing that way."

The tingling sensation didn't follow. Apparently Karbin didn't want this to turn into an extended conversation.

Well, perhaps that was for the best. Aefric didn't want message spells to put Karbin at risk. He was the one out there alone, not semi-comfortable in a ship's cabin.

Aefric dressed in a strong, bright red wool tunic over dark brown leathers, with matching leather boots and belt. He reflexively checked his noble's dagger, pouch, and the wand Garram, to make sure they were in place, before taking the Brightstaff in hand and leaving his cabin. Under the dim light of a fishy-smelling oil lamp, he moved down the tight hall to the door at the end.

The salt wind that met him as he emerged was stiff and in his face, which meant it was with him. The rising sun was to his left, over a shoreline more distant than he expected. The sea the only sight in all other directions but up, where clouds smeared the lightening purple in their hurry.

Ahead of him, on the afterdeck, the clashing sounds and snark of knights getting in some practice. On the main decks around him, sailors rushed here and there about their business, calling to each other as they worked.

Aefric looked up. The sails billowed a bit, but weren't full. Not nearly full enough.

"Your grace!" Beornric called down from the afterdecks, then came swiftly and smoothly across a second deck and down the steep set of shallow steps to the main deck. "Good morning. Shall I ask about breakfast or Karbin first?"

"Karbin," Aefric said, and told him about the exchange.

"Well, good thing we're heading south then."

"We had to anyway, to maintain the illusion," Aefric said, frowning, "though I don't know how we're expected to evaluate ports we can't even see."

"Captain Ol'Vanett said the best way to do it was the sweep south, then come up the coast. And that's the route she logged at Ajenmoor."

"She knows that's not what we're doing though, yes?"

"She does," Beornric said with a nod. "But she insisted that making it look authentic to start would help us when we deviate from our route."

"Well, she's captain for a reason," Aefric said, frowning at the sails. The wind felt stiff enough on his face and blowing his hair about, but it wasn't enough. Not for the kind of speed he'd need to have any chance of catching up with those princesses.

Once more Beornric seemed to read his mind.

"You need food, your grace."

"I'll eat later," Aefric said, crossing the deck toward the stairs to the afterdecks.

"Those spells take a lot out of you," Beornric said, following right along. "By your own admission."

"My admission this past spring when I learned them," Aefric said, annoyed enough at the shallowness of each step that he considered just flying up the steep slope. "How do they tolerate these stairs?"

"Watch the sailors," Beornric said. "They take them four at a time on the way up, and come down them so fast they seem to leap."

"I've come a long way with Sirondfar's wind spells since springtime," Aefric said. "And we need the speed."

"You're not going to be talked out of this, are you?"

Aefric reached the next deck up. From here he could clearly see the knights sparring up on the afterdeck. All of them in their full plate armor, of course, except for Deirdre, who was whirling in the center of them like a maroon flame dancing about in a steel forge.

He realized then that she must've been sparring with all of Killian's knights, because his own Knights of the Lake all stood around the perimeter, catcalling the action.

The wheel was just to Aefric's right, and the captain herself piloting. Captain Paett Ol'Vanett. Swarthy and sea-hardened, she looked every bit as tough as her brother, Ser Joshen. Her graying dark hair hung in dreads to her shoulders, and she favored strong linen clothing. A bright pale blue for her tunic under a red doublet, but black pants tucked into hard-looking leather boots that came to her knee.

She wore a cutlass at her belt, along with at least four long daggers and a cleaver. All of them sheathed.

"Morning, captain," Aefric said, approaching.

"Morning, your grace," she said, watching something in the distance. "See any holes in my sails, be sure to tell me."

Puzzlement crossed his face before making it to his lips. And even though he hadn't said anything yet, she spoke as though he'd asked.

"Way your grace was looking at my sails. Like he'd caught them sleeping on watch."

"Not the sails, the wind," Aefric said. "Not strong enough."

"Be strong enough before midday," she said. "Is this where I get to hear my true destination?"

"Wulfport."

"Malimfar, eh? Fair piece of sea between here and there," she said, "but not too distant. Not nearly far enough to justify all the supplies we've taken on."

"Wulfport's our next destination, but not necessarily our last before we head home."

Captain Ol'Vanett gave Aefric an assessing look. Nodded abruptly, as though she'd concluded something.

"I'm going to see to our winds," he said.

She cocked a weathered eyebrow. "We in a hurry, your grace?"

"Lives hang in the balance," Aefric said. "A lot of lives."

"Should've known," she said with a sigh. "Nobody brings that many weapons onto a ship unless they're looking for a fight."

"Some fights are worth having."

Her eyes widened. She opened her mouth, then shook her head. Snapped her lips shut. Frowned.

"No," she finally said. "I don't know and I don't want to know. And I don't want any of your grace's people telling my crew. Not unless there's no other choice. Not if your grace is doing ... what I think he's doing."

"What do you think I'm doing?"

"I'm not going to say it, and I hope I'm wrong. But if I'm not, the truth will scare my crew, your grace. And your grace doesn't need that any more than I do. So ... whatever we're doing ... I'm going to ask that your grace and his people keep it to themselves until there's no other choice."

Aefric nodded. Turned to Beornric.

"I'll get the word around myself, your grace. Right now."

Beornric went off to do just that, and Captain Ol'Vanett lowered her voice.

"Your grace, are my people coming back from this?"

Aefric leaned in a little closer. "I'm going to fight like hell to get everyone on this ship back home in one piece."

Captain Ol'Vanett stared at Aefric a little longer than anyone would have considered polite. She nodded, once, then turned her attention back to whatever she was looking at on the horizon.

And he knew exactly what that nod meant. His words were good, and sincere. But doing something was a lot harder than saying it.

CONVENTIONAL WISDOM SAID THAT THE SAME SPELL WOULD BE CAST THE same way by every magic-user who used it.

As was often the case with conventional wisdom, it came close to the truth, but missed some essential elements.

First of all, the approach to casting varied greatly with the type of magic-user involved. Dweomerblades produced their magic without anything a wizard would identify as a spell. Warlocks lacked the technical aplomb of wizards, because they gained their powers a very different way.

But even among wizards, there was variance. After all. The structural design of spells came down to three elements: applied logic, a touch of artistry, and an understanding of the interrelationship of forces.

Wizards were masters of logic. And among themselves, their logic was entirely consistent, and a big part of the reason that they could learn spells even from ancient grimoires, penned by wizards whose philosophies and training had been entirely different from their own.

Artistry, for wizards, dealt more in the minutia and the details. It tended to run in lines, from master to apprentice. For example, every spell Aefric had found in the Soulfist grimoires — so far, at least — had shown the same basic artistic sensibility, even if it varied subtly through the generations.

Understanding of the interrelationships of forces, well, that was largely a matter of training and experience.

However, while the world at large believed Aefric to be a wizard — and in many ways, he functioned much like one — he himself knew the truth. He was a dweomerblood, the first of his kind. And while his sense of the artistry of magic was stronger and more distinct than any wizard he'd ever met — including Kainemorton himself — command of magic's internal logics did not work the same way for him as it did for wizards.

A fact that had caused his old teachers no end of frustration.

Aefric could learn spells from wizards. But when he did, he often found his way to mastery of a spell *despite* the way the wizard understood it, rather than because of.

The wind spells he'd learned from Sirondfar were a perfect example of this.

Sirondfar was not only a wizard, but a *ventavis*. A specialist in the magics of weather and birds. Those concepts underlay everything he did, and even how he thought about magic.

So the basic words of power he used for that particular wind spell — selected from the set of ancient words that tapped directly into primal forces and still handled much of the heavy lifting for most modern spell work — were a problem for Aefric from the beginning.

The ones Sirondfar used had ties to a long-forgotten god of birds. A god even Aefric only knew of because of an offhand comment from Kainemorton, a few years back.

And while those words of power might serve well a wizard whose magic focused so much on birds and weather, they did not perform nearly so well for Aefric. Which meant that the spell required a great deal more effort from him than it did from Sirondfar.

Effort that had, at first, left Aefric drained after maintaining the winds for a decent stretch of time.

So he'd experimented. Changed those core words out to others, ones with more personal resonance with the magic in his blood.

The difference was like going from carrying a full load of cord wood to carrying a half load of feathers. There was still a little effort there, but very different, and much less work.

The approach Sirondfar had taken to shaping the spell — chanting to the rhythm of an old kindaren song in praise of sweet winds — was fine, but adding certain na'shek gestures of assuming command worked better for Aefric, and removed the need to chant aloud.

Those gestures went all but unused these days by the na'shek themselves, except during the formal ascendance of a new leader. But they appealed greatly to the artist in Aefric.

In all, he got a good deal better results from the spell now than he'd been able to produce when he'd first learned it. And for a lot less work.

So Aefric took up a post behind the ship's wheel at just about dawn that first morning and worked his spells. Filling the sails of the *Swift Wave* with all the wind they could handle and speeding the ship south.

With the wind in place, Aefric sank into his spells and held them with a focus that allowed for no distractions. He spared no attention for thoughts of food, the passing of time, or activities on the deck around him, or even what might've been transpiring at sea. It could have rained on him and he wouldn't have known.

He had his spells, and his spells were enough. So he stood there, Brightstaff in one hand, augmenting his work with its own power, and he kept those winds gusting. Not across all of the sea, of course, but forming a tunnel around his ship.

A tunnel that began no more than a hundred feet or so behind the ship itself, and ended no more than a hundred feet ahead. Out to the sides, it didn't stretch more than fifty feet in either direction.

Far more precision than he could have managed even this past summer. But precision was one of the benefits of adding the na'shek gestures.

This wind blew for his ship and his ship alone.

Could Sirondfar have managed the same? Probably. Though not with the spell he'd taught Aefric. But then, he probably kept his best wind spells to himself and perhaps his own apprentice, Farondonic.

If so, Aefric couldn't blame him. There was always a sense of competition among magic-users, even when working toward a common purpose.

Or at least, if there was another reason Karbin *still* had not taught Aefric the secrets of teleportation, he couldn't guess it.

But that was nothing more than a small thought, flitting through the back of Aefric's mind while he held his spells. He'd learned over the years that, no matter how deep his focus, some part of his mind was always thinking.

The key was not to pay those thoughts the kind of attention that would distract him from what most of his mind was doing. And he was best served at the moment by keeping most of his focus on his spells. That way he could keep them going with the least effort, in terms of spending his power.

The more focus he used, the less effort he needed. One of the strange contradictions of magic.

It took a hand shaking his shoulder — hard — to finally bring Aefric's attention back to the world around him.

The sun rode high and warm in a bright blue sky. He dismissed his spell, but still wind filled the sails and the *Swift Wave* looked to be earning its name, cutting its way across the Risen Sea.

Aefric's face was covered in light perspiration, and he tasted of salt. The salt of the sea air, though. He wasn't sweating that much. Still, the taste of *anything* seemed to be enough to set his stomach rumbling. Hard.

He could hear the chaotic sounds of training coming from up on the afterdecks. Too many voices and too much steel to be the knights. Had to be the soldiers, taking their turn.

Aefric shook himself. Nodded at Beornric, who returned an assessing look before giving Aefric a nod of his own. Killian, standing beside Beornric, looked somewhere between fascinated and concerned.

The captain was no longer at the wheel. The pilot was a grizzled old sailor, who frowned at Aefric as though he'd been a child engaged in foolishness.

Then again, the winds *were* blowing strong enough now on their own...

"Just like the captain said," Beornric said, nodding at the sails. "Full enough now, even without your grace's spells. We're making good time."

"Honestly, Aefric," Killian said, frowning. "Were you just going to stand there all day casting that spell?"

"Holding it together, more than casting it," Aefric said. "If I hadn't, it wouldn't have lasted long past full sunrise. By midmorning, we might even have been becalmed."

"And it wouldn't have cost us much time," Beornric said. "Not with the wind we've had gathering since." And before Aefric could consider responding, Beornric added, "And the captain says we're likely to hold this wind through evening."

"Good," Aefric said, stretching while his joints popped from being held still so long. "I'll be able to get some research in this evening."

"We won't be playing cards then?" Killian asked.

"Cards?" Aefric asked, puzzled for a moment before he realized that Killian didn't have much to do during the voyage. "I shouldn't. I have a research project that might help us..." — he glanced at the pilot, who was clearly listening — "when we get where we're going."

Killian looked as though he was going to ask a question, but Beornric also spotted the listening pilot and cut in first.

"His highness has spent the morning going over the charts," Beornric said.

Killian gave a self-deprecating smile and shrugged one shoulder.

"Can't have the crew tripping over me," he said. "I know the rivers and lakes of Armyr well, but I'm still learning the ocean currents. To say nothing of the habits of the winds." He clapped Aefric on the shoulder. "But then, I'm no wizard."

"Few are," Aefric said, smiling. "But most find their way about by ship just fine all the same."

"Have lunch with me, both of you," Killian said, putting an arm each around Aefric and Beornric, and heading belowdecks. "And perhaps we can talk about how your ducal champion has been beating up my knights."

That evening, just as the sun was setting, Aefric returned to his rather cramped quarters to contact Karbin. He raised a finger to ignite his oil lamps with a gesture, then grimaced.

Whale oil. When burned it gave off a fishy smell would not set well with the taste of beef stew lingering in his mouth from dinner.

But then, he'd never cared for the smell of whale oil anyway. In fact, if he intended to sail the *Swift Wave* again, he'd have to make sure their lamps burned something else. Whatever they burned on the *Duke's Hand* would be fine. Or almost anything else, really.

So instead Aefric lit the room with a touch of his own magic. Just enough for a comfortably soft, white glow. Enough to read by.

He sat on his chest of clothes. Flared his nostrils in a deep breath. Cast the spell that would reach out to Karbin.

"Crew kept in the dark. I'm ensuring the wind. Captain says we'll reach Wulfport by tomorrow evening, latest. Killian may make a good navigator."

He waited then, with the tension of the spell tingling the air around him, for Karbin's words to return.

"Already at Wulfport. Dead end. Kidnappers took another route. Talk of war is spreading. Don't enter port. Contact me when near. I'll come to you."

Wulfport, a dead end? That was just about the worst thing Aefric could've heard. They'd already lost track of the kidnappers up in Hatay. Not that finding them would've been easy, with Hatay hiding the kidnapping.

Now the kidnappers in Malimfar had gotten away as well?

How could Karbin possibly be so certain that the kidnappers didn't go through Wulfport? He'd only had since dawn to poke around there, and only that long if he'd teleported.

Plus, Nelazzi was strong in Wulfport. Heck, she was even moving *slaves* through there. Surely moving a couple of princesses wouldn't be as hard to keep undetected as a full shipload of slaves. Surely the kidnappers would want to...

To what? The Wulfport route might be the *easiest* for Nelazzi's confederates, but it would also be the most obvious choice to those who knew anything about her organization. If the kidnappers were expecting pursuit — which they had to be — they likely planned a separate route well away from Nelazzi's usual business.

After all, there was a reason people called her the pirate queen. She was cautious, and had a habit of staying one step ahead of her pursuers.

All right. So — on top of whatever Karbin had learned — there was logic to the conclusion that the kidnappers had used a different port. Might not even have left the rivers yet, depending on where they were going.

Where would they be going?

To Nelazzi herself. They had to be. Surely royal captives were valuable enough to merit her personal attention.

So where would Nelazzi receive them?

Unproductive line of thought. Aefric wasn't going to reason his way through this. Not here and now. Tomorrow evening he could discuss the possibilities with Karbin, Beornric, Deirdre and ... Killian. Yes. If Killian had been studying sea routes, maybe he'd learned enough to make himself useful in this conversation.

The captain would be even more useful, of course. From the way she'd reacted that morning, she had to have guessed that they were after Nelazzi. Surely she had some idea of where the so-called pirate queen could be found...

Tomorrow's problem. And Aefric might have a solution in his pouch without even knowing it.

Speaking of which, it was time to get to his research.

He drew a deep breath, and thought about the gift from his majesty. The engraved teak box. He opened the black velvet pouch at his belt and there the box was, just inside the lip and ready for his hand.

The box was bigger, but only to the eye. That was the nature of the space-warping magics woven into the pouch by Jenbarjen. A gift that was part of her attempt to prove her value to her new baron.

That pouch carried significantly more than it looked, though not as much as the wonderful sack he'd kept hidden in a backpack, during his adventuring days. The sack that still held most of his old treasure. And like that sack, no matter how much the pouch contained, it never seemed weigh even a featherweight more than it did while empty.

The pouch had two other handy features, as well. The first was that it would bring to his fingertips any object inside it that he thought of. And the second, that it was designed specifically for Aefric. It wouldn't work for anyone but him.

A good gift. And now to see about this latest gift.

Aefric held up the teak box. The lettering was unfamiliar. The images involved two men...

No. Two humans, they could have been of either gender, or somewhere in between...

For that matter, they were human*oid*. One head, two arms, two legs. The engraver who'd worked so hard on the lettering hadn't bothered to give the figures enough character to make clear if they were intended to represent humans, na'shek, eldrani ... or even dybbungstad, for that matter.

No way to tell.

And what they were supposed to be doing was a puzzle unto itself. Could've been a kind of dance, or perhaps a ritual.

No simple answers, just looking the box over. But then, he hadn't really expected any. Not when generations of wizards had been unable to solve the riddle of the box.

Aefric looked over the letters again. He'd thought at first that they might've been Ancient Hwalish, but no. The letters sloped the wrong direction. Left, instead of right. And they lacked the sharpness on crossing movements, or the small ligature marks that indicated vowels, aspiration and other sound modifiers.

The images and letters were only on the one side of the box. The side of opening. And nowhere on the box itself was an image of a box, either open, closed, or opening or closing.

No hints there.

The magic of the box was just as slippery now as it had been out on Aefric's balcony in the...

...in the sun.

He was holding the box now. But the light of his magic was unchanged. He set the box down on the chest in front of him. Picked it back up.

No change. No dimming. So it was sunlight the box dimmed. Not magical light. Or was it just that it didn't dim *magical* light?

Aefric put the box back into pouch, picked up the Brightstaff, and went out on deck.

A gentle rain fell, but only in the general area of the ship. About half the sky was still clear, with at least a share of starlight. To say nothing of the oil lamps of the watch.

"All right, your grace?" a watch sailor called to him.

"Fine," Aefric said. "Just wanted a little air."

The sailor's attention was already off of Aefric and on to something else.

Aefric found a private spot nearish the rail and allowed his eyes to finish adjusting to the dim starlight.

He pulled the box out of his pouch.

Starlight remained starlight. Lamplight remained lamplight. No dimming.

No change to the sounds about him, either. He could still hear the snap of the sails, the creak of the rigging. That hadn't been true on the balcony. Ocheda had called him three times before he'd heard her voice, and even then she'd sounded distant.

He put the box back into his pouch and returned to his cabin.

So it dimmed the light and sounds of the day, not the night.

Then again, perhaps the muting of the sounds had had more to do with his focus than the box. New magic always fascinated him.

He'd have to test that later, to be sure.

But for now, by the light of his spells, he sat again on a chest in his cabin. Cast the Soulfist linguistic spell, and looked at the lettering once more.

Meaning did not come. The letters remained nothing more than unrecognizable shapes.

Aefric's heart quickened. Tricky, this little box. Well, he had more tricks up his sleeve.

He went back to a different type of linguistic spell. This one taught to him by Kainemorton himself. It was only useful for reading, not speaking, but it had never failed him before.

It failed him now.

Well, not *failed*. The spell *worked*. It was just that the spell couldn't unriddle the secrets hidden in those letters. They remained the same meaningless shapes, instead of whispering their concepts straight into his mind, as though he understood them and could read them normally.

Aefric frowned through a deep breath. He'd used that latter spell countless times over the years. It had worked on crumbling bits of stone as well as faded bits of parchment.

There'd never been any written word that this spell could not read.

Any written *word*.

What if the "letters" weren't letters at all?

Ambiguous figures doing ambiguous things, underneath a row of symbols that looked like letters, but weren't.

There would be no logic to that.

Which would drive wizards crazy...

Aefric started laughing. Wizards always began and ended with logic. But what if the only logic to the secrets of this box was in the shape of the box itself? The general styling of its containment? Making it a fitting container for power, that could reveal its power...

...when? When could it reveal its power?

Killian had said not to open it in the sun. Which implied that others had opened it, without releasing its power. But that opening it in the sun was ... inadvisable for some reason.

He'd have to ask Killian about that.

Aefric tilted back the lid. The box opened smoothly to a ninety-degree angle, where its hinges caught and held.

The inside of the box was empty to the naked eye, but Aefric could feel that slippery power before him. Constrained by the box, even when the box stood open.

The feel right now was *exactly* the same as it was when the box was closed. Lid open, lid shut didn't matter to the power. Not so long as its riddle remained unsolved.

Now, following the logic of most enchanted objects, a box containing power should not open until and unless someone opens it the right way.

Which meant one of two things. The first possibility was that this box wasn't following conventional magical logic at all. Which could be true, if the letters weren't letters and the ambiguous figures were a kind of blind. A false lead.

The other possibility was simpler, in its way. Opening the lid wasn't really opening the box. This meant that the box itself was a false front. A distraction. And the true secret to the contained power "inside" the box required a different approach entirely.

The question at the moment, then, was which of the two possibilities — if either — was the right one.

Aefric settled down to study the spells of the box. Those involved in building the framework within it that would contain whatever powers it might hold. There had to be some clues in that structure.

Except that studying that structure was not so easy. It was every bit as slippery as the power the box contained.

Aefric worked at that until he developed a headache from the effort, only to discover that hours had passed — rung out by a bell on the deck — and he'd gotten exactly nowhere.

Frustrated, he went to sleep.

Aefric's second day aboard the *Swift Wave* started much the same way as the first. He rose at dawn.

There was no contact from Karbin that morning, but that was no surprise, because they were already planning to get together in person that evening. No point in contact by spell unless there was news.

So Aefric had gone up on deck and spent most of the morning ensuring the winds, until Captain Ol'Vanett got his attention to let him know they were in position to catch the trade winds, and no more spells would be needed to get them to Wulfport before sundown.

After lunch, he passed most of the afternoon placating Killian with a game of cards.

The game was Queens' Conspiracy, and though the description of it was all politics and maneuvering behind the scenes, the game itself involved accumulating powerful cards of each suit — anchored by a queen — or a queen with a strong enough combination of cards from the same suit (indicating influence with the masses).

The second-best combination was to hold four queens and an ace, which was called "Concordance."

The unbeatable combination, though, was to hold all four greater kings and a greater queen, which was officially called a "Queen Ascendant," and unofficially called an "Elysant," after an ancient queen who was said to have had several different kings dancing on her strings.

They played at the fixed table in Killian's cabin. Whatever wood had gone into making that table, it had been varnished and lacquered to an orange color that had nothing to do with the tree it was cut from.

Likely a pale softwood like fir or pine, given extra lacquer for something like strength. At least, that was Aefric's speculation.

Aefric and the prince faced each other on the fixed bench seats. Aefric with the Brightstaff standing beside him.

As they played cards, they drank a light sharabi — both in its green shade and its strength — that tasted of crisp, fresh cucumbers. A refreshing aftertaste to their lunch, which had been good Water's End venison that was almost criminally blackened by the ship's cook.

Their game was lit by the fish-smelling light of oil lamps, which was unfortunate, and not good for the taste of the sharabi. But the prince insisted.

Aefric wasn't surprised that Killian was a remarkable card player. He had a good mind for it. And, of course, plenty of practice for the same reason that Aefric was finally learning to play card and board games after a lifetime spent playing only chess. When he played any game at all.

Board games and card games were inevitably popular among nobles, and expected at courts across Qorunn.

Fortunately, Killian was a gracious winner, and happy to share some of the finer points of Queens' Conspiracy with Aefric, so that — as the hours passed — Aefric was starting to win ... well, if not his *share*, at least more often than he had been when they started.

And talking about the game was good. Because when he wasn't talking about the game, all Killian wanted to talk about was sex.

Oh, it started with a more general discussion of Aefric's prospective brides — especially Byrhta Ol'Caran — and where he stood on his own views of his future. But once it branched out into talk of Aefric's lers and knights and vassals, Killian wanted to talk about who among them were the sexiest — men and women both, though he focused more on women, as Aefric did.

But Killian still had plenty to discuss on the topic of women and sex, continuing on to those Killian knew at Armityr and Netar, in Merrek and Silverlake and other counties and baronies. Even his own bride-to-be, Princess Gitta.

It seemed that Killian liked Gitta well enough, but wasn't in love with her and didn't expect to be. Though he did think they could have a good partnership, which he seemed to consider more important.

And whenever the discussion quieted for a time, Killian inevitably began talking about Deirdre again. Not just her looks, though. He'd been stunned to learn that she'd beaten all of his knights at once yesterday morning.

Of course, it wasn't as though they'd all rushed her and she'd overcome their organized effort.

No, she'd been invited to participate in a free-for-all sparring skirmish with Killian's knights.

Not only was she the last one standing, but she was the one who took down each of the other six. Something Killian would have paid dearly to see, if he could bring himself to ask his knights to risk the embarrassment of it happening again.

It seemed that all of his knights had excuses for how they'd fallen. Some blaming one another, others claiming she'd used unfair magics counter to their agreement before beginning. One even blamed an unfortunate shift of the deck.

No matter the excuse or reason though, in the end, she had been the last one standing. And Killian was now thoroughly entranced with her.

"And to make matters worse," he said at one point, "she says she won't come to my cabin. Can you believe it?" Killian shook his head and poured more sharabi. "Says if she's going to bed a prince, she wants an actual bed. Silk sheets. Pillows. Not a hammock."

"We couldn't have taken a warship," Aefric said carefully. "You and I would've been more comfortable, but—"

"I know, I know," Killian said, waving the argument away. "We need a ship people will forget. I remember the discussion. It's just..."

He tossed back the glass of sharabi. "It's just that I wonder if she even *wants* to. I've never had to wonder that before, Aefric."

"What makes you think so?" Aefric asked, but he wasn't sure Killian even heard him.

"I'm a *prince*," he said. "The only one Armyr has. And let's be honest, I'm damned handsome. Sure, there've been times — not many, but a few — when I've been told no for one reason or another. But when it happens, I always see regret in their eyes. The missed opportunity. And often they'd offer, well, a lesser pleasure to soften the blow of refusal. And maybe to make sure I asked again sometime."

Killian shook his head. "I didn't get either from Deirdre."

"I don't think Deirdre believes in regret," Aefric said thoughtfully. "I think that once she decides to do or not something, she simply doesn't think about it again."

Killian frowned. "Do you think she doesn't believe in the lesser pleasures either? Is she one who wants only the most traditional method of chasing the bliss moment?"

"I don't think there's anything traditional about Deirdre," Aefric said with a chuckle. "Except maybe her sense of personal honor."

Killian thought about that as he poured himself more sharabi.

"Wait," he said, and started tapping the deck of cards with a fingertip. He smiled, and the smile turned into laughter.

"What?" Aefric asked.

Killian picked up the deck and started shuffling. "I get it now. How could I not have seen it?"

"Seen what?"

Killian dealt the cards. "It's so obvious. She wants her first time with a prince to be special. I can certainly understand that. And as for offering a lesser pleasure, I bet she figures making me wait for *anything* from her will drive me crazy with desire."

"If so," Aefric said, raising an eyebrow, "I think it's working."

"*Was* working," Killian said with a triumphant gleam in his eye. "Two can play that game. I'll act unimpressed with her. Or maybe bored. Or maybe I'll just dote on another knight. Vria's certainly pretty enough. Or Temat. Maybe Arras..."

"And all three are willing enough, I'd wager," Aefric said. "I don't know if making Deirdre jealous will work though."

"Oh, I'm not going for jealousy," Killian said, picking up his cards and tapping their edge on the table sharply. "But she's proud. Loves attention. I bet she *can't stand* being ignored, especially by someone important. Like, say, a prince."

"Well," Aefric admitted, "her pride may be her sticking point." He tapped the table. "Happy hunting."

"No," Killian said, smiling. "Hunting is Maev's game, and this Deirdre situation proves I'm not as good at it as my sister. If Maev were hunting Deirdre, she'd've had her already. But Deirdre seems the type to like a conquest. I'll just have to make sure she knows I'm most desirable conquest around."

Fortunately, Aefric's cards were a mess, and he was able to distract the prince by asking for help. And then they were playing cards again. And now that he had a plan for Deirdre, it seemed Killian was happy to be distracted from talk of sex.

Made for a better afternoon, if Aefric had to be playing cards when he would rather have been doing research.

Aefric had actually managed to win three games of Queens' Conspiracy in a row — a first — when the knock came on Killian's cabin door.

"Come!" Killian called. But didn't even look toward the door as he smiled at Aefric and said, "*Now*, you're getting it. We'll make a card player of you yet."

Beornric entered, and even though they were at sea, his face was as neatly shaved as the prince's — excluding Beornric's thick mustaches and the prince's mustache and goatee — and his armor looked as polished as ever.

Made Aefric's unshaven face feel scruffy.

"Your highness, your grace," Beornric said, "we're nearing Wulfport. Though as instructed, the pilot is not approaching the port. Holding a bearing closer to due south — as though we were heading for Varondam, rather than turning towards the southeast."

"How's the sun?" Aefric asked.

"Not even touching the horizon yet," Beornric said. "We've made excellent time."

"Good," Aefric said, then cast the spell that would contact Karbin.

"We're at sea outside Wulfport now. Bearing due south. Not heading for port. Come aboard as soon as you can."

Karbin could have said up to twenty-five words for his reply, but all he said this time was, "At once."

"We should head up on deck," Aefric said, standing and taking the Brightstaff in hand. "He'll be here anytime."

"What did he say?" Killian said, standing. "Does he have news?"

"Only that he's on his way," Aefric said. "Anything more we should know shortly."

The three of them went out onto the deck, where the sailors looked a bit irritated as they went on about their business. Likely because all the knights and soldiers were up taking the sea air at the moment, and likely at least a little in the way.

Beornric anticipated Aefric's question. "They have to spend enough time belowdecks, and not all of them have the bellies for sea travel. Good to give them time up top, even all at once. It's not for long. Once dinner comes, they know they're not allowed topside but in groups of ten or less."

Aefric nodded. The warriors had to be as anxious about this arrangement as the sailors. So long as no fights broke out, all would likely be fine. But the sooner they could get where they were going, the better.

And they had indeed made good time. Aefric could still see half again the span of his hand between the sun and the horizon.

"Your grace," Deirdre said, sauntering up and smiling. "I was starting to think his highness had spirited you away to a private love nest."

"He's too rugged," Killian said with a shake of his head. "I don't like many men, and the ones I do are prettier. No offense, Aefric."

"None taken," he replied absently.

Fortunately, before that conversation could go someplace Aefric wanted to avoid, Karbin slipped down out of the clear skies and landed on the deck.

Something in Aefric's guts relaxed. "Get into any trouble?"

"No," Karbin said. "You?"

"Only at cards."

"Your grace," the captain called down from the helm. "Bearing?"

Aefric looked at Karbin who gave a slight shake of his head.

"Hold us southbound for now," he called back to the captain. "I'll tell you more in a while." He turned to the others. "We need to talk in private."

"Captain's cabin?" Karbin asked.

"No," Aefric said. "She wants to stay in the dark until the last possible minute."

Karbin lowered his voice. "She's guessed what we're doing?"

"I think so. Either way, she wants to keep it from the crew."

"Let's use my cabin," Killian said. "I have the table."

"I'll fetch us some charts and maps," Deirdre said.

Figures. She not only invited herself to the meeting, she'd found a way to do so that guaranteed she'd bring something useful, even if only what she carried.

Killian led the way back into his cabin, but Aefric frowned at the oil lamps. "We may need more light for this."

Killian's nose flared in a sigh, but he nodded. Karbin caught the sigh, and gave Aefric a puzzled look.

Aefric gave his head a bare shake and cast a light spell.

Deirdre returned with an armload of rolled up maps and charts.

"Wasn't sure what we'd need," she said, "so I brought all I could carry."

She handed Beornric one map, and arranged the other rolls between one of the prince's chests and the wall while everyone took seats at the table. Karbin and Beornric on the inside, Aefric beside Karbin and Killian beside Beornric.

Beornric unrolled the map, which showed the Risen Sea and all the kingdoms bordering it.

Deirdre wedged in close beside Aefric.

"What did you learn in Wulfport?" Aefric.

"Most of Nelazzi's Wulfport contacts are in disarray right now," Karbin said. "Much of their Nelazzi business either came or went through Drake's Landing."

"And Kefthal slammed that door hard," Aefric said.

"Exactly," Karbin said. "It's a mess. Some of them are holding firm, waiting to hear from Nelazzi herself. Others are trying to open new businesses. Even trying to turn their operations legal, in some cases."

"In other words," Beornric said, "anyone trying to bring two princesses through Wulfport right now would find their allies unhelpful."

"Not just unhelpful," Karbin said. "Many are upset enough to try for a reward from Rethneryl."

"But this is all quite recent, yes?" Killian said. "Recent enough that Nelazzi could have *planned* to take the princesses through Wulfport, and her kidnappers might've had to change the plan at the last minute."

"Which means," Deirdre started, then frowned. "No. Never mind."

"Never mind what?" Aefric asked.

"Well, if I were working for Nelazzi, and I found one of her strongest ports in disarray, I might be thinking of trying to find another customer for my cargo." She shook her head. "But we're not talking about a shipment of gold or spices or some other trade good. We're talking about princesses."

"Hard to move," Beornric said. "Hard to hold onto securely

without ... well, without risking their value. And very hard to find a market for. Or at least one where you'll get the kind of compensation you might expect."

Deirdre nodded. "Even if one of Nelazzi's ports is shaky, still safer to get the princesses to her, get paid, and let her deal with whatever follows."

"So we all agree," Aefric said. "It's most likely that the kidnappers *are* on their way to Nelazzi, even if we don't know by what route."

Everyone knocked the table in agreement.

"All right," Aefric said. "The next question would be whether the Hatay-Shachan kidnappers are heading for Wulfport, but it's almost moot. We have no way to identify their ship, and when they see the state of Nelazzi's business there, they'll put back out to sea."

"And head for Nelazzi directly," Killian said. "Makes sense. Probably safe to say the same for Varondam's unspoken bastard. All of the kidnapped princesses going straight to Nelazzi."

"Which begs the question," Aefric said. "Where is Nelazzi?"

"Last I heard during my part of the investigation," Deirdre said, "was somewhere down around the Cape of Teeth."

"Sounds too remote to be accurate," Aefric said.

"That's why I didn't mention it before," Deirdre said. "Felt like the sort of thing people say because they think it sounds scary."

"Nothing scary about the Cape of Teeth," Karbin said. "Just a bunch of standing stones."

"You've been there?" Deirdre said.

Karbin nodded.

"Most haven't," she said. "Easier to make up stories about a place you've never been."

"I've asked about Nelazzi in a few ports," Killian said. "While making trade contacts for Father. Most say she has a private cove on an island that's not on any map."

"That's what they tell the tourists," Karbin said. "Remember I got to talk to some of her people after they'd fled Drake's Landing. Some who'd actually talk."

"Some who'd been to her base?" Beornric asked.

"No," Karbin admitted, "but they'd talked to sailors who had. Some said she has a private port down in Zhenderran. Others that she has a patron in Hayroun. Some local lord who's besotted with her."

"Sounds like the same kind of rumormongering," Killian said.

"I'd think so too," Karbin said, "but the two ideas were remarkably consistent."

"You think she has two bases?" Aefric asked. "One in each?"

"Safer than keeping all your gold in one pouch," Deirdre said.

"We all know the reputations of Zhenderran and Hayroun?" Karbin asked, with one eye on Killian.

"Neither as evil as *Kefthal*," Killian said, "but close. Zhenderran with their fell gods and foul rites. Hayroun, a writhing sea of chaos where the factions change with the winds, and the strong always punish the weak."

"Both the kind of places that might welcome someone like Nelazzi, if she brought in money."

Aefric considered that. "She'd need stability for her base. Hard to find that in Hayroun."

"Throw ten pebbles into a pond," Killian said. "They all cast ripples, but some of those ripples cancel each other out. Leave spots that don't move."

"If anyone could find a spot like that in Hayroun..." Deirdre said, not bothering to finish her sentence.

"And since she's gotten into slavery," Beornric said, "she could offer sacrifices to the Zhenderrites. Or whatever it is they need."

"So both are likely," Aefric said. "Is anyplace *more* likely?"

"Kefthal," Killian said.

"But we already know she isn't there," Aefric said.

"Unless that's what Kefthal wants you to think," Killian said, leaning forward. "Think about it. They're putting on a great show. But what if it's to hide what they're really doing?"

"If so," Karbin said doubtfully, "they're going to a lot of effort to make sure we believe it."

"They know how thorough you are, Aefric. They just don't want you looking their way until they've finished whatever they want with the princesses."

"But they aren't getting the princesses," Aefric said. "Nelazzi is."

"Unless she's only been hired to *acquire* them." Killian tapped his finger on the table. "Kefthal might be behind the whole thing. Some grand plan to gain influence in the courts in our region though magics laid on those princesses."

"Too shortsighted," Karbin said. "You have to remember. The Nine Beyond Death rule Kefthal, and they don't think in terms of a year or a generation or a lifetime. They think in terms of centuries and millennia."

"It's unlikely," Aefric said, then sighed. "But I'm not sure we can afford to rule it out."

"What we *need*," Deirdre said, "is a way to find Nelazzi herself. Her *favorite* hideaway. The most secure one she has. If we could do that, we wouldn't have to puzzle through who might be hiding her."

Aefric frowned. Something she'd just said tickled at the back of his mind, but he wasn't sure why.

"I think we all agree with that sentiment, Deirdre," Beornric said. "Do you have any suggestions for how we might go about *finding* her?"

"If we had one of her ships," Karbin muttered. "Or something we knew was hers. Maybe a tracer spell—"

"That's it!" Aefric slapped his hand down on the table, making everyone but Deirdre jump. "I've got a link. That copper pendant."

"The ward key?" Karbin asked, puzzled. "Useful when we find the wards, but not for finding her."

Aefric grinned. "Ah, but it *is* a ward key. Which means the spells are linked. And I know how to follow that link."

"You *do*?" Karbin sounded almost offended. "*I* don't know how to do that."

"Teach me to teleport sometime," Aefric teased, "and maybe I'll show you. But for now, I have a spell to cast."

Aefric tried to jump up from the crowded table in Killian's cabin, but Deirdre remained wedged in place beside him, showing no signs of budging.

"Deirdre," Aefric said, "this is the part where you move so I can return to my cabin and work the magic that will lead us to Nelazzi's lair."

"I don't think it is, your grace," Deirdre said simply. She looked around at Karbin, who sat beside Aefric, and Beornric and Killian who sat across the table. "Am I alone in this?"

"I think you are," Killian said.

"You're not alone, Deirdre," Beornric said, and Karbin knocked the table in agreement.

"Well," Aefric said, trying hard to be patient while his heart was pounding and excitement burned through his veins. "Would one of you mind explaining to me while I *shouldn't* go cast that spell right now?"

"Let me," Beornric said.

Karbin nodded and Deirdre gestured for him to go ahead, while Killian frowned.

"Your grace," Beornric said with infuriating calm, "we are moving on towards evening. Soon we will have dinner, and later we must sleep. Yourself included."

Aefric's turn to frown. He snorted. "All right. I admit. The spell I have in mind will give me direction and distance, not anything I can point to on a map. So yes, I'll have to remain up by the helm while we sail—"

"Someplace we likely couldn't reach before morning," Beornric said. "Which means that at least one good meal — preferably two — and a good night's sleep should be yours before you attempt this."

"And there's another factor that I doubt our good knight has considered," Karbin said.

"Go ahead," Beornric said.

"I'm not as good at that wind spell as you've become. Which means that if I'm the one maintaining the wind, I'll be more drained when we get where we're going than you would be. Whereas a tracer spell..."

"Takes less power," Aefric said, then huffed. "You just want me to teach you the secret without having to teach me teleportation."

Karbin grinned. "No. I'll teach you that anyway. You won't come close to mastering it before we go off to war — I doubt even Kainemorton mastered it that fast — but you might get good enough to at least teleport yourself home if everything goes wrong."

"How could anything go wrong?" Killian said. "Father is planning this war himself. He knows what he's doing."

"Dear gods do you need seasoning," Deirdre muttered.

"War is always risk, your highness," Beornric said. "Even the best-laid plans can fall apart. Weather. Conditions. Fortune. I agree that his grace should have an emergency means of evacuation. One that won't see him the target of arrows, like flying would."

"Worse comes to worst," Aefric said, "I can become lightning for one stroke. Cover a lot of distance that way."

"True," Killian said. "Assuming you haven't been separated from the Brightstaff in battle."

Aefric frowned but nodded. "All right. Good points all."

"There's another," Deirdre said, then looked at Beornric. "Shall I?"

"Please," Beornric said.

"We haven't discussed formal tactics of approach and engagement yet. We'd be fools to commit one or both of our wizards to attention-stealing spells without at least *trying* to plan what we'll do when we *find* Nelazzi's lair."

Aefric blinked at her. Smirked. "Are *you* actually chiding me for not planning sufficiently?"

"I *know*," Deirdre moaned. "I *hate* being the responsible one."

"I don't mind it, Deirdre," Beornric said with an indulgent smile. "You can leave it to me in the future."

"Thank the *gods*," she said. "Beornric, you're a treasure, and I'll fight anyone who says differently."

"So planning then?" Aefric said.

"And dinner," Beornric said. "And then a good night's sleep."

"All right," Aefric said. "But at the first light of dawn..."

"You eat breakfast," Beornric said firmly.

Killian laughed. It was so sudden and out of place that everyone stopped and stared at him, which didn't seem to bother him in the slightest.

"I'm sorry," Killian said, though he didn't look or sound sorry. He was still smiling broadly. "I don't think I'd really believed you, Beornric, when you said you were the grizzled old man henpecking Aefric these days. But if you have to press him into eating *breakfast*..."

Beornric started chuckling too.

"To be fair," Aefric said. "Eating an actual breakfast every day is a recent thing for me. Most days of my life, I'd just grab something quick and go."

"Life in the field can be like that," Beornric acknowledged, while Deirdre nodded agreement. "But *only* when it has to be. You have the option of a breakfast in the morning, and you should take it."

"Even I agree with that," Deirdre said. "And I'm hardly anyone's idea of a grizzled old man."

"Fine," Aefric said. "I'll have breakfast first thing. All right?"

The others all knocked the table in agreement. Even Killian, who looked entirely too amused about the whole thing.

"After breakfast you show me how to work your tracer magic using that pendant," Karbin said, "and we begin the hunt in earnest."

The dinner they ate was venison again, but the cook did a better job with it this time. As though lunch had been a warm-up. Slow-roasted with salt, pepper and cumin. Came out savory, if still a bit well done. The root vegetables were soggy from roasting in the deer's juices, but at least they were tasty. And the dessert of sliced pears and apples with honey certainly hit the spot.

Strangest thing about the meal was that they didn't have honeyed oat bread. Instead, aboard they ship they ate a dark rye. Fortunately, Aefric had a good dark beer to pair with it.

So they ate, and they planned, and by the time Aefric returned to his cabin that night, he felt a good deal better about their hunt.

Soon they would have Nelazzi. Right where they wanted her. Soon.

WHEN THE PLANNING SESSION WAS DONE, ADDRESSING AS MANY contingencies as they could think of, Aefric retired to his cabin. Still tasting the dark beer they'd continued to drink after their meal was eaten.

Their plans were good, but necessarily incomplete.

How many pirates would be at Nelazzi's lair? How many ships? How would they be armed? How would they be organized?

This couldn't turn into open battle. Aefric hadn't brought enough support for that. They were too likely to be outnumbered. And even the best knights could be overwhelmed, if the pirates had enough support.

No. There would be fighting. No way around that. But the fighting had to be contained. Quick. Strategic. With Aefric's and Karbin's magic guiding and assisting.

And speaking of magic, if Aefric could puzzle out that teak box tonight, he could have one more weapon in his arsenal when he needed it the most. One surprise that Nelazzi could never see coming, no matter how much she might've learned about him.

And the others were convinced she'd been studying Aefric.

Karbin had even suggested that she might have kidnapped the princesses to try to lure the adventurer in him into doing something foolhardy.

All the more reason to keep things organized. And to find one more trick to keep up his sleeve...

Trick up his sleeve. Was that Aefric's phrase? Or Keifer's?

He shook away the thought. Didn't matter. Not unless he spoke it aloud in front of witnesses.

Aefric sat on a chest, and stood the Brightstaff beside him, with its yellow diamond lighting up the room.

He pulled the teak box out of his belt pouch...

Sighed. He'd had *all afternoon* to ask Killian what happened when someone had tried opening the box in the sunlight, and he hadn't done it. He'd been too distracted by Killian's fixation on talking about sex.

The box would've been a perfect distraction too. Ah well. No point mourning a spent coin. Gone was gone. Might as well lament that he didn't have the resources of his magic laboratory at his disposal. Pointless to even think about.

Aefric held the box and considered it. Last night he'd approached it starting from its shape and form. Killian had made him so paranoid about its power that he'd been hesitant to touch its magic the way he knew he'd have to. Sooner or later.

Later might not come. Sooner it was.

Aefric closed his eyes. Focused through his breath.

He projected a part of himself outward into the flows of Qorunn's magic. The ebb and flow of those forces that were simply part of the world around him.

From there, he tried to follow those flows into the magics of the box, expecting them to lead him into the magics involved in containing the power that was bound into the box.

That was how truly studying an enchanted item worked. Not as fast as the spell adventurers used in the field, but far truer, more certain, and more informative.

But for the first time in Aefric's life, it didn't work.

He followed the flows of Qorunn's magic all right. But they didn't move into the box at all. Not into the foundational structure that would allow the containment in the first place. Not into the containment itself. Not even into the power held within.

Qorunn's magic slipped right around the box as though it were not there at all.

Aefric felt a wash of cold through his guts. The magic of this box — all of it, both containment and contained power — it wasn't part of Qorunn's magic. It was something else. Something he'd never encountered before. Not even while traveling with Kainemorton.

And yet, Aefric *could* sense it. So whatever the power in this box was, it was of a *similar* nature to the arcane magics that he used, if not entirely the *same*.

Where was Kainemorton when Aefric needed him?

Well, he wasn't *here*, and the box was. So Aefric would have to do his best.

All right. So the power was not part of Qorunn's magic. That might mean it wasn't native to Qorunn. Perhaps that the box, and its magic, came from another plane of existence?

There were many, after all. Earth, to name only one, but there were plenty of others that were known of here. The astral plane, the thirteen hells, the six heavens, the Abyss, the planes and sub-planes devoted to the elements.

All right. Stop there.

Aefric knew this was not power associated with any of the elemental planes and subplanes. Their magic was all too easy to pick out.

This power was not of the thirteen hells, either, nor the Abyss. He'd encountered demons and devils before. He knew the feel of their power.

Well, to be more precise, he knew the feel of their power in *Qorunn*. And when they brought or formed or claimed bodies here, it filtered their magic through that of Qorunn's.

This magic was unfiltered...

No. This magic was in an unfiltered *state*. Because it was contained. And the containment was unfiltered, because it wasn't interacting with anything in this world.

All right. Stop. Back up.

This magic was magic from another plane. That much seemed to be clear. So look at it again with that in mind.

Aefric drew a deep breath and opened his eyes.

The figures still looked nondescriptly humanoid. Could've come from anywhere. Though they did lack horns or wings, but that didn't necessarily mean anything.

The lettering — assuming it was lettering and not a false front — that could be the language of another world...

No. No it couldn't. The linguistic spell Aefric had learned from Kainemorton worked on languages from other worlds. That was why Kainemorton had taught it to him. He thought it might come in handy someday, if Aefric started traveling the planes.

So, still more likely that the letters, and possibly the figures, were a blind. A lead down a false trail.

The box had been found in a dybbungstad lair. And the dybbungstad and their demon twins were known to travel between Qorunn and Za'Kazazak, the Realm of Shadows. The eighth hell...

No. Aefric might never have fought the dybbungstad himself, but he'd faced shadow demons before. And their magic was familiar too...

Or was it?

It was familiar to him while filtered through *Qorunn's* magic. But this ... whatever it was in the box ... was raw. Shaped, most certainly, but unfiltered by Qorunn. And he couldn't really grasp it with his power, to sense it properly.

And if it dimmed the sunlight, wasn't that shadow magic?

No. Shadow magic would dim *all* light. Even magical light. Or at least, magic native to Za'Kazazak would.

He needed a way to get a real sense of ... some part of it. The foundation, the containment, *something*.

But how?

Naturally, this was when someone had the audacity to knock on Aefric's door.

Just when Aefric felt he was beginning to make some progress into his research on this strange teak box, someone dared to knock on his door?

Hadn't he told the others that he had research to do?

Yes. Yes he had. True, he hadn't mentioned what he was researching, but that didn't really matter.

He had important magical research to conduct. Research that might make the difference in their assault on Nelazzi.

And someone had the gall to come knocking on his cabin door? *His* door? He was a duke, for crying out loud. Surely that meant that...

There was a prince on board. And while the others might leave him to his research, Killian's title gave him freedom, and he didn't care much for magic.

So *of course* Killian would come knocking. Possibly looking for a nightcap. Or perhaps to talk about whether or not his new Deirdre tactic was working.

Perhaps if Aefric ignored the knock, he could persuade the prince that he was asleep. It was worth a try.

A moment later, the knock returned, just a little bit harder, and Aefric realized that the light from his Brightstaff's yellow diamond was likely visible in the cracks around his door. So Killian wouldn't believe him asleep.

Aefric huffed out a sigh and put the box back into his pouch. He almost said *Come in, Killian*, but the prince would have attributed Aefric's guess to magic, rather than logic, and might've misliked it.

"Come," Aefric said instead.

The door opened. Deirdre entered, smirking.

"Interesting choice of invitation words, your grace," she said. "Are you aware of the way they use that word down in Sartis?" Her smirk widened into a grin. "Oh. Yes. You must be. Being *from* Sartis and all."

Irritated as he wanted to be with her for interrupting him, Aefric couldn't stop himself from smiling, half in exasperation.

"I haven't lived in Sartis in nearly two decades," he said. "And I think you know that's how I pretty much always answer a knock."

"I do," Deirdre said, looking about, grin still in place as she closed the door behind her. "I just like to hear you say it."

"What can I do for you, Deirdre?"

She met his eyes. "Would you like a list?"

Aefric laughed before he could stop himself. Her smile beamed and her jade eyes danced.

"I'm trying to do research in here, you know. Something important, that may aid us against Nelazzi."

"Truly?" she said curiously. "And your grace thinks he can complete this research in a single night, does he? While still allowing himself the kind of sleep he's *supposed* to get tonight?"

"I ... might stay up a little late, if that's what it takes."

Deirdre shook her head. Mocked shaking a finger at him. "No good, your grace. I can just imagine what Beornric would say. Especially after *you agreed* to his plan of sleep and meals."

"But this research—"

"There's always more research, your grace," she said, no humor in her voice this time, or even her posture. "Always more magic to learn. For me too, and I'm only a dweomerblade."

"There's nothing *only* about dweomerblades," Aefric said, cocking an eyebrow. "And *especially* not about you."

She gave him a lopsided smile. "Don't distract me with sweet talk. Your grace needs his sleep."

Aefric held that eyebrow high. "And that's all you're here to do, is it? Tuck me in?"

"Don't be silly," she said. "I want your grace to get a *good* night's sleep. And I don't know about you, but *I* sleep best after a good bliss moment."

"I thought you favored beds over hammocks," Aefric said.

"That prince does like to talk, doesn't he?" Deirdre said, undaunted. "Much as I would *love* a chance to slip between silk sheets with your grace — with *you, Aefric* — who knows when that chance will come? Better to take what I can get now, and let later sort itself out."

She gave him an impish grin. "Besides, the rocking of the hammock might prove quite interesting."

Aefric gave her a wistful smile.

"I feel like you're getting shorted," he said. "I promised you a proper night when we could really explore each other. Tonight can't be that. Not if we're both going to get much sleep. Assuming we could even *manage* much variety in a cramped hammock, in a cabin that smells of varnish and lacquer and sea air."

"Oh," Deirdre said softly, "this doesn't let you off the hook for that full night, Aefric. Not even if you let me sleep here afterwards. But I know I want a bliss moment before the hunt begins tomorrow. And if you're going to send me back to the knights, I'll pick one of them for it. But I know who my first choice would be, and I'm looking at him."

The frankness of her expression cut straight through him. The humor was gone now, and Aefric found himself responding to the gorgeous knight in her maroon leathers.

"Am I ever going to see your hair unbraided?" he asked, voice low.

"I'll let you unbraid it yourself, when we have the time," she said, sauntering closer. "But not tonight."

"We'll need nysta tea," Aefric said.

"I'll go fetch it," she said. "You ... stay right there." She touched her chin and tilted her head. "Maybe take your clothes off. Wouldn't want to risk damaging them if I do it."

Aefric chuckled, but started pulling off his tunic. Deirdre stopped and watched. He cleared his throat. "The tea?"

"Oh! Right!"

She slipped out the door.

By the time she returned, Aefric had had enough time to not only get undressed, but start shivering from the cold of sitting there naked. He'd even had enough time to consider and discard thoughts of draping a cloak or blanket around his shoulders, deciding a little discomfort was worth the better presentation.

She came back in carrying a tray, a teapot, and two small, copper cups.

"No matter what he tells you," Deirdre said, closing the door with her hip and putting the tray down on a chest, "the cook was bruised when I found him. Fell out of his hammock, I think."

She looked up at Aefric, who stood naked in the middle of the cabin, facing her. Words seemed to fall right out of her mouth.

"I'm lying. He didn't want to get up and show me where he kept the nysta tea, so I encouraged him a bit roughly. But it's his own fault, really."

Aefric laughed. "A confession?" he said, stepping closer while her gaze roved hungrily over his body. "From you? I'm shocked."

"My mother always told me not to lie in the presence of something beautiful."

"Me?" Aefric scoffed, pouring the tea. "Hardly. Pleasant enough to look on, I'll agree to. And I keep myself fit enough. But hardly—"

"Beautiful," Deirdre said. "And I'll fight anyone who says differently." She frowned. "No. Come to think of it, I won't. Wallowing in their foolish ignorance is punishment enough."

"Speaking of beauty," he said, picking up the steaming cups of bitter tea and handing her one, "I'd love to watch you take that armor off."

She sniffed the tea. Tossed the contents of her cup onto the deck. "Needs to steep a little longer for full strength."

Aefric emptied his cup the same way.

"But as long as we must wait a moment," she said, smiling, "I might as well indulge you, Aefric."

Her leathers had quite a few straps. And while she didn't dance around, or try to make a formal show out of it, she kept up a teasing smile and slowly, achingly slowly, undid each and every one of those straps. Only removing any piece of armor once all its straps were done.

And the armor was only the outer layer. Underneath, she wore a light, sleeveless white silk top and white silk underwear. Not the kind of frilly, fancy things Keifer had seen on Earth — the sort that minimized their actual use of fabric — but something more practical to protect delicate skin from chafing under all that tight leather.

And honestly, her silks were all the more enticing because of the woman wearing them.

Somewhere in there, Aefric had stopped shivering. In fact, the simplicity of her disrobing had his blood running hot.

Her silk undertop followed, and her underwear fell last. Finally naked, she stretched a bit, now obviously showing off her trim, lithe body.

She looked over at him. Smiled at the most obvious sign of his arousal.

"I think our tea is ready," she said.

"Good," Aefric said.

6

———

Aefric was dreaming something about a hunt in a deep forest ... near an ocean ... where he was both hunting and being hunted.

But for some reason, the hunt also had something to do with globes of colored glass hidden among the trees.

No. Not quite among the trees themselves, but among *logs* of *fallen* trees. Well, they were and weren't logs. There was something off about them. Something that looked wrong in the forest but he couldn't quite put his finger on why.

Which was when the red-crested woodpecker flew up, and started pecking at his collarbone...

Aefric awoke to the sensation of Deirdre tapping rapidly on his collarbone. They were both still naked. Her mostly on top of him — with a soft wool blanket covering them both — and a rather cramped, creaking hammock underneath.

All was still dark. But then, there were no portholes in this cabin, and he'd extinguished the Brightstaff before he went to sleep. Though he'd left it standing beside the hammock.

He made a sound — wasn't quite a grunt, but wasn't quite a word either — to show that he was awake, and with a thought illuminated the large yellow diamond embedded in the top of the Brightstaff.

"Hey!" Deirdre protested, hiding her eyes in his neck. "Warn a girl before you do something like that."

"Sorry," Aefric said, stroking her cheek. "I don't think well when I'm pecked awake by a woodpecker."

"Woodpecker? I've been called a lot of names in my day, but—"

"In my dream a woodpecker started tapping on my collarbone and woke me up."

"Well, I'd've been happy to wake you up a number of other ways, but they'd all lead to ... delays." She blinked and winced at the light as she pulled back from the hollow of his neck. "It will be dawn soon, and we have a lot to do."

"We do." Aefric sighed. "Would one more kiss be out of the question?"

"If I ever say no to that, Aefric," she said with a smile, "it means I'm possessed."

She put one hand to his cheek and kissed him hard, as though trying to work a lifetime of kisses into a single kiss.

He had to shake himself slightly when she pulled back.

"I thought you weren't trying to start anything," he said.

"If I were trying to start something," Deirdre said with a coy smile, "you'd know it."

She rolled out of the hammock and landed in a crouch on the deck. She straightened and stretched and twisted.

"Definitely not as good as a bed," she said with a final stretch that used her whole body. "But better than the alternatives." She smirked when she noticed him watching. "Oh. Have I *distracted* you, your grace?"

Aefric growled. "You *know* we don't have time for that."

"I know," she replied with a grin. "But I like knowing you aren't done with me yet."

"Not even close," Aefric said, getting out of the hammock himself. "Although I must admit, I have yet to feel ruined for all other women, as you said I would."

"Give me a *proper* chance instead of these quick jaunts and I will *absolutely* ruin you for other women," she said confidently, as she began dressing. "You've only the barest inkling what I can do for you, Aefric Brightstaff."

Aefric dressed in dark colors that day, in case stealth was needed. A black wool tunic, over black leathers, black boots, and a black belt with its usual accouterments.

Deirdre gave the look a nod of approval, then said, "I'll send Karbin in with your breakfast, so you can start the teaching while you eat."

That breakfast was a hot porridge with shredded beef — not very flavorful, but not bad — along with rolls of rye bread, an orange, and water to drink.

And as he and Karbin — who chose his usual colors of dusk and sand over any extra concerns for stealth — sat on chests in Aefric's cabin and ate their breakfasts, Aefric explained his approach to tracing one spell through another that was connected to it.

"For a ward key to work properly," he said, "its spells must be cast by the same wizard who cast the wards. You know this much."

"Know it," Karbin scoffed. "I'm the one who taught *you* that."

"Yes," Aefric agreed, blowing on a spoonful of porridge to cool it a bit. "But you missed the implications. The ward key and the wards are actually two parts of the same spell."

"They're not, though," Karbin said. "The wards are complete unto themselves by definition. The key is no more a part of the wards themselves than a physical key is part of a physical lock. It merely fits right, and causes the right reaction when triggered."

"You're looking at the logic," Aefric said, "not the art."

"Not this again," Karbin said with a sigh. "Look. I haven't forgotten your theory about the three components of all magic. And I admit, it isn't without interesting implications. If true. But it remains unproven. At least, to any great extent."

"Unproven by wizards, you mean," Aefric said patiently.

"Of all the magic-users across or under the surface of Qorunn," Karbin said, just as patiently, "wizards are the past-masters of magic. Because we alone can develop new spells and techniques and teach them to others."

"I can develop new spells and techniques and teach them to others," Aefric said. "And yet if I'm a wizard—"

"You ... what you are ... is the exception that proves the rule," Karbin said pointedly. "Though I won't pretend to understand how exactly magic works for you. *Especially* when the spell you're casting, itself, should not."

"Because you, my dear Karbin, share one unfortunate trait with every other wizard I've ever met," Aefric said. "You all want to give logic primacy."

"Because artistry is just *flair*. Style. It does not change the magic itself. You and I could cast the same flame-bolt spell, and though our spells would vary in color, sound and style, they would produce remarkably similar effects because they are functionally *the same spell*."

"Do you want to learn my ward-key tracer technique or not?"

Karbin sighed. "This conversation has me half-convinced I won't be able to. This might be one of those weird things you do that only works for you."

"Then let's not get distracted with another theory argument," Aefric said. "My technique for this works. Let that settle into the logical part of your brain. If *I* can produce this effect, then there must be some way you can too. If you're wizard enough."

Aefric didn't even try to keep the smile out of his voice over those last words, and Karbin's eyes blazed at the challenge.

"Boy," he said, "I've *forgotten* more magic than you've ever learned. If you can do this, so can I."

"Then try listening first, and see if you can find your way to my conclusions, all right?"

Karbin sighed again, but nodded.

"Consider *the possibility* that the ward and the key are part of the same spell. Can you do that much?"

Karbin gave a terse nod.

"Then the ward key wants to return to the ward as much as a vial of your blood wants to return to you."

"Your blood doesn't *want* anything," Karbin said. "It was part of you, so it..."

He trailed off when he saw the impatient look Aefric was giving him.

"Fine," Karbin said, holding up his hands in surrender. "Of course your blood wants to return to your veins. Might not be logical, but it sounds *artistically* true. So, sure, the ward key would want to return to the ward the same..."

He sighed and hung his head.

"No," he said. "The blood was part of you. For the ward key to be as connected to the ward as your blood was to your body, the ward key would have to have been designed and cast at the same time. It would have to have once been part of the ward as the blood was once part of your body."

"Too much logic," Aefric said. "Not enough art."

"But your theory is a house of cards!" Karbin said, slapping the back of one hand against his other palm. "If I cast wards and create a ward key for them, *I can change that ward key.* The old one won't work anymore, and the new one would. How does *that* compare to blood?"

Aefric drew a long, slow breath through his nostrils, and let it out the same way.

"It doesn't," he said. "Not if you remove art from the equation."

"And you *must*," Karbin said, "because art and equations are *antithetical*." He shook his head. "Will this trick of yours work if the ward key was changed?"

"Assuming the wards weren't entirely taken down and replaced, yes," Aefric said simply. "If the wards have been entirely changed, my spell will fail. But if all that was rewoven was the portion dealing with the ward key, the base spell would be intact, and my tracer should work."

"See," Karbin said, "that doesn't make sense either. If the key is no longer any good, how does that not sever it from the wards entirely?"

"Because the spells of the ward key are still connected to the spells of the wards," Aefric said, then shook his head. "This isn't going to work."

Karbin sighed and shook his head. "If you really can do this, I can probably figure out a way to do it too. But it'll take me more time than we have."

"You'll have to handle the winds then," Aefric said. "I'll cast the tracer myself."

"I may not be much good when we get there, then," Karbin said, shaking his head. "I'm hardly a *ventavis*, and I don't have magic burning through my blood."

"Let me tell you about the changes I made to Sirondfar's spells. Maybe some of them will help you."

Karbin sighed heavily. "At the moment I doubt it. But it's worth a shot."

FINDING SOMETHING USEFUL FOR KARBIN IN THE MODIFICATIONS AEFRIC had made to Sirondfar's wind spells took longer than either of them would have liked, but when they finally emerged onto the deck that morning, he sounded encouraged.

"Now see, some of your work *there* was inspired," Karbin said happily. "These changes should cut at least thirty percent from my required power output."

"I hate it when you talk like that," Aefric said. "You make it all sound so—"

"Logical?" Karbin said, smiling. "Does have its advantages."

"Good morning, your grace!" Beornric's voice, coming from the helm deck.

"Has its limitations, too, but I'm done arguing with you for one morning," Aefric said to Karbin, then turned to call to Beornric. "We're on our way up."

The day was heavily overcast, and already tossing down a sprinkle of fresh rain. But the only flashes of lightning were — to judge by their thunder — at least a dozen miles east. A direction they weren't likely going.

As they'd planned, no knights and soldiers up on deck yet. Only the sailors, calling to one another as they went about their business. Always seemed to be more sailors hard at work than Aefric could imagine tasks for them.

As he approached the stairs, though, Aefric couldn't bring himself to bother with all those shallow steps. Not today. Not when he was already feeling some edginess in his guts. Anticipation.

He flew directly up to the helm deck, where Beornric had been talking with Captain Ol'Vanett, who handled the wheel this morning herself.

Beornric had thrown an oilskinned cloak over his full plate armor, hood down so far, and today his gauntlets hung from his belt beside his sword. The captain wore heavy, dark linens under an oilskin of her own.

Aefric landed only to realize that half the crew had watched him fly while Karbin had taken the stairs.

Captain Ol'Vanett raised an eyebrow in disapproval.

"Never good to hurry on a ship, your grace," she said. "Causes accidents."

"I can control my flight, thank you."

"I don't doubt it, your grace. Not always the one rushing about gets into the accident."

She nodded at the sailors who were only just returning to their duties.

"I hadn't realized," Aefric said. "My mistake."

The captain nodded and returned her attention to the horizon ahead of her.

"I'll send someone for your grace's oilskin," Beornric said. "I know your grace has a spell that keeps him dry, but—"

"But I may need all my magic before we're through," Aefric said, nodding. "Fine."

Beornric lowered his voice. Easy to do under the wind, which was southerly and picking up. "I've told the captain what we're doing. She doesn't want the crew informed until Karbin starts giving us directions. Just in case—"

"In case the spell doesn't work," Aefric said, quirking a half-smile.

"You sound like Karbin. Which is why I'll be the one casting the tracer."

"So Karbin will ensure the wind?"

"If we're going south, won't need his help until at least midmorning," Captain Ol'Vanett said in a normal voice, as though she were part of the conversation, while Karbin stepped up and joined them.

"Good," he said. "Even with the modifications we discussed, the less I have to use those spells, the better."

"Don't suppose I can talk your grace out of this," Captain Ol'Vanett said wearily. "Won't be the first to try her, and likely won't be the last."

"She must fall," Aefric said definitively. "And now is as good a time as any, and better than most."

Captain Ol'Vanett shook her head, but said nothing.

"Knights and soldiers know what the plans are?" Aefric asked.

"Deirdre is down there right now," Beornric said. "Making sure of the arrangements."

"You sure that's wise?" Karbin asked. "She's a marvelous knight, but—"

"Deirdre's been to war," Beornric said. "She knows the importance of clear, accurate orders and the flow of information. She'll make sure each group knows what it's doing, and when, exactly as we planned it."

"I'm still not entirely clear about what *I'm* supposed to do."

That last came from Killian, who was coming down a ladder from the afterdecks. He wore a full breastplate, front and back today. With leathers underneath to protect his arms and legs, and a pointed, steel half-helm on his head.

No rapier and dueling dagger for him today, though. He wore a hand-and-a-half sword at his side, and was carrying a round shield that he set down as he approached.

"Stay near me, your highness," Beornric said. "You don't have to be in the front rank to be part of the fighting."

"Shouldn't be fighting at all," the captain said, only just loudly enough to be heard over the wind. Though whether or not she knew she could be heard, Aefric couldn't tell. "Bringing the *crown prince* into battle against *Nelazzi*. Ought to turn this ship around."

Aefric was going to let the captain's grumbling go, but Killian didn't.

"If you do," he said loudly, "you'll be the one facing charges of treason. For make no mistake. The crown backs his grace in this."

That was so untrue Aefric was surprised that the sheer weight of the lie didn't sink them. But Captain Ol'Vanett merely said, "Of course, your highness. My apologies."

She even sounded at least a little sorry.

Killian gave Aefric a firm nod, and said too softly for the captain to hear, "If we die today, it won't matter. And if we live, Father will back you. So it's true enough for me."

He winked at Aefric, and Aefric smiled and shook his head.

"Well," he said, "let's be about it then."

He pretended to dig into the velvet pouch at his belt, rather than let on that the bronze pendant was at his fingertips the moment he thought of it.

"Moment of truth," he muttered, and began the spell that would trace the spells on the pendant — the ward key itself — back to the wards it was connected to.

For whatever Karbin argued about logic, that the ward and the key were intrinsically connected was *artistically* true. And that, Aefric knew, made a difference.

So long as Nelazzi's wards remained essentially the same. If she'd had them taken down and recast — especially if another wizard had done the casting — then this was all for nothing.

But either of those latter choices would be more expensive, and more work. Not to mention insulting the wizard who'd cast the first wards. Assuming he or she still lived.

So Aefric could only hope...

He regarded the pendant, now dangling from his hand by its cheap leather thong. A bronze sextant of no particular value.

Wasn't even good bronze. And it had been cast, not forged, showing even less attention had been paid to its making.

In all, it looked like something bought by a tourist for less than a handful of coppers.

Certainly not something that could house a decent enchantment. So even most spellcasters would not bother checking the pendant for magic.

And for those magic-users who did inspect it — especially if they used the quick method so popular with adventurers — they would find little to interest them. Three incomplete wind spells. Decent ones, but useless unless the bearer knew the right words and gestures to complete the spells. *And* supplied his own power.

At which point most would have abandoned the pendant as trash. And why not? Cheaply made, and nothing but incomplete spells that would be more effort to puzzle out than they'd give back in value.

Certainly no reason to expect that the pendant concealed anything more.

But sitting in his personal magic laboratory at Water's End, Aefric had given the pendant his entire attention. And through his careful study, he'd realized there was something off about those three spells. Something he couldn't even put his finger on...

At least, until he tried regarding them not as *three incomplete* spells, but as *one complete* spell. Only then did the truths of this bronze sextant begin to open up for him.

There were not three spells on the pendant. There were only two.

The first was an illusion. Brilliant work. Made itself look like those three incomplete spells. And did one other thing besides. It hid a deeper enchantment within the pendant.

The ward key. The true secret of the pendant.

The bearer of this pendant — and the ship they sailed — could pass through the right set of magical defenses. Wards. So long as the bearer knew the key phrase, which Aefric had found hidden in the structure of the spell.

"Safe haven" was that phrase, spoken in the common tongue.

Magnificent spellwork. Too good for the wizard Aefric took it from — Gwawl, who was competent enough to be dangerous, but lacking in subtlety. And far too good to be contained long by such a cheap work of cast bronze.

However, the diamond flakes and their tiny gold housing *inside* the cast bronze were another matter. Those minuscule diamond chips — when viewed under the highest quality of jeweler's loops — could be even seen to form a capital "N" for Nelazzi, set in high-quality gold.

The work of a *master* jewel smith, and the perfect housing for two such excellent spells.

Aefric had let Calder and Gwawl believe he'd considered the pendant useless. Made sure they heard that he'd discarded it in disgust.

Soon enough, he'd know if his deception had worked.

Either way, Karbin was right about one thing. This tracer spell didn't work the way other tracer spells did.

Most tracer spells worked by connecting a spellcaster's *sense* of a target — usually through a physical connection, but sometimes through knowledge of the target alone, then following that sense to the source. Like a bloodhound.

With connected spells this way, it didn't work quite the same.

What Aefric needed to do was reach through the pendant's magic — the ward key — to find the rest of its spell — the wards.

It wasn't about power. And really, Aefric didn't think of the spell as difficult — assuming the spellcaster could assume the right frame of mind.

The ward key and the wards *wanted* to be together. And so, Aefric needed only a pulse of magic — in the form of an ancient power word he wove into an eldrani song of longing — to persuade the ward key that it needed to rejoin the ward.

Then, Aefric would need only a part of his concentration to maintain the spell.

Aefric sang the song, shunting just enough power through it.

The pendant swung towards the south, possibly south-southwest.

And they were off.

THEY SAILED SOUTH LONG ENOUGH THAT MORNING THAT ALL SIGHT OF the coastline fell away to the west. And around the time that land was lost to sight, they lost the trade winds along with it.

The storms that had been blowing out east came their way around midmorning, calling Karbin into action earlier than they'd hoped.

The storm was blowing crosswind, and too strongly wrong to make tacking worth the effort. So Karbin called up winds to keep the *Swift Wave* following the right course.

Or near enough. Because he couldn't *overcome* the storm winds, only counter them with a strong wind of his own. So instead of a true south at that point, they'd traveled more to the southwest and would have to correct later.

Leaving the proper course felt like ants crawling all over Aefric's skin. An unpleasant combination with the rain coming down on them hard enough that the seas roiled and plenty of sailors were bailing preventatively.

At least, Aefric hoped it was preventative. He didn't bother asking. And anyway, Captain Ol'Vanett was too busy shouting orders and berating any tardiness she saw — not to mention holding her course as best she could — to bother answering what she'd likely consider a stupid question.

And rightfully so.

Cold came with the storm — even with his oilskin cloak — but wet and shivering had never stopped Aefric from keeping a spell going before, and it wasn't going to slow him now.

By midday, the storms were gone and they were back on a proper course.

The sun was out by then, and Beornric insisted on lunch. So Aefric and Karbin ate oranges and trenchers of shredded beef that was likely intercepted on its way into a stew. But a meal that could be eaten easily enough by hand on deck.

Reasonably tasty, too, especially with the cheddar melted across the top of the beef. And accompanied by a decent enough day beer to wash it down. The orange made a sweet dessert.

Karbin moved about the helm deck as he ate, stretching and doing some replenishing exercises that always seemed to work better for him than they did for Aefric.

Aefric stayed toward the back of that deck, leaning against the bulkhead near the door to the captain's cabin.

"How are we doing?" he asked Beornric between bites. "How much did we lose to the storm?"

"If you ask the captain," Beornric said, shaking his head, "the storm didn't cost us time. But then, she expected us to lose a full day to getting blown off course. I think Karbin did something a little different there than you usually do."

"Probably found a way to shield us from the worst of the cross-winds. I wouldn't know how to do that. How's the crew holding up?"

"This is their business," Beornric said with a half-hearted shrug. "Even the worst of the roiling waves didn't trouble them. Which is more than I can say for some of our knights and soldiers."

"Don't name names," Aefric said, "but how bad is it?"

"I've seen worse. That their keeping lunch down is good. Micham is helping."

Micham, having grown up the son of Ajenmoor's mayor, seemed to know just about everything about ships and life aboard them. Including how to stave off and deal with seasickness. At least, as much as could be done, for those suffering from it.

"Any way to tell how close we've gotten?" Beornric asked.

"I can feel it," Aefric said. "We've covered more of the distance between us and those wards than I expected. We may be there by tonight."

"How drained is this making you?" Beornric asked in a low tone. "Do you need rest?"

"This is nothing," Aefric said. "More about focus than power, and I've got more focus than I know what to do with anyway."

Beornric chuckled. "So you promise me that if I let you stay at this through the afternoon, you won't be burned out if we get there by dusk?"

"I promise. Any sense of how Karbin's holding up?"

"He's ... doing things differently than either you or Sirondfar, so far as I can tell." Beornric frowned. "Seems to be using that obsidian rod of his, as much as anything else."

"It acts as a kind of amplifier for him, I think," Aefric said. "He's conserving more of his personal strength, at the cost of what he could do later with the rod."

"How much will that slow him when the fight comes?" Beornric asked quietly.

"More than he'll admit, and less than you'd fear." Aefric snorted. "Remember, he makes me as crazy as I make him. Part of the reason we've stayed friends all these years."

After the brief break for lunch, Karbin took up his post and summoned his winds while Aefric resumed his tracer, making sure both Karbin and the captain — who remained at the helm — kept them on course.

They hadn't been at it long before the lookout called down from the rika's nest.

"Sails, ho! I make a ship our size ... thirty degrees off starboard bow. Westbound."

"Keep an eye on 'er," Captain Ol'Vanett called up. "She shifts to follow, I want to know." In a more normal voice, she said to Aefric, "Probably just a merchant. No more interested in us than we are in him. Odd course, though. Most merchants cross the Risen well north of here this time of year. Better currents and better wind. A good payday at the other end, though, would make his course worth the effort."

"Am I mistaken," Aefric asked, "or do I hear an unspoken second possibility?"

Captain Ol'Vanett frowned. "Some pirates like to crisscross the trade routes on the hunt."

Much as Aefric wanted to turn and keep an eye on that ship, that would be going too far. Letting himself worry about a threat not yet manifest could distract him and cost him the tracer.

Sometime later the lookout called down, "Strange sails gone. Last known course west-northwest."

"West-northwest," Captain Ol'Vanett said. "Heading for southern Malimfar, maybe Varondam, or maybe the Free Baronies."

"Merchant then?" Beornric asked.

"Merchant. A pirate wouldn't have left us alone. Not heading on a strange course the way we are."

A strange course that continued due south-southwest for a time.

Around mid-afternoon they passed the Hundred Islands. Of which there *might've* been a hundred, if one counted every speck of land that showed a large enough face above the sea — when the tides were right — for a person to stand on.

Far as Aefric was concerned the Dozen Islands or maybe the Twenty Islands was closer to the truth. But the mapmakers never consulted him. And he had to admit, the Hundred Islands did sound more poetic.

Plus, more of the smaller islands were inhabited now than had been the last time Aefric passed this way.

"Going to look funny," Captain Ol'Vanett groused. "Coming this near the islands and not stopping. Whipping along with an unnatural wind. Your grace wants to avoid attention—"

"I'll concede half of that," Aefric said, then raised his voice for a moment. "Karbin take a break." Turning back to the captain he said, "But we can't take time to dock."

"I know," she said. "This way's still better. This way we're not likely to get some curious fool after us, assuming we're carrying treasure or something."

Giving up the wind spells slowed them for a time, though the captain and crew did an impressive job of tacking to what wind there was and staying close to the right course.

"Last of the islands is gone," the lookout finally called down. "No sails either."

With that, they resumed the wind and continued on. On through the heat of the afternoon sun, unbroken now by rainclouds.

The shift of sailors changed sometime during the afternoon, but their work continued. Calling to each other as they handled the sails, the rigging, and the ship itself. Captain Ol'Vanett refused a break at the helm, and Aefric couldn't remember if she'd even taken lunch.

Asking, though, would have insulted the captain. And he wasn't willing to go that far.

So he followed the pull of the pendant, which grew stronger and stronger as the day wore on. He became more and more convinced that they would reach their goal before full dark.

Karbin began to take a rhythm of casting without maintaining. So that he'd call up a wind, then let it ease its way to nothing over the hour or so that followed, conserving even what little power that maintaining the wind would have used up.

Of course, had Aefric been doing it, maintaining the wind would've taken less effort than recasting it every hour or so. But Karbin knew his business, so Aefric didn't question him.

Not now, at least. Later. He'd have to remember to ask about it later, so he could try to understand how it all worked for Karbin.

But Karbin did his work, Aefric did his, and the sailors did theirs. And by the time the sun approached the horizon, it did so ahead of them.

And landfall was dead ahead.

WHETHER BECAUSE OF THE DISTANCE OR THE GLARE FROM THE SETTING sun, Aefric couldn't see land yet. But the call had come down from the rika's nest — *Land ho!* — and the crew of the *Swift Wave* had begun buzzing about to make ready for port.

Assuming there was a port.

He knew one thing, though. The pull of the ward key was strong enough that he could say with certainty that they had almost reached the wards it would open. Or, rather, grant passage through.

They were helped by the tides now. Karbin was no longer needed for wind. He joined Aefric and Beornric back behind the wheel, where Beornric was forcing a skinned orange on Aefric and had one ready for Karbin too.

"The rest of us already ate," Beornric said. "You two need at least one more thing in your bellies before it all comes down."

"The others stand ready for our arrival?" Karbin asked, taking his orange while Aefric started on his own. Fresh and juicy and not at all what he was used to eating before action.

Then again, he wasn't used to eating *anything* before action. But that was the price of running with knights and soldiers. They always took their sleep and their food whenever they could, and so it was expected that he do so as well.

He did share a small smile with Karbin though, while Beornric answered the question.

"Deirdre's down below, getting everyone organized and going over last-minute instructions. They'll be ready when the time comes."

"You still feel," Killian said, walking up, "that they're better waiting down below than being ready on deck? What if we're attacked?"

"If we're attacked unexpectedly," Beornric said patiently, as though he'd answered this question before, "your highness will be most pleased to see how quickly and efficiently two doors can disgorge a *lot* of knights and soldiers."

"In the meantime," Aefric added between bites, "observers won't have any reason to think we're hiding a fighting force."

"And the closer we get to land," Karbin added, "the greater the chances of *someone* watching."

"I still think there ought to be a better way," Killian said, frowning. "Couldn't you hide them under an illusion?"

"And have my crew bumping into knights they can't see?" Captain Ol'Vanett said. "Begging your pardon, your highness, but I think Ser Beornric is right to keep them belowdecks for now."

"I suppose," Killian said sourly, still plainly trying to come up with a better plan.

"Simplicity, your highness," Beornric said softly, "is often the best route in war. It's a matter of efficiency. Fewer *chances* for mistakes mean fewer mistakes."

"Does the crew know what's going on?" Aefric softly asked Beornric.

It was the captain who answered. The woman had to have the ears of guard dog.

"My first mate put the word around," she said. "Won't pretend they're not scared, but if it comes to that, so am I. But we'll do our jobs, your grace. You and yours take the fight to Nelazzi, and I and mine will keep this ship clear and ready to sail when you need us."

"Thank you, captain," Aefric said.

"Still think this is madness, myself," she said. "But we'll back you, your grace. You've been a good duke so far, and gods know you've got a rep for pulling miracles. I just hope you've got at least one more up your sleeve."

"So do I," he muttered. Louder he added, "Where are we? Hayroun? Zhenderran?"

"Hayroun's a little more than a hundred miles from us, more or less due west," Captain Ol'Vanett said. "You've found us an island that's not on the maps, your grace. And I can't imagine anyone coming here without some kind of magic moving their ship. We're well off the trade winds, and even the currents were fighting each other only maybe three or four miles behind us. Getting here would've taken a hell of a lot of work, without those wind spells."

"Sounds like a perfect pirate hideaway to me," Beornric said.

"If it is, then either Nelazzi knows a few tricks of sailing that I don't, or she likes to lean pretty heavy on her wizards. Because no captain in their right mind is going to break out the oars unless they already know this island's here."

"We already know Nelazzi likes her magic," Karbin said, nodding at the pendant, then gave Aefric a lopsided grin. "I may not be able to handle your reasoning, but I can't argue with your results."

"We're not through those wards yet," Aefric said. "If they've been rewoven, we'll have our work cut out for us."

Karbin scoffed. "I was breaking wards when you were still a street rat. If that pendant can't get us through, I will."

Aefric could just make out the island on the horizon now. Or at least, some lumps that might've been hills. Without anything big enough to qualify as a mountain or volcano.

Odd. One island all alone would tend to suggest a nearby volcano.

Aefric pulled his own spyglass out of his belt pouch.

Yes. The swells of some low mountains. Looked to have lots of growth. Couldn't tell the type yet...

He handed the spyglass around. Too soon to learn much, but everyone wanted to take a turn looking.

Twice Aefric considered lending the ship a little speed with a wind. The second time he got as far as suggesting it before the captain said, "Any sailor who lives on that island knows the winds like you know your clothes, your grace. They see us coming in too fast, they'll sound the alarm."

And so he could do nothing.

Nothing but wait.

This was different waiting, though, than the kind he usually did as a duke. This wasn't waiting for aetts or seasons. No. This was the *old* waiting. This was minutes. No more than an hour. And at the end of the wait, not just a message and more waiting.

No. At the end of this wait would come action.

And that thought was enough to get the good tension of anticipation building again. In his belly. In his legs and arms and shoulders. Enough to make him roll those shoulders and move about a bit, even twirl the Brightstaff in his hands.

"Might want to throw a cloak over that, your grace," Captain Ol'Vanett said. "A length of white thunderwood, topped by a yellow diamond big as half my thumb might get spotted by a lookout."

She hadn't even finished explaining before Beornric had tossed Aefric an oilskin cloak to cover his signature weapon.

"Should I get below as well?" Killian asked.

"You look like a noble," Aefric said, "but without crests or a sigil

— and especially without us flying certain flags — no one's going to spot you as the Crown Prince of Armyr. Not unless they've seen you before."

Minutes passed. The dark lump on the horizon came slowly clearer, but without details just yet.

And the wait seemed to be getting to Killian.

"Shouldn't Deirdre be back by now? How long does it take to organize knights and soldiers?"

"She was finished with that some time ago, your highness," Beornric said in a placating tone that would have irritated Aefric, but Killian seemed to take in stride. "But a woman in maroon leathers wearing her hair in a long, dark red braid? Carrying herself like a warrior? Kind of stands out."

Killian scoffed. "You think they'd recognize her?"

"Some would," Aefric said. "And that's too much risk for this. So she knows to stay belowdecks until we arrive."

"Well, what about—"

"No one ever recognizes *me*," Aefric said. "They recognize the Brightstaff." He turned to Karbin and raised an eyebrow. "You, on the other hand."

"I suppose you're right," Karbin said with a sigh, and cast an illusion that had always impressed Aefric, until he'd learned its secret.

The spell appeared to alter one's features, so Karbin went from being a bald, clean-shaven man to a weathered man with skin closer to mahogany brown — a more common shade in this region than Karbin's own blue-black skin — with unruly brown hair and beard.

The secret of the illusion was simple enough. It wasn't that Karbin had selected this precise look and conjured it about him as an artist would a painting. It was that the spell made him nondescript. A blank that every viewer would fill in with features that fit the setting.

Karbin was currently on a ship, with sailors, so the spell made him look to Aefric the way Aefric expected sailors to look. Weathered. Unkempt. Even his clothes now looked like dark brown linens. Over-all, a look that would make Karbin fit in with the rest of the crew. He wouldn't even be mistaken for an officer, since officers tended to be better groomed, if not always better dressed.

"Impressive," Killian said, nodding. He frowned. "Why not just do that with Deirdre, too?"

"She'd never stand for it," Beornric said. "Not unless it was *absolutely* necessary. And it's not, so long as she stays below."

Killian started pacing.

"How do you stand the *waiting*?"

"Because you have to," Beornric said. "Remember, your highness. Others will look to you for their example. If you're nervous, they'll be nervous. If you're calm — visibly, at least — they'll be calm."

Killian stopped and turned. "I should stop pacing then, shouldn't I."

"I'd suggest it," Beornric said. "Look to his grace. Movements to loosen up for battle. Nothing more."

Killian nodded.

And together they all watched their approach to Nelazzi's lair.

THE ISLAND WASN'T LARGE. BY THE CAPTAIN'S ESTIMATE, NO MORE than five miles across, and probably not as long. Lots of jungle across the hills. Tropical type, which suited the humid, lingering warmth of the late afternoon, with sunset no more than an hour away.

Something lighter than wool might've been a better choice for his tunic.

Aefric noted both palm trees and rubber trees through his spyglass, and that was only at a glance.

More important was the "natural" dock a few hundred yards away. A jut of flat red-gray rock that stuck out from a white sand beach for maybe fifty feet.

"Don't see that every day," Captain Ol'Vanett said about it.

"That's because it's not every day some wizard shapes rock that way," Karbin said.

"You think it's a wizard then?" Beornric said. "Rather than, say, a warlock?"

"The work on the wards was too fine for anything but a wizard," Aefric said, mentally adding *or maybe me, with practice.* "Likely the same wizard handled that as well."

"Speaking of those wards," Captain Ol'Vanett said. "Your grace can get us through them, right?"

"That's the plan," Aefric said, stifling his worries.

"Maybe another forty yards," Karbin said, just as Aefric stretched out with his senses and determined the same thing.

Wards came in a few different varieties. Most common were those that stood firm and clear, like walls or domes. Edges so precise you could stand a handspan away and not risk touching them.

These wards, though, were a more dangerous type. More like mist, even to Aefric's magical senses. The type that wouldn't look like much, at first. Hard to even focus on. And by the time they were plain, they were all around you and doing their work. Which was all too likely fatal.

Aefric didn't wait until they reached the first wisps of those wards to hold up the pendant and whisper, "Safe haven."

The words seemed to vibrate through the sextant. A vibration that shivered swiftly through Aefric's body as it passed outward from him. Making everyone in sight shiver as the vibrations moved through them as well, out to the edges of the ship and beyond.

Even the sails seemed to tremble as those words echoed through them.

"It's working," Karbin said at once.

Aefric looked back toward the wards and realized that the vibrations had formed a tunnel in the mists, just large enough to allow the *Swift Wave* to pass safely through.

"Not to sound ungrateful, your grace," Captain Ol'Vanett said, "but it occurs to me that if you die we might not to be able to leave again."

"Wards like these are only dangerous on entry," Karbin said, while Aefric held his focus on the wards and their key. Just in case something unexpected happened. "In fact, wards in general tend to be one-way."

"And these *definitely* are?" Captain Ol'Vanett pressed.

"Given the key phrase to activate them, yes," Karbin said. "Besides, why would Nelazzi want to kill people *leaving* her lair?"

"I suppose," Captain Ol'Vanett said, sounding unconvinced. But then her eyes widened and she said softly, "Ulna bless me."

Here and there around the ship, sailors gave cries of wonder. Even Killian said, "Well, will you look at *that.*"

"Illusion on the ward key," Karbin said, "illusion on the wards. Clever."

Aefric looked up from the pendant then, and understood.

As the ship emerged from the tunnel of warding mist, the island ahead of them looked completely different.

Well, not *completely*. It was about the same size. But a fair amount of that size was taken up in the middle now by a volcano that jutted a few hundred feet up. It might've been dead, though. Or at least, it wasn't smoking.

The jungle looked much the same, too, but there was less of it. Instead, there was a ship on one side of that rock pier — a big three-masted beast — and a handful of wooden buildings in a cleared area past the beach.

At the back of the buildings, one stood taller. Though that wasn't saying much. It was two stories tall, while the others were only one.

Smoke from a few chimneys. Cooking fires, most likely.

"Well," Captain Ol'Vanett said, "I was going to ask if we should sail around to someplace we could put in unobserved, but I don't think that's an option."

Sure enough, someone had emerged from one of the smaller buildings. Human by the look of him. On the heavy and shaggy side. Carrying a clipboard, as though he might be the dockmaster of a single dock.

"All right," Aefric said. "Looks like they intend to let us dock. Put in—"

"Docking, I know how to do," Captain Ol'Vanett said. Then

added, "Your grace," almost as an afterthought before she started hollering orders at her crew.

To her credit as a captain, whatever fears or reservations the sailors might've been feeling, they treated this just like putting in to any other port. From throwing soft sacks over the side to prevent damaging the hull on the dock, to handling the sails and rigging as though they might actually intend to stay a while.

As soon as the gangplank was down and the ship was tied off, the man who seemed to be the dockmaster approached the gangplank and called up, "Ahoy, there. What's your cargo?"

"Spices and silks by the ton," Karbin called back, pretending to be the first mate. "Gonna need help offloading."

"I don't usually talk to mates," the dockmaster said with disdain. "Something wrong with your captain?"

"Bad shellfish," Karbin said, tapping his throat. "Still gettin' over it. Crew's thrilled she can barely yell at 'em."

"Movement on the other ship," Captain Ol'Vanett said softly.

"I see it," Aefric answered the same way. Handful of armed pirates, staying low to the decks and trying not to draw attention.

"Can't say I remember this ship," the dockmaster said with a frown. "When were you last here?"

"Before Midsummer," Karbin answered. "Now you gonna get us a hand or do we have to break our backs getting Nelazzi her cut?"

For just a moment, something seemed to sharpen in the dockmaster's manner. But just as quickly, it was gone.

"Not until you gather your officers and come down to the office," the dockmaster said.

It might've been Aefric's imagination, but he thought the dockmaster said that louder than he'd said everything else.

"What's this gash?" Karbin complained. "We're just here to drop off, resupply as we can, and put back out. The crew is due shore time in Aleff's Bay."

Aefric had to fight not to smile at that one. Aleff's Bay was a particularly notorious port in Hayroun.

"Rules are rules," the dockmaster said, "and you know who makes 'em. You ain't been here since the seasons turned, so you gotta check your officers against our records."

"That's bilge!" Karbin said. "When did this place grow a bureaucracy?"

"Been some leaks in the hull," the dockmaster said. "Gotta caulk it and check the hatches, and this is how it's done. Now. You comin' down?"

"Can't we handle it on the docks?" Karbin said. "The tides wait for no one."

"Like I'd know the names of the officers on the *Swift Wave*," the dockmaster said, but before he said anything else, a boatswain's whistle blew three sharp blasts from the other docked ship.

The dockmaster dropped his clipboard and dove straight into the water.

The attack began.

***

At the sound of the boatswain's whistle, Aefric turned to face the other docked ship. A score of armed pirates rushed down its gangplank with murder in their eyes. All of them shouting their fury and waving cutlasses or longswords.

Even worse, more pirates, armed with crossbows, popped up at the rail. Aefric had exactly enough time to shout, *"Down!"* before they loosed.

Sailors on the *Swift Wave* dove for cover. Killian snatched up his round shield.

All of them were slower than flying crossbow bolts.

Screams of pain from a sailor or two.

Three bolts bounced off an invisible shield conjured by Karbin.

Another hit the wheel beside the ducking captain. Two more each came for Aefric and Killian, but were turned aside by the magic of their protective bracers and sank into the deck around them.

Bellowing *"Deepwater!"* Deirdre led the charge of knights and soldiers onto the deck to meet the onrushing sailors. Her rapier and dagger limned with red light as she leapt high in the air in a flying somersault.

Every knight or soldier following her shouted either "Deepwater!" or "Armyr!" as they charged. The knights armored to their helms and gauntlets, bearing swords, axes or warhammers. The soldiers behind them all in their chainmail with pikes at the ready and swords at their sides.

But someone had to stop those crossbows before they reloaded.

Karbin hit three of the crossbow pirates with fiery bolts of magic that left them screaming and falling to the decks.

Aefric didn't think that small. Throwing the oilskin off the Brightstaff, he used his favorite tool to call down mighty, booming strokes of lightning on those archers and their ship.

Three. Four. Five blasts in quick succession. Devastating enemies, deck, masts and more. Brilliant flashes of light. Booms of thunder that left even Aefric's ears buzzing.

From there, the fight didn't last long. His lightning had thrown off the charging pirates, while his own people had been warned to expect it.

Led by the whirlwind that was Deirdre, the knights cut through those pirates like cheap quintains. In moments, all that remained of their attack was a burning, groaning hulk of a ship, sinking on the other side of the pier.

"They were ready for us," Captain Ol'Vanett said.

"Not ready enough," Killian said with a grin, but Beornric shot Aefric a grim look. He nodded.

That attack. It didn't feel right. Wasn't enough.

Could be they just kept ready in case *any* strange ship showed up. Planned a fight against undisciplined — or at least *less* disciplined — sailors.

But even so, that wasn't much of a fight...

Karbin — his illusory disguise gone now — called, "We better get moving."

"Right," Aefric called back. Louder, to Deirdre, he shouted a code phrase, "Watch out for traps."

She nodded acknowledgment.

"Soldiers," Beornric ordered. "Fan out and lead the way."

The soldiers took the front, and spread out into two ranks of twelve, while the knights fell in as one rank behind them, with Deirdre alone between the two groups.

Beornric, Killian, Karbin and Aefric brought up the rear.

"Sails, ho!" the lookout cried from the *Swift Wave*.

Aefric started to turn, but Beornric grabbed his shoulder.

"Leave the ship to Captain Ol'Vanett. She'll signal if she needs help."

Aefric frowned, but nodded.

As they approached the pack of small buildings, the soldiers and knights split into small units. Two soldiers for every knight, and Deirdre moving among them freely, checking for both magic in general and — because of the code phrase — illusions in particular while the others checked for threats.

Aefric's group reached the white sand — loose enough at first to make walking an effort — and waited for the calls back.

"Empty," came call after call.

"No magic," Deirdre called back. "Not among these." She pointed with her rapier toward the large house at the back. "I'm betting that'll be different."

Aefric pointed to a couple of chimneys that still issued smoke. "Those houses empty too?"

"Checked each myself," Deirdre said. "Old fires that look left to burn themselves out."

"Or make us think these buildings were in use," Beornric said darkly.

"This whole situation feels more and more like a trap," Karbin said.

"I agree," Beornric said, turning to Aefric. "Perhaps you and his highness should hang back."

"We move as one or we fall as many," Aefric said. "We proceed."

"Right into their hands?" Beornric asked, but Karbin was looking back out into the bay.

"If I'm Nelazzi," he said, "I have the princesses on that ship. Keeps you from sinking it, and ensures my getaway."

"I disagree," Aefric said. "If the princesses are on that ship, I'm free to burn her whole safe haven."

"Safe haven's probably worthless to her now anyway," Karbin said. "It's been found and breached."

"A lot of investment to throw away, though. And likely a good portion of her career's wealth, which won't move so fast or easy. Whereas if she kills us, she solves the problem."

"If she *can* kill us," Killian said.

"Pointless argument," Beornric said. "We have no way of knowing what's on that ship. Not without deviating from the plan." He looked at Aefric. "Do we do that? Send you or Karbin, *alone*, back to investigate the ship?"

"No," Aefric said. "The lookout didn't see sails until after the fight. Could be they were on the other side of the wards, where the illusion hid the whole battle. Could be just another pirate ship coming to offload, hanging back because of fire at the pier."

He drew a fast, deep breath and blew it out. "We proceed."

"Move out," Beornric called.

Deirdre took the lead now, with the knights three abreast behind her, with a soldier flanking on each side, and the rest of the soldiers back forming a ring around Aefric's smaller group.

They were walking now on rock and hard-packed sand. The sultry wind hardly more than a breeze, but smelling of decaying vegetation from the nearby jungle.

The *nearby* jungle. But the bird calls and other animal sounds weren't so close as they should've been...

"Should be more noise," Aefric said softly. "Birds, monkeys, that kind of thing."

There wasn't though. It was as though the portion of jungle nearest them was holding its breath.

Aefric raised his hands and cast a spell to break illusions at the jungle.

Half the nearby jungle disappeared. A cleared area more than a hundred yards across now separated the buildings from the jungle. Even extending onto the first, low slopes of the volcano, back behind the big house.

Killian shook his head. "What's the point of that?"

"Depends on who might be hiding in the jungle," Karbin said. "Under cover of illusion, they could have assembled a horde of pirates there, armed to the teeth and ready to charge, without us knowing it."

"Should Deirdre have spotted that illusion?" Beornric asked softly.

"No," Aefric answered the same way. "She's checking only her immediate area."

"That jungle's still pretty quiet though," Karbin said. "Think it was the lightning?"

"Hope so," Aefric said, as they reached the big house.

The big house was two stories tall and painted a shade of red that suggested they'd used pomegranate seeds for the pigment. It had white shutters open to show glass windows on the second floor, but none on the first.

No smoke coming from the chimney, either.

Beornric nodded to the jungle in both directions. A good hundred yards of cleared, hard-packed dirt away, and still quiet. Maybe because the animals had been spooked by Aefric's lightning. Or maybe because of something else.

Of course, there was always the chance that most birds and animals slept through the worst of the late-afternoon heat, even during autumn. But Aefric certainly couldn't count on that.

"If I'm Nelazzi," Beornric said, "and I expected unwanted guests, I've got a host waiting in that jungle. They'd be moving up right now, but you got rid of their cover. So they're waiting for us to move in here."

Beornric nodded at the house.

"No windows on the first floor. Probably no stairs up. We go in. The pirates converge. Bar us in and set fire to the place."

"No smell of pitch," Deirdre called from the front, as though she'd heard him. "Just paint."

"Doesn't make it less of a trap," Beornric said.

"Fine," Aefric said. "We check the jungle first."

Beornric split the knights and soldiers into two groups, and sent them to check the nearby parts of the jungle. Karbin went with the left-hand group to check for illusions and magic. Deirdre went with the right-hand group to do the same.

Aefric couldn't help glancing back out into the harbor to see what had become of that ship. But it hadn't docked. Not yet. It was coming in... slow...

Of course it was. Half the pier was blocked by the *Swift Wave*, and the other half by a burning, sinking hulk.

Well, whoever they were, they certainly had to know that something was wrong.

He turned his attention back, to see both groups go into the jungle.

What bird and animal sounds there were, all stopped.

Beornric loosened his sword. Killian followed suit.

Minutes passed. Sweat trickled down Aefric's brow, and not all of it from the heavy, humid warmth.

Karbin's group emerged from the jungle. Didn't say anything until they reached reasonable conversation distance, but even on approach they didn't look worried.

"Just looks like jungle," Karbin said, "and thick at that. "Nothing out of the ordinary, and a hard place to sneak a large group."

Wardius, behind Karbin, said, "Lots of undergrowth. Doubt any large groups *could*—"

Something screamed off to the right.

Aefric turned, adrenaline already spiking. Killian drew his longsword. Beornric grabbed each by a shoulder.

"Patience," he said. "That was not a cry for help. Trust your people."

Karbin's group hustled back to wait anxiously alongside Aefric and the others. All of them straining to hear more.

Aefric prayed he didn't hear a weak cry for help...

Deirdre's group came out from the treeline, buzzing with talk. Some of them even smiling. Deirdre herself looked to have a little extra swagger in her step that went well with her smile.

"Mandatok," she said, which was a kind of strange, half-cat-half-serpent thing with both poisonous fangs *and* a stinger. "Tried to make a meal of us, but we cut it to ribbons."

She nodded to the soldiers. "Good men and women with pikes, your grace. They move fast, and contained it while I dealt the death blow."

"*Insisted* on dealing the death blow is more like it," Vria grumbled. "Flipping in over its striking stinger so you could cut off its head."

"Enough," Beornric said. "There's time for stories later. I take it there was no sign of pirate activity?"

"None," Micham said, and one of Killian's knights — a big man Aefric believed to be Oudin Ol'Maquill — added, "Too thick for troop movements. Unless they're that good in the trees."

"Sailors can certainly scramble the rigging like monkeys," Killian said.

"Rigging and trees aren't as alike as your highness might think," Micham said, but before he could continue, Beornric cut him off.

"Speculation isn't evidence," he said. "And we have work to do."

Killian looked toward the jungle as though he was half-considering going to see if there were any more mandatoks, but Aefric cleared his throat.

"All right," Aefric said. "We try knocking first. Always a chance our hostess will want to talk."

"You think?" Deirdre asked, sounding disappointed in the idea.

"Have to give her the chance."

"Fine," she said, then took the lead and knocked with so much sarcastic formality and politeness that Aefric couldn't fight down a smile.

"It appears, your grace," she said in mock formal tones, "that our hostess is refusing us the proper hospitality due our ranks and stations. May I knock with more intention then?"

"Wait," Aefric said, then stepped forward.

He held the Brightstaff in front of him, so he could look through its yellow diamond at the door and surrounding wall. He whispered the right words of power, then gazed through the diamond.

He saw five images of the door and the area around it. All of them a good, clear yellow which meant there was no mechanical or magical trap waiting for them.

If it were trapped, one or more of the images would have glowed red. The more red, the more dangerous the trap.

"No traps," Aefric said. "Well, none on or around the door, anyway."

"Do love that *fascinating* tune you hum when you cast that spell, your grace," Deirdre said in a tone too intimate for the situation. "But I don't believe I know it."

He'd been called on that tune before, because its origins were nowhere in Qorunn. But as Keifer, he known it from a children's show when he was growing up. Once an episode it would play while the hostess would look at the camera through a "magic" faceted lens. Pretending to look through the television screen, she would call out the names some of the children she saw watching the show.

"Just a nothing tune from childhood," Aefric said, resuming his place toward the back, while the knights and soldiers resumed their own formation. "For some reason it comes to me when I look for traps."

Deirdre determined that the door was locked, then kicked it open. Inside was dark, but she caused her sword's blue glow to brighten.

Nevertheless. "Darkness protocol," Aefric said.

A half-dozen knights and soldiers — which ones had been determined in advance by Beornric — held up their weapons, and Aefric lit them up with bright white spell light.

He then caused the yellow diamond on the Brightstaff to shine out as well.

"Hallway," Deirdre called back. "Two sets of doors on each side. One door at the end."

Beornric muttered something Aefric couldn't quite make out. Given the older knight's expression, he wasn't expecting anything good.

"Let me check it," Aefric said, then came up to check for traps.

Again, all clear and yellow through the diamond. He resumed his place in the formation.

Deirdre led the way, checking for magic and illusion as she went. Soldiers then knights rotating behind her, two by two, with Aefric's smaller group in the center and more knights and soldiers behind them. Two of Killian's knights on rear guard, one of whom now carried a glowing warhammer.

"She has to know we're here by now," Karbin said. "Is she just going to give us free rein?"

"Could be she's not even home," Killian said. "We could be chasing echoes while she's off sailing somewhere."

Aefric didn't think so, and he doubted Karbin or Deirdre believed that either. He had a gut sense that Nelazzi was here somewhere. Waiting for him.

He didn't expect the soldiers and other knights to understand though. They'd never been adventurers. They didn't know what this kind of hunt was like. It had a way of honing a kind of extra sense.

Nelazzi was here. He would have bet his duchy on it.

***

THE SIDE DOORS WERE NOTHING. THE FIRST TWO LED TO STORAGE rooms, and Aefric didn't bother with the crates and barrels they contained. Perhaps later, if there was time. They were real, not trapped, and without magic, so they could wait.

Aefric had the soldiers test those rooms themselves with the butts of their pikes. Checking for hollow spots that might mean hidden nooks or concealed doors along the walls, or even on the floor.

Nothing yet, but he made sure the soldiers kept checking every room and hallway as the group continued on.

The house itself smelled recently aired. Aefric had been expecting dust and mildew, but someone had cleaned in the last day or so, even sweeping the storerooms.

Second door on the right was a well-stocked kitchen. Even cleaner than the storerooms. Trapdoor at one end led to a cellar for roots and wine.

Last door on the left led to stairs up.

"There's no way she's up there," Beornric said. "If she is, I'll personally clean the castle middens for a month."

She wasn't.

Sitting room at the top of the stairs. Simple, but well used. Mostly wooden furniture, but one chair upholstered in purple and padded along the seat, back, and even the arms.

"Seems she gave herself a throne," Killian said, taking the time to slash the padding with his noble's dagger while the others continued the search.

Bedroom upstairs at the front of the house on the left, with a sumptuous bed, four large, fancy teak armoires, a freestanding full-length mirror, and a broad assortment of clothing for both men and women. Though most of it didn't look like usual pirate wear.

"Seems *someone* has interesting tastes," Deirdre said, trying for her usual tease, but not quite making it. She was clearly feeling the same tension that was singing through Aefric's muscles, and keeping the others tight and quiet.

They were somewhere in the eye of the storm right now. The question wasn't *if* the storm would hit them, but *when*.

The right side of the upstairs was one big room, clearly used for meetings. A large, pale wood table in the center. A dozen seats around it, more seats along the wall.

At one end of the table, another throne upholstered in purple. Killian slashed the padding on that one too.

On the long inside wall, a massive map painting of the Risen Sea and the kingdoms around it.

But nothing hidden. And no sign yet of Nelazzi.

"Only one door left," Beornric said, when the soldiers had finished checking for any hidden nooks or doors. "Can't be that simple."

"You said simple is better," Killian said.

"In war, simple is better," Beornric said. "But while we're bringing war to Nelazzi, she's not meeting us in kind."

"She's a pirate," Karbin said, "not a soldier. She knows she can't meet us on equal footing."

"And if I were her," Aefric said, "I'd have my wizard listening to everything we're saying."

"You have the scrying itch?" Karbin asked. "I don't."

The scrying itch wasn't really an itch. That was just the conventional term for how most spellcasters could tell without being able to describe how, when someone tried to scry them. But it was an unreliable sense, unless one was relaxed. At peace.

Which none of them were at the moment.

Aefric shook his head.

"I'm calm enough to get it," Deirdre said. "I don't feel it."

Karbin shot Aefric a look that needed no words. Good at her form of magic as Deirdre was, she was still a dweomerblade. Not nearly as sensitive to the finer magics as a wizard like Karbin, or someone who had magic in his very blood, like Aefric.

"Well," Aefric said, "whether she can hear us or not, at best we're wasting daylight. Back to that final door."

The resumed their formation and retreated to the hallway downstairs. Aefric had already checked that door at the end of the hall for traps and determined there were none. A fact that didn't make him feel any better.

Deirdre tried the latch, and the door swung inward smoothly and almost soundlessly.

"Stairs down into rock," Deirdre said. "Looks like a long haul. Lit by hanging oil lamps."

"We're never going to see Ol'Vanett's signal from here," Beornric said.

"Right," Aefric said, nodding to Karbin, who cast a contact spell.

"Captain Ol'Vanett," he said. "We'll be out of sight for a time. I'll check with you by spell every so often. How are things out there?"

A moment later, Karbin nodded. "She reports all quiet topside. That new ship is just sitting out there in the harbor. No attempt at contact."

He frowned. "Might be waiting for a signal of their own."

"No help for it," Aefric said. "We proceed."

"Pikes up front," Beornric said.

Deirdre frowned, but didn't object as the two nearest soldiers took her place, to lead the way with their pikes, and two more took up position behind them.

Likely Deirdre understood the order as well as Aefric.

Anything could be waiting for them down there. The extra reach of a pike in front might save lives.

The walls of the stairwell were like a mine. Hewn into the rock, and buttressed.

"I'm thinking we're going to find more than a storeroom at the bottom," Karbin said.

Aefric nodded. This made more sense. No way those crates and barrels in the "storeroom" held any of Nelazzi's wealth. They were just too accessible.

She might have an entire personal castle down here.

"Magic," Karbin said softly, interrupting Aefric's speculation about the layout ahead of them. "Subtle stuff. Don't think it's a threat, though."

Aefric could have kicked himself for not noticing it first, but Karbin was right. There was a subtle sense of magic all around them. Not latent or waiting, but ... complete.

"Feels like the tunnel," Aefric said. "Spell shaped?"

"That's what I'm thinking. But why the buttresses then?"

"Wait," Aefric called to the line, then turned to Karbin. "We need to know."

Aefric hated to admit it, but Karbin was faster at puzzling through strange magic than he was. Of course, Karbin had been doing so for two or three times as long as Aefric had been alive.

Karbin also insisted that being an actual wizard helped the process, though Aefric doubted that part.

"Clay and stone magic," Karbin confirmed. "Don't think it's precise enough to be *vohlcairn* work, but still impressive. Shaped the tunnel and holds it in place against volcanic activity."

Deirdre, who'd been examining the buttresses, said, "Ha!"

She pressed something that clicked, and a panel in the buttress slid open, showing a waiting longsword on hooks.

"Emergency armory," she said with a grin. "Every beam likely hides a weapon."

"Well spotted," Aefric said, "but I don't think we need her swords. Let's go."

THE LAMPS ABOVE THOSE ROCK-HEWN STAIRS WERE BURNING WHALE OIL, lending an unpleasant fishy smell to air that was warmer than it should've been.

Most times Aefric had gone delving — mines and ancient passages — the way hadn't been *cool* exactly, but it hadn't been overly warm either.

And yet, the air was definitely getting warmer as they descended that long, long staircase.

"Explains the spellwork," Karbin muttered. "If they wanted to go down that ... far..." He winced. "And it's getting warmer."

"I know," Aefric replied, just as quietly. "There may be magma in our future."

"I *hate* fighting around magma."

"You and me both, old friend."

The buttresses quit after the first few hundred steps, and the oil lamps hung on hooks instead. But even then, there was no sign of an end to those stairs.

"I feel like I'm back at Water's End," Killian grumbled. "Takes forever to get anywhere in a castle that big, you know. Stairways there are *endless*."

"Hush, your highness," Beornric said, more respectfully than Aefric would have. "Think of morale."

Their boots scraped and clomped on the rock, with enough tight echoes to kill any hope of hearing much from whatever lay at the end of the stairs.

And though the ceiling was comfortably high enough for walking, it wasn't designed for marching with pikes. The soldiers had to keep their pikes ready instead of shouldered.

Not good. Those soldiers were already tense. Probably gripping their pikes harder than they had to. The extra effort of holding those pikes ready instead of shouldered on this long march down the stairs, it might tax their muscles. Slow them when the time to fight came.

Nothing Aefric could do about that though. Not now. Later he could mention it to Beornric, since they were soldiers of the ducal guard, and technically his responsibility. Perhaps he could think of a way to train them for a scenario like this one. In case there was a next time.

As those stairs went on and on, oddly enough, Aefric found himself hungry. He didn't usually think about food at moments like this one. Maybe that last orange was to blame. Maybe it had thrown off his normal rhythm.

Either way, even some of that overcooked venison would have tasted good to him right then.

But the march went on. And thoughts of food fell off to the side after no more than another hundred steps.

Older habits of thought kicked in.

Noise and light. Friends and enemies both to an adventurer.

Noise was the best way to get warnings about what might by lying in wait. Scrapes, clacks, ticks, taps, hearing any of those things could make the difference between being ready when the ambush came and being caught in it.

On the flip side, *making* noise in situations like this one gave warning to the enemy. Allowed them to prepare that ambush. And to be waiting in perfect silence while they monitored their kill zone...

Light was the same way. A pair of glowing eyes in the darkness, or really, any kind of glow in the darkness. That could be as important a warning as any sound. While *carrying* light into dark places was a necessary evil.

Borogs and na'shek might not need light. Some said the taroks and certain of the eldrani could do without it too. But humans *relied* on it.

This group was all human — save for a certain amount of nonhuman heritage in Vria and maybe one or two others — so light they had to have.

And with only two exceptions — not including himself of course — these people were not adventurers. They were soldiers and knights and a prince. They might be *capable* of stealth, under the right circumstances, but not while decked out head to toe in all that metal. Rustling chainmail. Clinking full plate armor.

Not to mention the heavy steps of their boots.

No. Aefric might hate the fact that his group was giving all the warning Nelazzi could possibly ask for, but he saw little he could do about it. Not without casting a spell to *enforce* silence. But that could be disastrous if an attack came.

No. Nothing Aefric could do about it, except reassure himself that Nelazzi already knew they were there anyway. So, in a sense, it really didn't matter how much light they shed and noise they made along the way.

And he did have some small consolations. The smelly oil lamps were casting enough light that his own light spells — though still active — weren't making a difference. And the tight echoes of the tunnel around the stairs might disguise their exact numbers.

Not much in the way of consolations, really, but he had to take what he could get, while this long march down those stairs continued.

On and down those stairs went. They had to have passed the

thousandth step by now. Even Water's End only had this many steps in the Great Spires.

So many stairs that Beornric finally called a break. Not a long break, and he didn't let anyone sit. In fact, though he didn't say so, Aefric suspected that Beornric called that break to give the soldiers a chance to set down their pikes for a moment. Rest their hands and stretch their arms.

The break was just long enough for Beornric to go speak privately with each knight and soldier. Perhaps with more tactical ideas, or perhaps only with thoughts about maintaining readiness on a seemingly endless stairway like this one.

"Could this whole stairway be illusion?" Killian asked. "I can't believe—"

"Nope," Deirdre said, doing some stretching of her own that Killian watched with interest. "Checked as soon as I saw it, and I check again every hundred stairs or so. The stairs are real, and no illusions hiding doors in the rock."

"Think we should be tapping the sides?" Killian asked. "To make sure?"

"Won't help," Aefric, Karbin and Deirdre all said at the same time. Aefric nodded for Karbin to continue. Deirdre shrugged.

"Rock is rock," Karbin said. "Even rock that works as a sliding door will be too thick to sound hollow to a knock."

"I haven't seen anything," Vria said. "I've been checking for any odd cracks or seams that might indicate a hidden door or trigger. If any are there, I haven't seen them."

"I've been checking too," Wardius said, and a couple of other knights indicated that they'd been checking as well.

And Aefric himself hadn't. Almost enough to make him blush.

"I'll check in with the captain," Karbin said. He'd done so every few hundred steps, just in case the *Swift Wave* needed aid. A moment later he said, "Still no change. That ship in the harbor dropped anchor and sits there watching. Or maybe waiting."

"All right," Beornric said. "Break over. Back in formation. Let's move."

And on down the stairs they went. But Aefric noticed now that the soldiers shifted their grips every so often, sometimes using one hand and a wrist, and found ways to adjust how they held their pikes that wouldn't hit either the ceiling, the walls, or each other.

"I apologize for the delay, your grace," Beornric said softly, "but the way they handled those pikes was bothering me. They've clearly trained to *use* those things, but not how to carry them long distances, when needed. I'll see to it that their training broadens when we return."

"Thank you," Aefric said, appreciating both the sentiment and the confidence that all of those soldiers would return alive, for more training.

Mercifully, after another only few hundred stairs, the stairway's end finally came into view.

* * *

"Halt here," Beornric called when it became clear that the endless staircase down through a tunnel of rock was finally proving to have an end after all.

By the light of those fishy oil lamps, Aefric could see that after only another fifty steps or so the tunnel mouth opened into a chamber of some kind, with a floor of black igneous rock.

"Deirdre," Beornric said, but before he could issue his order, Aefric cut in.

"Wait."

When Aefric had everyone's attention, he gestured for the knights and soldiers ahead of him to move to one side.

He extinguished his unneeded light atop the Brightstaff and looked through its large yellow diamond as he whispered the right words of power.

Five clear yellow images of the stairs ahead and the tunnel mouth opening at the end, including the flat rock flooring.

"No traps," he said.

"Depends on how you define a trap."

That was a woman's voice, and not one Aefric recognized. Strong, clear, confident. Raised and echoing as though carrying some distance, even though the speaker had obviously heard what Aefric had said in a conversational voice.

"Might as well come on down, Brightstaff," the voice said. "You and whoever you brought to back you. Not like I don't know you're here. And obviously you know I'm here. So enough with the foreplay. Let's get to it."

"Stick to the plan," Beornric said to the knights and soldiers. "Nothing's changed."

That brought a rough laugh from voice of the woman who had to be Nelazzi.

"Can I just go kill her, your grace?" Deirdre said. "I mean, if she's done with the foreplay, I'll be happy to jump straight to the climax."

"That's not Deirdre Ol'Miri is it?" Nelazzi laughed again. "Gods. Haven't seen you since you were a girl. What the hell are you doing bowing to the Brightstaff?"

Deirdre gave Aefric the first truly stunned look he'd ever seen on her face.

"I have no idea what she's talking about," she said, and Aefric could only nod to show he believed her.

Oddly though, Killian's expression was suspicious as he looked at Deirdre now. As though he actually worried she might be secretly working for the pirate queen.

"Let's go," Aefric said, anxious to rush down there, but forcing himself to be patient. "You all heard your captain."

The knights and soldiers resumed formation. All of them with ready weapons. Even Killian had his sword in hand and shield ready.

They reached the flooring and began to spread out.

Finally Aefric reached the flooring as well, and he could see what the new situation was.

A high, arching ceiling — easily a hundred feet at its apex — of black volcanic rock with only a few stalactites. Two of which stretched all the way down to meet two of the few stalagmites reaching up from the flooring.

No lamps down here, but there was light. Magical light. White and sourceless enough to prevent shadows, but not overly bright.

Interesting that there was magical light down here...

The cavern was too round to be natural — Aefric could feel that same vague thrum of clay and stone magic behind it — and probably two hundred feet across. A series of round wooden doors around the outside. None of them all that close together.

In the center of the cavern, a pool of boiling magma surrounded by a waist-high wall of black rock.

Sitting casually against that wall was the room's only visible occupant. The pirate queen. Nelazzi.

For a brief moment, Aefric almost thought she was too young to be Nelazzi. She looked only a handful of years older than he was. Dressed in a heavily embroidered bright blue silk shirt over tight brown leathers that disappeared inside calf-high black leather boots.

A gold buckle on the black leather belt that held her cutlass. Gold rings on each of her fingers, and all of them sparkling with gemstones. Sapphires, rubies, diamonds and emeralds. More gold in the necklace that disappeared into her shirt, and yet more gold in the three rings dangling from each ear.

Her black hair, loose and wild. Her brown eyes as arrogant as her smile. Not a scar or tattoo visible on her.

She might've been pretty, if she were anybody else. But that didn't matter anyway, because her appearance could've been as much of a lie as her age.

Nelazzi was a wizard. And a good one. The moment Aefric sensed her power he knew she was the one who had cast those wards and created their key. Even likely the one who'd done the clay and stone magic that formed that tunnel and stairs, as well as this cavern.

So she had power and subtlety. A dangerous combination.

"I see you understand," Nelazzi said, nodding. "Good. I hate explanations."

"Well I still want one," Deirdre said. "What the hell do you mean you know me?"

Nelazzi laughed. "Ask your mother sometime about what she

used to do for a living. Back before your daddy the knight made a *respectable* woman of her."

She made the word "respectable" sound like an insult.

Deirdre frowned. Shook her head. "No need. I'd believe Mom used to be a pirate."

"Used to be a damn good boatswain," Nelazzi said. "Back when I was sailing under another name." She nodded at Deirdre. "You look so much like her. And you don't belong with *them*. You're wild as I am. As your mother was. Come join me and live a better way."

Deirdre spat.

"Pity," Nelazzi said. "Hate to kill Moira's kid."

"Come try," Deirdre said, but Nelazzi had turned her attention back to Aefric.

"Knew this day would come soon as I heard some fool gave you a coastline. Trick was getting you here on my terms..."

She kept talking, but Aefric wasn't listening. Something was wrong with this scenario. Her tunnel. Her cavern. All her magic. And magma boiling, ready. She could turn this whole chamber into a deathtrap pretty quickly. Might even have a magical lynch pin waiting to be pulled.

That would kill *her* though...

No. Not necessarily. Not if she had a way to get to that ship, waiting in the harbor...

A ship that clearly had orders to drop anchor and wait in *just the right spot.*

"She can teleport," Aefric muttered to Karbin. "Ship's her escape hatch. Kill it."

Without a word Karbin teleported in a flash of light. And the moment he was gone, Aefric cast a special spell he'd learned from a Soulfist grimoire, but never had a reason to use himself.

It seemed that Duchess Arinda's great grandfather, Duke Arenott, had been frustrated that he'd never figured out how to teleport — none of the Soulfists ever did — so he figured out how to stop others from doing it in his presence. Just in case.

His spell created a ward against teleportation that would fit naturally into anyplace that had defined borders. The walls of his great hall worked for Duke Arenott, and this cavern would certainly work well enough for Aefric.

Nelazzi caught on too late. Tried to counter him, but Aefric had the words and gestures out before she could even *try* to break the power he'd quickly massed.

"No one's leaving until the party's over," Aefric said.

"Foolish boy," Nelazzi said. "The party's just starting."

Nelazzi stuck two fingers into her mouth and blew a piercing whistle.

———

AT THE SOUND OF NELAZZI'S PIERCING WHISTLE, TWO THINGS HAPPENED at the same time.

Doors burst open around the outside of the cavern, and pirates came charging out. At least two score of them, all carrying swords and shields, and wearing chainmail shirts and coifs. Shouting war cries that all blended into a white noise roar.

But the other thing was worse.

Out of the magma pool crawled four gammagan, humanoid creatures that looked twice too thick to be anything natural, and made of living lava. Or perhaps living igneous rock — for their torsos, limbs and featureless heads were all black, veined stone — but within their veins and cracks flowed steaming lava. And everywhere they touched, they dripped more lava.

"*Knights on the monsters,*" Beornric boomed out over the howls of the onrushing pirates. "*Soldiers with me on the pirates!*"

Unspoken went the obvious. Aefric would fight Nelazzi himself. With the Brightstaff in his right hand and the wand Garram in his left, he took to the air.

Nelazzi pulled her "cutlass," which turned out to be blunt and made of a blue-green stone Aefric had never seen before. Clearly more of a magic rod than a sword, but a weapon nonetheless.

She took to the air as well.

Below the clash of steel and shouts of combat began.

"Tell you what, boy," Nelazzi taunted loudly, "any of your people still living after I kill you will get to join my crew."

"And I'll tell *you* what," Aefric called back. "You and yours lay down arms and surrender, and I'll see you all get fair trials in Armyr."

Nelazzi laughed, and waved her stone cutlass. A waft of vivid green flames shot at Aefric. He countered them with a sheet of ice from his wand, and finished the movement by shooting more ice at the back of one of the gammagan.

The green flames didn't just melt the ice. They corroded it away. But the ice that hit the gammagan created an opening for one of Killian's knights to get in a good shot at its gut with a battleaxe.

"Afraid to use your lightning down here?" she shouted and laughed. This time a series of blue-green orbs shot out of the stone cutlass.

Oh, those were bad. Aefric knew that spell, or at least a variation on it. Whether the orbs would strike like hammers, burn like acid or fire, freeze like ice, or something else besides, they were a bad, bad thing. And unfortunately, that lovely protective bracer Aefric wore wouldn't do a bit of good against them.

The orbs swirled and wove as they flew at Aefric. He had to spin and juke in the air to try to keep them away. But each time he avoided one, it unerringly curved in the air until it was back on course, coming for him once more.

Just as he'd thought. They'd keep coming until they hit him.

Or at least, until they hit *something*.

He led them among the stalactites. And it worked. An orb hit a stalactite with a resounding *crack*, loud even over the echoing roar of the battle below.

Then the stalactite broke off and plunged down into the melee.

Shocked, Aefric twisted around to try to see what he'd done.

The distraction cost him. Orbs began to strike.

Hammer blows felt better than those orbs. Four of them pounded into his ribs and hips. Pain spiked all through his body, bad enough to redden his vision.

Worse, Nelazzi laughed triumphantly and sent more of those orbs after him. A dozen now, coming from all directions once more.

A dozen. He couldn't take a dozen more of those hits. And if he took the time to strike at her, they'd start pounding him to death.

He could summon a shield — like Karbin had with the crossbow bolts — but that would stop three or four at most before it fell. Not nearly enough.

The orbs homed in like flying death.

He had only one option. He angled himself to point at Nelazzi and trigged a power of the Brightstaff.

Aefric became a bolt of white lightning. Flashed through the cavern at Nelazzi, thunder in his wake.

Unfortunately, she must've had reflexes like Deirdre, because he didn't hit Nelazzi full on. Grazed her. And a graze wasn't enough to stop him. He slammed into the rock at the far end of the cavern, blasting it apart before becoming human once more.

Silence.

The sound and concussion of the blast left all the human combatants below momentarily stunned.

Too dangerous a situation for the knights, because the gammagan swung fists into chests, sending knights sprawling while their chest plates sizzled.

Aefric flew outward from the hole he'd put in the wall. Nelazzi's orbs were gone. They'd either struck rock, or vanished completely when their target disappeared.

Nelazzi. Somewhere in this cavern Nelazzi was momentarily stunned and vulnerable.

Aefric could end this fight right now...

But his knights were exposed. And the gammagan were closing in. Going for Nelazzi now meant letting knights die.

No. His knights were more important.

Aefric soared closer and channeled as much power as he could risk — including some of the magic flowing through his very veins — into the wand Garram's ice powers.

He hit all four gammagan with a volley of devastating ice shards the size of spears. Dozens of them slamming into each of the lava creatures.

The gammagan dried out, cracked, and crumbled apart, but the effort left Aefric sweaty and panting.

Still in the fight, though.

He looked about for his enemy. Saw the state of the battlefield. A number of pirates were down, but so were a few of his soldiers. But now, with the gammagan out of the way, the knights wasted no time joining the soldiers. With Beornric shouting commands, and Deirdre acting as a one-woman flanking force, Aefric felt confident they'd soon turn the battle into a route.

So where was Nelazzi?

She couldn't have *fled*...

Aefric almost cast a spell to contact Karbin, but then he spotted her.

Alas, she hadn't been killed by the lightning strike.

Admittedly, Aefric never really thought she *would* be, but there was always a *chance*. Unfortunately, not only was she very much alive, she hardly looked much more than badly *singed* as she took to the air again, fury in her eyes.

But then she held up her magic stone cutlass. Or rather, what remained of it.

Most of that blue-green stone was gone. What she held now was little more than a golden hilt with a bit of blue-green stem sticking out. No magic left to it at all.

With an angry roar she threw the useless junk aside.

Aefric smiled.

"You destroyed my cutlass!" she screamed. "That's it. You get my special treat!"

She reached into her shirt.

Aefric unleashed a powerful firebolt from his wand.

Damn her reflexes. She managed to dodge most of that as well. Though he was pretty sure he at least caught her along the hips.

Out of her shirt she pulled a small onyx figurine.

She flung it in the air, crying out a word Aefric didn't recognize. Not a word of power then, but a trigger word for the figurine.

In the air the figurine became a bat demon. Ten feet tall, onyx black, and hairy through its thick, muscled body. With glowing red eyes and spittle dripping acid.

Aefric started to dodge to one side, preparing a bolt of lightning from the Brightstaff, but then he recognized something.

Aefric had spent a good deal of time studying that ward key. The magic of the ward passage part, yes, but more importantly just now, the illusion work that had disguised that passage part.

He knew the feel of that illusion — and the identifying characteristics of the wizard who'd cast it — nearly as well as he knew the work of say, Karbin or Kainemorton.

And he felt that same sense of illusion right now.

He broke the bat-demon illusion with a single word of power focused straight into the spell's lynchpin.

The bat-demon popped out of existence.

Nelazzi edged away a little. Aefric moved forward to counter. Just in case she tried to flee.

"You forget," he said with a smirk. "I know your illusions."

"I forget nothing," Nelazzi said with a grin. "And now you're *right* where I want you."

Aefric realized then that the fighting — and especially his efforts with the gammagan — had brought him right back into the center of the cavern.

Right above the pool of magma.

Magma that came shooting up at him.

Aefric had made the fool's mistake of flying right over a pool of boiling magma. Even knowing that Nelazzi had mastered enough of the magic of clay and stone to use it against him.

And now that whole pool of magma came blasting up at him like a fountain.

No time to get away. No chance of using that lightning trick again. He could only do it once between sunrises. He could create walls or shields out of thin air, but they'd be no help. The shields wouldn't even slow the magma down. The walls would, but force of the magma's momentum would use his own wall to crush him against the ceiling.

He knew a spell that could allow him to walk through solid rock, but that was useless against magma.

One advantage to old adventuring reflexes though. All those ideas flashed into and out of his thoughts so fast they took no time at all. Leaving him with exactly enough time to try one thing.

He curled in as tightly as he could and threw all of his remaining power through the wand Garram, to create a huge sphere of thick, solid ice. Completely encasing him. Barely leaving him room to breathe.

The magma hit.

He was thrown upwards like a ball, even as the boiling magma began melting away the ice. As though it were hungry to reach his tender flesh.

Cracking sounds everywhere as Aefric battled to hold on to consciousness against expending so much power so fast.

His ice sphere smashed into the ceiling. Cracks formed behind him from the shock of the blow. More cracks ahead of him, as wet, icy chunks melted free.

Now Aefric was falling through the air. Surrounded by more falling ice.

But the magma. It was falling too. Ahead of him.

That was bad.

Wait. No. That was good. If the magma was *there* and he was *here*, it wasn't burning him. That was good.

No. No. Bad was right. Because the falling magma might hit the ground *first*, but he was right behind it.

And he wasn't just going to hit the ground. Hard. No. He was going to hit a *pool of magma*. Hard.

Yeah. Aefric was looking at his death.

And he'd never—

No.

Not like this.

There had to be *something* he could do. Some way to save himself. Always had been before. Problem was, he couldn't think straight. His mind, it just moved *so slowly*. And he felt like he was down to his last drop of power. If that.

And he was so *wet*. Positively *soaked*. And strangely cold, for some reason.

Oh. Right. The ice.

That slow fall spell. How did that—

Something slammed into Aefric's back and side. Right in one of the places an orb had struck him. He cried out from the pain.

What hit him? Some Nelazzi spell? No. No. Whatever hit him was still clinging to him.

A person then?

No.

Yes?

Maybe?

If so, it was a person wearing one *hell* of a lot of metal. Even wrapped a metal arm and hand around Aefric's head.

Oh! A *knight*!

That made sense. Most knights ran around wearing a hell of a lot of metal.

Heh. That was a funny thought. Hell. When he'd been falling into magma.

One of the thirteen hells had lots of magma. Or was it lava there? There was a difference between the two, but—

Aefric's side slammed *hard* into the rocky ground. His head hit too, but it hit that metal arm and hand. Which hurt, but wasn't nearly as bad as all the pain coming from his ribs and back and butt and waist and...

Breathing. Breathing would be nice. Why was there no air here?

Was this one of the thirteen hells? Certainly hot enough...

Aefric shook his head, getting at least some of his sense back.

He'd had the wind knocked out of him. All right. He could deal with that. He'd bruised or broken some bones too. Not good, but livable.

Someone was moaning in pain. No. *Two* people were moaning in pain. One was him. The other was...

Oh. That person in all the metal, lying half-atop him. Sounded like ... Vria?

But where was...

There. Nelazzi. Floating high in the air. Coming down slowly from the ceiling right above him.

"I must thank you, Brightstaff," she said. "I'll miss my stone cutlass, but you killed some useless bastards for me out on the pier. And you and yours taught the others here a lesson the survivors will remember for quite some time."

Aefric would have loved a snappy comeback. But he didn't have the air. And he couldn't think of one anyway.

All he could think to do was roll Vria off of him, so whatever Nelazzi did didn't hit her too.

Vria started getting to her feet. Moving as though she intended to shield Aefric with her body.

Nelazzi waved a hand and threw his knight-savior aside.

No more sounds of combat. Moans from the wounded and dying. Boots on rock, too. A few shouts, but they didn't matter.

Nelazzi mattered.

So many spells Aefric knew. But he couldn't get enough breath to even whisper any. Plus, he was pretty sure he was tapped out after that ice sphere.

Some he could have cast in silence, but the only ones that would have hurt that arrogant pirate required more focus and power than he could manage just then.

Even the Brightstaff's powers were beyond him at the moment.

He tried a spell anyway. Tried to set her clothes on fire with the little nothing magic he'd first used to light candles as an apprentice.

Hey. His left hand was empty. Where was his wand?

Nelazzi dispersed his feeble attempt at a spell with a derisive laugh as she floated down above him, descending oh so slowly.

"I know, I know," she said. "There's still Karbin to deal with, and he'll put up a fight." She smiled. "But on the other hand, after I finish off your minions here, I'll have the Brightstaff to help me."

Aefric realized then that his people had brought no ranged weapons. All those pikes and no spears. All those swords, and no bows.

Was Nelazzi right? Was killing off his knights, his soldiers, his *prince* now just a matter of time for her?

A maroon blur through the air said otherwise.

From out of nowhere, Deirdre came leaping to land on Nelazzi's back.

Nelazzi swore. Went for a dagger.

Too late. Deirdre hadn't bothered with her sword, and her red-limned dueling dagger was poised at Nelazzi's throat.

"Surrender," Deirdre said, "or I'll personally make sure your head gets a tour of every port on the Risen Sea."

Nelazzi hesitated.

"Do you really want to test the nerve of Moira's daughter?" Deirdre asked.

Nelazzi threw down her dagger in disgust and surrendered.

***

By the time Aefric managed to sit up on the black rock floor of Nelazzi's cavern, the situation seemed to be well in hand.

The gammagan were hardly more than crumbling chunks of dried rock.

The pirates were dead or fleeing. Some through side doors, others up the stairs.

Up the stairs? Aefric snorted. *That* would be a long run.

Nelazzi herself was now on her knees, bound by her own belt, with her wrists and ankles strapped tightly together behind her. Deirdre stood over her, red-limned dagger in hand, making sure the fallen pirate queen didn't try any spells.

Killian and two of his knights stood near her. The prince looked upset about something. Or maybe he was just angry at Nelazzi. But there was blood on his sword — and on his sword arm — so he couldn't complain he'd been kept out of the fighting.

Of course, if Killian wanted to trade wounds, Aefric would've been willing.

Pretty much every part of his body hurt, and not just a little. In fact, the only spot that didn't was under his left shoulder. Why that alone should have escaped the battering punishment that the rest of his body complained of, Aefric didn't know. But he suspected that the contrast with *one unharmed* bit of his body made everything else feel that much worse.

One good thing about the Brightstaff, though. Even apart from its magic, it was a staff. Which made it useful at times like this to help him get to his feet, and stay on his feet.

"How are you holding up?" Beornric asked as he approached. The older knight's eyes were wary as he looked Aefric over.

"Well, I can breathe again, and I think only one of my ribs is broken." Aefric shook his head. "Hurt like hell, though. Where do we stand?"

"Thirty pirates dead or wounded. Fifteen more fleeing. Easy enough to catch, if we want to put in the time to hunt them down."

"Any of ours?"

Beornric nodded grimly. "Among the soldiers, five dead, ten more wounded badly. They all have some hurt, though."

"Who are the dead?"

"Dartan, Olin, Pohl, Zel, and Khora."

"Gods, Zel and Olin weren't much more than a year into their majority. And—"

"They knew the risks, your grace," Beornric said gently. "As did we all. They fought honorably and died well, doing something worth doing for a liege they believed in. Their spirits will be content."

"Their families won't."

"Their families will mourn them even more than we do. It's true. But we're going to *war* soon, your grace."

"And soldiers die in war, I know. I'm just not used to being the one giving the orders."

"Then consider this your first taste of a bitter fruit you'll have to swallow from time to time. There's no way around it."

Aefric sighed and nodded, but his guts had tied themselves into a knot they wouldn't ease anytime soon. And he knew it.

He drew a deep breath and blew it out. "What of our knights?"

"The knights came off much better. We all have bruises or small cuts or both, of course. And some have sprains, or bruised or broken ribs from those lava monsters. But the worst off is Vria."

"How is she?"

"Hit her head when she landed with you. She's regained consciousness, but got her bell rung pretty hard. Good thing she had her helmet on though, or it would've been a lot worse."

"How'd she save me?"

"Grabbed a pike off the ground and used it like a catapult arm with her as the missile. Carried her right into you." Beornric shook his head. "Never seen anything like it."

"I'll be sure to thank her," Aefric said, wincing as a twitching muscle lanced another round of pain through his torso. "I don't suppose you saw what happened to my wand? I dropped it ... somewhere in there."

"Someone find the duke's wand," Beornric called out, and some of the soldiers who were not busy with the wounded or the dead began to search for it.

"Now," Aefric said, "we need to deal with Nelazzi."

Beornric nodded. Fell into step beside Aefric and the two walked over.

"Good to see you up and moving, your grace," Deirdre said without looking. "Can't believe Vria got to you first."

"I'm sure she'll tease you about it later," Aefric said with a smile that faded like the sunset as he turned to Nelazzi.

"So," she said. "Will I get that trial you offered? I did surrender, after all. Or was that just talk?"

"You'll get your trial," Aefric said, nodding and immediately wishing he didn't. Pain in his neck spread through his skull. He grimaced and leaned a little harder on the Brightstaff.

"Good to see you at least came out of this worse for wear, Brightstaff," Nelazzi taunted. "Hope your joints make you remember me when it rains."

"Enough of this," Aefric said. "Where are they?"

Nelazzi did her best to shrug. "Who? The scum who went running before the fight was done?"

"The princesses," Aefric said. "Where have you hidden them?"

Nelazzi started laughing.

"No games," Aefric said. "You're beaten. Give them up."

"You think I stole them for *me*?" Nelazzi said, still laughing. "You think I want to listen to pampered quiffs moan about how they miss their silk sheets and fancy food?"

"Where?" Aefric said, undaunted.

"I'm a *pirate*, you fool!" Nelazzi said. "They were just cargo. Sold before they were even stolen."

"Sold to *whom*?" Aefric said.

"Like I'm going to tell *you*," she said.

"You'll tell me or you'll tell the justiciar. Easier on you if you tell me now."

"Justiciar," Nelazzi scoffed. "By the time you get me under a three-edged sword, won't matter what I know. Client'll already have done ... whatever they want those princesses for."

"Maybe we can make a deal," Aefric said.

"You don't have the authority," Killian said suddenly.

Nelazzi turned her head to look at Killian for the first time. As she looked him over, one of Aefric's soldiers handed him the wand Garram, which made Aefric relax a bit. He'd been half-afraid it had fallen into the magma. He slipped the wand back into its sheath at his belt.

"So *that's* who you are," Nelazzi said to Killian. "Thought you looked like just another pampered quiff yourself. But you're that pretty prince I've been hearing about."

Deirdre, however, wouldn't let Nelazzi change the subject.

"She's not your prisoner, your highness," Deirdre said carefully. "She's the duke's prisoner. If the duke wants to offer a deal, he has the right."

"How about I finish a sentence, Killian," Aefric said. "How would that be?"

Killian frowned and narrowed his eyes, but he nodded.

Nelazzi laughed. "Run a tight ship, don't you, Brightstaff? Gods. If one of my captains were this sloppy, I'd work him over so hard he'd be *grateful* when I finally got around to the keel-haul."

"Here's the deal," Aefric said. "You tell me who you sold those princesses to, and I won't throw your grimoires into that magma pool."

"You wouldn't," Nelazzi said. "They're too valuable to you. And anyway, you'll never find them."

"I've cracked the secrets of your illusions," Aefric said. "I'll find them easily enough. And as for their value, well, I look at it this way. Right now I'm betting that you think you're getting out of this. That you've got enough friends — or at least enough people wanting to kiss your ass — that you figure someone will help you escape justice. Like Calder did for Gwawl."

Nelazzi didn't say anything, but she smiled, certainty shining in her eyes.

"Yeah, you have a lot of friends," Aefric said. "Eyes in every port, so they say."

"Not just seaports either," she said. "Rivers. Lakes. Wherever there's a port, I have friends."

"Exactly," Aefric said. "So I'm betting that you figure on not only escaping, but stealing back your grimoires from me. Maybe adding my own, if you can."

Nelazzi didn't say anything, but she didn't have to.

"But if I throw your grimoires into the magma right in front of you—"

"Well," Nelazzi said, "then you'd have to be fool enough to think I don't have copies stashed somewhere for safe keeping."

She sounded confident. But was that *just* a hint of uncertainty in her eyes? Was she bluffing?

Karbin flew into the cavern and didn't land until he was beside Aefric.

He looked pained. And he had the stubs of two crossbow bolts sticking out of him. One in his left thigh and the other on the right side of his ribs. In both places, his robes were wet with blood.

"Couldn't teleport ... straight here," he said, sounding about as weary as Aefric had heard him in some time.

"Sorry," Aefric said. "The block's still up."

Karbin nodded.

Nelazzi looked him over.

"You sank *The Squid's Revenge*?" she asked.

Karbin nodded.

"Did Gwawl escape?"

"Why should I tell you?" Karbin asked.

"Just a second," Aefric said. "Nelazzi was just about to tell me who she sold the princesses to, to prevent me from throwing her grimoires into that magma pool."

"Do it," she said. "If I have to start fresh, I'll—"

Her words were cut off because Killian Stronghand, Crown Prince of Armyr, thrust his sword through her chest.

For a moment, even Deirdre was too shocked to do anything more than stand there while Killian withdrew his sword from the dying form of Nelazzi, former pirate queen of the Risen Sea.

About five people, including Aefric, Beornric and Karbin, got as far as, "*What*—" before the cavern started rumbling.

"Dead man spell," Karbin said quickly.

"Grab the wounded!" Aefric yelled. "Run for the stairs. Everyone! Out! Now!"

Dust started falling from the cavern ceiling. Cracks spiderwebbed their way across the dome of black rock.

One of Killian's knights shouldered Nelazzi's corpse while Karbin summoned a pair of *Nester's platters*, great silvery floating discs that could carry quite a bit of weight.

Aefric raised a hand to summon one of his own, but Beornric grabbed that hand.

"You're *spent*, Beornric said. "Can you even fly?"

"No," he admitted, "but—"

Chunks of rock started falling.

"Move!" Beornric said. "Get yourself out. I'll see to the rest."

"But—"

"I've got him," Deirdre said, grabbing Aefric and swinging him over her shoulder like a sack of wheat.

One of Aefric's cracked ribs broke, and fresh pain tore through his system as Deirdre began sprinting for the stairs.

And then the race was on. All of them fleeing for the stairs as the cavern began to cave in on itself.

But the stairs weren't much better. Because the rumbling came from the tunnel all around them. More dust began to fall.

Aefric tried to hold on against the pain. But with Deirdre running up the stairs, he bounced with every stride. And every bounce was a fresh volley of pain.

The world gained a sheen of red. His heartbeat thundered in his ears. He started feeling even hotter than that pool of magma...

That was the last thing Aefric noticed before he passed out.

<hr>

Aefric woke with someone gently slapping his cheek over and over.

He groaned to show he was awake. His head pounded like Nelazzi's orbs were hitting it. Pretty much every part of his body was screaming at him that whatever it had done, it was sorry, and would he please just stop all the pain.

Didn't help that he was lying on hard-packed sand. What he would have given for his nice, comfy bed right then.

Weather would've been better, too, at Water's End. It was still too warm here. And stifling, with the humidity.

People were shouting at each other, but Aefric couldn't quite make sense of whatever they were yelling about.

He managed to flutter his eyes open. The skies were dark, but there was light. That generalized, unfocused light that only came from spells.

His?

No. He'd been unconscious for a while. Had to be Karbin's work then.

The slaps had come from Arras, who knelt over Aefric, helm off, and her short black hair matted with sweat and at least a little blood. She nodded as Aefric and said, "Micham."

Micham, who'd been standing over her, gave a whistle so loud and sharp it cut through the yelling.

"His grace is awake," Arras said, and helped Aefric to his feet.

Standing. Standing was a bad idea. Just changing angles hurt so much that every breath seemed to cue a dozen daggers to stab him. And his right leg didn't want to support him at all.

But he was needed. He knew that. So he called on the focusing techniques that let him cast difficult spells, even under the worst conditions.

And Aefric straightened himself up on one leg as best he could.

The Brightstaff was suddenly there, beside him, waiting for his hand. It helped, but he did still lean on Arras as he took in the situation.

The knights were facing off. Beornric and Oudin at the heart of it — standing over the body of Nelazzi — each with the expected knights supporting him.

Killian stood between them, just to one side, arms crossed. Facing him, Deirdre, looking fit for murder.

No one had drawn weapons. That much was good.

Karbin sagged more than stood, and well off to the side. Most of his remaining focus likely on just maintaining those *platters* that held the wounded. The dead soldiers lay on the ground near him.

If he needed this much focus to maintain two spells as simple as *Nester's platter*, he was near the end of his tether himself.

"All right," Aefric said heavily. "What's the yelling about?"

"Where shall we start?" Deirdre asked.

"It all comes down to Nelazzi," Killian said.

"Yes," Aefric said. "Nelazzi. The prisoner you murdered."

For a moment it was quiet enough to hear the breeze. And apparently some very loud insects buzzing from the nearby jungles.

Nearby?

Ah. They were standing just outside what had once been Nelazzi's house. Out behind it, the nearest foothills were now a very big sinkhole.

The rest of her little buildings stood between them and the pier.

"I executed a pirate," Killian said with disdain in his voice.

"No," Aefric said. "You do not have the right of high justice. You do not have the authority to execute anyone. Even if we *were* in Armyr, which we are not at the moment."

"She was a prisoner of Armyr, and we both know she was going to be found guilty and executed. I just saved us time and money."

"No," Aefric said, with diminishing patience. He wanted food. And sleep. And ideally a cleric of Nilasah. "You see, your highness, you denied her a fair — and might I add, *very public* — trial. You denied *any* of the populace she'd terrorized the right to *see* their bogeyman executed."

"Details," Killian said.

"And now you're about caught up," Beornric grumbled.

"You've done her a favor," Aefric said. "By murdering her in cold blood this way—"

"I most certainly did *not*."

"*You executed a bound prisoner who had given her surrender.*"

"I executed a prisoner who was on her way to the gallows anyway."

"That wasn't your call to make."

"I'm the prince of Armyr. Absent my father's presence—"

"I am a duke and a peer of the realm."

"You don't outrank me, Aefric."

Aefric wasn't convinced of that, and almost insisted on his courtesy there. Had to bite down on his cheek to keep from driving a permanent wedge between him and the man who would one day be his king.

Even if that man was turning out to be an arrogant fool.

"Do you remember the conversation we had before I agreed to allow you to come along on this venture?" Aefric asked, voice tense enough that his tension spread through the knights.

"Of course," Killian said.

"Then whose venture is this? Who is in charge?"

Killian stifled a sigh, but nodded. "You are."

"I am." He pointed to the corpse. "Which makes her *my* prisoner. Not yours. Not your father's. Mine."

Killian didn't say anything, which had to have meant he agreed. Or at least knew he'd lose the argument there if he objected.

"As such, if anyone was going to execute her here and now, it should have been me. *My* choice. *My* call to make. Correct?"

Killian frowned and looked away.

"Am I correct?" Aefric said.

Killian gave a rough nod.

"Which means..."

"Very well, Aefric," Killian said. "You're like a dog with a bone when you've got a point to make, aren't you? All right. I should have asked your permission first. Which means I suppose I owe you an apology."

Killian didn't get it. For one reason or another, he honestly didn't see why what he did was wrong.

Yes, Nelazzi was just about as guilty and evil as they came. But to simply murder her that way. That wasn't any better.

Clearly King Colm had doted too much on his son. Failed to impart some critical lessons about the truths of justice.

But Aefric could correct none of that right now. They all had to get on the ship, and get that ship in motion. If the princesses weren't here, he'd accomplished only half of his objective, and still had the other half to worry about.

Plus, oh, yes, that *war* he was supposed to fight in just about two aetts.

"All right," Aefric said. "We're all tired, hungry and hurting. We all need to get aboard the ship. At least we have her body to display. Grisly a thought as that is, it may help keep rumors from spreading that she still lives."

Oudin picked up the corpse of Nelazzi, while soldiers gathered their own dead. Karbin started the *platters* towards the ship, and they all began moving that way.

Deirdre — apparently the least hurt of everyone — took over for Arras in helping support Aefric on his way back to the ship.

To Aefric's surprise, Killian fell into step on his other side.

"I *am* sorry, Aefric," he said. "I didn't think you'd be so upset."

Aefric bit down his first response. "Why did you do it? The real reason."

Killian grimaced.

"I know, I know," he said quietly. "All that prisoner-surrender stuff. I know all that. Technically, you're right, too. Even if you, yourself, admitted she was likely to escape before she ever saw the executioner's block."

"I admitted no such thing," Aefric said. "I was playing to her vanity to gain information."

"Perhaps. But you must admit that escape was a serious threat in her case. So, in that sense, I only ensured that justice was done."

Aefric didn't trust himself to say anything to that one. And beside him, he could hear Deirdre quietly scoffing at the prince.

"But I think, just between the two of us," Killian said, apparently ignoring Deirdre's presence, "I can admit that I had another reason as well."

"I suspected as much," Aefric said, in as neutral a tone as he could manage.

"I got into *some* of the fighting down there," Killian said. "Which was good. But really, I didn't *do* much. Killed only *one* pirate before I took that slice to the arm, and wasn't much good for the rest of the fight."

He shook his head. Held up the arm. Showed free movement with it.

"Wasn't much more than a scratch, either," he said. "Hardly touched the meat. But at the time, it felt like I was going to bleed to death. And my hand just *did not* want to cooperate." He shook his head. "If I hadn't had my shield, I might not've survived."

"Wimp," Deirdre whispered, and Aefric had to bite down to keep from smiling.

"So I traveled all this way," Killian said. "Got into a big battle with pirates, and that's all I came away with? One kill? A scratch that won't even scar? Hardly much of a story in that, is there? Not something I could build a reputation around, you know?"

There was no way Aefric could've phrased his question without including the words *murder* and *prisoner*, so he held his tongue. But it wasn't easy.

Or necessary, as it turned out, because Killian answered him anyway.

"But now..." He smiled an altogether inappropriate smile. "Now *I'm* the man who killed the pirate queen Nelazzi. *That* is a story to start building my name on."

"It's a *lie*," Deirdre said, tight rage in her voice. "*His grace* fought her to a standstill, allowing *me* to capture her. All *you* did was shove a sword through the chest of a helpless, beaten woman."

"Ah, but I can swear under the three-edged sword that I killed her," Killian said, apparently considerably less worried about Deirdre's tone — not to mention the look in those jade green eyes — than Aefric thought he should've been.

"I'm prince now," Killian continued, "and later I'll be king. I can tell whatever story I want, safe in the confidence that even the test of a justiciar will confirm that I'm the one who killed her. And because of my rank, when I tell my story with the confidence that comes from underpinnings of truth, no one will *dare* risk testing me. Which means I'm free to invent the rest of the details as I choose."

He rubbed his hands together. "Oh, it will make a thrilling tale. You'll back me in it, won't you, Aefric?"

He clapped Aefric on the shoulder. Aefric moaned as a fresh wave of pain whisked through him.

"Please don't do that," he said through gritted teeth. "Perhaps you've escaped serious injury, but I'm hurt pretty much everywhere."

In fact, the only place Aefric wasn't hurting was under that left shoulder still. Which meant that Deirdre's supporting him didn't hurt.

Which was about the only good thing Aefric could think of at the moment.

BACK ON THE SHIP, BEORNRIC AND DEIRDRE BOTH TRIED TO CONVINCE Aefric to go straight to his cabin, as Killian had done.

Aefric wouldn't hear of it.

He still needed support, but even before the *Swift Wave* finished casting off, he went to every knight and soldier on that ship.

He began with the dead. Taking a moment to say a few words and honor each of them there and then, though the full funeral service he had in mind would have to wait until they returned to Water's End.

Then, on to the living.

His soldiers and knights were nearly all wounded, so he started with the worst off among the soldiers. He sat with each for a time, listening to their tale of the battle. Offering what little help he could in his own pained state.

He thanked them for their fierceness in battle that day. And made sure they knew what a difference they'd made in the lives of the citizens first of his own coastline, and then throughout all the ports on the Risen Sea.

He worked his way through all of the soldiers that way first. Then he went to Killian's knights, who were a little more close-mouthed about the battle. And their wounds.

Looked to Aefric as though they didn't like what their prince had done, but wouldn't speak against him. So they compromised by trying to hold their silence entirely.

Aefric thanked them each individually all the same. And made his point about all the people they'd helped in doing what they'd done that day.

His Knights of the Lake were next, starting with Vria, who had to be forced to rest by the others.

"Head blows are no laughing matter," Temat said. "You'll stay in your hammock or I'll sit on you."

They were all laughing about that image when Aefric approached, with Deirdre still supporting.

"Every time I think I know what to expect from you six," he said, smiling, "you exceed my expectations. Every single time."

He let Deirdre ease him to a sitting position on a crate, while the other knights gathered around.

"Tell me how the fight went for all of you."

"Those lava monsters," Wardius said to start. "They were worse than those stone men in the Dragonscar."

The others all agreed.

"I dulled two good blades on them," Arras said. "And I'm not sure I ever really hurt them."

"Cut them and they bleed lava on your sword," Leppina complained. "We'll all need new weapons when we get back."

"And I'll be paying for them, don't doubt it," Aefric said.

"And they hit like a *lance*," Micham said.

"Like Wardius, on his charger," Temat said.

"Harder," Vria said, to a round of agreement.

"And my lance never did more than *dent* your armor," Wardius said, gesturing to his scarred breastplate.

"Lucky thing that lava cooled fast," Leppina said. "We'd've *all* been dead."

"We would've anyway," Vria said. "If your grace hadn't rained a holy hell of ice on them."

The knights were all agreeing, but Aefric shook his head.

"*I* didn't beat them," he said. "*We* did. I couldn't have done any of it without you. Without all of you. We fight as one, and we win as one."

He gave them the knight's salute and they bowed to him.

"And never forget," he said. "We didn't just stop Nelazzi today. We saved towns and cities all around the Risen Sea from her attacks and plunder. To say nothing of countless ships."

"Does your grace really think her organization will die with her?"

"I think without her keeping her captains in line, they'll fight each other over what remains of an organization that had already been dealt a deep wound. There will always be pirates. And gods know another Nelazzi will rise one day. But for now, we've done some good."

He gave them a moment to acknowledge that.

"Now I've been trying to help people with their wounds—"

"Go rest, your grace," Micham said. "You're worse off than any of us."

"Maybe not worse off than Vria," Temat said.

"I'm *fine*," Vria insisted. "Don't make me prove it."

"Vria," Aefric said, and waited until she finished glaring at Temat and turned her attention to him.

"Your grace," she said.

"I'm going to go eat, and rest, and heal. And I expect you to do the same without an argument."

"Yes, your grace."

"And when we get back, I'll figure out some way to give you a commendation for your quick thinking with that pike. You saved my life. Don't doubt it. And I won't forget it."

"Only doing my duty, your grace, and proud to serve."

He gave her a salute of her own, then let Deirdre guide him out. His legs were on the verge of giving up entirely.

"Your cabin?" she asked, and before he could answer, she added, "Karbin's already sworn to go straight to sleep as soon as the ship's surgeon's done with him. You can thank him in the morning."

"There's still Beornric."

Beornric, it turned out, was waiting on the deck for Aefric's return.

"I cannot believe you're still up and moving, your grace," he said. "Deirdre, I was *sure* you'd have him in bed by now."

"In his current state? I'd probably just hurt... Oh. You meant resting."

"If you can stand the idea."

"He's still awake and talking, you know," Aefric said.

"I know," Beornric said. "And I know what you're doing. But my bruises aren't that bad. My story can keep. I know I have your thanks. I know who all we helped today. Now go to your cabin and I'll bring you some food."

"And I'll see that he eats it," Deirdre said.

Aefric chuckled. "Never pictured you as a nursemaid."

"For good reason," she said.

Together she and the Brightstaff got him back to his cabin. She was reaching for the oil lamps when he lit up the Brightstaff's diamond.

"Hate the smell of burning whale oil," Aefric said, groaning as he eased down onto his hammock.

It seemed as though every ache in his body approved of the change for a moment, then began a fresh round of complaints about how much every inch of him hurt.

"It's not ideal, I admit," Deirdre said, looking him over. Sighed. "We need to get you out of those clothes, but you should probably eat first."

"Right," Aefric said with a weak smile. "Dinner first."

Deirdre shot him a lopsided grin. "I believe that's my line, your grace."

"True," he said, "but I won't be good for much beyond conversation for a while anyway."

"Nonsense," she said. "We'll have you on your feet before you know it."

A knock on the door. Beornric's knock.

"Come," Aefric called, which brought a smirk from Deirdre.

Beornric entered carrying a bowl of savory beef stew, along with a rye roll and a skin of beer.

"What about Deirdre?" Aefric asked, but Deirdre answered before Beornric could.

"A knight brings his wounded liege a meal, he's just doing his duty," she said. "He carries a meal for someone else at the same time, he's doing servant work."

She accepted the food from Beornric, who nodded and left.

Deirdre came over, shoving a chest closer with one boot.

"What about you?" Aefric asked.

"I'll eat in a bit. When you're sleeping."

"I can't sleep yet," Aefric said, trying to sit up. "I—"

"Hush, Aefric," Deirdre said softly. "Whatever it is, it can wait. We have to take care of *you* first."

"I can feed myself at least."

"Or," she said casually, "you can be quiet and enjoy something I don't do for many."

She actually began spooning the thick soup into his mouth. It was good. Better than the previous. The beef was tastier, and the carrots, peas and potatoes too.

Must've been a fresh-made batch.

As she fed him, Deirdre spoke.

"The last person I did this for was my mother," she said quietly. "This was years ago. When I'd returned, fresh from training, and about to go out into the world and seek my fortune. Gods, I was young and stupid.

"But I was smart enough to go home one more time first. Mom was down with something. Healer'd already been there. Dad said the cause was gone, but Mom had waited too long before agreeing to see the healer.

"She never did trust them." Deirdre smirked. "Probably the pirate in her. Anyway, I'd arrived just in time. The healer'd done her work and swore she'd recover. *If* she lived through the night.

"She was so weak." Deirdre shook her head. "I couldn't believe it. She'd always been so strong. Like nothing could touch her. Ever meet someone like that?"

Aefric cocked an eyebrow at her. "A name does come to mind."

Deirdre gave him a small smile.

"Anyway," she said, and by now the soup was gone and she was tearing up his roll for him, interspersed with sips of rich, dark beer. "I sat with her all night. Fed her. Washed her. Told her stories. Got pretty bad not long before dawn. She started sweating and shaking like her insides were fighting to get out.

"But she made it through." Deirdre shook her head in wonder. "Sometimes I think that woman could survive anything."

"I'd like to meet her someday," Aefric said.

"Maybe," Deirdre said with a shrug. "If I can guarantee she'll behave."

"Her daughter doesn't," Aefric said, chuckling around the last of the roll. "Why should she?"

"I will *not* have my mother seducing you," Deirdre said firmly. "That would just be *too* weird."

Aefric choked out bits of roll. "Seducing?"

"Oh, I doubt she would," Deirdre said. "She's *devoted* to Dad. But technically she's a knight's wife, which makes her a noble, and in Armyr…"

"Well, if she tries I'll say no."

"I don't think you appreciate how persuasive my mother can be."

"I'll … try to keep it in mind."

"All right," Deirdre said, rubbing her hands together. "Dinner's all eaten, yes?"

Aefric nodded.

"Let's get you out of those clothes."

And despite her teasing tone, she was remarkably quick and efficient in stripping Aefric. Not to mention gentle. And once he was naked, she looked him over in a very different way than she usually did.

She touched him here and there. Each place a pain, but never the worst of his pains. And as she did, she muttered something and nodded to herself.

"You're *not* going to tell me you're a healer," Aefric said.

"No," she said with a grimace. "But I've seen my share of fights, and learned a few things. Plus" — she wiggled her eyebrows — "I have a few secrets of my own."

From a leather pouch at her belt she pulled a small jar. She unscrewed the top, and a surprisingly pleasant herbal smell wafted out.

"What's that?" Aefric asked.

"This," she said, holding it up, "is an excellent excuse to put my hands *all over* your body." She fluttered her lashes. "Purely for medicinal reasons, of course."

She began rubbing that unguent onto him. Not slathering it on, either, but only using small amounts. Nevertheless, everywhere the unguent touched him, relief began to spread.

It was too much. The pure relief overwhelmed him and he passed out before she even finished his chest.

———

THE NEXT TIME AEFRIC'S EYES OPENED, HE FELT GOOD.

Really good.

Better than he'd felt in days. And thinking clearer, too.

He was even hungry again.

Aefric lay naked under a blanket in the hammock in his cabin aboard the *Swift Wave*. The smells of wood, varnish and creosote overlay the sea air.

He sat up. The Brightstaff still stood beside his hammock, filling the cabin with a warm glow from its diamond.

He saw Deirdre. She'd moved a chest against the door, and fallen asleep sitting on that chest with her rapier across her lap.

She looked surprisingly peaceful for someone who clearly expected trouble.

"Deirdre," Aefric said softly.

Her eyes snapped open and suddenly she was on her feet. Didn't stand. Didn't hop. Just one moment she was asleep, seated, leaning against the cabin door. The next moment she was on her feet, eyes assessing for threats.

She nodded to herself and turned to Aefric, sheathing her rapier.

"While I appreciate your standing guard last night," he said, "I must ask why you felt it necessary."

"Two reasons, your grace," she said, walking closer as she spoke. "First, I wasn't altogether happy with the attitudes of Prince Killian's knights when we got back to the ship last night. They acted like plotters. And I wanted to make sure they weren't plotting against *you*."

"I think they were just upset after watching their prince murder a prisoner. It couldn't have sat well with them."

"Most likely," Deirdre said. "But I wanted *certainty*."

"Fair enough," Aefric said. "What's the other reason?"

"Oh, I'd've thought that obvious."

When it clearly wasn't, she frowned, and said, "Oh. Right. You did take at least one blow to the head in the middle of all that." She cocked her head slightly and touched her chin. "Probably should've used more unguent on your scalp."

"I feel fine," Aefric said. "But I'm clearly missing something."

"About fifteen somethings," Deirdre said.

"The escaping pirates," Aefric said. "You think some of them might've snuck aboard? Without the crew knowing?"

"Again," she said with a shrug. "Not likely. But I prefer certainty where your grace's safety is concerned."

"Thank you," Aefric said.

"Anytime, your grace."

"I haven't gotten to hear how the fight went for you."

"Hardly much to tell," she said with a shrug. "Beornric told me in advance that he wanted me keeping our royal fool alive, so I didn't get to do much. Mostly kill any pirates that were stupid enough to pose a real threat to him."

"How many?"

"After the fourth they stopped trying."

"Smarter than I thought."

"I think they were Nelazzi's elite." She shook her head. "*Four gammagan* and I didn't even get to fight *one*. Didn't even get to really open up on the pirates until the knights joined the fray."

"I take it you didn't get hurt?"

"Against nothing more than a few pirates?" She snorted.

"Well, at least—"

"I know what good we did, your grace. And I know who we helped."

"Will you at least let me thank you?"

"Always, your grace," Deirdre said with a smile. "And even if you only mean with words, I still like to hear them from your lips."

"Then on behalf of everyone you helped yesterday, and most of all on my own behalf, I thank you most sincerely, Deirdre Ol'Miri."

"You're most welcome, your grace," Deirdre said with a bow.

"That unguent of yours is impressive," he said. "Reminds me a bit of potions I used to carry from time to time, when I could get a cleric to make them for me."

"It's the same stuff, though a different recipe. Much easier to carry, doing the kinds of things I do." She looked him over. "And if your grace is feeling better—"

Someone knocked on the door. Aefric didn't recognize the knock.

"Come," Aefric said, and Deirdre muttered something under her breath.

Killian entered, followed by an irritated-looking sailor, carrying a tray of food.

"Good, you're awake!" Killian said, then crinkled his eyebrows in puzzlement at the sight of Aefric's clearly unbruised chest.

"What's this?" he asked. "I thought you'd been battered within an inch of your life. And here I brought you breakfast."

The sailor set the tray down on a chest and left without a word, which got a frown from Killian and an amused look from Deirdre.

"My healing is Deirdre's handiwork," Aefric said, before Killian could say anything about the sailor leaving without being dismissed.

"I know a few tricks, your highness," Deirdre said, and Aefric noted that she had yet to bow to the prince since he'd entered.

"I'm sure you do," Killian said with a smirk, then shook his head. "Honestly, Aefric. She's gorgeous. A brilliant fighter. Handy with the magic, and clearly devoted to you. I mean, she carried you *all the way* up those stairs."

"Believe me," Aefric said, looking at Deirdre, who looked back at him as though the prince weren't even present. "I know."

"What I don't understand," Killian continued, "is why you haven't named her as a bridal candidate. I mean, yes, she's certainly unconventional. And there might be a bit of scandal at first, but—"

"His grace knows better than to consider me a bridal candidate," she said, speaking right over Killian. "I'd never say yes. The wife of a duke? Me?"

"Aefric himself was low-born," Killian said. "If any duke could marry you, I daresay he could. You don't seem the type put off by a bit of scandal. And his reputation could certainly survive the hit."

"You're not listening, your highness," she said. "If I married his grace, I'd have to give up my sword and armor for *dresses*, because his majesty would *forbid* us from entering the hazard together. And I certainly couldn't ask *his grace* to play the house cat. So it would mean no more fighting. No more investigating. What's more, I'd be required to *socialize regularly* with people I'd rather stab than talk to. And worst of all, thanks to Armyrian tradition, I'd have to put up with every powdered puff in the latest frippery thinking she has as much right to share *my* husband's bed as *I* do."

Deirdre shook her head, and her eyes shone as she turned to Aefric.

"No," she said. "Marrying Aefric Brightstaff the adventurer, that would be a dream. But marrying the Duke of Deepwater?" She shook her head. "A nightmare."

"Deirdre," Aefric said, "I—"

"I do get one consolation, though," she said, smiling now even though her eyes were still quite shiny. "Whoever *does* marry his grace will have to put up with the fact that *I'll* be in his bed every chance I get. Setting a standard she will *never* be able to match."

Killian laughed openly at that. Aefric laughed too — because she clearly wanted him to — but his laugh was tinged with sadness. Because she was right.

He'd never ask her to give up being the magnificent knight that she was. And even if she volunteered — and talked him into letting her — she'd hate court life as much as it would hate her.

Which meant that, over time, she'd chafe. Then, well, something bad would follow…

"Now be fair, Deirdre," Killian said, smiling and shaking a finger at her. "Some of those 'powdered puffs' can be exquisite lovers."

"Oh, I'm sure whoever marries his grace will be capable enough," Deirdre said with a dismissive wave. "Maybe even creative enough to keep him from growing bored with her."

She shook her head. Poised and sure of herself once more, and no trace of pain in her eyes as she continued.

"But only someone who has spat in the eye of death *truly* knows how to celebrate being alive. I've done it." She nodded at Aefric. "He's done it. But most of the people you find in any court never will."

Killian frowned as he thought about that.

"And now," Deirdre said, "if you will both excuse me, I'll see about my own breakfast."

"Of course," Aefric said, not caring what Killian said just then. "I'll need to talk to you later, though."

"I'm yours whenever you want me, your grace," Deirdre said with a bow, and left.

"Does love to tease, doesn't she?" Killian asked.

It was true. She did. But underneath her tone this time, Aefric heard something more. Some of it was pain. Some of it, he thought, was regret that they hadn't met a year ago. And more than that besides.

It wasn't fair. Deirdre had gone above and beyond for him again last night. Saved his life. Saved the lives of everyone who'd been down in that cavern facing Nelazzi. And then she'd carried him out herself. Treated his hurts with her unguent, and guarded him while he slept.

He could thank her for all that. He could reward her, too.

But there was no unguent to treat her pain. And he couldn't think of a single thing he could do about that.

BREAKFAST WITH KILLIAN WAS AN EXERCISE IN FRUSTRATION.

Not because of the breakfast itself. That was good enough. Sure, it was simple. A bland but meaty porridge with leftover rye rolls from last night, served with water. Hungry as Aefric was, though, he finished his and considered seeking seconds.

Killian, though, was another matter.

First, he'd insisted on remaining while Aefric dressed. Not to watch. Just because the idea that Aefric might've preferred privacy didn't seem to occur to him.

So Aefric had just yanked back on the same clothes he'd worn the day before, rather than find something more appropriate.

The prince himself wore a red silk shirt with gold brocade, over sage green hose and low, soft leather shoes with turned-down collars.

Next, Killian complained about the breakfast, wondering why Aefric hadn't broken into his personal stores so the two of them could have enjoyed something better.

Aefric's answer — he hadn't brought much that either of them would have thought of as breakfast foods — was met with indifference and a launch into Killian's real topic of conversation.

The story he was concocting about how he saved the day by killing the pirate queen, Nelazzi.

It was quite a reimagining of events.

To hear Killian tell it, he, not Aefric, had been in charge of the whole operation. And he'd commandeered Aefric's ship for it.

"I'm royalty, after all," he said by way of explanation. "I'm expected to lead, not follow."

Which was the same poor excuse he gave when he told how he, not Beornric, had organized the tactics of the knights and soldiers.

The number of pirates he killed personally varied as he worked through the details.

"I don't want to be *unfair* to the knights and soldiers," he said. "No one must believe they didn't do their part. It's just that it will be good for the people to know that their prince is a force to be reckoned with on the battlefield."

In the end, he settled on four pirates. Plus he distracted the gammagan — being quite vague on the details there — while Aefric froze them solid and the knights shattered them.

Stirring imagery, if pure invention.

And then, on to Nelazzi herself.

Killian wasn't willing to go so far as to cut Aefric out of that fight entirely. Which he seemed to think was magnanimous of him.

He gave Aefric credit for countering her magic and battling her spells, creating the opening for Killian to leap into the fray.

It was sword-to-sword then with her enchanted cutlass until she mis-stepped and he stabbed her straight through the chest.

He kept the detail about the cavern collapsing.

"Fantastic bit of drama there," he said, smiling and rubbing his hands together. "How my quick thinking enabled us all to escape with no further casualties."

Once Killian had gone over and over his story until he was happy with the way it worked out, Aefric finally asked a question.

"Do you expect me to tell that same story?"

"Well ... come now, Aefric," Killian said, cajoling. "We're *friends*. And you have *so many* deeds already. Surely it won't hurt you to give me this one."

Aefric drew a long, slow breath through his nose, fighting not to show anger.

"And Beornric?" he asked. "He has so many deeds to his name that he should cede to you his tactical brilliance yesterday?"

"Well..." Killian said, frowning. "I suppose I can give him a larger part in my story. So long as everyone understands that I *oversaw* his tactics, and could have changed them if I disagreed."

He rubbed his chin. "Perhaps if he handled most of the battlefield command, but I gave a key order that swung the fight our way. We *were* outnumbered, after all."

"If you undercut your knights," Aefric said bluntly, "how can you ever expect them to fight for you?"

"You're right," Killian said. "I should play up the role of the knights in the fight with the gammagan, and how they helped me turn the battle against the pirate forces—"

"And tell all your knights that you'll claim credit for their work," Aefric said. "Because they may never say a word to your face, but I saw how your knights reacted when we got back to the ship. Word will spread that you're a glory-thief, and *that's* not a reputation you want."

"Oh, *fine*," Killian said, rolling his eyes. "I'll leave the main battle the way it was. And I'll give good Ser Beornric Ol'Sandallas full marks for his tactical genius."

"And?"

"And I'll leave out the part about distracting the gammagan." Killian frowned. "Wasn't too clear on how I was going to describe that anyway. I mean, how *does* one distract a lava monster?"

"And?"

"All right," Killian said with a sigh. "It was *your* venture. You organized it. I ... merely oversaw everything in my capacity as Prince of Armyr. And *that* you cannot gainsay."

"But you're going to hold to your story about Nelazzi, aren't you?"

"Not a story," Killian said. "The truth. I killed her. You fought her magic to a standstill, and I killed her. Anything in between is an unimportant detail."

"So that *Deirdre captured her* is an unimportant detail?"

"Oh, I don't think Deirdre cares what stories people tell about her. You heard her. She can't stand court politics. She'll never even have to know."

"Deirdre pulled off a move yesterday that any adventurer would be proud of," Aefric said. "And if you think she won't tell the story over drinks with her fellows, you're sadly mistaken."

"And I'm sure she'll embellish her version," Killian said, looking as though he'd made a masterful move on a chessboard. "As I've embellished my own."

"There's a difference," Aefric said, "between telling a good story, and claiming a deed you *didn't do*."

"But I *did* kill Nelazzi."

"You killed her after she was beaten. While she was *bound* and *helpless*. You make it sound as though you bested the pirate queen on the battlefield, but all you did was *murder* a *prisoner*."

"If she was so helpless," Killian said, "why did Deirdre keep a dagger on her?"

"Nelazzi was still a wizard," Aefric said. "And there might've been spells she'd mastered well enough to cast even while trussed up and gagged."

"So, *not* helpless then," Killian said.

"You're playing games with semantics."

"And you're fighting me over *nothing*," Killian said. "*Details.* And the minuscule kind that never bother historians anyway."

"Come now," Aefric said. "You've met Elkari."

"I have," Killian said, undaunted. "And believe me, she's the exception, not the rule. Most historians know the golden rule of history. The truth doesn't matter. Only what the *winners* say."

Killian clapped Aefric on the shoulder. "I'm the Prince of Armyr, and I say I killed the pirate queen, Nelazzi. And I can say it under the three-edged sword, because it was *my* blade, driven by *my* hand that took her life."

He gave Aefric's shoulder a little shake.

"And you can believe," he continued, "that Armyr's historians will write it the way I tell it. And I'll tell the story at Armityr so many times that it will grow in the telling. Others will add details to my deed. And *no one* will care what others are saying way out in Deepwater."

Killian smiled. "Go along with me on this, Aefric. It's best for everyone."

Aefric sucked in a slow breath and blew it out just as slowly.

"I guess I don't have a choice," he lied.

AFTER BREAKFAST, KILLIAN WANTED AEFRIC TO COME PLAY CARDS, BUT Aefric begged off.

"Deirdre's healing was a marvelous thing, but she's still no cleric of Nilasah," he said, affecting a tired smile. "I'm afraid she's left me worn out."

"I don't doubt it," Killian said suggestively. "Wish she'd wear *me* out that way sometime. I'd *love* to see if she's as good as she claims."

Aefric fought down his first three responses. "I'm just going to nap for a while."

"All right," Killian said as Aefric climbed up onto his hammock. "I'll tell Beornric not to let anyone disturb you."

"No need," Aefric said. "Just tell him I'm resting. He'll know what's worth disturbing me for and what isn't."

"I envy you your relationship with your knights," Killian said. "I look forward to the day I can command such devotion."

He left the cabin, and when the door was closed behind him Aefric muttered, "I hope you learn to *earn* it someday."

But then, he had ideas about how to see about that.

He hopped down off his hammock, and dug through a chest for parchment and his special pen. It was enchanted just for him. A quill that needed neither ink nor sand to draw a good, steady, unblotted line.

He began his first letter with the king's courtesies, then continued on to tell his majesty the whole story, plain and simple. How and why he had heard about the kidnapped princesses. The reasoning that led him to believe Nelazzi had them. How and why he ended up bringing Killian along. The hunt. The island. The ships. The battle. The capturing of Nelazzi and, most important, her death.

He went on to explain Killian's reasoning — as Aefric understood it — and Killian's plans to claim undeserved glory.

Aefric made certain to underscore his own opinion of what Killian had done, and the many flaws he saw in Killian's logic.

He finished...

...please note, your majesty, that I take no pleasure in writing this letter. I know full well that I have gone against your explicit orders in hunting

down the pirate queen. But I have done so with the intention of aiding our relationship with our allies, and securing my own coastline before going off to war in Caiperas.

Though I have not accomplished the former, I believe I have accomplished the latter. As well as removed a foul presence from the sea lanes and avenged the harms done to Deepwater by both Nelazzi and Calder, in her name.

As a final note, your majesty, I am sealing this letter before giving it to my courier, Ser Deirdre Ol'Miri. She has not been told the contents of this letter, though I don't doubt she'll guess their general nature.

I tell your majesty this as an invitation to ask Deirdre any questions he wishes about the hunt for Nelazzi, how she was taken down, and how she was murdered. I suspect Deirdre will even volunteer to answer questions on the matter before a justiciar, should your majesty so wish it.

I am confident that she will confirm everything I have written here.

Though you might question this at the moment, I assure your majesty that I remain

Your most loyal and true vassal,

Aefric Brightstaff

Duke of Deepwater and Baron of Netar

Aefric was sealing the king's letter when Beornric finally knocked and entered. He wore his full plate again today.

"Ah," he said as he watched Aefric cooling the wax with a gesture. "So that's it. I wondered, when Deirdre pointed out that you should be fully rested."

"Killian intends to go ahead with his mad plan of claiming credit. He even plans to see his version made official Armyrian history."

"Shameful," Beornric said with a look of distaste. "I fully agree. But it won't be the first bold lie passed down as truth in a history book."

"He wants to build his name on this," Aefric said. "He'll be undercutting anything he ever *actually* does, because word will have spread already about—"

"And tell me, Aefric," Beornric said gently. "Does Killian strike you as the type to ever really *do* anything?"

"What do you mean? He'll be king. One day he may need—"

"To lead his troops to war, yes." Beornric shook his head and took a seat on a chest facing Aefric. "But he won't be the first king to 'lead' from the comfort and safety of a tent at the rear while someone else plans and executes his battles. And he certainly won't be the last."

"That's not his father's way. I remember King Colm at the Battle of Deepwater."

"One of the reasons Colm was a joy to serve under," Beornric said. "But I was at Armityr when Killian was off for page training in Silverlake. I heard the king complain about the letters Duke Wylyn kept sending. Talking about how the boy was just this side of useless with bow and blade and hammer. Didn't think fast enough. Couldn't move, and didn't feel motivated to train half so hard as he should."

"Wylyn put up with that?"

"This was the crown prince," Beornric said. "What choice did he have?"

"And the king wasn't bothered?"

"Duke Wylyn's an old adventurer, like you. I believe the king felt that his duke was thinking like an adventurer. That Killian might've been doing just fine, even if he wasn't up to the standard of those old warriors who once accompanied Wylyn into hellish places."

"Ah," Aefric said.

"And that's not all," Beornric said. "His majesty thought the duke was overselling the prince's ... let's say indolence. Maybe even trying to lower the king's expectations, so when his son came back an excellent hand with the sword, it'd look as though Wylyn had pulled off a near-miracle."

"But when Killian returned, the king learned the truth."

"He did," Beornric said with a sigh. "Tried giving him to three different knights to finish his training. Didn't do any good."

Beornric frowned. "Well, I shouldn't say *any*. He's not the worst I've seen. But he's far from the best."

"Which is why you had Deirdre watch his back against the pirates."

"He'd've been dead for sure if she hadn't kept him alive."

"Wonderful."

"He'll do all right as king," Beornric said. "When he tries, he has a pretty good mind. And despite what we saw yesterday, a decent sense of justice. Most of the time, at least."

"If he can set justice aside whenever it pleases him, he has no sense of justice at all."

"I think he was caught up in the moment."

"And if he isn't called on it," Aefric said, "this won't be the last time that happens."

"And by that letter in your hand, I presume you mean to call him on it?"

"Where's Nelazzi's body?"

"Packed in ice, and stored below. Cook's none too pleased, either."

"Anyone guarding the body?"

"No," Beornric said, as though disturbed by the question. "Why?"

"I'm sending Deirdre to Armityr," Aefric said. "With the body and this letter. The king is going to hear the truth before the prince gets to start spinning his lies."

***

Didn't take too long to arrange. Getting the Knights of the Lake sparring with Killian's knights was enough spectacle to bring the prince out to watch.

Killian wouldn't have wanted to stay cooped up in his cabin anyway. The day was bright, the sun was warm, and the sultry winds were giving the crew enough to tack to on their way back north towards home.

Aefric begged off the show, saying he had matters he needed to discuss with his court wizard, and met Karbin on the helm deck behind a nervous young pilot who kept sneaking glances at them over her shoulder.

"What are we meeting about?" Karbin asked, once the clash of steel and taunts and jibes started up on the afterdeck.

"Well, I do want to hear how things went with that ship. *The Squid's Revenge.* But mostly I'm killing time."

"Thought you might be." Karbin gave Aefric a knowing smile. "And you were right. Nelazzi had a big teleportation landing circle on the main deck. Clearly she knew the spell, but had never quite mastered it."

"You and Kainemorton have both made it sound tricky."

"Yes, but with your natural talent, I'm sure you'll find a way." Karbin drew a deep breath. "Crew were ready for me. Or at least, ready for one of us to show up. Filled the air with quarrels as soon as they saw me. Lucky to only get hit by two before I got a barrier up."

"I doubt luck had much to do with it."

"Hey, now!" Someone cried from up above. "If she gets two swords, I want a shield!"

"Guess Arras is up," Karbin said. "Ship was spell-hardened, so I had to do more fighting than I wanted to, while I figured out how best to take it down. Plus, Gwawl was there, trying to catch me with battle spells of his own."

The clash of swords turned into a round of cheers from up above, including shouts that sounded like Leppina and Wardius. Arras must've scored or won her match.

"How'd you finally take it down?" Aefric asked Karbin.

"Well, I'm better than Gwawl," he said. "So it was really just a matter of time and effort."

"I hear a 'but' coming," Aefric said with a smile.

Karbin nodded.

"But I spotted a part of the hull, down below the water line, where the patch-work was temporary. Short-term stuff done with spells, and not yet reinforced with wood."

Aefric chuckled. "So after you rained acid, fire, ice and ramming force on that thing, in the end you just undid the patch?"

"Wasn't *all* I did," Karbin said, smiling, "but yes. That was the key."

"What about Gwawl? Did he get away?" Aefric asked, as Beornric and Deirdre came up the stairs from the main deck.

Up on the afterdeck, another mock duel started.

"Didn't see him when the ship was sinking," Karbin said. "Don't know for sure. I know I hit him hard a couple of times, but I'm not ready to count him out. Figure he knows a few good water breathing and swimming spells. Maybe even a fishy shape-change. We might see him again sometime."

"Or he'll be smart enough to stay well clear of Armyr," Deirdre said as she and Beornric joined them.

Aefric greeted them, then looked his question to Beornric.

"It's being done right now," Beornric said softly. "Two of the soldiers. They're bringing it where we discussed, and making sure it's well-wrapped."

Good. Another mast between them and Killian. Just in case.

"What's all the secrecy?" Deirdre asked, clearly enjoying being involved. "What subterfuge are we about?"

"Not a subterfuge, really," Aefric said. "I just need you to play courier, and I don't want Killian finding out until it's too late to stop you."

"Where am I going?" she asked. "And how?"

"Where is Armityr, directly to the king and no one else." Aefric pulled his rolled-up and sealed letter from within his black velvet pouch. "You're bringing him this and the body of Nelazzi, which is being fetched right now."

He handed her the letter and she tucked it into her belt without looking at it. "I'll set the body in front of him myself, your grace, and put this letter in his hands."

"He may have questions after he reads it."

"Am I to answer them?"

"Of course."

"Then I shall do so to the best of my ability."

"I know you will," Aefric said, giving her a small smile that she returned.

"How am I to get there?" she asked.

"With this." Aefric reached into his pouch and pulled out an oblong, squared-off white crystal. "It will summon my *magari*."

"Really?" Her eyes lit up. "I've *always* wanted to fly one of those."

He leaned in and whispered in her ear. "The keyword is *Nastaya*."

She nodded as she took the crystal. "Am I to return immediately? Or is there more?"

"Return to me at Water's End as soon as his majesty gives you permission."

"He will not keep me long from your side, your grace."

Beornric cleared his throat. Nodded down to where a soldier was surreptitiously waving from behind the mast.

Aefric took a step forward, but Deirdre stopped him with a hand on his chest. "I have my mission, your grace. Leave it to me."

With feline grace she leapt backwards from the helm deck to the rigging and found a halyard she could slide down to the foot of the the mainmast, where the soldiers were waiting.

Moments later flame red horses leading a fiery chariot appeared on the deck.

Sailors immediately began screaming about fire.

The clash of steel on the afterdeck stopped. In its place, cries of wonder and curiosity as Deirdre took to the air, whisking away in the *magari*.

The cries of "Fire!" from the crew stopped.

"I think we should have warned the captain," Beornric said.

"I'll go apologize to her now." Aefric said, turning toward the stairs.

"Aefric," Killian called down, and he didn't continue until he had Aefric's attention. "Was that Deirdre I saw at the reins of that ... fire chariot?"

"Yes," Aefric said. "She's about a mission for me."

"But I wanted to watch her duel some of my knights this afternoon."

"Well," Aefric said, "I don't expect her to be back in time for that. But if she is, I'll send her up."

"What's she doing?"

"Nothing I want to yell about across an open deck," Aefric said, laughing. "Come down to my cabin and I'll tell you."

"Later," Killian said. "Come watch the knights."

"I have to talk to the captain first. Then I'll come up."

"You work too much, Aefric." Killian laughed, then turned back to his show.

"We could use more speed," Karbin said. "Want me to work the first shift of winds?"

"Are you up to it?" Aefric asked.

"Who are you asking, apprentice?" Karbin said, cocking an eyebrow.

"All right," Aefric said, chuckling. "It's a good idea. The sooner we get back, the better. I'll take the next shift when you're ready."

With that agreed, Aefric went to find the captain, and apologize for terrifying her crew.

* * *

During the three-day trip home, Aefric did his best to keep Killian happy. Went through more from his stash of finer foods, even though it meant not having enough to share a meal with the officers and wounded as Aefric would have *preferred* to do at least once on the voyage.

He played cards with Killian. Watched with him, while the knights sparred. Participated with the sparring himself, though he couldn't talk Killian joining him.

Aefric even went so far as to spend a *great* deal more time discussing his bridal candidates over those three days than he usually tolerated over the course of several aetts.

Frankly, Aefric found himself looking forward to his shifts ensuring the winds. Just for the break from all the "fun."

Certainly Aefric wasn't getting any time to do research on that teak box, which was more than a little frustrating. Though he did at least get to survey the port towns and cities along his coastline — though from too far a distance for it to be considered a true check of their readiness to stand against trouble.

From what he could see through his spyglass, though, Aefric at least felt that they were making good progress towards rebuilding. They might not be *finished* before winter hit, but they'd be close enough that no one should go without housing or food.

Though it was difficult to be certain, because Killian seemed to begrudge even the time Aefric spent looking through his spyglass.

Strangely, though, the prince never asked again about Deirdre.

Well, no. That wasn't true. He asked about her fighting. About where she trained. About what a dweomerblade *really* was. What it might mean that her mother was apparently a pirate.

And, of course, Killian wondered often about Deirdre in other ways that Aefric was less eager to discuss. Though the fact that Aefric hadn't wanted to discuss those details about his bridal candidates either seemed to keep Killian from pressing too hard on the subject.

Usually those attempts on Killian's part ended with him chuckling and saying, "In some ways, you're still very much a foreigner, Aefric."

But he never once asked about the mission that saw her flying away on a *magari*. It was as though he'd forgotten about it completely.

Beornric didn't seem to think that was strange, though.

"You sent a knight on a mission. That's done all the time. And most often those missions aren't anything that would interest him all that much. He probably assumes it has to do with the hunt for the princesses."

"And he doesn't really care about that, does he?"

"Oh, he *does*," Beornric said, as they discussed this question in Aefric's cabin late one night before they turned in. "In theory. But he's probably convinced they're in Caiperas, as he's said all along. And since he feels he knows the answer, your looking into the question doesn't interest him."

"Do you think they *are* in Caiperas?" Aefric asked.

"I can't help but wonder how a landlocked country would come to work with a pirate like Nelazzi for something like this."

"Maybe they're more likely to hire a pirate because they have no coastline of their own to worry about."

"Maybe," Beornric admitted. "And certainly Nelazzi bragged that she has eyes in every river port. So that would seem to imply that she could contact Caiperas if she wanted. And rivers were certainly involved in the kidnappings."

"There's something about it that bothers me, though," Aefric said, irritated. "I just don't know what. Maybe that a country without a coastline has little to *offer* a pirate."

"Little beyond money, you mean?"

"I suppose there's that."

"Who else could it be, then? Malimfar?" Beornric asked. "They're the only other country in the conversation that didn't have a princess stolen. And they certainly have a coastline."

"I don't know," Aefric said. "I'll have to think about it."

And then it was sleep, time ensuring the winds, and time entertaining Killian, until they finally passed Ajenmoor, made their way up the Searun River, and finally down the Deepwater to Water's End.

At last.

7

———————

AEFRIC EMERGED FROM HIS CABIN INTO THE JOYOUSLY CLEAN SMELL OF fresh lake air. Not the salt of sea air. Not the wood and varnish and creosote of his cabin. Not the fishy smell of all those lamps.

Just a good, strong, southern lake breeze. Even carried a refreshing hint of coming rain.

A moment worth enjoying through a long, slow breath with his eyes closed. The feel of that breeze on his skin. Savoring the scent as it filled his lungs and diaphragm.

Good enough to ease some tension out of his shoulders and back.

His chests were packed. His clothes and person freshly spell-cleaned. Which meant he stepped into the cool evening air clad in black hose, a royal blue shirt, gold sash belt and low, soft doeskin boots.

Aefric opened his eyes. Spotted Killian. Already standing on the forecastle, gazing ahead at the lights of Water's End, not so distant now.

He looked considerably more rumpled and less fresh after their voyage, despite his clean white silk shirt — embroidered with gold thread — over forest green leggings and soft, doeskin shoes. Possibly something his sister had made for him, after a hunt.

Three people converged on Aefric as he started across the deck: Karbin, Beornric and Captain Ol'Vanett.

The captain spoke first, gesturing vaguely at the many sailors scrambling here and there about the deck and rigging, calling to each other as they worked.

"I understand your grace wishes a word before we start through the reef. I trust he'll be brief, as I'm sure he knows I have a good deal of work to do."

"Of course," Aefric said. "I'd intended to share a meal with you and your officers during the voyage, but didn't get a chance. To make up for that, you and your crew are all invited to dine in my castle tonight. Your choice whether it's with or without my company."

The captain started to say something, then checked it and gave Aefric a lopsided smile.

"Without, if it please your grace," she said. "While your grace's presence would honor us, I think my crew would feel more comfortable — and certainly have more fun — if they felt free to be themselves."

"They won't wreck my dining room, will they?" Aefric asked with a grin of his own.

"I'll make sure they know that anyone who abuses your grace's hospitality pays for it in lashes." She gave a firm nod. "That'll keep them under control."

"Been a pleasure sailing with you, captain. I won't keep you further."

"The pleasure's mine, your grace." She leaned in a little closer. "I still can't believe you pulled it off. But I'm proud that me and mine were part of it."

Aefric clapped her on the shoulder, then she bowed, turned and started yelling orders before she'd even taken a step.

"Call that line tied? Get it right before I tie it with your guts!"

"I like her," Beornric said with a nod. "She's got style."

"Mind if I take off?" Karbin asked. "I've had all the ship travel I care to anytime soon."

"Go ahead. I'll see you at the morning meeting," Aefric said, and Karbin flew off into the darkening evening sky.

"Sounds like you don't plan to dine with your court tonight," Beornric said.

"I'm not ready to play politics, or games about who wants to share my bed." Aefric shook his head. "What I'd like *most* is a chance to research that teak box. I have ideas about how to crack it, but I haven't had a chance to try them because—"

"Your grace!" a crisp, baritone voice called.

"—I keep getting interrupted."

In this case, the interruption came from Ser Leon Ol'Barre. The tallest person on the ship — easily two hands taller than even Aefric himself — Leon strode quickly across the deck from the fore, clad in the uniform of most knights, full plate armor. Longsword at his side.

Even busy sailors cleared a path for him.

Leon was likely the oldest of Killian's knights, his hair completely white and his dark face well-lined. But he remained a fierce fighter, with plenty of strength yet in those long limbs.

As usual, he schooled his expression and gray eyes to share no hint of whatever he thought or felt.

He stopped, only two paces away. Bowed to Aefric. Nodded to Beornric.

"Your grace," Leon said in an even tone, "his highness requests the pleasure of your company on the forecastle."

Aefric twisted a smile. "What did he actually say?"

"His highness said," Leon said without any hint of humor, "'Leon, please tell Aefric to come have some fun before he works himself to death.'"

Beornric snorted.

"I'll be along in a moment," Aefric said, turning to Beornric.

Leon continued to stand where he was, waiting.

"Is there something else?" Aefric asked, turning back.

"No, your grace. I have no further instructions from his highness, and nothing further to say of my own. Certainly I have nothing to say on the subject of Nelazzi's body, nor its current whereabouts. I have nothing to speculate about the reasons Ser Deirdre Ol'Miri left this ship aboard a *magari*, nor any guesses to make about her destination or purpose."

"You're not saying quite a bit," Beornric said quietly.

"I'm not finished not talking," Leon said. "I am not offering any opinions on the subject of Nelazzi's death, nor the version of events his highness wishes to put forward."

"Yes," Aefric said. "I imagine none of you want to offer any opinions about that."

"Indeed," Leon said. "Finally, I am not thanking your grace for including us in the action against the criminal Nelazzi, nor am I offering any support for your grace, should he choose to put forward a view of the related events that ... conflicts with that of his highness."

"And you're not speaking on your own behalf?" Beornric asked.

"Well, I'm certainly not speaking on behalf of all the knights aboard this ship sworn in service to his highness."

"I understand," Aefric said.

"I'm not sure that's possible, your grace," Leon said with a bow. "I haven't said a word."

With that, Leon turned and walked away.

"Knew they had to be chafing against what Killian did," Beornric said, shaking his head. "His majesty wouldn't assign his son anything less than his most honorable knights."

"That not-speak," Aefric said. "That's a capital thing?"

Beornric nodded. "Only when speaking could be really dangerous, but you can't quite keep your mouth shut."

"I'm glad you don't have to live that way anymore," Aefric said, clapping Beornric on this steel-clad shoulder.

"As am I, your grace. As am I."

"Was there something you wanted before I go entertain the prince?"

"Nothing that won't keep, your grace. Especially if we're having our usual morning meeting."

"I think we'll need it."

"You're probably right."

A beautiful autumn evening on Lake Deepwater, made all the more beautiful by the fact that Aefric was almost home. His magnificent castle, all lit up and only minutes away.

"By all the gods, Aefric," Killian said, leaning on the forward rail as Aefric approached him on the forecastle. "I can never see Water's End without thinking about how amazing a castle it is. The sheer *scope* of it."

He turned as Aefric joined him. "Do you know, I tried to see every room of that castle while I sat regent, but didn't even get to finish the *keep*, let alone the Great Spires."

"Haven't seen it all yet myself," Aefric said. "There's always too much to do."

Killian scoffed. "You work too hard, Aefric. You have to let your advisers handle more of your load. That's what they're there for."

"I imagine I will someday," Aefric said, watching as the *Swift Wave* started navigating the harbor reef on the final approach to his pier.

Behind him, he could hear the beat of the drum and the calls to the rowers as they readied to fight the evening tides for the last part of the voyage.

"But you must remember," Aefric continued. "You've been raised to rule. I have a lot of catch-up to play if I'm going to *understand* everything I need to know about handling my lands and people. Let alone do a good job of it."

"I'm sure you do just fine," Killian said, then sighed. "Wish I could stay tonight. I could certainly do with a good meal, a tryst and a night's sleep in a bed that doesn't rock before heading back out."

"Lovely thoughts," Aefric said. "But if you aren't back in Armityr before the march to war begins, your father will *skin* me."

"Skin us *both*, you mean," Killian said, but then he smiled. "At least I'll get to see Father before he begins the march. I'll get to tell him all about our great victory over Nelazzi, and her death at my hands."

"I'm sure his reaction will be something to see," Aefric said.

"He'll probably throw a feast that very night." Killian straightened a little as his smile brightened. "I'll get a hero's welcome! Do you know I've never had a hero's welcome before?"

"Sometimes it can feel really good," Aefric said. "All those people cheering and screaming your name. Buying you drinks. Giving you gifts. Thanking you. And at times like that, just being *alive*, when you'd come so close to death. There's nothing like it."

He shook his head slowly.

"Other times though," he continued, "it tastes like ashes, because all you can think about are the friends and comrades you lost along the way. The ones who aren't there to celebrate with you. Or the people you had to kill, even though you had no choice. The families that will miss them."

"You can throw a wet blanket on anything, can't you?" Killian said, marveling. "A whole city celebrating me, and I'm not supposed to enjoy that?"

"I never said that," Aefric said. "You *should* enjoy it. When a city celebrates you, they *want* you to enjoy it. I'm just saying, it's not always an easy pleasure. It has two sides. And it's rare that you get one without the other."

Killian shook his head. "That's what being an adventurer is like? Doing amazing things, then *regretting* them?"

"No," Aefric said firmly. "Being an *adventurer* means going places others won't go, and doing the things that others can't do. But the deeds that get you called a *hero*, they're always hard. And all too often they come at a cost you wish you didn't have to pay."

"I don't understand you at all," Killian said with a frown.

"I know."

"I bet *Deirdre* would love a hero's welcome. No matter *what* she had to do to get it."

"Deirdre enjoys being the center of attention," Aefric said. "For a time. But if she had to sit around and let a crowd of townspeople or courtiers laud her, she'd grow bored quickly."

"I doubt that a great deal," Killian said with a smirk.

Aefric shook his head. "Trust me. When Deirdre celebrates, she prefers to do so with those she knows *understand* all the things I'm talking about."

"Those who've spat in the eye of death, eh?"

Aefric nodded.

"Well," Killian said confidently, "I've done that now, and lived to tell the tale."

"No, your highness," Aefric said. "You haven't."

Killian didn't even hear him.

"And I'm not so *morose* about it. Come *on*, Aefric. Cheer *up!* You're *home!* You get to spend tonight in the soft arms of some lovely who wants to hear all about our great deeds on this voyage."

"Actually, tonight I need to arrange funerals for the four men and one woman who died in the fight with Nelazzi's pirates. Dartan, Olin, Pohl, Zel, and Khora. And I need to see to what compensation we can give the families who would much rather have their sons and daughter back."

Actually, Kentigern and Garnotin — by their own request — would handle most of that. But Aefric wanted to drive home that the price of taking down Nelazzi had been paid in blood.

Not that the Crown Prince of Armyr seemed to care.

"Hopeless," Killian said with a grimace.

Down below, with the help of dockworkers on the red and green coral pier, the *Swift Wave* eased into its slip and began tying off.

"Your highness, your grace," Beornric called from a respectable distance behind them. "We've arrived."

Killian shook his head again.

"I like you, Aefric," he said, "but you're really far too dour. I hope you find a bride who can put a smile on your face."

"I'm sure that's the answer," Aefric said, as they turned to make their way toward the gangplank.

"Oudin," Killian called to his knight. "Be sure to see that Nelazzi's body is moved to our ship right away and packed in ice again. I want it fresh as possible when we reach Armityr."

"That might be difficult, your highness," Oudin said. "A few minutes ago I asked a couple of sailors to have the body prepared, and now they tell me it's missing."

"Missing?" Killian said. "You're saying they've *lost* it? Do they sail with *that* much ice?"

"No, your highness," Oudin said. He gave Aefric an unreadable look as he continued, "I suspect—"

"The body isn't there," Aefric said, not willing to make the knight deliver the news. "In fact, by now it's likely been at Armityr for nearly two days."

Killian turned a shocked look on Aefric. "Deirdre. *That's* what she was doing?"

Aefric nodded.

"I thought you just sent her off on some quest to find those princesses." He huffed out a soundless laugh. "Well why didn't you let me go with her? My arrival would've been *legendary*. And..."

Realization crossed his face.

"You *do* plan to support me in this, don't you, Aefric? As we talked about?"

"If it was only my deed you were claiming," Aefric said, "I might. But Deirdre deserves to have the world know what she did. So does Vria. And Beornric. And *all* the knights and soldiers — your own included — and *especially* those who died in the battle. They *all* deserve to have history reflect the *truth* of what they did on this voyage. And I *won't* let their deeds be diminished for another's glory. Not even yours."

"What about *me*, Aefric?" Killian asked angrily. "What about *my* deed? *My* glory? *I killed the pirate queen Nelazzi! I* did. With *these two hands.*"

"Believe me. I have no intention of hiding that fact."

Killian's eyes widened. He paled, which for him was quite a trick.

"You ... you told *Father*," Killian said. "You sent a letter with Deirdre, didn't you?"

Aefric nodded.

"And you told Father ... you told him what ... what Nelazzi was doing when I killed her."

Aefric nodded.

"You're going to make it sound—"

"I've done nothing to slant it one way or the other," Aefric said. "I told only the truth in my letter. At least, the truth as I understand it."

"Well," Killian said, stroking his chin, "it's still my word against yours…"

He snapped an angry look at Aefric.

"That's why you sent *Deirdre* instead of your wizard. He wasn't down there for the fighting. But if Father has his justiciar ask Deirdre how Nelazzi was defeated… *Before* I have a chance to…"

Aefric nodded.

"Oh, *Aefric*," he said. "I'll get you for this. Don't doubt that I will." He started to turn away, then turned back. "I presume it goes without saying that you are no longer permitted to call me by name."

"I already guessed that, your highness."

"Why…" Killian started, expression pained, then grimaced and shook his head. "Never mind. You'll just spout some pablum about honor or duty, absent the *truth* of the way the world works."

"The world works the way we make it work, your highness."

"This won't *change* anything, you know," Killian said harshly. "The histories will say what *I* want them to say. Reflect the *truth* that it was *I* who killed the pirate queen Nelazzi. *Absent* any *needless* details of your insertion. Even if I have to wait until I'm *king* to ensure this."

"If you say so, your highness."

"Come, my knights," Killian said, taking in all of his knights at a glance. "We have a long way to sail yet, and I wish this place to be *well* behind me before the dawn."

He marched off, with his knights falling in behind him.

The last in line was Leon, who gave Aefric a single nod before he left.

Twilight was just beginning to ease its way into night, held back aboard the deck of the *Swift Wave* by oil lamps burning that lamentable whale oil with its fishy odor.

Late season night gulls squawked up above, hunting for fish or refuse — possibly drawn by the lamps.

The lake breeze was growing chillier and a little stronger. And with the clouds moving down from the north, rain would be likely before midnight.

Aefric turned from the skies to watch Prince Killian make a show of getting his people and possessions off of this ship and onto his own as fast as possible. He even snapped at porters if he felt they weren't moving swiftly enough to suit him.

Beornric and the Knights of the Lake joined Aefric, to watch with him.

"He complained on the trip here that the crew of his ship could get drunk during a two-hour stopover," Aefric said.

"Likely exaggeration," Beornric said. "Or those sailors were done for the day."

"Well I hope his crew is shipshape and ready to cast off now." Aefric sighed. "That captain is going to catch all thirteen hells if our prince is kept waiting on the dock when he wants to make a dramatic exit."

"*What do you mean half the crew are in taverns?*" Prince Killian shouted from the pier. "*I want them back here at once! We sail before moonrise if I have to hoist our sails myself!*"

"I'd pay to watch that," Temat said, keeping his voice low.

"I wouldn't," Leppina said with a frown as a pack of sailors from the prince's ship hustled down the pier toward the city to recover their fellows. "He'd make a mess of it then get angry at the delay while real sailors straightened things out."

"No, he wouldn't," Micham said. "I sailed with him when he was regent here. He can handle himself aboard a ship, when he feels like working. And right now, I'd say his highness is motivated."

Garnotin and Kentigern, down on the pier — accompanied by the dozen porters waiting to work the *Swift Wave's* cargo — looked shocked at the turn of events. They leaned towards each other in close conversation. Likely discussing whether they should get involved or stay out of the way.

"Well, one thing is certain," Beornric said, as they watched the prince harangue his captain. "By morning word will have spread all through Water's End that you've had a fight with the prince."

"No avoiding that," Aefric said. "Don't know if you heard, but he's promised to 'get' me."

"I imagine you're shaking in your boots."

"I'm more concerned that he'll do something stupid."

From the deck of his ship, Prince Killian was issuing dire threats if they missed the evening tide.

"You had to know he wouldn't take it well," Beornric said.

"I did," Aefric said, shaking his head. "But I hoped I could make him see reason."

"Well he has the whole trip to Armityr to cool off." Beornric gave a nod. "And his knights will work on him. Try to cool his blood. Talk sense to him, when no one can hear them. And, of course, their majesties will have a few things to say. By the time all is said and done, our prince may finally understand why you did what you did."

"He might understand, but he'll still feel betrayed." Aefric sighed. "He'll try *something*. If only to keep his word."

"Look at the bright side, your grace," Micham said, a smile not quite reaching his lips. "Deirdre wasn't nearby when his highness threatened you."

Beornric groaned. "Thank the gods for small favors."

"Please," Aefric said. "Deirdre's impulsive, there's no denying it. But she's far too smart to attack the prince."

"She's ducal champion," Wardius said.

The other knights nodded as though that were a complete answer. And all of them thought, in this case, that fact spelled trouble.

"What does that tell you that it's not telling me?"

"I'll answer that," Beornric said. "What precisely did the prince say?"

"I believe it was, 'I'll get you for this. Don't doubt that I will.'"

"That's what I thought," Beornric said grimly. "That is an overt threat. As your champion Deirdre would be empowered to answer it."

"Wouldn't she have to check with me?"

"A cool-headed champion would ask your grace if a threat had been issued, or perhaps if his highness' words were something your grace felt the need to answer. Give you a path out that wouldn't stain your honor."

"But since it was clearly *intended* as a threat, Deirdre wouldn't ask, would she?"

"A threat that clear? Issued to *you*?" Beornric shook his head. "She'd answer it."

"At *once*," Wardius said.

"Especially since it came from someone arguably your grace's equal in rank," Vria said.

"Possibly before the words were all the way out of his highness' mouth," Temat said.

The knights all slapped their hilts in agreement.

"What, exactly, do you think she'd do?"

"Well," Beornric said, "it's hard to be certain with Deirdre. But my bet is, she'd step forward and say something like, 'As his grace's champion, I accept this challenge on his behalf. We may duel whenever your highness is ready.'"

The knights slapped their hilts again.

"His highness, of course, would pick one of his knights to stand champion," Arras said.

"A knight that Deirdre had recently both sparred with, and seen fight for real," Leppina said. "And she can learn your moves so fast it's frightening."

"Really?" Aefric said, surprised to see an honestly disturbed look in Leppina's eyes.

"Frightening," she repeated, and several of the other knights nodded.

"Even so, it wouldn't have to be a lethal duel," Aefric said. "I'm sure first blood would suffice."

"First blood can be fatal," Leppina said, "if it's drawn from the right spot."

"And Deirdre might want to make an example of this duel," Beornric said. "To make sure everyone knows not to challenge you."

Aefric whistled, low and long.

"Exactly," Beornric said. "Prince Killian would feel twice-shamed and blame you for both."

"Well, I'll count my blessings then," Aefric said, then frowned at Vria. "How's the head?"

"I'm fine," Vria insisted.

"I'll see to it she visits the healer, your grace," Temat said.

"We have *actual* wounded in the hold," Vria said. "Soldiers held together with little more than spit and bandages. *They* need the healer, not me."

"Vria," Aefric said.

She closed her eyes. Her mouth formed a tight line for a moment, then she let out a breath, opened her eyes, and bowed to Aefric. "Your grace?"

"You suffered a severe blow to the head while saving my life. Do you deny it?"

"No, your grace."

"Am I a thoughtless or ungrateful liege?"

"*No*, your grace," she said, sounding shocked at the question.

"Then you must agree that it is proper for me to arrange your healing at the hands of nothing less than my own ducal cleric of Nilasah."

"I ... yes, your grace."

"As such, you will visit my ducal healer with the rest of my wounded tonight. You will remain there until she has evaluated you, and given you any healing that she, *in her sole judgment*, decides is necessary. And you *will* accept this healing, including following any instructions she gives you to the letter. Am I understood?"

"You are understood, your grace. I swear it shall be done."

"I'll keep you company," Temat said with a lopsided smile. "So you don't get bored."

"And now," Aefric said, "let's get moving. I suspect his highness doesn't want me waiting around to wave goodbye as he departs."

AEFRIC AND BEORNRIC DESCENDED THE GANGPLANK TO THE CORAL PIER. The Knights of the Lake followed only a few steps behind.

Aefric suspected they were keeping one eye on the prince's ship, which was waiting for part of its crew to return from the nearby taverns. As though his knights thought the prince's temper might boil over into ... something regrettable.

The soldiers of Aefric's personal guard followed last, helping their wounded and carrying the five bodies of their dead fellows.

It bothered Aefric that he wasn't helping there, when he could easily have called forth two or three *platters* to carry those who couldn't walk on their own. But it had been emphasized to him over and over since he was created duke that he needed to let people do such things for themselves, rather than shortcutting with magic.

Which made it a shame that he had let Karbin leave the ship early. As court wizard, *he* could have helped without it coming across as inappropriate.

Porters filed past to offload the *Swift Wave*. Aefric and Beornric stopped on the pier beside Garnotin and Kentigern. Both of whom made a point of looking at the dead and wounded being carried and helped down the gangplank.

"That must've been *some* tour of the ports, your grace," Garnotin said, one eyebrow high. He wore a shirt of deep blue silk over woolen trousers of dark orange. His warhammer, of course, was strapped to his back.

"Truly, your grace," Kentigern said. "The *winds* must've been *fierce*." Kentigern was dressed in his preferred black silks. This time a robe, embroidered with silver thread, over matching black slippers.

"Neither one of you are fools," Aefric said. "I withheld from you that I was going after Nelazzi *only* to shield you from possible blame if all went poorly."

"You were worried the king would test us with his justiciar?" Garnotin asked.

"I had to take the crown prince with me on a mission for which I was expressly denied royal permission," Aefric said. "If I fell, I didn't want to bring you two down with me."

Both regarded him in silence for a moment.

Aefric felt the pressure of those things he needed done, but he owed them that time to think. So he forced himself to wait. Though he did wave his soldiers to move on with the dead and wounded.

"No other reason?" Kentigern asked finally.

"None whatsoever," Aefric said.

"We have your grace's word on that?" Garnotin asked.

Aefric looked back and forth between them — meeting the eyes of both — as he spoke.

"I swear in the name of Kalinda, goddess of magic, that I trust you both. I further swear that I withheld information from you both before I last left Water's End for the sole purpose of protecting you from what I saw as the possible consequences of my actions."

Kentigern and Garnotin looked at each other. Nodded.

"Thank you, your grace," they both said, not quite in sync.

"However," Kentigern said, "I would ask, in the future, that if your grace wishes to take such a risk, he give me the opportunity to take it with him."

"Exactly what I was about to say," Garnotin said firmly. "I didn't become a knight to avoid risk. And it isn't as though your grace were about something foolish."

"Let that judgment wait until we've seen how his majesty reacts." Aefric started walking. Garnotin, Kentigern and Beornric kept pace, and the others followed behind. "Is Deirdre back yet?"

"Not that I've seen, your grace," Kentigern said.

"Should she be?" Garnotin asked.

"She'll be returning from Armityr aboard my *magari*. You won't miss her."

Kentigern started to ask a question, but Aefric reached into his black velvet pouch and pulled out several scrolls, bound together with a small length of red cord.

He handed the bundle to his seneschal.

"Two of these go to Ashling and Wylyn, one to Countess Faenella, one to Baron Osmaer, one to Mayor Vagran over in Ajenmoor, Raedwaru down in Kivash, and the other is for Elkari. You'll know which is which. I want the messengers dispatched *tonight*, with priority going to Ashling and Wylyn. The sooner Fyrcloch and Stormsent get these letters, the better."

"Of course, your grace," Kentigern said, and was likely about to say more, but Aefric spoke first.

"What's been going on here?"

"Your grace," Garnotin said, "couldn't we hear about your venture first? And perhaps those letters?"

"The two are related," Aefric said. "We tracked Nelazzi to her lair. She was waiting. We had a big battle. Beat her forces and captured her. Then our dear prince shoved a sword through her chest while I was trying to get information out of her."

"He did *what?*"

Aefric wasn't sure which of them asked that. Might've been both.

"You heard me," he said. "Murdered a bound prisoner in cold blood, after he'd heard me promise her a fair trial. You might've noticed some tension between us?"

They glanced at each other.

"We did rather think something was amiss," Kentigern said.

"Well, the prince wants to make it sound as though he's a great hero, stealing glory from knights and soldiers alike in the process."

"Not to mention from your grace," Beornric said.

"So I sent Deirdre to Armityr with Nelazzi's corpse and a letter, telling the king what really happened before the prince gets a chance to spin his lies."

Both Garnotin and Kentigern looked as though they wanted to say something but weren't sure what.

"As you might've guessed, I managed to keep that little fact from the prince until we docked. He'd not best pleased with me."

"I imagine not," Garnotin said weakly.

"I need the peers to know the full truth as soon as I can get it to them. And I need the ports to know that Nelazzi is dead."

"Are you certain, your grace," Kentigern said slowly, "that informing the peers should not be the act of his majesty?"

"Ashling and Wylyn both know me well enough. They can judge my words for themselves against whatever story finally makes it out of Armityr."

"You think his majesty will support the prince?" Garnotin asked. "Even in the murder of a captive?"

"I think his majesty has doted on the prince to excess," Aefric said. "While I'd like to think this will serve as the warning shot that makes him *see* that, I cannot *trust* that he won't indulge the prince now."

"Were there witnesses of concern?" Garnotin asked.

"Besides myself and Beornric, Deirdre, the Knights of the Lake and the prince's own knights."

"Too many honorable men and women," Garnotin said. "The king can't risk supporting the prince in this. He'd undercut the faith and loyalty of his knights on the eve of war."

"Unless he withholds the information entirely until *after* the war," Kentigern said. "Gives him time to maneuver. Find some way to tell the truth without making it sound so *base*."

"But if the ports all know," Garnotin said. "Word will spread quickly. His majesty may not be able to stop it."

"Either way," Aefric said, "the prince wants revenge for my not supporting him in his lies. He'll move against me. And since his weapon will likely be politics, I need the peers to know the truth as soon as possible. In case he tries to poison them against me."

"Never happen," Beornric said. "They're both too savvy for the prince."

"Only if he goes to them directly," Kentigern said. "Smarter way would be working through their courts. Plenty of lesser nobles to manipulate."

"That about covers the basics for now," Aefric said. "The details you can hear later. What about here? Anything I should know about before the morning meeting?"

"Nothing that competes with that," Garnotin said.

"Quiet enough," Kentigern said. "We've had arrivals for the festival, of course. Nobility, mostly. Oh, and Countess Faenella, so I can get her letter to her tonight. But the populace has also begun descending on the inns of Water's End, or setting up tents outside the walls."

"Yrsa growls a lot," Garnotin said, "but in between complaints she sounds as though she'll have Deepwater's armies ready to march on time. Though those of some vassals will have to be collected along the way."

"That's fine," Aefric said. "Has word been sent to the Dragonscar yet?"

"No, your grace," Garnotin said. "I believe Yrsa is waiting until the last possible moment."

"Probably the right move," Aefric said. "She knows borogs even better than I do. And they never exactly need long to prepare for a fight."

"Will your grace be dining with his court tonight?" Kentigern asked. "I believe dinner is due soon, but it could be held if your grace wishes to clean up."

He ran a sharp eye over Aefric. "Not that he needs it."

"No," Aefric said. "I've had a long trip, and I want to go to my rooms. Have my dinner sent there."

"Of course, your grace," Kentigern said.

"Oh," Garnotin said. "Did you learn anything about what's happened with those princesses?"

"Yes," Aefric said. "Nelazzi stole them all right. But she sold them before they were even captured."

"Sold them to who?"

"I don't know," Aefric said. "His highness murdered her before I could get the answer."

Too many stairs, but Aefric took them all. Didn't seem right for him to simply fly up to his apartments. Not when he had wounded and dead being carried in.

He was still alive, and healthy enough to walk under his own power. The least he could do was do so.

Garnotin and Kentigern didn't follow. Both had too much to do. Leppina and Wardius did follow, because they were now on duty. The other Knights of the Lake were either headed to see Bebara with Vria, or about their own homecoming business for the night.

Beornric, of course, stayed by Aefric's side all the way to the door of his apartments. And he might've come in, but Aefric turned to him before his guards opened the door.

"Go," he said. "If nothing else, I know you want see Yrsa."

Beornric smiled and bowed. "See you in the morning, your grace."

"Would that we could all sleep in," Aefric said with a sigh. "But first thing it is. Good night."

Finally entering his apartments, Aefric was caught between a lack of surprise and a touch of wonder that Dajen stood waiting inside the doorway. Posture crisp, white hair perfect.

The complete lack of surprise was thanks to Dajen's habit of *always* being right there and waiting, whenever Aefric arrived. No matter how he arrived. If he'd flown to the balcony, Dajen would have been waiting just inside the balcony doors. Tonight Aefric came to the main apartment doors, so of course Dajen was there instead.

The wonder was that he did this *all the time*. He never guessed wrong. He was never one step out of place, or only just arriving as Aefric entered.

No. He was right there. Waiting. Every single time.

"Welcome home, your grace," Dajen said, while guards closed the door behind Aefric. "Dinner shall arrive soon. Would your grace care for a drink while he waits?"

"No," Aefric said, "that's not necessary."

He crossed the white oak floorboards to find a seat on one of the several large, comfortable couches in his sitting area. He chose the dark blue couch tonight. The one under the large tapestry depicting ship traffic around Behal, where the Deepwater fed into the Haven River.

"Perhaps a story then, while your grace waits?" Dajen said, having unobtrusively followed.

"A story?"

"I don't believe your grace is aware of this," Dajen said, "but in his youth, King Colm — then Prince Colm, of course — spent a good deal of time here at Water's End."

"He did?"

"Oh, yes. As often as he could. He was quite smitten with the daughter of our Duke Arallan."

"Arinda?"

"Naturally. And she was quite taken with him. And so they went riding together, hunting together, sailing together. Water's End became quite a fashionable destination for nobles from all across Armyr. Especially those who hoped to develop a good relationship with their future king."

"But wasn't Prince Colm promised to Princess Zinerva of Retheryl?"

"Princess Zinerva Haltallan," Dajen said. "That's quite correct, your grace. She who would later become mother to our current prince and princess. A very beautiful and clever woman. She made a very popular queen."

"And she didn't mind her betrothed becoming so attached to another woman?"

"She had no reason to fear, your grace. A duke's daughter could not begin to compete with a princess of the royal blood of Rethneryl. Not in terms of marriage. And so she could afford to let the infatuation burn itself out. Might even have indulged herself in a similar fashion."

"Arinda never married," Aefric said.

"Ah, I believe your grace begins to understand," Dajen said. "She had many suitors, of course. Even though, at the time, she was not to inherit."

"No? I didn't know she had a sibling."

"An older brother, in fact. Alaric. Fine. Strong. A bit hot-tempered, perhaps. He and Prince Colm were close, for a time."

Cold understanding seeped through Aefric.

"They were close until Arinda started losing suitors because she ignored them in favor of Prince Colm. Is that it?"

"Entirely," Dajen said. "Arinda tried to persuade her lover to cast aside his promised bride and marry her instead. He refused, of course, putting his duty to Armyr ahead of his love for her. Alaric came close to challenging Prince Colm to a duel."

"What stopped him?"

"His father. Duke Arallan sent him off to deal with some problems caused by piracy along the southern coast of Deepwater."

"Nelazzi," Aefric said.

"A name that did not yet strike terror into sailors, but yes, your grace. It was her."

"And Alaric never returned."

"Not alive, your grace, no. Though his body was returned for burial."

"Arinda and Prince Colm probably stopped seeing each other. Arinda took up the duchy in her brother's place, and the prince went on to become king?"

"A king who blames a pirate for the loss of his friend Alaric, his love, Arinda, and the goodwill he'd built up in Deepwater. Goodwill he has had a great deal of difficulty rebuilding. The Soulfist family was well-loved here."

"Which is one reason he gave the duchy to the Hero of Deepwater," Aefric said. "He hoped I would be a popular choice, work well with him, and help him rebuild that goodwill."

"It's worked quite well so far, your grace."

"But why wouldn't he let me go after Nelazzi? I'd think he'd burn for revenge."

"It could be that he did once, your grace. But that fire has grown cold over the years. Now, I suspect that what his majesty remembers most is the pain and loss that the pirate caused him. And he has refused all requests to hunt her down to avoid losing even more to her."

"She's dead now."

"I rather suspected, your grace. Well done."

"There may be … complications."

"There often are following great deeds, your grace. Especially when there can be disputes about credit or the division of any gains brought about by the deed. Such as land, wealth or the like."

Aefric chuckled breathlessly. "You already know about my quarrel with the prince."

"Very little happens at Water's End that escapes either my attention or Ocheda's, your grace."

"Do you also know what the quarrel's about?"

"Not the particulars, your grace. But I suspect they do not matter."

"No?"

"What happens when we are young, your grace, is formative. Events leave a much stronger impression on youth than they do on those who have reached maturity, much less exceeded it."

"You think Nelazzi was King Colm's personal bogeyman?"

"And now she is dead. And whatever the details, there can be no question that your grace is largely responsible for her downfall. Whatever difficulty now stands between your grace and his highness, I suspect his majesty will force you both to set it aside in favor of what really matters to him. The pirate who killed his friend and soured his love is no longer among the living."

"I hope you're right."

"Does your grace doubt that I had ample time to study his majesty, during his many visits?"

Aefric laughed. "I wouldn't *dare*."

Dajen didn't smile, but his eyes did twinkle a little.

"There is another factor to my story that your grace appears to have overlooked, in favor of its more immediate implications."

Aefric frowned for a moment. "Arinda never married."

"Her grace was a wonderful duchess in many ways," Dajen said.

"But she never forgave the crown for spurning her and causing the death of her brother and father."

"Her father?"

"Duke Arallan is said to have died of a sickness, but most believe his heart gave out after the loss of his beloved son."

"And Arinda never forgave Colm."

"No, your grace," Dajen said. "That is not what I am saying."

"I don't understand."

"Though she never said so directly to me, I suspect that Duchess Arinda died believing that her lover, Colm Stronghand the man, would have married her in a heartbeat. But for the duties he owed Armyr."

"She blamed his father then? For not being willing to break the engagement to Princess Zinerva?"

"No, your grace. I mean she never forgave the crown of Armyr. The monarch, regardless of who filled the role. It was the crown who denied her marriage to the man she loved. The threat of reprisals from the crown — should Alaric have taken the expected action against Prince Colm — that sent her brother on his last and fatal mission."

"And she believed that mission took her father as well, if indirectly."

Dajen nodded.

"So ... she never married ... to punish the crown?"

"I believe, your grace, that she never married, nor acknowledged any offspring, to ensure that she was the last Soulfist in Armyr. To deny the crown the strength and leadership of any more Soulfists."

"She wanted to abandon the crown, as she felt abandoned?"

"Essentially."

"Seems a bit extreme."

"She was a woman of great passion, your grace."

Aefric narrowed his eyes at Dajen. "Why are you emphasizing this part?"

"That Duchess Arinda died unmarried and officially childless was a deliberate choice on her part. Your grace takes a great many risks with his life, but so far as I know he has made no similar decision."

"I swear I'll—" Then it clicked. "There's someone waiting for me upstairs, isn't there?"

"If your grace wishes to dine alone, I will see to it. But I believe that atop the stairs awaits company he will be pleased with."

"All right," Aefric said, standing slowly. Sitting on so comfortable a couch had been a mistake. His body didn't want to stand. As though all his recent exertions were descending on him at the same time. "But if you're wrong, I won't let you forget it anytime soon."

"I would expect nothing less, your grace."

Aefric started across the room to the stairs, but one last point from Dajen's story bothered him. He turned back to see Dajen watching him. Waiting.

"One last thing…"

"Your grace?"

"You've emphasized that Arinda never *acknowledged* any bastards."

"That's quite correct, your grace."

"It's often said that one of my knights, Arras, bears a strong resemblance to Arinda."

"Anyone who has seen them both would say so, your grace."

"Arras is only a couple of years older than our prince and princess."

"Both of whom were conceived shortly after the wedding of then-Prince Colm to then-Princess Zinerva. A wedding that took place while Arinda was away from Deepwater, and had been for about two seasons."

"You don't suppose Arras' father was…"

"Duchess Arinda never acknowledged any bastards, your grace, which renders the question moot."

"I guess it does," Aefric said.

"Though your grace should keep in mind that bastardy bears no stigma in Armyr."

"So you think she would have acknowledged Arras if she hadn't decided to be the last Soulfist?"

"Not the point I wish to make, your grace."

Aefric frowned at him.

"Your grace has no heir, and goes off to war in a matter of days."

Aefric raised a halting hand. Didn't trust himself to say anything else. Just turned and ascended the curving staircase.

———

As Aefric ascended the carved, curved staircase from the public floor of his apartments to the first private floor — the floor with his personal living space — he wondered just whom Dajen had permitted up to wait for him.

Kentigern had mentioned that nobles had been arriving for Harvest Day, which meant it could've been Sighild, or one of his vassals, or—

The moment he reached the top of the stairs, he caught a glimpse and knew at once.

Of course. Byrhta Ol'Caran.

She sat casually on one of the two maroon, overstuffed couches in his smaller, private sitting room. The ones that were long enough to sleep on, and formed a triangle with an equally overstuffed chair at the apex.

The third side of the triangle was a hearth, where a merry fire crackled away at cherry wood, lending its scent to the air.

She faced away from him, her attention in a book. He could see little more than a bared shoulder draped in long, lush hair of dark forest green.

That didn't matter. There was no mistaking her.

Her beauty and presence seemed to suffuse the very air around her. As though she literally brightened the room simply by sitting and reading in it.

Just that glimpse was enough to take some of the tiredness from his limbs. Though perhaps not so much that night as it might have normally.

"Byrhta," he said, and she turned and stood at once, smiling to see him.

The full effect of her beauty, even clothed in a simple sleeveless gown of dark red, was beyond breathtaking. The utter magnificence of her face and form. Those large amber eyes, flecked with canary yellow.

In a world filled with beauties the likes of which Keifer McShane had seen only in magazines and movies, Byrhta Ol'Caran towered above them all. More like the perfectly executed pinnacle work of some legendary painter.

If there was a living exemplar of physical beauty, it had to be Byrhta Ol'Caran.

She rarely bothered with much jewelry, but tonight she wore the amber brooch he'd given her.

Her smile became teasing.

"Aefric," she said, "are you just going to stand there looking at me? Or are you going to come greet me properly?"

Aefric tried for a smile, but didn't quite make it. "I'm tempted to just stand here and look at you for a moment."

"A *moment,* you've had," she teased, but then she frowned. As though she'd seen something distressing in his mien. When she spoke again, her voice was soft. "I heard about what happened on the docks. Would you like to talk about it?"

He crossed the thick rugs to her in three long steps and took her in his arms. She dropped her book as she returned his hug.

She didn't say anything at first. Just held him. Comforting, while he buried his face in her neck and hair and took in her familiar scent, still both exotic and spicy in a way he could never quite describe.

After a time, he realized she was repeating something, so softly he could barely hear it. In High Eldrani.

"Quarrels are storms.
They strike us like foes.
Drive us apart.

Drive us apart.
Quarrels are storms.
We first see their harm.
Fire and flood.
Fire and flood.
Quarrels are storms.
They clear the dead growth.
Make room for new.
Make room for new.
Quarrels are storms.
Their water brings life.
They make us strong.
They make us strong."

After he'd been aware of hearing it through three times, Aefric eased back from the hug. Gave her a wistful smile.

"I've never heard that before," he said.

"My grandmother used to chant it for Taeric and me. When we were children and came crying to her, after fighting with each other or our friends." She stroked his hair. Switched to High Eldrani. *"I still find it comforting."*

"As do I," he said in that same language, gesturing for her to sit with him on the couch. He switched to the common tongue as he continued, "I take it you've heard about what happened on the docks."

"Even if I hadn't," she said, "you left the Brightstaff by the stairs when you came to me." She arched an eyebrow. "Usually that only happens when I'm naked."

"I don't think anyone would blame me for that."

"Certainly not me," she said. "Would you like to talk about what happened?"

And so he told her. At length. All about the princesses, the voyage, Nelazzi, the prince, all of it. And as he told the story, Dajen brought in dinner — fresh, delicious spiced lake trout, a light salad of mixed greens with cucumbers and peppers, a sweet sharabi, and a dessert of chocolate pudding with cream.

Dajen even brought in a silver teapot filled with steaming nysta tea, and two cups, along with a small plate of cookies. Though he specifically set that tray to one side, and gave Aefric a look that seemed to suggest that he hoped Aefric would not drink his tea that night.

Aefric, however, was too concerned with his retelling to worry about Dajen and his own thoughts about the ducal lineage.

It was funny, in a way. Aefric had retold the events themselves several times as he'd written all those letters. And yet, it was only now, after *this* retelling, that he felt unburdened. More at ease.

Admittedly, the version he told Byrhta was more complete than any of those letters save the one he'd sent to the king. But that wasn't it. He felt safe enough with her to allow himself to be vulnerable.

If Byrhta judged him at all for anything he said, it didn't show. She listened with sympathy, and even more understanding than he expected. Then again, she was the daughter of a count, and had grown up far more used to court politics than a street rat from Sartis.

"Dajen doesn't seem to think his majesty will punish me over-much," Aefric said, as he finished his tale. "That his majesty's own past with Nelazzi will make him so grateful that she's dead that he might be willing to overlook that I took her down against his orders."

"And you don't think so," she said. "Why not?"

"If it were just about me, he might," Aefric said. "But his son murdered a bound prisoner. I left that detail out of most of the letters I sent, but still. There were witnesses. Word will get out, and the crown might need to ... assert its preferred narrative."

"And you think this might ... cast an unkind light on your role?"

"If Killian has any say, it will. And Killian will be king one day."

"But if his majesty is no fool, he will know that his legacy depends greatly on the *kind* of king the prince makes. Which means the prince must learn that even *his* actions have consequences."

"I suppose," Aefric said, unconvinced.

"And no matter how thoroughly they tell a conflicting story," she continued, "word of the truth will spread among the knights."

"Not if all the witnesses just *happened* to die in the coming war."

Byrhta frowned. "You know his majesty better than I do. Would he do something so base?"

"I don't think he'd kill them outright," Aefric said. "But I can't help that think about the fact that, in war, there are always some missions more dangerous than others. And the more honorable the knight, the more likely they take such a mission without question."

"And only the honorable knights would present a danger to the prince's version of events? Is that it?"

"It doesn't sound out of the realm of possibility to me."

Byrhta considered that, and nodded.

"Is there any way you and I can figure out the truth here and now?" she asked. "Are there recent histories that would help us? Events we might discuss that could allow us to eliminate some possibilities in favor of others?"

"Not that I know of," Aefric said. "Short of inviting others, like Elkari, into the conversation."

"I'd really rather we didn't."

"I agree. They can wait for morning."

"Good," she said. "And for tonight, would you agree that we have taken this subject as far as we profitably can?"

Aefric thought about that for a moment. Nodded. "I think so."

"Then perhaps I could turn your attention to something more pleasant?"

Her expression was so blatantly full of false innocence he laughed.

"What did you have in mind?"

"Well," she said, arching an eyebrow again. "Let me think." She raised one finger. "I haven't seen you in several aetts." She raised a second finger. "You have no more duties pulling at you before dawn, yes?"

True, he could have gone upstairs to do research on the teak box, but if this conversation was going where he thought it was going, that seemed like the inferior option.

He nodded.

She raised a third finger.

"So many nobles are descending on Water's End that by midday tomorrow, the demands on your time will seem endless."

She raised a fourth finger and smiled.

"We have a perfectly good pot of nysta tea right here."

She lowered her hand and adjusted her position so that she was sitting properly, instead of comfortably.

"Now," she said. "Given those four points, what do *you* think I have in mind?"

"Pour the tea."

THERE WERE NIGHTS WHEN AEFRIC LAMENTED ARMYR'S PRACTICE OF the noble privilege. That he felt pressured by his nobility to take women to bed, even on nights when he would rather have slept alone. Because it was expected of him, because he was a stranger to Armyr before he had been named duke, and because the nobles needed to know that he was participating in their traditions.

It's not that he was ever pressured to take any *particular* woman to his bed, or even to do so on any particular night. It was just that if he started sleeping alone even a third as many nights he had company, his court got anxious.

A stark change, for the man who'd slept alone far more often than he had with company through most of his life. And strangely, one of the harder things to acclimate to about being duke.

Tonight, however, was not one of those nights.

This was not just some pretty noblewoman he barely knew among the silk sheets of his oversized bed. It was Byrhta.

And not just because the full effect of her naked beauty was staggering. Overwhelming. Nearly divine in its glory.

No. Far more important than her looks or charisma was the woman herself. The woman he'd come to know over the past couple of seasons. Who had shared her hopes and fears, as well as her joys and laughters. Who had proven to be far more clever and insightful than most would notice, because they never looked past the surface. Not even her own family.

This was a woman he cared for deeply, and who cared for him just as much. And he got to take her to his bed without any concerns over possible social ramifications for either of them, because this was Armyr.

With her, the bliss was not so transitory as with most. It lingered in every touch they shared. In every caress. In every kiss. In every way they came together, and in every way they sought to please each other.

And their culmination, each time it washed over them, was all the more fulfilling for that it was shared between them.

With Byrhta, he did not feel the need to guard his thoughts, nor his words. He was free to be himself. To express himself. As free as he hoped she felt with him.

Yes, Aefric had learned to find pleasure in the arms of many women, since coming to Armyr. But Byrhta was one of the few who could also bring him peace. And true delight.

In fact, it was that true comfort that led him to tell her something he hadn't intended to, as they lay together among the tangles of his sheets. Sheened with perspiration and smiling as they drew out the kiss that had begun as bliss overwhelmed them, and lingered even after the moment itself had passed.

When the kiss parted — for the moment, at least — he said, "You know, Dajen did everything but directly ask me to put a bastard in you tonight."

"I wondered if he had something like that in mind," she said. "Usually when I have to wait for you, he brings me nysta tea early, so the bitter taste fades before I get to kiss you. Tonight, I think he didn't want to bring it out at all."

"I wouldn't ask something like that of you, of course."

"Why not?" she asked, sounding only curious, which surprised Aefric.

"You wouldn't find it an offensive request?"

"I don't see why." She shrugged one shoulder. "I can think of worse things than giving you a child. If you acknowledge the bastard, I'd be mother to the next duke or duchess of Deepwater. And if you don't—"

"If we had a bastard together, I'd acknowledge the child."

"So much the better then."

"Wouldn't it hurt your marital prospects?"

"Certainly wouldn't hinder my first choice," she said, and nipped at his shoulder. "But if I must settle for a lesser husband, few would care that I had a bastard by the duke of Deepwater. The child would never be a threat to their own bloodline or inheritance."

Something about this logic sat wrong with Aefric, but he couldn't put his finger on why.

"If anything," she continued, "an acknowledged bastard would hurt *your* marital prospects. All those princesses, daydreaming about being wed to the dashing Duke of Deepwater would have to face the fact that their own bloodline would likely never rule here. Even if they fell for you, they'd likely have to walk away."

"Assuming any of them are even still alive."

"If they are, I'm sure you'll save them," Byrhta said simply. "It's your nature." She cocked her head. "Of course, if you wanted to marry Duchess Ashling, then having a bastard by *me* would clean up a lot of the extant issues that could be holding you back."

"What makes you think I'd want to wed Ashling?"

"She's beautiful. She's clever. She's—"

"Both terms that apply to you, you'll note."

"She's *powerful*, which I am not. A duchess. She has a far older, wealthier and more influential family than I have, all factors that could set your vassals at ease and help anchor you firmly in Armyr."

"I hate that I have to worry about that."

"It's not that you have to *worry* about their opinion, but you can't *ignore* it either."

"Not as much difference between the two as I'd like."

"A chafe felt by every ranking noble from time to time, I assure you," Byrhta said, and gave him a quick kiss. "As a team, you and Duchess Ashling would be something to fear. And if you think his highness will move against you, solidifying your alliance with her through marriage might be the best way to go."

"I'm not choosing a wife to stop some kind of political move."

"Noble marriages have been created for less," she said, shrugging again. "But we both know that's not why you won't marry her."

"Because she prefers women?"

"Hardly," Byrhta said. "Duchess Ashling Fyrenn is not the sort to let a little thing like her sexual preference get in the way of her ambition. You can't tell me she hasn't offered to bring women to bed for the two of you to share."

"I think she's hoping I'll share you with her."

Byrhta shook her head. "When you want me in your bed, it has to be just the two of us."

"I never said yes to her offer, nor even implied I'd consider it."

"I figured as much," she said. "I just wanted to make my position on the topic clear, in case you ever find similar thoughts occurring to you. And you're changing the subject."

"The subject was why I wouldn't marry Ashling. But I'm not sure what reason you're thinking of."

"The same reason you haven't picked Zoleen Fyrenn, or Sighild Ol'Masarkor, or any of the other noblewomen who have their eye on you. Myself included. The same reason you won't pick any of those foreign princesses either."

"Oh?" Aefric rolled over on top of her, while she adjusted to accommodate. "And just what is this reason?"

"None of us are Princess Maev, and you still hope for her."

Her words were simple, but hiding in those amber eyes was pain.

Aefric stroked her cheek.

She gave him a wistful smile.

"Not even naked in bed with me, one movement away from being inside me again, can you lie to me about it."

"I don't lie to you," he said. "I've never lied to you."

"I know," she said, running her hands over his shoulders. "In this one instance, I almost wish you would. But the princess has managed to capture your heart in a way I can't touch, hasn't she?"

"I can't explain it," he said. "I think—"

"Don't," she said softly. "Not now. Not here. Tell me later, if you want to. But right now, I'd like to kick good Princess Maev back out of this bed. Right now, I'd like to have you to myself, for just a little while."

Aefric leaned down and kissed her. Tried to tell her with that kiss just how much she meant to him. How deeply he cared for her. Loved her even. And Byrhta, she kissed back with equal fervor.

And they kissed until nothing existed but the two of them again. Only then, at her urging, did they seek bliss once more.

8

———————

AEFRIC AROSE BEFORE DAWN THE NEXT MORNING. PERHAPS NOT HAVING had as much sleep as would be considered ideal, but certainly all the more refreshed for his company.

In fact, under other circumstances, he would have woken Byrhta. They would have bathed together — even though that would delay his duties — and lingered over breakfast before his morning meeting.

But this morning could not risk such delays. And besides. In the gentle light of Ocheda's candle — for it was she who'd woken him at the appointed time — Byrhta looked so sweet and content, sleeping among the silk sheets, that he couldn't bring himself to disturb her.

So he slipped into the simple linen dressing gown Ocheda handed him, took the Brightstaff in hand, and followed her into the bath room to wash up for the day.

He didn't indulge himself in a full bath. Only hot water — scented with something woodsy — soap and towels as he stood. But as he cleaned himself, he thought over a moment of conversation from his night with Byrhta.

Maev. Was Byrhta right? Was he really not giving any of these other women a chance, simply because part of him held out hope for Maev?

If so, what was it about her that got to him so?

Her contempt for some of the noble niceties? The little ways she kept surprising him? That she knew the sorts of skills he was accustomed to finding only in other adventurers?

No. Nothing he could delineate so simply. It was just that the two of them connected on such a basic level...

Or was it?

Or was it just that the two of them had this strong connection — that had never gotten to play itself out in the bedroom?

For all the women Aefric had shared his bed with in his time in Armyr, Maev had never been one of them. At first, because he was too new a noble and he feared she might reject him. Then, when it was clearly what they both wanted, they were kept apart by duty. The likelihood of her marrying King Dalius down in Varondam.

And Varondam looked down on the noble privilege. Once she became an official bridal candidate for their king, they would never have tolerated her sharing pleasure with Aefric.

A requirement enforced by King Colm and especially by Queen Eppida.

But what if they had? Would he still feel this strong pull toward Maev? Or could it be as simple as desire for the one woman he couldn't have?

One thing was certain. If marriage to Maev *did* become a possibility, they would have to share a bed a few times first...

Aefric laughed as he toweled dry, then drew back on the dressing gown and took up the Brightstaff again.

Such a thought! Requiring that he have sex with her before considering marriage. Only a year ago — less than that — would a requirement like that even have occurred to him?

Certainly not.

Oh, it might have been that he would have slept with the woman he later wanted to marry. Life as an adventurer was such that marital options were few, and most often among those he traveled with.

And facing death with people, well, it occasionally led to frantically shared bliss moments.

But marriage was something different. And the way he'd been raised in the south, had he retired to some village. Opened an inn. Looked for a wife among the locals. Well, it would never have occurred to him to require sharing pleasure before contemplating marriage.

Or at least, it would never have occurred to *Aefric Brightstaff*. But that sort of thought certainly would have occurred to Keifer McShane. After all, he and Andi had been sleeping together regularly for more than two years before getting engaged, let alone married.

So that he had such a thought that morning may well have been more about his two lives coming together that day in Kainemorton's tower than it was a response to Armyrian sexual habits.

Either way, it was an interesting question, and one he pondered as he followed Ocheda into his closet, where she directed his body servants to dress him in jewel tones that day. A silk shirt of emerald green, over hose of sapphire blue. Soft leather shoes dyed to match the shirt, and a brown leather belt with a gold buckle, to hold his noble's dagger, velvet belt pouch, and sheathe for the wand, Garram.

Then he merely had to hold still while another servant took silver combs to turn the night's knots into something more presentable in a hairstyle.

He didn't go straight downstairs to his meeting room, though. No. There was something he'd really wanted to do last night, but had decided it could wait once he saw Byrhta in his private sitting room.

And given one of their later conversations of the night, he was glad he'd decided to wait.

Instead of going down the stairs, he went into his meditation chamber. A simple room, intended more for general contemplation by the duke than for any of the other purposes of formal meditation that might be employed by a magic-user.

White oak floorboards uncarpeted. Plastered walls painted a gentle gray, but otherwise unadorned. A small, simple teak desk — no drawers — with matching chair. On the desk, a small pile of parchment, a quill and inkpot.

Against one wall, a teak couch that was about as comfortable as it could get without padding or spellwork. Against the other wall, a deep, thick couch upholstered in the same gray color as the paint on the walls.

Aefric spoke the word to light the room gently, and closed the door behind him. The door, on this side, had been painted to match the walls.

He faced south, and cast the spell that would carry his words to Maev.

"I've led an assault and taken down Nelazzi. Expected to find kidnapped princesses. Found none. She'd already sold them. Real threat still extant. Stay safe."

Tension tingled in the air as he waited for her reply. Usually it came within a span of a few heartbeats.

That morning, the tension of the waiting magic seemed to strengthen as the wait stretched.

Finally, though, an answer came.

"Nelazzi! Wish I'd gone with you. Can't wait to hear the story. Stop worrying, though. Some reports are false. No Varondam princesses kidnapped. Miss you."

Wait. No Varondam princesses kidnapped? Was she saying that because Kiala wasn't considered a true princess? Or was it a false report that Kiala was taken in the first place?

He had to know. So he broke the rule they'd agreed to back when he first began keeping in touch with her by magic.

He cast the spell a second time, without letting a day or two pass first.

"Please forgive me for breaking our rule, sweet Maev, but I must know. Do you mean Kiala is no princess? Or not kidnapped?"

Her answer came back swiftly, but her voice was teasing.

"You break our rule to ask about another woman? Oh, the indignity. Rest assured. Princess Kiala is here, as she has been since my arrival."

Kiala wasn't kidnapped? Hadn't left the capital?

But he had more than reports from sailors in ports. King Colm himself had sent a letter, telling him...

Realization swept through him, doing more to shock him fully awake than a plunge into icy waters could have.

————————

When Aefric reached the black oak room for his morning meeting, he found the typical Armyrian breakfast arrayed on the buffet at the near wall. But despite his exertions of the night before, he had no appetite.

His advisers stood in their usual places. Beornric and Yrsa, in simple tunics and hose. Dark brown over dark red for him, dark green over dark brown for her. Garnotin in purple silk and Kentigern in black. Elkari in simple browns — likely linen — and Karbin clad as he so favored.

And all of them gave Aefric worried looks as he stood beside his chair.

"What's happened?" Beornric asked.

Aefric frowned. Sat. Gestured for them all to do the same.

"Deirdre arrived last night," Garnotin said. "She's to join us—"

Beornric waved him to silence, his focus still on Aefric. "Your grace?"

"I think you all know that I keep in touch with Princess Maev by spell, from time to time."

"I still think that's a bad idea," Yrsa said. "You're distracting her from her proper work. Not to mention the distraction it causes—"

She was good enough to stop when Aefric raised a forestalling hand.

"That's as may be," he said. "But I've told her about the princesses, and how I went after Nelazzi, and the frustration of finding Nelazzi had already sold them."

"Well," Garnotin said. "I believe we can trust her highness' discretion."

"You don't understand," Aefric said. "When she answered, she told me I'd had a false report. About Princess Kiala."

"That's certainly *possible*," Karbin said, "though it doesn't seem very likely. Some ports are better than others about such information, and I was—"

"I know," Aefric said, cutting in before Karbin felt the need to explain his process further. "I'm not questioning you. I'm telling you that Maev herself just told me that Princess Kiala is there with her at Vaaran Tir."

"At the Varondami royal palace?" Kentigern asked. "Then whom did the kidnappers steal, thinking they were snatching her?"

"No," Beornric said, understanding. "That's not what he's saying."

"I'm confused," Elkari said, frowning, which looked more extreme than normal because of the position of an ink stain on her cheek. "Was it not his majesty who informed you that Princess Kiala was on her way here?"

"*That's* my point," Aefric said. "King Dalius had formally approached King Colm for permission to have Princess Kiala come pay court to me. Permission our king granted, before he even sent Prince Killian to us. Which means she should have arrived before now. And yet, according to Maev, Kiala has never left Vaaran Tir."

"Risky," Kentigern said. "Not sending her, after getting formal permission. No way to interpret that as anything but an insult. And they couldn't expect us not to find out, given that we know Princess Maev mentions her in letters."

"Letters she must rely on rikas or Varondami messengers to deliver," Yrsa said. "Very easy for those letters to 'go astray.'"

"You think Varondam has the princesses," Karbin said.

"It makes sense to me," Aefric said. "But I don't understand it. What would be the point?"

"Hatay and Shachan have a loose alliance with us," Yrsa said, "and each has had a princess captured."

"Rethernyl has a *strong* alliance with us," Beornric said, "and they've had *two* princesses captured."

"And Princess Maev is in their hands already," Karbin said.

"Combine all that with what Malimfar told us," Beornric said. "That Varondam and Caiperas are allied."

"Malimfar would see that alliance whether it was there or not," Garnotin said.

"True," Yrsa said. "But just because one suspects every ship from the west of being a pirate does not mean pirates will never come from the west."

"Wait," Aefric said, turning to Kentigern and Elkari. "*Are* Varondam and Caiperas allied?"

"Not currently," Kentigern said. "I don't believe they've been formally allied since before the Godswalk Wars."

"That's correct," Elkari said. "But the precedents of alliance between them are many. Over the last ... five hundred years, Varondam and Caiperas have made and broken eight alliances of ... forty years or more. And ... three that lasted less than ten years. That I can think of offhand."

"A secret alliance could exist then," Beornric said, "which fits the sorts of activities we're talking about."

"And is entirely based on speculation on our part, and suspicion on Malimfar's part," Elkari said.

"All right," Aefric said. "Assume for a moment that such a secret alliance *does* exist. What would be the point of capturing those princesses?"

"They know," Yrsa said suddenly. "I don't know *how* they know, but they know."

"Know what?" Elkari asked. "And by 'they' do you mean Varondam?"

"Yes," Yrsa said, distracted, before turning her attention back to Aefric. "They know it's not Malimfar we're going after. It's Caiperas."

"But King Colm has been so clear," Kentigern said. "Every report I've had from—"

"Doesn't matter," Yrsa said. "Maybe their spies are just that good."

"Or maybe they already knew that Caiperas was behind the assassination attempts," Beornric said, "and deduced the rest."

"I didn't hear any rumors that would support this hypothesis during my investigation," Karbin said skeptically.

"Your grace," Yrsa said. "I know more about warfare than anyone else at this table. And my every instinct is telling me that Varondam knows Armyr is after Caiperas, not Malimfar."

Aefric thought about that for a moment.

"Suppose they do know," he said. "What's their endgame?"

"Invasion," she said without a moment's hesitation. "Any alliance they have with Caiperas is secret, so none of their neighbors could judge them for abandoning it."

She thumped the heavy, blackwood table with her fist.

"They're only waiting for us to march off to war in Caiperas with the bulk of our forces. And then, they'll invade our coastline. Steal it from us. Maybe even sail up the Searun and try for Water's End."

"Water's End would hold," Garnotin said.

"Perhaps," Yrsa allowed, "but would Behal? Lachedran? What about the rest of Deepwater? With the bulk of our knights and soldiers nearly a *thousand* miles away and winter descending in a matter of aetts?"

"And once Varondam held the lake," Beornric said, "Goldenfall would topple quickly, as would Motte. Giving them the Threepeaks and most of our mines."

"What about Merrek?" Aefric asked. "Would Varondam hit them too?"

"Too much trouble," Yrsa said. "Smaller coastline, and the only major river access is the Indecisive. They'll focus on what they'll see as the softer target and the faster victory. The size and shape of Deepwater work against us here."

"Besides," Beornric said. "Leaving Merrek untouched maintains a buffer between their newly captured land and Malimfar."

"Well, why not add Malimfar to this imaginary alliance?" Garnotin asked. "Merrek's forces will be off to war as well. Why not imagine Malimfar invading again, while we're at it?"

"Because we already know Malimfar is too weak to even try it right now," Aefric said. "And this is not just wild imagining. This is speculation with a point."

"Is it?" Garnotin asked. "Because it sounds to me as though we're spinning in unproductive circles when the one thing we *know* is that we're off to war in an *aett*."

"What fools game is Colm playing anyway," Yrsa said furiously. "Starting a *war* after midautumn. First the worries about Nelazzi, now this?"

"It was the assassination attempts," Beornric said. "They pushed him to the brink. The rest just … tipped him over."

"Wait." Kentigern said. "*That's* why Varondam would want the princesses? To accelerate the time frame of the coming war, and have our armies away through the winter?"

"That's one good reason," Yrsa said, "and it worked. Another is that they'll be holding high-value prisoners when Armyr and its allies want to come for revenge."

"This raises another concern," Beornric said, and Yrsa alone seemed to immediately spot his point.

"Have they warned Caiperas?" She said, and ran one finger down her major scar while she considered the question.

Aefric had never seen her do that before. Was it because she was thinking quickly?

"If they have," Aefric said, "then the question becomes *how much* Varondam knows. Knowing we'll invade Caiperas is one thing. Knowing about the split forces, the vectors of approach, the timing. It could turn the invasion into a trap."

"I don't think so," Yrsa said finally. "It's worse for their own invasion plans if Caiperas is ready."

"Why?" Kentigern asked.

"They want our armies as far from home as possible," Yrsa said. "And taking as many losses as possible. Their best bet for both is a prolonged conflict. With our armies plunging *deep* into the heart of Caiperas. Preferably laying siege to their cities and keeps and holding there while winter descends."

"If Caiperas is ready for us," Beornric said, again seeming right there with Yrsa, "they could turn us back at the border. We'd have no choice but to retreat. It's too late in the year to stall armies at our own border. Foraging among our own lands, taking food our own people need."

"If we *must* discuss this," Garnotin said, "then we must acknowledge that either way is good for Varondam. If Caiperas is ready for us, we'll likely sustain heavy losses because they'll hit us when and where we won't be expecting resistance."

He turned to Elkari. "What about that Malimfari report? Anything in it that would prove a current alliance between Varondam and Caiperas?"

"Had there been, I would have said so earlier," Elkari said. "The report does not address that question. It concerns only Malimfar's attempts to minimize the blame its crown should receive for the events of this past spring. The closest it comes is the scanty evidence it presents that can be interpreted to suggest that Caiperas supported Arl Reynar in the hiring of mercenaries."

"It almost doesn't matter if the alliance is real," Aefric said.

Beornric narrowed his eyes at Aefric. Nodded. "What matters is that they may know we plan to invade Caiperas soon, and intend to invade us while we're gone."

"Which is information we have to bring to the king," Aefric said. "This is too big."

"We're due to march in little more than an *aett*," Garnotin said. "It's a little late to change his plans now."

"That's not for me to say," Aefric said.

Beornric gave Aefric a thoughtful look.

"It's killing you, isn't it? Sitting here talking with us when you believe the princess is in trouble."

"Not as much as I expected," Aefric said, frowning. "Yes, I'm worried about her. And yes, part of me wishes I were in the air, flying south to her rescue."

He shook his head. "But this ... this is too big a problem for an adventurer. It may even be too big a problem for a duke. But a duke is what I am now, and I'm going to do everything in my power to keep my people safe from invasion. And that starts by exerting whatever influence I have left with the king."

"Well, before we consider sending a messenger to Armityr," Kentigern said, "we should probably first hear what word Ser Deirdre brings back from his majesty."

Aefric wanted to do a good deal more than send a messenger, but his seneschal was right.

Though before he could even go to the door to send for her, one of his knights — sounded like Temat — knocked on the meeting room door.

"Speak of an evil," Garnotion muttered, "and lo, it shall come."

DEIRDRE SAUNTERED INTO THE BLACK OAK MEETING ROOM LOOKING cool and confident as ever. Her dark red hair back in its customary long braid over her maroon leathers. Rapier on one hip, dueling dagger on the other.

But she stopped no more than three steps into the room. Frowned at the looks on the faces around the table. Tilted her head as though she were about to ask a question, but shook it away and dropped to one knee before Aefric.

"Your grace, I have returned to your side as swiftly as his majesty permitted. I would have come to you last night, but your castellan would not permit it."

She turned a look on Garnotin, but Aefric cut in before either of them said more.

"Thank you, Deirdre," he said, gesturing for her to rise. "Have a seat. I'll explain the tension in the room in a bit, but first I need to hear how his majesty reacted to my letter."

Before she stood, she held out the white, oblong crystal he had loaned her.

"I must return this first, your grace," she said with a small smile. "With my thanks. Your grace's *magari* was a joy to drive."

"I trust I won't be receiving reports of you flying low over signal towers or keep walls?"

"I certainly hope not, your grace," she said, which wasn't nearly as reassuring an answer as he would have liked.

He slipped the crystal into his belt pouch.

"But to deliver his majesty's reaction," she said, standing, "I must ask your grace to stand. And to please bear in mind, that I am only following the orders of his majesty to the letter, and even then only because one of those orders pleases me."

"You should follow *all* orders from his majesty," Garnotin said.

"As I'm sure you would without hesitation, Garn," Deirdre said, as Aefric stood before her, "but *some* of us are not blind followers."

"Please," Aefric said, raising his hands, before that back-and-forth could continue. "The message from his majesty."

"This is the first part, your grace." She stepped behind Aefric and gave him a swift kick in the behind.

Shocking, certainly, but not too hard. And she didn't point her toes, which in those boots of hers would have been quite painful.

Beornric chuckled at the kick, but Yrsa laughed aloud, thumping the table as though this were the most amusing thing she'd seen in quite some time.

Aefric gave her a dark look.

Yrsa, entirely unabashed, tried to speak through her laughter and failed.

"I believe," Beornric said, losing a fight against a smirk, "that our dear general is trying to say that you can't deny you had that coming, after disobeying an order from your king."

When Aefric looked for Deirdre again, she was right in front of him. Close enough that he reflexively started to raise his hands.

He stopped though. If she were going to strike him, he was nowhere near fast enough to stop her. Not at this range.

"This is the second part."

She grabbed his face with both hands and kissed him, hard and deep.

After the kiss had gone on for a moment — somewhere in there

Aefric and Deirdre had put their arms around each other. When had that happened? — Beornric cleared his throat noisily.

Deirdre held Aefric tighter and showed no signs of stopping their kiss.

"Deirdre," Beornric said.

She ignored him. Aefric wasn't feeling all that rushed to end it either. Deirdre certainly knew how to kiss.

"Deirdre," Yrsa said. "If you make me stand up and separate you, I swear I'm going to throw you in the lake."

Deirdre finally pulled back from the kiss. Turned to Yrsa. "Killjoy."

"This is a *meeting*," Yrsa said. "If you want to chase the bliss moment with his grace, do it on your own time."

"I must say," Beornric said, one eyebrow high, "you were *supposed* to be delivering the message from his majesty."

"Oh, but I *am*," Deirdre said with a wide smile. "His majesty was quite clear. I was instructed to give his grace a swift kick in the back-side for going against his orders. And only after I'd done so, was I to give his grace a kiss for ending Nelazzi once and for all."

"I'm fairly certain that wasn't the kind of kiss his majesty had in mind," Garnotin said.

"His majesty was not specific about the type of kiss or its dura-tion," Deirdre said, then brought one hand to her chest. "*I* believe he meant for me to express not only his own gratitude, but the gratitude of all Armyr, not to mention every port city on the Risen Sea."

She gave Aefric a smile. "In fact, I believe a few ports got left out. If I could only—"

"Sit," Beornric said, indicating the lone empty chair at the table. "And *tell* us anything else his majesty had to say."

She sighed as she took the indicated chair. "You people really need to have more fun."

Sitting wasn't quite as comfortable as Aefric would have liked, but he did his best not to show it.

"The message that accompanied the kick and kiss is this. 'Aefric, I'll let you get away with disobeying me this once, because I wanted Nelazzi dead every bit as much as you did. And because you both gave my son some much-needed field experience, and kept him alive through it. But make no mistake. Disobey me again at your own peril. And expect no kisses for any fortuitous results that stem from disobedience.'"

"What about my letter?" Aefric asked. "What did he have to say about how Nelazzi died, and what the prince intends?"

Deirdre grimaced and sighed through her nose.

"He forgives his son his ... 'impulsive deed' as he forgives your grace for his," she said, shaking her head. "Though he promises a stern talk with 'the boy.' Further, though his majesty will not allow his highness to claim a great deed out of what he did, neither will he allow others to call him the slayer of a helpless prisoner."

"Here it comes," Yrsa growled.

"Officially, it was your grace's expedition — under your grace's command and with full royal sanction — that captured Nelazzi," Deirdre said. "Karbin, myself, Ser Beornric, and all other knights and soldiers involved are to receive full credit for our deeds and contributions. Including that it was I who actually captured her.

"What about the *Swift Wave*?"

"Her captain and sailors are to receive full credit for their work as well."

"But..." Beornric said.

"But officially his highness did not slay a helpless prisoner. His highness noticed that the pirate queen Nelazzi, despite being bound and *apparently* helpless, wore a Necklace of Fire under her shirt. She was beginning to invoke its powers against us when, lacking any other option, good Crown Prince Killian slew her before she could wipe us all out."

"A *Necklace of Fire*," Aefric said.

"That's correct, your grace," Deirdre said.

"A *powerful* item," Karbin said, "that somehow you, Aefric and I all failed to notice?"

"It had been concealed under her shirt until she was bound. You, Karbin, were off dealing with the *Squid's Revenge*. Your grace was said to have been distracted by both the blows he'd taken during the fighting, and the 'general aura of magic' from Nelazzi's nearby treasure trove."

"Which was sadly buried, of course," Yrsa growled, "and thus undisprovable."

"And yet," Aefric said to Deirdre, "*you* still are supposed to have overlooked it? While *guarding* her?"

"That I was the one guarding Nelazzi when the prince struck is to be left out of the story. Prince Killian himself 'volunteered' to guard the valuable prisoner."

"Putting him alone in the perfect position to both see the necklace and kill her, I suppose."

Deirdre gave a sour nod.

"Does his majesty appreciate how much power a Necklace of Fire represents?" Karbin asked.

"Apparently his majesty has had one in the family vaults for generations."

"He seems to have quite a bit of magic in those vaults," Karbin muttered.

"And I take it he's going to *reward* his son with the necklace?" Aefric asked. "For his quick thinking?"

"No, your grace," she said. She reached down into the pouch at her belt.

He felt its fire magic the moment she pulled the necklace out. And yet, he'd felt nothing of that magic while the necklace had been in the pouch.

Clever bit of enchanting there. Likely any item put into that pouch would have its power masked.

Karbin murmured something appreciative as well. Which meant that even *he* hadn't known the necklace was in that pouch.

She held it up. A thick chain of gold, including gold settings that featured nine large rubies, the biggest of which was the size of the Brightstaff's yellow diamond.

"Gaudy thing, isn't it?" Karbin said, wrinkling his nose.

"And now, your grace," Deirdre said, setting it on the round, blackwood table, "it is *your* gaudy thing."

She slid it across the table to him.

"A bribe," Yrsa scoffed. "To make sure you uphold the story."

"I suppose his majesty expects me to wear this," Aefric said, looking down at it, "and tell the story whenever anyone asks about it. Including the role of the prince."

"He did not *explicitly* say so, your grace," Deirdre said, "but that was certainly implied."

"Well, then the next guest in my magic lab can ask me about the necklace hanging on the wall," Aefric said.

"Since when have you started taking guests into your lab?" Karbin asked.

Aefric raised an eyebrow at him.

Karbin chuckled, followed by a couple of others around the table.

"Still, if it's that powerful," Yrsa started, but stopped when she saw Aefric shaking his head.

"It's impressive, all right," he said. "But nothing on what the wand Garram can do in my hands. On me that necklace would only attract the sort of attention I don't need. What about you, Karbin?"

"A wizard who walks around wearing that thing is asking for trouble."

"Fair enough," Aefric said, then took in the rest of his advisers with a glance. "Anyone who knows me or Karbin or Deirdre — or even much about magic — will doubt that story. That the prince, who is *not* trained in magic, would spot an item like this while all three of us *overlooked* it?"

"Won't matter," Kentigern said. "There will always be questions asked about such stories."

"And inconsistencies," Elkari added. "If anything, the unlikelihood will make it feel truer to many."

"That doesn't make sense," Aefric said.

"I know, your grace," she agreed. "I find it most frustrating, myself."

"What matters here," Beornric said, "is that Killian won't get to spread his lies."

"No," Deirdre said. "He'll spread his father's."

"Which we all must keep as well," Beornric said, urgently. "Make no mistake, your grace. If we don't uphold that story—"

"We will," Aefric said, reassuringly. "Not because of a bribe, or out of fear of punishment. We'll do it because credit has not been stolen from those who followed me in that venture. That matters to me more than anything else. Let the prince claim he killed her before she surprised us with magic that no one in their right mind would believe we'd overlook. The matter is settled, and we can move on to something much more important."

"Does this mean I get to find out why you all looked so upset when I came in?" Deirdre asked.

So Aefric told her.

ONCE AEFRIC CAUGHT DEIRDRE UP ON WHAT HE AND HIS ADVISERS HAD been discussing before her arrival, silence descended on the room. The sheer weight of what they knew — and what it meant — seemed almost too much for so small a room to contain.

It was Deirdre who broke that silence.

"His majesty has no idea," she said.

Everyone looked at her.

"I got to speak with him more than once, and at some length," she said. "And he did not send me away when questions came in about war preparations."

"Did you discuss the princess with him?" Aefric asked.

"She's not my preferred topic of conversation, your grace," Deirdre said, one dark red eyebrow high. "But I did overhear the queen complaining that her highness was late sending the last report about progress towards marriage."

"Is it to be marriage then?" Beornric asked.

"Marriage... alliance..." Deirdre yawned. "They sounded like the same word on her lips. And I confess the topic did not hold my attention."

"Surprise, surprise," Garnotin said.

"We can't all be spinsters, Garn, worried only about who the local children will marry. I'm afraid you'll just have to carry that load for the rest of us."

"The important point here," Aefric said quickly, "is that Maev has been out of touch with Armityr. And for long enough that it's been noticed."

"In fairness," Beornric said, "Queen Eppida would *notice* if the report were even a day late."

"No," Deirdre said with a sigh. Possibly because they were still talking about Maev. "I heard that much. I *couldn't help* but hear that much. Her majesty's voice can be piercing when she's angry."

"How long overdue?" Yrsa asked.

"An aett. Perhaps two."

"What did his majesty say in response?" Aefric asked.

Deirdre started to say something — likely something sharp from the look on her face — but then she frowned and tossed those first words aside.

"His majesty said something to the effect of, 'Knowing Maev, she's finalizing arrangements, and holding her report for the good news."

"He's not concerned yet," Kentigern said.

"He doesn't think he has reason to be," Aefric said. "He doesn't know what we know."

"What we *think* we know," Elkari said. "There could still be a misunderstanding here. King Dalius might intend to send Princess Kiala to us in springtime, and perhaps failed to make that clear."

"I doubt it," Aefric said. "His majesty's letter seemed to imply that King Dalius wanted Varondami competition here when the other princesses arrived."

"Indeed it did," Elkari agreed. "But implications are not state-ments, let alone facts. We *know* from Princess Maev that Princess Kiala remains at Vaaran Tir. We have only *rumor* that she ever left Varondam by ship, much less that she was captured at sea."

"Rumor confirmed in several places," Karbin said.

"Rumor nonetheless," Elkari said. "Forgive me, good wizard. I do not disparage your methods. I only point out that your conclusion is *likely*, but not *certain*."

"You're missing my point," Karbin said.

Elkari adjusted attentively in her chair.

"The consistency and content of those rumors — across multiple ports — confirm that *someone* was kidnapped. Someone who could reasonably be mistaken for Princess Kiala, aboard an appropriate ship with an appropriate escort."

"So *someone* wanted people to believe that Princess Kiala was kidnapped on her way here, as the other princesses were," Yrsa said.

"Exactly," Karbin said. "Which means that if Varondam *isn't* behind it, why haven't they told the world it's not true?"

"There's no way they haven't heard the rumor by now," Beornric said. "And allowing it to stand as a falsehood — that a member of their royal family was taken—"

"An upspoken bastard," Elkari said.

"But *Varondam's* unspoken bastard," Beornric said. "The least valuable member of their royal family, yes, but it still makes them look weak. Vulnerable."

"Which means," Yrsa said, "they wouldn't let such a rumor *stand* unless they benefited by doing so."

"By keeping our attention on Caiperas," Garnotin said, apparently finally coming around to the idea. "Right where they want it."

"Either way, this changes nothing," Aefric said, which brought a bit of confusion around the table, save from Deirdre, who seemed to be enjoying the turn of conversation.

"If Varondam denied the rumor at all," Aefric said, "Armityr would hear about it first."

"They haven't, your grace," Deirdre said. "Or certainly the king still seemed concerned about it when I left, shortly after midday yesterday."

"If *our king* hasn't heard yet," Kentigern said, "Varondam has said nothing. They've had more than enough time to get word to the capital by messenger, let alone by rika."

"What about Hatay and Shachan?" Elkari asked. "Neither of them has said anything about their own kidnapped princesses."

"Precisely," Beornric said. "They've suppressed even *rumors* that would make them look weak, while they conduct their own investigation."

"Which supports the idea of Varondam being behind it all," Karbin said. "They would have been expecting word to spread about princesses being captured from Hatay and Shachan as well as Rethneryl, proving that Rethneryl was not the sole target. That word did not spread, and suddenly Varondam has a princess captured as well? One that never left its royal palace?"

"Makes sense," Yrsa said. "Increases both the scope of the threat and the urgency to act."

"My point," Aefric said standing, "is that I'm going to Armityr. I'm going to carry this word to the king myself. He needs to know what we know."

"What about Duchess Ashling?" Kentigern said suddenly. And when everyone's attention was on him, he frowned. "It's just that — or perhaps I've lost track — but are we still not concerned that Caiperas might be preparing to ambush our armies when we invade?"

"Ashling's gone to meet with King Makarios," Aefric said. "Do we have any idea how that meeting went? Or even if it's over?"

"I've heard nothing about it from Fyrcloch," Kentigern said. "Which suggests that she hasn't returned yet."

"And she might be in trouble, if Caiperas is expecting us," Garnotin said. "Is that it?"

Kentigern nodded.

"Well, what do you expect us to do about it?" Garnotin asked. "We'll be in Caiperas soon enough anyway."

Aefric though, worried at one lip while looking at Karbin. He knew what he *ought* to do, but—

"Her life may be in danger, Aefric," Karbin said softly. "I think she'd agree that's enough reason."

"Fine," Aefric said. "While I do, you try to reach Sirondfar."

They each cast their spell of contact. Aefric didn't hear what Karbin said, because he was too busy putting together the words his spell would carry to Ashling.

"Ashling. Please forgive me for reaching out this way. Caiperas might know our plans. Do you need help?"

But there was no tense tingle in the air, while he waited for a reply. Which could mean only one thing.

"Blocked," Karbin said. "I can't reach Sirondfar."

"I can't reach Ashling."

"What could cause that?" Yrsa asked.

"Wards," Aefric said. "Enough weight of stone or metal, yes, but unless those two have gone someplace a good distance underground, wards are the likely answer."

"Unfortunately," Karbin said with a sigh, "that doesn't give us information one way or the other."

"Wouldn't that mean they were imprisoned?" Garnotin asked.

"Not necessarily," Aefric said. "Armyr is a new ally, and controlling the magic available to visitors from a new ally isn't the most unreasonable idea I've heard. Especially if one of those visitors is a wizard of Sirondfar's caliber."

"We have ... such warded facilities among the guest quarters here," Kentigern said. "I can assure your grace that the entourages from Malimfar and Caiperas stayed under such wards when their princesses visited this past summer."

"Why is this the first I'm hearing about them?" Garnotin asked.

"Well," Kentigern said patiently, "I trust you realize that this is rather a large castle, and you've had quite a bit to do in taking up your duties—"

"Don't blame yourself, Garn," Aefric said. "I didn't know either."

"Neither did I," Karbin said archly, "though as court wizard I should have."

"Well," Kentigern said, still surprisingly patient, "the next time you remain here at the castle for a *full aett*, I'll try to go over as many of its magical secrets with you as we can find time for."

"All of that can wait," Aefric said, and Kentigern nodded as though those very words were the reason Garnotin and Karbin had not known. "I must leave for the capital at once."

"Put barding on your horse," Kentigern said. "You can meet your armies there."

"I'm not going with full entourage," Aefric said. "I'm taking my *magari*. Beornric, Yrsa, I need you with me when I talk to his majesty."

"You need a guard," Beornric said. "At least one. For form, if nothing else."

"I volunteer," Deirdre said quickly.

"It should be a Knight of the Lake," Garnotin said, cocking an eyebrow at Deirdre. "You know, Deirdre. One of the knights sworn specifically to protect our duke?"

"I'm his champion," Deirdre started, but this time Yrsa cut in by slapping her open hand on the table.

"His grace can take only three passengers on that fiery chariot of his. If Beornric and I are going, and I agree we should, that means exactly one more. And Deirdre, no one doubts your willingness or qualifications to protect his grace, but we're going to the *capital*. A bodyguard there will need to *look* and *act* like a bodyguard *at all times*."

"Beornric." Aefric said the name simply, but the question was implied.

"Leppina," Beornric said.

Deirdre frowned. Her nostrils flared in a quick breath. She nodded.

"Leppina's a good choice, if it can't be me. But—"

"Deirdre, you'll be busy," Aefric said. "You and Karbin both."

The two of them shared a smile.

"We do make a good team," she said.

"What are we investigating?" Karbin asked.

"If Varondam plans invasion by sea," Aefric said, "then their navy must be making ready as well as their armies. I need you two to find out if they're preparing for war, and get word to me as quickly as possible. Whatever you need to do to make that happen."

"Oh, I love a broad mandate," Deirdre said slowly.

"Try not to start a war," Garnotin said.

"I need to know," Aefric said, cutting short the Deirdre and Garnotin show. "Everything may hinge on what you two can find out."

"We won't let you down, your grace" Deirdre said with a small bow while Karbin gave a firm nod.

"Then let's get started," Aefric said. "We all have a lot to do."

INTERESTINGLY, THE PRESENCE OF YRSA ABOARD THE *MAGARI* SEEMED TO help Beornric with his fear of flying. Instead of staying at the back, clutching the chariot's sides, he stood with her in the middle, behind Aefric. Even appeared to be looking around, from time to time.

Something good about this trip, at least, to help lighten Aefric's mood.

Delays, delays, delays. The life of a duke sometimes seemed to be nothing but delays before he could *do* anything.

Even this. Even an urgent flight to the royal palace — with questions of war and the fate of princesses in the balance — and had he gotten to leave as soon as he'd cleared the doorway of his meeting room?

Of course not.

Leppina had not been on duty, so she'd had to be fetched, while Beornric explained to Temat and Arras — who *had* been on duty — why he was choosing Leppina over either of them for this mission.

Not that Aefric got to hear the reason. Because at the insistence of *all* of his advisers — even Deirdre agreed with this — he had to go change for the flight.

Didn't matter that his rooms in the royal palace had clothes that fit him well. Didn't matter that he wasn't planning on sticking around to play politics, or really anything beyond talking with the king and getting back into the air as soon as he could.

No. He was a peer of the realm traveling to the royal palace, and he was expected to look the part.

So while the three knights accompanying him kitted themselves for battle in full plate, Aefric was dressed for a freaking ball.

A silk shirt of navy blue, embroidered with silver along the cuffs and trim. Hose of Deepwater gray. Low, soft doeskin shoes dyed to match the shirt and laced with cloth-of-silver laces. A doeskin belt dyed to match the hose.

The ring he'd been given by the queen — featuring a large emerald set into sixteen strands of gold, each a different shade — on his left hand. On his right, the gold ring that featured his personal sigil — a staff with two bolts of lightning coming from it, one upward and to the left, the other upward to the right.

And weighing heavily on his neck, that awful, gaudy Necklace of Fire. Because it was a new gift from the king, and not wearing it for this visit would *absolutely* be taken as an insult.

Aefric tried to argue against this, but the others all formed a united front. And when Elkari began citing past incidents caused by the poor reception of a gift by a ranking noble, he knew he had no choice but acquiescence.

He at least took some comfort from the fact that no one would deny him the wand at his belt or the Brightstaff in his hand. And more, that his cloak matched the others. Navy blue silk, lined with Deepwater gray wool.

Not that he really needed a cloak aboard a *magari*. The fires of the horses and chariot might've been phantasmal, but they still seemed to abate the chill of wind during flight.

Still, a change of garment was not the only delay. Beornric insisted Aefric have breakfast — appetite or not — and Yrsa supported him immediately.

That battle Aefric surrendered before any more allies jumped into the fray against him.

He didn't eat much. Some slices of turkey and good sharp cheese.

Chunks of nava fruit, apple, and casaba melon. A buttered roll of honeyed oat bread.

That was about all his anxious stomach could handle. And anxiety seemed to afflict him more as a duke than it ever had as an adventurer.

But then, as an adventurer, he'd only *really* had to worry about himself. Now, though, the lives and fortunes of many *thousands* of people depended on what he said and did.

With all the delays, it seemed that at least an hour must have passed between the time that Aefric had urgently exited his meeting room and the time he and the others finally took off from his public floor balcony.

Admittedly, though. While he would have felt just fine about leaving Water's End in riding leathers and a simple linen tunic, as the hours passed on the long flight from Water's End to Armityr, he was glad of the food in his belly. Kept his concentration up.

He was grateful, too, for the *magari's* speed — it flew much faster than he could by spell alone — and that steering it took considerably less effort than flying without it.

They crossed the Kerrik Forest sometime around midmorning, the great fork in the Kingsroad by about midday, and shortly after that came the approach to Armityr.

Few aetts had passed since Aefric was last at the capital, but more had changed than he expected.

For one thing, his majesty had already begun to gather his troops. The chaotic tent cities filled with merchants and laborers outside the western city walls of Armityr were joined on the north side by the organized and structured camps of a good many troops.

"I make three thousand," Yrsa said, before Aefric could even consider counting. "That's about half of all that should be inbound from the royal lands."

"I saw troops coming down from the north," Beornric said. "Couldn't spot the banners, but they'll be some of the numbers you're expecting."

"None to the south, though," Leppina said. "And I looked."

"Part of the illusion," Yrsa said. "The southern troops are likely mustering farther south to keep selling Caiperas on the idea that we'll be invading Malimfar."

The massive city itself — nearly half-again larger even than Water's End — was still rebuilding after the assaults it had taken during the Godswalk Wars. But repairs looked to be coming along well.

The outer walls — white and gray stone like the palace itself — were repaired, though the gatehouse at the new southern gate was still being built.

The sinkholes Aefric had seen during his last visit were largely repaired as well, which suggested na'shek work. And the sections of the city worst hit looked to be most of the way to rebuilt. Certainly their buildings would be complete before winter set in.

And the brilliant stonework of the royal palace itself — the oldest and largest construction anywhere on Qorunn that was said to be built entirely by human hands — stood tall and strong and fine again.

All six of its towers stretched to heights of two or three hundred feet once more, with no sign that many of them had been collapsed and one listing only two seasons ago.

And the main keep itself — easily a hundred-fifty feet tall and five hundred wide — had yet been only perhaps three-fourths intact when Aefric visited a few aetts past.

Nevertheless, the keep looked good as new, from the mortarless fit of its stonework to the patrolled crenellations of its walls.

For the first time, Aefric was seeing the palace in all its true glory, and the sight was stirring enough to make him whistle appreciation.

"Built by human hands," Beornric said, "but supported by wizardry."

"I know," he said, still hearing awe in his own voice. "I was told of how it could self-repair. But to see it work so well, so *fast*."

"It builds speed, the less it has to do," Beornric said. "The more it repairs, the less its power to do so is split among its many needs."

Aefric raised his eyebrows at hearing a magical explanation from Beornric.

The older knight shrugged. "I asked Nayoria about it once. She's made a study of its magic."

"I don't doubt it," Aefric said, easing the *magari* down now. "I hope to make a similar study of Water's End one day."

But Beornric wasn't listening. Apparently even a gentle descent was too much to ask of his new appreciation for flying. He'd moved to the back of the chariot, closed his eyes, and held the sides while Yrsa spoke softly to him.

Aefric did his best to land softly on the green and gold painted tile courtyard just outside the tall, arched main palace doors.

Nevertheless, guards — oddly including a young battle wizard in quilted robes — approached warily. Menacing pikes in the guards' hands, and a spell etching orange readiness around the fingers of the battle wizard.

A fire blast? He was readying a fire blast? Good thing for him Aefric wasn't an enemy.

"Peace," Yrsa called. "Ser Aefric Brightstaff, Duke of Deepwater and Baron of Netar, Hero of the Battles of Deepwater and Frozen Ridge and Vanquisher of the Pirate Queen Nelazzi, comes to bring urgent news to your king. Conduct us to the royal presence at once!"

Aefric wasn't sure which surprised him more, that Yrsa had acted as herald instead of Beornric, or that she'd given him a new title.

AEFRIC AND HIS KNIGHTS WERE CONDUCTED THROUGH BEAUTIFUL HALLS and up a grand, marble staircase to a waiting room on the third floor, at the back of the keep.

But it was clearly one of the better waiting rooms.

The flooring was tiled in sea green marble, with swirls of white, like foam. The walls and ceiling were tiled in sky blue marble, also swirled with white, but these like clouds.

Low along the walls had been painted a handful of ships, a beautiful mermaid, sunning on a rock, and the coils of a distant sea serpent. On the ceiling, in the center, a large yellow and orange sun.

The sun was enchanted to give off light, when necessary, but it wasn't lit up just then. Plenty of light came in through the three arched, glass-paned windows along the outside wall.

Out the windows, a view of a courtyard below, where young warhorses were finishing training for the coming conflict.

The room featured in its center a pair of couches, spaced and angled so that both vaguely pointed across a long, low table at a pair of chairs. All of the furniture looked to have been made from well-worn wood that had once been part of ships.

Aefric and Beornric sat on one couch while they waited. Yrsa and Leppina sat on the other. A servant brought them a light white wine, served in crystal goblets and poured from a crystal pitcher, which he left on the table, beside a wide silver platter covered in chocolate candies.

Leppina helped herself to the candies, but she was the only one. Well, Aefric allowed himself one, but his stomach was too unsettled by his news. Even the excellent chocolate didn't set well within him, and he decided that the wine was a bad idea.

He was alone in declining the wine.

The wait felt eternal, but the three windows gave that feeling the lie. The shadows outside had not lengthened overmuch, nor the warhorses finished training for the day, before the room's one door — which also looked to have been part of a ship once upon a time — opened, and a servant called in, "Their majesties, your king and queen."

Aefric and the others got to their feet at once, of course, then knelt on the hard tiles as their majesties approached.

Looking fit and ready for battle, King Colm had cut his graying black hair battlefield short, and wore a simple white silk shirt — hardly any gold trim, even — over cream hose. A token rapier at his side, and his diamond wedding ring on the middle finger of his right hand.

Queen Eppida looked far more ready for a ball herself, in a complex, long-sleeved gown of sapphire blue, to match her eyes, with her golden curls down and dancing around her shoulders. She wore her own wedding ring on the same finger, an enchanted, protective golden torc around her neck, and a rapier of her own at her side.

Aefric offered his right hand. The king didn't hesitate to kiss it. The queen — as she always seemed to do with Aefric, though not with everyone — kissed his hand as well.

"Rise and be seated," King Colm said, which they did — after their majesties took the two chairs — save for Leppina, who moved to stand guard behind where Aefric sat.

"Good to see you, Aefric, Beornric, Yrsa," the king said. "And ... Ser Leppina, I think, isn't it?"

"Yes, your majesty," Leppina said, bowing again from the neck.

"Didn't you fight for my sister during the wars?" Queen Eppida asked.

"Your majesty, I did," Leppina said, "albeit briefly. But I stood with General Yrsa during the Battle of Deepwater, which was how I came to swear myself to his grace."

"You do have a knack for inspiring loyalty, don't you, Aefric?" Queen Eppida said, though not as though she expected an answer. "Knights and borogs alike all rally to your banner."

"If they do so, your majesty, it only makes me a better vassal in your service."

She chuckled, and he knew the look in her eye and the words that followed in her mind, if not spoken aloud this time. *Yes, you are learning the noble's games, aren't you?*

"If a *willful* vassal betimes," King Colm said with half a smile. "But let us not linger on such thoughts. That you come here now with urgent news worries me. Does it concern my son?"

"Your majesty, it does not," Aefric said. "I haven't seen the prince since he departed Water's End by ship yesterday morning."

Queen Eppida arched an eyebrow. "And tell me, your grace, how did things stand between you when you parted?"

"I don't need an answer to that to know they quarreled," King Colm said, waving a dismissive hand. "No point in making him say so. Get to this news then. If it's not about Killian, what is it?"

Telling the king the direct, unmodified truth meant admitting that Aefric had kept in touch with Maev by spell since she'd left for Varondam this past spring. But the most important parts of the story would not hold up if he withheld that detail.

So he told it all. He began with how he'd conducted his own investigation into the attempt on his life, and what he'd learned from it — including the kidnappings of Princess Raedrun Al'Trener of Hatay and Princess Jodis Ol'Nariss of Shachan.

He briefly covered the assault on Nelazzi to explain what she had told him about her sale of the princesses. And then he had to admit how he'd kept in touch with Maev, to explain how he'd warned her to be careful.

He pushed on quickly into how Maev had told him that Princess Kiala had never left Vaaran Tir, and what that fact seemed to imply about everything else that was going on. The kidnappings of the princesses. The war with Caiperas. The likely assault on his coastline. Even the delay in Maev's latest report.

As Aefric's tale progressed, the king looked more and more concerned. The queen, on the other hand, grew impassive. Expressionless as a clear sky.

And Aefric held nothing back. He told them everything he knew and everything he speculated. And he did his best to make clear which was which.

He also made sure both Beornric and Yrsa contributed to the telling, because there were points those two could drive home far more cleanly than Aefric could hope to.

"...which was how I came to be here now, your majesties," Aefric finished. "Obviously such information could not be withheld from the crown so much as a heartbeat longer than it had to be."

The king frowned. "You mention that you believe Varondam to hold princesses from Hatay and Shachan as well, yes?"

Aefric nodded. "Your majesty, Karbin's evidence on this point was convincing."

"Strange then," his majesty said, "that *I* have heard no word of this before now."

"Your majesty," Beornric said, "we believe Hatay and Shachan conceal these kidnappings in order to avoid looking weak while they conduct their own investigation."

"And yet," Queen Eppida said, "Rethneryl freely admits their own loss."

"Your majesty," Yrsa said, "Rethneryl has less to fear from looking weak. It is stronger than either Hatay or Shachan, and has us as its staunch ally."

"And Rethneryl has publicly declared that it has identified the culprit and is taking action to rectify the situation," Beornric added.

"I see," the king said. "Speaking of action, Aefric, tell me. What action have *you* taken on this information already?"

"Your majesty, very little. I came here as soon as I could. But the one thing I did before leaving was task my court wizard, Karbin, and one of my strongest investigators, Ser Deirdre Ol'Miri, to determine whether or not Varondam is preparing for war. Obviously—"

"You *what?*" Queen Eppida snapped. "You sit there claiming to be a loyal vassal, but sent agents to *spy* on Varondam while *alliance negotiations* are underway? Recall them! At once!"

"Peace, Ep," King Colm said, raising a calming hand. "I understand the boy's instinct."

"But—"

"*Peace,*" he said again. "Or I'll have to ask you to leave the room. This concerns the war and there is little time to determine my proper course of action."

The queen looked for all the world as though she had about a dozen more objections to make, but firmed her mouth into a line and shot death at the king with her eyes.

Not for the first time was Aefric glad that Eppida Fyrenn had never studied magic. The only death she could glare was figurative.

"I am handling it," King Colm said, voice low.

Queen Eppida huffed, but sat back in her chair. "Well *handle* it then."

"As I was saying," King Colm said, turning back to Aefric. "I understand your instinct, but she's right. You must recall your agents at once."

"Of course, your majesty," Aefric said, "though may I ask—"

"You may in a moment," the king said, arching an imperial eyebrow. "*After* you've recalled your agents. Don't pretend you cannot do so here and now, Aefric. You've certainly had no trouble contacting my *daughter* with your magic."

"Of course, your majesty," Aefric said, bowing. He cast his contact spell twice then. The version that did not allow for a response. To both Karbin and Deirdre he said the same thing.

"By order of the king, your mission is canceled. Return to Water's End at once."

"Oh, so no pretense of royal sanction this time?" Queen Eppida said softly once Aefric was finished.

The king ignored the jibe.

"There is no need for your agents," he said, addressing Aefric's unasked question. "My own court wizard should be able to determine easily enough if Maev is in trouble, and if Varondam is preparing for war."

"Of course," Queen Eppida said softly. "Why send a vassal's spies when you can send you own."

"Not at all," King Colm said with a smile. "The princess' report is late, and I've waited as long for it as possible, considering that we have battle plans to finalize. Naturally I need to know the status of our alliance negotiations before I march into Malimfar."

"All right," Eppida acknowledged. "That *is* believable."

"Give me *some* credit, Ep. I may not be a Fyrenn, but I do know a thing or two about politics."

Aefric finally snuck a glance at Beornric, but from the expression on the older knight's face he couldn't believe it either. That their majesties were openly quarreling in front of a vassal.

Yes, it was a private room, but it was still a shocking sight.

"Now," King Colm said. "As soon as we're done here, I'll send Nayoria to Vaaran Tir. She should be back with an answer by tonight."

"And if that answer is that I'm right?" Aefric asked.

"If you're right, then your forces will stay behind and defend your coastline. But Caiperas must still answer for its crimes."

"Please, your majesty," Yrsa said. "Wait until spring."

"What about Rethneryl?" Aefric asked, making the king frown. But the queen saw where he was going.

"He's right, Colm," she said. "Rethneryl burns for Caiperan blood not just for our sake, but for the sake of their princesses. And if those princesses are in *Varondam*, we owe it to King Edan to tell him."

"Which will shift his priority," Colm said, punching his fist into his other palm. He calmed himself through a deep breath. "All right, Aefric. Beornric. Yrsa. If Nayoria proves you right, I'll hold off the war for spring, in favor of … well, that will have to be determined."

"We'll have to be careful at that point," Queen Eppida said. "If his grace is right, then Varondam is no ally. Might be working with Caiperas. And then they'd need only Malimfar to present a united front against us."

"An unlikely alliance," King Colm said.

"As an alliance, yes. But if they turn from us and split Malimfar between them?"

"If they do, then at the very least we'll seize the other half of the Indecisive River Valley and still come out ahead." He smiled at Aefric. "I believe we hold part of Malimfar's territory there even now."

"That's not my point," Queen Eppida said.

"Nor mine," King Colm said. "For it does not address either the crimes of Caiperas nor the deceit of Varondam. But one step at a time."

"Colm—"

"Hold a moment, beloved," King Colm said, and called for a page. When the young man came in, clad all in gold and green livery, his majesty continued, "See the duke and his entourage to their rooms to freshen up after their journey."

"Are we staying here tonight, your majesty?" Aefric asked hesitantly.

"I haven't decided yet."

AEFRIC'S APARTMENTS IN THE ROYAL PALACE MIGHT NOT HAVE STOOD beside his own in Water's End, but he couldn't deny that they were spacious. Even by the standard to which he was becoming accustomed. Further, they were very well appointed, and left no doubt — from the colors of rugs and paint to the subjects of the tapestries and paintings — that these rooms were reserved for Deepwater's duke.

Ordinarily, Aefric would have enjoyed the chance to relax for a time in surroundings more sumptuous than even his apartments in Behal.

But in his head he felt the time passing, and the need to act building with each breath. Each heartbeat.

How much more confirmation could his majesty want?

Beornric and Yrsa didn't help matters. They both paced as well, and spoke of nothing but what sorts of actions his majesty might countenance, once Nayoria obtained final proof.

"A rescue," Yrsa said. "Perhaps with multiple assault teams on the main targets, while others create a smokescreen."

"No," Beornric said. "A political solution is better. Contact Hatay, Shachan and Rethneryl for support then blockade Varondam until all princesses are returned, safe and sound."

"A blockade this time of year?" Yrsa scoffed. "How many ships do you want to lose to the winter storms?"

They went back and forth like this while Aefric distracted himself by writing a letter to his castellan at the Iron Keep in Netar. There was little to say in the letter though, beyond that Netar would, of course, support his majesty's military actions, and that Netar's troops would join with Deepwater's before crossing Armyr's borders.

After he sealed the letter, he gave it to a page to send by messenger. And then there was little to do beside pace, or get involved in the debate with Yrsa and Beornric. Neither of which sounded like profitable courses of action.

Aefric was contemplating the value of taking a bath when he realized he had an answer right there in his pouch.

The teak box.

Thanks to Deepwater's long tradition of magic-using nobles, the ducal apartments here at Water's End included a simple yet functional laboratory.

"All right, you two," Aefric said. "While you worry away at the question of what we'll be doing tomorrow, I'm going to go get some research—"

A knock on the door. Leppina's knock.

"—done."

Leppina opened the door and leaned in. "Your grace, her majesty is here."

Of course she was.

Aefric frowned, while Beornric and Yrsa looked at each other as though sharing thoughts as easily as words.

"Well," Aefric said, forcing a smile, "by all means, don't keep her majesty waiting on my doorstep. Admit her."

"Her majesty, the queen," Leppina said, as Queen Eppida entered.

Fortunately everyone in the room was already standing. Aefric began to kneel, but she cut him off.

"Don't bother with the formalities just now, Aefric." She took in Yrsa and Beornric with a glance. "You two. Out."

"At once, your majesty," Beornric said with a bow.

"Of course, your majesty," Yrsa said with a bow of her own.

And then Aefric was alone with the queen.

"May I offer refreshment?" Aefric asked. "The servants are in their waiting room. I think all the pacing was making them nervous."

Queen Eppida quirked a smile. "Suppose I'm here for the noble privilege? After all, if your grace doesn't stay here tonight, now might be my only opportunity."

"That's certainly possible, of course," Aefric said. "And quite a compliment, if so. But I don't believe it to be the case."

"And why not?" she asked, giving her hips a touch of swing as she took a few steps closer.

"Because we both know how your majesty prefers to have me remove her clothes at such times. And yet she has arrived not clad in an expendable linen dressing gown, but in a beautiful and valuable silk dress. One I doubt she would wish to see magically torn to shreds."

"Honestly," Queen Eppida said, casting an eye over her own gown, "it will be out of fashion soon. But you're quite right. That's not why I'm here."

She gestured to a well-padded couch of Deepwater gray.

"Sit with me, Aefric, and let us talk."

"Of course, your majesty," Aefric said.

He stood the Brightstaff beside the couch and sat down, straight and proper, while Queen Eppida lounged beside him as though she might be reconsidering the noble privilege.

"Do relax, Aefric," she said. "We can send for wine, if it will help."

"It wouldn't, I'm afraid," he said. "I ... have been a man of action all my life. The waiting a noble must endure. I find it ... trying."

She smiled. "One of the qualities you share with Colm, and one of the things I like about you. He puts up a very good front, but I can tell you that he's worried enough about his daughter to consider marching his armies straight through Malimfar all the way to Vaaran Tir. If that's what's needed."

"But if Varondam and Caiperas *are* allied..." Aefric started, but the queen finished for him.

"...Caiperas might be ready to march right down Armyr's waiting throat, while its armies were elsewhere. Yes."

"It seems that war is only practical if you're otherwise surrounded by allies."

"Oh, it's not so simple as that," Queen Eppida said, waving a dismissive hand. "Deals can be brokered short-term to avoid such complications. And the threat of repercussions prevents weaker kingdoms from trying to take advantage of such openings."

She tilted her head thoughtfully. "Which you must know instinctively on some level, because you've expressed no concern about Malimfar trying to invade again, once my sister's armies march away from their shared river valley."

"I've heard a good deal about how long it will be before Malimfar could risk another war."

"Exactly," she said. "Taking land is one thing. But *holding* land is another matter entirely. A farmer might try to take fields he believes abandoned by his ranching neighbor, only to find himself facing quite a problem when that rancher and his family return."

"And our armies would return battle-tested and ready to fight for their homes. Is that it?"

"Part of it," Queen Eppida said, "but I have another question of more importance. Have you heard from my sister?"

"Zoleen or Ashling?"

"I was thinking of Ashling, but I'm now curious about Zoleen as well."

"I haven't heard from Zoleen since before she left on her new assignment."

Queen Eppida's brow darkened and her nostrils flared in a calming breath.

"And Ashling," Aefric continued quickly, "I haven't heard from since before she left for Caiperas."

"Neither have I," Queen Eppida said. "Which might not mean anything. She's likely to finish her work at Reyvenue before telling me about it. But if Varondam knows our plans and has warned Caiperas..."

She shook her head.

"Tell me, Aefric," she said, leaning forward urgently. "That contact spell you used earlier. Nayoria tells me it is only possible to contact someone that way when the wizard is 'sufficiently acquainted' with them. But she's been maddeningly unclear about what 'sufficiently acquainted' means."

"It could be thought of as a kind of sliding scale, where contact goes from—"

"I don't care about the details," she said, waving away what he was saying. "I need to know if *you* are 'sufficiently acquainted' with *Ashling* to contact her by that spell. Because Nayoria is not."

"I am," Aefric said. "And I tried this morning. I failed to reach her."

The queen sighed and closed her eyes as though preparing for a blow. "Does the failure mean she's dead?"

"No," Aefric said. "Most likely her guest accommodations are behind wards preventing such contact."

She frowned, but opened her eyes. "I could see that. I wouldn't be surprised if we have similar arrangements."

"Karbin attempted to contact Sirondfar the same way, with the same result."

"And I doubt anything could kill that old bastard," she muttered. Nodded. "Thank you, Aefric. That helps."

"I hope she leaves their palace at Reyvenue before we invade."

"Obviously," Queen Eppida said in a droll tone. "I doubt she'll remain there that long, though. She knows she has her own warfare preparations to make. Even if she isn't aware of the accelerated timeline."

Aefric wasn't sure what to say to that, but the queen gave him a slant look.

"So," she said. "How do *you* feel about Zoleen's new assignment?"

"Obviously, such an important post for someone so young is—"

"A great compliment, yes, yes," she said, leaning a little closer. "I'm not asking the *duke's* opinion of the posting. I'm asking the *man* how he feels about having Zoleen sent so far away from him."

"I'll miss her, of course. And I hate that I didn't even get to say goodbye."

"There are many ways to miss someone. Do you miss her in a way that makes you imagine never having to miss her again?"

Aefric considered that through a long, slow breath.

"If I had to decide here and now whether or not I would ask her to marry me, then the answer is no. I would not."

"Why not?"

"Because if I'm going to marry someone, I want to feel certain about them. And I don't feel that certain about Zoleen."

The queen considered that for a moment. Nodded.

"Fair," she said. "And all the more reason for me to be angry with Colm for denying Zoleen the chance to bring you that certainty."

"I'm sorry."

"Don't be," she said, with a shake of her head. "While I'm sorry to hear Zoleen will not be making you part of the family, I never want you to feel the need to hide the truth from me. We're going to be working together for a very long time, and our working relationship is more important to me than whom you marry."

"Thank you, your majesty."

She arched an eyebrow. "And I believe that's the last time I wish to hear my courtesy from your lips over the next few hours."

Aefric had to check himself from using that courtesy again immediately. "Oh?"

"I am both anxious and at loose ends, Aefric. A combination I deplore. Colm is busy, and will be until close to dinner. And so my choices are to seethe about being excluded from his deliberations — I *love* the man, but I *hate* that he will not hear my thoughts on war — or to find a distraction that will pass the time pleasantly."

She smiled. "And I believe you, my man of action, could do with a more vigorous activity than pacing."

"But," Aefric said, while she stood and faced him with her arms extended to her sides, "what about your dress?"

"I told you. It will be out of fashion soon anyway."

ALTHOUGH RESEARCHING THE TEAK BOX WOULD HAVE BEEN A MORE *profitable* use of Aefric's time, he had to admit that the queen's choice of activities was a good one.

Yes, there were times when Aefric understood Armyr's embrace of the noble privilege. And this was definitely one of them.

Eppida — for he twasn't to think of her as the queen at times like this — wasn't just an active lover, but aggressive. She gave his tense muscles a needed workout while diverting his busy mind with pleasure.

They passed the afternoon this way, right up until the call came for them to prepare for dinner. Then they shared one more kiss, and waited for a servant to fetch her a dressing gown and cloak.

After that kiss, still naked, Queen Eppida — and he knew without being told that she was *Queen* Eppida again — rose from the shambles of the bed and dug through the tattered remains of her silk dress for a pouch he hadn't noticed on her belt.

From it, she withdrew a small jar of a salve he had only previously been given by the king himself.

She smiled and held it up, posing just a bit, so he had to work to keep his attention on her eyes.

"I know Colm usually gives you this for the little marks I leave behind."

Little marks. Try countless scratches and bite marks. At least she never actually left a wound.

She tossed the jar to Aefric and he caught it.

"I thought you hadn't planned on the noble privilege," he said.

The serving girl came in then, and the queen spoke as the girl helped her into a simple, white linen dressing gown and forest green cloak, with gold trim.

"I hadn't. But one thing to keep in mind, my dear duke. Although it is impossible to plan for the unexpected, a clever noble prepares for the unlikely." She winked at him. "See you at dinner."

She left then, but the serving girl remained, and stood waiting for his attention.

"Is there something else?" Aefric asked. "Because if you're expecting to help wash me, I can assure you I'll handle that detail myself."

"Very good, your grace," she said with a bow. "In that case I should inform your grace that, once he has finished washing up, a page awaits without to conduct him to the presence of the king."

Aefric winced. "Directly?"

"Yes, your grace."

"You don't meant the king is waiting for me."

"I believe he is, your grace."

"Please find Sers Beornric and Yrsa and have them meet me in my sitting room," Aefric said, kicking away the sheets to jump out of bed.

"Forgive me, your grace," the serving girl said — eyes widening as she watched Aefric clean himself up with a quick spell — "but I am told Sers Beornric and Yrsa have already been conducted to the royal presence."

"They're *all* waiting on me?"

"I believe so, your grace."

"How long ago was that page sent to fetch me?"

"Only—"

"In terms of royal patience."

"Oh," she said, blushing. "Well ... I'm not certain I'm the best—"

"I swear that I need only to know how much trouble I'm in for keeping the king waiting, and not trying to trap you into speaking against his majesty."

"Then may I suggest that your grace hurry?"

"Help me dress?"

She did so, with quick efficiency, and between them Aefric was clad once more in his clothes from earlier. Much faster, in fact, than he could have dressed himself.

"Oh," Aefric said, while she gave his hair a quick comb through, "why was the page kept waiting? Why wasn't I informed of his arrival sooner?"

"Her majesty left orders that if she decided to seek the noble privilege with your grace, she was not to be interrupted until the time came to prepare for dinner."

He sighed. The serving girl gave him a sympathetic look.

"You realize," he said, "this is all likely some game they're playing between themselves. Her wanting the noble privilege. The timing. All of it."

"Far be it for me to speculate, your grace."

"Well," he said, calling the Brightstaff to his hand, "if you ever have the choice, do try to avoid coming between them."

"May the hand of Vera always will it so," she said, and made a warding gesture.

The page waiting for Aefric in his sitting room was a woman with dark blonde hair. In fact, she didn't even look like a young woman on the cusp of her majority, but a woman grown. Perhaps close to his own age. He wouldn't have even thought her a page, were she not wearing royal livery.

A woman grown, serving as a page? That was odd.

Aefric almost asked about it, but shook the question away. He had no time to waste.

"Please," he said, "conduct me to the king. And if you know any shortcuts, please take them."

"I might know a few," the page said with a sly smile.

They called Leppina in from the hallway beyond, and the three of them left in a hurry.

The page led Aefric and Leppina over to a cabinet, where she twisted the knobs of three drawers. One counterclockwise, and the next two clockwise.

One side of the cabinet slid forward in an arc, revealing a narrow stone passage. A torch a few steps down the passage sprang to life with silent, heatless fire.

"This way, your grace," she said, and led Aefric swiftly through a series of passages, down two different sets of tight stairs, and up a third.

The passageway smelled like lit beeswax candles, which was a bit maddening, because obviously even the torches weren't burning with actual fire.

The passages were cool and breezy as well, which seemed even stranger, and made Aefric lament that he couldn't stop and study the touch of magic he felt all about him through the passages.

They passed doors from time to time, and a handful of younger pages.

After the third time they passed another page, Aefric couldn't hold back his curiosity any further.

"May I ask your name?"

"Of course, your grace. I am Rashien Ol'Ofaris, third child and second daughter of Ler Nadell Ol'Ofaris."

"Well, Rashien, I don't believe I've met a page who's come of age before."

"There aren't many of us, your grace," she said. "Usually there must be some compelling reason to remain a page after one comes of age."

"Would it be prying to ask about your compelling reason?"

"Well, I don't know that most would find my reasons *compelling*, as it were, but being a senior page in the royal palace is more exciting than life at Father's castle." She gave Aefric a quick smile. "And it helps that I'm something of a favorite of his majesty's."

"I could see where you'd find those reasons compelling."

"And now, your grace," she said stopping outside one particular door, "we're as close as we dare come by shortcut."

She opened that door — the other side looked like bare wall — and Aefric found himself in a hallway that lacked any marble at all.

White stonework and blackwood paneling made for a stark contrast as Rashien led him past busts of past kings and queens and paintings of a military nature to a door at the end of the hall.

She knocked.

The king's muffled voice answered.

"If that's not the duke of Deepwater, whoever knocks had better have a good reason."

She opened the door and announced him.

***

The room Aefric entered was smaller than he expected. Not much larger than his black oak meeting room back at Water's End. A comparison he could not help making because, like that meeting room, this room was entirely paneled — floor, walls and ceiling, even the cabinets along the walls and the door in the corner — in black oak.

It smelled of wood oil, and was lit by the soft white glow of ... yes, Nayoria's spellwork.

The table in the center, though, was large, rectangular, and made of teak. And it was currently covered in maps, including markers representing troops across Armyr and Rethneryl, as well as certain others in Caiperas.

The king stood at one end of the table, looking irritated. He hadn't changed for dinner, but wore the same clothes from earlier. Which made Aefric glad he hadn't changed either.

Yrsa and Beornric stood together — and Aefric noted that neither of them wore a weapon. They looked over troop placements in Deepwater, making adjustments, though they paused in this as Aefric entered.

Ser Beatritz Ol'Teraak, captain of the Knights of the Crown, stood near the king, muttering something to him.

Ser Beatritz was short, but made up in muscle what she lacked in height. Her graying chestnut braid was currently draped over her right shoulder, calling attention to the old arrow scar along that side of her jaw, and the bit of earlobe she was missing. She wore her full plate armor, as well as the only weapon in the room not carried by Aefric — a greatsword, strapped to her back.

Across the table from Beornric and Yrsa, looking up from an apparent conversation about Caiperan troop deployment, were two women Aefric didn't know. Both of them magic-users of some stripe.

The first had the feel of a strong dweomerblade, and was easily the oldest person in the room. She stood tall and lean in a dark yellow silk shirt over dark orange hose. Her battlefield-short hair was snow white, her skin tanned and lined, and she had a single visible scar, straight across the tip of her chin.

Aefric had a feeling that the quick glance she gave him had assessed him in terms of threat potential.

The other woman felt more like a wizard, and a reasonably good one. She appeared to be perhaps a decade older than Aefric. With the kind of smooth, pale skin that marked her as a noble as surely as her bearing. Her wavy black hair teased down past her shoulders, and she wore a gown of soft white silk that looked too low-cut for what appeared to be a war council.

Then again, her fine gold chain belt, with its series of small carnelians seemed out of place in the room as well.

And yet, it was she who gave Aefric a shocked look. "How *dare* you come armed into the royal presence?"

"Peace, good Gwenellia," King Colm said, though he sounded more irritated than peaceable himself. "Our dear duke here has more than earned the right to carry weapons in my presence."

He clapped his hands once for attention.

"As not all of you have met, let us dispense with that part quickly." He gestured to Aefric. "This, of course, is his grace, Ser Aefric Brightstaff, Duke of Deepwater and so on."

His majesty gestured to the mollified, yet uncertain woman. "Aefric, this is her grace, Gwenellia Quinnian, Duchess of Neastall, and emissary from the crown Rethneryl."

They bowed to each other with a quick greeting.

"And this, of course, is my general. That legendary knight, Ser Paic Ol'Shenquill."

Paic Ol'Shenquill? Slayer of the Kohl Manticore? Holder of Olan's Pass against an entire horde of tarok?

As Keifer, of course, he knew her from the sourcebooks, and from references in at least three different adventures. But she was one of those great, established heroes of Qorunn. Like Kainemorton.

She might even have been one of the Silver Arrows, when she was younger. He couldn't remember.

Growing up as Aefric, though, he'd heard so many stories attached to that name that he'd come to believe she was a fictional creation. An amalgamation of several knights, not an actual woman.

The irony of this was not lost on him.

As she bowed to Aefric, he gave her the salute of a noble to a knight.

"Your reputation precedes you," he said.

"As does yours, your grace," she said in reply.

"All right," King Colm said, "let's not get distracted with war stories. We've delayed too long as it is."

"Please forgive my tardiness, your majesty—"

"I believe I can guess the reason for it," the king said dryly. "So let us move on from that as well."

"What word from Nayoria then?" Aefric asked, stepping up to the table.

"None," the king said, shaking his head. "And overdue."

"I don't know her well enough to reach her by spell," Aefric said. "And in case your majesty wonders, I do know Ashling well enough. In fact, I attempted to contact her this morning while my ducal wizard attempted to contact her wizard. Both attempts failed, most likely due to them being behind wards at Reyvenue."

"Unfortunate," the king said. "But that does answer my next question."

"I don't believe there's reason for concern about Nayoria," Duchess Gwenellia said. "The Varondami can be expansive in their formality. Your wizard might not yet be in a position to return without giving offense."

"She's acting as a messenger," Paic said, "not a visiting noble. She should be afforded a messenger's freedom of movement. Which means she should have returned by now."

"I agree with Paic," Beatritz said. "Several of us have known Nayoria a very long time. Tardiness is not a trait I associate with her."

"And yet," Duchess Gwenellia said, "messenger or not, she remains the Royal Court Wizard of Armyr. They may fear that not giving her full accolades could be taken as an insult."

She raised an eyebrow to Aefric. "I often find that those who lack the gift for spellwork fear giving offense to those who possess it. Would you not agree?"

"I would," Aefric said. "But I should point out that my own ducal wizard has — over his own objections — been required to serve as messenger for me a time or two. And he has always been accorded the freedoms associated with that role."

"Nayoria's role as messenger might be the very cause of her delay," Beornric said, drawing everyone's attention. "For example, when his grace recently dispatched Ser Deirdre Ol'Miri to Armityr carrying a message to the king, I believe we expected her to return immediately."

"And yet," King Colm said thoughtfully, "I kept her here for more than a day, while I considered the message I wanted her to return with. Is that it, Beornric? You think Dalius is holding Nayoria while he considers a message for me?"

"She was officially dispatched to learn the status of alliance negotiations," Beornric said. "Would it not be reasonable to delay her, if King Dalius stands of the brink of a final decision one way or the other?"

"Not in this case," Paic said with a note of finality. "We stand of the eve of a march to war. That much is known publicly, even if our true target is concealed."

She glanced at Aefric. "Or believed to be concealed." She turned back to the king. "Whatever the standing of negotiations — be they nearly complete or a distant hope or even broken down — bringing that status to us is critical and can brook no delay."

"And yet," Duchess Gwenellia said, "if King Dalius insists on certain formalities, your majesty's wizard might well be delayed into the evening. A delay the Varondami may consider reasonable."

"I still say," Paic said, "there is no *good* reason for such a delay."

"In the mind of a woman of war, no," the duchess answered. "But in the mind of a youthful king who loves his ceremonies?"

"Your majesty," Aefric said, which stalled the argument as attention turned to him. "Do you possess a personal means of contacting Nayoria?"

King Colm's nostrils flared in a sharp breath, but he gave a rough nod.

"I do. I cannot reach her ... by that means. I was hoping your spell would prove more effective."

"Nayoria designed this means of contact?" Aefric asked.

King Colm nodded.

"Then my spell, had I been able to cast it, would likely have failed as well. And for the same reason."

"Wards?" Beornric asked Aefric.

"Certainly my first thought. But that would be strange, given..." he trailed off, not sure he should admit to having contacted Maev in front of the emissary.

"Given that there is someone else at Vaaran Tir you've been able to reach by spell," King Colm said. He pointed to the door in the corner. "A small room for quick, private conversations."

Aefric crossed to the door and entered. More black oak, and a soft yellow light emerged from the ceiling once the door closed behind him.

Three could not have stood in here and talked, without all three feeling crowded. Two would have felt close. Even alone, Aefric felt a bit confined. And he wondered at the resurgence of that beeswax smell.

He guessed the direction of south, faced it, and cast his contact spell.

"My sweet Maev, I reach out now at the behest of your father. You may think your response if you're not alone. Is Nayoria there?"

But no tingling tension followed.

His spell had failed.

THERE WAS NO POINT IN TRYING AGAIN. IT WASN'T AS THOUGH AEFRIC could possibly have miscast a spell he had cast *countless* times over the years.

Nevertheless, he tried again. Twice more.

The second and third attempts proved no more successful than the first.

He emerged from that little closet back into the planning room, to see an eager look on the king's face, and concern already on the faces of Yrsa and Beornric. Paic looked doubtful and Duchess Gwenellia merely looked curious.

"The spell could not reach its target," Aefric said.

"I hesitate to ask for fear of giving insult..." King Colm started.

"There's no need to ask," Aefric said. "I could not have miscast the spell, yet I tried it twice more all the same.

"And you have contacted ... this person ... by spell before?" Duchess Gwenellia asked, one dark eyebrow high. "While they were at Vaaran Tir?"

"I have. Several times. Including this very morning."

"Of course," she said, "the connection *can* be refused. If the timing would have been ... awkward."

"That may be true of the version taught among the courts," Aefric said. "But the version I learned as an adventurer was, shall we say, less considerate. Declining contact was not an option. Not *responding* was an option, but I know what that feels like. And this was a complete lack of contact. The spell never reached its target."

"Wards then?" she asked.

"That would be my guess," Aefric said. "And we're talking about a person who has not been behind wards during any previous contact attempts."

"What time of day do you customarily contact ... this person?" Paic asked.

"Most often quite late at night. Occasionally quite early in the morning."

"So this person could spend a good deal of time each day behind wards that prevented contact," Paic said reasonably, "and you might never have known it."

Aefric's turn to raise an eyebrow.

"General, if you had a secret means of contacting someone behind enemy lines, what times of day would be safest to do so?"

"Ah, good point," Paic said with a nod. "Which suggests that if ... this person is behind wards at all, they would be so warded at the obvious prime times for such contact, late at night and early in the morning."

"Well, *enemy* is a strong word at this stage," Duchess Gwenellia said. "But I'll concede that — assuming this individual is part of Princess Maev's entourage — as the member of a foreign government and possible spy, it would not make sense to keep him or her behind anti-contact wards for part of the day and not the whole of the day."

"In short," King Colm said in a dark tone, "this is a new development. And one that should concern us."

"Your majesty, I believe so," Aefric said. "In fact, I consider it corroborating evidence that Varondam works against us."

"On what basis do you conclude that?" Duchess Gwenellia asked. "It could merely be the case that talks are going poorly, and the move to quarters behind wards is simply a stratagem on the part of King Dalius."

"No," King Colm said. "That's not the way Dalius maneuvers. If talks were going poorly he would *want* us in contact with Maev — even through a member of her entourage — so that she could be pressured to find common ground. He knows I want the alliance."

So the king *didn't* want Rethneryl to know Aefric kept in touch with Maev. Worth noting.

"Assuming Varondam wants the alliance with Armyr at all," Duchess Gwenellia said. "For all we know they pretend interest to allow them time to prepare and attack Malimfar themselves while it's weak. Without having to share any gains with new allies."

"Forgive me, your grace," Paic said gently, "but I believe you've forgotten that Varondam *should* believe *we're* about to attack Malimfar. If they wish to attack Malimfar as well, they would benefit from immediate alliance, so that we could coordinate. And give them support, if needed."

"In fact," Yrsa said softly, "as Nayoria would have emphasized that our assault on Malimfar is imminent, if King Dalius has any designs on Malimfari land himself, he should send her back at speed with an alliance agreement. If only for the current conflict."

"I agree," Paic said. "Which makes the delay all the more concerning."

"Your majesty?" Aefric asked.

The king stared at the map and troop markers, but not as though he was seeing them.

"How easy is it to trap a wizard?" he asked.

"Easy is not the word I would choose," Duchess Gwenellia said.

"It depends on what is known about the wizard," Aefric said. "And the amount of time one has to prepare. About—"

"Your majesty," Paic said, "if I wanted to capture Nayoria I would distract her with an interesting sight and knock her unconscious."

"Well..." Duchess Gwenellia began, but Paic wasn't done talking.

"I would take her grace down much the same way," she said, nodding to indicate Gwenellia. And as the duchess began to huff indignantly Paic continued, louder. "*And for much* the same reason."

She turned to Gwenellia. "Forgive me, your grace, but you have led a soft life. You did not march in the wars, and so far as I know, you have never faced death with nothing but your cunning and your spells to keep you alive."

"Nayoria fought in the Godswalk Wars," King Colm said.

"She did," Paic allowed, "but she did so from great distance, and never entered the hazard herself."

"Your point?" Duchess Gwenellia said in a curt tone.

"There are instincts that a battle-tested warrior develops that others do not. Instincts that render one much more difficult to take from surprise. His grace possesses those instincts. Beatritz, Beornric, Colm, Yrsa of course, and I all do as well."

She bowed to the duchess. "But you, your grace, have never had to develop them." She turned back to the king. "Nor has Nayoria."

"And this matters because..." Duchess Gwenellia said.

"Because Nayoria knows we wait for her," Paic said. "And as a messenger, she would have every right — even when dealing with Varondami pomp and ceremony — to ask for a moment outside of wards to send word back. *At least* of her delay."

"If I were acting as messenger in such a position," Aefric said, "I would certainly ask to warn your majesty of my delay."

"And yet your majesty has already said that his personal means of communication with Nayoria remains silent."

Interesting choice of words. Made Aefric wonder just what this means was.

"Wait," the king said. Frowning, he turned to Aefric. "You once delivered into my hands by magic a formal, written message, which did not disappear, but remains to this day."

"How in Kalinda's name to you do *that*?" Duchess Gwenellia asked, seeming almost offended at the very idea.

"Wasn't easy," Aefric said to her, because he didn't have time for the whole explanation. "That's correct, your grace. The paper and ink written on it were all as real as any delivered by hand. Only the delivery method involved magic."

"I take it the body of Nelazzi could not be sent this way?" Paic asked.

"I didn't want to take chances with so important a corpse," Aefric said. "It is a new technique of my own invention, and requires ... refinement."

"I should be very interested in learning the method," the duchess said.

"Could you reach through wards with it?" King Colm asked. "Perhaps into Vaaran Tir?"

"I don't know," Aefric said. "But even if I tried and it worked, the communication would have to be one-way. No response would be possible. And potentially dangerous for the receiver, if they were observed when the message arrived. Unlike a normal spell of contact, once delivered, the parchment would open for anyone to read. Just like any other delivered message."

"Nevertheless," Duchess Gwenellia said, "I wish to learn this technique, once your grace has refined it."

"That may not help," Aefric said. "Are you acquainted with Karbin?"

"Only by reputation."

"Well, I explained to him how I developed the method, and he became furious because he insists it shouldn't work. The nearest we can figure out is that it works for me because my relationship with magic is ... unusual."

"What relationship?" the duchess scoffed. "Magic is power. You could no more have a relationship with magic than I could have with my title."

"All magic is part of Kalinda," Aefric said, "and so—"

"Enough," King Colm said, slapping the table. "I did not bring you here to debate magic theory."

"My apologies, your majesty," Aefric said, while the duchess mumbled something that might have been apologetic.

"So what you're saying is that even if you managed to send written messages to both Ashling at Reyvenue and my daughter's entourage at Vaaran Tir — messages that left no need for reply — we could still be not only informing our enemies of our capability to send such messages, but also warning them of our plans."

"Your majesty, I'm afraid so," Aefric said. "With no way to confirm any of it."

"Then the question is settled," King Colm said. "Aefric, I think we have to proceed with the assumption that you're right. Gwenellia, I'm afraid it seems that Varondam is holding your two missing princesses, as well as my own, and apparently two others from Hatay and Shachan."

Gwenellia's eyes rounded wide. "And your majesty has waited this long to say so?"

"It was unconfirmed, and I did not wish to spread rumor."

"So your majesty was *not* going to withhold it while we marched into Caiperas beside him?"

"No, I was *not*," he said sharply. "And let us move on to the far more important question. What shall we do about it?"

———

FULL DARK HAD RISEN BEFORE AEFRIC, BEORNRIC, YRSA AND LEPPINA once more boarded his *magari* and took to the air.

The clear sky was full of stars, with a rising moon almost full. The night winds carried a chill, but the magic of the *magari* held it at bay.

Aefric and the others had not dined with the royal court. They'd gnawed on roast chicken and tara with honeyed oat rolls and a good, dark beer while going over maps and discussing and discarding dozens of plans with the king and his military council. Including input from the duchess from Rethneryl.

And now they had their plans.

Or at the very least, Aefric had his task. He expected that other parts of the king's plans were still being finalized and detailed.

Duchess Gwenellia never seemed entirely happy with Rethneryl's part of the plan. Partially because it meant keeping their own armies in the dark about their princesses and proceeding into Caiperas as though they suspected nothing about Varondam. But mostly — in Aefric's opinion — because she wanted to be part of the mission to rescue those princesses.

Unfortunately, she was alone in thinking she should come along. It seemed that Paic's earlier mention of the duchess' soft life had worked against this being her first venture into the field.

But by the time Aefric and his party had left, the duchess was still continuing her arguments.

One of which, in Aefric's mind, raised a solid point. Rethneryl deserved a presence on the rescue team. After all, they'd still be sending in all the troops they'd agreed to. But Armyr would be holding back a portion of its own troops.

Of the forces from Deepwater, one soldier from every ten, and one battle wizard from every three would be held back for another mission.

The same would be true of Merrek.

No troops at all would be coming from Silverlake. It was deemed too distant for Varondam's spies to be bothering with. Which gave them greater numbers to provide for that other mission.

The king had wanted to spend some of Merrek's troops to hold their southern border against the possibility that Varondam would try a lightning assault across Malimfar and into Armyr, to be coordinated with whatever might be coming by sea.

Neither Aefric nor Yrsa believed that was likely — Paic questioned it as well — but his majesty would not allow the possibility to be ignored.

Fortunately, Aefric had talked him out of spending troops to prepare for such an invasion, by pointing out that he had another way to shore up southern defenses against Varondam. And his plan there brought a smile to the king's face.

However.

The other mission for those held-back troops and battle wizards would combine them with the naval forces of Merrek, Silverlake and Deepwater, under Yrsa's command.

They were to filter out of the ports in small enough numbers to avoid drawing attention, and meet up at sea. They would then sail south and hunt down Varondam's incoming ships. If possible, blockade them in their ports, and keep them from ever setting sail.

Which, Paic argued, should be possible, because even if Varondam's spies were highly placed, their ships should not be expecting to sail for another aett. That would fit the last timeline they would have known about.

Which was part of the reason that the armies from Deepwater and Merrek would be seen beginning their march only one day after Harvest Day. The second morning hence.

Meanwhile, the armies already gathered near Armityr — and those in place in Rethneryl — would not wait. They would begin the march at pressing speed and assault early.

So, while Rethneryl's armies wouldn't be *alone* marching into Caiperas, they wouldn't have anything like the level of support they expected.

Though they would, at least, have company in their ignorance about the princesses. Because that information was being withheld strictly to those who *had* to know it.

Further, the duchess was *somewhat* mollified that the movement into Caiperas would not be a true assault. Only a front, to keep Varondami spies from learning about the rescue mission and warning Vaaran Tir. And a test, to see if an ambush awaited them.

If an ambush came, it proved that Varondam was working with Caiperas. If not, that Varondam was merely taking advantage of the situation.

What would happen from that point, well, Aefric was much less certain of that. Paic and the king were still discussing options when the time came for him to leave.

After all. Aefric had to fly back to Water's End tonight, get something like a good night's sleep, and get his part of the plan in motion with the dawn.

Not to mention dispatching messages by rika and messenger to more places than Aefric even wanted to think about.

The messages would be part of Yrsa's job. She was now acting as Royal Fleet Admiral of Armyr. A temporary title, to be sure, but a title all the same, and one she looked proud and excited to be bearing.

Which was why, behind where Aefric stood with the reins, she, Beornric and even Leppina discussed the coming battle fronts. Distribution of ships and troops. How quickly they could set sail. What approaches they should take, and more.

Aefric, however tried to keep his focus on flying. Pushing the *magaunts* that pulled the chariot through the skies above the Armyrian landscape. Even though *magaunts* could not truly be pushed. They had the appearance of fiery red spirit horses, but not the emotions, personalities, nor flexibility of true horses.

They were *constructs* in the *seeming* of horses. Nothing more. They did not tire, but neither could they be pushed to fly faster than their limit. They did what they were capable of, and nothing more.

As he flew, Aefric envied the *magaunts* their inability to worry. His thoughts kept drifting to Maev. The clever, surprising, beautiful woman he'd kept in steady contact with since spring.

But who was now, suddenly, behind wards that prevented such contact.

Well, one form of it. They did write each other regular letters as well. Though given the tardiness of her report to Armityr, they probably didn't want her writing Aefric at the moment, either. Not that there would be time to exchange letters.

A line of thought he'd followed only to try to stave off key questions that now came flooding into his mind.

Was Maev languishing in some dungeon cell? Chained to a wall, alongside the other prisoner princesses? Or was she still living the pampered life of a royal guest? Ignorant of her change of circumstances? Perhaps taken hunting by Kiala while Varondam's court wizard cast wards about her rooms, rendering them little more than a comfortable cage? Given excuses to keep her in those rooms, denying her freedom of the castle and grounds?

And what of her forest lynx, Sylkanis? Would the poor thing suffer some kind of "accident" to prevent her from aiding Maev at some key moment? Or perhaps be imprisoned over some invented slight, and murdered once away from Maev's side?

Wait.

Maev wasn't just some messenger or part of an entourage. She was a visiting princess brokering an alliance, and possibly a marriage.

Even if her guest apartments were warded, certainly the whole of the castle would not be. And Maev was accustomed to dealing with Vaaran Tir's court and courtiers on a regular basis. Dining in its main hall. Roaming freely outside when she hunted, or simply walked among the gardens.

So for Maev to be behind wards close to a likely dinner time, that meant that whether she was chained to a cell wall or lounging on a padded sofa, she was held prisoner. And knew it.

She'd try to escape on her own.

Oh, that could complicate everything.

***

ONCE THEY RETURNED TO WATER'S END, YRSA AND BEORNRIC BOTH took off to see about sending messages and rikas, and generally doing as much as they could to get the great war machine in motion before sunup.

Though Aefric suspected they knew that even they would have to arrange some sleep for themselves in there somewhere.

Aefric's entire job was to sleep. Just go to his rooms — accompanied by Leppina, who considered herself on duty through the dawn — and sleep.

He was not to invite company to his bed. Not to pace and worry. Not even to take time to research that teak box.

Just ... sleep.

As though it were that simple.

Somewhere in the castle at Vaaran Tir, Maev would have figured out by now that she was a prisoner. And likely already be seeing about rescuing herself.

That was the great irony of it all, really. Armyr was the kingdom mounting this great rescue attempt. Not Hatay or Shachan, who refused to acknowledge that their own princesses had been taken. Not even Rethneryl, who was helping provide the smokescreen for the attempt, but not sending along personnel or resources themselves. Even though they were the only kingdom to have had *two* princesses taken.

No. The rescue mission was to be conducted entirely by Armyr.

And here, Armyr's princess was the most likely to rescue herself.

How would King Dalius respond to that? If Maev's guards — whether that meant soldiers or his unspoken bastard sister — checked on her and found her gone. Would they risk killing her in hunting her down?

She was a forester. And a damned good one. She'd mastered forestry secrets she shouldn't even have had access to. Secrets the eldrani and kindaren never shared outside their own races. Yet somehow, they'd shared those secrets with Maev.

The Keifer part of Aefric found that amusing. Maev would be the kind of rule-breaking non-player character in a *Torn Kingdoms* sourcebook that infuriated some players.

But life as Aefric had proven something he'd always suspected. NPCs were people too. Every bit as much as the player characters. And when NPCs broke the rules, well, there was usually a very good reason for it.

In Maev's case, she must have done some amazing things during the Godswalk Wars herself. Helped the eldrani and kindaren in ways that made them regard her as one of their own.

Stories she wouldn't commit to parchment in a letter, but he looked forward to hearing from her someday.

Yes. If anyone could escape Vaaran Tir on her own, it would be Maev.

But that wouldn't help the other princesses. So even if Maev made it out on her own, Aefric would still have to go ahead with the rescue mission. Saving women he didn't know, instead of the one he wanted to help.

This was the very essence of being a duke, it seemed to him sometimes.

Life seemed so much simpler when he'd been just another adventurer.

Aefric was in his bedroom, as he thought about all this. Wearing nothing but his dressing gown and pacing by the bed. He wasn't even carrying the Brightstaff, though it followed at his heels like an impatient puppy.

The only light came from the fire in his hearth. Casting shadows in the darkness that looked for all the world like spear-carrying guards on the hunt for Maev, through castle corridors, where she would still be at risk.

Once she made it outside, they'd be hard-pressed to *find* her, let alone capture her.

But if they'd separated her from Sylkanis, freeing her forest lynx would be her first priority. And that choice that might get her caught again.

Not only would it be predictable, but it would lead her into an area easier to guard against her skill set. Plus—

"Your grace?"

Dajen's voice, coming from the doorway. Dajen's silhouette and shadow, when Aefric turned to look.

"What is it, Dajen?"

"Midnight has come and gone, your grace. And I suspect the coming dawn carries a great weight of responsibility and activity."

"That's one way to put it," Aefric said.

"Which makes sleep all the more important."

"I can't sleep. All I can think about is—"

"Oh, I see," Dajen said, and unless Aefric was greatly mistaken, his head valet's voice carried an undercurrent of sarcasm. "I'd been given to understand that those who practice the magical arts required the ability to clear their thoughts and center themselves, even in the midst of chaos."

"Well, yes, but—"

"And *certainly* I would expect that such a skill could be used to banish troublesome thoughts when sleep is of the essence. As I believe it is even now, unless your grace wishes to tell me otherwise?"

Aefric sighed, then gave a breathless chuckle.

"You're a terror when you have a point to make, aren't you, Dajen?"

"Not in the least, your grace. However, as the Duke of Deepwater's chief nighttime valet, his health is of paramount importance to me. And that begins with sleep."

"All right, all right," Aefric said, holding up one hand in surrender. "I'll employ those very skills right now and get some sleep."

"Very good, your grace. I am pleased to know that I shall not have to resort to sterner measures."

Disturbing thought, that. But some perverse part of Aefric required him to ask even though he doubted he really wanted to know.

"Just what are these sterner measures?"

"With permission, your grace, I would prefer not to divulge them until such time as they become necessary."

"I think perhaps that's best."

"Thank you, your grace. And your grace?"

"Yes, Dajen?"

"Good night."

"Good night, Dajen."

9

———————

Aefric awoke early the next morning, without anyone waking him. Instead, he used a trick he'd figured out back when he was an apprentice, and more than mastered during his adventuring days. Even if he hadn't made use of it at all as a duke until that morning.

It was based up the decay rates of local spells when crossed with the amount of effort used to establish them and the amount of power invested in them.

Simplicity itself to cast such a spell that had two parts. The first would whisper in his ear that it was time to wake. The second would prevent the first from happening.

There were other timing techniques of course, most of which were more common among magic-users. Methods that were arguably more elegant. But they were also more complex, and required a hint more power.

The technique Aefric used that night, on the other hand, would have felt simple even to most apprentices, if they figured it out.

The right amount of effort into the whisper and a *hair* less into the preventer and Aefric had a spell that could wake him exactly when he wished.

And that morning, he wished one hour before the dawn.

Once awake, he moved about in darkness, naked and holding only the Brightstaff. Trusting to his months of living at Water's End to remind him where everything was.

Of course, it helped that Dajen and Ocheda kept everything in its place.

In darkness he entered his bath room and washed up at the ewer. Just as he would have when he was still an adventurer and didn't have large, fancy bathtubs available to him every night.

From there, he wandered into his closets.

A small, soft glow from the Brightstaff's yellow diamond then. Not enough to wake the two body servants who napped as they sat their stools and waited to do their duty. Only enough to let him find and don the right accouterments.

A simple red, linen tunic. Dark brown leathers, tucked into high, hard boots of matching leather. A leather belt, with a simple gold buckle.

From his weapons closet, his old longsword. In case he needed it. And he emerged from his closets — into the darkness of his private sitting room, still only lit by the soft glow he'd allowed the Brightstaff — dressed as he used to during his adventuring days. Sword and wand at his belt, along with the belt pouch.

He'd almost skipped his noble's dagger. For what he was doing felt more like something from the old days than something a duke ought to be doing. But he was still a duke of Armyr. And he might find a use for a silver-edged blade before all was said and done.

By the soft glow of the Brightstaff, he stalked silently up the carved, curving staircase to the third floor, where his magic lab was waiting.

"Good morning, your grace," Ocheda said, the moment he came into view at the top of the stairs. "I understand there is to be no morning meeting today. Would your grace like his breakfast on his private balcony? There may be a touch of chill, but I know how he enjoys the sunrise over the lake and mountains."

"How could you *possibly* have known to expect me here?"

"Simplicity itself," she said. "Your grace rarely chooses to awaken by means of his spells. I presumed that if he did so this morning, he likely did so for the same reason that his predecessors often did. To begin the day with some kind of spellwork before their more expected duties interfered."

"Not *quite* the case, but close enough," Aefric said, shaking his head as he made his way up the last steps to the small landing.

"Does this mean your grace wishes to dine on his private balcony this morning?"

"Doubt I'll have time. I'm sailing with Yrsa at dawn."

"And will your grace's magic consume the whole of the time between now and then?"

"Shouldn't," Aefric said.

"Then I shall see to it that his breakfast is ready and waiting when he emerges from his laboratory."

"Thank you, Ocheda."

"Of course, your grace," she said with a crisp bow, and started down the stairs.

"Oh," he called after her, "and I'll need enough clothes for a few days sent down to that ship as well."

"Already handled, your grace," she called without looking back.

Aefric almost asked about that, but he really didn't have the time.

AEFRIC'S MAGIC LABORATORY AT WATER'S END WAS WONDERFUL. Always a joy, and a bit of a relief, to enter.

A gesture lit the blocky white candles in sconces around the room, bathing the simple whitewashed stone of the walls and floor in gentle light that would add no possible magical interference.

No windows in this room. No tapestries. No hearth, even. And certainly no soft, overstuffed furniture.

It was a functional room. Not built for decoration.

His spell research desk in a near corner. Big and heavy, with many drawers, but only a simple wooden stool for sitting.

Notes and diagrams and sketches were spell-tacked to the walls around the desk. Some the work of Aefric himself, but others of his predecessors.

And on six shelves above that big desk, many, many grimoires. Some of them Aefric's own, both those he'd carried for years, and another he'd begun since arriving here. Others, he'd captured along the way, such as the Hrafntonn grimoires taken from his castle in Kivash.

Most of them, though, were the old Soulfist grimoires, from which Aefric had been able to expand his understanding of magic and gained more than a few spells, even though he was still working his way through them.

So much to learn from those books. If only he had the time.

It was from one of those shelves that the Necklace of Fire dangled, though Aefric didn't consider bringing it along.

Speaking of items he wasn't bringing along. The greenwood staff he'd taken from the former Ducal Wizard of Silverlake leaned against that desk, waiting for Aefric to explore its mysteries as well, when he found time.

Time, time, time. Never enough of it.

On the opposite corner, a similar desk, with a similar set of spell-tacked notes and diagrams on the walls around it. And a similar set of books on the six shelves above it.

A table stood beside that other desk, covered in various forms of paraphernalia such as the alembics and burners and mortars and pestles.

Like the desk in that corner and the books and notes, that table and its contents — as well as those stored in the cabinet below it — were dedicated to the twin arts of alchemy and potion-making.

Along the center of the rectangular room were several magic circles inset into the floor with rose gold, along with similarly inset triangle, hexagram and heptagram.

Finally, the double-door closet on one long wall, where more supplies waited.

Once more, Aefric felt the itch to do research. He was soon to cast a tricky spell, after all. Why not take the time to refine it?

Because he didn't have time to risk making a mistake by deviating far from what he knew would work. He would have to make do what had worked last time. Or a derivation thereof, since these weren't *exactly* the same circumstances, nor the same target.

And so he sat at his spell research desk, and he wrote a letter. He then rolled up that letter, sealed it with navy blue wax, and used a quick touch of magic to impress it with the Deepwater seal.

He carried that letter into the center of the room, to the magic circle whose glyphs and runes best worked with summonings. And even though what he was going to do was more-or-less the reverse of a summoning, this was still the circle most congruent with his intentions.

And he would need all the help he could get.

Logic. Art. The interrelationship of forces. The three pillars of magic, no matter how Karbin might disagree with Aefric on this point.

The summoning circle he'd chosen was all three, in some ways. The forces he intended to apply all related to magics that carried something from one place to another. Of course, logic insisted that those things not involve people from this world, but creatures from *other* worlds.

But artistically, there was connection. And a proven connection, because it had worked once before.

He had his letter, which would serve as both the object to be ... unsummoned? He liked the sound of that. And that the word pleased him would only help. He placed the letter in the middle of the circle, then closed and activated the circle by chanting certain ancient words with the right inflections and rhythms to bring them more tightly into alignment with his purpose.

These words in particular worked even better for him than they did for most wizards. Something to do with the magic in his blood.

Bright red power crackled first around the edges of the circle — where it brightened further and seemed to thicken as it swirled through the glyphs and runes, then added a patina of itself across the floor within the circle as well, including the scroll.

Two songs came next. One was na'shek, drawing power from the land beneath him. The other was a kindaren song, in praise of the skies and stars, calling their power too into the mixture.

As those powers came in answer to his call, he wove them together into what he'd already raised in the circle.

Twin hums then, like the final peals from ringing bells. One of them high and clear and beautiful, the other deep and resonant enough to ache in his bones.

As the hums faded, the power within the circle shifted to deep orange, sparked with blue.

Next, he considered his target. A princess. A member of royalty, even as Aefric was a member of nobility. Authority connected them both. And his authority as duke came from a king. Same as the role and authority of a princess.

A connection through peerage. Both logical and artistic.

For the third pillar there, bringing the other two into balance, he struck the na'shek pose of authority. A new addition to the spell, but it caused the power to flare hot, begging for release.

Aefric held that pose, while the heat of the power began to well and shake within him. Even as bright blue and scalding orange rose and crashed together within the circle.

He held that pose while the power seemed to stretch and cover him as well, imploring him for release. He felt both orange and blue. Tasted them. Sunlight and shadow. Lavender and orange blossom.

He held that pose while power built to a crescendo that made him sweat a waterfall and clench every muscle in his body to hold out, while the power in the circle built higher and higher. The blue and orange mixing and swirling now.

But he had to hold out until he felt the peak.

He *had* to hold out.

Hold out.

HOLD OUT.

Finally, the artist in him knew he'd hit that highest peak.

He broke the pose, flinging the power outward as he cried out the words of command that had worked the last time he'd tried this.

A crack sounded. So loud that, for a moment, Aefric thought a wall had given out.

But no. It was only the spell.

And the scroll was gone from the circle.

THE LETTER AEFRIC SENT:

To her royal highness, Astrid Eadredsdottir, Crown Princess of Malimfar:

Please forgive this rather unusual delivery method. I promise that I will not make a habit of using it. In fact, I would not have employed it in this instance, but what I have to say is important, and time presses.

First, I must inform your highness that Armyr has no plans to invade Malimfar. We have given the appearance of preparing to do so to lull Caiperas into complacency.

It is Caiperas our armies will begin invading later today. For while we have not yet confirmed that Caiperas supported Malimfar's arls this past spring, as your highness has alleged, we have proven conclusively that Caiperas was behind assassination attempts made against members of our royal family this past summer.

Caiperas will be made to pay for these crimes against our sovereignty.

Second, I must warn your highness that Varondam might invade you. Soon. As your highness might suspect from my choice of words, I do not know with certainty that this will happen. I do, however, have compelling reason to believe that they intend to invade my coastline during the coming war with Caiperas.

Some of our military minds believe that Varondam might try a second front of war, invading by land. First through Malimfar at lightning speeds, and then, if possible, extending into Armyr.

Neither I nor my own general believe this is likely, as it would overextend their military, and hurt their ability to maintain supply lines and support.

However.

It cannot be denied that Varondam has warfare on the mind. Which means that if your highness possesses any high-value targets near their border, or even areas of your shared border under frequent dispute, I would advise your highness to watch them carefully. And to be prepared, just in case.

I would warn your highness also that Caiperas might be planning to invade, but I suspect your highness already watches them for the possibility.

Now, I realize that some advisers will tell your highness that I am dissembling. Attempting to soften Malimfari defenses for the Armyrian invasion that doubtless many sources have warned your highness of over the past several aetts.

I can only tell your highness why I send this letter, and trust to her assessment of my character to know that I am telling her the truth.

I promised your highness once that I would keep an open mind regarding the royal family of Malimfar. I have attempted to do so, which has made me note the following.

Your highness did not have to come herself to deliver both that report and those gifts these few aetts past. Nor, once it was clear that my king would not permit me to receive her, did she have to host me for lunch aboard her own ship.

And yet, your highness did both of these things. Even to the point of disavowing the words and threats of a royal adviser who took offense at your highness' treatment.

Throughout that lunch we shared, your highness made clear that, despite the events of this past spring, she holds out hope that friendship might yet blossom between us.

I too hold out such hope.

Your highness should know that the contents of this letter will be confirmed through normal channels by your own ambassador to Armityr.

However, if Varondam does indeed possess designs on Malimfari targets, that confirmation will come too late to help your highness prepare.

Thus, it is in the spirit of our shared hope of friendship that I write to your highness now. And employ a methodology of delivering this letter that it both difficult and personally costly, but timely.

Written most sincerely by the hand of his grace,

Aefric Brightstaff
Duke of Deepwater, Baron of Netar, and Arl of Storbakki

BY THE TIME DAWN CRESTED THE HORIZON ON HARVEST DAY, AEFRIC had cleaned himself up after his spell, dined quickly on a traditional Armyrian breakfast — heavy on honey-roasted turkey, fresh pears, and strawberries — and boarded the *Swift Wave*.

He'd left the castle on foot, wearing a dull gray cloak with the hood up. To throw off anyone who might be watching for him, he carried the Brightstaff tucked safely into his velvet belt pouch.

The first time he had ever employed such a deception.

For this voyage, his cabin was the one he'd previously ceded to the prince. The cabin with that fixed wooden table and benches attached to one wall. It had more room, as well, not that he needed it. He'd be leaving the ship soon enough, and passing these quarters to Yrsa.

The fishy smell of the whale oil lamps was a touch dispiriting. He'd hoped not to deal with it again anytime soon. But the *Duke's Hand* couldn't be seen to be leaving the pier, or there'd be no doubt who was aboard it.

Aefric sat waiting at that table, with its wood an orangish color from too much varnish or lacquer.

Deirdre was the first to arrive, followed quickly by Karbin. Both dressed as they preferred, and both looking ready for action. Though Karbin had in hand a white staff approximately six feet in length, with a pale leather wrap in the right spot, and a faceted piece of yellow glass embedded in the tip.

"Not bad," Aefric said, looking over the staff, then at the true Brightstaff, which stood just behind him. "Should be close enough to fool distant observers. Especially if you fake throwing lightning from it."

"I still think I should be part of the rescue attempt," Karbin grumbled. "You might need me. After all, you never mastered invisibility."

"I need you out in the harbor," Aefric said, "and visible as me. If my fleet is there, but I am not—"

"Yes, yes," Karbin said. "They may start looking for you in their castle, which could ruin the whole rescue operation. I still say you *should* be with your fleet. You're the duke. Let *me* be the one going in with the rescue team."

A token knock on the door before Beornric and Yrsa entered.

"Paic suggested that," Aefric said to Karbin. "So that a peer of the realm would not be entering the hazard. Rethneryl objected, officially requesting the Hero of Deepwater and Frozen Ridge to be the one leading the rescue operation. Since they had more princesses at stake, the king acceded to that request."

"Partially," Beornric said, as he and Yrsa crossed the cabin. "He only partially agreed because of the number of princesses involved. He also agreed to placate Duchess Gwenellia, who was still fighting to go on the mission herself."

"Which would be a fool's errand," Yrsa said, then looked at the table. "Not enough space here for all of us."

"Yes there is," Deirdre said, quickly getting up and wedging in close beside Aefric. "As long as Beornric is on the other side, we'll be fine."

Yrsa looked at the line of Deirdre's body pressed against Aefric's side and shook her head, but took her seat.

"I think I can take the edge and give you more space."

"I'm good," Deirdre said.

Muffled cries from up on deck, then the feeling of motion. The *Swift Wave* had cast off.

"Is everything ready?" Aefric asked.

"Yes," Yrsa said. "Countess Faenella knows the plan, and will take command of the armies and lead the march on the morrow."

"Wish she could be coming with us," Aefric said. "A Blessed Knight with adventuring experience would be a boon."

"Too big and clunky," Deirdre said. "We need speed and stealth."

"Doesn't matter anyway," Beornric said. "With the official word being that you left for Armityr by air before dawn, if there's no ranking noble leading your armies, observers—"

"Meaning spies," Deirdre said.

"—will wonder where Yrsa is. This way, they'll assume she left with you for Armityr, to coordinate forces nearer the border."

"What word has been spread about the *Swift Wave*?" Aefric asked.

"That your grace misses the taste of pineapples, and is sending one of your personal ships to Sartis to fetch some and bring them to him at Armityr."

Aefric frowned. "That's believable?"

"For a man settling into his powers and wealth as a duke?" Beornric asked. "It's not excessive."

"Well, as long as it works."

"It will work," Yrsa said. "And all other orders have gone out. Ships will be gathering at the appointed place, and then we can proceed on schedule."

"What if Varondam gets word that we've marched and launches early?"

"Too risky for them," Yrsa said. "If they're seen launching a north-bound armada, word might reach us before our armies have gone too far to recall." She shook her head. "No. They won't launch until our armies have *at least* passed Kerrik Forest. By then, our whole fleet will have gathered and be southbound to meet them. Possibly in place in time to blockade their ships at port."

"How long until we leave?" Deirdre asked, indicating herself and Aefric.

"I suggest tomorrow evening," Beornric said. "We have one of our battle wizards on wind duty, so we'll reach the second checkpoint by then. That should give you an angle of approach that won't cross Malimfari borders, and should minimize your exposure."

"That will also give them time to respond to the news about our troops marching early. Assuming Varondam's spies have a swift enough means of communication."

"Assume they do," Aefric said.

Someone knocked on the cabin door. A knock Aefric didn't recognize.

"Are we expecting anyone?" Aefric asked.

"No," Yrsa said. "In fact, I gave orders that we were not to be disturbed."

She stood, drawing one of her maces as part of the movement. She crossed the cabin floor in four quick strides, readied her mace, and yanked open the door.

Standing in the doorway was Gwenellia Quinnian, Duchess of Neastall and Royal Emissary from Rethneryl.

Duchess Gwenellia was dressed in a dark brown silk tunic, over riding leathers only a few shades lighter. Her calf-high leather boots were the same shade as her shirt. Her black hair was tied back with a red leather thong.

Tucked into her belt, beside her belt pouch and noble's dagger, three wands of not-inconsiderable power. Aefric also sensed a protective bracer under her left sleeve, and some kind of magic on a pendant tucked inside her shirt.

The duchess raised an eyebrow at Yrsa and her ready mace.

"If you're going to use that thing, good ser knight, by all means do so. I'm *quite* sure King Colm wouldn't mind your damaging relations with his staunchest ally at this critical juncture."

Yrsa lowered her mace and put it away. She bowed to the duchess. "We were not expecting you, your grace."

"Of course not," the duchess said archly. "Your king seems to think I should be glad to sit in safety, perhaps drinking sharabi and dancing, while my troops go off to fight and my princesses are in peril."

She looked past Yrsa to Aefric.

"Am I to be invited in, your grace? Or must I continue to stand here?"

"Please do come in, your grace, and join us," Aefric said, and Yrsa stood aside to let the duchess enter.

With casual wave of her hand and hardly more effort visible in her aspect, she caused a chest to slide across the deck to serve her as a chair at the end of the table.

Once the door was closed and all were sitting again, Aefric said, "I should warn your grace that I have not brought along any of the little niceties that most nobles are accustomed to having available when they travel."

"My people will be sleeping on rocky ground and eating camp food," she said. "Perhaps it's time I learned to live without those niceties now and again."

Deirdre nodded approval. "First field mission, your grace?"

"Excuse me," Aefric said. "Your grace, you've already met acting-Royal Fleet Admiral Ser Yrsa Azenai and the captain of my Knights of the Lake, Ser Beornric Ol'Sandallas. These other two are Karbin, Ducal Court Wizard of Deepwater, and Ser Deirdre Ol'Miri, Ducal Champion of Deepwater."

"I've heard a good deal about you both," Duchess Gwenellia said. "A pleasure to meet you in person. And to answer your question, good ser knight, it is indeed."

"And what, exactly, do you see that mission being?" Yrsa asked before Aefric could.

"I intend to join the rescue mission, of course," Duchess Gwenellia said. "I will accompany your grace's team, infiltrate Vaaran Tir, rescue the princesses, and help them escape."

Silence descended on the table for a moment.

Aefric stood. Walked to the center of the cabin. A low enough ceiling to feel a bit cramped for a tall man like him, and not enough room any direction — despite only four chests taking up space. But it would do.

"Your grace," he said, "please stand and face me."

"All right," she said suspiciously.

She did so, leaving about two paces between them.

"Your grace," he said, "do you know how to bring forth a protective shield?"

"I *have* dueled before, your grace," she said, sounding slightly offended. "And *won*."

"Good," Aefric said. "Cast such a shield now, if you would be so kind."

She tried, but Aefric stopped her with a single pulse of power and thrust of his hand.

Deirdre looked away, biting her knuckle to keep from laughing. Karbin grimly shook his head. Yrsa and Beornric watched stoically.

"Hardly fair," Duchess Gwenellia said. "You knew what I was going to do."

"All right," Aefric said patiently. "Well, let us reverse the role then. I shall bring forth a shield, and you shall try to stop me. Fair?"

Still suspicious, she nodded.

Aefric cast his spell before she could stop him, bringing forth a shimmering transparent field of force that would protect him from many kinds of attacks.

He dismissed it.

"What is the point of this?" the duchess demanded. "It is well known that your grace is an experienced and powerful wizard. I do not claim the ability to compete with his power."

"This was not a test of power," Aefric said calmly. "This was a test of training."

"And your grace has more than I? Well I do not deny it."

"That's not my point," Aefric said, shaking his head once, slowly. "Your grace tells me she has dueled. Well, duels are all well and good. But they are structured. Organized. Dueling is nothing like fighting."

Aefric took a deep breath. Gave the duchess a chance to think about that before he continued.

"I know your grace is court-trained," he said. "But what I didn't know was whether that training included any work with battle wizards."

"I know a good many battle spells, thank you," Duchess Gwenellia said. "Shall I list them?"

"Not at this time," Aefric said, "though I am glad to know it. But if your grace had trained with battle wizards, she would have learned the difference between laboratory speed and battle speed. She would know that, however good her spells, they would be useless in the field *if she cannot cast them fast enough.*"

"I'm faster with some spells than others."

"Very well," Aefric said with a nod. "Pick any attacking spell you know. Your best. And hit me with it whenever you're ready."

She decided on her spell when he said the word "best." He saw it in her eyes. She began casting as soon as he said "whenever." Looked to be a variation on that orb spell Nelazzi had used so effectively.

He stopped the duchess' spell before he reached the word "you're."

He finished the sentence only out of politeness.

Duchess Gwenellia clenched her teeth. Her nostrils flared in a deep breath.

She tried a quick, simple spell then. Some kind of fire-lighting spell. Likely something she used every day on candles, hearths and the like.

Wouldn't have accomplished anything more than setting fire to a corner of Aefric's red linen tunic.

He stopped her anyway.

She hung her head through a breath, then drew herself proudly erect.

"What of my wands?" she asked, though with less defiance in her voice. "I have practiced with them."

"The issue is in trained reflexes," Aefric said. "Working by tool and not spell changes nothing. I could prove it, if your grace would like, but—"

"But what your grace is saying is that, for all my magic, I would be useless to him on this rescue mission."

"No. I am saying that your grace's coming on this rescue mission would accomplish little beyond hastening her own death." He took a step closer. "I applaud your grace's courage. Few would throw themselves into the hazard the way she wishes to. But your grace is not ready."

"I will not return to Armityr," she said firmly. "I am no silly woman to sit idly by, gossiping and politicking while others go to war. I did not fight while the gods walked because Father *forbade* me. I was the heir and not to be risked. Well, now *I* am the duchess. And I will *not* be *useless.*"

"I *never* said you were useless," Aefric said harshly, closing the gap between them. "Your grace is a clever woman and a wizard. And I understand you know battle spells?"

"A good dozen," she said slowly, looking at Aefric a little differently now. "I'm best at the *detonating flames.*"

"Ooh," Deirdre said, smiling. "I've always loved that one. I mean, not when I'm near the detonation point. But still."

"Excellent," Aefric said, smiling. "I don't know the large-scale version of that one myself. Only a smaller version that I found useful in, shall we say, confined spaces. But I wouldn't mind having your grace teach me the battlefield version sometime."

"Perhaps," the duchess said with a smile more evident in her eyes than on her lips. "If your grace would help me train my reflexes the way he speaks of."

"That can be arranged," Aefric said with a smile. "Now, let's return to the table and discuss what battle spells you've mastered, and how they may be useful during the coming blockade and likely naval battle."

"Oh, yes," Karbin said. "Reflex speed in battles like those is less important than timing. Timing is *crucial.*"

Yrsa met Aefric's eye and gave him a small nod of approval.

AEFRIC AND THE OTHERS DISCUSSED PLANS AND OPTIONS THROUGH lunch and for some time into the afternoon. But there came a point where the discussion could accomplish little more than retreading covered ground.

And when that point came, the duchess said, "I think I'll take a stroll on deck. See how far we've come."

"I'd offer to join you," Aefric said, "but I can't be seen on deck. I have to stay below until it's time for the rescue attempt."

"Trapped below?" Duchess Gwenellia asked. "With only the smells of caulk and varnish and burning whale oil?" She grimaced. "Perhaps your grace should not suffer alone."

"No. Please. By all means. Enjoy your stroll. I'm going to take the opportunity to get some research time in."

"Anything interesting?"

"Might be, if it yields fruit."

"Ah, yes," she said with the first sincere smile he'd seen from her. "I know the stage you're at. May Kalinda bless your efforts."

"Thank you, your grace."

"Gwenellia," she said. "Please."

"And you must call me Aefric," he said in return.

She left the room then, followed by the knights. Even Deirdre, though Deirdre arranged to be the last one out the door. And before she left she gave Aefric a lopsided grin.

"I myself find ship travel boring. So if your grace desires *distraction* later, I shall be most happy to provide it."

"Thank you, Deirdre. I'll keep that in mind."

She left then, and Aefric added a simple spell-lock to the door. The kind that could be forced easily enough, but would prevent him from being otherwise interrupted.

He pulled the teak box out of his velvet pouch.

The two humanoid figures, engaged in their dance, or ritual, or whatever they were supposed to be doing.

The markings that looked so much like Ancient Hwalish lettering, but were not. In fact, were not letters in any language, but only markings in the seeming of letters. Perhaps as a blind, to help conceal the truth of the box's powers.

The lamplight of the cabin didn't dim while he held the box, but he no longer expected it to. The box dimmed sunny daylight, but no other light.

Of course, on his balcony it had muted sounds as well, while he held it...

No. By concentrating, Aefric could hear the muffled calls of sailors about their work. Distant, but no more distant than they had been before he picked up the box.

He never had gotten to ask Prince Killian why he'd advised Aefric not to open the box in sunlight. Now, well, he might never get a good answer out of the prince. Perhaps he could ask the king sometime. Or even Nayoria, after the rescue.

Assuming Nayoria was still alive. There was value in keeping the princesses alive, but Armyr's Royal Wizard? She might be too dangerous. Pose too great a threat through the possibility of escape.

Poor Nayoria. Her name had hardly come up in the discussion of the rescue attempt, in favor of focusing on the princesses. But if she lived, she was a prisoner every bit as much as they were. And while King Colm would be more worried about getting his daughter back, doubtless he was worried as well about the court wizard he'd known most of his life.

Well, Aefric had not forgotten her. And he would not...

He was getting distracted.

Returned his attention to the box. To that slippery magic that seemed to be *in* Qorunn, but somehow not *of* Qorunn. Untouched by the ebbs and flows of the magics native to this world.

So far as Qorunn's natural magical energies were concerned, this box and its spells did not exist.

Which was still just weird to think about.

His best guess so far was that this was a work of magic from some other world — some other plane of existence — that somehow existed here in Qorunn in an *unfiltered* state. Unlike the normal way that summoned creatures and the beings and objects of other worlds seemed to take part of Qorunn into themselves to manifest here. A kind of filtration...

So, that suggested that perhaps this box contained something *un*manifested. Something, perhaps, caught between another world and this one.

A power half-summoned?

But the *box* was physical enough. That was undeniable. He could hold it. Tap it. Might even be able to damage it, though he hadn't tried...

Wait.

This box was old. Very, very old. Killian had said it had been in the Stronghand family vaults for — well, Aefric didn't remember exactly, but definitely more than a hundred years. And it had been recovered from an underground dybbungstad lair. A recovery that involved a great deal of combat.

And yet, this box showed not so much as a scratch, nor the slightest fading of age.

Aefric set the box down on the deck.

He drew his sword.

Stopped himself.

What was he *doing*? Striking the box with a *sword* just to test? To see if it could be damaged?

What if it *could* be?

What if striking the box with a sword shattered it? Released all its contained power in the form of a sudden blast?

That happened, sometimes with enchanted items. Especially the staves. Breaking them risked releasing all their bound power in a single explosive moment.

Not a risk worth taking.

Instead of swinging the sword, then, he tried prodding the box. Gouging into its surface.

Nothing.

Aefric tried harder.

Still nothing.

He leaned his shoulder into it.

Wait.

Looking down, while leaning his whole body weight behind the tip of his longsword, Aefric realized something.

The tip hadn't so much as broken the surface of the wood. Not the slightest nick. The sharp tip held there at the lid of the box as though...

...As though it simply refused to budge any further...

Aefric withdrew the sword tip.

With a gesture, he moved the box...

The box didn't budge.

He frowned. Tried again.

Nothing.

Frowning harder now, he tested his technique and the same level of effort on the chest Gwenellia had used as a chair.

The chest slid easily across the cabin to stop at the wall.

Aefric leaned down with his empty hand leading, and picked up the box.

Easy.

He set it back down. Nudged it with his boot.

It slid a fingerwidth across the deck.

He tried to move it with magic again.

Nothing.

Impervious to magic? No. No. It couldn't be, or he couldn't store it in the velvet pouch.

Then again...

The magic of the pouch was *in* the pouch. Not trying to affect the box. That the box could be placed in the pouch only proved that the box was not *anti*-magic.

Aefric tried his personal version of the fire-lighting spell Gwenellia had attempted earlier. Just enough to char the lid a little.

The fire flared for a moment and was gone.

The box remained pristine.

Aefric nudged the teak box across the deck with his boot, until the hinges rested against the bulkhead.

He checked his angle. Made sure not to hit anything else with his stroke, then swung his longsword into the side of the box at full combat speed.

The blade stopped at the side of the box.

No impact. No jarring sensation through his hand and wrist and arm. The blade simply stopped, as though...

...as though the energy of the strike had been sapped away in an instant.

Aefric sheathed his sword.

Did his best to examine the slippery power of the box again.

Was there more now? Had it absorbed power from the strike?

Frustratingly, there was no way to tell. He simply could not get a strong enough fix on that so-slippery power. He needed some way to connect it to the power of Qorunn, so that he could work with it.

At the moment, he knew only that — in its current state — it seemed to mute or absorb...

...anything that might harm it?

Daytime sunlight. Not something most would think of as harmful, but expose wood to it daily over time, and watch how the color of the wood changes.

If only he knew what happened when the box was exposed to sunlight.

If only he could go up on deck right then and find out. But no, he had to stay belowdecks. As they'd planned. Invisible to anyone with a spyglass.

So all he could do, for now, was sit with the box and try to find some way for his mind and magic to get a fix on the powers contained within.

And that was what he did.

EVEN AEFRIC KNEW HE COULDN'T SPEND HIS WHOLE TIME ABOARD THE *Swift Wave* enmeshed in his research. First, because it was too taxing, and he needed to be fresh and ready when the time came to leave the ship.

And second, and more frustrating, he *wasn't getting anywhere.*

The teak box was maddening. He'd tried every trick he could

think of to reach its power. Improvised dozens of new spells that might've detected any number of cross-planar anomalies.

Nothing worked.

The box remained a mystery.

And the most frustrating thing about it all was that, based on what he *could* figure out, *it shouldn't work.*

If the power was not part of Qorunn's magic — as *every* test so far had confirmed — then its power should not be able to *influence* or *affect* anything here in Qorunn.

At least, not in its *current* state.

And yet, there was that strange resistance to both physical and magical damage. Which meant its power *was* affecting things here in Qorunn. Even in its current state.

Which *should. Not. Work.*

Was this what Karbin felt like, when dealing with some of Aefric's more ... singular ideas and conclusions?

Well, if so, maybe he knew how that felt, but he could be buoyed by the knowledge that his own spells that shouldn't work *did*, and so obviously the only thing between him and understanding the power of that box was some missing key.

Some missing key...

Was that it? Was it that the box was not complete unto itself, but lacked a second component? Something intended to be put *inside* the box, which would then connect the bound power to the magic of Qorunn, provide a kind of filter, and finally allow it to be understood and used?

Made sense.

And so, frustrated but hopeful, Aefric opened himself up to company. Shared dinner with Gwenellia and Deirdre. Beornric, Karbin and Yrsa were dining with the captain that night, as they discussed plans for the coming battle.

"And you're sure you don't need to be there for this?" Aefric asked.

"No," Gwenellia said, opening a bottle of white wine and pouring into three copper mugs. "I've had enough of planning meetings for now. And I doubt they'll give any of my ideas much consideration anyway, given that this will be my first sea battle."

"But you have the best knowledge of your own battle magic," Deirdre said — either being polite or trying to get alone time with Aefric — "and so you could contribute to that degree."

"Karbin has it covered," Gwenellia said, shaking her head as she looked at Aefric. "You know, until recently I thought I was a pretty good wizard. But compared to you and him, I'm still an apprentice."

"It's all about the type of wizardry you've studied," Aefric said.

"And the way your grace has lived," Deirdre said. "His grace and Karbin — and myself, for that matter, though of course I'm a dweomerblade, not a wizard — have had to refine our magic in combat. Gives us an intuitive sense of where and how our magic is best-used."

Gwenellia asked Deirdre about being a dweomerblade then, and Deirdre began regaling the duchess with stories, while a pair of sailors brought in a spicy clam chowder, served with rolls of rye bread.

"Sure your graces don't want beer for this?" one of the sailors asked.

"Never developed a taste for it," Gwenellia said.

"The wine will do," Aefric said, and Deirdre nodded, before turning to the duchess. "Gods, I can't imagine having to *develop* a taste for beer."

"I think you've spent more time in taverns than I have," Gwenellia said with a laugh.

And then the stories were flying. First about taverns — both Aefric and Deirdre contributing. Then about adventuring, with those same two leading. Then Gwenellia spoke for a time about growing up in Rethneryl, though to be honest Aefric couldn't tell how that sounded much different than growing up in the noble household of any ranking Armyrian family.

It was an experience he couldn't quite identify with. And he knew Deirdre felt the same way, because during one of Gwenellia's stories

— this one about a boar hunt that had led to the discovery of silver in the middle of a forest — she gave him a subtle wink.

"And so," Gwenellia said, laughing, "we ended up with a new silver mine. All because that stupid boar refused to die."

"Think of it as a gift from the spirit of the boar," Deirdre said, smiling. "A reward for a good hunt."

"Oh, I do," Gwenellia said. "Soon as I came of age, I renamed it the Boar's Head Mine. And I've cut down on the amount of boar hunting allowed in those woods as a thank you."

"Cut down, but not stopped?" Aefric said. "Think the boars take that as much of a thank-you?"

"They breed too fast there," she said. "If I stopped all hunting in those woods, the boars would pose a threat to the mining operation."

"Now that *is* odd," Deirdre said, and sipped her wine. "I'd think the mining camp would be enough to keep them away."

"I know," Gwenellia said, sounding exasperated. "But it *doesn't*. And if we didn't keep their numbers low, I swear they'd kick us right out of that forest."

Deirdre gave Aefric a look he understood.

Something else was going on in those woods. A local spirit, power or creature was influencing those boars. And when Aefric was an adventurer, he would probably have looked into it.

"I think we have more pressing work on the table than odd boar breeding practices," Aefric said to Deirdre, which made her laugh.

"Oh, *no*," Gwenellia said, laughing herself. "I wasn't asking you to come deal with my boars."

"We know, your grace," Deirdre said. "But if your grace drops a mystery like that on the table, his grace and I — through long practice and inclination — feel an urge to pick it up and look it over."

"Really? Just hearing about it is enough to draw your attention?"

"I admit an urge to investigate it," Aefric said.

"So," Gwenellia teased, "if I told you of the mystery of our hot waterfall, you might have to come visit Neastall?"

"That does sound like something I might have to see. As you

might wish to see the giant dragon skeleton at the end of the Dragon-scar, in the northern part of my duchy."

"That's *real*?" Gwenellia asked. "I thought it was just a story."

"Oh, it's real enough," Deirdre said. "I've climbed it myself."

"I would like to see it."

"Then when all this is over," Aefric said, "you'll have to come for a visit."

"Most definitely," Gwenellia said.

And so the conversation ran on for a time. And Aefric broke out a bottle of honsach, to share. The honey and caramel taste of the liqueur made for an excellent dessert.

They shared that for a time, though not too much of it, and more laughter, until finally Gwenellia said, "Aefric, you're a marvelous host, even to an unexpected guest."

"Thank you, Gwenellia."

"You may call me Gwen, if you like."

"Thank you, Gwen."

"In fact," she said with a half-smile. "Were we in a proper castle, with proper beds and proper baths and proper smells, I might wish to share the noble privilege with so handsome and worldly a duke such as yourself."

"Then I lament that we are here," Aefric said gallantly.

"Yes," Gwen said with a sigh. "Here, where the beds are nothing but rough rope hammocks and the only thing worse than smell of caulk and varnish is the odor of those damnable lamps."

"Foul, isn't it?" Deirdre said.

"And so," Gwen said, standing. "I shall take my leave instead, and seek sleep. Deirdre?"

"Oh, if his grace will have me, I'm staying. Fishy smells and rope burns notwithstanding."

Gwen tilted her head as she thought about that.

"You mean you *could*?" she asked Deirdre. "Even in surroundings like these?"

"For a chance to lie with his grace," Deirdre said, "I'd suffer far worse."

Gwen shook her head.

"Aefric," she said. "You're handsome. But you're not *that* handsome. Good night to you both."

"Good night," Aefric said, chuckling.

"Good night, your grace," Deirdre said, and as soon as Gwen had closed the door behind her, turned to Aefric. Wiggled her eyebrows. "More the fool, her. If you'll have me tonight."

"This is the eve of battle for us," Aefric said. "I'm not going to send you away tonight."

───────

"ONE OF THESE DAYS, AEFRIC," DEIRDRE SAID, YAWNING AND stretching atop him in the most intriguing fashion. "You and I are going to get to share a proper bed. Do all the things to each other that we're always talking about."

"I still owe you that promised night," Aefric said, fighting back a yawn himself. "This doesn't count."

"I agree," she said, and kissed him.

Without the lamps burning or any magical light, he couldn't see her clearly, but he could tell she was smiling.

And without the lamps burning, the caulk and varnish smell of the cabin could be ignored in favor of the cleaner — or at least more pleasant — scent of sea air.

He reached out, picked up her ponytail and gently smacked her naked backside with it.

"And when that night comes…"

"My hair will be unbound," Deirdre said with a nod. "A promise of my own."

It was sometime close to midmorning. Aefric was sure of that much without casting a spell, but—

"Midday is two bells away," she said, laying her head back down on his shoulder. "And we don't have to depart until after dark. Surely we can stay here a while longer."

"You know I need to check on the plans, the turnout of ships so far, and all of that. Plus, I should probably have lunch with the duchess."

"Don't you mean with *Gwen*?" she teased.

"Yes, I—"

"Oh, Gwen, it's so *nice* to enjoy a *proper* lunch with you. Oh, Aefric, it's *ever* so lovely. Would that we had truffles and jam and…"

She dissolved into a fit of giggles and tucked her face against his chest.

Aefric was so shocked at Deirdre *giggling* that for a moment all he could do was stare at her in the dim grayness until she was breathing again, in great gasps.

"Got that out of your system?" he asked.

"I'm sorry," Deirdre said, not exactly sounding contrite. "She's really a fairly pleasant woman, for a powdered puff. But she's just so *obvious*. Soon as you taught her a little lesson in magic she practically started *drooling*."

"Oh, she didn't."

"Well, maybe not *drooling*, but she definitely *reassessed* the duke of Deepwater."

"She's married," Aefric said. "In Rethneryl they only wear a simple band on the smallfinger, but—"

"And you're telling me she doesn't have sisters and cousins she wants to set you up with?" Deirdre asked. "Hells, I bet half the reason she wants to bed you is so she can bring back a report."

Deirdre started laughing then, and Aefric let her laugh herself out.

"Finished?" he asked at last.

"I think so." She patted him on the chest and sounded far more serious when she next spoke. "See, Aefric. This is why I could never be a bridal candidate for you. I could never live my life taking people like her seriously."

She ran her hands over his chest. "Imagine. Turning down a chance to be with a man you *want*, just because of a fishy odor and the threat of rope burns."

"Well—"

"In fact," she said pensively, her hands playing with his scars now. "I wouldn't mind risking another rope burn..."

"Don't start something," Aefric said. "It's time to get up."

"Time for *one* of us to get up," she mumbled and began to nibble his throat. Which felt entirely too good, considering he couldn't afford to give in.

"Deirdre," he said, and his tone of voice was enough to make her stop. She sighed.

"Back to the world outside?" she said.

He nodded. "Back to the world outside."

"Tell me one thing, Aefric. If you were still just an adventurer—"

He touched her face. "In a heartbeat."

He felt her smile more than saw it.

They got up then, and he cleaned himself with magic by the light of the Brightstaff. Once more, though, she declined his offer to do the same for her. Though she did allow him to clean her leathers and silken undergarments that way at least.

He dressed in a black linen tunic over black leathers, with matching belt and boots. The buckle was even black steel, and the cloak he pulled out to go with outfit was black as well.

He made sure his sword and wand were positioned for easy drawing, if necessary.

"I like that look on you," she said, fingertips on her chin. "Naked is better, but this is good. Very ready-for-trouble."

"All right," he said, rubbing his hands together, "I want to try something before we open the door."

Suddenly Deirdre was all business once more.

"Then I shall stand guard, your grace," she said, drawing her rapier and dagger and facing the door.

This was probably a wasted bit of magic, but he had to try. He couldn't help thinking that Maev might've managed at least enough of a self-rescue to get outside the wards, even if she was probably hiding and hunted on the castle grounds or in the city.

So Aefric cast his spell of contact once more.

"Dalius has the princesses. You're in danger. We're coming to your rescue this evening. I'll need any help you can give me, to find you."

He'd girded himself against that sense of emptiness that he expected to follow. As though his magic had been sucked down a whirlpool.

Not literally, of course. But it felt *somewhat* like that to cast a spell of contact that failed to reach its target for some reason. His sense of the magic would just fade and fade until it was gone.

But this time, he felt the tingling tension.

Contact!

Followed quickly by Maev's voice.

"Aefric, thank the gods! Fools thought they could stick me in identical rooms and I wouldn't notice they were *a half-floor higher*. I need—"

In her rush, she'd forgotten the twenty-five-word limit of the main version of that spell. But that didn't matter. He could cast it again and again.

What mattered was that Maev was alive. Maev was safe.

The rest, they would figure out.

A SHORT TIME LATER, AEFRIC GATHERED PEOPLE IN HIS CABIN, TO EAT lunch and discuss the latest changes to their plans in light of his piecemeal conversation with Maev.

Yrsa and Beornric, Deirdre and Karbin and Gwen, all gathered around the orange table with Aefric. This time Beornric took the chest at the end, putting Karbin and Yrsa on one side, and Deirdre, Aefric and Gwen on the other.

Aefric began as soon as they were seated, rather than waiting for their food.

"All right," he said. "I tried once more to contact Maev this morning—"

"*Maev?*" Gwen said. "Are you saying that the member of Princess

Maev Stronghand's entourage that you've been magically communicating with for nearly two seasons—"

"—is the princess herself," Aefric said. "That's right. I'm not sure I'm supposed to divulge that, but we don't have time for word games."

Gwen thought about that for a moment, then nodded.

"I think it's safe for me to keep that secret. If she were negotiating something with us, or one of our allies it might be different. But we have no part of Varondam. And frankly, knowing this explains a few things I've been wondering about."

"Thank you," Aefric said.

"Your graces," Yrsa said, "if I might ask you to set aside further discussion of this issue for another time, we have more pressing matters on us."

"Of course," Gwen said. "I'm sorry. Do continue, Aefric."

"The point is that I reached her. It turns out that they'd moved her behind wards by moving her into identical quarters while she was out hunting with the king, and thought that returning her by different stairs would hide that those quarters were something like a half-floor higher. Though I'm not sure how that could work."

"Clever architecture," Gwen said. "Some castle designs allow for half-floor spacing that affords nearly identical views. I've seen it in our own royal palace."

"Princess Maev is a forester," Beornric said. "Change her view of some trees, and she'll know it in an instant."

"Ah, then it was the orchards of Vaaran Tir that gave away the game," Gwen said.

Everyone looked at her.

"You knew about those?" Aefric asked. "I only learned of them from Maev."

Gwen frowned.

"Am I the only one here who's actually *been* to Vaaran Tir?" She made show of looking around the table. "Knight. Knight-Admiral. Former adventurer and newly appointed Court Wizard. Wandering troublemaker knight and newly appointed Ducal Champion. Former adventurer and newly created Duke." She nodded. "I guess I am."

Aefric chuckled. "I think you, Deirdre and I have a great deal to discuss about Vaaran Tir before this evening."

"I'd say so. You really don't know anything about that castle?"

"My historian gave me a sense of the castle's layout, to help me find the princesses, and a sense of where it stands in the city, to help me plan my route in and out. But her notes about the castle grounds said nothing about any orchards."

"Ah, too recent. They were planted after the Godswalk Wars, in honor of the Green Lord. Saplings grown quickly to mature trees through the blessings of one of His clerics. I saw them when I was there one summer past."

"Excellent," Beornric said. "But for the moment, we should perhaps return to what the princess had to say?"

"Right," Aefric said. "The point is that the change of apartments — without any mention of it from her hosts — indicated to her that she was now a prisoner."

"Why?" Gwen asked.

"I'd previously warned her it was a possibility."

Gwen nodded.

"Fortunately," Aefric continued, "that she was hunting meant she had her bow and a quiver of arrows, in addition to her rapier and hunting dagger. And Sylkanis was with her. Doubtless Dalius intended to take all those things away overnight, while she slept. But the moment she was alone, she knew her priority was escape. Even though it meant leaving her luggage and entourage behind."

"Naturally," Gwen said. "How did she manage it?"

"I left that question for later."

"Probably went out the window and down the castle walls," Deirdre said, "with that great forest lynx of hers on her back."

"Her quarters were likely at least four floors up," Gwen objected. "Possibly higher."

"Wouldn't slow her down," Beornric said.

"The point is," Aefric said, "she got out of the castle and city, and into a forest in the nearby hills. But she had no friendly place to go for hundreds of miles. She considered simply making her way north, but she didn't like the idea of just abandoning her friends and servants."

"Well," Karbin said, "at least extracting her will be easy enough. Did you arrange a meeting place?"

"Yes ... and no," Aefric said.

"Oh, you *didn't*," Beornric said, looking pained.

"As I said, she didn't like the idea of abandoning her entourage—"

"She's our *princess*!" Beornric said. "You know, the primary reason good King Colm agreed to send us on this rescue mission?"

"What am I missing?" Gwen said.

"What they haven't said aloud," Yrsa said, "is that dear Princess Maev isn't content to have us extract her before the main rescue mission. She wishes to *partake* of this rescue mission."

Yrsa looked at Aefric. "Am I correct?"

"She insisted on it. And she had a compelling argument for why she should come along."

"And *she*, of course, got to serve as a scout in the wars," Gwen grumbled. "So *she* gets to go."

"And just *what*, your grace, was this compelling argument?" Beornric asked.

"She can gain us entry into the castle through the servants' backway."

"I'm sold," Deirdre said. "She can come."

"Yes," Beornric said with a sigh. "Even I can't argue that. But you better bring her back alive, Aefric, or the king won't forgive you this time."

Gwen visibly caught Beornric's use of Aefric's name, but said nothing about it.

"It won't be our duke who must bring her back alive," Karbin said quietly. "That will be my responsibility. For I must take his place on the mission now."

Silence hit the table like a catapult-flung boulder.

Aefric forced himself to take a long, slow breath before he answered that.

"How do you calculate that?" he asked, impressed at how calm he sounded.

"Simple," Karbin said. "I was never sold on your planned extraction method in the first place. Packing five princesses into a *magari's* chariot? Even with lightfall spells to resolve the weight capacity problem, it—"

"It will work," Aefric said.

"It *might* have," Karbin conceded. "But now you have a whole entourage to deal with. And possibly their luggage. How do you plan to extract them all? Tow a *platter* or two?"

Gwen said something then, but Aefric missed it. He was too angry at Karbin.

"I'll wedge them all into a cart if I have to and carry it with magic."

Gwen might've said something then, too. Aefric wasn't sure. He was too focused on Karbin's answer.

"Don't be foolish. This *requires* teleportation. And I'm the only one here who can—"

"I said I can teleport!"

With five words, spoken loudly and clearly, Gwen had finally broken through the pattern of old arguments renewed.

Both Aefric and Karbin looked at her, confused. What she'd said was so unexpected, Aefric wasn't sure he'd parsed it correctly.

It was Deirdre, oddly enough, who spoke next.

"Really, your grace? I hope you'll forgive us all for assuming you couldn't. It's a rare spell, and one that few ... truly master."

"Few are descended from Quinn the Slippery," Gwen said, practically biting off her words.

Quinn the Slippery. Not just a powerful wizard of his time, but a member of the Silver Arrows — that group known widely as the greatest and most powerful heroes in all Qorunn.

"Forgive me, Gwen, please," Aefric said. "I did not mean to ignore you when you spoke. It was the result of a bad habit of long years. Karbin was my master of old — my *first* master of magic — and argument for us is as natural as swimming to a fish."

She looked only slightly mollified by his apology, but she nodded. Then arched an eyebrow.

"Honestly," she said, looking around the table. "Did none of you wonder how I came to be here on your ship?"

"I assumed you flew," Aefric said.

"I did. That last part. Appearances, you know. But ask yourself this. Did I arriving looking as though I'd been flying all night?"

Aefric chuckled and shook his head, which seemed to please her.

"Quinn," Karbin said, "called the Slippery, might have been the most elusive of the Silver Arrows in his day. But he was never known to have used teleportation."

"Of course not," Gwen said smugly. "He would famously grouse in public that Kainemorton refused to teach it to him, and that he couldn't find another teacher worth learning it from."

"Then how—"

"Because he learned the secret from the Goddess of Magic Herself. I mean Astryma, of course. This was long before the gods walked and Kalinda replaced Her."

"Then why—"

"Why do you think? It's common practice for enemies to prepare for wizards based on their known powers. If all believed that Quinn could not teleport — while he, at the same time, quite famously made frequent use of other spells of movement and escape — then teleportation blocks were rarely, if ever, employed against him. He used the spell sparingly, carefully, and in ways that none would suspect."

"And your family kept up that tradition," Aefric said.

Gwen nodded. "Every direct member of my family who has the talent for magic — and especially we who hold the family title — is required to master teleportation, to practice it regularly, and to keep it secret. I would not have used it to come here, but I was so *irritated* with Colm for excluding me from his battle plans."

"He excludes his own queen, as well," Beornric said. "He excludes any who have not actually fought in battles."

"In any event," she said with a sigh, "I am the first of us to break that secret. But the lives of our princesses hang in the balance."

"We will keep your secret," Aefric said. "No one outside this cabin will learn of this."

A chorus of ascent around the table.

"Good," she said. "And thank you. But now, as Rethneryl's ambassador, I must point out that your king has agreed that the Hero of Deepwater and Frozen Ridge must lead the rescue attempt. So Aefric is going."

"And now your grace wishes to accompany him after all?" Karbin asked.

"No," Gwen said. "Aefric's illustration of why I should not was quite clear." She smiled. "*I* will be the extraction team."

10

———————

The fleet was gathering a little slower than Yrsa expected — which rankled her visibly when she spoke about it — but more ships were coming in by the hour.

At this rate, they might not be ready to sail south by nightfall and in place at Varondam's three major ports before midnight, but close enough that Aefric felt the difference was not worthy of concern.

So the seaborne portion of the plan was coming together well. But the rescue mission looked to be coming together even better.

Gwen might not've been in a battle before, but it turned out she had an excellent head for spaces and layouts. She'd spent only two aetts in Vaaran Tir, and those over a year ago, but she remembered more about its layout and surroundings than Elkari had been able to tell Aefric.

In all, the afternoon planning session had been more profitable than Aefric expected.

Then, evening came. A quick but hearty dinner of spicy beef stew with rye rolls and red wine, and then it was time to go.

Aefric and Deirdre would go in first, contacting Gwen by spell when they were in position, so she could join them.

Deirdre didn't look right with a long black woolen cloak covering all her maroon leather, but she needed it for the same reason Aefric once again stashed the Brightstaff in his pouch.

Each was simply too visible and distinctive.

Flying in from the west was bad enough. They had to wait until the sun was barely visible above the sea — and the skies above them purpling toward black, with the first stars showing up in the east — before they could take to the air.

Deirdre, of course, could not fly on her own. And taking Aefric's *magari* would have been the opposite of a stealthy approach. The whole city would have wondered at the fiery flying chariot pulled by red, fiery horses.

Aefric would have to fly for both of them. Deirdre, lightened by a lightfall spell — which would also help if she lost her grip — would cling to his back.

Of course, he hadn't expected her to curl her legs around his and tuck her face in close to his neck, but he couldn't say he objected to the position. And certainly she'd have an easier time holding on that way.

What *didn't* help were her teasing comments like "Faster, horsey!" and "Higher, horsey!" and "Hyah! Hyah!"

He could only hope she didn't notice him laughing. If she did, she might never let him forget it.

Flying high was not the plan anyway.

Aefric flew low, skimming close to the surface of the water. Close enough that they caught cold salty spray carried on even colder wind.

They came in just outside the northern edge of the city harbor. Using the lights on ships and the city walls to navigate before entering the city itself.

Vaaran Tir was an old city, and looked the part. The innermost section, closest to the harbor, was all gray stone, from the cobbles on the streets to the buildings themselves, where there were no sharp edges to be seen. All stonework had been worn to rounded edges by time and wind.

Like a tree, the age of Vaaran Tir could be seen in its rings. Each ring — semicircles, really, for they were all cut off by the harbor — bordered by what had once been a city wall. Seven in all.

Aefric had no time to see or worry about the walls or the buildings, though. His attention was all on sightlines, and quick, furtive flights from one shadowed spot or high roof to the next.

Deirdre was a big help here. She understood sightlines even better than he did, and was able to give him constant warnings of "high window right" or "wall patrol left" to keep him from crossing sightlines he hadn't caught.

Together, they moved like a shadow deeper into the city. Where the buildings and walls grew taller.

The great palace at Vaaran Tir was near the back edge of the fifth ring. Or rather, taking up much of the central portion of the fifth ring.

Aefric and Deirdre found a hidden spot high on a gray stone watch tower to look over the palace, and orient what they'd been told of it with what they now saw.

It was a surprisingly simple castle, but of an odd design.

Most of the city had been built from stone that was gray or dully whitish or a shade of brown.

The palace had been built from red stone. But dull red, not gleaming, and with a porous look, as though it might not stand up to assault by catapult.

Aefric didn't believe that for a moment. And not just because he could sense magical defenses woven into the castle walls. There was just something about the stonework that suggested strength.

The palace itself had low outer walls that seemed mostly token, beside the taller walls of its ring. No one even patrolled them...

"No one on the walls?" Deirdre asked quietly. "Doesn't that seem suspicious to you?"

"Maybe Vaaran Tir has no thieves?" Aefric suggested.

Deirdre snorted.

"Could be a guard change, I suppose," she said.

The main part of the square keep itself looked to stand only about four stories, but it was wide in both directions. Easily a hundred-fifty feet to a side.

After the fourth level, there looked to be a public area on the roof. A flower garden, with benches and gazebos and the like.

At the four corners stood what *could* have qualified as towers. Technically. But each was squared and fifty feet on a side, and stood another ... four or five stories. Hard to tell from the window positioning. Certainly at least sixty feet.

The towers looked like standing keeps unto themselves, that just happened to have been built up out of an existing squared keep, instead of finding new ground.

The towers were connected — along the perimeter, not the diagonal — by suspension bridges at three levels.

"There are your guards," Aefric muttered. Two on each bridge, armed with crossbows and carrying lanterns.

Deirdre snorted again. "They better be *amazing* shots at that distance. Assuming they could even *see* someone going over that low wall after dusk."

"Well," Aefric said, "in any event, this is exactly what Gwen told us to expect. Still think it looks odd."

"Says the man with all those giant towers, *thrusting* high into the sky. Including his ... *Spike*."

"Oh, come on," Aefric said.

"You come on," Deirdre countered. "Are you seriously telling me you never looked at those huge, *erect* towers and thought, 'Hey, that looks like a—"

"No," he said. "I never did. And anyway, I didn't design Water's End."

"Does the Spike make you feel inadequate?"

"Can we get back to the rescue?"

"Anytime you're done staring at towers." She shook her head. "Some men are so distractable."

"Well, I haven't heard *you*—"

"There's our entry point," she said, pointing down along the right-hand outer wall. "The southeast tower will largely block the view of the watchers, the street is dead, and once we're over the wall we shouldn't be more than two dozen steps from the nearest grove. Oranges, if Gwen was right."

Aefric stared at her. "When did you notice that?"

"The moment we set down. But you were busy studying the castle like you needed to memorize it."

He shook his head. "Let's go."

Now that they weren't flying, or up high, Aefric learned quickly that Maev hadn't been kidding.

Varondam was a hot, sultry place.

A few seconds out of the breeze and already he could feel sweat starting under his collar and down his back. Deirdre, entirely encased in leather, must've had it even worse.

Strangely, though, the place didn't *smell* the way he expected a hot, sultry city to smell.

By now, even the Keifer part of Aefric had come to understand that cities in Qorunn didn't have the ... odor problems he would have expected from medieval cities. Because they *weren't* medieval cities. Thanks to magic, and other innovations, their sanitation was far, far advanced by comparison.

Still, even for a city in Qorunn, the dark, gray stone street just outside the low castle wall smelled ... good.

Like ... hibiscus. That was strange.

Not what he needed to focus on, though.

"Oh," Deirdre muttered. "Well, I guess we couldn't have expected it to be *too* easy, could we?"

Aefric knew what she meant at once. For while the wall was low — only perhaps eight feet tall — and unpatrolled by people, it wasn't *unguarded*.

The wards were faint. Subtle. But there. Woven into the gray stonework.

"They cover the walls," she said.

"They extend above as well," Aefric said, "by..."

He sighed. "Fifty feet."

"So, well into both viewing and firing range of those crossbows."

"Yep. At *best* flying over will likely alert the whole castle."

"I can't quite tell what they do," she said. "The wards, I mean. I know it's more than detection ... and some kind of alarm ... but there's some odd third thing. It doesn't quite feel *aggressive*, but..."

She shook her head. "I can't get it."

"The alarm is practically a klaxon, to make sure no one misses it. And the part you're having trouble reading gives you the *flickers*."

"Oh, I *hate* that," she said. "What color?"

"Bright green."

"Even worse," she said, grimacing.

The *flickers* were a kind of magical targeting device. What they did, quite simply, was limn the target in a bright, flickering corona that looked like trapped lightning. Quite visible in darkness or light, and *very* good for setting someone up for archers.

"So the guards just stand those bridges, waiting for the klaxon to alert them to targets, and shoot anything with the *flickers*," Aefric said. "Not bad."

"For them," Deirdre said. "Not bad *for them*. Unless those wards aren't defensive. In which case, not bad *for us*."

"What do you mean?" Aefric asked.

"Those wards," she said. "You can read them clearer than I can. Are they, themselves, protected?"

"You mean against dispelling?"

"Or against direct assault."

"They're not designed to *receive* direct assault," Aefric said, frowning. "It's not their nature. Magic that works against magic would work on them, but it's not as though you could slash them with a knife."

"As a matter of fact," Deirdre said with a grin, "that's *exactly* what I intend to do. Assuming they won't explode if I try it."

Aefric took a moment. Focused in and studied their structure. The wards weren't easy to spot at first, too subtle in design and application. But now that he knew they were there, it was simplicity itself to read them.

"No," he said a moment later. "It would be safe to dispel them — which would take me longer than we want to spend here — so it must be safe to do ... whatever you're going to do."

She drew her dueling dagger and transferred it to her right hand. "Pick me up. Lift me to the top of the wall."

Aefric put his arms around her middle and held her tight. Using just the right amount of flight, he lifted them just high enough for her to reach the top edge of the wall.

"Could we have flown like this the whole way? Because—"

"Focus, Deirdre."

"Right. Wards first." She grinned at him over her shoulder. "You didn't train with the Iron Wands long enough to learn this trick, and we don't like to advertise that we can do it."

Mumbling softly under her breath, she reached out with her dagger and cut a hole in the wards.

All around that hole — which was just under three feet in diameter — the wards were strong and complete. But within that hole, nothing but empty space.

"Wow," Aefric said.

"Let's get over that wall," Deirdre said, "then you can admire me all you want."

He carried them through the hole quickly and set down on the other side.

Here the grounds were grassy. The first grass he'd seen inside the city, come to think of it. Not that he'd been looking hard for grass while flying them in.

No lights, where they were. But ahead and to the right were the shadowed orchards, beginning with the oranges, just as Gwen had said.

Farther ahead that direction, left of the shadowy trees, was a lit area. Walking gardens, with small globes of light on spikes along the paths. And what looked to be a hedge maze beyond.

The keep itself was maybe fifty, seventy-five steps from the wall where they were. And nothing of it was lit below the second level. Not that Aefric could see from here.

"Study architecture later," Deirdre whispered.

"Right," Aefric said.

Deirdre led on from there, having better night vision than he did. He followed her along the wall — one step away to ensure they didn't stray into the wards, which oddly extended to the wall on this side — and into the trees.

The fresh, citrus smell of the trees gave Aefric an unexpected lift. And the oranges that grew looked fat and happy.

"Which one again?" Deirdre whispered.

"Toward the back of the grove," Aefric said, "Where—"

The mewing sound was too bass for a housecat, and Aefric recognized it immediately.

Then Sylkanis was there. Only shades of gray in the darkness, Aefric couldn't check her markings, but he knew that great forest lynx all the same. And the lynx knew him, nuzzling his knee with her head, and bumping his legs hard enough to stagger him.

Deirdre had already stopped moving.

Sylkanis took Aefric's sleeve in her mouth and tugged.

"This way, I think," Aefric said.

"Are you *sure*?" Deirdre mocked.

They followed Sylkanis toward the back of the trees.

Suddenly Aefric was hugged tightly by a woman about half a handspan taller than Deirdre. He couldn't even see this woman properly yet, beyond her loose and wild black hair, but he knew that hug. And that honeysuckle smell.

Maev.

"Thank the gods," Maev said, when she released him. "Being here alone and unable to act. I hate it."

Aefric's eyes had adjusted enough to see dimly in the grayness. He could see that Maev was dressed in buckskin, from her shirt and pants to her belt and calf-high boots. All likely her own work, from a buck she'd hunted. Rapier and hunting dagger on her belt. She picked up her longbow from where it had lain against at tree.

"Wait," she said, sounding shocked. "Where's the Brightstaff?"

"Concealed," Aefric said, patting his pouch, "so it didn't give me away."

"Good thinking," she said, turning now to see who was with him. "And you ... *Deirdre*? I almost didn't recognize you under that cloak."

"Rather the point of it, your highness."

The two embraced.

"Barely seen you since the wars," Maev said.

"We've both been a bit busy."

"Can't tell you how glad I am to have you along." Maev clapped a hand on her shoulder. "Now. Extraction through those wards will be tricky."

"Covered," Aefric said, then frowned. "Wait. How did *you* get past those wards?"

Maev clucked her tongue, as though the answer should've been obvious.

Aefric scoffed. "Am I the only one here who would have had to *work* to get past those wards?"

"Which is why you need us," Deirdre said smugly.

"One reason, anyway," Maev said, but when Deirdre chuckled suggestively, Maev immediately added, "I meant on the rescue."

"Sure you did," Deirdre said.

"We still have to figure out extraction," Maev said. "I've found a covered wagon that will work for what we talked about, but it still sounds slow and awkward."

"Handled," Aefric said. "We just need to get to a lemon tree with a knot that looks like a face."

"I know the one," Maev said, and then led them swiftly and close to silently among the grass and trees — well, everyone else moved silently, Aefric *tried* to — past the end of the orange grove and into the lemon grove to a small, unlit sitting area.

Moonlight bathed the open area, and showed that the tree in question had a knot that looked like an old man, weeping.

This was too exposed a place for Aefric's liking. The moonlight. The nearby walking path bordered by more spiked globes of light. But it was definitely the spot Gwen had spoken of.

He cleared the other two and the now plainly reddish-brown lynx from the area just in front of the tree.

He cast his spell of contact. Said softly, "We're in position."

A moment later Gwen appeared. Still clad in the same finery, though someone had found her a black cloak.

"Gwen?" Maev said.

"Surprise," Gwen said with a grin.

The two embraced quickly.

"I didn't know you could teleport," Maev said she pulled back.

"And I'd like you to pretend to keep it that way," Gwen said, putting one finger to her lips and winking.

"Of course," Maev said with a smile.

"All right," Aefric said. "Gwen stays here, ready to extract everyone we bring back. Maev, time to get us into that castle."

"Good," she said.

Aefric expected Maev and Sylkanis to lead him and Deirdre to some spot along the back of the wide main keep.

He'd already been considering spells of magical darkness to help cloak their approach, and weighing their value versus pure speed when crossing the most visible areas, when he realized he was wrong.

She was leading them through the groves. With the castle well to their left. They passed grapefruit trees and apples trees. Pear trees and plum trees and prune trees.

Only then did she begin cutting left — between leafy trees heavy with fragrant purple fruit — toward the north side of the castle.

When they reached the edge of the grove, Aefric could see that the lights of the sitting area and walking paths were a good fifty paces or so to his left. And not far to his right, the hedge maze. Which was oddly unlit.

The question must've been obvious on his face, because Maev whispered, "Any who want to use the maze at night are expected to carry their light. Something about the interplay of shadows."

"Fascinating," Deirdre said drolly.

"As mazes go, it's not bad. And if we get stuck, there's a bolt hole in it. Has exits at the outer edges of the fifth, sixth, and seventh rings."

"So that's how you got past the wards," Aefric said.

"No," she said. "But it *is* how I got out the first time. They didn't know I'd found it. Now the passage is guarded, but between the two of you, those guards won't be a problem. If we need that route."

Maev led them over to the edge of the maze, then along its near side, before cutting quickly over to the castle wall. Another dozen paces along that wall she stopped.

"Here we go," she said softly. "Where did I leave that trigger?"

Sylkanis pawed at a spot about knee-height.

"Thank you, Sylkanis," Maev said, scratching the lynx behind her ears. She adjusted her grip on her bow and knocked an arrow.

Deirdre drew her rapier and dueling dagger, both limned with red light, currently faint.

Aefric pulled the Brightstaff out of his pouch.

Maev lifted a boot toward the trigger.

"Wait," Aefric said, then cast a quick spell and gazed, humming, through the facets of the yellow diamond. "All clear. No traps."

"Why would it be trapped?" Maev asked. "Servants use this door."

"And now *we're* using it. If they expect you to come back for your entourage..."

"Fair enough," she said. "But it's safe?"

He nodded.

She tapped the trigger spot with her boot.

With a click, a slender portion of wall pulled inward. With a soft grinding sound, it slid right, revealing a dark passage.

"In before light," Maev said softly. "Trigger to close is on the left, inside. Sylkanis and I will be on the stairs, waiting."

Then she and her forest lynx slipped into the darkness. Deirdre bumped Aefric with her shoulder, so he entered next, checking his footing with the butt of the Brightstaff to avoid stumbling.

His boots scuffed stone. He smelled cold stone and oil and something vaguely metallic. Iron, maybe. Little light came into the narrow passage from outside though. His eyes needed time to adjust.

Then the soft grinding sound came again, and even the little light from outside vanished.

"In?" Maev's soft voice, from somewhere above and ahead.

"In," Deirdre confirmed, no louder, from behind Aefric.

"As little light as you can tolerate," Maev said.

Aefric caused the Brightstaff's yellow diamond to emit a glow no stronger than a single candle flame.

The passage height was reasonable, but the gray stone walls hemmed in closer on his sides than Aefric liked. Gray stone flooring, too.

Perfectly normal door to his right, but Maev had said something about stairs...

There. Beginning only about a dozen steps ahead of him, stairs leading up. He could see Sylkanis looking back at him from about the edge of the candlelight.

Aefric and Deirdre caught up, first with Sylkanis, then the three of them joined Maev, who leaned against the wall close to the top of the stairs, an arrow nocked and ready and pointing down the passage ahead of her.

She didn't look back, but he didn't expect her to. Likely she was using the Cat's Eyes, and didn't want to risk getting blinded by even his dim light.

"If we encounter any servants," Aefric said, "let me put them to sleep."

"Agreed," Maev said. "I was kept in the southeast tower. I expect the other princesses will be there as well, for both ease of guarding and to minimize the risk of courtiers discovering what their king was up to. Because I guarantee Dalius' court has no idea about this."

"Servants gossip," Deirdre said.

"Which means those servants probably never leave that tower either," Aefric said. "Or at least, haven't lately."

"All right," Maev said. "I'm thinking the best route is up stairs to the fourth floor this way, then across to the southeast tower and up."

"Agreed," Aefric said, and Deirdre nodded.

Maev found them more stairs then, and they ascended swiftly. Twice they encountered candle-bearing servants, and both times Aefric needed only a quick spell to put each into a sleep they wouldn't wake from before morning.

And, of course, a mere gesture to extinguish their candle.

The servants slowed them, though. Because Maev may have been shutting her eyes as fast as possible when their candlelight came into view, but she still needed at least a dozen breaths to recover her sight.

They reached the fourth floor of the main keep through the servants' backway without any real difficulties. Just before Maev opened the door that would lead to the backway passage she wanted, Deirdre reached past Aefric and put a hand on her shoulder.

Maev stopped, but didn't look back. "Yes?"

"Drop the Cat's Eyes before we emerge onto the fourth floor."

"Why?"

"Because if the servants aren't allowed out of that tower, the rest of the staff isn't allowed in."

"You think there'll be a guard station?" Aefric asked.

"And a lot more light than a single candle."

Aefric extinguished the Brightstaff as well, just in case.

Maev readied her bow. Deirdre readied her weapons.

With a gesture, Aefric opened that door.

This passage was wider, like a regular hall. Easily four strides wide. And tall, too. Twice Aefric's height. Still bare stone though.

Worse than all the room, there was light. Bright light. Down at the far end of the passage. Four guards in chainmail, carrying spears and shields.

The good? That the aura of their light didn't extend more than a quarter-way down the hall. Likely those guards had no idea Aefric and the others were here.

"Can you put them to sleep?" Maev whispered. "Like the servants?"

"Yes, but I have to get closer. Maybe a third the way down the hall I should be able to catch all four at once."

She nodded. "Softly then."

Maev's steps were as soundless as her cat's as they passed through the doorway, followed by Deirdre and Aefric.

Which was when Aefric noticed the bad. That vaguely itchy sensation between his shoulder blades.

"Crap," Deirdre said at the same moment, which meant that it wasn't just Aefric's imagination.

Oh, he hadn't *believed* it *was.* Just a vague hope.

"What?" Maev whispered.

"Scrying," Aefric said. "Someone knows we're here."

MAEV FROZE MID-STEP. HER LYNX LOOKED UP QUIZZICALLY. DEIRDRE swore softly.

"Keep going," Aefric whispered. "We knew they'd find us out sooner or later anyway."

"Right," Maev said, then accelerated, Sylkanis by her side. Oh, they weren't running full out, but considering they still made *no noise at all*, it certainly felt as though they were.

Even Deirdre, following in their wake, made more noise. And Aefric could barely hear *her.*

So he didn't bother walking. He knew all too well how loud the scrape and clop of his boots would sound if he tried to keep up. He took to the air instead.

Fortunate for him, it turned out. Because the floor turned to mud when they were halfway down the hall.

Sylkanis gave a kind of harsh scream. Maev and Deirdre both cried out in alarm, already calf-deep in the floor and sinking quickly.

Down at the end of the hall, the guards shouted alarm and started moving.

Aefric couldn't twaste time on the guards. Not yet. He summoned a glowing orange *Nester's platter* and started yanking his companions onto it by magic. Maev first, then Deirdre, then Sylkanis.

The hallway gloom suddenly glared into bright daylight. Someone had activated its magical light.

The guards down at the end threw spears, but those spears fell well short of the *platter*. Landed point-first in the mud and began to sink.

Unfortunately, the guards had more spears handy.

Maev, crouching on the *platter*, put an arrow in the neck of one of those guards. He fell with a strangled cry.

"Closer?" Aefric asked.

"Let me finish them," Maev said, taking down a second guard with an arrow in the back as he picked up a spear.

The other two held spears now, but crouched behind their shields.

"Closer," Deirdre said, and Aefric raised the *platter* higher toward the ceiling, putting the energies of its disc-shaped bottom between its passengers and any more spears. He slid it swiftly through the air toward the end of the hall, following in its wake.

Some kind of missile struck him from behind. Acid burned through his cloak, scalding his back. He cried out in pain.

A split second to decide. Give up the *platter* or fall.

He fell into the mud. It was surprisingly warm, and smelled like regular mud, not melted stone.

"Aefric!"

Maev's cry of concern, but he'd turned to see where that missile came from.

An old wizard floated on a cushion of bluish power, perhaps halfway between Aefric and the other end of the hall.

The old wizard had lined, deeply tanned skin. His dark gray hair was cut short, his chin was shaved clean, and his bare arms were covered with tattoos that swirled with reddish-orange power. He wore a red silk vest with purple trim, and matching, billowing pants.

He held a wand casually in his left hand, but with his right he was reaching toward the floor...

He was going to turn it back to stone, with Aefric half-buried in it!

Gritting his teeth against the fiery pain of that acid, Aefric took to the air again. But he couldn't risk splitting his focus with an attack, because—

"Kill the *platter*!" Deirdre's voice from behind him. They must've reached the safe place at the end of the hall.

"Go on!" Aefric called, dismissing the *platter*. "I'll follow in a moment."

"Will you?" the old wizard asked, musing. "I should hardly think so."

"You must be Varondam's court wizard."

"And you must be an interfering fool." He snapped his fingers.

Instinct made Aefric swerve toward the ceiling.

Two rocky hands, each the size of his head, barely missed him with their grab. The hands grasped from rocky arms, extending straight out of the walls.

"This is *my* place," the old wizard said, throwing an odd, swirling kind of gray missile at Aefric. "You're overmatched here."

Aefric managed to duck that odd missile, which struck the ceiling and sizzled.

Ah. That would be the same spell that burned him with acid, earlier. Well, it wouldn't burn all the way through the ceiling. It had already stopped trying to burn through his skin.

Not that its aftereffects were *pleasant*. His back still pained him with every move he made, though it no longer felt as though someone were trying to roast him over a fire.

Using the Brightstaff, Aefric threw a bolt of lightning at the old wizard. Not because he expected it to strike home, but because he knew his foe was ready for it. And he wanted to see how the old wizard responded.

Which turned out to be by catching the bolt on his wand, where it remained, crackling all around its length.

Interesting.

"Easier than recharging it myself," the old wizard said with a smile. Then flicked the wand at Aefric, sending that lightning right back.

If anything, the return blast looked stronger now.

But throwing lightning at the Brightstaff was like throwing rain at a storm.

Aefric used his namesake to split that bolt in two and destroy those grasping stone arms.

The old wizard nodded. "Not bad. I admit, I didn't expect that."

"Most people know better than to throw lightning at me."

Aefric sent another bolt of lightning at the old wizard, who frowned while he caught it on his wand. But Aefric followed immediately with a spell he called the *geyser*, because it shot a blast of water from his hand.

In and of itself, the spell wasn't particularly damaging. More of an annoyance, really. He'd developed it to both shame and awaken Lauszen, after the great oaf had gotten particularly drunk.

But Lauszen never been holding a handful of lightning when it drenched him...

The old wizard screamed as shock yanked his body straight. It also spoiled his floating cushion, and he fell into the mud that had been the hallway floor.

Aefric shoved him deep into the mud with a gesture, then used the wand Garram to cover the hallway floor in a thick sheet of ice.

He floated. Waiting. Raised a shimmering shield in front of himself, just in case.

Yes, many would have drowned quickly and awfully in that mud. But many were not wizards.

Well, he would know soon enough. Because even a wizard can live only so long, drowning in mud...

With a thunderous crash, a mighty bolt of pure force shattered the ice outward. Thick shards bounced off Aefric's shield as the furious wizard emerged, flying, completely covered in mud.

His hands empty of that wand.

Aefric immediately hit him with more lightning. Then fire from his own wand. Then more lightning. Then ice.

He kept this up, even while the old wizard was falling into the mud once more. He kept it up as the old wizard sank into that mud, apparently lifeless.

Once the old wizard was fully submerged, Aefric covered the mud in a thick sheet of ice once more. He resummoned his shield, and waited.

A dozen heartbeats.

Two dozen.

Three dozen.

By the time Aefric had counted his tenth dozen of heartbeats, he decided that was the end of Varondam's court wizard.

"What a waste," Aefric muttered, letting his shield drop. He used a quick spell to clean himself up.

If only he could do the same for the floor. But he didn't know how deep the mud was. After all, how thick was the stone of the castle floor? A question he'd never thought to ask.

He considered finding out, but what if Deirdre and Maev needed him? Better not to risk dallying here.

So Aefric added more ice to his sheet, doing his best to make it gritty. Not too slippery.

He turned and flew down the passage, to see where Maev and Deirdre had gone.

Past the door at the end of the passage, Aefric found a large, open room that looked to be outside the servants' backway. Here, the stone floor was covered with maple hardwood, and the plastered walls painted a soft, violet color.

There were tapestries on the walls, but Aefric was more interested in the dozen dead guards scattered around the floor. Dead of sword strokes, puncture wounds, claw-raked faces.

Swift, painful deaths.

His friends had been busy.

Aefric cast a contact spell. "Maev, I've beaten their wizard and am on my way to you. Where are you?"

Nothing. No contact.

Were the wards here that subtle?

A quick check told him they weren't. He could feel the wards on the outer castle walls, strengthening the stone, but nothing that would stop him from magically contacting another.

So his spell wasn't stopped by wards around *him*. Which meant the wards were around Maev and Deirdre.

Lovely.

Well, only one door was open, so that had to be the way to go. It led into a tight passage. More servants' backway then. How had Maev found all the...

Of course. She'd been raised in a bigger, older castle than this one, and she was the type to make a habit of finding every concealed door and hidden passage she could.

Really easy to imagine that being her favorite pastime as a little girl. Probably got her into all sorts of trouble, but not enough to stop her.

The image brought a smile to Aefric's face.

Guided by a soft light from the Brightstaff, he closed the passage door behind him and proceeded through the tight confines and up the stairs. They'd left one door open to mark their route. Doubtless they'd leave more.

Sure enough. As he reached the third floor of the tower, a door stood open, leading off the stairs. He followed another tight passage on the other side, then heard voices. Women's voices. Most of them he didn't know, but...

Yes. One of them was Maev. And it sounded as though she were taking charge.

He sped down the passage now, to the first open door he found.

An overdecorated room with a very high ceiling, and in the center ... what was the word Zoleen had chosen? Ah, yes. In the center, a gaggle of princesses.

Seeing them, in this moment, he understood why she chose that word. The four — two from Rethneryl, one from Hatay, one from Shachan — flocked like goslings around Maev, their goose. No older, but wiser, and confident.

All of them beautiful in their plumage. All of them harried. And all of them trying to talk at the same time.

Servants and noble attendants worried around the outside of the inner circle, possibly caught between trying to be helpful and trying not to get in the way.

Deirdre stood off to one side, a portrait of exasperation.

Aefric shut the door behind him, but it slid closed with a soft click, not a loud slam.

Deirdre looked up at him. Smiled. Whistled. Not a shrill, piercing tone, but a high, steady note that continued until she drew attention.

And once the attention began to shift her way, it snowballed quickly until all the talking stopped and every princess, Maev included, was looking at Deirdre.

Deirdre pointed at Aefric. "He's here."

Aefric held up a hand to forestall what looked to be a stampede of gratitude.

"I don't see Nayoria," he said. "Where is she?"

"Nayoria?" Maev asked. "She hasn't been here that I know of."

"All right, well, we have to get you all out of here first. Before more guards come. I'll return for Nayoria once you're all safe. So. Single file line. Maev and Deirdre — with Sylkanis, of course — leading. I'll handle rear guard."

"Right," Maev said. "Princesses at the front. Attendants next, then servants. Form up."

They were slow to form up. Deirdre huffed and began physically moving women into place.

"A warning," Aefric said to Maev and Deirdre. "That fourth-floor hall is still mud. I've covered it with ice. Tried to keep it from being too slippery, but—"

"We'll manage, your grace," Deirdre said.

He nodded.

"Let's move," Maev said.

"Quietly," Deirdre said. "Anyone starts *talking*, I'll kill her myself."

The nearest princess swallowed, eyes wide, looking thoroughly convinced that Deirdre wasn't joking.

Which was good, because Aefric doubted she was.

"Move out," he said, and the princess procession began.

Amusingly, they were all light on their feet. Yes, most of them were wearing soft shoes or silk slippers, but still. Apparently stealth was not unknown among royalty and its attendants.

All the same, moving quietly meant moving slowly enough that Aefric had a moment before he'd need to worry about taking up rear guard.

After all, with Maev's entourage included — and what had to be an incomplete selection from her luggage — there were twenty women in all.

Which meant Maev was right. The cart idea would never have worked. Not without two or three, and that would have been hard to manage, even with magic.

Maybe with illusions, he could have disguised them. But it would have been slow, and chancy...

The last of the servants stepped through the doorway. Aefric moved to do the same.

"Oh, don't leave *yet*, Brightstaff. Getting *you* here was the whole point."

The voice came from behind him. Male. Something vaguely familiar about it, but Aefric wasn't sure what.

He turned and immediately recognized the speaker.

The short, greasy hair. The pale, blotchy skin. The dirty, sea-green robes.

Gwawl.

"Really?" Aefric asked, trying to stall for time so the others could get away. "The *whole* point?"

"Well," Gwawl said. "Wasn't the point of stealing the princesses. That was King Dalius' thing. Don't know why he wanted them. Don't care, really. But once word spread about you taking down Nelazzi, he was worried she'd give him up, and you'd come in to rain vengeance."

"So he asked you for help?"

"Asked?" Gwawl spat. "*Paid.* Handsomely. Wasn't too careful with his wording, though. Told me I was to 'stop you.' Didn't get specific on what that meant."

"How do *you* interpret it?"

By now, at the pace Maev would set, her group might've reached the fourth floor of the main keep. There might be more guards, but Deirdre could handle those...

"The way I see it," Gwawl said, "I don't have to give a piss for whether those silly bints escape. Hell, if they do, maybe somebody *else* will pay me to steal them again."

He grinned evilly. "But *you*, Brightstaff. *You* are another matter. It's *your* fault Nelazzi's dead. *Your* work that broke her organization."

"It *is* broken then?" Aefric asked. "Good. Hard to be sure about these things."

"Oh, between killing Nelazzi, destroying her favorite base, burying her treasure, and the Purge of Kefthal — also your fault, I understand — her organization is *quite* dead."

"Pirates always find someone to follow," Aefric said.

The princess procession had to have crossed the ice by now. Might even be close to out of the building...

No. Couldn't risk it. Had to buy more time.

"Oh, I'll get them all to fall into line again," Gwawl said. "Eventually. But it'll take time."

"They won't follow *you*," Aefric scoffed. "You need a captain for that."

"And I'll find one with a strong enough personality to get the others to follow, and a big enough brain to acknowledge that *I'm* the man in charge."

"And where does Nayoria fit into all this?"

"Who?" Gwawl said, and he both looked and sounded honestly puzzled.

"Armyr's Royal Wizard. She came here only days ago to find out why the princess' most recent report was late."

"Well, bad luck for her then," Gwawl said with a shrug. "She never got here."

"I'd think you're lying, but I don't see why you would."

"Think what you like, but you're the only wizard to arrive at this castle in the last aett. Maybe longer. And you can *believe* I've been looking."

Aefric considered that through a breath, but couldn't spare it any more thought. If Gwawl was playing some kind of game, Aefric needed to play it too. If only until the princesses and Maev's entourage were safe.

Worries about Nayoria would have to wait.

"Well, man in charge," he said, "you did all this to ... what? Have your chance to deal with me yourself? Get your vengeance on me? Is that it?"

"Of course."

"Weren't you taking a pretty big risk there? I mean, what if the local royal wizard had beaten me and stolen your thunder? Not a very satisfying victory."

Gwawl spat. "If that arrogant, court-trained fool managed to kill you, you didn't deserve to die by my hand." He rubbed his hands together. "Now I have a chance to eliminate you as a future threat. Might even be enough to open Kefthal's ports to me again. If I bring them your head."

"And you think you can?" Aefric said. "Even though I bested you last time?"

"You don't have me by surprise this time, Brightstaff. Karbin tried and failed, and he's better than you."

"You didn't *beat* Karbin. You *escaped* him. And anyway, Karbin had a whole ship to worry about, including some impressive archers. I don't have any distractions."

"Oh, no?" Gwawl said mockingly. "Well..."

He clapped his hands.

Aefric raised the Brightstaff and looked about for guards. Or maybe pirates.

But no.

Instead, an invisibility field dropped. One good enough that even Aefric hadn't spotted it. And it wasn't just invisibility to sight.

The sense of both overwhelming power and overwhelming evil washed over him first. Then the strong odor of brimstone.

Then he saw the demon.

It was huge. Maybe twice Aefric's height, and three, maybe four times his width. All of it muscle. Skin on the dark side of red, but constantly shifting, as though flames burned within.

No horns on its head, but at the tips of its immense bat wings. Feet, not cloven hooves, though Aefric wasn't sure if feet *that* size were any better. Sexless, which was a plus. Aefric didn't want to imagine any other options there.

Its fingers ended in wicked-looking claws though.

"I did manage to prepare *one* distraction for you, Brightstaff," Gwawl said. "Hope you enjoy it."

"*KELKAZIKZ*," GWAWL SAID, "*NIK ATAL AF-RIIK BRYSTAFFUR!*"

Aefric recognized that as one of the demon languages, but he didn't know which.

Sadly, the demon — likely Kelkazikz — understood.

It lifted a hand and sent a blast of wind at Aefric.

Thinking quickly, Aefric used flight. Not to counter the wind, but to work with it. Alter the direction just enough that he slammed not into a wall, but a window.

Glass shattered. Cut him in several places. But Aefric was out of that room and into the night sky.

Plus the demon was much bigger than the window. Maybe—

The wall exploded outward as the demon flew *through* it.

Dear gods that thing was strong. And it flew fast.

Thinking quickly, Aefric hit it with the *flicker*, coating the demon in bright green sparking lightning that might not have harmed it, but made the demon much easier to see in the night sky.

Green. He hoped he remembered that color right...

This was ridiculous! A demon? Gwawl didn't have the *power* to summon and bind a demon. Nor did he have the training. Demonologist wizards, they carried an aura every bit as distinctive as that of a necromancer, and Aefric had *not* sensed such an aura around Gwawl.

He had to have a *token* of some kind. Could be he bought the spell from someone, but more likely a ring, or a pendant, or—

Demon!

Out of seemingly nowhere, twin claws grabbed for him.

Cursing himself for losing focus, Aefric twisted and juked to evade those claws, but they raked at him all the same…

Tore gouges across his chest and back, but…

But nothing deeper?

Even through the searing pain, Aefric could kiss Yrsa and Beornric for insisting he get into the habit of wearing that protective bracer. Must've helped turn the demon's strike from lethal to survivable.

Good thing, too. He was already reeling from that acid on his back, and bleeding from countless small cuts from the window glass. If those claws had dug in, he'd be *finished*.

Of course, he *was* bleeding profusely from those gouges. Still, at least he wasn't dead.

Yet.

Aefric drew the wand Garram and flung an ice bolt at the demon's face.

It ducked the blast.

Then the struggle became an aerial race above the fruit orchards. With Aefric ducking and weaving. Flinging ice bolts when he could. The demon evading every shot, while Aefric managed to stay *just* out of reach of its claws.

With a howl of fury that could probably have been heard in Lachedran, the demon fell back and flung eight balls of fire at Aefric, each the size of its own huge head.

Aefric used Garram to turn their fire into a shield between himself and the demon.

Didn't help. The demon flew through the fire entirely unharmed.

Naturally. This *would* be a demon from one of the hells that made it immune to fire. Probably fairly immune to lightning too, given that Gwawl knew he'd need this demon against Aefric.

Speaking of Gwawl, the green-robed bastard had taken to the air as well. He'd started shaping handfuls of fire and throwing *them* at Aefric, too. But his fire wasn't a problem, so much as a nuisance.

The scant moments he spent turning Gwawl's fire balls about and sending them back at their caster were moments he couldn't spend attacking the demon.

Which meant he was doing little more on that front than evading. Hardly a way to win a fight.

He couldn't *outfly* the demon. It had quickly proven to be at least as fast and maneuverable in the air as he was. Fire was useless against it, of course. Likely lightning too, though that had yet to be tested.

Ice might've been his best bet, but ice bolts seemed too slow to strike it.

Shouts down below.

The princesses — still here?

He couldn't afford to look. Couldn't risk taking that much attention away from the demon.

Worse, he could see Gwawl looking down.

The demon threw a concave wall of fire into the air in front of Aefric, trying to hem him in. Aefric punched a hole with his wand and slipped through.

"Go!" Aefric shouted down frantically. Hoping Gwen could hear him. "Get them to safety! Go!"

More shouts. Different direction. Men's voices.

Guards?

Finally!

Aefric swooped away from the orchard, between the nearest towers, and over the main keep itself. Now to find out if his guess was right.

Crossbows started launching bolts into the air...

...and none of them came at Aefric!

Yes! Gwawl hadn't let anyone in on his little plan, and instinct had taken over. The guards with their crossbows saw the *flicker* around the demon — and he must've remembered right that green was the color — but not around Aefric.

That made the demon the interloper and Aefric the one they should help. So they started shooting at their obvious target.

Of course, those bolts weren't nearly enough to get through the hide of a demon, but they did distract it for a moment.

Buying Aefric a chance to hit it full in the face with a powerful ice blast.

Staggered the demon in the air.

It roared loud enough to shake the towers.

Bells started ringing. More and more shouts down below.

"Fools!" Gwawl screamed at the reloading guards. "The demon is *on your side. Help* the demon!"

No, they kept shooting at the demon. But its focus was on Aefric again. Hit him with a gust of wind that flung him at a tower.

And those towers were some fifty feet wide.

Using what he could manage with his flying spell, Aefric redirected a decent portion of the blow's force, but he still slammed into the wall and rolled across the stone.

Gods, not more bruised and broken ribs. He felt as though he'd just gotten those healed from the last time...

Demon incoming!

Aefric dropped straight down, and the demon flew headlong into the wall where he'd been.

A section of tower collapsed as the demon burst through.

But the bridges between the towers. All of them. On fire. And Gwawl. Screaming at the guards. Throwing more flame at them.

No. That was too much. Those guards didn't deserve this. Not for trying to defend their castle against a demon.

A position *Aefric* had put them in.

He slipped his wand into its sheath and became a mighty bolt of lightning, blasting straight at Gwawl.

Gwawl wasn't ready. No chance to save himself. Took the hit full-on.

Aefric resumed his human form in time to see the blackened and burnt corpse of Gwawl falling from the sky. Along with whatever item had let him summon that demon.

The demon emerged from the crumbled section of tower and took to the air. Very much still present. And now very much uncontrolled.

AEFRIC FLOATED IN THE AIR A MOMENT, REORIENTING IN HIS OWN BODY after striking as a bolt of lightning. Usually he needed only a rapid heartbeat or two, but this time he needed several breaths.

Definitely took more out of him than usual. Had he ever before used that power when he was already so badly hurt?

Certainly he was in no shape to continue fighting this demon. Between blood loss from gouges and cuts, whatever hell that acid had played on his back, countless bruises, and possibly broken ribs from slamming into that tower, he just didn't have much left.

Every breath seemed to set fire to his chest, both from inside and outside. He was having trouble maintaining his focus enough to even fly, let alone counterattack.

He could smell fire and smoke.

For that matter, he could *hear* fire from those burning bridges, and countless shouts and screams. But they all sounded distant. Too distant. And vaguely metallic.

He found himself thinking of telephones, of all things. Aefric didn't know them, but Keifer did. And when a phone line had a problem, sometimes it muffled sounds like this. Even added that touch of metal to the sound in a way he'd always found hard to—

No!

Aefric shook away that line of thought so hard that he dropped ten feet in the air before he stopped himself.

Demon. There was still that demon around here somewhere. And maybe Gwawl was no longer commanding it to kill Aefric, but it was here. In Qorunn. Where it shouldn't be.

Nothing good could come of that.

He had to banish it. Or failing to banish it, he had to destroy its current form. That shape it assumed as its power filtered from its native hell into this plane of existence.

Where though?

Screams. Shouts. So many. How could he...

Oh. There. That sense of overwhelming power and evil. From that hole in a tower. Where people were screaming.

But then, where weren't they screaming? Seemed like—

He shook his head. Must've been more hurt than he thought. Too much trouble keeping his focus where he needed it.

A quick mental exercise managed to get something like coherent thought going through Aefric's head again.

Brightstaff leading the way, he flew toward that tower.

As he got closer, he picked a word out of the screams.

Children.

Aefric pushed himself to fly faster. Into the hole and closer to that sense of power and evil. The wand Garram in one hand again, Brightstaff in the other.

Fancy décor on fire all around him. Stairs. Men and women screaming...

Up the stairs.

There. Past a slick mound of shredded guards. The demon, tearing apart still more soldiers, who spent their lives valiantly to protect whatever children lay behind them.

"*Kelkazikz!*" Aefric shouted.

The demon turned.

Aefric blasted it with lightning and ice in the same movement.

The lightning did almost nothing, even though that blast could have done major damage to even this warded tower.

But the ice blast made the demon fall backward with a cry of pain, before straightening and staring hatred at Aefric.

Aefric stared it right back. Raised both staff and wand.

"You will have no more of these people while I live," he said.

"Then die," the demon growled. Whipping outward with one clawed hand, it flung fire at Aefric.

He was ready for that. Caught the fire on the wand Garram.

"Pathetic," he said, letting the flames dissolve. "Now I understand how even a fool like Gwawl mastered you. *Anyone* could. I bet the reason you seek those children is that even they pose a threat to you. Any of them could overmatch *your* meager will, and—"

With a scream of rage that nearly burst Aefric's eardrums, the demon came soaring down the stairs at him.

Aefric was ready as he could be. Led the demon a merry chase back out into the night sky while he worked to hear past the buzzing in his ears. He tried to shoot ice back at the demon, but he didn't have enough focus to do more than loose his bolts in vaguely the right direction.

Not one of them struck home.

Pain and exertion were wearing away his focus. He couldn't sustain this fight much longer. All he could really do at this point was buy time. Karbin couldn't teleport here. He'd never been here. He'd have to fly in, and that would take time.

Karbin would be fresh, though. Maybe he could—

A blast of wind caught Aefric. But this time it didn't fling him into the tower.

In fact, for a split-second, Aefric thought he'd just forgotten to keep flying. But no, he was still willing his movement away from the demon. The problem was that no movement took place.

Too much to think about. He put away his wand. Focused on the fist of air holding him where he was. Gathered his power...

Suddenly that fist of air vanished. Before Aefric could even attempt to break its grip.

Karbin?

The demon's claws grabbed his arms at the shoulder.

Oh. Not Karbin then.

The grip was intensely painful. But instead of ripping him apart, the demon decided to crush him.

His shoulders began to compress inward, grinding bones.

"Mortal fool," the demon said, and Aefric heard it. "I shall feast on your arrogance and wallow in your magic, before I carry your soul back to Ulzinazk with me."

Of course. Ulzinazk. The fifth hell, and full of fire. Made sense.

At least as much as anything made sense.

Then pain blasted away coherent thought. Those claws dug deeply into his shoulders. And where they broke the skin, fire seemed to seep in through his pores and burn him from the inside.

The scream wasn't Aefric's choice, but it came out of his throat all the same.

He wanted to fight back, but he had nothing left to give.

Nothing for escape.

Nothing for counterattack.

And no Vria to save him this time.

Not even a way to save those children. The demon would feast on them all. And their guardians. And anyone else it fancied.

Pain sheened the world red, at the same time it seemed to begin tunneling down, leaving darkness in its wake.

The sky ... fading ... gone.

The towers ... fading ... gone.

The ground below him ... fading ... gone.

Those screams and shouts, softer and softer now. Softer and softer until he couldn't hear them anymore.

The sound of the demon's taunts faded out the same way.

Even that strong odor of brimstone. Couldn't smell that anymore either.

Small blessing there.

The pain, that was fading out too. Another blessing. Couldn't feel those acid burns or claw gouges. Couldn't even feel those awful, crushing hands anymore, and the fire they seemed to spread *under* his skin.

Nothing left but that narrowing tunnel of the world, tightening down around the demon's face, visible only through a hazy sheen of red over red.

And the tunnel began shrinking smaller still. Soon, even that hideous face would be gone.

Nothing more for Aefric to do. Nothing but wait for death.

No.

Aefric refused to just *die*. Not when his death meant that the demon would roam free, killing at will.

There had to be *something* he could do. Some way to at least take the demon with him. Some way to...

Wait.

What was that?

There, in the middle of that darkening tunnel.

A pair of silver eyes.

Tinkling laughter. He couldn't hear anything else, but he could hear tinkling laughter. He couldn't even feel those demon hands crushing him anymore, but he could feel a shiver down where his spine should've been.

A laughing voice, sweeter than a drop of honsach on the tongue after a full morning's sparring with his knights.

"Tell me, Aefric," that voice said, "*how ever* did you earn that namesake relic of yours?"

The laughter faded. The silver eyes faded.

No divine salvation for him this time.

But the world returned. Pain erupted in from everywhere, most of all his shoulders. The foul stench of brimstone, so strong he felt the urge to vomit. The sounds of distant screams and shouts, and the closer taunts of the demon.

"...your eyeballs, while with your tongue I'll..."

And somehow, through all this, even with his body on the edge of failing him completely, Aefric realized he still held the Brightstaff in his hands.

And he remembered. He remembered the battle with that supremely powerful lich, Nez'karak. How Aefric had been flung from the battle up a side passage.

How he'd tried to get back to the fight through the magical darkness that defied his spells, but his hand on the tunnel wall found the trigger of a hidden door.

He remembered the room beyond, where a second lich

demanded his business. Called him a coward, fleeing the battle. How Aefric had defied that second lich. That strange guardian. Challenged it.

And he remembered how that lich had challenged *him*. To master its staff and return to the battle, or die in the attempt.

That staff. The Brightstaff.

The challenge, its...

Its *cold white flames*.

Flames that were not fire, but burned all the same. Burning something else entirely. Astral ... aetheric ... will ... the soul itself, perhaps. But whatever they burned, those flames tested Aefric.

And Aefric passed.

He had mastered the white fire of the Brightstaff. Those flames that burned not with heat, nor truly cold, but something else besides...

Aefric threw the rest of whatever power he still had left into the Brightstaff. Summoned its white fire to engulf them both, as it had once engulfed Aefric and that lich-guardian.

The demon screamed. Thrashed as it tried to release Aefric. But it could not escape the white fire of the Brightstaff.

In Aefric, that fire burned away all distractions. Even those caused by his many, many hurts. The longer it burned, the sharper and clearer his focus grew. The stronger he felt.

But the demon became frantic. Desperate. Looked about as though for aid. Its mouth moved, perhaps offering bargains.

Aefric spared no attention for its words. Wanted no bargains with the likes of hellspawn.

Aefric held to the Brightstaff, to its white fire and the ever-sharpening focus it gave him.

He could see the demon for what it was, now. Burning coal and smoldering ash, given form and shape by power and personality filtered into this world from a creature in another plane of existence.

He could even see through that filter, to the connection between this huge, muscled form and the true demon behind it.

Aefric channeled the white fire through that connection to burn the demon's true form.

The demon became the very manifestation of pure panic then. Trying to fly. Trying to kick. Trying to bite. Trying everything it could think of. But it could not touch nor harm Aefric. Not now. Not while the white fire engulfed them both.

Aefric knew the Brightstaff was testing him. And once more he passed.

The Brightstaff tested the demon too, but its powers were never meant to be held by such a thing.

The white fire burned that demon away. Not merely the form of coal and ash here in Qorunn, but through that connection to the true demon in Ulzinazk.

And then the demon was no more.

THE MOMENT THE DEMON VANISHED, SO DID THE WHITE FIRE.

Sadly, so did Aefric's perfect focus.

All his pain and exhaustion hit him at once, and that was it for any more flying.

Aefric fell from the night sky. Plunging downward toward that rooftop garden on the main keep of the royal palace at Vaaran Tir.

There was a crowd down below, pointing up at him. Shouting. And there were bells ringing somewhere. Many somewheres.

The crowd though. Below him. That was bad because...

Because...

Oh. Right. He shouldn't come crashing into them.

Wincing through intense pain and exhaustion, he managed a lightfall spell, that arrested his momentum and started him drifting slowly down, no faster than a maple leaf falling from a branch.

Why were there so many guards down there?

The demon. Probably because of the demon.

Plus, well, this was Varondam. And there was that matter of the princesses.

Yeah. Those guards were probably going to kill him when he landed. Or arrest him. But spent and aching as Aefric felt, maybe that wouldn't be so bad either way. If they killed him, all the pain would stop. And if they arrested him, at least they'd have to let him sleep.

Wouldn't they?

Did they have the Geneva Convention in this world?

No. No. That was the other world. Whatever it was called. From Keifer's life.

Someone grabbed him out of the air. A moment of intense pain, even worse than breathing.

Vria?

"I've got you, Aefric."

Oh. Deirdre. Good.

"I'm really glad to see you," he managed, and she chuckled.

She must've been swinging on a rope. That really fit her. He could imagine her swinging from a chandelier, too. Maybe fighting the cardinal's guard.

No. Wait. That was the other world. Qorunn didn't have cardinals. Though it had plenty of guards. She could probably find some to fight while swinging from a chandelier.

Deirdre was sliding down that rope with him now. And people below were shouting, but it was just too much. He couldn't pay attention to it all.

"They're going to kill us, aren't they?" Aefric said.

Deirdre scoffed. "I'll kill every one of them before I'll let them touch you."

"Don't let them touch you either. You're too good to die."

She didn't say anything to that, but they reached the bottom of the rope. They fell a short distance then, slowed by his spell.

The moment they were on the red stone, she set him down and drew her weapons.

Down was probably good. Not any less painful, really, but probably good all the same. The red stone was cool, and that was kind of nice. Really, anything that wasn't burning was an improvement.

"His grace is under my protection," Deirdre said. "Any of you who attempt him harm will soon regret your foolishness in the afterlife."

"He is under *my* protection as well." That voice. Aefric had heard it before, but not sounding so ... authoritative.

He tilted his head to look and saw Gwen standing near Deirdre. Knees bent, arms out, and red power coruscating around her hands.

"Hi, Gwen," Aefric said.

Her gaze flicked to him, but quickly back to the crowd.

Aefric forced himself to sit up. The claw gouges on his chest and back — plus the acid burns — all screamed as he did, but they dulled to a roar again once he was sitting.

He looked over the threat. About two dozen soldiers. Some with crossbows, but most with spear and shield. And all of them in chainmail.

Not just guards there, either. Nobles. At least a dozen of them. All in their finery, and all of them looking scared and excited and ... something else. Aefric couldn't tell what. But he doubted it was good.

"Gwen," he said, "I don't want to be here. Can you teleport us out of here?"

"Done too much of that already," she said softly. "Not used to doing it more than once in a day. I'm *spent*. Can't do much more now than fly a little, and maybe throw some fire."

The burbling crowd quieted as one of the nobles stepped to the fore. A slender man. Not very tall. Long, curly black hair, and a goatee slicked to curl inward. Fancy purple silk shirt, embroidered in gold, over similarly embroidered red hose. Pale leather belt held his rapier and dueling dagger. Pale leather shoes matched it, and belt and shoes were both buckled with more gold.

Glittering gemstone rings on three fingers, two of which held some magic. One felt defensive. The other ... Aefric just didn't have the focus to tell for sure.

"You must be Aefric Brightstaff," the lead noble said, appearing to ignore both Deirdre and Gwen.

Aefric gritted his teeth through a deep breath so he could speak with some volume.

"And you must be Dalius Swiftblade."

"I am *King* Dalius Swiftblade, and you will address me as 'your majesty.'"

"You didn't give *me* my titles or courtesies, so no. I won't."

"I'm not even sure I want to call you *Swiftblade*," Deirdre said. "Though you're welcome to come prove that you deserve the name."

"Too far, Deirdre," Gwen said softly.

Dalius' face darkened to match his shirt. But he steadied himself.

"Obviously you have all committed acts of war, and are now my prisoners," he said. He nodded to Aefric. "You summoned a demon to destroy my castle, and you two aided him."

A sergeant of the guard leaned in and said something quietly to his king. Aefric couldn't pick out his words over the roar of blood past his ears.

How much blood did he have left to roar past his ears? He'd been bleeding for a *while* now. All his clothes — where they weren't torn — were sopping, and it wasn't all sweat. Even in this hot, muggy place.

"I don't care what you *think* you saw," Dalius said. "*I* say he summoned—"

"*Gwawl* summoned your demon," Aefric said, then frowned. "His charred body's around here somewhere, but I'm sure you remember that pirate wizard. You hired him, after all, to keep me from freeing the princesses you kidnapped."

That set a buzz through the assembled nobles that Dalius didn't like at all.

"Lies," he said quickly. "It is well known that I have no business with pirates. While lies are stock-in-trade to an upjumped commoner like *him*."

But the mood of Dalius' nobles wasn't supporting him. And his guards looked hesitant. One of them spoke up.

"It was that wizard in green, setting fire to the bridges. And Duke Brightstaff here stopped it by killing him."

"Aye!" another said. "Turned into a bolt of lightning. Saw it with me own eyes."

"And that wizard in green," another said, "he were telling us the demon was our *friend*. A *demon!*"

A chorus of assent.

"This is all well and good," Aefric said, "but has anyone called for a healer? I really need one."

One of the soldiers nodded and turned as though to fetch a healer for Aefric. That was the final coin for Dalius.

"Kill him!" he screamed at his guards. "Kill him now!"

Deirdre adjusted her grips.

"Stop!" Maev's voice, from somewhere in the air nearby. "Armyr has already blockaded Varondam's ports over King Dalius' crimes. Murder my duke and our fleet will *destroy* those ports and whatever ships dock there. I swear it in the name of my father, King Colm Stronghand."

One of the guards dropped his crossbow to clatter on the red stone and put up his hands, as though she'd called for his surrender. Some of the other guards started dropping their weapons too, though no one else raised their hands in surrender, and that first guard sheepishly lowered his.

Karbin landed then, with Maev beside him.

Wait. Karbin could fly them both without holding her? How did he—

"*This madman summoned a demon to destroy my castle!*" Dalius shouted.

"He did no such thing," Maev said calmly, coming to stand between Aefric and the king. "I know because I was with him right up until the demon appeared."

Before Dalius could reply, she looked past him and addressed his courtiers.

"You all have come to know me over the past two seasons. And I tell you my rooms were moved only days ago to put them behind *isolating* wards..."

While she continued, Karbin leaned down. "Her highness can distract them for a moment with truth, but it won't last."

"I can't fight anymore today," Aefric said.

"I know. Where's your *magari* crystal?"

Gritting against the pain of movement, Aefric pulled it from his pouch and offered it up with a shaky hand. Karbin slipped the crystal into Deirdre's dagger hand. "Get ready. I'll put up a wall, and you get the princess and the duchess out of here. I'll handle our duke."

She nodded.

The wall Karbin conjured was thick, gray stone. Some fifty feet long and thirty feet high, and all of it between them and the Varondami.

Deirdre sheathed her weapons and summoned Aefric's *magari*.

Karbin put a hand on a relatively unwounded spot on Aefric's chest and teleported them away.

The world swirled and compressed Aefric in ways that should have been horribly painful, but were only uncomfortable.

A moment later, instead of bleeding all over the porous red stone of Vaaran Tir's keep, he now found himself bleeding all over the white covers of his private hospital bed, back in Water's End.

Small, white room, lit by magic. Large, high arching windows showed the dark night outside. The comforting smell of sweet herbs and rain.

Soft, welcoming bed. Fine red calinwood nightstand to one side, and matching chair to the other.

A large rendering of the Deepwater sigil faced him from the other wall, near the open doorway.

Karbin hurried out that doorway, calling for Bebara.

She answered quickly, and came rushing into the room. Her steely gray hair messier than usual, but her yellow clerical robes pristine and her sense of ageless vibrancy fully intact.

She was followed by a harried-looking apprentice. A shaven-headed youth in pale robes.

Karbin entered last, but Bebara's hands were already poking and prodding Aefric in ways he really didn't want to be poked and prodded.

He hissed with pain like a newly forged sword thrust into a bucket of water to cool.

"Some of these cuts aren't too bad," Bebara said, turning Aefric in ways he didn't want to turn. "Don't like the look of these acid burns, though. And the bruises. And whatever made these gouges?"

"A demon," Aefric said.

"I thought as much." She reached up and smacked Aefric's forehead with her palm.

He went right to sleep.

11

Aefric awoke late the next morning, still in his hospital bed. Daylight streamed into his room, glinting off the shining, full plate armor of six angry knights.

The Knights of the Lake.

Arras spoke for them.

"Good morning, your grace," she said with a bow every bit as formal and frosty as her tone. "I am pleased to see that your grace is awake, and appears to be healing well, thanks to the ministrations of his cleric. Would your grace agree with that assessment?"

"Yes," he said, carefully.

"Then your grace would agree that his ducal cleric successfully performed the functions of her office?"

"I would," he said, afraid he saw where this was going.

"And Karbin, your grace's court wizard. Would your grace agree that he performed his duties well when he teleported your grace here last night?"

"I should think so."

"And the state your grace arrived in. Would your grace say that he arrived whole and uninjured? Or would it be more accurate to say that your grace barely survived a mighty struggle, and came all too close to death?"

He sighed, which at least didn't hurt him physically. "The latter."

"And when your grace faced the hazard, how many of the Knights of the Lake stood with him?"

"None," he said.

"None," she said. "Well, then where were they? Those knights sworn to give their lives in protecting the life and person of the Duke of Deepwater?"

"Back here at Water's End, waiting for me to return."

"Back here at Water's End," Arras said. "Tell me, your grace. Have the Knights of the Lake failed in their charge? Have they displeased the duke with their work?"

"Not in the least," Aefric said firmly, meeting all six challenging glares. "I am quite proud of all of you, and proud to have you in my service."

"Why then, your grace — for I feel we've earned the right to ask this — were we left behind when your grace *deliberately* entered the hazard?"

"Politics," Aefric said. "No other reason."

"Perhaps your grace would be so good as to explain his meaning there?" she asked. "I understand that he would be within his rights to refuse this request, but—"

"I was specifically ordered by our king to sneak into the royal palace at Vaaran Tir and free princesses kidnapped by agents of King Dalius. I was to do this with the smallest infiltration team possible, and to cause as little havoc in the process as I could."

He gave a soft chuckle of chagrin. "Failed a bit there."

Aefric sat up, heedless of how the covers fell to his waist revealing the new scars across his naked chest. His knights noticed those scars though.

"Your grace," Arras began, but Aefric raised a forestalling hand.

"Please, Arras," he said. "Let me finish."

Her nostrils flared in a quick breath, but she nodded.

"We were to be swift, silent, and few," he said. "That meant no plate armor. That meant no formal assault. The *minimum* team I could take. So I included only one other. And I don't think any of you would dispute that Deirdre is better in melee than any other knight."

None of them denied that. But they didn't offer to confirm it either.

"When the true fight came, when I would've loved the aid of my Knights of the Lake, I doubt you could have helped me anyway. It was aerial combat against a demon, and none of you can fly."

"Does your grace question our skill with the longbow?" Arras asked.

"Not in the least. But I question the power of a longbow to penetrate the hide of—"

"Its eyes are not its hide. Its open mouth is not its hide. Its ear holes are not its hide. A good archer might not *kill* a demon, but could *hurt* one. And surely that would have aided your grace in his struggle."

"The wizard who summoned the demon was throwing fire at any archers he saw."

"The hide of wizards is far less proof against arrows."

"True," Aefric said.

"Where was Deirdre when you needed her?" Arras asked.

"She was following my orders and making sure the princesses got to safety. That was the priority. Not my life. The moment those princesses were safe, she found a way back to my aid. The demon was dead by that time, but King Dalius had a crowd of guards. She stood between me and them."

Arras frowned.

"My knights," Aefric said, "please accept my deepest apology. I would not have excluded you from this mission, but I felt I had no choice. Both because of the king's orders — and I was already in trouble with the king for going after Nelazzi, so I didn't think defying him again was a wise course of action — and because it might have affected our relations with Rethneryl."

"Will your grace do everything in his power to not exclude us again?"

"I swear I will," Aefric said. "You have *all* more than earned my trust and faith. And I will do all I can to keep you by my side, whenever the hazard finds me again."

That seemed to mollify them a bit. And finally one spoke who wasn't Arras.

"Your grace certainly never seems far from the hazard's embrace," Temat said.

The others laughed then, and Aefric drew his first relaxed breath. Not a full breath by any means — he was still nervous about trying that — but deep enough to confirm that his ribs had been healed.

"All right, all right," Bebara said, hustling into the room. "Enough badgering my patient for the time being."

"Am I still your patient?" Aefric asked.

"Your grace is my patient until Nilasah tells me his healing is complete," Bebara said, sparing him a glance and a token movement that *could* have been construed as a bow. By someone looking for a movement to call a bow.

Before Aefric could reply, though, she turned back to the knights.

"Now, two of you are supposed to be here on duty, yes?"

"I am," Arras said, "and Wardius."

"Fine. Then you two may stay if you must, though I'd prefer you on the other side of that door. The rest of you, *out*."

Vria, Temat, Leppina and Micham all bowed to Aefric. His tired limbs managed to give them a proper salute in reply before they left.

"I would prefer us to remain within the room," Arras said to Bebara. "We may be expecting a response from Varondam, and—"

"Fine," Bebara said, shooing them back, "then against the wall with you while I'm working."

She turned back to Aefric. "Deep breath. Deepest you can."

Aefric inhaled slowly and deeply, but the breath was only half-drawn when fiery pain lanced outward from his shoulders through his whole chest.

He coughed that breath back out, which didn't feel any better.

"I thought as much," Bebara said, shaking her head. "Damage from demons never heals neatly. Too corrupting by nature."

She smacked Aefric on the forehead with her palm, and he crumpled back, asleep.

THE NEXT TIME AEFRIC AWOKE, HE WAS FIRST AWARE OF HEARING THE soft, dulcet tones of a harper playing *Je Sinlo Osoch Fa*, an eldrani song about lovers torn apart by war, and spending their next hundred fifty years tracking each other down across two continents.

So many eldrani songs had similar themes. The idea that true love transcended time and could surmount any difficulty.

It was the sound and song of the harp, even more than the subtle scent of something exotic and spicy that told him Byrhta was with him.

She played well, and favored songs taught her by her grandmother, Lylasalaas, who was not only full eldrani, but reputed to be the most beautiful eldrani woman in all Qorunn.

How odd it seemed, that both Byrhta and her grandmother were famous beauties, and yet Aefric had never heard anyone talk about her mother...

His eyes fluttered open. Bright morning light flooded in through the high, arching windows. The sun was still visible, meaning it was early, but not too close to dawn.

Rain clouds looked to be coming in from the north, though.

The Brightstaff stood near the windows. As though waiting for his hand.

A slow, deep inhalation led to some pain, fiery in character, but a mere smoldering coal beside the burning of the last time Aefric had tried taking a deep breath.

Good sign: the breath didn't make him cough.

Better sign: he was hungry.

As he turned from with windows to see Byrhta, sitting in the visitor chair, his eyes passed Vria and Micham in their full plate, standing guard near the rendering of the Deepwater sigil on the wall opposite the bed.

They both smiled and nodded, but did not speak. Perhaps not wanting to interrupt the harper.

Today Byrhta wore a light gown of canary yellow silk, to bring out the flakes in her amber eyes. Arms bared to the shoulder, likely to avoid getting in the way of her playing, but a modest neckline and a strand of amber around her throat. She wore her long, dark, forest green hair pinned back in three places, creating a tiered effect.

Even here and now, Aefric sighed to look upon her.

Her focus was entirely on her playing. He could probably have sat up and she wouldn't have noticed. But Aefric merely lay there and watched her play. The steady, skillful way her long fingers danced across the strings. Strumming here, plucking there. Always precise, yet expressive at the same time.

The harp she played was old. Vivid white ivorywood, inlaid with gold. Designs, mostly, but the inlay included her name, as rendered in the characters of High Eldrani.

Interesting to see her name that way. Aefric had never thought of what "Byrhta" might mean, because the common pronunciation was a corruption. A common tongue elision over the proper syllables. But now that he saw it written out in High Eldrani — *Byy yrh taah* — he knew it meant, "the beauty of seeing the first ray of dawn glint on fresh water, when one has thirsted near the point of death."

As she finished the song, Aefric said, in High Eldrani, *"Your skill brings fresh joy to an old song, Byy yrh taah."*

She answered with an old eldrani saying. *"Music can treat the soul as Nilasah treats the body."*

"But a harper can bring healing where no wound was known," Vria said softly.

Byrhta nodded her thanks at the praise, then frowned as she looked over Aefric's face. "Though I think you may need more music."

"I've got armies on the march, and I don't know if they're going to war. I've got navies blockading ports. Possibly fighting a sea war as we speak. Princesses stuck on a ship in the middle of it all, and—"

"Hush, Aefric," Bryhta said softly. "I can at least reassure you about the princesses. Ser Beornric, with the aid of your ducal wizard and Ser Deirdre, brought them back last night aboard a pair of *magaris*. All of them are here in the castle, Maev included."

Hearing Byrhta use Maev's name made Aefric's eyebrows rise of their own accord.

She gave him a lopsided smile. "Yes. Our dear princess gave me the right to call her by name following a ... rather interesting discussion the two of us had about you."

She reached down and gently smoothed some hair away from Aefric's forehead.

"So there was no knife fight then," he said, quirking a smile of his own. "I worried."

"Oh, no," she said. "Though if you're fishing for information, you may as well stop. We both agreed to keep the content of that conversation between the two of us."

"Tell me this much, at least," he said. "*Should* I be worried?"

Her smile widened and mischief danced in her eyes. "Depends on what worries you."

Bebara marched into the room then, looking irritated. No apprentice followed her this time.

"Back," she said, making a shooing motion at Byrhta. "I need to see how our duke is faring this morning." She stopped a step shy of Aefric. "I've got a passel of princesses, a Rethneryli duchess, a wizard and a pair of impatient knights, all clamoring to get to your grace right away. As though—"

"I'm sorry about that," Aefric said, making a gentling motion with his hand. "A great deal is happening, and—"

"Oh, *really*, your grace?" Bebara said, voice dripping with sarcasm. "I'd *never* have guessed."

"—and it's not a good time for me to be laid up in bed."

"Well," she said, cocking an aggressive eyebrow, "perhaps your grace should *consider* that the next time he goes tangling with a demon all on his lonesome."

"It was that or let it slaughter children, Bebara. And maybe worse than slaughter."

That stole some of the wind from her sails.

"Well," she said again, but much more gently at least, "then I suppose I won't show you the resources I've had to expend to heal your grace this time. But I will more certainly remind your seneschal, when he next prepares the castle budgets. For now, at least let me make sure you're ready to be on your feet."

"I won't leave this bed until you permit it," Aefric said.

"Oh," Bebara said, chuckling, "your grace is lucky I'm not the sort of healer to abuse that."

She ran her hands through the air above Aefric's body, beginning with his toes and ending with the top of his head, mumbling all the while.

There was magic to that. Of a sort. Aefric knew it. Her healing was proof enough. But he could never sense so much as a drachm of power while she worked. Apart from any purely physical sensations from the healing, anyway. The same as anyone else might notice.

Bebara frowned on finishing at his head, then poked and prodded Aefric various places on his chest.

Uncomfortable, but tolerable.

She jabbed harder, right in the middle of one of his new scars.

"Ouch," he complained.

"Then show me no brave fronts just because a pretty lady is watching," Bebara said, cocking an eyebrow again. "Tell me when something I do hurts."

"That last thing you did hurt," Aefric said. "Before that, what you were doing was merely ... uncomfortable."

Bebara muttered something about ex-adventurers and pain tolerance — likely unflattering — and rolled him onto his side so she could get at his back.

"If those new scars of his need some attention—" Byrhta started, but Bebara cut her off.

"Not *that* kind of attention, they don't." She turned and frowned at Byrhta. "Those are *demon* scars, girl. And they're not so healed yet they can't spread a little corruption."

She turned back and shook a finger at Aefric. "So none of that noble privilege business for you, your grace. Not until you can slap one of those scars and not have it feel any worse than ... well ... any worse than one of your many other scars."

Aefric started to say something, but Bebara shook her head.

"Least the acid burns are gone," she continued. "Hope you don't mind I didn't let *them* scar you too. Know how all you action-happy types love to soil your skin with—"

"That's fine, Bebara," Aefric said. "Sooner I can forget about that acid, the better. And as for the demon scars—"

"Yes, I can do something about them. The corruption, anyway." Bebara dug a small jar of ointment out of her pouch. "Your grace must *swear* to me that he'll have this put on his demon scars — front *and* back — twice every day until those scars just feel like any of his others."

"Twice a day," Aefric said with a nod. "I swear it."

"And I mean once in the morning and once at night, your grace. No playing games with my wording and trying to double up when it's convenient. Am I clear?"

"You are clear, my good cleric."

"I'll help with that," Byrhta said.

"I'm sure you will," Bebara said. "But if you do — if *anyone* does it but your grace himself — I want them *wearing gloves* and *slathering* the ointment on. Not making some kind of *sexy game* out of it. Understood?"

"Will leather gloves do?" Byrhta asked, sounding serious enough that Bebara did a double take, then shook her head.

"No, they won't," she said, and dug into the nightstand, pulling out a pair of big, thick linen gloves. She tossed them to Byrhta. "You'll use linen. No animal skin, or the corruption goes right through it."

"It won't go through linen?" Micham asked.

Bebara frowned at him. Spoke as though addressing a child. "No. Because demons corrupt people and animals. Not plants. Don't ask me why, because I can't spare the rest of the day to give you a lesson in planar cosmology."

"Sorry," Micham said.

"Ah," Bebara said, "no need for that. I just don't like having impatient people trying to get into my hospital. Puts me on edge. All you really need to know is that the Green Lord won't allow demons to corrupt His flora."

Aefric *almost* asked about why the Green Lord permitted the corruption of animals, but Byrhta spoke first. Which was probably for the best.

"Does the corruption extend beyond the scars?" Byrhta asked.

Bebara gave her a considering look. Shook her head. Sighed.

"No. There's no danger anywhere but those scars. So, yes, you can safely kiss him on his lips." She cocked an eyebrow. "Or anywhere else you're thinking of kissing him. But I mean it. No skin-to-skin contact with those scars. Not with bellies, lips, hands, breasts, *anything*. And *especially* not through perspiration. Acts as a catalyst. You show up here with signs you touched those scars—"

Bebara turned to Aefric. "—or *anyone else* does—"

She turned back to Byrhta, "—I'll slap you before I heal you. And then I'll slap his grace."

"You don't want that," Micham said softly. "I've been slapped by Bebara."

"And for good reason, too," Bebara said, giving him a frown that was still on her face when she turned back to Byrhta. "Well? Put the gloves on. We haven't got all day, and I need to see if you're fit to do the job, or if I need to assign a novice to see that it's done *right*."

Byrhta nodded and put on the gloves.

It was a good thing that Bebara was there watching when Byrhta applied the first batch of ointment to Aefric's scars. Because thick as she slathered it on, the scars soaked it up like a band of successful adventurers with a barrel of ale.

"No, you don't need to add more," Bebara said as Byrhta reached into the jar a second time. "That's what's supposed to happen. On your belly now, your grace, so she can get the back."

The ointment itself was odd. Well, not that it felt cool. That made sense, especially countering the heat of the demon. But as Byrhta applied the ointment, Aefric both smelled and tasted cinnamon and cumin, and kept tasting both until the scars finished soaking it up.

"Now sit up," Bebara said, once the back scars were finished.

Aefric did that on his own, and felt cheered that doing so didn't hurt. He felt tired — more tired than he had before the ointment — but other than that, he felt pretty good.

"See these smaller scars around his shoulders?" Bebara said. "His grace never said so, but those are demon scars too."

"I can't be held responsible for what I don't say when I'm unconscious," he said.

"I asked you about the gouges," Bebara said. "That would have been the time to make sure I didn't miss the shoulders."

"Right," Aefric said, cocking an eyebrow at the healer. "Next time I've bled half my life away and am lying here in intense pain, I'll try to be more thorough in cataloging my hurts."

"Was it really that bad?" Byrhta quietly asked the cleric.

Bebara nodded. "Maybe even worse. So, all right, I suppose that's fair, your grace." Turning back to Byrhta, she said, "Point is, make sure you get the five gouges around each shoulder the same way."

Byrhta did. The taste of cinnamon and cumin faded. Aefric sighed deeply and shook his head.

Bebara leaned in and looked him in the eye. Nodded.

"All right. This is good. Now." She slapped her hands together. "You test those scars yourself before each application. Any discomfort beyond what you'd get from any other scar — and yes, I want you to poke *at least* one for comparison — and you need another dose of ointment. I don't expect that jar to run out, but if it does and you aren't done, *you better* come back for more."

"I will," Aefric said.

She turned to his knights. "You see that he does. You're sworn to safeguard his life and person, and you'll be failing if you don't."

Both Vria and Micham slapped their hilts.

"Is that a yes?" Bebara asked.

"It is," Aefric said.

Bebara sighed. "Knights." Shook her head. Turned back to Aefric. "Right. Your valet sent down some clothes. Might as well put them on."

"May I help with that?" Byrhta asked.

Bebara gave her an approving look for asking. Nodded. "Long as you're careful not to touch those scars, or it'll be slaps for both of you."

"I'll be careful."

Bebara gave her a considering look. "Fine then." Turned back to Aefric. Bowed formally. "I hereby clear your grace to leave his bed and my hospital. So long as he remembers his promise about the ointment."

"I will remember it," Aefric said.

"We'll remind him, if circumstances push it from his mind," Vria said.

Bebara growled — actually growled — then shook her head and left.

"I know where the clothing is," Byrhta said, and left the room.

Aefric turned to his knights. "I can't meet that crowd here. Bebara would throw a fit. Would one of you be so kind as to tell Beornric, Deirdre and Karbin that I'll see them in my morning meeting room as soon as I can arrive? Then tell the princesses that I will meet with each of them afterwards, and the duchess after the princesses?"

"The princesses won't like waiting," Micham said.

"I know," Aefric said. "Which is why, if one of you is willing to carry this message for me, I'd like you to apologize in my name for the wait, but concerns about the war status *must* come first."

"I'd *think* they'd understand that," Vria said.

"Then *you* can play messenger," Micham said.

"Why big, bad Micham," she teased. "Afraid of a few princesses are you?"

"Damn right," he said. "I never piss off royalty when I can avoid it."

"That's fair," Aefric said. "Send for a page, and—"

"No need, your grace," Vria said with both a smirk and a bow. "I have no fear of pretty girls in fancy dresses, whether their veins flow with royal blood or not."

"That's not fair—" Micham protested.

"Don't worry, Micham," Vria said. "I'll protect you from the pretty girls."

"I—"

"Your grace," Vria said with a bow, and sauntered out of the room while Byrhta came back in.

"We're not talking about pretty girls, your grace," Micham said. "We're talking about *royalty*. We're talking about—"

"Did you know, Ser Micham," Byrhta said, as she laid out Aefric's clothes on the bed and organized them, "that I have been courted by no fewer than two kings?"

"No," he said, suspiciously.

"That's right. Two. I wasn't even of age yet." She held up the silk undergarment and gave Aefric a knowing smile. "I'd best let you don this one yourself, or we'll be delayed."

Aefric chuckled and slipped it on.

"And one thing I learned," Byrhta continued as she held up a pair of dark red hose. Muttered, "Not the color I would have chosen," and helped Aefric into them as she continued telling her story.

"Royalty are like normal people in nine circumstances out of ten. It's just that the tenth circumstance carries with it such weight that it seems to overbalance the rest."

She carefully helped Aefric into a dark blue silk shirt, handling the buttons herself. "Oh, that's much better. Reached to smooth it down, then paused. "I better ask the cleric about that before I leave. Make sure it's safe to touch you through a shirt."

"Should be safe through silk," Aefric said, donning a sash belt of cloth-of-gold that could still hold his noble's dagger, black velvet belt pouch, and sheath for the wand, Garram. "But asking is probably the smart way to go."

"Those princesses will know and understand better than most," she continued, adjusting Aefric's belt for him, "how important information about the war is. They'll accept the delay readily. Though they'll be frustrated, and may use that frustration as a conversational tool later."

She slipped Aefric's soft, dark leather shoes onto his feet, and adjusted their cloth-of-gold spats.

"And that's the key to remember," Byrhta said, nodding and turning back to Micham. "They will phrase many things in terms of that tenth circumstance, when doing so is to their advantage. But you must keep in mind what the true circumstances are."

Micham frowned. "But as a mere knight, I don't have the standing to push back, if they insist on a context I don't agree with."

Byrhta favored him with a smile. "As a knight, they'll consider arguing with you beneath them. If you deliver a message they don't like, the worst you'll likely have to tolerate are some cold looks and a cutting comment or two."

"You don't think they'd remember me and hold it against me?"

"Of course they'd remember you," Byrhta said. "Royalty remembers everyone. But they'll only hold a past incident against you, again, when they see advantage in doing so."

Aefric stood. Byrhta carefully tugged at the shirt and belt for a final adjustment, then stroked his cheek.

"I disagree with your valet about the hose, but otherwise, perfect."

"Thank you, Byrhta."

"Of course, Aefric." She gave him a saucy smile. "And if you decide against the hose, I'll be happy to help you out of them again."

Aefric chuckled and kissed her.

THE TREK UP FROM HIS HOSPITAL BED — ON ONE OF THE FIRST FLOORS of the main keep — was long enough that Aefric found himself wondering if he needed to start taking advantage of his other meeting rooms. After all, he had several, scattered throughout

Water's End. No reason he had to keep returning to the one in his apartments. No reason apart from habit.

Still, it felt good to walk, and climb stairs. Get his legs and hips moving again after sprawling in bed for ... two days? Maybe three?

"How long was I in that bed?" he asked Vria and Micham, who flanked him one pace behind, through the sweeping marble hallways and up the beautiful stairways, with their expansive window views and bright sunlight.

"Two days, your grace," Micham said.

"Three, if you include this morning," Vria said. "Though your grace arrived late enough and left early enough that I don't think it would be fair to say three full days."

"So ... two then," Micham said.

"Oh, let it go, Micham," Vria said. "I've already stopped with the pretty-girls thing."

"Which reminds me," Aefric said as they rounded a corner and started up another stairwell, passing a trio of servants laden with what looked like laundry. "How did their highnesses take the news?"

"Well enough, overall," she said. "I think one of them — I couldn't tell you which — had thoughts of objecting, but Princess Maev cut in and said, 'We've stolen enough of his grace's attention from the war effort, I think. The least we can do is let him get his updates before we thank him for quite literally flying to our rescue.'"

"Smooth," Micham said. "Wish her highness indulged in the noble privilege more often."

"What difference would it make if she did?" Vria said. "She's not just a pretty girl, Micham. She's *royalty*. I mean, yes, I can think of *one* way you could please her from a bowing position, if you bowed low enough, but *eventually* she'd tire of that pleasure and want you to move on the main event."

"All right," Micham said.

"I mean, if nothing else, your tongue would—"

"*I yield*," Micham said, putting one hand on his breastplate and raising the other with a bent elbow.

Vria chuckled.

"And I think I could handle her highness just fine," Micham mumbled.

"I know you could," Vria said, reassuringly. "But you leave an opening like that, you have to expect the attack to come."

They kept up this way the whole walk up to the public floor of Aefric's apartments. Admittedly, anytime there was the least unexpected sound, or anyone else entered the hall or stairs, they were all business and watching for threats.

But the moment the potential threat passed, they were back to bantering together, playing games with combat metaphors.

Aefric was leaning on the Brightstaff more than he wanted to admit — with perspiration breaking out on his brow — when he finally entered his public floor sitting room.

"Your grace," Ocheda said, greeting him with a bow. Crisp as usual in her Deepwater livery. "The dual advisers have gathered and await in your grace's morning meeting room, along with his breakfast."

She looked over Aefric with an eye so critical he practically *felt* her gaze. "Your grace *has* been cleared to leave his hospital bed?"

"I have," he said, trying not to sound a little winded. "But the treatment for my demon scars seems to take a bit out of me."

"Then may I suggest that your grace not stint on the meats, when he takes his breakfast?"

"Thank you, Ocheda." Aefric stopped himself mid-step and turned back to her. "Did you choose these hose to go with this shirt?"

Ocheda looked over the combination. Frowned. "Those are not the hose I selected. Those are not *bad*, but I'd chosen the maroon. I'll have a talk with your grace's body servants. Would your grace care to change?"

"The look is still good enough?"

"Good enough to meet with the ducal advisers, certainly. But I'd suggest changing before meeting with princesses, your grace. And perhaps adding a touch of jewelry."

"I'll have to add my coronet. That'll be enough. Especially with the sash belt and spats."

"As you wish, your grace."

"I agree about the hose, though," he said. "Have the others ready and waiting, along with the coronet, and I'll change after my meeting."

Such a weird thought. Just a few seasons ago, Aefric would have spent as little attention on the color of his ... well, he wouldn't have worn hose anyway. He'd have worn leathers, or a robe. Either way, he'd've given their color less concern than he would've the color of saddle he put on his steed.

Now look at him. Worrying about clothing combinations. Seemed that he was settling into ducal life after all. He was even in the habit of changing for dinner now.

Aefric shook such thoughts away, and took in instead the lift he felt at seeing his apartments again. The many waiting couches of his public sitting room. The glass of the patio doors, no more than a dozen or so steps away. The fresh scent of sweet herbs in the air.

The sights and smells of home.

And now, his morning meeting room.

He opened the door and entered. Smiling at all the black oak of the walls, the buffet, the cabinets and drawers. The ornate blackwood table and matching chairs. The soft magic light, thanks to some past Soulfist enchantment. The rich scent of the wood.

And around that table stood his advisers.

Beornric in his full plate, looking ready for war. Garnotin in *his* full plate, for a change, looking ready for a battle himself. Deirdre, in her maroon leathers, smiling to see him up and about. Ink-stained Elkari, in her brown linen tunic and breeches, a stack of books and scrolls beside her. Kentigern, wearing black velvet — including that harbinger hat of his — but his thick brown beard freshly trimmed. And Karbin, in his colors of sand and dusk.

Yrsa, absent of course. She was down with the fleet, blockading Varondam.

"Your grace," Deirdre said, as Aefric began piling a silver plate with fruits, cheeses, sliced meats, and rolls of honeyed oat bread. "May I be the first to say how good it is to see you up and about."

The rest of his advisers all knocked the table in agreement, while Aefric smiled and nodded his thanks. He filled a silver goblet with water. Both plate and goblet followed him through the air at his bidding, while he stood the Brightstaff beside his chair and took his seat, allowing the others to take theirs.

"Garnotin," he said, "I think this is the first time I've seen you in armor."

"Certainly looks untested," Deirdre said.

For once, Garnotin didn't rise to her bait, while Aefric started in on slices of roast beef and honeydew melon.

"I was uncertain that your grace would be able to take his proper place with his forces," Garnotin said. "And I wished to make clear I am ready to stand in his stead, should he wish it."

"Which begs the question," Beornric said. "How *are* you, your grace? Are you well enough to go to war, if needed?"

"I am," Aefric said. "Though I do possess scars from that demon that are not fully healed, and must have ointment applied twice a day."

"Has that task been assigned, your grace?" Deirdre asked.

"Byrhta has volunteered for it, if I remain in the castle. Which remains to be seen."

"Demonic corruption is nothing to play with," Karbin said. "I would suggest your staying in the castle until those wounds are fully healed."

"Well," Aefric said, "we'll have to see. I have the ointment and, if necessary, I can handle its application myself. Though not as well as I could with aid."

"You'd have aid in the field," Beornric said. "Even if I had to handle the task myself."

Deirdre started to say something, but Aefric raised a hand for silence.

"The future, we will deal with soon enough. First I must learn of the recent past. What's been happening since..." He shook his head. "No. What don't I know that I need to, from recent events?"

"I'll start," Beornric said. "Our blockade is in place, and shutting down Varondam's shipping entirely."

"Have they tried to breach it?" Garnotin asked.

"Once, but we had the advantage of position and preparation. Sank the oncoming warship before it could pose a serious threat."

"Has Yrsa begun the bombardments?" Aefric asked, before taking a bite of a fresh honeyed oat roll, still warm from the oven.

"Not as of the time I left. We're due for a report from Yrsa though. She's written the capital for permission to proceed."

"From the *field*?" Deirdre asked, shocked.

"She had no choice," Beornric said. "With Nayoria's whereabouts unknown, Princess Maev ordered the bombardments delayed until the royal wizard's fate is discovered."

"And Yrsa can't overrule Maev without the king's approval," Aefric said, sipping some water and slicing up some honey roasted turkey for easy chewing. "Well, that bought Varondam time we'd rather they don't have. What word from the Caiperas front?"

"First rika came in yesterday," Kentigern said. "A small party of Rethnerylli soldiers was able to take out the Caiperan scouts above the Pass of Dayor Ol'Tain. This was coordinated with a swift move down that pass by Armyr. That Caiperan border castle known as Caer Ylfarai was caught with its gate down. Armyrian forces overwhelmed and took the castle, giving us control of the pass."

Deirdre gave a low whistle.

"Yes," Garnotin said. "That gives us full control of the primary route between Caiperas and Rethneryl."

"King Colm will likely cede Caer Ylfarai to Rethneryl," Beornric said. "Give them a major early spoil from the war, to make up for the lack of support they're getting from Armyrian forces right now overall."

"It's not close to our border anyway," Deirdre said. "Be a pain to keep it ourselves. But it's still a princely gift."

"Especially if we end up taking more of their northwestern land," Garnotin said. "That would connect the pass to our new border."

"What matters more right now," Aefric said, taking a break from his breakfast, "is what Caiperas knows about it. Were the castellan or seneschal able to get a messenger or rika away before the castle fell?"

"Definitely no messenger," Kentigern said. "But possibly a rika."

"Then Ashling is in danger," Aefric said. "Unless we've gotten word about her?"

Everyone shook their head. Well, except Deirdre, who merely shrugged.

"Perhaps there's something in that letter from Princess Astrid," Garnotin said.

"What letter?" Aefric asked.

"This one," Kentigern said, setting a scroll on the table. Aefric could see that its wax seal remained unbroken. "Arrived the second day after your grace sailed south with the armada."

"Your grace's seneschal *refused* to let me read it," Garnotin said. "Even though its information might've been timely, and I stood in his stead while his grace was away."

"The messenger who delivered it made clear that the letter is to be opened *only* by his grace. Not his castellan."

"But his grace could have been *dead*, for all we knew."

"And until we received confirmation of that death," Kentigern said casually, "I would continue to withhold the letter. Only after confirmation was received would you, Garnotin, ascend to the status of Duke Regent — which status you'd only keep until his majesty assigned another — at which time I would give you access to this letter."

Aefric cleared his throat.

"Oh, excuse me," Kentigern said, holding up the document in question. "Your letter, your grace."

Aefric brought the scroll to his hand by magic, broke the seal, and unrolled it.

A clean, white handkerchief fell out.

Aefric frowned at that, but began to read the letter.

My dear Duke of Deepwater,

I cannot say which surprises me more, the content of your grace's letter, or its means of conveyance. That your grace is able to transmit a physical object into my presence by means of a spell is a matter I find myself hard-pressed not to find threatening.

Save for the content of that letter.

For surely, if your grace meant me ill, he would not have revealed this heretofore hidden power for so innocuous a reason as delivering a letter of warning, unless he had no interest in surprising me with a more, shall we say, aggressive transmission at some later date?

Nonetheless, our royal wizard is, even now, attempting to ward Svarturvigi against any further such transmissions. For while your grace represents that matters between us stand as friendly, Father says, and I find I quite agree, that we cannot count on remaining in your grace's good graces. If might be forgiven for the inadvertent pun.

Which brings me to the content of your grace's letter.

I find rather extraordinary the notion that, following more than a season of hearing about how Armyr intended to wage war on us, that we are not, in fact, the true object of Armyr's military intentions, but rather that Caiperas should fill that role.

Caiperas, who has been gathering armies of their own with the clear intention of invading our eastern border.

I cannot pretend that we could stand against either Armyr or Caiperas individually at this time, much less a coordinated assault by both. And so, obviously, I would wish very greatly that your grace's words were as true as though they'd fallen directly from the lips of Taesark Himself.

The question, of course, is how can I trust what your grace tells me?

Ironic, really, in that it was only a few aetts past that I sat down to lunch with your grace for the expressed purpose of convincing him that the truth of our difficulties last spring lay along inobvious lines despite apparently overwhelming evidence to the contrary.

And now here, your grace sends me a letter, telling me to look for an inobvious truth in the face of overwhelming evidence to the contrary.

When our positions were reversed, your grace told me that he needed time for his own agents — as well as those of his king — to verify the truths I'd presented to him.

And so, I trust that your grace will not be surprised to learn that I, too, must verify for myself the contents of your grace's letter.

Until each item written of in that letter is confirmed, Malimfar shall take no action upon that item. And each item shall be tested independently.

I must say, I do hope that your grace has written only truth to me. For this would mean that we may, in fact, grow in friendship in the years to come. A thing I myself devoutly wish for.

Of course, if your grace has written lies, then this friendship cannot come to pass. But I'm sure your grace knows this already. May even lament it, if he has written me lies under orders from his king.

But with an eye toward the hope of friendship, I reveal to your grace the following truth.

The Royal Wizard of Armyr, one Nayoria, was caught flying over Malimfari land. She was, of course, captured as a spy. In fact, she was to have the question put to her when I received your grace's letter.

In hopes that your grace has written only truths to me, I have persuaded Father to at least postpone formal interrogation of her until such time as we know with certainty whether or not we are at to be invaded by Armyr.

If such an invasion comes, she will be treated as a spy. A noble spy, but a spy nonetheless. I trust I need not provide details about what this means.

If the invasion does not, in fact, come, if Armyr is in truth warring with Caiperas instead, we shall, of course, release her unharmed.

Until we have full and complete confirmation of our status in this matter, however, the Royal Wizard of Armyr shall remain in a wizard-proof cell, and behind the thickest wards our own Royal Wizard can conjure.

I suspect that your grace would not be able to reach her even by the rather extreme methods he used to deliver his letter to me. Of course, if your grace were to attempt contact her or send her aid by this means, I would take his action as a poor sign regarding relations between us.

Her inaccessibility to your grace's magic, however, does motivate me to provide proof that we do indeed hold this Nayoria. Thus do I present to your grace a handkerchief, taken from her person. Our royal wizard assures me that either your grace or his ducal wizard shall be able to test this handkerchief with magic, to confirm that it was indeed taken from the Royal Wizard of Armyr, and recently.

I assure your grace again that she is being treated well at this time, and shall continue to be treated as a noble guest — albeit a guest whose movements are necessarily restricted — until and unless we achieve a final determination regarding Armyr's military intentions.

I wish very much to believe your grace. I look forward to confirmation of his words.

Written with hope, by the hand of

Astrid Eadredsdottir

Crown Princess of Malimfar

Postscript:

I trust your grace has noticed that I address him in this letter not by his proper due as Arl of Storbakki, but by his primary Armyrian title. I presume I need not explain the reasons for this.

<hr>

AEFRIC SET THE LETTER DOWN AND LOOKED AROUND AT HIS ADVISERS.

"Well," he said. "King Colm did a terrific job of convincing Malimfar that we've been preparing to invade."

"Her highness didn't believe you then?" Beornric asked.

"She must've," Deirdre said. "She sent him her favor."

"This" — Aefric raised the handkerchief — "isn't her favor. This is proof that Malimfar is holding Nayoria."

That set his advisers buzzing. Aefric slapped the table for attention. When he had it, he tossed the handkerchief to Karbin.

"Confirm it's hers, would you?"

Karbin caught the handkerchief, but raised a dark eyebrow.

"My day may grow very long," Aefric said. "I better save energy wherever I can."

Karbin nodded. Held the handkerchief and mumbled for a moment, a faraway look coming into his eyes.

"Hers," he said a moment later. "Taken from her less than an aett ago." He tossed it back to Aefric, who held it up when he caught it.

"Confirmed then. Malimfar has Nayoria. Apparently they caught her flying on her way to Vaaran Tir. Princess Astrid writes that my letter convinced her to persuade her father to at least postpone *putting the question* to our royal wizard for the time being. At least until they have confirmation that we're not invading."

"They took her for a spy?" Kentigern asked, shocked.

"Yet another reason for wizards not to play messenger," Karbin said.

"They did," Aefric said. "And if they see any sign of invasion from us, she'll get the full spy treatment. For now, though, they've got her in a wizard-proof cell—"

Karbin scoffed.

"—where she'll stay until Malimfar knows one way or the other. They promise to release her unharmed when the invasion doesn't come."

"Would our good wizard care to try a night in one of *our* wizard-poof cells?" Garnotin asked. "Since he seems to feel that no cell is wizard-proof?"

"I've already checked our cells," Karbin said. "I'm not sure anyone short of *Kainemorton* could break out of them. At least, without outside aid. But the *Soulfists* designed those cells personally, and improved them over the years. I simply doubt that the ones at Svarturvigi are as well-designed."

"We must assume they are," Aefric said, "given that Nayoria hasn't returned."

He frowned the question at Kentigern.

"Still missing, officially," he answered. "Though I will, of course, send word of this to Armityr as soon as this meeting is done."

"And to Yrsa," Aefric said, "so she knows she can proceed as originally ordered."

"Of course, your grace," Kentigern said.

"So to answer Beornric's question from before," Aefric said, "no. Princess Astrid didn't believe me. She threw in my face the fact that we didn't take *her* at *her* word when she was here recently, but have been seeking independent verification of her report."

"She had to know we would," Elkari said.

"It's just an excuse," Beornric said. "We couldn't expect them to believe you on the strength of one letter. Not after how hard his majesty has worked to make sure Caiperas wouldn't see us coming."

"We had to try," Aefric said.

"I agree," Beornric said. "And we had to warn them about Varondam."

"I doubt Varondam wants to invade anyone right now," Deirdre said. "Their plans have blown up in their face."

"They might already have ordered their armies to begin," Garnotin said. "They'd need to be moving before their navy left dock anyway."

The ducal advisers began debating Varondam's possible military movements.

Aefric slapped the table for attention. When he had it, he said, "This is a fruitless direction for this meeting. Where are my troops?"

"The Deepwater detachment called to the war effort should be halfway between Kerrik and the great Kingsroad fork," Garnotin said.

"Netar's troops are likely bivouacked in the conquered castle," Kentigern said. "Though I can seek confirmation, if your grace wishes."

"I do," Aefric said. "And I need to know where his majesty wants me. With the navy, with my armies, or here at Water's End."

"This was just supposed to be a token invasion," Beornric said. "Deepwater's troops should be sent back soon. And likely Netar's will return once Rethneryl is handed possession of Caer Ylfarai."

"Assuming his majesty doesn't wish to plunge deeper into Caiperas while they aren't looking," Deirdre said.

"And find out if there's any word about Ashling," Aefric said to Kentigern. "Far as we know, she and Sirondfar are still at Reyvenue, which means two valuable prisoners, once Caiperas learns what's happening."

"One, really," Beornric said. "As prisoners go, the duchess herself is far more valuable."

"I'll find out, your grace," Kentigern said.

"Anything else pressing?" Aefric asked. "Anything local? How did Harvest Day go?"

"Quite well, all things considered," Garnotin said. "If anything, the celebrations were more ... intense than usual, as word had spread that we were on the cusp of war. Your grace's presence, of course, was missed, though I doubt that many found it surprising."

"One of Baron Osmaer's Green Lord clerics came to preside over the religious portions," Kentigern said. "Which may make winter easier for us all."

"Good," Aefric said. "What word from the coast?"

"The forces your grace has dispatched to shore up coastal defenses are all in place," Kentigern said. "Though with the Varondami fleet stymied, the question is sure to come if those forces need to remain through the winter."

"Without Nelazzi to control them," Aefric said, "the Risen Sea pirates may be more ... chaotic than usual through the coming year. Better to keep those forces in place, just in case they're needed."

"Other than that," Kentigern said, "only the usual things to report."

"Armityr has been updated about the princesses?"

"Yes," Kentigern said. "Princess Maev wrote the capital, and each princess wrote home herself. Both quick letters that could be sent by rika, and full letters which have already been dispatched by messenger. Hatay, Shachan and Rethneryl will all know soon who captured their princesses, who held them, and most importantly, who rescued them."

"I hope they don't give me too much credit there," Aefric said. "It was hardly something I did on my own."

"Your grace was in charge," Garnotin said. "He deserves primary credit."

"Try fawning a little harder there, Garn," Deirdre said.

"All the same," Aefric said. "I'll have to send each monarch a letter, explaining the operation and ensuring that all credit goes where it's due."

"You might want to get royal permission for that, your grace," Kentigern said. "His majesty might wish to have those kingdoms focus their gratitude on you."

"Has he said so?" Aefric asked. "Officially?"

"Well, no, but—"

"Then so far as I know, I have no reason to *not* write those letters. So I will."

"Of course, your grace," Kentigern said.

"His majesty is focused on the war anyway," Beornric said. "I doubt he'll quibble. Especially since you brought his daughter back."

"Good enough," Aefric said. "Anything else? Anything pressing, I mean?"

"Locally there are concerns about our soldiers going off to war this late in the year," Garnotin said. "Otherwise, nothing unusual."

"All right," Aefric said. "Let's adjourn for now. I've got royalty to meet formally."

WITH A CHANGE OF HOSE AND HIS CORONET ON HIS HEAD, AEFRIC awaited Maev in his public floor solarium.

The whole of the outside wall in this large room seemed at first glance to be missing entirely. But in truth it had been rendered invisible from the inside, to provide an unrestricted view of the lake, and beyond. This was a wall thrice Aefric's height, and easily a dozen good strides long. The invisibility worked with illusion enchantments on the ceiling — which displayed the skies directly above — to create the effect of being exposed to the elements, while still entirely indoors.

The rest of the walls formed a single curve, but Aefric wasn't sure exactly what the designers wanted by that. To make the room feel like a cave or a bowl, perhaps? But the shape wasn't quite right for a bowl, with the floor included. And with the smooth, plastered walls painted a soft blue, they hardly looked like a cave either.

There were two rows of very comfortable, padded chairs — black oak, upholstered in navy blue and bearing the Deepwater sigil in gold — two seats in the front row, and six in the second.

Between every two chairs, a fine, black oak side table.

Aefric sat in the right-hand forward chair — the Brightstaff standing to his right. He watched the swiftly moving storm clouds overhead. Wondered when their rains would burst forth.

He'd just gotten to the point of drawing an analogy between the storm clouds and the war fronts when a page cried out, "Her highness, Princess Maev Stronghand."

Aefric got to his feet, smiling as he turned.

Maev was in her buckskins again. Not the same ones he'd seen before, though. These were a darker shade. Also, her tunic was sleeveless, and far too low cut to be practical when hunting. In much the same way, her breeches looked even tighter than she usually wore — emphasizing her shapely legs — and stopped at mid-calf. Her shoes came no higher than her ankles.

Her long hair, so black its highlights were blue, she wore loose and wild as the smile in her soft gray eyes.

The reddish-brown coat of Sylkanis, who entered beside Maev, looked to have been recently washed and brushed.

"Alone at last," Maev said, stalking forward. "I'm tempted to insist on having this conversation in your bedroom."

"Not an option, I'm afraid," he said with a grimace. "I have demon scars, and until the corruption is gone, I'm not allowed the noble privilege."

Maev stopped so abruptly that Sylkanis looked up in alarm.

"You must be joking," she said.

"I wish I were," Aefric said with a sigh. "The scars are on my chest, back, and shoulders. And my healer has forbade me from letting those scars touch *anyone's* skin until the corruption is fully purged. Apparently it spreads easily."

"Well," she said, frowning, "I *suppose* I could tolerate your wearing a dressing gown. If absolutely necessary."

"Dressing gown's not enough," he said. "Silk isn't safe either. Thick linen only."

"Well…"

"And if I sweat through it, the protection of even thick linen becomes useless."

"And if you're not sweating, we're not doing it right," Maev said with a sour turn of her face. She sighed. "So *nothing* then?"

"The lesser pleasures would be an option," he said. "Our hands. Our mouths. So long as you don't come near the scars."

"Suppose I sat astride you—"

"And you could guarantee that you wouldn't lean on my chest, or collapse atop me when we finished?"

Her shoulders slumped and she shook her head.

"I was thinking that it might be possible with you on all fours and me behind you, but—"

"But *you'd* have to fight the temptation to lean forward, or collapse atop *me* afterward." She shook her head. "Not at the risk of demonic corruption."

"So it's the lesser pleasures or nothing for a while."

"Then it's nothing from me, for the time being," Maev said, tone crisp as she closed the gap between them. "The first time I bed you, Aefric Brightstaff, I don't want any restrictions about what we do."

"Agreed."

She cocked an eyebrow. "It's safe to kiss you at least?"

"Should be if—"

"If I don't touch your chest. *Damn it.*" She threw herself into the left chair in the front row, making it scrape a handspan backward across the red oak floorboards. She folded her arms across her chest. "*Seasons* we've been waiting. I should've made Deirdre rescue the others while I threw you down on the grass and had my way with you."

Aefric sighed as he took the chair next to her and Sylkanis

stretched out in front of her. "She never would've made it past that fourth-floor hall."

Maev cocked an eyebrow at him. "Don't spoil the fantasy."

"Sorry," Aefric said, quirking a half-smile. "Would've been grand, though, wouldn't it?"

"Yes, it would've" she said with a smile. "The threat of discovery by guards would've made it all the hotter."

"Might've rushed us though."

"I might not've needed long," she said. "The Varondami don't practice the noble privilege, after all."

"You mean you've been without—"

"No touch but my own," she said. "And then *you* had to go and get wounded by a demon."

"Thoughtless of me."

"Well," Maev said, "I guess I'm staying here at Water's End until the corruption is gone. That's all there is to it."

"Even if the king wants you to come scout for him?"

"He's really invading Caiperas? This time of year?"

"They've already taken the castle at the end of the pass from Rethneryl."

"The Pass of Dayor Ol'Tain. That would be Caer Ylfarai." Maev pondered that a moment. "Caiperas' armies *should* be massed well southwest of there. But they'll be motivated to return at speed. Pure folly for Father to push farther before spring."

"Will he be able to hold that castle?"

"As I recall," she said, "Caer Ylfarai is less defensible to the south. Which would work against him. Still, *less* defensible is not *in*defensible. And they should have stocked for the winter before now. Which means that, if the conquerors dig in the way they *should*, and fortify their positions, they'll be better able to survive a siege through winter than the besiegers."

She shook her head. "Did Father tell you what his plan is?"

Aefric told her what he knew. The feint to set up Varondam, and the blockade and barrage that would follow.

"And here I've stopped the barrage," Maev said.

"Delayed it only," Aefric said. "Malimfar captured Nayoria, mistaking her for a spy."

"A *spy*?"

"Yes," Aefric said, then explained about the exchange of letters he'd had with Princess Astrid. "So we've already sent word to Yrsa that the reason for delay is gone."

"Well done," Maev said. "What's the goal in Varondam?"

"Primary goal was to get you out of there. Secondary to get the other princesses. Tertiary, I think, to punish King Dalius for the kidnappings."

"That's not a good goal for warfare," Maev said.

"Your father's angry."

"Father needs to have someone talk sense to him."

"Others have tried."

"Others are not me," Maev said with a shrug. "I need to get to the capital. Quickly. Take me there?"

Aefric almost teased her about her promise not to leave Water's End, but this was too important.

"We'll leave at first light. You'll be there by midday."

"Excellent," she said, gently touching his arm. She was close enough for a moment that he could thrill to her honeysuckle scent. "Thank you."

"There's no need for thanks."

She gave him a small, wistful smile. "And here I made this top with you in mind."

"It's been driving me crazy since you walked into the room."

"That helps," she said, smiling a little wider.

They quietly gazed into each other's eyes for a timeless moment. Maev finally broke it.

"I better go," she said, "or I'll need to be treated for demonic corruption."

"We can't have that."

"I don't know," she said softly. "Might be worth it."

"Bebara will slap us both before she treats you."

To his surprise, Maev burst out laughing. Hard enough that

Sylkanis jumped to her feet and looked about to see what was going on.

"What?" Aefric asked, but Maev was still laughing. "Come on, tell me."

Finally she managed to get hold of herself, though such deep breaths that Aefric fought not to let her low-cut top distract him.

"She slapped Killian once," she said. "While he sat duke regent here. Spent a whole letter complaining about it. At least two of the paragraphs were about how much it hurt."

Aefric chuckled, then told her about their quarrel.

She listened patiently, frowning now, shaking her head then, and finally wincing at word of the final dispute on the deck of the *Swift Wave*.

"Father will set him straight," she said, standing. "I don't think he did Killian any favors, keeping him out of the wars."

"Does sound that way," Aefric said.

"Oh," she said, gesturing to the coronet. "You might not want to wear that to meet the others. I know that *officially* you're supposed to every time you greet royalty. But they don't have their diadems, so skipping the coronet would be considerate of you."

"They don't have their diadems?"

"All four were snatched from their ships with only what they were wearing. They didn't even get a change of clothes until they got to Varondam."

"Right," Aefric said, removing it so quickly that Maev chuckled.

They parted with nothing more than a touch of their hands, but even that tingled harder than a contact spell waiting to deliver its reply.

AEFRIC REMAINED IN HIS PUBLIC FLOOR SOLARIUM AS HE AWAITED THE first of the visiting princesses. He did have Ocheda take away his coronet — complete with an explanation about why he wanted her to do so — and arrange for tea service. A steaming, sweet jasmine tea from the Free Baronies, along with an assortment of shortbread cookies.

He wandered over to the invisible wall as he waited. Outside, the rains had begun. They even appeared to drum down on the illusory ceiling as though it were glass, and not just the stone between this floor and his private floor.

The rain was hardly more than a sprinkle, though, compared to the downpours he'd seen only…

Was it an aett ago? Two?

Fall seemed to be flying past. Winter would be on them all too soon, and if this war of King Colm's were not resolved, or at least *banked*—

A page announced, "Their highnesses, Princesses Brigit and Adsaluta Haltallan of Rethneryl, Princess Raedrun Al'Trener of Hatay, and Princess Jodis Ol'Nariss of Shachan."

Aefric whirled around, unable to conceal his surprise. All four at once? He was supposed to meet them one at a time. Now they had him outnumbered. Now…

Then Aefric remembered Vria's teasing of Micham about pretty girls, and Byrhta's discussion of how royalty were just like everyone else in nine circumstances out of ten.

So he steadied himself, spread his arms wide, and smiled at his guests.

"Such a dazzling array of beauty," he said. "The mere sight of you drives protocol right out of my head. I'm not even sure whom I should greet first."

His answer came from the taller of Rethneryl's two princesses — easily spotted, for both wore gowns of burgundy velvet, with the rampant unicorn of Rethneryl embroidered above their hearts in gold thread.

"I should think that Armyr's oldest and staunchest ally deserves the right of first greeting. Would you not agree, cousins?"

A question clearly not addressed to Rethneryl's other princess, but to those from Hatay and Shachan.

"That seems fair to me." That had to have been Princess Raedrun

Al'Trener of Hatay speaking. She wore a gown of dusty rose silk, with Hatay's mermaid sigil embroidered in sea green above her heart.

"So long as you don't dominate our host's time, cousin." And that would be Princess Jodis Ol'Nariss of Shachan, in the gown of dark brown velvet, with the Shachan sigil — a white wyvern — embroidered above her heart.

All four dresses must've been made quickly after the princesses arrived, for they weren't what any of them were wearing earlier. But they all fit well. And they all had similar cuts. Modest necklines, long sleeves, but slashed at the sleeves and skirts with the color of their embroidery.

The two in burgundy bowed deeply to Aefric, requiring him to match the depth of their bow when they straightened. But he'd been ready for that. This past summer, Princesses Astrid and Xenia had practically made him touch his head to the floor, they'd bowed so deep.

Rethneryl was a strong ally, and deserved a little more courtesy than a simple bow in return. But before Aefric could provide it, he needed a question answered first.

"Forgive me," he said, "but I've not been told which of you is Princess Brigit and which Princess Adsaluta."

"I am Brigit, the elder by two seasons," the taller one said. She had a tumble of black curls that fell past her shoulders, eyes of bright hazel, a willowy frame, and posture that made Aefric suspect she was an excellent dancer.

"I am Adsaluta," the shorter one said. Not quite as slender as her … cousin? Sister? … but certainly no less shapely. Her ornately styled hair was a deep auburn, and there was a smile lurking somewhere in her pale blue eyes. "The closer to the throne by six steps."

"Hardly fair, Addy," Brigit said. "That interpretation relies on which of our uncles is given primacy by the peers—"

Jodis cleared her throat.

"Point acknowledged, Jodis," Brigit said. "Discussions of succession can wait for another time."

"Especially since *neither* of you are closer to the throne than *twenty* steps, by *any* reckoning," Jodis said with a smile.

Aefric stepped in close to Brigit before she could respond.

"Princess Brigit," he said, taking her hand. He kissed her cheek, taking in as he did her scent of willow bark. "It is my pleasure to make your acquaintance, and to welcome you to Water's End."

"The pleasure is mine, your grace," she said, returning the kiss the same way. "Thank you for welcoming me to your home."

He repeated the welcome for Princess Adsaluta, who favored the scent of vanilla. Princess Adsaluta made a point of letting her own lips linger a beat longer on Aefric's cheek than Brigit's had, before pulling back and saying the formal words of greeting.

Princess Raedrun was next in line, so Aefric went to her next. She wore her dark blonde curls in a waterfall, cascading halfway down her back. Her eyes seemed to match the sea green of the mermaid sigil on her chest.

Princess Raedrun bowed deeper than her Rethneryli cousins. Aefric bowed just as deep in response.

He opened his mouth to offer her a formal greeting, but she raised her hand for him to take, clearly expecting a kiss on the cheek.

Technically that was not a requirement, as Hatay wasn't as strong an ally. So the question was, would he be offering the greater insult to Rethneryl by kissing Princess Raedrun's cheek? Or to Hatay by *not* giving her the kiss?

Hoping he was making the right choice, Aefric erred on the side of gallantry. He took Princess Raedrun's hand and stepped in close.

"Princess Raedrun." He kissed her on the cheek, and noting her scent of black cherries. "It is my pleasure to make your acquaintance, and to welcome you to Water's End."

"The pleasure is mine, your grace," she said, giving him a kiss in return that lingered just a breath longer than Princess Adsalutas'. "Thank you for welcoming me into your home. I must say, the journey here has been far longer than I would have dreamed."

"But you have arrived," he said, "and that is what matters most."

Princess Jodis had a touch of eldrani heritage, visible in the bright orange highlights in her otherwise reddish-brown hair, and the blue-flecked lavender of her eyes.

Aefric wasn't surprised in the least that Princess Jodis bowed deeper still, and let her lips linger yet longer when her turn came to kiss Aefric on the cheek. The scent she favored was rhododendron.

Once the greetings were finished, Aefric waved a hand to arrange five of the chairs in a circle around a triangle of tables, with their silver tea service and shortbread cookies.

"Won't you please make yourselves comfortable?" he asked.

The few hours Aefric spent in that solarium, playing host to four princesses felt like something between a study in politics and a plunge into cold warfare.

Most of their actual conversation was light chit-chat. The sort that might occur at any gathering. The weather. The recent news. No talk at all about their kidnappings, nor their recent rescue.

Aefric found himself wondering if they'd met beforehand and established ground rules for this meeting without anyone telling him.

If any one of them even *looked* as though she were raising a point of political significance — or anything that might give one of them a, well, matrimonial edge over the others — the other three immediately shot arch glares and the subject changed. Often mid-sentence.

With the result that they all drank their tea and ate their cookies, and behaved with near-perfect decorum through the whole of their gathering.

It was, in many ways, one of the most frightening things Aefric had ever seen. For it quickly became clear to him that the four princesses were playing a game on a deeper level than he could begin to comprehend.

It reminded him of the time he'd watched Karbin duel with the wizard Tulvaquil by potion-making. Aefric had been little more than a child at the time. Barely into his apprenticeship. He'd only just touched on potion-making, when the duel took place.

The entire conflict had looked like nothing more impressive than watching two men grind, decant and blend ingredients at a common desk before finally activating them with the proper words to turn their bottled, stoppered brews into potions.

He'd had no idea why Karbin had smiled so triumphantly over his jet blue concoction, nor why Tulvaquil had turned away with slumped shoulders and left without so much as another word. After, of course, placing the disputed magic ring — the duel's prize — on the counter next to his cloudy, pale blue product.

The way Karbin explained it later: "You are too young yet to understand the nuances of mortar and pestle. Of alembic and athanor. To comprehend the small signs that indicate when you should separate which ingredients with your lead dagger, and when to use your sharp, white-handled steel. But I defeated Tulvaquil long before those potions were activated. And the best part was that he knew it, even if he gave no sign."

"Then why did he finish?" Aefric had asked. "Why didn't he simply give up once it was clear he was beaten?"

"Because to admit defeat early would have been the greater loss of esteem. What is begun should be completed. Especially when it comes to potions."

Tea with the princesses that day made Aefric feel like that young apprentice once again, struggling to understand the duel being fought before him.

In a way, tea with the princesses was even stranger. Because he was participating this time. One of them would ask a question, such as, "How do you find the hunting in the Forest of Souls, your grace?"

He'd give what seemed to him a fairly innocuous answer. Discussing how during the summer, the elk were plentiful there and it seemed that a hunt of even a single day might provide enough meat for the whole of his usual table at Water's End. And that a hunt of less than an aett would provide for an entire meal for all of his court, including visitors.

Seemed ordinary enough, in that sense.

But the follow-up questions. The way the princesses alternated.

What weapon did he favor for hunting elk? Did he prefer to hunt with dogs or without? Did he insist on being the only hunter, or did he bring a full party? If he were hunting elk and he found boar, would he hunt the boar as well, or push on for the elk?

After the third such barrage of questions — the same sort he might get at any gathering, had they been less deliberately timed and phrased — he began to notice that whoever asked the question that got the longest or most involved answer seemed to take it as a point of pride.

Made him self-conscious about how he responded to them. How many words was he using? Was he showing the same amount of enthusiasm for this topic as for the previous? And what did it meant to them if he did?

Instead of being a pleasant, breezy conversation about small topics, it became as tricky and intense for him as though he were improvising a magic ritual with lives depending on his success.

But this was a ritual in a language he didn't quite speak. And it involved spirits of a type he'd never dealt with before.

Thoroughly exhausting. And so stressful he finally gave up on the tea, because he'd noticed his grip on his cup had become white-knuckled. And the acidity had begun to irritate his stomach more than shortbread cookies could mitigate.

They'd moved on to the topic of whether they should call for a late lunch or an early dinner when Ocheda stepped into the room.

She stood just inside the doorway, posture perfect, and waited until Jodis finished asking her question about the difference between sailing the Deepwater in the *Duke's Hand* versus one of his warships, such as the *Calming Influence*, to interrupt.

"Your grace, your highnesses," Ocheda said with a deep bow, "I fear I must crave your pardon for this interruption. But there has been a development on the war front that his grace must be made aware of as soon as possible."

"Oh?" Aefric asked, standing a little too quickly and taking the Brightstaff in hand.

"Ser Beornric awaits your grace in his black oak meeting room."

Ocheda turned to the princesses. "I fear his grace may be some time dealing with this matter. If your highnesses would be so good as to come with me, I shall see to the question of a late lunch or early supper, should your highnesses so choose, or see to your highnesses' entertainment until it is time to dine with the court."

"I feel as though we only just sat down," Princess Jodis said with a sigh.

"The war must come first, cousin," Princess Brigit said. "Were his grace not so fine a military man, the four of us would yet be captives of Varondam."

"Too true," Princess Raedrun said, stepping in close enough to take Aefric's hand and kiss him on the cheek. "Only the smallest of down payments on the debt both I and Hatay owe to your grace."

That seemed to open the door, and each of the other three princesses followed with their own kiss on Aefric's cheek — once more each kiss was longer than the kiss preceding it, if only by a heartbeat or a breath — and reference to that kiss as a down payment on the debt owed Aefric by themselves and their kingdoms.

Finally, though, they were escorted out of the solarium by Ocheda, and Aefric could swiftly move though his sitting room and into his black oak meeting room, where he found Beornric leaning casually against the blackwood table.

The moment the door was closed behind Aefric, Beornric smiled.

Aefric frowned. "What's the development on the war front?"

"That my duke will be useless to his king if he collapses into a pile of nerves."

Aefric managed a breathless bark of uncertain laughter. "You mean—"

"I mean that Bebara's ointment takes something out of you, and that the servants told Ocheda that your meeting with the princesses didn't look so much relaxing for you as..."

He frowned. "How did they put it?" He smiled. "Oh, yes. As though your grace were a trapped rabbit, surrounded by four *very* hungry wolves. Ocheda sent word to me, and well, now you're here."

Aefric slumped forward through his first relaxed breath in what seemed like *hours*. "I've never seen anything like it. I swear, they were fighting some kind of deadly duel, disguised as little discussions about hunting and the weather."

"There are some drawbacks to being new to nobility," Beornric said. "You've been raised to fight a hundred different ways. But so have they. Only most of their weapons are nothing like yours."

"I started tracking how many words I used every time I spoke," Aefric said, leaning back against the currently empty buffet. "How much feeling I put into each answer."

"Wrong approach," Beornric said, raising a finger to emphasize his point. "You aren't raised to their game, so don't play it. Be yourself with them."

"But what does it *mean* if I enjoy one answer more than another?"

"I realize this is a strange situation for you," Beornric said. "These women may be princesses, but remember that they've been sent to you as potential brides. They want to know more about you, and you *must* learn more about them."

"But ... the interplay between them. I don't think I could've learned *anything* from that gathering. They seem to have set up ground rules."

"Likely they did," Beornric said. "But *you* didn't agree to those rules, and you don't have to play their game. Be yourself. Make *them* respond to *you*, not each other. Otherwise, the next thing you know, they'll negotiate one of themselves to be your bride, and you'll be married before you know what's happened."

Aefric drew a deep breath, and blew it out slowly.

"Take a little time to recover yourself," Beornric said. "And when you're ready, the Duchess of Neastall is waiting in your art gallery."

Aefric chuckled. "I'd forgotten I *had* an art gallery in my apartments."

"Once the current crisis is over, we'll have to talk about finding more time for yourself."

"Assuming we ever get a break."

"We will," Beornric said. "And I'm going to insist that you take one now, before meeting with the duchess."

"Good idea," Aefric said, pulling out his customary chair and taking a seat. "I think the knots in my shoulders have grown tight enough to bind an ogre."

"Oof," Beornric said, taking his customary seat beside Aefric. "Reminds me, though. Has Deirdre ever told you the story of how she singlehandedly defeated the Ogre of Threepeaks?"

"I've heard references to it, but not the story."

"I'll leave it to her, then," Beornric said. "It's her story anyway, and she tells it better than I could." He pulled out a deck of cards. "Care for a game of Queen's Conspiracy?"

IF OCHEDA WAS AMUSED THAT SHE HAD TO GIVE AEFRIC DIRECTIONS TO his own art gallery, she gave no sign of it. Turned out to be only one room and a short hallway away from his formal temple. But then, he rarely used that either.

The art gallery itself had no door, but a wide, arched entryway, framed in ornate descriptions of beauty, truth and love in dozens of languages.

The gallery was designed to have a great deal of natural light, with many large, arched windows along three walls. Though the effect was diminished that day by the rain, which had strengthened into a small storm. So instead the room was lit brightly by old spells of the Soulfists' working.

The stone flooring, walls and ceiling of the gallery were all plastered and painted a neutral, whitish tone, so as to reflect more light and not detract from the art.

In much the same way, sweet herbs had scented the air, but only enough to calm the nose. Not enough to attract attention to themselves. Which was for the best, at the moment, for Aefric's stomach was still unbalanced by the tea and princesses, and he didn't need any strong odors anytime too soon.

Paintings were hung from the four sides of a dozen, evenly spaced pillars in two rows down the long center of the gallery. Around the outside were many smaller pedestals, each featuring a statue of some kind.

The paintings were not all done by human hand. Many were clearly the work of eldrani artists, or derekek, or kindaren, or na'shek. A series of land and seascapes, arranged to depict the different ways the various major races viewed such things.

The statuary, Aefric could not begin to guess at, in terms of who the artists were. But there were works done in several varieties of stone, as well as three of more expensive woods, and at least a dozen in metals ranging from iron to platinum.

The statuary showed no consistent theme. There were depictions of gods here, but mere mortals there. Three dragons, but also a manticore and a great serpent, done in green soapstone, that wrapped entirely around its pedestal.

Aefric resolved to take some time to go through his gallery properly, and appreciate each of the many fine works.

For now, though, he turned his attention to the woman in the gown of emerald silk slashed with ruby. She wore her wavy black hair bound back in three gentle tiers behind her head.

Gwenellia Quinnian, Duchess of Neastall.

Gwen did wear her three wands at her belt, beside her pouch and noble's dagger. And she seemed focused on a topaz statue of a woman rising up high and strong out of her own corpse. And the new version of the woman had silver eyes.

As Aefric approached, Gwen spoke without looking up. "Do you think that's supposed to represent the ascension of Kalinda to godhood?"

"That's how I'd interpret it," he said, coming to a stop beside her. "Especially with the silver eyes."

Gwen turned to look at him. Something pensive in her eyes.

"I've been told that your grace has seen her eyes. At the Battle of Frozen Ridge."

"I did," he said. "After I overextended myself trying to defeat the massed armies of Malimfar." He drew a deep breath. "And I believe I saw them again at Vaaran Tir."

"Truly?" Gwen said, interest lighting up her face. "Did she save you there, as she was said to have done at Frozen Ridge?"

"Yes, and no," he said, frowning. "At Frozen Ridge, after that great spell, I should've fallen to my death. But I didn't. The only explanation I can think of comes back to the sight of those silver eyes. The sense of Her kiss on my forehead."

"Did She kiss you again at Vaaran Tir?"

"No," he said with a chuckle and perhaps half a smile. "She laughed at me and asked how I ever managed to win my staff."

Gwen looked at the staff in his hand. "I haven't heard that story."

"It tests those who'd wield it with a kind of white fire that isn't fire. Only those it deems worthy survive. The goddess was telling me to call the white fire while the demon tried to crush the life out of me."

"So that's what that was," Gwen said, frowning. "There was a white blaze in the air, visible even from the ship. Karbin said it was trouble. I teleported before he finished his sentence."

"Thank you," Aefric said.

"Thank *you*," Gwen said. "That venture to Vaaran Tir was the most exciting, harrowing, and insane thing I've done in my life."

"And you want to do it again?" Aefric said with a smile.

"Not in the least," Gwen said firmly. "Don't get me wrong. I'm glad I was able to help. But I had no sense of what I was doing, how much I could accomplish before my magic began to fail me. Even focusing on spells was harder than it had ever been before. I—"

"It's not for everyone," Aefric said. "Adventuring, I mean."

"And I shall leave it to others," Gwen said. "While I focus on those things I'm best at. Which is what I need to talk to you about."

"What do you need?"

"To return to Armityr at once. I've been away too long, and Rethneryl needs me in your king's war room, making sure *our* interests are tended as well as Armyr's in this conflict."

"I understand," Aefric said, then snapped his fingers. "Would you be willing to take Maev with you?"

"She's not staying?" Gwen asked with a sly smile. "I felt certain she wouldn't want to leave you alone with those other princesses."

"She knows I need to head to Armityr as well."

"I can transport three almost as easily as two."

"I appreciate the thought," Aefric said with a smile, "but I'll have to bring at least some bodyguards with me or the Knights of the Lake will revolt. And I can't ask you to teleport so many."

"It almost doesn't matter," Gwen said with a sigh. "I'll be giving up the family secret anyway."

"Wait," Aefric said, with a smile. "I see a way to keep your secret and get us all to Armityr."

"Oh?"

"If you don't mind bringing along two of my knights…"

"That would be the limit I could teleport safely."

"…then on arrival we can claim that I did it. That I'd found a scroll containing the spell in Nelazzi's lair and claimed it, intending to transcribe it and learn its secrets. Instead, I had to expend it, for the war effort."

"I like it," Gwen said, with a conspiratory smile. "It *sounds* like something you'd do, and this way no one will even *consider* that I did it."

She kissed him on the cheek. "Thus endeth my adventuring career."

"Successfully, which puts you ahead of many adventurers," Aefric said. "And make no mistake. I'm glad you came along. I'm not sure we could have rescued everyone without you."

"You would have found a way," Gwen said.

"Gwen," Aefric said seriously.

"Yes?" she asked with a puzzled frown.

"Please don't denigrate your efforts. If I hadn't known you were there, waiting to safely teleport those princesses to the ship, my attention would've been split and the demon would've killed me. Our efforts could well have failed *entirely* if not for you."

A slight flush colored her cheeks.

"Thank you, Aefric," she said softly.

"No, Gwen. Thank *you*."

A short time later, Aefric, Gwen, and Maev — Sylkanis beside her — gathered in his public floor sitting room, along with Beornric's selection for two knights to accompany them to Armityr: Arras and Micham.

Aefric noted that Maev had changed into another of her buckskin tunics, this one with a far more conservative neckline, and her usual half-sleeves. She'd also gathered some things from her luggage into a single pack at her feet that looked like something else made from the skin of an animal she'd hunted. Her bow was unstrung and in one hand, and she wore her quiver of arrows over her shoulder.

With her looking ready to hunt, and Aefric having his old leather backpack at his feet, he felt almost as though they were off on another adventure.

"All right," Gwen said. "I hope this is everyone, because I'm not sure I could handle a sixth."

"This is plenty, Gwen," Aefric said, "and thank you."

"All right," she said again, visibly nervous. "Now, I realize that the rooms you know best at Armityr are your ducal apartments, but I've never seen them. So—"

"Wherever you can take us will be fine," Aefric said. "I'll make excuses if I need to."

"I was thinking of going straight to the war room."

Aefric chuckled. "Well, I admit I might do that if I were in a hurry."

"Which you are," Maev said, "because I insisted. I can even insist on that arrival point, if it helps."

"It might," Gwen said, then drew a quick, deep breath. "All right. Everyone in close and touching."

"Mind the demon scars," Aefric reminded them. "Stick to my arms, elbow down."

Aefric slipped his backpack over one shoulder and held up his empty, untouched left hand as though holding a scroll up where he could read it.

Gwen cast her spell.

That moment of strange, uncomfortable compression and darkness, then they were standing in the war room at Armityr.

Plenty of black oak on the walls, ceiling and floor. A large, oblong table covered in maps, and small figures representing armies or navies. The smell of wine and roast chicken lingering in the air.

King Colm in gold-washed chainmail, looked up from where he'd been making a point to Beatritz, in her dinged-up full plate armor.

"*Maev!*" he shouted, smiling brightly as he pushed past his knight to come seize his daughter by the arms and twirl her laughing in the air while her bow clattered to the floorboards. "You're home and safe!"

"She'd rescued herself, your majesty," Aefric said with a smile. "Then stayed behind to help free the others." He gestured to Gwen. "Fortunately, the duchess had come along to facilitate getting them from Vaaran Tir to the ship."

"There's no time for that story," Maev said — though she was smiling at her father, who had yet to set her down. "Father we must talk about Caiperas and Varondam."

"I know, I know," he said, setting her down. "There's still no word from Ashling, and by now she may be Makarios' prisoner."

"That's only part of the problem, Father," Maev said, "and I know you know this."

"Hold," he said.

"But Father—"

"*Hold*, I said," King Colm said, raising one hand. "Your words have waited this long, they will keep a few minutes more."

Maev frowned and picked up her bow.

"Your grace," King Colm said, turning to Gwen. "Your absence has been a source of some trouble for me."

"A regrettable situation, to be sure," she answered. "But unavoidable, as I knew my king would expect *someone* from Rethneryl to go on that mission to rescue his nieces. Took a great deal of rushed flying, but I managed to catch up with his grace's ship."

"No small feat that," Aefric said with a smile. "Especially for one unused to the hazard. She comported herself well on the mission, and I must say that I question that we would have succeeded, had she not been along to render timely aid."

"Another story I wish to hear," King Colm said to Gwen, "but at a later time." He turned to Aefric. "Your forces from Netar help me hold Caer Ylfarai. I've already dispatched a messenger to send Deepwater's armies home. Their decoy work is complete. What is the latest word on the bombardments?"

"Begun," Aefric said, and explained about Nayoria.

"You were right to send that letter," King Colm said. "Thank you for talking me into letting you."

"It was necessary, even if they didn't have your wizard," Aefric said. "We needed them fighting Caiperas in the east, and they needed to know about the possibility of invasion from Varondam in the south."

"Speaking of Varondam," Maev said.

"In a moment," King Colm said. "Bide a little longer." He turned back to Aefric. "Malimfar is indeed fighting Caiperas in the east, but they are losing ground. They simply don't have the resources right now to repel invaders."

"Not until Caiperas gets word that we've taken Caer Ylfarai and the pass," Beatritz said, sounding as though she'd said those words — or words much like them — several times in the past hour.

"We don't know that," King Colm said. "Makarios may choose to cede the castle and pass to us through the winter, if we push no farther, in favor of gains in Malimfar."

"Which would be the height of foolishness," Beatritz said. "He'd leave us in position to strike deeply into his own kingdom while spending his troops to hold new land in Malimfar. *He will not do it.*"

"I agree with Beatritz," Maev said. "Makarios is no fool, despite his poor choice to come after us with assassins. If he maintains the attack against Malimfar *while knowing* we hold Caer Ylfarai, it can only be because he has another plan for retaking that castle."

"It is a castle built into a mountain?" Aefric asked.

"This is not what I wish to discuss right now," King Colm said.

"It is," Maev said. "Why does that matter?"

"I've been in more than one ruined castle built into a mountainside that proved to have secret tunnels running deep into the mountain. Tunnels that entered through hidden passageways that conquerors might not find until *after* raiding parties have stolen their food, or arms, or simply—"

"Enough!" King Colm barked. "We *do not know* that Makarios has learned the fate of Caer Ylfarai. If he *learns it*, then his most likely course of action is to make prisoners of Ashling and her entourage, and send word to us demanding we ransom them. Perhaps by abandoning the castle and retreating from their borders."

"Which you will not do," Beatritz.

"No, I will not. Caiperas owes us a debt of blood, and they will only compound their debt if they dare seize one of my peers."

"Have they been told of that?" Aefric asked, drawing all eyes to him. "We may have confirmed through a justiciar of Taesark that it was Caiperas behind those assassins from the Order of the Severed Dream. But does Caiperas *know* we know? We've been hiding it from them for a good while now."

"And it is hidden from them still," Beatritz said. "Which will only cause confusion among the other kingdoms, who may wonder at us suddenly assaulting an ally — a weak, recent ally, but an ally nonetheless — without so much as a word of warning."

"Confusion that will be made clear easily," King Colm said, "and after the fact."

"Father, there is the Varondam matter to discuss. And I wish—"

"Bide but a little longer, my sweet daughter, and you shall have my undivided attention." The king turned to Aefric. "I am not ready yet to dispatch you to Caer Ylfarai. Retire to your rooms, and I shall send for you soon."

"At your service, your majesty," Aefric said with a bow.

"Oh, and while you're there, try to contact Ashling and her wizard for me again, if you would."

"Your majesty, I shall try."

"Gwen," King Colm said, "I suggest you meet with your aides and get caught up on all recent developments, then rejoin me here. After dinner, if not sooner."

"I imagine I've missed quite a bit," Gwen said wryly. "I'll look forward to rejoining you then."

As Aefric left the room, Maev and Colm looked ready to do a kind of battle all their own.

AEFRIC WAS NOT LONG IN HIS SUMPTUOUS DUCAL APARTMENTS AT Armityr before the expected knock came. It was Arras' knock, and Arras' voice announcing his visitor.

"Her majesty the queen!"

Queen Eppida hardly allowed those words to finish forming — much less let Aefric finish standing and taking the Brightstaff in hand — before she stepped through the doorway. Her blonde curls were piled atop her head. She wore an aggressively cut dress of sapphire blue, with gold bracelets on each arm in addition to the torc around her neck. Tension seemed to crackle in the air about her.

"Sit down, Aefric," she said, crossing to where he stood by a navy blue couch. "We can skip the niceties today."

"As your majesty wishes," he said, standing the Brightstaff again and retaking his seat while she sat beside him.

"Have you heard anything from Ashling?" the queen asked immediately.

"Your majesty, I have not," he said. "And I tried again scarcely a few minutes before you arrived here. She still seems to be behind wards."

"What are the chances that she's dead?" Queen Eppida's sapphire eyes — so much like Ashling's and Zoleen's — bored into him. "Mince no words with me. I must know."

"Is Makarios a fool?"

She shook her head.

"Then she lives. He knows we'd seek vengeance for her death, even if he doesn't know we know he was behind the assassination attempts."

"But if he *suspects* us of knowing," she said. "And if he's received word of our invasion. He's vindictive enough to kill her, if he feels he has cause."

"And Ashling is clever enough to remind him of all the reasons he should keep her alive," Aefric said, then quirked a smile. "Or do you doubt your sister's ability to survive?"

Queen Eppida laughed, shaking her head, and the tension broke.

"No," she said finally, through a sigh. "No. That woman could talk the Flayer Himself into refusing the mar the perfection of her skin."

"Perhaps she'll talk King Makarios into surrendering?"

Queen Eppida lifted an imperious eyebrow. "She lacks your facility with miracles."

"I'm sorry I can offer no better reassurance than that," Aefric said. "Is there anything else I can do?"

"Why, your grace," the queen said with a small smile. "If I didn't know better, I would think you were propositioning me."

"Something I cannot do right now," Aefric said, and explained about the demon scars.

Oddly, her reaction to that was laughter. And not just a little chuckle, either. No, it was loud, sincere laughter that verged on out of control.

Aefric wasn't sure how to handle that, so he tried to sit still and ride it out.

That took a while.

When Queen Eppida finally seemed to have herself under control again, albeit gasping for breath, she first managed to say, "I'm sorry."

But nothing followed those words — apart from her efforts to contain her breathing — for long enough that Aefric finally said, "Your majesty is forgiven?"

She chuckled again, then gulped a deep breath and sat back.

"Oh," she said. "I haven't laughed like that since before this war began." She shook her head, and realized that three curls had broken free from the pins that kept them in their place so that they fell down near her face.

She toyed with them a moment, then decided to leave them be.

Aefric couldn't deny it was a fetching look on her.

"No," she said, "I'm not laughing at you, Aefric." She patted his thigh. "That was what I was apologizing for, in case I gave that impression."

"I hadn't realized demon scars were so funny," Aefric said, still not sure what she'd been laughing about.

"Oh, they aren't," Queen Eppida said, patting his thigh again, and giving it a small squeeze. "Not in the least. No. The source of my laughter was much simpler, and a bit childish, I'm afraid."

"Do I get to know what it was?"

"Maev, of course," Queen Eppida said, appearing to suppress another round of laughter. "*Seasons* that woman's been wanting to bed you. I've stopped her. Her father has stopped her. Dalius' *mother* has stopped her. And all because of the possibility of her marrying Dalius."

She started chuckling, then slapped her thigh stop the laughter from overwhelming her again.

"But now," she said, then took a slow, controlling breath. "Now when it's clear she won't have to marry Dalius. Now that she's finally free to hop into your bed. *She can't! Because of demon scars!*"

Queen Eppida burst into laughter again, but if she'd hoped Aefric would join her, she was sadly mistaken. He didn't see anything funny about it. And not just because the delay annoyed him too.

No, it seemed to Aefric a mark of *cruelty* that Queen Eppida could find so much humor in Maev's frustration. Made her feel cold. Hard. Possibly heartless. Certainly nowhere near as attractive as she'd been only a short time ago.

He sat patiently waiting for the queen to control herself.

When she finally did, smiling as though she expected to see Aefric smiling back at her, he said, "May I offer your majesty refreshment?"

"Oh, come now, Aefric," she said. "Surely you can't be so bitter at the delay that you can deny how *funny* this is."

"It feels no more funny to me than the assignment of Zoleen to that diplomatic post."

Queen Eppida shook her head. "I thought *sure* you had a better sense of humor than that. The one is a political maneuver intended to prevent a joining of houses. Nothing funny there. The other, though, is the anticipation of satisfaction following *seasons* of patience, only to see *yet another delay*."

Aefric didn't laugh.

"Come," she cajoled, "frustration of desire and expectation is the very *essence* of humor."

"In this instance, I'm afraid, it just feels cruel."

The queen nodded. Sighed. "Well, a queen must be cruel sometimes. I'll just have to hope you understand enough of politics to understand that."

"I'd say I've learned more about politics in the last day than I had in the season before it."

"Good," she said. "These are lessons you must learn."

She reached out to touch his shoulder. Her intercepted her hand.

Her eyebrows shot up.

"Demon scars," Aefric said. "They're on both shoulders, as well as my chest and back. Touching them isn't safe, even through silk."

"So many," the queen said thoughtfully. "I can see how they'd prevent seeking the bliss moment, then."

She stood.

"Aefric," she said, "I hope you will not judge me too harshly. Maev and I, we've been sparring since her father and I first got involved. My laughter is nothing more than a continuance of that."

He nodded. "I can understand that."

She raised an eyebrow again. "You can't tell me she speaks well of me."

"We ... do not speak of your majesty often."

She chuckled. "You..."

But Aefric missed the rest of what she said because he was

receiving a spell of contact. He raised a forestalling hand as he listened to the words.

Not Sirondfar's voice though, nor Karbin's.

Jenbarjen?

"Your lordship! I am thrilled to announce that I have completed work on the flying ship your lordship requested. When may I schedule the launch?"

"Launch it at once," Aefric said, as soon as he felt the tingling sensation that it was his chance to reply. "I am at Armityr. Bring it to me here. I look forward to seeing what you have for me."

Once the sensation faded, he turned to his curious queen.

"Forgive me, your majesty. I just received word from my baronial wizard that she has completed a task I wasn't sure she could accomplish."

"Oh?" she asked as he stood.

"Yes," he said with a smile. "And I must see the king at once."

THE SUN WAS HANGING LOW AND HEAVY IN THE WEST, TURNING THE skies a variety of orange shades. The winds blew blustery down from the north, but the closest rains had already passed them by.

Aefric stood on the gray and white parapets of Armityr, along with their majesties, Beatritz and a dozen of the Knights of the Crown, Maev, Prince Killian, Gwen, Arras and Micham. All of them watching the northeast skies, towards Netar.

Prince Killian looked disgruntled, and Aefric had not yet had a chance to speak with him.

"There," the king said. "I see it."

He pointed, though he didn't really need to. Any of them could have seen those pinprick lights in the sky above a shadowed form, which grew larger even while his majesty spoke. That had to be the incoming airship.

At least, Aefric *hoped* it was the airship. Because the only two other options that leapt to mind for something that size, flying that fast, were a roc or a dragon. Not exactly welcome options.

Then again, Aefric had never heard of a roc or dragon with small lights on its dorsal side.

A moment later, the complete lack of wings became certain when Aefric could pick out the silhouette of a ship bottom against the darkening blue of that patch of sky.

Could that silhouette be a trick of the eye, though? If not, it was a *beast* of a ship. Perhaps the size of the *Calming Influence* or the *Lake Monster*.

And fast. If Aefric remembered the distance between Armityr and Netarritan as well as he thought he did, that ship must've been flying faster even than a *magari*.

"Look at the *size* of it," Queen Eppida said a moment later. "I'm not sure even *Ashling* has a ship that large in her *fleet*."

The queen was right. That airship wasn't a beast, it was a *mammoth*. Gigantic. Easily the largest ship Aefric had ever seen. Were it a seafaring vessel, it could have supported four masts. Maybe five. Dozens of sails. Possibly *miles* of rope for its rigging.

And yet, the airship had no masts at all. No sails. No rigging. And all the wood of the sides and bottom had been painted a sky blue. In fact, were the ship not approaching in a darkening sky, she might've blended with the background.

A clever touch.

Otherwise, though, the airship had a prow, and a warship's shape. And spaced along the port side, a series of what looked like ten trapdoors.

"What comes out of a trapdoor that size?" King Colm asked.

"A dozen na'shek at a time?" Beatritz suggested.

"Small assault vessels?" Arras said.

"I can't wait to find out," Aefric said, then cast a contact spell to reach Karbin. "I'm at the royal palace. You should get out here at best speed. You need to see this. And bring Beornric and Deirdre."

He didn't give Karbin the opportunity to respond to that. No need to chance his ducal wizard objecting.

The airship eased to a hovering halt in the skies about three hundred feet above the tallest spire of the royal palace. A longboat launched from the afterdecks, sailing downward through the air toward them.

King Colm turned to Aefric. "I want one."

"Let me find out what's involved, your majesty."

"Aefric, you have the *best* toys," Maev said with a smile.

Aefric met her smile, then looked back up at the descending longboat.

No rowers, of course. It had no more need of rowers than the main ship had of sails. In fact, there was only one person in the longboat.

One very short, slender person — obviously kindaren — wearing robes of muted green and brown. She had three pebbles circling her head, close to her short brown hair. Each featured the dull orange light of a rune. The ironwood rod tucked into her belt glowed with many graven red runes.

Jenbarjen.

She brought the longboat in close enough to the parapet that Aefric could have walked aboard from a crenel.

"Your lordship," she said with a bow, addressing him by his baronial title for she was his baronial vassal. "Your majesties, your highnesses, and you other fine nobles I do not know, may I offer you all greetings."

"You may," King Colm said.

"For those of you who do not know her," Aefric said, "this is Jenbarjen, Baronial Wizard of Netar." He turned to Jenbarjen, and introduced Gwen and Beatritz, but was stopped there by a cautionary nod from Maev, or he would have introduced all of the knights.

"And I am to understand that this magnificent flying vessel," King Colm said, "is entirely of your own design?"

"Your majesty," Jenbarjen said with a bow, "the ship itself, of course, is not. Its design involved the finest shipbuilders I could gather, along with their full crews and additional hired hands.

However, the many enchantments carved into it beam by beam and nail by nail are every bit the product of my own, tireless work."

"I very much look forward to the story of how you accomplished this all so quickly," Aefric said.

"Oh, by resolving multiple problems at the same time, your lordship," Jenbarjen said with a smile. "In the finest tradition of wizards everywhere."

He chuckled appreciatively.

"The details, of course," she continued, "should likely wait until after the formal viewing, when your lordship takes full possession of his new airship."

"No time like the present," Aefric said, turning to their majesties. "May I invite you all aboard for the viewing?" Then quickly turned to Jenbarjen. "The longboat can accommodate us all?"

"It can carry thirty easily, your lordship, even if all thirty are outfitted for battle, complete with their supplies. Forty such might push its limits."

"Then we won't come close to that," King Colm said. "Beatritz, pick two each from the Knights of the Crown. The rest shall remain down here."

She quickly chose two guards for each of their majesties and highnesses, and then boarding began. The king and queen first, followed by the prince and princess, then their guards. Aefric invited Gwen to board next. He was about to board himself when he noticed Karbin, Beornric and Deirdre swiftly approaching along the parapet.

"She did it," Beornric said, amazed. "And so swiftly."

"I've never seen anything like it," Karbin said.

"We get to fly it, right?" Deirdre said. "Tell me we didn't just come here to look."

"I wouldn't be so cruel," Aefric said with a smile. "Of course you'll be along for its maiden voyage."

He boarded then, flanked by Arras and Micham, with the others following in his wake. He made sure everyone was seated, then joined Jenbarjen at the back of the longboat.

"Whoever holds the rudder can control the longboat by intention," she said. "Like flying."

"Then take us up," Aefric said, settling onto the bench seat beside her.

Aefric took a moment to savor the excitement flavoring his every breath right now.

New magic. Was there anything better in life?

AS THE LONGBOAT STARTED TO ASCEND, AND MOST OF HIS GUESTS BEGAN talking among themselves in eager voices, Aefric turned to Jenbarjen and spoke only just loudly enough for her to hear him over the whipping winds.

"And tell me, how *did* you accomplish all this so quickly?"

Jenbarjen shot him a smile, before turning her attention back to her flying.

"By dedicated, efficient use of my time and other people's money," she said, matching his tone. "I built up a great deal of debt to the barony during my years of ... well, your lordship knows what I was doing. So I went to each of Netar's noble families — starting with those who'd hired me in the past — and told them that I was working on a special project for the baron. I gave them the opportunity to invest and gain the baron's goodwill. Many were *quite eager* to impress their new baron."

She gave him a chagrined look. "I trust I didn't exceed my bounds by too great a measure. With the war coming, I felt haste would be appreciated, and that your lordship would look favorably on those families who helped see this project to a speedy conclusion."

"You thought right," Aefric said. "And I will. Nothing improper, of course, but—"

"Of course not, your lordship," Jenbarjen said quickly. "Nor did I imply that they would gain ... *undue* influence."

"Good."

She grimaced. "I must say, though, that your lordship's investors will be less than thrilled to learn that the *Baron's Will* launched the first time without them aboard. I'm sure they expected a formal launch, with an appropriate feast."

"I will personally apologize for that, and ensure that we have just such a feast and formal launch where the investors are the guests of honor. In the meantime, if anyone asks, tell them the ship was needed for the war effort. Which I suspect will prove true, given the way his majesty is looking at it."

"Of course, your lordship."

"The *Baron's Will*, eh?" Aefric smiled. "I like it."

"I think your lordship will be even more pleased when he learns what it can do." Jenbarjen's smile faded into a frown, and her next words came out a little subdued. "Your lordship should know that Grond and Drien helped make sure every coin raised not only went toward the project, but was spent as effectively as possible."

"I don't doubt it," Aefric said. The two were his castellan and seneschal in Netar, and both had proven themselves trustworthy.

"Not only did I not profit from this project personally, but I think your lordship will find," Jenbarjen added, "that the funds I raised and invested in his ship shall not only *meet* the debt I owed, but exceed it."

"Once Grond confirms that, I'll consider your debt officially cleared. In the meantime, know that not only do you get to keep your job, you have managed to impress your baron greatly," he said, clapping her on the shoulder. "I look forward to learning everything about my new airship."

Jenbarjen smiled and concentrated on steering the flying longboat.

Aefric drew a relaxed breath, and realized that the *Baron's Will* was so thoroughly enchanted, he could feel the nearness of its many spells without even trying. They teased him with the urge to investigate their secrets, though he knew that doing so would be a project that might take an entire season.

Fortunately, seasons of living at Water's End had taught him to ignore the siren song of background magic, once he acknowledged it.

Ascending in the air-longboat was a fun, if windy experience.

Flying was always a little more pleasant when Aefric didn't have to constantly monitor his movement. He could enjoy just looking down at the royal palace, and the city of Armityr around it, bustling even at dusk.

The wind was certainly stronger up here though, tossing his blonde hair about his shoulders and buffeting his face.

Jenbarjen brought the longboat in close to the airship's sky blue port side, giving everyone a better look at the ten huge trapdoors set into the side of the ship.

"What are those trapdoors?" King Colm called back over the wind.

"They aren't trapdoors, your majesty," Jenbarjen called back. "They're shutters."

She pulled a silver whistle from a pocket in her robes and brought it to her lips. She blew two quick, shrill blasts.

With a loud clacking sound, all ten shutters opened, revealing the heads of ten ballista bolts. Five of them steel arrowheads, three of them stone balls, and two of them looked like clay.

"Ten ballistae?" Aefric said in disbelief. "Belowdecks, yet?"

"Ten on *this* side, your lordship," she said with a smile, then raised her voice as she continued. "The arrowheads and hammerheads should be obvious enough. The clay heads are filled with quicksleep."

Aefric chuckled. Quicksleep was an alchemical formula. Two drops of it into a cup of wine would be enough to send a good-sized man into a heavy sleep for six hours. But it had to be handled gently because, when agitated, it sublimated into gas that acted even faster, and might ensure sleep for as many as twelve hours.

"Quicksleep gas disperses too quickly to be useful in battle," he said.

"Unless it's thickened with marsh sap that has been rendered inert," Jenbarjen said and winked. "Then the gas hangs in the air for a full minute. Assuming the winds aren't too strong."

"I've never heard of marsh sap being used that way."

"Your lordship has never experimented with the marshes around Lake Fist."

"Fair enough."

Jenbarjen steered the longboat around the starboard side, to show off the other ten ballista ports, open and ready to fire.

She blew another two sharp blasts on her whistle and the shutter doors closed again.

Up the air-longboat went, and up farther still, until it finally crested the high rail above the fifth afterdeck of six at the back of the airship. Seen from above, the many decks of the ship all looked to be made from some dark hardwood and lit by hanging lanterns.

She set the air-longboat down near the port rail, beside one of its brothers. Two others were currently stowed near the starboard rail.

Plenty of room to store longboats up here. This deck was at least fifty feet wide, and thirty long. And this was only one of the afterdecks.

A crowd of sailors — if that was the right word — had gathered in ranks behind their captain and first mate. All of them wore Netar's colors, forest green and gold, with the golden acorn of Netar in the center of their chests.

The captain was a male human, thirtyish and so weathered he might've been born at sea. And there was something familiar about him...

Of course. His eyes. The set of his jaw. This man had to be one of the many cousins of Guimond Ol'Riel, Netar's historian.

His first mate was a male kindaren who bore more than a passing resemblance to Jenbarjen. Perhaps one of her cousins, too.

Well, so long as they knew their business.

As Aefric and his guests disembarked the longboat, the ship's boatswain blew a series of notes on his whistle, and the assembled sailors all saluted, right fists held high in the air.

The king, as though by reflex, acknowledged the salute with a nod, but they held that salute until Aefric himself gave them acknowledgment.

Only then did the sailors relax into an at-ease position, while their captain stepped forward.

"Your lordship," he said, "I am Karsten Ol'Riel, captain of the *Baron's Will*. I understand your lordship's wizard, Jenbarjen, wishes to conduct the first tour of the vessel herself. Does that meet with your lordship's approval?"

"It does," Aefric said. "She's responsible for it flying, after all. I say, let her show it off."

"Fair enough, your lordship," Captain Karsten said with a smile worthy of a sea devil. "Any orders during the tour?"

"Just hold her steady for the time being," Aefric said. "I imagine his majesty will want a short trip to see what she can do."

"Will we be firing the ballistae?"

"I doubt it. Not for this trip."

"Aye, your lordship. Enjoy the look around your new ship, and I'll be near the helm if you need anything."

"Thank you, captain," Aefric said, and the captain turned and dismissed his assembled crew, who began going about their business.

With the crew returning to their business, and his guests milling about the windy fifth deck, admiring the airship or the view it provided of the castle and city down below, Aefric returned to the king's side.

"I don't think we have enough time for a proper tour," King Colm said, looking about. "This thing's the size of a small keep, and I've got a war to fight. Not to mention dinner with my court, some of whom chafe at being excluded from my war council."

He shook his head. "Honestly, nobles can be like children sometimes."

"Well, we can save your majesty's full viewing for another time then," Aefric said, turning to Jenbarjen, who stood nearby. "Perhaps a couple of highlights for our guests?"

"I know just the two," she said. "If our esteemed guests would be so good as to follow me, the first is right this way."

Jenbarjen led them aft, to a wide, green circle between two sets of ladder rungs.

"Now. Of course the ladder rungs are a perfectly good way to go up and down decks," she said. "As has been proven aboard ships since time immemorial."

She clapped her hands once sharply.

"However!" Jenbarjen bowed to the queen, one hand extended as though presenting her. "Ladder rungs are hardly appropriate for one dressed in finery, such as her majesty's lovely gown."

Jenbarjen smiled at the queen, and gestured with a flourish at the green circle on the deck. "If your majesty would be so kind as to step into the circle and think, 'Up.'"

"Very well," Queen Eppida said, with only the slightest frown.

She stepped into the green circle and vanished.

"Well!" Queen Eppida said an instant later, looking down from the deck above. "I must say, *that* was a new experience."

"Teleportation!" King Colm exclaimed.

"Your majesty, not quite," Jenbarjen said. "True teleportation is a powerful means of traveling quite a distance in an instant, with little in the way of restriction. These circles — found in several places aboard the ship — are merely linked together in such a way that the right keyword will allow one to momentarily slip the space between and return swiftly and safely to its mate on the deck above or below."

"Impressive, nonetheless," King Colm said, stepping into the circle only to vanish and reappear on the deck above.

"I got the idea from your lordship's reference to linked teleportation circles as an option," Jenbarjen said. "I couldn't accomplish something that powerful without dedicating at least a full year to the project. But this little bit of play with space is related to magics I use often. Such as the enchantment on your grace's special pouch."

"Very well done indeed," Aefric said, making use of the circle himself. The sensation wasn't the compression of teleportation, but more of a momentary feeling of being stretched, followed by a not-unpleasant sort of *pop* all along the skin.

Immediately he noticed the wind was gone. He could still hear it. See it blowing the hair and clothes of the others, who had not yet come up. But here on the sixth afterdeck, nothing. He stepped closer to the nearest rail.

Ah! There. A wind ward along the borders of the deck. Clearly, Jenbarjen had covered as many details as she could think of.

As Aefric turned to look around, he realized quickly that the sixth afterdeck was designed for his personal use. There was a large, silver magic circle inscribed in the deck. One of the basic forms that would need to be tuned for certain specific types of magic, but would be an excellent place to gather and channel power for a great variety of effects without any tuning at all.

For example, he imagined it would be easy to throw some impressive battle magics from that circle.

"She's done something to the wind," King Colm said, smiling. "We can actually talk in normal voices up here."

He clapped Aefric on the back of the neck, and they turned to see what else there was to see.

There was a large deckhouse near the aft rail, and before it a set of eight wooden chairs built into the deck, in a circle. They had good backs and arms — and the Netar seal on the chairbacks — but only a single post connecting each seat to the deck.

"Those hardly look stable on an airship," Beornric said, and Beatritz nodded, frowning disapproval. Aefric looked about to see that his crowd was all gathered up here now, with Karbin and Deirdre discussing something near the silver circle, and Maev and Killian in conversation near the back rail.

"Your lordship," Jenbarjen said, loudly enough to draw everyone's attention. She bowed to Aefric before turning to bow to the king and queen. "Your majesties." She turned to Maev and Killian. "Your highnesses." She turned to Gwen. "Your grace. If you would all be so good as to take seats?"

At a nod from his majesty, Aefric took his seat first, and started laughing the moment he sat. Jenbarjen's eyes sparkled at his laughter, because she understood it. Likely even expected it.

For the moment he sat, he felt the way these chairs were linked directly into a primary structural beam of the ship's body. These chairs would not break free, nor would anyone fall out of them. Not unless the airship itself was destroyed and its primary beams snapped.

"What's that I feel?" King Colm asked as he took his seat.

"Your majesty," Jenbarjen said, "that sensation is the hug of those chairs. This is an airship, after all, and even should it roll in the air for some reason, anyone sitting in one of these chairs would remain safely seated."

"The magic follows intention," Aefric said, understanding the enchantment involved. "Should your majesty wish to stand, the chair will not stop him. But so long as he wishes to stay seated, no force could *pull* him from the chair."

"And as the seats are mounted on single posts," Jenbarjen said, "they can spin. Simply think the word 'unlock' and the chair can be spun to face any direction. Thinking 'lock' again will stop this at the new facing."

All six of them played with that a bit, Maev most of all. Deirdre gave the seats a longing look.

"Now," Jenbarjen said, moving to stand near the silver circle. "If your lordship would join me here?"

Aefric stood and walked over to her, while everyone else watched.

"Into the circle, if it please your lordship."

Aefric stepped into the circle.

"Your lordship may now take formal possession of this airship and all its magics by simply stating his name and titles."

Prince Killian stood from his chair.

"*All* titles or Armyrian titles?" Aefric asked.

"I should think Armyrian would suffice," Jenbarjen said, frowning.

"*I* should think Armyrian titles would suffice," King Colm said pointedly, but then laughed, allowing others to laugh as well. If not with all that much humor.

"I am Ser Aefric Brightstaff, Duke of Deepwater and Baron of Netar."

The circle flared, and Aefric felt a pulse of warm power sweep through him.

A sense of connection followed. Not entirely unlike what he felt with the Brightstaff, though certainly a lesser version. However, instead of merely feeling the magics of the ship as nearby enchantments, if he tried, he could feel them flowing through him as well.

"Your lordship no longer needs trinkets such as this whistle" — Jenbarjen held up her silver whistle — "or the aid of others to do something like open or close the ballista ports. Your lordship could now even overrule the helm regarding bearing, speed, or anything else. All of the magics of this ship now answer to your lordship first and foremost."

"They answer to Aefric himself," Prince Killian said, "or they answer to the Baron of Netar?"

"Those are one in the same," King Colm said archly.

"*At this time* they are the same, Father," Prince Killian said. "Which may make the point salient one day."

"They answer to his lordship as Netar's rightful baron," Jenbarjen said, plainly uncomfortable with the direction of this conversation.

"Then should Aefric be *replaced* as Netar's baron," Prince Killian said, "the ship would answer to the *new* baron."

"Killian," King Colm, Queen Eppida and Maev all said at the same time.

"It may become an important point one day," Prince Killian said. "And we should understand how this works."

Jenbarjen visibly struggled against squirming. "The ship is designed to serve Netar's rightful baron, once that baron has claimed it properly."

"So if Aefric were *removed* as baron—"

"For cause," Aefric said.

Prince Killian frowned at him.

"What he means—" Maev began, but the king silenced her with a gesture, then stepped over in front of his son while everyone else studiously looked away.

Well, everyone except for Queen Eppida, Maev and Deirdre.

Aefric tried not to watch, but found his peripheral vision keeping the king and prince in view.

"What that *peer of the realm* is reminding you," King Colm said firmly, "is that he, Aefric Brightstaff, will *remain* Netar's rightful baron until and unless he dies, or is removed from his post *for violating his oaths*. I take it my *crown prince* understands the distinction there?"

Prince Killian's nostrils flared in a sharp breath, but he nodded.

"Say it," King Colm said.

"Your majesty," Prince Killian said, "your crown prince understands the distinction."

"I recommend you mentally review a certain recent conversation of ours," King Colm said. "Lest I am *forced* to remind you of the potential consequences."

Prince Killian's eyes widened.

"Pray, good wizard," Queen Eppida said, standing and addressing Jenbarjen, "what other wonders are there to see on this deck?"

Jenbarjen cleared her throat.

"The deckhouse at the back certainly qualifies," she said. "It's warded as strongly against attack as I can make it. As strongly as any part of the ship. Should his lordship and any guests be up here when the weather turns, or should attack come, moving into that deckhouse will provide safety, as well as access to the decks below."

"Provisioned appropriately, I take it?" Beornric asked.

"Oh, of course," Jenbarjen said, sounding more comfortable now that the tension seemed to be passing. If somewhat slowly. "With comfortable couches and chairs, tables and the like. Plus excellent rations, if need be, and a selection of alcohols."

King Colm turned, smiling once more, though his son's expression was still dark.

"You're tempting me to see the whole ship," King Colm said.

"Would that we could spare the time," Queen Eppida said.

"We can't, of course," King Colm said, sighing. "In fact, I'll have to pass on seeing that deckhouse for now. Show us instead that other wonder you said was important, then most of us will have to head back down. There's much work to do."

"Of course, your majesty. The other thing I thought your majesty might wish to see is this way."

Jenbarjen led Aefric and his crowd back down the six afterdecks to the vast main deck and across, through the heavy winds. Passing little on the main deck except the occasional stack of crates, fastened down under rope nets.

Aefric assumed she was leading them to one of the six forward decks.

Along the way, she mentioned some of the other fine points of the ship. Not only did it have enough proper cabins to accommodate Aefric's typical entourage and guests, complete with guards — part of his requirement of her, after all — but there was room to bunk an extra hundred soldiers in reasonable comfort, and stables enough for at least an extra six dozen horses. Well beyond what he'd asked for.

"Though, of course, your lordship will want those horses blindfolded as they're brought aboard and disembarked, or they may not take too well to the heights."

"They can be trained for that," Prince Killian said, looking about.

"Of course, your highness," Jenbarjen said, and began talking about the sumptuous accommodations provided for not only Aefric, but for as many as six other ranking nobles, with lesser — "but still impressive" she insisted — accommodations for the knights and lesser nobles, before getting to the cabins for the servants and so forth.

Apparently, Aefric had his own galley, where his own cooks could prepare food for the nobility. Something he was less thrilled by himself, but he knew that other nobles would expect it.

"And, of course," she continued, "as I know your lordship loves his research as much as I do, I've set aside a cabin in his suite for research and experimentation. Warded every bit as much from the inside as from the out."

Aefric laughed appreciatively.

"We may never get him to *leave* this ship," Karbin said with a smile.

"Remember, your grace," Beornric said with a grin, "living here full-time is not an option for a duke *or* a baron."

"What about—" Beatritz started, but Jenbarjen raised a hand for silence.

"We're here," she said, although they were still on the main deck. The forward part of the main deck, but still...

Wait. There were no masts. No rigging. He could see some of the crew swabbing, but what else did they have to *do?* None of the typical shipboard jobs he thought of would have had a purpose aboard an airship like this one...

"Behind this door," Jenbarjen said, drawing his attention back as she patted the dark brown wood of the door in question, "lies the *war room.* Care to see it?"

"At once!" King Colm said, possibly even more excited about all this than Aefric was. Certainly Maev rolled her eyes at his reaction, though the queen merely smiled affectionately at him. Prince Killian scowled thoughtfully.

"Your lordship?" Jenbarjen asked.

"Please," Aefric said.

She opened the door.

Once more, a war room done in black oak. There had to be some sort of historical significance to the choice of wood. Aefric hoped he remembered to ask Elkari about it at some point, because it had certainly never been mentioned in any of Keifer's *Torn Kingdoms* setting books.

The ceiling in the war room was pleasantly high. Aefric didn't even feel the urge to hunch, which was unusual aboard a ship. And the magical light in here was soft and slightly yellow. As though from candle flames.

"In case you missed this," Karbin said softly to him, "those lanterns on the deck are magical. I doubt there's a drop of oil burning anywhere on the ship."

"Thank the gods," Aefric muttered, looking about the war room. "If I never smell burning whale oil again it'll be too soon."

And true enough, the main odor in the room was that of old varnish, and not very strong.

Technically the war room was large enough for all of the guests to crowd in, but for this first look, only their majesties, their highnesses, Gwen, Jenbarjen, Karbin, Beornric, Deirdre and Beatritz entered.

Along each of the port and starboard walls, a series of ten empty picture frames. The aft wall had the sigils of Armyr, Netar and Deepwater — Netar's done largest, of course. The fore wall held an immense, framed map of ... well, Armityr was clearly in the center, so to the left would be ... perhaps two hundred miles west and up another hundred miles north — all of it more of Armyr.

Yes, there was Kerrik Forest, and on into Deepwater to the west.

Which would make the stretch of map to the right of Armityr showing the two hundred miles east, extending into Rethneryl and Caiperas, and below, the hundred or so miles south. Including more of Caiperas to the southeast and the northern part of Malimfar to the southwest.

But the crown jewel of the war room was right there in the center. The round, blackwood table, roughly nine feet across.

This table wasn't *covered* with maps. It *was* a map. An illusory display in three dimensions that showed the *Baron's Will* in the center, floating above Armityr. Below it, the royal palace and the city around it, complete with the sections still under repair, and even...

Yes. Aefric could pick out people moving down below. And outside the walls, the tent city. And the sections of still-dented grass that until recently had been occupied by some of Armyr's armies, waiting to march.

"That..." King Colm said, then turned to Jenbarjen. "How accurate is it?"

"Your majesty, I would hesitate to call it *perfect,*" she answered with a bow. "It is scrying magic, and so it is largely good and accurate, but I would not suggest relying on it for fine details. And certainly it is not proof against counterspells."

"But good enough to get a troop count, if they were below us?"

"Good enough for a *close estimate*," Jenbarjen cautioned. "And for an accurate accounting of any accompanying larger threats, such as siege equipment."

"But we'd have to be careful using the ship that way around battle wizards," Aefric said. "At least, once word got out that we have that capability. The moment they began to sense our scrying out in the field, they'd pass word around and start searching the skies. Ready to turn their siege engines against *us*."

"A possibility," she said, then smiled slyly. "Tell me though, your lordship. Did *you* sense the scrying, while you stood on the parapets below?"

"No," Aefric said, frowning. He glanced at both Karbin and Deirdre, but they shook their heads.

"It's a *general* kind of scrying," Karbin said, understanding the details of that kind of magic better than Aefric did. "The sort least likely to draw attention because it cannot be used to target *anything*, let alone spells."

"Just so," Jenbarjen said with a bow.

"What about these frames?" Queen Eppida asked. "I assume they are not for decoration, and I suspect significance to their number and placement."

"Your majesty is most perspicacious," Jenbarjen said with another bow. She was clearly enjoying showing off to the king and queen. But then, she deserved to. "When the ballistae ports are open, these frames show a view of their targets."

"And this wall map," Deirdre said, over by the fore wall. "Does it move with the ship? Shifting its display?"

"Well spotted, good ser knight," Jenbarjen said with a smile. "It does indeed. Though, of course, it does not reflect people or armies, nor current views below, the way the map table does. But there are other resources aboard the ship to handle such things."

"Amazing," the king said, then leaned in over the table and began discussing something quietly with Beatritz.

Aefric turned and gazed at his baronial wizard in disbelief. "You had to have worked day and night on all this."

"Your lordship, I did," she said, and for a moment he could see the exhaustion in her aspect. "With the aid of my apprentice, and supplemented here and there by the use of scrolls prepared by the house wizards of certain Netari noble families."

"Even so…"

"This…" Jenbarjen said proudly, looking about. "This is my finest work. My crowning achievement."

"Truly," Aefric said softly, "you have outdone yourself. I still have so much more to see of this ship, and you've already exceeded my wildest hopes."

"Your lordship," she said, "while my financial decisions of the last several years have been … ill-considered, I must say that taking so many commissions for nobles taught me a great deal. Stretched both my speed and skill at enchantment. Perhaps even served as my own equivalent of your lordship's adventuring days."

"That might be."

Looking troubled, she leaned in closer and lowered her voice.

"But please don't ask me to make another of these. I don't think I could. I've … hit a snag."

"Oh?"

"That new technique I wrote of? Enchanting parts from separate trees and forests as though they were grown together?"

"Yes?"

"It failed. The enchantments were strong initially, but indicated a decay rate that, while better than anything I'd seen before, was insufficient for anything intended to be as lasting as this ship."

"But…"

"Your lordship, the nobles were *very* generous. And Grond … smoothed over the details. Allowing me to find a … workaround … for the issue. Sinking a nail into each board with the right rune graven into the head. All of the nails made from that one gold vein in your lordship's mines."

"That shouldn't make a difference," he said. "A single nail isn't enough."

"I'll write your lordship a full explanation as I understand it," she said, casting a worried glance at the king. "But for the moment, suffice to say that gold works with oak in this way, and only if the oak is specially treated and both board and nail are carved with the right runes within the right time frame, such that the end result is as fine, strong and enduring as though all the wood of this ship came from a single tree."

"And just how expensive is this 'special treatment?'"

"*Prohibitive* would be a gentle word, your lordship. And it was required by every board of the ship."

"I understand."

"That's not all. I suspect there was something *special* about that gold vein. Gold always holds enchantments well, but this—"

"Your grace," King Colm called over. "I and mine must return below. But I have a mission for you and this marvelous new ship of yours."

12

———————

The research room that Jenbarjen had built for Aefric aboard the *Baron's Will* was a neat bit of work.

Not so much physically, though it certainly looked good enough. The floors, walls and ceiling had all been sanded smooth and sealed with something that left them pale. Each board fitted together tight enough that a chalk line drawn across two boards would have no gap.

A basic circle and triangle had been burned into the wood and inset with copper. Not the metal Aefric would have chosen, but a good, neutral conductor of arcane energies, and therefore, good for a number of purposes.

A fine oak desk at one end, with plenty of drawers and small cabinets to provide a good stock of common reagents, as well as parchment, quills, and ink in five colors. An empty oak cabinet beside the desk, doubtless for Aefric to fill with whatever other reagents and tools he favored.

Magically, though, the research room was brilliant.

There was so much magic to this ship. Flight enchantments, after all, had been woven into every beam and board of the ship, so that every fingerwidth of it pulled its weight. And that didn't begin to include the transportation circles on every deck, the scrying of the war room and other places, and much more that he had yet to explore.

Further, this research room was an interior cabin, and so it had only minimal wards against damage from without, but included wards against sudden movement. Likely Aefric could carefully add individual grains of rackspen from a spoon to a flame with a steady hand, even while catapult shots assailed the ship.

But it was the way she'd used the *counter-wards*. Those wards that protected the rest of the ship from ... *mischance* occurring while Aefric experimented with spells.

She'd found a way to perfectly balance the forces protecting the outside from the inside with the forces protecting the inside from the outside. With the end result that this room was as magically neutral as it was possible for any cabin on a flying ship to be.

Even the smells of this room were largely absent. Hints of soap from a recent washing was all Aefric could pick out. Not even any varnish or lacquer.

Doubtless the reason he'd had to light the room by means of the Brightstaff's diamond, because even a small light spell graven into one of the ceiling boards would have spoiled the balance.

But the Brightstaff was more than up for the job, and familiar enough to be functionally neutral. And in the glow of its light, Aefric sat within that copper circle, examining the teak box, in hopes of finally puzzling through its secrets.

Some kind of power from another world, held in check. Constrained. Perhaps half-summoned, and lacking a point of connection in this world to filter its power into useful presence. A combination that had rendered the teak box apparently impervious to harm or manipulation by magic.

But the teak box itself might be the answer.

Aefric had gotten the idea from what Jenbarjen had started to say about the gold vein. She hadn't gotten to finish her explanation, but he hadn't really needed her to do so. He understood. Possibly better than she did. It was a phenomenon he'd run across before.

Once, while adventuring deep within the bowels of Mount

Ki'ek'teynah, somewhere south of Goldenmoon on the other side of the Risen Sea, he'd found a pool of strange water.

He'd expected the water to smell stagnant, but it hadn't. It had smelled fresh as a running stream. No sign of scum or other algae. Nothing swimming in it, or floating in it.

It was as though this small pool of water didn't belong there, deep within the mountain, but somewhere else entirely. A notion that had fired his imagination nearly beyond the tolerance of his adventuring partners.

Fortunately, the others were willing to camp in the cave that night, giving Aefric time with that pool. None of them were willing to drink from it, not that he'd asked them to. But they were all willing to let Aefric play with it, so long as he got his rest and didn't miss his turn on watch.

He'd summoned a watcher to handle his turn on guard duty, and devoted those hours — as well as all time before sleep — to figuring out what was strange about that pool.

Turned out not to be the water at all, but the rock bowl beneath it. The rock that formed that bowl — and perhaps as much as a stride all around it — had inherent magical properties beyond those of common rock.

Not *as* a source of power, but through an ability *to retain* power.

Unfortunately, by the time the watches were finished, everyone rested, and another meal in their bellies, Aefric was the only one who wanted to remain and spend more time studying the rock. Perhaps trying to chip away parts of it for experimentation.

The impatience of his group had made him abandon that rock bowl and its strangely fresh water. But the next time he'd seen Kainemorton, he'd pressed the great mage for anything he might know about the phenomenon.

Kainemorton, of course, parted with clear and concise knowledge the way a fog enabled clear and concise vision. But from the clues Aefric had picked up *despite* Kainemorton's manner of presentation, and based on research he'd managed here and there through the years that followed, Aefric had come to certain conclusions.

There were places in Qorunn that were natural crossing points of the planes.

Well ... no. That wasn't *quite* right. *Crossing points* implied the wrong idea. Nothing *crossed* them. It's more that those points themselves seemed to cross the worlds, in a way. They were spots that seemed to exist in multiple worlds at the same time.

Anchors, perhaps. Or nexus points. And whatever lay at one of these anchors or nexus points held more inherent magic than anything around it, which could show up in unexpected ways. Such as keeping water fresh that ought to be stagnant.

That rock pool had been such a nexus. And from the way Jenbarjen described the qualities of gold from that one vein, it was likely another. Which made sense, given that the borogs of the former Clan Blood Stone had smelled that vein from farther away than they should have.

And the teak of this box, it likely came from a tree that was a third such nexus point.

A detail that might be key.

The power constrained here was, after all, power of another world. What better natural container for it than a box fashioned from a tree that existed in more than one world?

Which meant that the box itself might be the perfect filter for the power contained in it. That this was likely the intention in constructing it in the first place — that the box itself become an item of enchantment, rather than merely a temporary means of containing this power until it was used — but something had interrupted the process. Stopped it shy of the final step that would have created the filter and turned the box into a true object of power.

All Aefric needed to do was figure out what that final step was, and how to complete it.

Yep. Made sense. That was all he needed to do.

Now. How in the name of Kalinda could he *do* it?

Sunlight. It had to have something to do with sunlight. After all, he knew that the box, when opened, *reacted* ... somehow ... to natural daytime sunlight. Therefore, natural, daytime sunlight *must* be part of the process.

But what was the *rest* of that process? How could he *complete* it? Because from the way Prince Killian had talked about it, opening the box in sunlight *without* activating seemed to be dangerous.

Which implied that it began accumulating power. Perhaps related to the way it dimmed light and sound even when Aefric was just holding it...

He looked closely at the carvings again.

Two figures, engaged in a kind of dance or ritual. Assuming for the moment that the figures did not represent a *blind*, a false lead, what *else* could they represent?

Harmony?

And above the figures, a series of symbols that *looked* like letters, but were *not*...

Glyphs?

They weren't glyphs of power in *this* world, but what about the other world? The world this power came from, it might have different magics, different glyphs.

And the *sun*. Surely the sun could be one of those nexus points between worlds. After all, how would anyone know? They had no other sun to compare it with.

Harmony. Glyphs of power from another world. The sun.

Then it hit him. What if those two figures weren't *two figures* at all, but *one figure*, rendered *twice*? In a way that represented movement in harmony...

And suddenly, Aefric had an idea of how he might solve the puzzle of the box.

Aefric finally accepted a late dinner with Beornric, Karbin, Deirdre and Jenbarjen, in the baronial dining room.

The ceiling was high enough in here to have an actual crystal chandelier dangling at a comfortable height. Not lit with candleflame, of course, but where normally candles would sit, small crystals dangled, each of which gleamed with magical candlelight, giving the room a soft, comforting glow.

The walls of the dining room were covered with paintings of landscapes depicting places in Netar. The Iron Keep. Lake Fist. The cliffside where all the baronial mines were. The Laughing Waterfall. Three different forests, none of which Aefric knew by name.

In the center of the room, a long, rectangular table made from burnished calinwood. Ornately tooled along the edges. Around it sat a dozen matching calinwood chairs.

Around that table were six others. Smaller. Round. Oak. Each with eight chairs. Aefric could host a reasonable dinner party in here, without anyone feeling too tightly packed in.

For an informal dinner like this one, Aefric would have preferred one of the smaller tables. But as this was his first dinner aboard the ship, he wanted to show appreciation for Jenbarjen's eye for detail. So he took the head of his baronial table, with Beornric and Karbin to his right, and Jenbarjen and Deirdre to his left.

For the repast, the cooks had roasted veal chops with peppers and onions, with a salad of mixed vegetables and a sweet, buttered wheat bread. Paired with a day beer, which seemed like an odd choice, but went quite well with the veal.

As they sat down to eat, Deirdre began the conversation.

"Your grace, has anyone treated your scars this evening?"

"Arras is going to handle it before I turn in." He tried a bite of the veal. Oh, he'd been unsure about the peppers and onions, but the the meat had a deliciously savory taste, with just enough bite to make each tender mouthful more interesting. And combined with the beer—

"Your lordship," Jenbarjen said, sounding hesitant. "Far be it for me to question his majesty, but—"

"But you think we're on a fool's errand," Karbin said. "I admit, the thought has occurred to me as well."

"Certainly, not the mission I would have chosen for this ship's maiden voyage," Beornric said.

Aefric swallowed his beer. Snuck another bite while the others continued their discussion.

"It's *risky*, to be sure," Deirdre said. "But you must admit that Reyvenue will never see us coming. Which will be literally true if we fly high enough."

"I'm talking about before we get to Reyvenue," Karbin said.

"I'm talking about all of it," Jenbarjen said. "Of course I wanted the *Baron's Will* to be able to defend itself, or perhaps strike at a target of opportunity, should it become necessary. But this is not intended as a warship."

"Then perhaps displaying the *war room* was the wrong choice," Beornric said gently.

"For something that's not a warship," Deirdre said, "it seems well designed for war."

"I just wanted the baron to be ready for all contingencies," Jenbarjen said, turning to Aefric. "I could imagine nothing worse than your lordship flying someplace only to be attacked from surprise. Perhaps by a wyvern or roc or dragon. Perhaps by fire from a suddenly unfriendly keep—"

"I understand," Aefric said, with a soothing gesture. "And I appreciate the thought. Further, I understand why you chose the war room. Easily accessed, and quite showy."

"But to bombard Caiperas' western forces, before turning toward Reyvenue." She shook her head. "We'll be slaughtering troops that aren't even fighting us yet."

"If they've left Malimfar," Deirdre said in a reasonable tone, "it can only be because they're marching north to see about Caer Ylfarai. Which means they're *on their way* to fight us, even if they haven't engaged us yet. They're fair targets in a time of war."

"But that's no reason to send *us* after them," Karbin said.

"I agree it's the wrong move," Beornric said. "I'd rather let Caiperas' troops march in the rain and mud. Let them forage on their own lands. Let them establish their siege, and suffer through the winter, if that's what King Makarios wants for them."

"Exactly," Karbin said. "Assaulting them from the skies accomplishes nothing but alerting the world that we have a flying warship."

"It's *not* a warship," Jenbarjen insisted.

"It is if it's used as one," Deirdre said.

"But—"

"She's right," Beornric said. "The world will *consider* it a warship, if we use it as a weapon of war."

"It's just supposed to serve the baron as transportation," Jenbarjen said plaintively.

"None of you were listening carefully enough to the king's orders," Aefric said.

"Oh, I was, your grace," Deirdre said. "I just prefer to err on the side of killing my enemies. And yours, come to think of it."

"The king was quite explicit," Karbin said. "We are to pick up Netar's soldiers from Caer Ylfarai, then fly southwest and assault any Capieran forces marching north from the Malimfar front."

"Exactly," Aefric said with a smile. "North."

"How else do you expect them to get to Caer Ylfarai," Jenbarjen asked.

"He's being clever," Beornric said, hiding a smile under his bushy mustache. "Caer Ylfarai will be *northeast* from their Malimfar front. Not north."

"Surely that's the same thing," Jenbarjen said.

"His majesty probably expects me to think so," Aefric said. "But there's an important distinction. If they march northeast, they are marching back into Caiperas, even if their eventual destination *might* be Caer Ylfarai. But if they march due north—"

"They're marching into Armyr," Beornric said. "With a potential destination of Armityr. Possibly hoping to assault our royal palace while we're looking at Caer Ylfarai. Is that it?"

"That would be my concern, if they turned north," Aefric said, spearing more veal on his fork.

"Wouldn't that be foolish, though?" Jenbarjen asked. "Where are Merrek's forces?"

"Mostly returning from a false move toward Malimfar," Aefric said. "Though I think some are probably at Caer Ylfarai, or involved in some other maneuver." He frowned. "Depends on what exactly the king wants to do in Caiperas."

"In other words," Deirdre said, "not far from intercepting any move toward Armityr. Possibly even dug in against the possibility."

"But I don't *know* that," Aefric said, gesturing with his forkful of veal. "All I know is that his majesty wants me to see what Caiperas' western forces are doing. To assault them if they turn north, and report their movements if they do not."

Aefric popped the bite into his mouth.

"Which you intend to interpret tightly," Karbin said. "Even knowing his majesty may want you to interpret it loosely."

"This is war," Beornric said. "If his majesty objects, his generals will remind him of the importance of precision in orders." He nodded. "I think we'll get away with it."

"I'm not sure we're getting away with anything," Aefric said. "I am not privy to all of his majesty's plans. He may be concerned about Caiperas' turning north toward the capital, and want us to assault and break such a march."

"And if they turn northeast?" Karbin asked.

"Then we'll follow orders. Scout them and send word back to the capital while we turn toward Reyvenue."

"So we'll still assault Reyvenue?" Beornric asked.

"I don't see any way around that," Aefric admitted.

They all considered the idea in silence for a time, as they ate.

IT WAS JENBARJEN WHO FINALLY BROKE THE SILENCE AROUND THE dinner table that night.

"How will we send word back?" she said. "About what we learn and do. Rikas? Or does your lordship have something faster in mind?"

"Funny you should ask," Aefric said with a smile. "How do you feel about shape-change magic?"

"I feel that the kindaren is the perfect shape, your lordship. For me, if not for others."

Aefric reached into his pouch for an amber, S-shaped crystal that he'd gotten from the former ducal wizard of Silverlake. He set it on the table.

"This crystal can allow the user to assume the form of a rika, and resume their own form when they choose."

Jenbarjen grimaced. "And your lordship wishes *me* to use his crystal, serving as the bird I'll look like? Even though this ship has a rookery full of rikas?"

"I imagine you'd be able to carry a great deal more information than can usually be tied to the leg of a rika," Aefric said.

Jenbarjen frowned, and ate as she thought about that. Aefric and the others indulged in more of their own dinner then, allowing the kindaren *zulim* to come to a decision.

She looked up suddenly with a bit of veal halfway to her lips.

"Your lordship will not *order* me to do this? I have free choice?"

"That's right," Aefric said. "I would like to be able to send more information back to his majesty than I can tie to the leg of a rika. But only if you're comfortable with the notion, and willing to undertake both the change and the flight."

She shook her head. "I'm sorry, your lordship. If it were the form of a crow, or a pekethrush, hells, even a pyltenius, I'd consider it. But flying over disputed territory in a form known to be used to convey messages. It just seems like asking to take an arrow."

"I understand," Aefric said, and put the crystal away.

"I'll do it," Deirdre said. "If it's important to your grace."

"Don't," Jenbarjen said. "Please don't." She set down her cutlery. "It's not that I'm afraid. I *am*, but that's not why I'm refusing."

"Go on," Aefric said.

She took a heavy slug from her goblet of beer, while Deirdre watched with a curious expression.

"Shape-change magic," Jenbarjen said, shaking her head. "I've ... I've seen it go wrong. And while I'm sure the spells on your lordship's crystal are good, the possibility of damage while in an alternate form implies risks that most don't understand."

"Theoretical risks," Karbin said.

"Everything is theory until you see it with your own eyes," Jenbarjen said.

"I'm missing something here," Aefric said. "Help me understand."

"To take the shape of a bird, and fly," she said. "People always think that the risk lies in losing yourself in the bird. But that's a misunderstanding of the real problem. Structural integrity."

"You mean beyond form and function, don't you," Karbin said softly.

"I do." Jenbarjen frowned. Finished her goblet of beer and spoke while Deirdre poured her more from a chased silver ewer. "You, your lordship, are human. And people think that implies something of your deeper nature, but it doesn't. The *essence* that poured into you at birth was not the essence of a human, but *your* essence, given human form."

"How are these not the same thing?" Deirdre asked.

"Because shape-change magic changes your *form*, but not your *essence*. Because *it doesn't need to*. If you take the shape of a housecat, then while in that shape you *are* a housecat. Your essence is you, but as you are when given feline form."

"Which is how you would not only be able to see in the dark, but also to stalk in silence, pounce, and so on without any practice," Karbin said.

"But there's *more*," Jenbarjen said. "While you are in that shape, it *is* your natural form. If you take the shape of a rika and your wing is injured, then you are a rika with an injured wing."

"But if you shift back to human," Karbin said, "or in your case, kindaren—"

"*That* is where the question comes in," Jenbarjen said. "Depending on the strength and skill of the enchanter who made that crystal, you may not *be able* to shift away from the rika form while injured."

"Why?" Deirdre asked.

"Because most of the time, such enchantments are designed to take a whole, uninjured person and give them a new whole, uninjured shape. All too often they couldn't shift a *wounded* shape into anything. They wouldn't be designed for it."

"Meaning that if you got hurt as a rika," Aefric said, "you'd be trapped in that form until healed."

"Which also suggests that if you healed *wrong* for some reason," Karbin said, "you might be *stuck* as a rika."

"There is the *possibility* that your lordship's crystal was built with a failsafe," Jenbarjen said. "If *I'd* handled the enchantment, I would have built one in. Something to approximate injuries across forms. But that takes a good deal more time, trouble and expense than a spell that only handles the hale and whole. Most wouldn't insist on it."

"I hadn't understood the risks," Aefric said.

"And there's more," Jenbarjen said. "What I was saying before about the shape-changed form being natural. If anything damages the *magic* of the shape-change — of the crystal in this case — the changed person doesn't revert. They *remain* a natural rika. Until and unless someone manages to use new shape-change magic to give them their old form."

"Assuming they even knew what that form was," Deirdre said.

"Not worth the risk," Aefric said with a sigh. "Thank you for telling me. Regular rikas will have to suffice."

"How much can you determine about that crystal through study?" Beornric asked Jenbarjen.

"If I might be forgiven for speaking bluntly," Jenbarjen said, "as I have focused my studies on enchantment for the whole of my career, I would dare say I could figure out more about the crystal than anyone else at this table."

"I wouldn't dispute that," Karbin said, shrugging one shoulder.

"Nor would I," Aefric said, pulling amber crystal back out of his pouch and passing it to her. "Find out more about its magic for me, if you would."

"Of course, your lordship," Jenbarjen said, taking the crystal.

"When you have time," Aefric said. "Don't consider this a top priority by any means."

"Thank you, your lordship," she said through a sigh. "I would dearly love to spend an aett or two catching up on my sleep."

"Well deserved, my good enchanter," Aefric said, "well deserved."

Beornric, Karbin and Deirdre all knocked the table in agreement.

DAWN THE NEXT MORNING SAW AEFRIC ALONE ON THE SIXTH AFTERDECK of the *Baron's Will*. His demon scars freshly treated by Micham and Arras, who, at his bidding, now waited one deck below while he did what he was going to do.

Aefric had bathed that morning in a copper tub that not only heated its water by magic, but both filled and emptied the same way. Not nearly as large or fancy as his tubs in either Behal or Water's End, but far better than he'd expected to find on any ship. Even *this* ship.

And his shave had been provided by a shaving mirror. Not his own hand, while looking into the mirror. No. All he'd had to do was look into the mirror and think "Clean shaven chin, cheeks and throat," and his overnight scruff was gone.

The amount of small, detailed magic Jenbarjen had added to this ship was truly staggering to think about.

After the bath, Aefric actually donned a robe that suited his morning plan. He'd worn robes at various points in his adventuring career, and he tended to choose them whenever he felt he was doing something exceptionally magical.

This robe — taken from the wardrobe in his personal stateroom — was forest green, embroidered with gold thread in the shapes of various magical symbols.

Not symbols that truly *carried* power, of course, but symbols that *represented* power. Stars with five, six, seven, eight, nine, ten and twelve points. The eleven-point star was excluded, of course, for its association with demonolatry. But triangles were included, and small representations of the major constellations.

He stood now on that sixth afterdeck. Facing west within the embedded silver circle, which he'd activated with the right pulse of power and the right words. He shivered a little from the morning chill, and still more from excitement.

Before him in the circle, the teak box sat on the deck. Closed. On the other side of the box, a full-length mirror stood steady, aided by a touch of Aefric's magic.

The first rays of the sun crested a gap between peaks of the Ulbardellis Mountains, which surrounded the *Baron's Will* that morning, as it flew swiftly and surely above the Pass of Dayor Ol'Tain, which led to Caer Ylfarai.

As those first rays of sun reflected back at him and the box through the mirror, he began.

First, he mimicked the poses depicted on the box front, seeing the way his own reflection took the role of the second dancer or ritualist.

He felt a slight hum of response from the power in the box.

So far, so good.

Once the poses were complete, he sank cross-legged into a sitting position, looked at the box.

One by one, left to right, he went through those symbols on the front of the box that were not letters. He sketched each of them in the air in bright red power. First, from left to right in the same order, exactly as they were depicted.

Then, below that first row, he repeated the symbols in dim green power. But this time, he reversed them, both in order and in shape. From right to left he worked, reproducing those symbols they would be seen in a mirror, if the box were held up to it.

In the air before him, red symbols as they were on the box above green symbols that were backwards. And in the mirror, the line of red glyphs looked like cross-color twins of the floating line of green glyphs, while the reflected green glyphs had the shapes of the floating red glyphs.

Once certain he had both lines correct both before him and in the mirror, Aefric picked up the box in both hands. Slowly, carefully, he lifted it up, so that he held it between both lines of glyphs and their reflections. Allowing him to only just see his own eyes over the top of the teak box.

He turned the box, so that its front faced the mirror.

He opened the box.

Within the circle, the sunlight darkened back to predawn gloom. Even though, all around the circle, Aefric could see the deck brightening every second.

Chanting. He heard chanting now. Low and distant, but seeming to come from everywhere at once.

"Zula ne, nula nee. Xilka besa xilka besa. Ohn nu a simak."

Over and over those words. In many voices. Never getting louder, but not fading either.

And within the teak box, the constrained power bucked. Bulged.

And not just there in the box. Aefric could feel those bucks and bulges in his head.

Each one of them hurt. The bucks felt like taking a mace to the skull. And the bulges, like his skull was being stretched like limbs on a rack. A comparison Aefric wished he could only make theoretically, but knew all too well.

The power. It was fighting him. Struggling.

No. Not fighting. Not struggling. Failing. Or perhaps flailing.

More bucks. More swells. Pain laced each breath, but he held his focus on those glyphs. Because unless he was mistaken, they were glowing brighter now. The only things within this circle that were, because everything else was darkening now towards midnight.

"Zula ne, nula nee. Xilka besa xilka besa. Ohn nu a simak," the chanting continued. Dozens of voices now, but never any louder.

Clearly, something was wrong. Was some part of this incomplete?

He grunted, wincing against another round of bucks and bulges from the power.

The contained power within the box was acting as though it were trying to complete itself, but somehow couldn't.

Aefric *had* to be missing something. Some key piece of the ritual. But what?

Had he gotten the colors wrong? They were a guess. Were the

glyphs off in some way? Was the image on the box the mirror version, and therefore he'd gotten both lines backwards?

"Zula ne, nula nee. Xilka besa xilka besa. Ohn nu a simak."

A hundred voices now. Men and women. All of them chanting...

The chant? Did he need to chant too?

Desperate, for each buck and bulge came searing through his head now, he tried.

"Zula ne, nula nee. Xilka besa xilka besa. Ohn nu a simak," he tried, repeating the chant in the fivefold rhythm the voices seemed to follow.

But the bucks and bulges continued. Beating at his psyche. His vision developed strange tendrils of pure blackness...

Wait!

The mirror. Reflections. What if the chant was backwards? Had to be revered in *this* world?

He listened through one more round, girding against the pain he endured while those black tendrils thickened. His heart beat now as though it were the only set of wings trying to keep this whole airship afloat.

He licked his sandy lips with a dry tongue, and did his best.

"Kahmees haa oon noh. Aseb aklix aseb aklix. Een aloon, ehn alooz."

Three repetitions, fighting to keep his voice strong through the pain of another round of bucks and bulges.

Five repetitions, and now those tendrils that thickened into branches.

Nine repetitions...

It wasn't working! But what else could he do?

Aefric kept going. Focused everything he had past the pain and into the words whose meaning he couldn't guess at.

On the fifteenth total repetition, everything stopped.

He noticed the missing pain first. Like sweet relief through his head. His heart lurched, and he gasped against the expectation of pain not felt.

He blinked a few times, but sure enough, those thick black

branches were gone from his vision. Not even tendrils remained. And the light inside the circle — the now-unpowered circle — was bright as the deck around it. And the glyphs...

The glyphs in the air...

Wait.

The glyphs *in the air* were gone, but the glyphs *in the mirror* remained.

And the teak box sat closed on the deck between Aefric and his reflection. Somewhere behind his reflection, an orange cat swished past.

Aefric's reflection smiled.

Aefric raised his eyebrows. His reflection didn't. But it did wink at him—

Suddenly it was just a reflection. Eyebrows high. No glyphs in front of it.

Aefric managed to lower the mirror gently to the deck before collapsing backwards in a sweaty heap.

Arras and Micham were there in an instant, checking for threats. Beornric, Deirdre, Karbin and Jenbarjen followed only steps behind.

"I do wish you'd *warn* me before you do something stupid," Karbin said.

"That'd leave him time in his day to do nothing else," Beornric said wryly.

"What the hells *was* that?" Jenbarjen demanded. "I haven't felt that kind of power surge ... *ever!*"

Deirdre eased Aefric's head off the deck and gave him a trickle of water from a waterskin while Karbin said something to Jenbarjen about power surges.

Aefric managed to drink the water without coughing. Smiled weakly at Deirdre.

"Thank you," he said.

"Always happy to help, your grace," Deirdre said with a smile. "Can you stand?"

"I think so." He reached out. The Brightstaff leapt into his hand. Between Deirdre and the staff, he was standing in a moment. He managed a deep breath, and tried something. He tried to bring the teak box to his hand with magic.

He smiled, as the teak box came to his hand.

<hr>

THE DECKHOUSE AT THE BACK OF THE SIXTH DECK WAS REALLY QUITE nice. A pleasant place to relax, after talking with the commanders at Caer Ylfarai and starting the process of taking Netar's troops aboard the *Baron's Will*.

The deckhouse had well-padded, comfortable chairs and couches. Tables that were the perfect height and shape for playing cards, or dice, or chess. Plenty of drawers and cabinets to hold almost anything Aefric could have asked for in a place to pass time while sailing the skies.

True, not quite as nice as his formal lounge a few decks down, but still. It was comfortable. The artwork on the walls involved pleasant depictions of scenes from Armyrian folktales. Shondi meeting Kheldran at Chhor. The race against the Withered Sprite. The eight suitors of Countess Idrina. And more. All done in soft watercolors.

The full-length mirror that Aefric had used in his ritual had been replaced on its hooks on one wall.

And, of course, a trapdoor led to stairs down into the belly of the ship.

Arras and Micham stood guard outside the main door.

Aefric lounged on one couch, while Deirdre matched him in a chair at the end of the coffee table. Karbin and Jenbarjen both sat straight on the couch facing Aefric, looking concerned.

Beornric sat casually in a chair opposite Deirdre, but Aefric could tell that he was as concerned as Karbin and Jenbarjen, even if he was trying to hide it.

On the coffee table, a bottle of dark green sharabi scented the air with peppermint. Five goblets had poured, but so far only Deirdre had touched hers.

In the center of the table sat the teak box.

Karbin and Jenbarjen seemed to take turns looking from Aefric to the box and back.

"Why don't you two vary your colors more?" Aefric asked. "You both always choose the same scheme. Why don't you try a dark red, Karbin? Or a strong purple? And Jenbarjen, what's wrong with a good burnt orange?"

"Tradition," Jenbarjen said.

"And it helps with recognition. Both when seeking it, and when avoiding it," Karbin said, breezing through his words. "Which I'd taught you long ago, even if the lesson never took."

"The only lessons that take with this one," Beornric said, "are the ones he likes."

"And I suppose you'd have me pick one style and stick with it?" Aefric asked Beornric. "You know as well as I do that if I wore the same clothes to dinner two days in a row, my court would talk of nothing else for an aett."

"Oh, they'd talk of plenty of other things as well," Beornric said. "But you're right. It would remain a common topic."

"I'm not interested in talking about clothes," Karbin said.

"Never thought you were," Aefric said, nodding. He looked over at Deirdre. "Then again, neither was I."

She snickered, and Aefric smiled.

"Is he drunk?" Jenbarjen asked Karbin softly.

"No," Karbin said, loudly and still looking at Aefric. "He's exhausted. Because he did something needless, risky and arguably stupid while recovering from demon scars."

Jenbarjen hissed in a breath, though Aefric wasn't sure she was reacting to the demon scars, or just to Karbin addressing his liege that way.

"To be fair," Beornric said, "the demon scars likely didn't influence him. He does risky, stupid things often enough that Yrsa—"

"All right," Aefric said. "Point made."

"The demon scars *do* complicate matters, though," Karbin said, before letting his tone grow wry. "I'd ask if you've been at least having them properly treated, but you wouldn't be so exhausted if you hadn't."

"I knew I could handle what I needed to do."

"Oh?" Karbin said. "And tell me, did you see the black tendrils?"

Aefric frowned.

"That's a yes," Karbin said to Jenbarjen before turning back to Aefric. "And did they thicken? Into branches? Trunks, perhaps?"

Aefric winced and admitted, "A few thickened into branches."

"Do you know why that happened?"

"No," Jenbarjen said, but Karbin was looking sharply at Aefric. And Deirdre was sitting up.

"Why?" Beornric asked, watching Aefric sharply as well.

"I need to know if *he* knows," Karbin said.

Aefric's nostrils flared in a long, slow breath. "Well, I don't *know*. But if I had to guess — based on your tone — that was the demon's corruption trying to seize me in a moment of weakness."

"I swear," Karbin grumbled, "even as my apprentice you learned more from my tone than you ever learned from me." Louder, he continued, "That's *exactly* what that was. And you just ensured several more days of treatment before the corruption is gone completely. Possibly an aett. Perhaps even a season."

"A *season*?" Deirdre said, shocked.

"Couldn't tell you for certain," Karbin said, one eyebrow high. "I'm not a cleric of Nilasah. And, of course, we don't have one aboard, do we."

"Do we?" Aefric asked hopefully. After all, the ship seemed to have everything else.

Jenbarjen shook her head.

"Well," Karbin said. "Then until we get back to one, I hope there's enough ointment in that jar."

"There should be," Aefric said. "I don't think Bebara trusts me."

"I'd worry more that she *knows* you," Beornric said.

"Well I, for one, think she trusts you *entirely*," Karbin said. "I think she trusts you to overextend yourself, as you do all too often."

Jenbarjen frowned at Aefric, perhaps drawing fresh conclusions about her new liege.

"Fine," Aefric said, raising one hand in surrender. And the truth was, he did feel tired. Just talking to the commander down below had felt *exhausting*. "You're all right. I probably should have waited. But I've been carrying that box and its temptingly incomplete magic around since before we went after Nelazzi, and I *finally* figured out how to unlock its powers. You couldn't ask me not to try to."

"It's scrying magic," Jenbarjen said. "Powerful stuff. And there's a second component, I think. Couldn't be sure, though, and I couldn't tell you the extent or nature of its scrying. Not without time and access to the box."

"You've *barely seen* it," Aefric said. "How could you even tell *that* much?"

"Enchantments are what I do," she said, shrugging one shoulder. "And that box is *powerful*. Of course I did what I could to figure out how it worked the moment I saw it."

"And have you learned more while we've been talking?"

"No, to be honest." Jenbarjen frowned. "And I should have. Something about that box makes it hard to focus on. Magically, I mean."

"Perhaps she should examine it more thoroughly," Beornric said softly.

"She should or I should," Karbin said. "You're in no shape to do so, Aefric."

"Which means Jenbarjen should," Deirdre said, then frowned. "I'm sorry, Karbin. You know how highly I esteem you—"

"No," Karbin said, "you're right. This is enchantment, her specialty. She should be the one to investigate its powers."

Aefric sat back against the couch. Shook his head.

"Do you have *any* idea how long and hard I've worked to figure out that box? To solve its puzzles and complete its enchantment? And you expect me just to let someone else take over?"

"Thick. Black. Tendrils," Karbin said flatly. "You've already seen them form branches. Next time, it'll be trunks. And then—"

"*All right,*" Aefric snapped. "But you'll study it together—"

"Your lordship," Jenbarjen said, "I really do work best alone."

"That may be," Aefric said, "but the teak box involves magic from other worlds. Cross-planar stuff."

"All the same, your lordship," Jenbarjen started, but Aefric cut her off with a gesture.

"This is not a debate. I freely admit that I would normally take the risks involved in investigating the box on my own. But since you all seem to feel that's a bad idea..."

He looked about. No one contradicted him. Not even Deirdre.

"...then I should listen to my advisers and delegate the task. And I don't feel comfortable asking *one* person to take the risks involved in puzzling through its cross-planar magics unless someone else is present to anchor and assist, if needed. Especially when the person I'd be assigning has been working too hard for a very long time herself."

He picked up the box.

"So it's either the two of you together, checking each other as you go, or I'll do it myself and damn the risks. What will it be?"

"I'm sure it will be a pleasure to work with you," Jenbarjen said to Karbin, who chuckled.

"I do love to watch an artist work," he said in return.

"Excellent," Aefric said, and passed them the box.

OH, THE JOYS OF A BIG, COMFORTABLE BED WITH SILK SHEETS, WHEN one is tired beyond reason. Aefric had only planned a brief nap. No more than shutting his eyes for perhaps one bell, before getting up and investigating more of the secrets of his new airship.

But he was fast asleep the moment his head hit that soft, soft pillow. The smell of lavender in the air, making him think of wild flowers...

The dream was simple enough, if not one he'd had recently.

He was Keifer again, dressed in cargo shorts and a Columbia

Sportswear shirt, hiking along the slopes and trails of Forest Park, back in Portland, Oregon. On Earth.

It was a hot, muggy day. September kind of weather. Still hints of the worst of the summer heat. The skies above *contemplated* rain, but weren't sure they wanted to put forth the effort.

The kind of day when the explosion of lush ferns all around the trail overpowered even the armies of Douglas firs with their scent.

This wasn't a memory. Couldn't have been. He was the only one on the trails. No middle-aged people with floppy hats and hiking poles getting their daily exercise. No business types trying to work off an indulgent lunch before heading back to the office. Not even any joggers or mountain bikers, attacking the trail with the zeal of a fanatic.

Just Aefric. Or rather, just Keifer.

And he was looking for something. Or someone. Whichever it was would be just around the next bend. Or the next one. Or the...

He rounded the wrong bend, and found the Witch's Castle.

The Witch's Castle shouldn't have been right around *any* bend. It was normally just sitting to the side of a long curve on the slope up the hill, beside a branch of the trail that went more sharply up the hill another direction.

It wasn't really a castle, of course. And likely a witch had never lived there. But that was what everyone Keifer knew called it. Mostly it looked like a half-built house. A concrete frame, with stairs, and a few standing walls and doorways and windows. Iron rails added to keep the foolish from hurting themselves. A single enclosed room on the lower level — well, as enclosed as it *could* be without a door — overflowing with graffiti.

The structure always looked sad to Keifer. Forlorn. As though standing vigil, waiting for its people to return, while time slowly wore it away.

He looked back down the trail behind him. Now it was the trail that led to that turnout and parking lot. The proper trail to see, standing beside the Witch's Castle. But a moment ago, he was sure he'd been hiking another trail, one that led up to the Pittock Mansion.

But that didn't make sense.

Then he remembered he was dreaming. Which, in theory, should've meant he could control the dream. But that had never worked right for him. Not as Keifer, and apparently not now, as Aefric. Not without magic.

So why was he here? He felt a seeking urge. That he was looking for something or someone, and—

There. Movement. At the top of the moss-covered stone steps, just inside the second story doorway of the Witch's Castle.

Was that a face?

Aefric — no, he was Keifer in the dream. Less muscled, and dressed in clothes that had never been seen in Qorunn. *Keifer* started cautiously for the stairs.

After all, that he was looking for something or someone, didn't mean that thing or person would be safe to find. And it didn't mean that he had no competition in the search.

A woodpecker alighted his shoulder. Not just a dark red crest on that woodpecker, but a crest that seemed to trail down the bird's back, splitting the maroon plumage.

The woodpecker leaned in and started pecking at his collarbone...

AEFRIC AWOKE IN HIS GRAND BED ABOARD THE *BARON'S WILL*, TO FIND Deirdre in her maroon leathers, tapping one finger on his collarbone.

"Of course you're the woodpecker," he said, chuckling up at her. "I should've known."

"I have to say," Deirdre said, crossing her arms, "I'm not sure how to feel about this. I mean, if I'm *going* to appear in your dreams—"

"Oh, hush," he said, sitting up and stretching as the sheets and blanket fell to his waist. "We both know it was just the way your tapping showed up in the dream before I woke."

She'd activated the room's magic lights, small crystals set into the tops of small candles that did their job pleasantly.

She sat cross-legged beside him. Easy to do, because the bed was large enough to comfortably sleep four. Which *did* make it smaller than his beds in either Water's End or Behal or Kivash — or his hunting cabin, come to think of it — but it was still larger than he had any right to expect aboard a ship.

And infinitely superior to sleeping in a rough, rope hammock again. Which Deirdre seemed to be contemplating, as she ran her fingers across the silk sheets.

Apart from the bed and its gilt frame, there was little else in this room of his cabin suite. A pair of matching oak nightstands, the closer of which held a silver ewer of water and a pair of goblets. Doors led to a privy, his clothes closet, and his salon.

The Brightstaff, of course, stood beside the bed. Waiting for him.

As Aefric filled his lungs with a deep, lavender-scented breath, his stomach growled loud enough that Deirdre should've chuckled. Or snickered, perhaps.

She did neither. She was looking at his demon scars.

"Should we apply more of the ointment?" she asked.

"Not until tonight," he said with a shake of his head. "Bebara was quite clear. Twice a day and no more. Once in the morning, once at night."

She frowned, but nodded.

"Looking for an excuse to fondle me?" he teased.

"Always," she said, with a ghost of her normal smile. "But concerned about this tendril-trunk business. If the wounds are worse, perhaps the treatment—"

"I don't think so," Aefric said. "As Karbin and Beornric both pointed out rather roughly, Bebara knows what to expect from me. Which means she likely knew I'd overextend myself, which means—"

"—she'd've given you instructions for what to do if, or rather *when*, you did."

"Exactly," Aefric said.

"Unless she was afraid that would just encourage you."

Aefric furrowed his brow as he considered that. Shook his head. "No. She'd prepare me for the contingency anyway."

"Or at least she'd tell Beornric," Deirdre agreed. "Speaking of whom. I awoke you because he figured you'd be hungry."

Aefric's empty stomach rumbled again.

"Oh. Yeah," he said. "Forgot to have breakfast this morning, didn't I?"

"Your grace must keep his strength up," Deirdre said with something closer to her normal smile.

"I should get dressed then."

Her smile broadened. "Would your grace care for any *assistance* with this?"

"Actually," Aefric said with a smile, "there are magical valets in the closet, for when I don't have body servants along."

She snorted a laugh. "Of course there are."

Naked, Aefric got out of bed and took the Brightstaff in hand.

"Probably for the best," Deirdre said, watching him with a sigh. "Enough people think I'm a corrupting influence without getting demon corruption involved."

He chuckled as he went to his closet.

"Your grace?" Deirdre asked, before he left the room.

"Yes?"

"What did you dream about? Anything interesting?"

"I dreamed I was looking for something," he said, frowning. "But I didn't know what."

"Then perhaps you'd already found it," she said. "You just hadn't realized it."

"That ... makes a kind of sense."

"I make all kinds of sense," Deirdre said with a bow. "To those with the wit to listen."

"Then I guess it says something good about me that I listen to you."

"I've always thought so."

Aefric laughed as he walked into his closet then, where he was surrounded by racks and racks of clothing and accessories.

"Valets," he said, and three ghostly young women appeared. All human in appearance, all clad in Netar colors, and all would be beautiful if they were less transparent.

They weren't ghosts, of course. They were illusory manifestations that accompanied the closet's ability to move clothes about and dress him. There was no reason they needed to be young women, or beautiful, except that Jenbarjen probably assumed he'd prefer that.

They were silent, of course. They didn't speak. To convey questions, they would hold something up and raise their eyebrows. For example, one immediately raised her eyebrows and held up a silver comb, and when he nodded she started combing out his hair.

To the other two, he said, "Silk shirt and hose, dark blue over dark orange. Maybe some silver trim in the shirt. Dark leather for the belt and boots, and I'll need my noble's dagger, my black velvet belt pouch, and the wand Garram in its sheath."

They dressed him with quick efficiency. The boots were low and soft, hardly reaching much past his ankles. Dyed calfskin, he thought, like the belt. The shirt had subtle silver trim at the cuffs and collar, and a line up the outside of his sleeves.

One of illusory valets held up a bycocket hat — dark blue with dark orange for the turned-up brim — and raised her eyebrows, but he shook his head. She put the hat away.

Thus clad, he and Deirdre returned to his dining room through wide wooden halls, decorated with paintings of hunting scenes.

Along the way, he asked her, "Where are Arras and Micham?"

"Resting. I told them I would handle your guard until evening, and Beornric approved."

"Thank you," he said. "If I'd known this would be a longer trip—"

"They know, your grace."

"Everything go all right with getting the soldiers aboard?"

"Aboard and berthed. And we're on our way southwest toward the Caiperas-Malimfar front. The captain has planned the route and speed so that we arrive after dawn tomorrow, taking full advantage of our paint for concealment as we scout."

"Good."

They reached the dining room, but before Aefric could reach for the door handle, Deirdre stopped him.

"I know one of your goals is to spend as few lives as you can in this conflict, your grace," she said softly. "It's commendable. But please keep in mind that the best way to save the most lives and prevent the most suffering is to bring this war to a speedy conclusion. Even if it means a skyborne ambush, where you must order the slaughter of hundreds or even thousands of enemy soldiers."

"There has to be a way to bring about that speedy conclusion *without* that slaughter," Aefric said. "And I'm going to find it."

"Then I wish your grace better luck than he had in his dream."

"In the dream you were the woodpecker waking me," he said with a half-smile. "But in *this* world, you're one of the greatest allies I could have. I'd say I have the advantage, now that I'm awake."

Deirdre's only answer to that was a small smile, but something fierce burned in her jade eyes.

BEORNRIC, KARBIN AND JENBARJEN WERE ALREADY IN THE DINING ROOM when Aefric and Deirdre entered. Dressed about the way they always were, especially lately. Beornric in his full plate, and the other two in their preferred colors. There was a sweet, herbal scent to the air, but nothing that suggested what lunch would be.

Karbin held the teak box, and he and Jenbarjen were discussing something about it in low tones, while Beornric watched, frowning.

Beornric was the first to notice Aefric, but before offering a greeting, he said something that made Karbin and Jenbarjen look up.

"If I didn't know better," Aefric said, "I'd say the three of you look guilty. What do you think, Deirdre?"

"I'd definitely say they're guilty of *something*, your grace."

"I take it there's trouble?" he asked.

"I'm not sure *trouble* is the right word," Beornric said.

"*I* am," Jenbarjen said. She smacked the teak box with the back of her hand. "Your lordship's new object of power *refuses* me."

"You make it sound as though it has a choice," Karbin said.

"And you're telling me you don't think it does." Anger made her seem much taller than her diminutive stature. Not easy to match tones with someone twice your height. "Which of us is the specialist here?"

"I may not be a specialist in enchantment," Karbin said, starting to heat up himself. "But I *have* seen intelligent items before. Swords that think, and can express those thoughts. Wands that have opinions about the right spell for a given situation." He tapped the box. "I sense no such mind in this."

"*But the evidence is plain,*" Jenbarjen insisted. "This box *actively evades* my attempts to investigate its powers."

"Yes, but—"

"*And yours,*" she added. "Don't you *dare* try to deny it. You've accomplished no more than I have. Less, even."

"I *don't* deny that," Karbin said. "What I *deny* is the conclusion you *insist* on."

"Stop," Aefric said, raising a halting hand. "Begin at the beginning."

"I'm pretty sure we're there already," Beornric said, frowning at Aefric. "Or at least, this is where *I* came into the conversation."

"Then begin *before* the beginning," Aefric said. He reached out his hand and the box leapt from Karbin's grasp to his own, while both court wizards watched, frowning. "How did this dispute begin?"

"We established ground rules for how to investigate," Jenbarjen said. "I trust that your lordship is familiar with the *proper* methods for investigating enchantment, not merely the adventurers' shortcut?"

"I taught him the method myself," Karbin said impatiently.

"Well, despite this handicap," Jenbarjen said, "did your lordship *learn* it?"

"*Enough,*" Aefric said sharply. "I won't stand here and listen to you fling insults at each other."

"Oh, I don't know," Deirdre began, but stopped when Aefric frowned at her.

"Right," he said. "Begin again. Stick to *facts*, not insults."

"I was to take the first turn probing the magics of the teak box," Jenbarjen said. "Karbin was to observe and be ready to render aid, if needed."

"Did you use a circle?"

"Yes," she said. "I designed a small magic room for myself, off of my own stateroom, for when I travel aboard the ship. I used the circle there."

"Go on."

"Now," she said, "I don't know how long it takes your lordship to explore the magic of an enchantment, but it doesn't take me long at all. I wouldn't say I'm *quite* as fast as the famous shortcut, but I come close. Normally."

"Normally?"

"Well, I don't work with planar magics much," she said, stroking her chin with one finger. "So I wanted to go slowly — for me — and make sure I didn't miss anything."

"But it evaded you?" Deirdre said.

"Exactly!" She smacked her palm with the back of her hand. "I had no trouble working my way *to* the teak box through the native magics of Qorunn. But when I tried to move my awareness *into* the box and its magics, it was as though they weren't there. More like ... sort of ... off to one side. As though I'd somehow ... missed."

"But," Aefric said, "that's not how it works."

"No," she agreed. "It *isn't*. Or it *shouldn't* be. But it seemed as though my every attempt to explore the magics of that teak box, well, *missed*."

"Missed," Aefric said.

"Missed," Karbin agreed. "She tried for a while, then had me try. I experienced almost the same thing."

"Almost?"

"I didn't ... *miss*, so much as fail to penetrate the outer layer of the box's magic."

"That shouldn't be possible either," Aefric said.

"No," Karbin said.

"Not unless some force within the box is *aware*," Jenbarjen insisted, "and *actively* resisting our investigation."

"There's another answer," Karbin said, and Jenbarjen growled.

"What?" Aefric asked.

"Lunacy," Jenbarjen said.

"No," Karbin said, gritting his teeth. He forced a quick, deep breath before continuing. "I posit that the teak box is a unique item, and bonded. Therefore, its magics *cannot* be explored by *any*. Except for the one it bonded to."

"Fairy tales," Jenbarjen said. "An item is only *unique* until a clever enchanter *duplicates* it. It's not some kind of grand, metaphysical statement of individuality."

"You say that," Karbin said, "but we're in the presence of a unique item right now."

"Circular logic," Jenbarjen said. "The teak box is unique because—"

"Not the teak box," Karbin said. "The Brightstaff."

"Legendary, certainly," Jenbarjen said, frowning at the object in question. "Unique, I'll grant only because I've never heard of anyone creating another. But if your lordship would let me study it, I imagine I could do so easily enough."

"If you'd please, your grace," Karbin said.

Aefric willed the Brightstaff to accept Jenbarjen's touch, and handed it to her.

"I don't have a circle," she said.

"A cursory investigation should be enough to prove me right or wrong," Karbin said.

She held the Brightstaff up. Closed her eyes.

Aefric counted five breaths while he waited.

Ten.

Fifteen.

"Well?" Karbin asked. "Surely by now you've completed a cursory—"

"It denies me too," Jenbarjen said, throwing the Brightstaff back at Aefric, who caught it easily with his free hand. She sighed and ran her hands over her face and gently slapped both cheeks several times. "I've *never* experienced this before, and now *twice in one day*?"

"Twice for the same reason," Karbin said. "Unique items."

"Unique," Aefric said, looking from the Brightstaff to the teak box and back. "Or perhaps made from a nexus point."

"A what?" Jenbarjen asked.

"Let's all take our seats and send for lunch," Aefric said. "This will require some explaining."

Lunch was a chowder of some kind of river fish, with potatoes and another root vegetable Aefric couldn't name. It was a good meal, though, served with day beer, rolls of honeyed oat bread, and a sweet rhubarb pie to follow.

And it took all through lunch for Aefric to explain to the others about the pool of strangely fresh water he'd found while adventuring. About the questions it had led to, and the investigations that had followed through the years, and finally what it had led him to suspect about the teak of the teak box, and perhaps even the sun itself.

When he finally finished — and Beornric was done with his second slice of rhubarb pie — Aefric looked around the dining table at the others. Karbin and Jenbarjen were clearly thinking hard. Beornric looked as though he were considering some kind of potential ramifications that had nothing to do with magic.

Only Deirdre looked relaxed. And she was the one to speak first.

"Makes sense to me," she said. "I think that great skeleton in the Dragonscar is the same kind of thing. A nexus. I think the dragon was in life, and his skeleton remains so in death."

"Why do you think so?" Karbin asked.

"Tried to carve my name on it once," she said, getting an of-course-you-did expression from Beornric. "Only time I've ever actually *ruined* a magic dagger. I mean, I've damaged a few—"

"It's not exactly *easy* to damage a magic weapon," Jenbarjen said, looking offended at the mere thought.

"I said only a *few*," Deirdre said, then turned back to Karbin and Aefric. "But when I tried hard to carve my name into a rib bone, and I mean using a couple of dweomerblade tricks, the attempt not only failed. It *wrecked* that dagger."

She sighed. "Took me *forever* to find a replacement. I loved that dagger."

"Clearly not enough," Jenbarjen said.

"That may not be proof," Karbin said. "Though I won't deny the possibility." He shook his head through a deep, heavy breath. "Leave it to Kainemorton to know something like this and keep it to himself."

"He's probably told the Silver Arrows all about it," Aefric said. "Though he made *me* piece it together, of course."

"Of *course*," Karbin said. "All right. Your conclusion about the teak box makes *logical* sense. Which means, coming from you, I have to treat it as suspect."

"That's hardly fair," Jenbarjen said.

"You don't know his grace like I do," Karbin said. "When it comes to magic, he and logic have only a passing acquaintance."

"I thought your lordship was a wizard," Jenbarjen said.

"It's complicated," Aefric said. "But my logic is often sound, even if it doesn't suit a theoretical structure that pleases my old mentor here."

"If by that," Karbin said, "you mean any theoretical structure with a sound basis and consistent construction, I agree."

"Doesn't really matter, does it?" Deirdre said, and everyone turned to look at her. "Nexus points. Unique items. They're just words. They aren't experiences."

"You don't understand," Karbin began, but Deirdre raised a hand to stop him.

"I do," she said. "I just don't agree that the point has value right now. Suppose the teak box and the Brightstaff are both some kind of nexus point or unique item. All right? Everyone got that in mind?"

She actually paused, until each of them gave her a nod, even if a couple of those nods were suspicious.

"Now, imagine they're not. That they're something else entirely. Something we don't have the vocabulary for. Now. How does the difference between these two possibilities help you? How does thinking of the box as a nexus point help you understand it in ways that you *wouldn't* understand it if it's something else?"

"I'm not sure I follow," Jenbarjen said. "I mean, if nexus points exist—"

"They do," Aefric said.

"Then understanding what they are could—"

"Could! Might! Possibly!" Deirdre shook her head in exasperation. "Wizards. I swear. You'll all think yourselves to *death*!"

"Where are you going with this?" Beornric asked.

"What do we know for sure?" she asked. "Experientially. Not theoretically."

Aefric opened his mouth, but Deirdre said softly, "Please, your grace. Let's see if the wizards can understand a foreign viewpoint."

"Well *that's* hardly fair," Karbin said.

"I think it is," Deirdre said. "You wizards think yourselves the masters of magic because you have the broadest array of powers, and theoretical explanations for everything under the heavens. But *I* can do things with magic that not *one* of you can do, no matter how many years you waste in study trying."

"Because you're born to it," Jenbarjen said. "All dweomerblades are."

"And you wizards think that has to do with our bloodlines or something." She shook her head. "It doesn't." She tapped her gut. "*Here* is the source of our magic. Instinct. Intuition. *Experience*. Not theory."

"All right, Deirdre," Karbin said. "Enough lecture then. What do you see that you think *we* don't?"

"You're looking for causes and logical consistency," she said. "When *experience* tells us what we most need to know."

"But how?" Jenbarjen said.

"The teak box eludes you the way the Brightstaff eludes you. And yet his grace commands the Brightstaff completely. Therefore…"

"He should be able to command the teak box completely," Karbin said. "But that wasn't in question. Of course he can. I don't see how this helps."

"Because you don't command the Brightstaff," Aefric said. "It's not like the wand Garram, or any other enchanted item I've ever possessed. It may not have a mind the way a talking sword does, but it certainly does act on its own from time to time. For example, the way it will follow me about, even when I'm unconscious."

"Which *could* indicate a sign of a specific enchantment within it," Karbin said, "not a mind."

"Which, experientially, makes no difference," Deirdre said.

"There's something else, too," Aefric said. "I've never needed to probe the Brightstaff's magics to understand it."

"Ridiculous," Jenbarjen said.

"No," Karbin said. "I think he's telling the truth. I was at that battle, when he acquired it. When the lich Nez'karak blasted him out of the chamber, Aefric was still clinging to his old staff. But when he came back into the fight, he was wielding the Brightstaff, and flinging white fire and lighting as though he'd been born with it in his hand."

"I'd had to *earn* the Brightstaff," Aefric said. "Through the test of its white fire. And once it accepted me, it offered up its powers freely."

"But the teak box didn't test you," Jenbarjen said. "It was just an incomplete enchantment. You said so yourself."

"Perhaps," Aefric said. "That was certainly how I thought of it at the time. But maybe I've been looking for answers that have been in front of me all along."

Deirdre gave Aefric a back-and-forth nod that said she'd accept this as a valid interpretation of his dream as well, which made him smile. If briefly.

Aefric picked up the teak box and wondered how to use it.

And just like that, the answers came to him.

It was all so simple — so *obvious* — he laughed. He couldn't help it.

"It *is* a scrying device," he said. "*And* a transportation device. It uses planar magics, and thus evades most kinds of wards that don't specifically guard against planar angles. And it can bring me to whatever place I scry."

"How does it work?" Jenbarjen asked.

"I can show you," Aefric said with a smile. "And I know just whom to scry on."

AEFRIC EMERGED THROUGH THE TRAPDOOR IN THE FLOOR, TAKING THOSE final few stairs into the deckhouse. Through the windows it looked as though it should've been raining, but rain didn't seem to reach the sixth afterdeck. He could see it falling hard and fast beyond the rails outside though.

Aefric stood, waiting while Deirdre followed him into the deckhouse, preceding Karbin, Jenbarjen and Beornric.

Excitement percolated in Aefric's belly. If this worked, it represented not only an amazing power, but a fantastic means of taking care of something that definitely needed doing.

But he needed an answer to something else first.

"I've been meaning to ask," Aefric said, once the others were all in the deckhouse. "Why a trapdoor and stairs there, instead of a transportation circle?"

"Two reasons," Jenbarjen answered. "First, it wasn't cost-effective to have those circles *everywhere*. Second, on the off-chance that something antimagical hit the deckhouse, I didn't want your lordship to be trapped here."

"Now *that*," Deirdre said, looking at Karbin but pointing at Jenbarjen, "is sound logic."

"Thank you," Jenbarjen said, sounding more pleased than Aefric expected.

He led them over to the mirror he'd used for his ritual that morning, and they gathered around.

"Now," he said, taking the teak box back out of his belt pouch. "It works like this. I think of a mirror I know, or a person I want to contact, and I open the box. The mirror here becomes a window to that place, or that person."

"What if that person isn't in front of a mirror?" Deirdre asked, and Jenbarjen nodded as though it were her question too.

"I'm pretty sure it just finds the mirror nearest the person in question. Which wouldn't be much help if they were in a dungeon."

He smiled at them. "Or *would* it?"

"It wouldn't," Jenbarjen said. "I've never heard of a dungeon anywhere that had mirrors for the prisoners."

"He's setting something up," Beornric told her.

"Transportation," Karbin said. "It doesn't just make the mirror a window. It makes it a *portal*."

"Just so," Aefric said. "The bearer can pass through the mirror to the destination shown. Or, if he wills it, he can allow someone else to pass through."

"How many someones?" Deirdre asked.

"Not sure," Aefric said, "but it feels open-ended. As long as the bearer wills the portal to work for others, and keeps the box lid open."

"Assume that's right for now then," Karbin said. "What do you have in mind?"

"Duchess Ashling," Beornric said. "You want to contact Duchess Ashling, don't you?"

"Of course," Aefric said, smiling broadly. "Who better to test it on?"

"Nayoria," Karbin said.

"No," Beornric said, "our duke is right. The peer of the realm takes priority."

"Besides," Aefric said. "If we rescue Nayoria, we'll only be proving to Malimfar that they can't trust me. And I don't think any of us want that."

"I'm not especially concerned about it one way or the other," Deirdre said with an eloquent shrug.

Jenbarjen actually giggled.

"Now," Aefric said, turning toward the mirror.

"Wait," Beornric said, putting one hand on his bicep.

Aefric turned back. Raised his eyebrows.

"You know you aren't going alone, right?" he asked quietly.

Aefric gave his knight-adviser a chagrined smile.

Beornric tightened his grip on Aefric's bicep and turned to the others.

"It seems our dear duke intends to do more than just *scry* our dear missing duchess. He intends to *rescue* her."

"Then I'm going along, of course," Deirdre said, stepping up.

"I should as well," Karbin said.

"I..." Jenbarjen sagged a bit. "I'm sorry, your lordship. I've never done anything like this. And I really am—"

"Spent," Aefric said. "Don't worry about it. I don't expect you to accompany me this time."

"Thank you, your lordship."

"Or you, Karbin."

"Now you're speaking nonsense," Karbin said. "You'll need me."

"No," Aefric said, taking the silver-edged noble's dagger from his belt and passing it to Karbin. "If something goes wrong, you're the only one I can trust to be able to use this for a connection and mount a rescue."

"Again with logic," Karbin said, as though it were an accusation. "We'll make a wizard of you yet."

"Oh don't," Deirdre said. "You'll ruin him."

"What *are* you then?" Jenbarjen asked, then quickly added, "Your lordship?"

"I told you," Aefric said. "It's complicated."

"Well Karbin may not be coming," Beornric said, "but I am."

"No," Aefric said. "I need you to command the mission in my absence."

Beornric gritted his teeth. "Karbin can—"

"Karbin's never been a soldier. He knows magic, not war. I need you *here*."

"Well, you aren't going with just Deirdre."

"*Just* Deirdre?" Deirdre asked, offended.

"There's nothing *just* about you," Aefric assured her, and Deirdre snickered at the double-meaning. He turned back to Beornric. "I'll take Arras and Micham with me then."

"I'll get them," Beornric said.

"And I'll see that he doesn't leave until you return," Karbin said.

Beornric didn't need long. Arras and Micham followed him through the trapdoor into the deckhouse, clad in their full plate, with weapons ready. Both of them looked better rested than Aefric expected.

"You know what we're doing?" Aefric asked.

Arras and Micham both gave firm nods.

"All right," Aefric said, turning back to the mirror. "Let's see how this goes."

He held up the teak box and flipped it open as he thought of Ashling. With her long black hair always styled just so, and her gowns always perfect. The clever intelligence in those sapphire blue eyes.

The mirror shifted. Filled for a moment with a soft, violet fog, that resolved itself into a closet.

Definitely a noblewoman's closet. Racks and racks of dresses and belts. A variety of shoes and boots and hats on shelves. Plastered walls painted a rich, brown color, but natural light coming in from somewhere to the left.

At least, it looked like natural light. Tough to be certain through the mirror.

The connection was made, and firm. Aefric knew that. The fog was gone entirely.

"Hello?" he tried. "Ashling? Are you near?"

No answer.

"Well," he said. "That settles it. We're going in."

Aefric started toward the mirror, but Beornric halted him with a hand on his arm. "No reason you should go through first."

"I just want to poke my head in and see if anyone's there."

Beornric shook his head. "Deirdre."

Deirdre stepped up. Checked her angle from the sides, then shook her head. "Clear as far as I can see without going through."

She leaned forward, but the portal didn't admit her.

"Sorry," Aefric said, then allowed the portal to open for her.

Deirdre dove through into a roll, coming up with rapier and dueling dagger in her hands. She vanished from view for a moment.

"Deirdre," Aefric said.

"Just checking the closet." Her voice came as clear as though she were standing next to him.

She returned to the mirror a moment later and nodded. "Clear, your grace. Nothing in here but frippery to please a powdered puff."

"Don't let Ashling hear you call her that," Aefric said, starting forward, but again Beornric stopped him with a hand on the arm.

"Arras. Micham. You next," Beornric said. "Just in case."

"Fine," Aefric said with a sigh.

His knights drew their swords — two in Arras' case — and stepped through. They moved somewhere out of sight, likely taking up guard positions.

Beornric nodded. "Your grace."

"Thank you," Aefric said archly, and stepped through the portal.

It was like stepping through a waterfall without getting wet. He could feel something streaming a line through him as he passed into the closet.

Once there, he looked back and forth. Saw the wide, arched window that was letting in late afternoon sunlight. Smelled clothes and the remains of some kind of flowery perfume.

No people in here though, except his own. Deirdre beside him, Arras and Micham flanking the only door, which was painted white and to his right.

"Voices," Arras said. "Women, I think. Not too near the door."

"Not approaching?" Aefric asked.

She shook her head, and so did Micham.

"I don't hear any footsteps," Micham said.

Aefric turned back to the portal. "Wish us luck," he said, and closed the box.

Aefric put the teak box back into his velvet belt pouch.

"All right," he said quietly, while he and Deirdre joined Micham and Arras beside the closet's only door. "That mirror is the closest to Ashling, but we don't know how close."

"Has to be a good sign that we only hear women's voices through the door, doesn't it?" Micham whispered.

"Perhaps not," Arras answered. "If Caiperas holds with tradition, they'll assign guards of the same sex as their noble prisoner. To reduce the chance of guards being seduced by charming nobles."

"Would it matter to them that Ashling prefers women?" Aefric asked.

"No," Arras said. "They'll assign guards that don't."

"So we can't tell from in here," Deirdre said.

"Then we have to be ready to fight when we open the door," Micham said, adjusting his grip.

"Not necessarily," Deirdre said with a grin. She nodded to the window.

"And outside that window, are there any guards who might be in a position to see a maroon-clad redhead clinging to the castle wall?" Aefric asked. "Or perhaps a floating man holding a big white stick?"

"Only a handful, down on the walls." Deirdre objected quietly. "And only if they happen to look up."

"If they do," Aefric said, "we'll alert people who could sound the alarm before we could stop them. No. We'll use the door."

"You've been hanging out with Karbin too long," Deirdre said with a grimace.

"Okay," Aefric said, taking up position beside Deirdre and facing the white door. "Micham, step back far enough to clear the door's arc. I'll open it by magic."

Micham adjusted his position.

"Deirdre goes through first," Aefric said. "By stealth, if possible. Arras, Micham, keep my line of fire clear until I say, then you're next through the door. You may need to kill guards, but avoid killing others, if possible. Targets should all be wearing the local red-and-white, either on their tabards or their livery, but if Ashling has noble guests, they won't be. So stay alert. Guards are first priority. Bringing down any potential runners or screamers is second."

"I've visited Duchess Ashling's court," Arras said softly. "I know most of her advisers on sight."

"Then you're on noble duty. Point out possible Caiperans to me."

She nodded.

"Everybody ready?" Aefric asked, and got three nods in return, one of which wasn't strictly necessary. Deirdre practically *vibrated* readiness.

He opened the door, and needed less than a breath to survey the room with a practiced eye.

It was a large rectangular room, with maple floorboards and enough couches and chairs to seat a dozen, split among three groups between here and that far wall full of windows. An empty stage to the right. The only people straight ahead, seated among the farthest group of red and white couches.

Three visible doors: two white, one glass. Glass door on the far wall looked to lead out onto a balcony under threatening skies. White doors to the left and right were near the far end of the room, past a series of tapestries depicting battle scenes.

Aefric smelled tea. Simple black tea. And some kind of sweet pastry.

One person in red and white livery that he could see. A young woman. Likely a page. She stood near the right-hand door.

Deirdre entered the room in silence, ducking low. She checked her new sightlines every step, hunting for more guards and servants, but didn't seem to spot any.

Aefric kept his eyes on that page, in case she showed any sign of noticing Deirdre. He listened sharply, but heard only the flow of quiet, indistinct conversation among those on the couches.

He did, however, pick out Ashling's voice among the speakers. She sounded ... well, she sounded like herself. Which was to say, not especially tense or under duress.

Deirdre passed the second group of couches. Still no sign that she'd been heard.

As she reached the third set of couches, Aefric put the page to sleep with a quick spell. She slumped to the floor where she stood.

Deirdre leapt to her feet, rapier and dueling dagger glowing bright red.

"Your grace," she said — presumably addressing Ashling — "are these three friends or foes?"

"Friends, Ser Deirdre," Ashling said quickly, standing and raising a calming hand towards the naked, enchanted steel. She looked about then, spotted Aefric, and smiled.

"Well," she said, raising one eyebrow while her friends whirled about in their seats, shocked expressions on their faces. Ashling posed a little, showing off in her gown of emerald silk, slashed and belted with cloth-of-gold. "I must be a lucky girl, if the Hero of Frozen Ridge himself flies once more to my rescue."

"Far be it for me to assume that the great Ashling Fyrenn is in need of rescue," Aefric said with a smile. He entered the room with Arras and Micham right behind him. Deirdre was already listening at the door behind the sleeping page. "This is merely a ... status check, if you will." He shook a finger at her. "You never write."

She laughed and bowed as though he'd scored a point, while her friends looked back and forth between two of Armyr's three peers, clearly uncertain what to make of this exchange.

"That I am a prisoner cannot be doubted," she said. "The last thing Sirondfar told me before they moved him to separate quarters was that the wards had been altered to avoid ... well, to avoid just this sort of happenstance, I presume."

"The normal rules don't apply to his grace," Deirdre said, coming back from the door. "I don't hear anyone close enough to overhear us."

"No, they don't," Ashling said, still smiling. "Which must be why he has such a talent for miracles."

The other three noblewomen stood, straightening their dresses with an air of expectation.

"Oh," Ashling said, "but where are my manners."

She gestured to a woman Aefric in crushed red velvet, slashed with orange. Aefric recognized her, not only by her shining light brown hair, but by the confidence in her eyes.

"You've met Countess Siburh Ol' Cynerstan, of course," Ashling said, "and no doubt you remember her daughter Cyneswith."

"Your grace," Countess Siburh said with a bow.

"Always a pleasure, your excellency," Aefric said. "And I hope you'll greet your daughter for me."

"She'll thrill to that," Ashling said with a smirk. "These other two I don't believe you've met."

She indicated the dark-skinned woman with long, ebony hair, who wore a gown of dark blue silk, slashed with crimson. "This is Ler Vashhal Altriett."

Ashling next indicated the palest woman present — which apart from Vasshal was saying something — whose fiery red hair contrasted sharply with her gown of bright yellow silk, slashed with azure. "And this is Ecgrun Ol'Masarkor. Of course, her cousin Baron Herewyn Ol'Norette is your vassal, and I believe you're very well acquainted with her younger cousin, Sighild."

"I am indeed," he said, while those two women bowed to him. "A pleasure to meet you both."

"My cousins both speak very highly of your grace," Ecgrun said.

"What?" Ashling teased. "Do I not speak highly enough of Aefric to suit you? Or do you not consider me cousin enough to include?"

"Be fair, Ashling," Vasshal said. "You're a far more distant cousin than either of those other two. One need only see your hair to know that."

"Either way," Aefric said to Ecgrun, "I thank you."

"Now," Ashling said, "on the subject of status, I assume Colm's blood ran hot and he started the war without giving me enough warning to leave?"

"I don't think it was *intended* that way—"

"That's all right, Aefric," Ashling said with a laugh. "Feel no need to defend him to me. I take it as a compliment that he felt I could take care of myself." She narrowed her eyes thoughtfully. "Which suggests that Eppida sent you."

"Her majesty *has* been frantic to reach you," Aefric said. "But I have no specific mission to come here. I found the means to do so, and came on my own."

"I'm flattered that you worried about me," she teased.

"We are friends, are we not?"

"We are," Ashling said with a nod, drawing raised eyebrows from her three companions. "Tell me what's going on with the war."

"Shouldn't we be getting you four out of here?" Aefric asked.

"No one will check on us until dinner, which is..." she looked to Vashhal.

"A conservative guess would be two hours," Vashhal said.

"...plenty of time, depending on how we use it," Ashling said. "Now. Tell me what's going on with the war."

"We might as well sit for this," Countess Siburh said, and so the noblewomen all sat on couches. Aefric took a chair at the end, with Arras and Micham flanking behind him, and Deirdre watching the door.

Aefric caught them up on everything as quickly as he could. Varondam. Malimfar. Caiperas. The troop deployments, and Rethneryl's involvement.

"That method you used to come here," Ashling said, looking thoughtful. "Wasn't teleportation, was it?"

"No. I found a way to use the mirror in your closet as a portal."

Her eyebrows rose. "Can you now use any mirror that way?"

"I'd prefer that not to become common knowledge."

"I'd think not." Ashling turned to the others. "As his grace is being good enough to come rescue us, I *presume* we will all keep his secret confined to *those in this room*?"

Countess Siburh took the longest to agree, but in the end she said the formal words of agreement, same as the other two.

"You brought these three through with you," Ashling said. "How many can you transport that way?"

"Enough to get you and your entourage out of here, one at a time."

"Oh," she said with a smile, "I'm not talking about leaving just yet. I want to know how many troops you can bring in through that closet."

"Why?"

"Because I have a plan, of course."

"I'm ... not sure his majesty would approve of this," Aefric said slowly.

"He'll approve it if I win his war for him," Ashling said. "And I know just how to do it."

"I don't know..."

"Aefric," Ashling said, sounding serious now. "Do you trust me?"

"My advisers might castigate me for admitting this aloud, but I do," he said. "And I have easy access to one hundred fifty soldiers, plus Ser Beornric and Karbin, my ducal wizard."

"More than enough," she said. "This is what we'll do."

ASHLING'S PLAN WAS FAIRLY SIMPLE TO EXPLAIN. WHICH WAS GOOD. Because they needed every minute they could get their hands on to organize Aefric's troops and ensure that everyone understood their orders.

Not to mention bringing them all, one by one, through the portal. Which was more effort than Aefric expected. Going through himself took next to nothing out of him. But holding the portal open for others, and willing the box to let them through, seemed to take just a little more effort with each person who needed to pass.

Which meant a hundred fifty soldiers, plus Beornric and Karbin. By the time he was done, Aefric wasn't quite *winded*, but his heart was pounding harder from the effort, and his brow was damp with sweat, and he was definitely glad of that nap and seafood chowder lunch he'd had earlier.

When someone finally knocked on the sitting room to announce dinner, everyone was in position. The soldiers — as well as Karbin and Beornric — were all wedged into Ashling's closets, bedroom, bath room and privy. It was a tight, uncomfortable fit, but they were hidden.

Ashling and her companions were seated on the couches, just as they'd been earlier. Aefric, Deirdre, Arras and Micham were crouched *behind* those couches, where they wouldn't be seen from the doorway.

That page from earlier was still asleep, and would be for some time. So she'd been moved to a comfortable couch near the back of the room, where she would be both out of the way and inobvious.

Whoever knocked did at least wait for Ashling's courtesy answer of "Enter," before coming in.

Aefric heard a stern woman's voice say, "Dinner will be served soon. I presume your grace and her companions are hungry?"

"We are," Ashling said, "but I have had enough of my confinement."

"I don't—"

"Your king told me he would not speak to me again unless it was to offer terms of surrender. You may tell him I am ready for just such a discussion, and wish to see him at once."

A moment of silence. Deirdre frowned impatiently, but Aefric made a reassuring gesture.

"I don't believe his majesty—"

Ashling stood. "Are you calling me a liar?"

"Of course not, your grace."

"Then you must accept that your king told me what *I just said* he told me."

"Well, I see that, your grace—"

"Which means that it is your *duty* — and I do mean your duty to the crown of Caiperas, not any misguided duty toward *me* should you have any — to go to King Makarios *at once* and tell him I am ready to discuss terms of surrender."

"But I don't see how your grace—"

"Do you intend to countermand the orders of your king?" Ashling said in loud, carrying tones.

"What's going on in here?" A different woman's voice. Higher, but sharper. And younger, Aefric thought.

"Tell her," Ashling ordered.

"Well," the first speaker said, "her grace claims—"

"Claims?"

"I mean her grace ... I-I mean the king ... I-I-I mean..."

"Oh, never mind, stupid woman," Ashling said. "Your king made clear he only wishes to speak to me if I am ready to discuss terms of surrender. I am ready. Either bring his majesty to me, or conduct me and my escort" — her three noble companions stood — "to his majesty. Either way, I expect this to be done *at once.*"

Impressive, how much command she could put into her voice. And when the younger woman spoke again, Aefric knew the tone he was hearing. It was the tone that clearly said, "This is a problem for someone with a lot more authority than I have."

Or, as Keifer would've put it, "This is above my pay grade."

"I shall conduct your grace and her escort to his majesty at once."

On cue, Aefric, Deirdre, Arras and Micham all stood. Though the only weapon in hand at the moment was the Brightstaff.

The guard in question was a strong-looking woman in chainmail, with the white cross on a red background of Caiperas on her tabard. She wore a half-helm on her head, with nose guard, and carried a spear in hand, with a sword at her side.

The moment Aefric and the others stood, she had that spear pointed and ready. She opened her mouth to call for support.

Ashling spoke first, and loud.

"These are my escort," she said. "As a duchess, I am entitled to them."

"That's Aefric Brightstaff," the soldier said, not lowering her spear.

"That's *his grace, Ser* Aefric Brightstaff," Ashling corrected him, "Duke of Deepwater, Baron of Netar, and I believe it's *Arl* of Storbakki." She raised unconcerned eyebrows at Aefric. "Yes?"

"That's right," Aefric said. "And Chieftain of Clan Thunder Stick, if you want to be complete."

"Well, by all means," Ashling said with a smile, "let us be complete. And nothing established in the customs of nobility disallows him as my escort, should he agree to the role. And you do, I believe, agree to the role. Do you not, your grace?"

"Readily," Aefric said, "your grace."

"Then there is nothing remaining but to conduct us to his majesty's presence at once," Ashling said. "Unless you wish to have Caiperas *violate* established custom."

The guard hesitated.

"Realize," Ashling said, "that once Caiperas violates custom in its treatment of a noble prisoner, there is nothing to hold his grace here in check. He would be free to devastate Reyvenue with lightning to his heart's content. And I suspect he would start with you. Would you not, your grace?"

"Your grace," Aefric said, "I do tend to punish first those who ask for punishment."

A bead of sweat trickled down the guard's forehead.

Aefric allowed white fire to play along the Brightstaff's length.

"Custom enforces your peaceful behavior?" the guard asked. Aefric wasn't sure whether she was asking him or Ashling — her eyes were on the Brightstaff — but it was Ashling who answered.

"As my escort, he would be obligated not to be the first to cause conflict."

The guard raised her spearhead.

"Follow me this way, if you would be so kind," the guard said, "your graces."

"I assure you," Ashling said, "nothing would please me more."

THE CAIPERAN GUARD DIDN'T ESCORT THEM ON HER OWN. SHE SENT A runner ahead, and soon was joined by eleven of her fellows — men and women both, and all similarly armed and armored. Together they surrounded Aefric and the others, and led them first through a pair of broad, bright halls. Once they descended the first set of long, narrow stairs, the halls became tighter. With ceilings that Aefric could have touched, if he'd tried.

He didn't, of course, though he was tempted. He was trying to affect a noble mien, which he'd never felt as though he managed well.

A close, old smell along here. As though these stairs and halls weren't cleaned or aired as much as the others.

Aefric and Ashling walked side-by-side within their circle of guards. Deirdre preceded them by a few steps, and Arras and Micham followed a few steps behind.

Along the way, they passed a good many servants — and a few nobles, unless Aefric was mistaken — but in each case his party was given a wide berth. Most others simply cleared out of the hall. Although Aefric couldn't help noticing that some of those in their wake buzzed with conversation.

Maple wood for the floorboards seemed a common theme here at Reyvenue. And many of the walls were papered, instead of plastered, but not with patterns. Mostly with Caiperan red and trimmed with white. Or in some places, with gold leaf.

No paintings or tapestries along these sets of halls and stairs, which suggested they were used mainly by guards and servants, rather than nobles and guests.

A page — this one a young man — approached at a run from down the hall ahead of them. The lead guard halted the procession, and spoke with the page in hushed tones before sending him running back the way he'd come.

"A good sign," Ashling whispered.

A short time later they were in their fifth corridor, following the fourth set of stairs, when Aefric felt the telltale ringing through his bones that told him to expect words carried by a contact spell.

Karbin's whispered voice. "I've found a spot outside the wards and in position. Ready."

"Understood," Aefric said in his mind alone, knowing that the spell would convey it as spoken to Karbin's ears.

He caught Ashling's eye and nodded. She smiled for only a moment, before resuming her haughty, put-upon expression.

Another two floors later they stopped outside a gilded white door at the end of a corridor that likely felt narrower than it was, because of the crowd.

The lead guard, the one they'd first spoken with, glanced back at Ashling and Aefric, and knocked three times on the door.

The door opened, revealing a wizard. Pale skin. Short brown hair. Robes of ruby red, and actual rubies in the black oak rod in his hand. He looked young enough to be just about the age of majority. As though he were an apprentice, which he clearly wasn't. Too much power about him for that, though nowhere near enough to intimidate Aefric.

In fact, that this wizard looked so young made Aefric feel a little contempt. It meant he was overcompensating with a newish spell, a sign of immaturity. Combined with what Aefric could sense of his power, this wizard probably wasn't more than a few years older than Aefric. If that.

And his rod wasn't enchanted. More of a focusing tool. Interesting.

"Ah," the ruby wizard said. "Duchess Ashling. So good to see you again, your grace, and in such fine health."

"Ulfrid," Ashling said, giving him no more greeting than that.

Aefric didn't recognize the name.

Ulfrid waited a moment, as though expecting Ashling to say more, but she was looking right past him into what looked like a smallish room, heavy on the gray stone.

"And this..." Ulfrid frowned for only a moment, before wedging a smile back into place. "This cannot be Duke Aefric Brightstaff, can it?"

"Who else?" Ashling asked, still not bothering to look at Ulfrid. "Unless you believe someone would be foolish enough to *impersonate* his grace."

"I ... had not been informed of your grace's arrival," Ulfrid said to Aefric, eyes narrowing above his forced smile.

"An oversight," Aefric said. "Nothing more. My arrival was both sudden and recent."

Ulfrid's eyes narrowed further. "Has your grace accepted the hospitality of the castle?"

A simple sounding question, but it made all the difference in whether or not Aefric was both protected and obligated by the guest-host relationship.

"It has not yet been offered," Aefric said.

"Then by all means," Ulfrid said, "allow me to—"

"You do not have the right to offer hospitality," Ashling said. "Reyvenue is not your castle, nor are you its seneschal or castellan."

Ulfrid gave a small nod, almost as though without thinking. Which was amusing, as he was clearly thinking quickly. He schooled his expression into false pleasantry.

"Your grace arrived without incident, I trust?" he asked Aefric.

"Entirely, I assure you."

"A necessary question, as I trust your grace understands. After all, your grace's reputation precedes him."

"Would that I could return the compliment ... Ulfrid, is it?"

Deirdre flashed him a quick smile.

"Yes, well, not all of us lead such *colorful* lives," Ulfrid said. "Rather we spend our time in more profitable *study*. I am indeed Ulfrid, and I trust I need not mention that I hold the post of Royal Wizard of Caiperas."

"You trust correctly."

"An impressive achievement for one so young, don't you think?" Ulfrid smiled as though sharing a joke with Aefric. As though he expected that only the two of them would know he was older than he appeared. And likely expecting that Aefric, too, was older than he seemed.

Deirdre yawned, which got her a dark look from Ulfrid.

She turned to Aefric and Ashling. "Please excuse me, your graces, but this sort of banter bores me so."

"Very well then," Ulfrid said sourly. "I must ask formally if his grace will confirm his willingness to stand escort to Duchess Ashling." He turned to Ashling. "I certainly have the right to ask *that*."

"You do," Ashling said with a nod.

"I so confirm," Aefric said.

"Excellent," Ulfrid said. "Then I shall admit you all to the royal presence once you've surrendered your weapons."

"We will *not*," Ashling said. "Custom allows—"

"*Peacetime* custom," Ulfrid said. "We are at war, after all."

"And yet," Ashling said, arching an imperious eyebrow, "I *remain* both the Duchess of Merrek and the official ambassador from Armyr. And as such, I am *entitled* to the security of *my own* armed escort, should I feel it necessary."

"Given your current status as a prisoner of war—"

"I am no prisoner of war," Ashling said. "That my movement has been restricted by order of your king cannot be doubted. As is appropriate in a time of war. But let it not be forgotten, I arrived here as an ambassador under writ of the king of Armyr. That war has begun does not change my status, and I have received no formal notification of imprisonment from your king. Until such time as I *do*—"

"Oh, very well," Ulfrid said with a slight nod. "Your knights may keep their swords. But a wizard carrying a powerful staff? Into the royal presence? Ridiculous."

"My wizard Sirondfar has served as my escort before. And *he* was not denied any magic he carried."

"Sirondfar does not carry a weapon like the Brightstaff, nor does he have the reputation of Duke Aefric for sheer destruction."

"He is an Armyrian peer."

"He is a jumped-up adventurer."

"He has played host to your own Princess Xenia," Ashling said, "who was sent to him by your own king. Therefore establishing the precedent of Caiperas according him his due as the ranking nobleman that he is."

"Holding that weapon he presents too great a threat," Ulfrid said. "He must surrender it if he is to serve as your grace's escort."

"It is *because* he stands as my escort," Ashling said, "that he need not surrender it. His status binds him not to be the first to bring conflict. As you knew full well when you asked him for confirmation."

"You ask too much," Ulfrid said.

"A moment," Aefric said, and waited until Ulfrid looked at him. "Duchess Ashling has the right to her escort. Custom permits her escort to come armed into the royal presence, when she acts in her role as ambassador. As she does now. I am officially part of her escort. What part of this progression escapes you?"

"Why, no part of it," Ulfrid said. "However—"

"However you wish to deny me the Brightstaff, correct?"

"I believe I have been quite clear on that point."

"And nothing else I carry is at issue?"

"I am not best pleased to see you carrying a wand like *that* one," Ulfrid said, nodding at the wand Garram. "But I can allow it, so long as it remains in its sheath."

"Then only the Brightstaff is under contention."

"Aefric..." Ashling said.

"It seems logic and custom go only so far, Ashling," Aefric said. "So let it become a matter of practicality."

He held up the Brightstaff in both hands, as though offering it. "Disarm me of it yourself, if you must. But let the consequences be on your own head."

"Attacking me would be in violation of your status," Ulfrid said. "And therefore, against the whole point of this conversation, would it not?"

"It would," Aefric said with a nod. "But I'm not talking about attacking you. I'm talking about how the Brightstaff will accept no touch but my own. And those who test this have found the consequences *dire*."

"Then your grace may leave it in this hallway, secure in the knowledge that it will await him on his return."

"Except that it will follow me."

"Through a closed door?"

"If need be. It has followed me farther, and through stone walls, in the past."

"And should I choose not to believe that?"

"Then I trust your king will not hold me accountable for the loss of his door. Or for the loss of any guards foolish enough to try preventing the Brightstaff from reaching my hand."

Aefric shrugged while Ulfrid considered that.

"Either way," Aefric said, "the end result will be the same. Me, in the royal presence, holding the Brightstaff. And behaving myself properly, as befits Duchess Ashling's escort."

"Unless you are determined to rescind his status and violate custom," Ashling said. "Freeing his grace to behave in whatever way he sees fit. Here within Reyvenue. While our two kingdoms are, as you pointed out, at war."

"And let us not forget Ser Deirdre," Aefric said. "I don't think she would take well to your abrogating custom here."

Deirdre smiled an evil smile.

"Ser Deirdre ... Ol'Miri?" Ulfrid asked, sounding ill, as he looked her over. But not as though he were looking at a woman. More the way he might checking the markings of a deadly snake or spider.

"I am she," Deirdre said. "And I *do* hope you violate custom."

"Not to mention that you have yet to take into account the excellent knights behind me," Ashling said. "They are Knights of the Lake, you know. Some of the best that his grace has at his disposal."

She waited while Ulfrid looked at Arras and Micham, who gave him very dark looks in response.

"I choose my escort well, do I not?" Ashling said with a smile. "Shall we proceed to the royal presence?"

"I need a moment," Ulfrid said, and started to close the door.

"You do *not*," Ashling said sharply. "We have played your game and addressed your concerns. Now. You will conduct me to his majesty, or you will give me no choice but conduct *myself* to his presence."

Ulfrid grimaced. "Very well."

———

THE ROOM ON THE OTHER SIDE OF THAT GILDED WHITE DOOR LOOKED more or less the way Aefric had expected, from his glimpses during Ulfrid's delays.

Smallish, gray stone room. Rectangular, but not by much. Maybe … seven good strides across, and nine long. Reasonably high ceiling, with a chandelier filled with perhaps a hundred lit candles.

Lit candles. Not light magic. Interesting. A statement?

Cool in here. A large fire in a gray stone hearth dried the air more than warmed it.

The floor was covered with a checkerboard of red and white rugs, woven and dyed from rushes. The air smelled of hickory from the fire, and sweet herbs from under the rushes.

Large banners on the walls, all of them the white cross on a red background.

At one end of the room, a small dais, with seven steps leading up, and a squat, gray stone throne. So this was *a* throne room, but obviously not *the* throne room. Secondary or tertiary, at least.

Two doors in here, not including from the one they'd come in through. Both of them white and gilded. One in the center of the wall opposite the throne, and one on the dais, behind the throne and to its right.

"His majesty will be along shortly," Ulfrid said, and departed through the door on the dais.

Aefric turned to Ashling. Said quietly, "Do we trust that?"

"For now," Ashling said. "Makarios will make us wait, to remind us that he's king."

Deirdre, Arras and Micham took up equidistant positions around the two peers, while the dozen guards who'd brought them here spread out around them — three along each of the side and rear walls, and three in front of the dais. All dozen with their spears at parade rest.

There was little magic to this room, and what there was, was built into the dais. Wards. Not active, but cast and ready to be activated at a word, the way a light spell could be.

Wait. There *was* something else. A small ward on the whole room. It prevented...

Communication.

Well. *That* could be a problem.

How long ago had they left Ashling's rooms? The hike down here took a while, but living in Water's End had hurt Aefric's judgment of such trips. He'd gotten too used to having to cover a good deal of ground to get anywhere in his castle. Stopped thinking about how long such trips took.

And then there was the delay by Ulfrid. How long had that taken? Felt like *forever*, but surely it wasn't more than ... a few minutes? Ten? Fifteen?

Could half an hour have passed already? That would be the mark on the candle left behind, which means the other part of the plan would be underway...

Another dozen guards came in, through the rear door, doubling the number that surrounded them. These new guards were a mix of men and women, which likely had some significance that Elkari would have recognized.

One of the new guards — a woman with a sergeant's look about her — stepped forward. "It will be just another moment, your graces. His majesty is hearing reports from the front."

Aefric almost asked which front, but Ashling stopped him with a tiny shake of her head.

"Thank you," she said, then smiled. "Although I trust that if his majesty keeps us waiting long, he'll at least provide refreshment."

"I doubt it will be so long as that, your grace," the guard said with a bow, and resumed her post.

Another delay. In a room where he couldn't send the counter-order if he needed to. Or even receive word about the plan's progress.

Concern fluttered in Aefric's stomach. Right now, the rest of their plan could be failing completely...

The door on the dais opened. Four knights in shining, gold-washed plate armor — helms on and visors down — entered and took up positions on the corners of the dais.

Once they were in position, each drew a greatsword from the sheath on his or her back, and clasped it in both gauntlets, point up.

The front knight, to Aefric's right, said in a deep, male voice, "His majesty, Makarios Zaredes, King of Caiperas, Defeater of the Demon, Scourge of the Flayer, and *rightful* King of Malimfar."

Rightful King of Malimfar? That was a new one to Aefric. But now that he thought about it...

Hadn't there been something about that back in the third edition of the *Torn Kingdoms* setting?

Yes! In adventure-sourcebook P88, *Two Crowns for One Kingdom.*

Keifer had never gotten to play that one, only read it. His gaming group didn't like political games.

King Makarios entered through the door on the dais. Perhaps a decade older than King Colm, King Makarios was taller even than Aefric, and broader than Beornric. A large enough man to arm-wrestle with Ge'rek and stand a chance of winning. An old scar on his right cheek, and another on the back of his left hand.

He wore gold-washed chainmail, and a broadsword over his shoulder. His crown was gold, and each of its nine points featured some valuable gem. A small red silk cloth fell from the back and sides of the crown, reaching just to his shoulders. Not quite hiding the gray in his black hair.

Lots of magic about this man. His armor was enchanted to diminish the power of hits he took. His sword, for sharpness and accuracy. His crown, to discern lies.

That one almost made Aefric laugh. He knew that spell. Wasn't *bad.* Saw right through direct lies. But it couldn't spot half-truths, lies of omission, or any of the other manipulations and deviations that a justiciar would see right through.

Probably good enough to help him with most people. But someone like Ashling could likely spend all day functionally lying to

King Makarios, and never once have his crown suggest she told less than the truth.

King Makarios looked over his own arrangement of guards, then Ashling's escort, and finally sat on his throne. Ulfrid came in behind him and stood over his right shoulder, black oak rod in hand.

"Well, your grace," the king said in a strong voice, "I must say I didn't expect to hear from you."

"I can't imagine why," Ashling said. "Surely your majesty would not expect me to sit idle in my rooms."

"No," King Makarios said, glancing at Aefric before looking back as Ashling. "I see you've kept *quite* busy. You'll have to tell me sometime how you managed to smuggle a duke into my castle."

"I did no such thing," Ashling said.

King Makarios frowned, likely because his crown confirmed the truth of her words. He adjusted unhappily in his seat, while Ulfrid whispered something to him.

King Makarios shook away his adviser.

"And yet, here he stands," he said, turning to look Aefric over. "The duke of Deepwater, here at Reyvenue. How ever did you accomplish this, your grace?"

"Forgive me, your majesty," Ashling said quickly, "but I would remind you that Aefric is here as my *escort*, not my peer or adviser, nor as your majesty's guest."

King Makarios chuckled. "And thus, my speaking to him directly becomes inappropriate. For the moment." He nodded. "All right, Ashling. We'll play your game for now. I can't *wait* to see where it leads."

"I think your majesty will find that we have more profitable directions for this conversation than simple matters of travel."

"Yes," King Makarios said with a sly smile. "A page told me you're ready to surrender. And as I hear you've been *insisting* on your status as ambassador from your treacherous kingdom, I can only presume you wish to surrender on your king's behalf?"

"I dispute your majesty's characterization of Armyr as 'treacherous.'"

"Colm has not only failed and refused to invade Malimfar," King Makarios said angrily, "but he has had the *audacity* to seize Caer Ylfarai!"

"As your majesty's adviser pointed out to me a short time ago," Ashling said calmly, "we are at war. Taking land and the occasional castle—"

"*You yourself came here to coordinate our invasion of Malimfar!*"

"I certainly recall discussing your majesty's invasion plans with him, and assisting in the preparation of those plans. However—"

King Makarios stood, pointing an angry finger at her. "*It had already been established that our mutual target was Malimfar.*"

"I was never under the impression that Armyr intended to invade Malimfar."

King Makarios turned purple with rage then. Likely because his crown had just confirmed that Ashling spoke the truth. He opened his mouth, but before he could speak, Ashling's sharp words cut through the air.

"*Your majesty, I remind you we are here to formally discuss terms of surrender.*"

That stalled him. He looked her over suspiciously. Shot a glance at Ulfrid, who looked nervous, but nodded.

"That *is* what she told the guards, according to the page." Ulfrid lowered his voice, and said something more. Aefric picked out the word *crown*.

King Makarios nodded. His wide nose showed off a forest of nostril hair in a deep breath. Nodded again. Turned to Ashling. "Say it again."

"Your majesty," Ashling said slowly, her tone verging on disrespectful, "I remind you we are here to formally discuss terms of surrender."

King Makarios tilted his head and frowned. As though trying to spot some lie that his crown had missed.

Finally, he scoffed. "Even if your king supported your surrender, which I doubt he—"

"Your majesty misunderstands me," Ashling said.

King Makarios raised an eyebrow, and the look was effective enough that Aefric wondered if he'd *ever* be able to match it. He doubted it. Maybe his great, great, great grandchildren would one day learn to cock an eyebrow the way people like King Colm and King Makarios and Ashling could. It seemed like the kind of thing that required *generations* of practice.

Then again, Aefric *would* likely live that long...

Assuming he left this room alive.

"Explain," King Makarios said.

"I am indeed here to discuss terms of surrender," Ashling said. "But the surrender I speak of is yours."

THE SMALL THRONE ROOM GREW STILL AFTER ASHLING'S DECLARATION. The only sound, the crackling of the fire to Aefric's left. The source of the hickory scent overlaying the sweet herb smell from under the carpets.

Aefric found himself reflexively checking their guards, but the soldiers all stared slack jawed.

Up on the dais, the four knights in gold-washed plate armor didn't move. Just held their swords at the ready, faces unreadable behind closed visors.

King Makarios stood on the dais before his stone throne, staring down at Ashling. Perhaps stunned for a moment into incomprehension. Behind the throne, Ulfrid glanced at the closed door behind him, as though checking something.

Deirdre, Arras and Micham — arrayed between Aefric and those two dozen guards — made small movements, likely readying themselves in case of attack. He was pretty sure Deirdre was fighting not to draw her weapons.

For Aefric's part, he held the Brightstaff loose and ready in his right hand. His left was ready to go for the wand Garram, if needed. But he already had his first move in mind, and it wouldn't use either weapon.

King Makarios started laughing. A booming laugh, but it didn't seem to spread humor to anyone, least of all himself. For there was nothing amused about the anger in his dark eyes.

"I must say, Ashling," the king said, "I never expected you to be so funny."

"There's nothing humorous about my statement," Ashling said. "Believe me."

"Oh, I'm confident that you mean your offer most sincerely," he said, smiling a humorless smile. "But that's what makes it all the funnier. Because you've tipped your hand. Yes, Colm has managed to seize Caer Ylfarai and the Pass of Dayor Ol'Tain while I was looking west. But he errs if he thinks this will spook me into jumping at shadows."

He laughed again, and this time his laughter sounded vicious.

"Obviously Colm, or perhaps one of his forefathers, discovered some secret way into my castle years ago. And now he's exploited that knowledge to send a small team to you" — he gestured at Aefric and his knights — "carrying instructions that you demand my surrender. Perhaps counting on the sudden appearance of his dreaded attack dog to inspire fear."

Dreaded attack dog? Did he mean Aefric? Was that how they saw him here?

King Makarios shook his head and smiled wide enough to show many, large teeth.

"All of this clearly means that Colm has played his best trick, but figured out that whatever he had planned as a follow-up will fail, because he's lost the element of surprise." King Makarios sat on his throne once more. "Of course, even Colm's great trick will soon prove meaningless. Caer Ylfarai will be back in my hands before winter. And the pass will follow, of course, for whoever holds that castle holds the pass."

"Nevertheless—" Ashling started.

"Colm has betrayed our alliance," the king continued. "All of our neighbors know that now, or will soon enough. His other allies will turn their backs on him, if they haven't already."

"There has been no alliance between Armyr and Caiperas since you sent assassins after our royal family," Ashling said. "As all of our neighbors do *indeed* know."

King Makarios paused, his brow furrowing. "What in the name of Vera are you talking about?"

It was a good act. King Makarios certainly looked confused at the accusation. But Ulfrid's eyes narrowed just a little as he looked at his king...

He didn't know. The Royal Wizard of Caiperas didn't know about the assassination attempts. But he clearly suspected something. And he *did* know about the crown's ability to sense truth.

Ulfrid started to lean in to ask his liege a question, but was waved back like an irritating fly.

"I am talking about assassins from the Order of the Severed Dream," Ashling said. "Making attempts on the lives of King Colm, Queen Eppida, Crown Prince Killian and Princess Maev."

King Makarios scoffed. "What has that to do with me?"

"A justiciar of Taesark confirmed that the crown of Caiperas was behind those attempts."

"Not a very creative lie, Ashling," the king said, "for one with your reputation."

But he said it too quickly. Clearly not using the crown's power to sense truths, even though he should've been concerned that she believed it.

Aefric quickly met Ulfrid's eye. "I swear in the name of Kalinda that she's telling the truth."

"Your escort speaks unbidden," King Makarios said. "Does he wish to participate in the conversation then?"

"He does *not*," Ashling said firmly. "And he will not speak again."

But Aefric was still locking eyes with Ulfrid, who gave a small nod.

"It matters little," King Makarios said, shrugging one shoulder. "His lie adds no value to yours."

"Your majesty knows I am not lying," Ashling said. "And I now wish to discuss the terms under which Armyr will accept his surrender."

"There will be no surrender," King Colm said. "You and your escort are now all prisoners of war." He turned to his court wizard. "See them disarmed, and taken to appropriate cells."

Deirdre, Arras and Micham all drew their weapons.

Aefric raised the Brightstaff.

The four golden knights stepped protectively close to their king.

Bells began to toll in the background.

Everyone hesitated at the sound of the bells.

"You!" the king called to one of his soldiers near the far door. "Go see what's—"

A terrified page burst through that door.

"Your majesty!" he cried, rushing forward. "We're under attack!"

"Impossible," King Makarios said, standing. "There've been no reports of any approaching armies."

"But, your majesty—"

"It's more than possible," Ashling said calmly. "It's happening. The attack your page is talking about is coming from within your castle."

The king's eyes widened. He held up a forestalling hand to the page.

"What have you done, Ashling?"

"I told you I was not one to sit idle," she said with a small smile. "I've smuggled in more than a hundred soldiers, who've been quite busy. By now they've cut off access to your armory, treasury, and food stores, and I *believe* taken your wife and children hostage?"

Here she raised her eyebrows at Aefric.

"I don't know for sure," he said. "This room is warded against spells of contact."

"She's right, your majesty," the page said. "Queen Omphale and Princess Xenia — along with several noblewomen — were captured at the stables as they returned from their daily ride."

"And Crown Prince Acastos?" King Makarios asked.

"Taken from his gallery, along with—"

"Kill them!" The king shouted, pointing at Ashling and Aefric with both hands. *"Kill them now!"*

Aefric raised his empty left hand, a spell on his lips.

"Wait!" Ulfrid said, and though he only spoke the word, the rubies on his black oak rod flashed and his word carried with it the force of a compulsion spell.

The spell didn't touch Aefric's will of course, but he'd never been its intended target anyway. He held his hand high and his spell ready, in case he needed it.

He didn't. Yet. None of the guards around him got further than lowering their spears before halting their movement.

Now *that* was an impressive bit of magic. Aefric couldn't have cast a spell like that so quickly and still affected so many. He wasn't sure Karbin could've either...

"How dare you?" King Makarios snarled at his wizard.

"Your majesty, *please*," Ulfrid said. "Enemy soldiers now hold your *wife* and *children*. Execute their leaders, and you create a standoff those soldiers *cannot* escape from. You will be as good as ordering the deaths of your own family."

King Makarios growled.

"Not to mention the deaths of several important nobles, I suspect," Ashling said casually. "Don't the two eldest daughters of Duke Stavrek join the queen and princess for their daily ride?"

The only person in Aefric's group who wasn't armed, and yet she didn't look as though she'd ever felt under threat. Unbelievable, this woman.

King Makarios drew in a breath so deep Aefric was surprised the hearth and chandelier didn't extinguish for lack of air.

The king blew out that breath slowly, while alarm bells continued to toll in the background.

"Very well," he said, turning to his soldiers. "I formally rescind the order to terminate these people at this time."

"And the order to disarm and imprison us," Ashling said. "Is that rescinded as well?"

"On the contrary," King Makarios said. "As my prisoners—"

Aefric made his gesture and cast his spell.

The *detonating flames* were a well-known spell. But they had an inherent problem. *Anyone* could be caught in their explosion. So, many years ago, Karbin had figured out a way of getting around that — under the right circumstances — and he'd taught it to his young apprentice.

So the flames detonated *around* Aefric and his group, leaving the center of the explosion untouched. A momentary flare of bright red fire that plunged the room into darkness.

Aefric lit up the Brightstaff's yellow diamond at the same moment that reddish light came from Ulfrid's rod, up on the dais.

Aefric, Ashling, Deirdre, Arras and Micham had gone untouched by the spell. Never even felt a brush of its heat. The dozen Caiperan guards around them, though, were all burnt to a crisp. The checkerboard carpeting of rushes they'd stood on, nothing but ash. The same could be said for the tapestries on the scorched stone walls. Up above, the twisted and molten remains of the chandelier dangled from links of iron chain. In the charred hearth, nothing but smoke.

The page, it seemed, had been fortunate enough to be standing between Aefric and Deirdre, and went untouched. Though he did faint dead away.

Up on the dais — as Aefric had expected — Ulfrid had activated the wards. He, King Makarios, and the four golden knights all went untouched by the flames, and the air shimmered protectively around the edges of the dais.

Deirdre gave Aefric a sour glare. Muttered, "At least you left me the knights."

Aefric's attention, though, was on the king.

"I have no intention of being taken prisoner," he said. "And if you choose to press the issue, you'll find those wards will not protect you."

The king's eyes widened as the crown confirmed the truth of Aefric's words. For while the wards protecting the king were impressive, they began at the *top* of the dais. Destroying the dais would ruin them, and that would be all too easy.

"Ah," King Makarios said, "but I have a wizard of my own."

Ulfrid leaned in and whispered something fast and harsh. The king glared in response.

"You will if I say you will," the king said.

"Your majesty," Ulfrid said, "Those wards are my *best*. You know how long they took me. If he really can destroy them here and now—"

"Enough!" King Makarios growled.

"We're *beaten*," Ulfrid said. "What choice do—"

"*I said, 'enough,'*" King Makarios snapped.

"Excellent," Ashling said with a bright smile. "Then I trust your majesty is ready to discuss the terms of his surrender?"

Formalizing the full terms of the surrender took well into the night. Fortunately, once word spread through the castle that the war was over and Caiperas was surrendering, the locals all took the surrender honorably.

The first thing that meant was that they were able to have assistance moving the talks to a room that didn't stink of recent fire and death. Smells that Aefric purged from himself and his party with a quick clean-up spell, while Ulfrid did the same for himself and his king. Though oddly, not for the golden knights.

Ashling chose the room they'd use. A sitting room hardly more than a few hundred steps away down a wide hall.

This square sitting room was easily thrice as big as that small throne room had been. More than enough space for a small forest of couches and tables in a rainbow of colors. High, large windows along three walls showed that rain had begun sprinkling down along with the oncoming dusk, and the fourth featured a large, blazing hearth.

The chandeliers above went unused, because this room was lit by magic. Felt like Ulfrid's work, and the light carried a tinge of orange. The flooring was maple, but largely covered by thick carpets with interesting, geometric designs in the style popular in Sartis.

Portraits along the walls displayed past members of the royal family, and above the hearth, a great banner featured the white stag of Caiperas — rampant and facing to the dexter — on a red background.

Ashling had the banner taken down for the talks. She also had servants move most of the seating spaces to one side. The chairs she ordered brought over for their use were the ones upholstered in dark green — likely the closest she could get to Armyr's forest green. The large table she'd chosen was black, with gold leaf.

Once that was done, Queen Omphale, Prince Acastos and Princess Xenia were all brought in, so that the royal family could be together for the talks. With the secondary effect that that each would know the others were alive and unharmed.

The other nobles who'd been captured were brought in as well and given comfortable seats where they could watch the proceedings, under a guard of Netari soldiers.

The four golden knights had surrendered their swords to Arras and Micham, and sat silently in one far corner.

Beornric presided over the guards, and had runners keeping him informed about the other groups of soldiers. Just in case.

Karbin sent word to Jenbarjen aboard the *Baron's Will* to halt the scouting venture and send rikas to Armityr and Caer Ylfarai to inform them that Caiperas was surrendering. Then he took up position just behind Aefric and Ashling, ready to contact Aefric's other groups of soldiers by magic, if needed.

The local seneschal was brought in as well. A thick-built woman with dark hair and an angry glare that looked more likely a permanent fixture than a product of circumstances. She stood steadfastly to her king's left — Ulfrid stood to his right — and whispered advice into his ear.

The queen and princess sat to King Makarios' left, and the crown prince sat to his right.

Food and drink were brought in over the course of the evening, as needed.

Ashling proved to be an absolute *terror* at the negotiating table.

She pressed hard, and gave little, if any quarter. Aefric couldn't help but wonder if she was always like this, or if she'd taken it personally that King Makarios had sent an assassin after her sister.

Given what Aefric had heard about Fyrenn family loyalty, probably a mixture of both.

For his part, King Makarios railed and swore about each term she presented, but Ashling merely sat still through his ranting. Implacable, in the face of his impotent fury. And each time he finished, she said the same thing.

"Realize that we have captured and hold you, your family, your nobles, your castle and your treasury. If you will not surrender formally, you leave us no choice but to slaughter you and begin taking spoils." She'd leave those words hanging for a moment, before finishing, "Shall I continue?"

Each time, the king growled, but told her to continue.

After the third time Ashling ran through her litany, Queen Omphale — a short, beautiful, fine-bonded older woman with streaks of white in her dark brown hair — moved the seneschal back and whispered something into her husband's ear.

King Makarios tried to whisper back, but he was too angry. His words were audible.

"I tell you, I don't know why Colm betrayed our alliance, and I don't know why he's put us in this position."

"Yes you do, your majesty," Aefric said, and the queen looked over at him with thoughtful eyes. "It's all been retribution for the assassins you sent after our royal family."

That sent a buzz through the watching noble prisoners. Prince Acastos — who looked the strong, handsome image of his father in his youth, albeit clad in an ice blue silk shirt over dark orange hose rather than gold-washed chainmail — turned a shocked look on the king.

"Father, you *didn't*."

"He didn't," the seneschal said. "The fool is lying."

"His grace is no fool," Princess Xenia said, watching Aefric's face. The princess had her mother's height and hair — minus the white —

but fortunately she'd turned her father's bone structure into a heart-shaped face and appealing curves that filled out her lavender velvet dress quite well. "And he isn't lying. I don't need my father's crown to read the truth plain on his face."

"Oh, Kari," Queen Omphale said to her husband. "What were you thinking?"

"I tell you this man is lying," the seneschal said. "Your king would never—"

"Oh, *enough,*" Queen Omphale said. "It may have been your idea. And *obviously* you handled the details. But you're too much of a glory hound to order it without getting your king's approval in advance. You'd never risk someone else taking credit for your work."

King Makarios glared at his seneschal.

"But your majesty—" The seneschal began, looking back and forth between the two monarchs, but Ashling cut in.

"That the crown of Caiperas was behind the attempts has been confirmed by a justiciar of Taesark."

The buzz among the nobles grew louder until King Makarios glared at them. It quieted then, but did not still completely.

"Will you attest to that?" the queen asked Ashling.

"Phale!" King Makarios objected, but the queen's attention was on Ashling.

"I have read the findings myself," Ashling said, "and can swear that their conclusion is as we have told you."

Ashling got to read the findings? Should Aefric have gotten to read the findings?

But Ashling was still talking. "And I can have a copy of the justiciar's findings sent to you after I return to Armityr."

"I would appreciate that," Queen Omphale said. "For our records. In the meantime, please do me the favor of having your guards escort my seneschal to a cell."

"*What?*" the seneschal cried out. She reached for a dagger, but Ulfrid froze her in place.

Aefric nodded approval. "Beornric."

"I'll see it done, your grace," Beornric said, hefting the seneschal's frozen form and carrying her to one side.

"Now," Queen Omphale said. "Enough posturing. Give us your terms. I assume they include my husband's abdication?"

"They do," Ashling said.

"Then as they must be signed before my son can be crowned..." She frowned at Ashling. "I presume there is no objection to my son succeeding his father to the throne?"

"None at all," Ashling said, raising a casual eyebrow at the prince. "His ignorance in the key matter is quite plain."

"Then present your terms and I shall sign them."

King Makarios objected. He and Queen Omphale went back and forth a few times, but in the end, she won. He sulked while Ashling went over the terms of surrender.

Those terms were pretty harsh.

First, that the crown of Caiperas would write a letter taking formal responsibility for the assassination attempts, and send copies of that letter — including an appropriate apology to the royal family of Armyr — to all kingdoms in this region of Qorunn. With five copies being sent to Armityr, for King Colm to keep or distribute as he saw fit.

(Ashling acceded that this letter could wait until Queen Omphale reviewed the justiciar's findings, but it had to be received at Armityr by Midwinter.)

Second, that Caiperas would harbor no grudge against Armyr and its royal family for this conflict, nor against any Armyrian or Rethneryli nobles for their actions during the conflict.

(Aefric thought that one would be hard to enforce, but he was told later that it was standard.)

Third, that Caiperas would not raise up arms against Armyr for a period of not less than fifty years.

Fourth, that Caiperas would neither wage nor abed economic war, nor any other kind of war, on Armyr for that same period.

And now we got into the harsh stuff.

Fifth, that all the Caiperan land north and west of the River

Sulquill — comprising nearly a fifth of Caiperas — be ceded to Armyr.

Sixth, that any and all ranking Caiperan nobles whose titles were tied to those lands would be given a free choice. They could either change their allegiance to Armyr, or they could abandon their lands for such compensatory lands as could be provided by the crown of Caiperas.

Seventh, that Caiperas pay financial reparations. And while their treasury wouldn't be *beggared*, Ashling did demand a hefty sum be paid. Immediately.

Eighth, that Princess Xenia be married to an Armyrian noble of King Colm's choosing.

(This one Queen Omphale pushed back on. She wanted to require King Colm to choose a spouse from among the peerage. Ashling flatly refused, but agreed to concede that the princess' husband would have to at least stand to inherit a county.)

Ninth was an agreement that the royal family and major noble families of Caiperas all foster children with Armyrian nobles. In other words, that they provide hostages against their behavior.

Tenth, that the seneschal — and anyone who aided her — be executed for the attempted assassinations.

Eleventh, that as his personal apology and reparation to King Colm Stronghand for the attempts, King Makarios Zaredes would surrender his family sword, Kaerdwan.

A chill went through the room when they reached that one. Prince Acostos visibly winced at the concession. The king began objecting again. Loudly.

Queen Omphale finally shut her husband down by shouting, *"You are a king who was caught sending assassins after another king, his wife, and his children!* If we don't pay a *hefty* price for that, we encourage others to do the same. And next time, *we* may be the targets."

She turned to Ashling, and in the queen's eyes Aefric saw that, while she believed what she said, she would remember the steep penalty Ashling demanded of them.

"Agreed," Queen Omphale said. "What next?"

But there was only one more term remaining. The twelfth and final. That King Makarios Zaredes abdicate his throne at once, and that he never again hold any formal post — even in an advisory capacity — in Caiperas.

ONCE THAT FINAL TERM WAS AGREED TO, KING MAKARIOS STOOD. HIS chair caught on the edge of a rug and fell backwards. For a moment, its clattering was the only sound heard above the soft patter of rain on the windows and the crackling of the fire in the hearth.

He reached over his shoulder for the hilt of his sword. Hissed intakes of breath came from here and there around the room.

Deirdre was suddenly there, standing between Aefric's chair and Ashling's. Aefric hadn't even known she was nearby until that moment. But she didn't reach for her weapons. Merely stood there. Ready.

King Makarios drew his broadsword. It was a beautiful blade. Blued steel, with a coating of gold along the fuller. Its hilt was gold as well, and featured a single large ruby on each side.

He looked at the blade through a long breath, then tossed it down on the table.

"No mention was made of its scabbard," he said, and Ashling nodded as though it hadn't been an oversight on her part.

King Makarios drew himself straight, shoulders back and head held high. In a ringing voice, he announced, "Let everyone here stand as witness. I, Makarios Zaredes, King of Caiperas, Defeater of the Demon, Scourge of the Flayer, and *rightful* King of Malimfar, do hereby abdicate my throne in favor of my son, Acastos Zaredes.

He removed his crown and set it gently on the table in front of his son.

"I'll tell you the same thing my father told me," he said to his son. "Wear it better than I did." He turned to Ashling. "I presume there is now no need for me to remain?"

"None," Ashling said.

"Then I bid you all good night." He turned and left the room.

After that, things went fairly smoothly. Although there was so much to do that they were still busy late into the night. Drafting and signing copies of the formal articles of surrender. Raiding the treasury — or rather, *collecting the reparations* — arranging and formalizing the delivery of the hostages. Or rather, the *children* to be *fostered* in Armyr.

Ashling ran it all, of course, with Queen Omphale ensuring everything was done. Aefric tried to watch and learn from Ashling, in case he ever had to do this himself, but there were so many small details. He was sure he missed a few. And she had clearly prepared for this in advance.

For example, she already had on her person — drafted perhaps while Aefric had been bringing through troops — a list of the children to be fostered, as well as agreements about when those children would be provided, and what penalties Caiperas would pay for missing any and all deadlines involved.

She just kept applying pressure the whole time. Absolutely merciless.

It all took so long that Beornric finally pressed Aefric to go aside with Deirdre and have her don the thick linen gloves and apply ointment to his scars.

Testing showed that the demon scars were, indeed, more sensitive than they should've been. But Aefric couldn't feel regret about that. Unlocking the secrets of that teak box had led to a quick end to the war. And victory, as well. A resolution worth going a little longer without the noble privilege.

The ointment took too much out of him, though. He sacked out on a couch, while Deirdre stood guard. By the time he jolted awake, morning was dawning and they were all ready to leave.

Aefric made sure everyone — his knights and troops, Karbin, Ashling's retainers and retinue and, of course, Ashling herself — went back to Ashling's rooms for their exit. Let the locals all think there was some hidden door here they couldn't find.

He brought out the teak box, then, and sent everyone back to the

Baron's Will, through the deckhouse mirror. Karbin and Beornric went through first, to get things organized. Then Aefric's troops followed. Then Ashling's retainers, troops and retinue, including Sirondfar, who looked on in frank amazement at what Aefric was doing.

Oh, but it was taxing work. He'd had plenty of decent food, but not enough sleep. And that ointment was taking it out of him. Now, holding the mirror portal open for over two hundred people?

He knew full well he'd need to go back to bed when he came through.

Finally, only three remained. Ashling, Deirdre, and Aefric.

"After ... you, Ash," Aefric said, sweaty and panting for breath, and leaning on the Brightstaff to stay upright.

"I really must find a way to thank you for this, Aefric," she said, touching his cheek. "Not only did you come to my rescue, but you brought everything we needed to win Colm's foolish war."

"Right now ... you can thank me most ... by stepping through."

"As you wish," she said with a smile.

"I think you'll like his airship, your grace," Deirdre said.

"Airship?" Ashling asked, eyebrows high.

"Please ... through," Aefric said.

Ashling looked closer at him, gave him a worried nod, turned and stepped through the mirror portal.

"Now you," Aefric said, waving away Deirdre's objections. "Can't ... hold it much longer."

Deirdre grabbed him by the belt, stepped through, and yanked him after her.

That was functionally two at once. Just too much for him. Aefric collapsed unconscious on the deckhouse floor.

13

———————

A woman's soft voice woke Aefric, though whatever her words were, he missed them.

He didn't want to wake. He was warm and comfortable. Lying between silk sheets...

Woman's voice? Silk sheets? His scars!

Aefric sat bolt upright, eyes snapping awake.

He was in his bed, in the bedroom in his cabin aboard the *Baron's Will*. The soft, magical light crystals had been activated. He was naked, but no woman lay beside him.

He sagged with a sigh. Just a...

"Forgive me, your grace. I didn't mean to startle you."

Arras, there in the doorway, dressed in...

Not much.

Oh, she wasn't exactly *naked*, but she wore only a shirt of white silk, long-sleeved, and so light it was translucent. The same could be said of her white silk hose. These were the scant clothes she usually wore under her armor. Far too revealing to be worn while just walking around. In fact, the last time Aefric saw her clad so temptingly, she was giving him a smoldering look while removing her armor in his rooms in Water's End...

He shook away the image. Obviously that wasn't why she was here.

"Quite all right, Arras," he said.

"I hope your grace will forgive my attire," she said, gesturing to herself. "But even I need a break from the armor once in a while."

She must've seen his next question in his eyes, because she continued.

"I am, technically, on guard duty. But Beornric said that so long as your grace continued to sleep, your guardian knight could ... relax somewhat. The war is over and we seem quite safe aboard this ship, given the many soldiers and wizards running about."

"How many wizards are we talking about?"

"Karbin and Jenbarjen, of course. Sirondfar. And I *think* I saw Karbin talking to Kainemorton at one point, but I'm not sure."

"Assume you did," Aefric said, shaking his head. He still felt sleepy, and ravenously hungry, but surprisingly clear-headed. "With Kainemorton, it's always safer to assume you *did* see him than that you didn't." He stretched, causing a series of pleasant pops along his spine. "Gods. So much for keeping that box's powers a secret."

"Is that important, your grace?" she asked.

"Probably not. At least, I hope not." He frowned. Through his connection to the ship's magic, he could feel that they were flying ... north-by-northwest. Yes. "Where are we? What's our situation?"

"Not far from the border now, and arriving soon at Armityr. I'm afraid your grace has slept through the journey. Have no fear, though. Micham, Deirdre and I have been applying the ointment twice a day, even while your grace slept. Speaking of which."

Aefric nodded, and she retrieved the thick linen gloves and jar of ointment from a nightstand drawer, along with a small dowel. The teak box sat on that nightstand, and the Brightstaff stood nearby.

"Did the box follow me?"

"No, your grace," Arras said, donning the gloves, "only the Brightstaff followed. Karbin brought the box."

She handed Aefric the dowel. "The scar test, if your grace would be so kind. None of us were able to properly perform it while you slept, of course, though we did try. But now that you're awake..."

"I should follow my healer's orders to the letter, yes," he said, then poked a normal scar on his calf, followed by a demon scar on his chest. Then frowned in puzzlement.

"Verdict?" she asked. "How much worse is the demon scar?"

"I'm not sure it is," he said. "It's pretty close."

He poked three different normal scars, then three different demon scars. First with the same amount of force, then applying a little extra to the demon scars.

"I *may* be done," he said, "but I'm not sure. They feel *almost* the same, but not entirely. Let's do today, to be safe. Though I don't see how—"

"Rest," Beornric said, walking into the room. Clad in his full plate, he was the only one fully dressed. "I spoke with Bebara before we left. She told me that the main thing you needed, apart from the ointment, was rest. Apparently sleeping for nearly two days straight has helped you more than your experiment with the box hurt you."

"Two days?"

"What did you expect?" Beornric asked, while Arras began applying the ointment. "Obviously using the teak box takes something out of you. Add to that the stress of what we did in Caiperas, plus—"

"Speaking of what we did," Aefric said. "I never got a casualty report."

"None among ours," Beornric said proudly. "On the other side, only the dozen soldiers killed by your grace."

"Don't remind me," Aefric said with a grimace. "I should've found some other way—"

"Deirdre told me exactly how it went," Beornric said. "And both Arras and Micham confirmed."

Arras made a point of nodding where Aefric could see her.

"Had you done anything less showy or fatal," Beornric continued, "you would probably have had to kill a lot more than a dozen soldiers before Makarios surrendered."

Aefric considered that a moment. "You're sure there were no casualties apart from those?"

"Oh, there were some injuries, of course. Far more on their side than ours, but nothing major either way. No lost limbs, and no one likely to die. They had no idea we were coming, and we struck quickly while surprise was on our side."

Aefric smiled. Nodded.

"Knew that would perk you up," Beornric said. "Now finish up here and get dressed. If you hurry, we can get you fed before we land."

As they would soon be reaching the royal palace, Aefric decided he'd better look as though he belonged there. So he dressed in a navy blue silk shirt with embroidered silver trim, and the image of Lake Deepwater rendered in silver thread over his heart. He chose hose of Deepwater gray, and belt and boots of soft calfskin, dyed nearly black.

On his belt he wore his noble's dagger — apparently returned by Karbin when he brought in the teak box — his enchanted black velvet pouch — which once again *contained* said teak box — and the wand Garram in its sheath.

With the Brightstaff in hand, Aefric ran a critical eye over the ensemble in the mirror held up by a pretty body servant who didn't really exist. The look would do.

He reminded himself to thank Jenbarjen later for making sure his closet contained clothes appropriate to his ducal title, not only his baronial title.

By the time he finished dressing, Arras was in her full plate again, with her twin longswords strapped to her sides.

It was she who escorted him to the baronial dining room. Where enough diners stood waiting for him that some of the round tables would actually see use this time.

Aefric sat at the head of his rectangular, central table, of course.

Ashling on his right hand, followed by pale Siburh and dark Vashhal. Beornric sat at his left hand, followed by Ecgrun with her fiery hair.

Beornric wore his full plate — Aefric doubted he had anything else with him, given the way they'd rushed to Armityr — but the noblewomen had all changed into finery from their luggage. Fine silks and velvets for their dresses, and the occasional glitter of gold and jewels, but otherwise Aefric's eyes glossed over the details there, because as soon as all were seated, servants in red and gold Merrek livery began bringing in food.

And nothing was more important than food at the moment. He hadn't felt so completely famished since his rations were ruined in the Mines of Mortauk, and he'd had to push himself nonstop for two days. Desperate to find food before he collapsed from hunger.

Two long days, riding his *magaunt* along the muddy remains of a long-disused road. Fighting to hold the phantom horse's spells together against exhaustion and starvation.

The inn he'd finally reached had nothing for him but day-old roast mutton, but it had tasted like divine fruit. And the next time he'd seen Karbin, he'd begged him for the secrets of flying magic so that he might never again risk death over a little thing like distance.

Aboard the *Baron's Will*, though, the servants weren't bringing in anything as filling as mutton. Or at least, not yet. Currently, their silver platters carried chased silver goblets of water and palate wine. The only food Aefric saw so far was some kind of garden salad.

His belly rumbled protest at being offered nothing but a mixture of lettuce and simple vegetables. He tried reassuring it that more would follow, but it wasn't listening. So he forced himself to pay at least a little attention to his surroundings.

Karbin, Jenbarjen and Sirondfar sat together at a nearby round table, off to his left. Farther away, to his right, Deirdre, Arras and Micham sat with four knights Aefric didn't recognize, but had to be Ashling's.

The palate wine was so light as to be almost flavorless. Intended to clear away any lingering tastes from earlier food. Aefric tosses his down anyway, for form's sake, tasting little more than wetness.

Then a salad was placed in front of him and Aefric took his first bite. Surprisingly crisp and tasty, and flavored with the tang of a spiced oil. But his stomach still felt as though it were being mocked.

"I trust you'll forgive my impertinence, Aefric," Ashling said, once the other diners began on their salads. "Properly speaking, I should have asked if you wished the aid of my servants before sending them to your cook. But—"

"It was quite thoughtful of you, Ash," Aefric said, and Siburh's eyes widened at the familiarity, "and I was indisposed. I should be thanking you, not forgiving you."

"I believe it's *we* who should be thanking your grace," Siburh said. "Such a dramatic rescue. Swooping in to win the war, then carrying us away on an *airship*. Cyneswith will swoon when she hears of it."

Aefric washed down a mouthful of salad with a taste of light white wine that carried an undercurrent of citrus.

"I may have arrived with the means," he said, "but it was Ashling who forged the plan that led to our success. And it was Ashling who had the foresight to learn the routines of the royal family, as well as the locations of those places we needed to take, to quickly seize control of the castle."

"And let us not forget the brave soldiers who executed the plan," Beornric said.

"Nor those who led them through it," Ashling said, giving Beornric a smile and a nod before turning back to Siburh. "Don't worry. Your own role will not go unremembered."

Ashling nodded to Vashhal and Ecgrun. "Nor will either of yours. You three were instrumental in checking my information about the royal routines, and especially the location of the treasury. As well as other ways you aided."

"I believe there will be plenty of glory to go around," Beornric said.

"But let us return to our means of escape," Ashling said, turning a smile on Aefric, who hoped he didn't know where this was leading. "This *magnificent* vessel. I've hardly had time to explore and already I've seen such wonders! Wherever did you get it?"

"My baronial wizard, Jenbarjen, is the creative and magical force behind this ship," Aefric said with a smile.

"*Baronial* wizard?" Siburh asked.

"Careful, Aefric," Ashling teased. "This one might try to steal her. I'd be tempted myself, to get my hands on such a ship."

"Then I'm afraid you'd both be as disappointed as the king," Aefric said. "For this ship cannot be duplicated. Its design relied on the special properties inherent in some of its materials. Properties that did not become clear until construction was underway."

"Special properties?" Ecgrun asked. "Might I inquire about their nature?"

Aefric waited a moment while servants cleared away the empty salad plates. He hardly remembered eating his — certainly his stomach didn't feel convinced that he'd eaten anything — but began to smell the joy of good roast venison. He pushed to speak quickly before his plate arrived and distracted him.

"This is difficult to explain to one who is not versed in magical theory," he said, glad Karbin wasn't involved in the conversation. Karbin knew how to heckle him without saying a word. "But suffice to say that there are certain ... places and objects that exist simultaneously in more than one world."

"How is that possible?" Vashhal asked. "As I understand it, the worlds are separated by a kind of planar veil. If, say, a tree were to exist in more than one world, it would have to exist *across* that veil. Which would mean it could be climbed up in one world and down in another."

"This is mostly theory," Aefric said. "To explain a kind of unusual phenomenon in which certain objects and places appear to possess inherent magical qualities that are both different and stronger than their surroundings."

"So no one has attempted to climb such a tree?" Ecgrun asked.

"Not to the best of my knowledge, no. The closest I've come was finding a pool of startlingly fresh water far underground, where by all rights it should have been stale. At best. But I didn't try swimming in it."

"And a good thing, too," Ashling said with a smile, while chased silver plates were placed before them, each featuring venison, garlic mashed potatoes and rolls of honeyed oat bread. Their goblets were replaced with fresh ones, these filled with a rich, dark red wine. "Otherwise you might've gotten lost in some other world and we'd never have had our duke."

She was trying to change the subject. Interesting. But Siburh wasn't ready to surrender it. Which meant Aefric couldn't start on his venison yet. Despite the watering of his mouth and rumbling of his belly.

"So your grace suggests that this ship was constructed from ... what ... wood from such a multi-planar tree?"

"Wood," Aefric said, "or some other element of its construction."

"Let the man have *some* secrets, Sib," Ecgrun teased. "It's a wonderful ship. Let's just enjoy it while we're here."

"And let the poor man *eat*," Vashhal said with a smile. "I can hear his stomach begging from here."

They all laughed then, even Aefric, who happily took his first bite of roast venison.

Roasted medium rare with just the right amount of salt and pepper.

Perfect.

The conversation quelled a bit while they ate their hearty lunch in the baronial dining room of the *Baron's Will*. At least, conversation quelled at the main table. The three wizards at their table continued some kind of discussion in steady, measured voices. And the knights' table verged closer to raucous than was probably appropriate for the setting. Aefric didn't need to hear much to know they were sharing stories.

But around him at the main table, it seemed that Ashling, Beornric, Ecgrun, Vashhal and even Siburh were all content to let their poor, half-starved host enjoy his meal.

But once the venison was finished, they'd all eaten they would of their garlic mashed potatoes and honeyed oat rolls, and sat sipping their rich, dark red wine, the conversation began again while servants in Merrek livery cleared away their dishes.

Naturally enough, the conversation restarted with the victory over Caiperas.

"So we've gained *all* the territory north and west of the River Sulquill," Siburh said.

"Yes," Ashling said, and sighed. "Pity we encouraged Makarios invade Malimfar so far south. We could've gained even *more* land."

"Assuming King Colm didn't hand that portion right back to Malimfar," Beornric said. "As a gesture of goodwill."

"A Stronghand? Give away land he has a claim to?" Ashling sounded positively scandalized at the thought. "We'll all be long dead before such a day dawns."

"Including me?" Aefric asked, for magic-users were known to lead *very* long lives.

"Given your grace's habit of throwing himself into the hazard?" Beornric asked through a chuckle.

Aefric was spared having to answer that when the servants brought out small, silver plates with portions of raspberry crumble.

"Even so," Siburh said, while the dishes were passed about. "What we *have* gained still represents a *significant* increase in the Armyrian borders. The largest since—"

"Silverlake," Ashling said. "Which was more than four hundred years ago now."

Aefric took his first bite of the crumble. Delightful. Full of flavor, without being too sweet. As the others joined him in the dessert, they continued their discussion between bites.

"And I believe our new lands represent an even greater total area than Silverlake," Vashhal said. "His majesty could even create a new duke or duchess, if he had a mind to."

"There would be some logic to that," Ecgrun said. "A single vassal, overseeing the new southeastern border."

"*Some* logic, yes," Ashling allowed, "but not enough to merit creating a new peer. Not when his current peers give him more than enough grief." She smiled at Aefric. "Even his new favorite."

Her sapphire eyes danced as her smile widened.

She knew. Somehow she knew — or she'd guessed — that Aefric had gone after Nelazzi without permission. No matter what story had come out of Armityr afterward.

"Well, if his majesty will not create a new peer," Siburh said, "then one cannot help but wonder how the new lands will be apportioned among the nobility."

Ashling favored her with a small smile. "A decision our dear monarch will give a great deal of attention to, of course."

"Of course," Siburh replied.

"Come now, Ashling," Ecgrun said. "I think we all know his majesty will hear your opinion before he makes his decision. There's no harm in sharing it with us."

"Nor is there any point. His majesty has not been best pleased with me of late. Should he learn my thoughts on the subject, he'd reject them for the sole reason that they're mine."

"It is true that you are *undoubtedly* his most troublesome peer," Siburh said, and to Aefric's surprise, she shared a smile with Ashling.

"You've just played a major role in winning his latest war," Aefric said. "If that's not enough to regain his favor, I can't imagine what would be."

"Oh, I'll be forgiven my transgressions," Ashling said. "But not before my sins are called to account. Gods forfend that Colm forgive a Fyrenn before he must. And I suspect I'll pay a price in land this time."

"That may depend on how matters stand with Varondam," Beornric said. "If his head is still in war—"

"Maev had something to say to him about that," Aefric said. "She may be speeding resolution on that front."

"And doubtless whatever her gains from Varondam might be," Vashhal said to Ashling, "they'll be less than yours in Caiperas."

"And for less of a price," Ecgrun added. "Considering how long

Varondam kept the prospect of marriage and alliance dangling before their plans were found out."

"You mean before they were discovered by his favorite," Ashling said, nodding at Aefric. "Who will also get the dragon's share of credit for Caiperas."

"I will not stand for anyone giving me another's glory," Aefric said, drawing a smile from Ashling, raised eyebrows from Ecgrun and Vashhal, and a studious look from Siburh. "I will insist on his majesty giving appropriate credit to everyone involved."

"Which is a lovely sentiment," Ashling said patiently. "And will likely lead to every soldier and knight on this ship being toasted until they can hardly stand. But among the nobility, your intentions will mean little. And to Colm, they'll mean even less."

"But—"

"Insist all you wish, Aefric," Ashling said. "And know that your words will be heard and appreciated, and that they will be reflected in the glory and accolades heaped on all of us. In public."

"But once the crowds have gone home..." Siburh said.

"His majesty will hand out his rewards exactly and only as *he* sees fit. Which, in this case, will include land."

"Even the queen will have only so much influence with him in this regard," Vashhal said to Aefric.

"Of course," Ashling said. "He may love her, but she's still a Fyrenn."

"It's not just your name," Siburh said, shaking her head. "It's your attitude. Always has been. You could have a much better relationship with his majesty if you wanted to. Only your pride stands in your way, Ashling."

"I am a peer of the realm and will have my due," Ashling said. "I'm sure my sister kneels for him often enough. He doesn't need me doing it too."

Aefric frowned. "You *are* speaking *metaphorically*, yes?"

All four women laughed, but none actually answered.

Beornric shot him an *I'll-tell-you-later* look.

"Well, whatever happens with the spoils," Ecgrun said, "at least we'll all be going home."

"*Yes*," Ashling said, with feeling. "Feels like a year since I last saw Fyrcloch."

From there, the conversation devolved into discussions of home. But Aefric doubted he'd be going home yet. Not until Vardonam was resolved.

AEFRIC AND HIS LUNCH GUESTS WERE LINGERING OVER THE LAST OF their raspberry crumble and discussing the things they missed most about home when a sailor in Netar's green and gold entered the dining room.

He played a trio of notes on a whistle.

One he had everyone's attention, he said, "Please forgive my intrusion, your lordship, noble guests, but I bring a message from the captain. We are on approach to Armityr and will reach the royal palace shortly."

"Thank you," Aefric said to the sailor, who raised his right fist high in salute, and left. Aefric stood. "Good people, I suggest we disperse to see to any final preparations we must make prior to arrival."

"If I might linger a moment, Aefric," Ashling said, as the others all stood.

"Of course, Ash," Aefric said, and the two of them waited while Ashling's companions left, then the wizards, and finally Beornric and the knights.

Once Aefric and Ashling were alone in the dining room, which still smelled of raspberry crumble, he smiled and said, "Not a problem with your accommodations, I trust."

"Tease," she said. "You know this ship is the stuff of dreams. No. I wanted to talk with you privately about rewards and the new landgain."

Four servants filed in and began cleaning up. Aefric looked at them pointedly. Ashling glanced at them, then gave Aefric a smile.

"I appreciate the thought, but they're fine," she said. "The ones Siburh, Vashhal and Ecgrun have spying for them have all been assigned to see to the packing today."

"Quite coincidentally, of course," Aefric said.

"Of course," Ashling said, and the false innocence in her voice faded as she continued in soft tones. "As you are still new to nobility, I didn't want you misled by the lunch conversation. Siburh, of course, hopes to gain some of that new land herself. Ecgrun and Vashhal doubtless have hopes along similar lines, but only Siburh is ambitious enough to push. And while I might publicly praise their assistance, in truth they did little more than keep me company and act as my spies."

"Spying is certainly a contribution to the war effort that should not be ignored," Aefric said.

"Nor should it be overstated," Ashling said. "They deserve some reward, certainly. But *not land*. Most likely they'll be given some small portion of the reparations paid by Caiperas."

"Part of the reason you demanded so much," Aefric said.

"Very good," Ashling said with a smile. "But when it comes to the *land*, I can tell you here and now how it will be distributed, with some degree of accuracy."

Aefric raised an eyebrow at her, fully aware that the effect was *nothing*, compared to what she could achieve with the same movement.

"Which is why you chose *that* portion of land," he said.

"Naturally," Ashling said, and now her smile sparkled. "Though, to be fair, it was only logical to take land already connected to Armyr. Even if I demanded significantly more than they expected me to ask."

"So how do you see it being distributed?"

"Easily," she said. "The land north and west of the River Sulquill is already apportioned into four counties."

She looked at Aefric expectantly. He frowned, but needed only a moment to realize what she meant.

"There are four peers in Armyr," he said. "The crown and the duchies."

"Just so," she said with a nod.

"But what about Rethneryl?" Aefric asked. "They certainly came to our aid."

"They did," Ashling agreed. "Which is why Colm might give them Caer Ylfarai and the Pass of Dayor Ol'Tain. One could argue that it was *we* who helped *them* take it, after all, while asking nothing in return. Fairly generous of us, really. Whereas Rethneryl contributed nothing to our efforts at Reyvenue, and certainly should not expect to profit by them."

"Do you believe this?" Aefric asked. "Or is this simply how you think our king will sell it to theirs?"

"Either way amounts to the same thing," she said, shrugging one shoulder. "And happy as King Edan is with us for rescuing his two lost princesses, Colm might not need to give them *that* much."

"All right," Aefric said. "So if he keeps those counties for the peers, what then?"

"Colm will evaluate them for relative value. The least, he'll give to Wylyn. With the excuse that while Wylyn played almost no role in Caiperas, his armies stood ready to do whatever was asked. Also, his navy answered the call quickly to oppose Varondam."

"You say 'excuse,'" Aefric said. "You don't mean this will be the king's excuse not to split even his *least valuable* new county among the knights and lesser nobles. The ones who *materially contributed* to our victory."

"That's *exactly* what I mean," Ashling said firmly. "Aefric, you must understand this. Splitting up an existing county would create problems for the common folk *well beyond* what they'd face from a mere change of count. It would be *disastrous*. In an area where we must have strong, consistent leadership *right now*."

"We'll be dealing with unrest in those counties for a while, won't we?" Aefric said.

"We should expect to," Ashling said. "Depending on how happy the common folk have been with Makarios, and whatever count or countess they're used to. Not to mention whatever rumors they've heard about *us*."

"Makarios called me our king's attack dog," Aefric said.

"Colorful," Ashling said, "but hardly an accurate depiction."

"Could be a troublesome reputation though."

"Oh, that's not your reputation," she said, waving away the idea. "And anyway, the common folk's experience of you will count for more than any rumors or reputations. Handled properly, any unrest we find should fade within a year."

"What about the counts and countesses who already hold those lands? What happens if they decide to remain, and shift allegiance to Armyr?"

"Then we'll have an easier time with the common folk, and deal with our new vassals as best we can. You did well enough handling Deepwater's vassals when you ascended to your duchy. I'm sure you'll do fine with whatever Colm gives you."

"So, potential unrest is the reason none of the counties could go to lesser nobles?"

"Any noble should be able to handle unrest," Ashling said, waving away that concern. "No. In theory, Colm *could* give a county to some castellan or landless knight. But we're not talking about some lerdom or barony, here. We're talking about a *county*. And there's only one petty noble Colm could argue would deserve *that* much land and power as a reward right now. Especially when *all* the peers contributed to his efforts in Caiperas and Varondam. I'm talking, of course, about his general."

"Paic Ol'Shenquill," Aefric said.

"That's her," Ashling said, then shook her head. "I doubt she'd take it if he offered it. She's never shown any interest in ruling, and her current role suits her too well."

"There's really no one else? What about—"

"Before you complete that sentence, ask yourself how that person's contributions and *reputation* compare with *Paic Ol'Shenquill*."

That was a tall order. Even Beatritz, Yrsa and Beornric fell shy of *that* measure...

"Exactly," Ashling said. "Now. Properly speaking, Colm should take the *next* least valuable county for himself."

"Because he dug this hole, but we got him out of it?"

"Not to mention that it was I who helped sell his lie to Caiperas in the first place," she said, then shook her head. "Nevertheless, he won't. He'll give Wylyn the least valuable, because giving *me* so little would be an insult. But he'll give the next least valuable to me, as the cost of absolving me of my sins."

"What exactly have you done to upset him?" Aefric asked.

"Oh, who keeps track? He feels he must assert himself from time to time over us 'grasping Fyrenns,' and I often irritate him by reminding him just how much he needs us."

"Not to mention who has the older family?"

"Oh, he doesn't need *me* to remind him of that," Ashling said with a smirk. "He wakes up next to *that* reminder every morning."

Aefric chuckled. "What about the last two counties?"

"He *should* give you the most valuable." She raised a hand against the objection on Aefric's lips. "Yes, it was my plan, as you're sweet enough to let no one forget. But it relied *entirely* on not only the forces and magic you brought with you, but also your reputation. Had you been anyone else, we might well have failed even if we had *twice* as many troops. And Colm will know that without being told."

"Just what *is* my reputation?" Aefric asked.

"I should have thought that was obvious," Ashling said. "To stand between you and your goal is to court destruction."

She reached up and stroked his cheek fondly while he absorbed those words.

"And now I have things I must see to before we land. Please do see me again before you leave Armityr."

"Of course," he said absently.

Halfway to the dining room doors, she snapped her fingers and turned around.

"Oh," she said. "Before I forget. Your Malimfari land is Storbakki, yes?"

"That's right," Aefric said, frowning at the change of conversation.

"I thought so. If you haven't been there yet, you should know it's right on the southern bank of the Indecisive River," she said. "A short distance from Kivash, where you now have your own shipping company. Could be a lucrative combination."

"*I* haven't had time to give Storbakki a thought yet," Aefric said, chuckling in disbelief. "And here *you* are already seeing the advantages in it."

"Naturally," she said with a bow that made her look more like a skald receiving applause than a noble offering a courtesy. "But remember, this is what I've been trained to do." She winked. "Don't worry, though. You're clever enough. You'll learn."

She left then, and Aefric stood there, alone with the cleaning staff, wondering about life as a noble, and what his reputation really meant.

AEFRIC HAD HALF-EXPECTED THAT THEIR ARRIVAL AT ARMITYR WOULD be met with bands and speeches and cheering crowds. But rain poured down from blackened skies. Under the light of occasional lanterns, the gray and white stone of the castle parapets looked empty of any but a handful of forlorn guards, doing their duty.

Good.

Oh, celebration was important. It had its place, and it would come. But not yet. Not when there was so much left to do.

Varondam, of course, was a viper's nest of unanswered questions. What was happening there? Was he needed? How quickly could it be resolved, and what could he do to help?

So many questions and concerns that he could hardly spare attention for the other matter that had been picking at his brain since he woke from his two-day nap.

Aefric felt he *finally* knew the answer to a question that had been plaguing him for *seasons*. Not that he would get to act on that answer anytime soon.

So it was to the sound of only whipping wind that Aefric and a longboat full of nobles, knights and wizards descended through the air from the *Baron's Will* to the parapets of the royal palace.

Fortunately, though, Jenbarjen had enchanted the longboats against rain, so those whipping winds were the worst Aefric and the others had to deal with on the ride down.

Alas though, they were met on the parapets by that downpour, as well as a pair of pages who split them into two groups. Those from Merrek and those from Deepwater. Which technically did not include Jenbarjen, but Aefric made sure she felt invited along.

Other pages waited in a rain-sheltered section of the parapets, while more longboats made the trip down with Ashling's entourage and both Merrek's and Netar's soldiers.

Aefric and his group were given only a small amount of time to refresh themselves in the sumptuous Deepwater residence — fortunately, between himself, Karbin and Jenbarjen, cleaning and drying everyone with magic took almost no time — before another page returned to escort Aefric to the royal presence.

This page was a young, coltish woman with long brown hair. Aefric recognized her immediately.

"Pleasure to see you again, Nesta," he said, as she bowed. "I trust you've been keeping well?"

"Quite well, your grace," she said, fighting down a blush. "And grateful at being remembered."

"You'll be one of my lers in Netar soon enough," Aefric said with a chuckle. "What kind of baron would I be if I forgot you?"

"The most common kind," Beornric said wryly. "Unless you were intent on sharing the noble privilege with her."

Poor Nesta lost her battle then and flushed bright red.

Aefric almost chided Beornric for embarrassing Nesta, but decided that might make things worse.

"I believe his majesty awaits us," he said instead. "Who may I bring with me?"

"Oh, forgive me, your grace," Nesta said, recovering herself, even if her cheeks and forehead were still quite pink. She bowed again. "Your grace is welcome to bring his adviser, Ser Beornric

Ol'Sandallas, should he so choose. I should have said so straight away."

Aefric nodded, and Beornric stepped forward.

"No others?" Aefric asked.

"Your grace, the only mention his majesty made of others," Nesta said apologetically, "concerns your grace's Knights of the Lake. I have been told that your grace's security within the castle has been assured."

"In other words," Beornric said with a smile, "don't insult the crown by walking around the royal palace with armed guards."

"Fair enough, I suppose," Aefric said, turning to Arras and Micham. "Looks as though you two get a break." He turned to Deirdre. Raised a suspicious eyebrow. "I know you're prone to restlessness..."

"Restlessness, your grace?" Deirdre said, fingers to her chest in mock innocence. "Me?"

Beornric cleared his throat.

"Yes, well, if you're going to bring *that* up," she said with a small chuckle, then gave Aefric a smile. "Don't worry, your grace. I'll be good."

"We'll keep an eye on her, your grace," Arras said.

"Hey," Deirdre objected. "I *said* I'd be good."

Arras, Micham and Beornric all started talking at the same time. Aefric tapped the butt of the Brightstaff on the maple floorboards and let loose a small clap of thunder.

Everyone looked at him.

"She is my champion, and she says she will behave herself," Aefric said. "That's enough for me."

Grateful was too weak a word for the look Deirdre gave him then. There were too many other emotions in those jade eyes.

It was too much. Aefric had to look away, so he turned to his wizards. "And as for you two—"

"We're at liberty drink and talk magic," Karbin said with a smile, "so long as we stay here. In case we're needed. Yes?"

"That's right," Aefric said.

Jenbarjen looked as though she'd rather have been escorted to see the king, but sighed and said, "Hope there's some decent honsach."

"Plenty," Aefric said, then turned to Nesta. "Let's not keep his majesty waiting."

"Their majesties," Nesta said. "Both will be present."

She bowed again, and led him and Beornric out the door and down the beautiful marble hallway.

This was a part of the palace devoted to the apartments set aside for the peers, and looked the part. Every inch was gleaming marble. Every half-dozen paces, a fresh vase of red roses. Plenty of arching windows that would normally have let in sunshine or moonlight, but now offered views of the downpour over the dim lights of the city.

The light in the hallway came from interwoven enchantments on those vases. Subtle work, that gave the light a sourceless look and feel that Aefric approved of.

They had to descend only two broad sets of stairs and cross only one more wide hall before they reached an arching double door. Both doors made from a dark oak, but they'd been intricately carved in elegant designs, with the carvings highlighted with gold leaf.

Nesta knocked twice on the door. It was opened by another page Aefric recognized, as much by her age — she was about his own age — as her dark blonde hair and pretty features. Rashien Ol'Ofaris.

"Ah, Nesta. Good," Rashien said. "I'll take them from here."

Nesta actually bowed, which Aefric had never seen one page do for another before. Even weirder in this case, because Nesta would one day inherit her family lerdom, while Rashien would not. Which meant that Nesta outranked her.

Apparently, though, deference from other pages was one of the advantages of being a senior page at Armityr. Which made Aefric wonder if there were any senior pages at one of his castles...

As befit her role, Nesta left without saying goodbye. Doubtless about her next task.

Rashien bowed to Aefric and Beornric, then opened the door and admitted them into a small, narrow corridor. Floorboards and wall panels of pale white oak. White stone for the ceiling, and magical light provided by two empty candle sconces.

The corridor didn't last five paces, and at the end was another double-door that was the twin of the one they'd just come through.

He realized, though, that he could hear hints of music and muffled voices from beyond that doorway now, which had not been true out in the hall. So perhaps that was the reason for this little corridor?

Rashien knocked twice on the door, then opened it and led them into the royal presence.

———

"His grace, Ser Aefric Brightstaff," Rashien called into the room ahead of him. "Duke of Deepwater, Baron of Netar, Vanquisher of the Pirate Queen Nelazzi, Hero of the Battles of Deepwater, Frozen Ridge, and Reyvenue."

Wait. So they were calling what he'd done in Caiperas the Battle of Reyvnue? And naming him its hero?

Oh, come *on*. That wasn't even *close* to accurate.

"His grace is accompanied by his chief adviser," Rashien continued, "Ser Beornric Ol'Sandallas."

Rashien led them then into a small throne room. Well, small was a relative term, of course. The room was square in shape, and would have taken Aefric at least a dozen steps to cross.

Certainly, though, it was small compared to the great hall down below, where their majesties' main thrones sat. But this was a throne room made for company, not proclamations or adjudication.

The thrones themselves were simple, but beautiful. Black oak, with cross-connections from points on the back and the arms and legs that made Aefric suspect they'd both been carved from the same great tree, and never quite separated.

The thrones sat on a small, white oak dais, only one step up from the white oak floorboards.

The walls and ceiling had been plastered. The walls were painted forest green, and the ceiling gold. The magical light in the room was tied to an enchantment in the ceiling, but didn't shine out from a specific spot.

Four curved couches formed a semi-circle in front of the thrones, leaving a path down the center from the door. All of them backless, made from black oak, and upholstered in burgundy velvet.

To Aefric's left as he entered, a small triangular stage in the corner featured an eldrani harpist, plucking a soft, gentle tune on a harp that looked to be made of cherry wood. It was a song Aefric didn't recognize.

Along the righthand wall, a serving man somewhere in middle-age stood beside a small series of cabinets. He held a silver platter in front of his chest, as though keeping it ready. Just in case.

Their majesties were on their thrones. King Colm clad in a white shirt that looked surprisingly stiff and set off the battlefield tan he'd somehow held onto. No crown atop his short, graying black hair today. Under his cloth-of-gold sash belt, he wore dark brown hose and matching shoes with cloth-of-gold spats.

Queen Eppida wore a cream-colored gown that looked simple at first glance, but shimmered in the light in ways that suggested it wasn't so simple as it appeared. She wore thin gold bracelets on each wrist, matching the enchanted golden torc at her pale throat. She wore her golden curls down and dancing about her bare shoulders.

Gwen stood near a couch to Aefric's left. Her silk gown was dark blue today, and she emphasized her low neckline with a ruby pendant set in gold. Like the queen, she wore her wavy black hair down and loose.

Both their majesties stood as Aefric and Beornric approached. Both of them smiling at Aefric.

King Colm raised both hands as though a skald declaiming to someone on the balcony.

"There he is," the king said in a booming voice. "The hero of the day, come forth at last."

"I am honored, your majesty," Aefric said, stepping up to the dais. But he was stopped short of kneeling by a gesture from the king.

"None of that today, Aefric," he said, and embraced Aefric like a brother. "You've won me another war, and brought back land and riches with you."

"Hardly all my own doing, your majesty," Aefric said. But before he could continue the queen embraced him tightly.

"You brought me back my *sister*," she said softly. "Consider any wrongs you've done me righted. And know that neither I, nor any of the Fyrenn family, will *ever* forget what you've done for us."

"Your majesties are too kind," Aefric said, after the queen released him. "But I was hardly alone in any of it. I brought soldiers and magic, but it was Ashling—"

"We'll have plenty of time to discuss the details of your triumph later," King Colm said, reclaiming his throne. "And don't worry, I promise to listen while you heap too much credit on every knight and soldier, while trying to avoid taking any for yourself."

"Well," Queen Eppida said, reclaiming her own throne, "I, for one, would like to hear what his grace was going to say about our peer from Merrek."

"Later, later," King Colm said, and Aefric saw a frustrated gleam enter the queen's eyes.

Rather than get drawn in there, he turned to Gwen. Offered his hand to shake, as they were of equal rank. "Good to see you again, Gwen."

"The pleasure is mine, Aefric," Gwen said with a smile as she shook his hand. "And congratulations on your victory. Though I must say my own king will have mixed feelings about it."

"Oh?" Aefric asked.

"Edan would *love* to have invaded," King Colm said, almost laughing, but not quite. "Doubtless he'd've taken a fair amount of northern Caiperas, including some very valuable mines. Thanks no small amount to my own deception, of course. But even his gains would have cost him lives and time, and there's no guarantee he could have held them."

"Instead," Gwen said, "I believe he'll gain a pass and a castle at very little cost indeed."

"We'll see, we'll see," King Colm said. "I haven't had a chance to evaluate the gains yet. And I certainly won't shortchange the hero of the day in that regard. But now sit, all of you."

Gwen sat once more on the first couch to Aefric's left, closer to in front of the king than in front of the queen. As there was plenty of room, Aefric joined her there, and Beornric sat to his right.

"Now," King Colm said, but the queen interrupted him.

"Shouldn't we wait for Ashling?"

The king frowned, then sighed. "Oh, I suppose. So long as your sister doesn't take too long."

"We *should* have given her time for a proper bath. This rain—"

"She's got her wizard with her, so she's got no excuse."

"This is very much like the discussion they were having before your arrival," Gwen said softly.

There was a knock on the door.

"Finally," King Colm said, then louder, "Come!"

Rashien called into the room, "Her grace, Ashling Fyrenn, Duchess of Merrek, and Vanquisher of the Third Skull."

Aefric, Beornric and Gwen all stood as Ashling entered. She looked resplendent to the point of aggression in a crimson gown, set off here and there with emeralds. She wore her long, jet black hair up in a complicated style, held in place with gold combs.

Both the king and queen stayed seated this time. Though the queen looked as though just seeing her older sister gave her a lift.

"I was beginning to wonder if you'd chosen to ignore my invitation," King Colm said.

"And give your majesty an excuse to have me brought before him by force?" Ashling said. "Never."

"Now, I wouldn't go that far," the king said, but he was smiling.

"Of course not, your majesty," Ashling said, matching his smile. "Never is a very long time."

King Colm chuckled.

Ashling approached then, but she didn't kneel. She did offer her hand to the king, who kissed it. Though she didn't press her forehead to his knuckles in return, but reclaimed her hand and addressed her sister.

"I know you're my queen these days," Ashling said, "but I'd very much like to embrace my—"

Queen Eppida practically leapt into her sister's arms and they clasped each other tightly. Both whispering to each other for a time before they parted.

And when they did, Aefric noticed that the queen's eyes glistened.

"Aefric," Ashling said with a smile, sounding as though she hadn't seen him in ages. She shook hands with him, then kissed him on both cheeks, which drew a small, surprised sound from Gwen.

"Always a pleasure, Ashling," Aefric said, returning the gesture.

"Good to see you, Gwen," Ashling said, and the two shook hands. "Hope King Edan isn't too unhappy with us."

"I think he'll survive," Gwen said.

"I should hope," Ashling said, then turned to Beornric. "Good Beornric, would you be so kind as to let me sit with my peers?"

"Of course, your grace," Beornric said with a bow, before moving to ... stand behind the couch?

"You don't have to—" Aefric started, but the king broke in.

"I have no objections if you wish to sit, Beornric. Although if you wish to stand behind your liege, ready to offer advice, I will of course permit that as well."

"Which is my preference, your majesty," Beornric said with a deep bow.

"Then by all means," King Colm said, "let us take our seats and positions, and we can discuss the reason I've called you here."

———

AEFRIC KNEW HE WAS SUPPOSED TO WAIT FOR THE KING AND QUEEN TO take their seats before him. That part was easy. But Ashling and Gwen, they were of the same rank he was. So what was the protocol there?

The Keifer part of Aefric wanted to let them sit first, because they were ladies, and that was polite. Where Keifer came from. Or at least, he had been raised to consider that polite behavior. Not everyone agreed that it was, though.

But here in Armyr, gender wasn't really a factor in matters like who should sit first. Rank was the primary consideration. So since dukes and duchesses were the same rank, were they all supposed to sit at the same time? Was there some subtle pecking order to their ranks that came first? Gwen was the foreign duchess, but Ashling might've held her title longest...

He looked to Beornric, standing behind the couch, but he couldn't read whatever his knight-adviser was trying to say with his eyes.

Ashling caught Aefric's eye, though, and gave him a subtle nod. Which was even worse, because he had no idea if that meant he should sit or wait or...

But then he realized that Gwen and Ashling were moving into position to take their seats on the maroon velvet of the backless couch they'd three share. But they were not sitting yet.

So Aefric took the same position.

They sat together.

Aefric tried to pretend there wasn't a drop of sweat rolling down his forehead.

Queen Eppida clapped her hands twice. "Sharabi, I should think."

"An excellent choice, my dear," King Colm said.

The serving man near the back dug into the cabinets for a bottle and goblets. The sound of his rustling an odd counterpoint to the soft playing of the eldrani harpist.

The sharabi was served in crystal goblets, not silver. Likely to highlight its dark green shade. This vintage smelled of sage. Ashling swirled hers, while looking intently into the goblet.

Aefric had no idea what she was looking for, but she nodded as though she'd seen it.

"To our victory in Caiperas," Queen Eppida said, raising her goblet, "and all who made it possible."

"And to the hero of the day," King Colm added, raising his own, "which has once again has proven to be our newest peer, Aefric Brightstaff."

"He does seem to be making a habit of it," Queen Eppida said.

The others all raised their goblets in confirmation of the toast — Aefric slowest of them all — and drank.

This sharabi had a complex, slightly sweet taste. Hints of nutmeg and something kind of like strawberries, underlying other tastes Aefric couldn't pick out quickly.

He decided he liked it.

"Now," the king said, "to the matter at hand. Varondam."

"A complex situation," Ashling said. "Dalius has managed to offend not only our two kingdoms, but also Hatay and Shachan, who will no doubt want their own measure of blood before the matter is settled."

"True," King Colm said, "but it is we who have our boot solidly on the throat of Varondami shipping right now. So it is we who control the outcome."

"A circumstance I myself played a role in bringing about," Gwen said. "A fact which I can assure your majesty is not lost on my king."

"Your larger role," King Colm said, "was in freeing the princesses. For which we — as well as Hatay and Shachan — owe you our thanks. But our own thanks in that matter must be held in measure, for — though I am given to understand that your role was important — the greater role in that rescue belongs to his grace here, to his knight, Ser Deirdre Ol'Miri, and, of course, to my own daughter."

"And let it not go overlooked," Queen Eppida added, "that while Princess Raedrun Al'Trener of Hatay and Princess Jodis Ol'Nariss of Shachan both needed rescuing, Rethneryl had not one, but *two* princesses sharing their dire straits. Brigit and Adsaluta Haltallan."

"Without the key, timely assistance of her grace of Neastall," Aefric said, "the entire operation might well have failed. And I myself might've died, or been captured by Varondam."

"Surely you exaggerate the peril," Queen Eppida said.

"I don't believe so," Aefric said. "Although your majesties are, of course, welcome to ask Ser Deirdre, who is here at Armityr, for her opinion on the subject. Or, for that matter, his majesty might ask his own daughter."

"If only Maev were here to give her testimony," Queen Eppida said.

"We will discuss my daughter and her mission shortly," King Colm said. "First, it seems, we must lay to rest the matter of the rescue. Aefric, no one questions the important role that our dear Rethneryli ambassador played. But it is simply *unreasonable* to give her anything approaching equal credit to your own. We all know it was *your* ships carrying you down there, *your* knight infiltrating with you, *your* skills, experience and magic leading the way, and *your* plan behind it all."

"To be clear," Gwen said. "I in no way seek equal credit with his grace of Deepwater in this matter. But I will certainly insist on the contributions of Rethneryl being acknowledged in both word *and* deed."

If Aefric understood that right, she was saying that if there was a reward for the rescue, Rethneryl wanted its cut. Which was more than fair.

"Then consider it so acknowledged in word," King Colm said. "As for in deed, that is a matter to take up with my cousins from Rethneryl, Hatay and Shachan."

"Your majesty's point is well made on the subject of the rescue," Gwen said. "But on the subject of the blockade, Rethneryl's contribution has yet to be acknowledged."

"Ah," King Colm said, shaking a finger. "But there I must question what contribution Rethneryl *made*, beyond the presence of its duchess on one of my duke's ships."

"If I might answer that question?" Aefric asked.

"I might have known you would," King Colm said, smiling but shaking his head. "Go ahead, your grace."

"In the plans leading up to the establishment of the current blockade, her grace of Neastall agreed to lend her battle magic to that of my ducal wizard, Karbin. Despite not having entered the hazard before herself, she stood ready to fling the most powerful spells she knows in defense of not only my own ships, but those of her grace of Merrek and his grace of Silverlake. Indeed, in defense of the entire Armyrian fleet."

"'Stood ready to,' you said," Queen Eppida said. "Did I hear you correctly, your grace?"

"Your majesty, you did," Aefric said.

"Now, I am no magic-user," the queen said. "And I am myself a complete stranger to the hazard. But even I am well aware that there is a not insignificant difference between *standing ready* to do something and *doing* it."

"If a soldier stands a quiet watch," Aefric said, "has he failed? Or has he done his duty and earned his pay?"

"A better question, I believe," Ashling said, "is why her grace was not called upon to do the duties she'd agreed to perform?"

"Because I was called into the rescue effort," Gwen said. "And afterwards, deemed it the priority of my king to see his nieces to safety myself."

"Ah," King Colm said, addressing Gwen. "Then your grace *did* play a part in establishing the blockade. However, I believe this role was, in *fact*, smaller than that of even the least sailor on any of the blockading ships. For duty overrode your grace's role before she could ever be called upon to act. Is that not the case?"

Gwen looked as though she'd gotten a taste of bad sharabi. She cleared her expression through a breath and said, "Your majesty's summation comes close enough to the truth that I see no point in disputing him."

"Excellent," King Colm said with a smile. "Then let me assure your grace that Rethneryl's contribution to the blockade shall not be forgotten. But neither shall it be overstated."

"Which brings us back to Varondam," Queen Eppida said.

"Unless something else presses for my attention?" King Colm asked, looking from duchess to duke to duchess to his queen. He even spared a glance for Beornric, standing behind Aefric.

No questions came.

"Excellent, then," King Colm said. "Varondam."

"If I might begin," Ashling said, "I have thoughts regarding a resolution in this matter."

"It never occurred to me that you wouldn't, Ashling," King Colm said. "Go—"

"Begging your majesty's pardon," Gwen said, "and with only the sincerest respect for her grace of Merrek, I wish to speak first on this topic, if I may. For I am confident that what I have to say will affect anything decided here today."

"I have no objection, your grace," Ashling said, inclining her head. "Please, precede me. If his majesty so wills, of course."

"I am certainly intrigued," King Colm said, and nodded at Gwen. "Go ahead, your grace."

"Once the safe return of the kidnapped princesses was established, and Hatay and Shachan ceased their denials, my king reached out to their monarchs."

"Did he?" Queen Eppida said, but not as though she expected an answer.

"Your majesty, he did," Gwen said anyway. "For while Armyr had been placed in a singularly undesirable position regarding Varondam's treatment of its own princess, the princesses taken from our three kingdoms shared the same complaint. Each was snatched from a ship at the behest of the pirate queen, whom we now know to have been in the employ of Varondam."

"Unquestionably," Aefric said.

"As our three kingdoms were dealt the same blow, King Edan felt we should come to accord in regard to how Varondam should make us whole. With Rethneryl taking the lead in this matter, for we were doubly harmed."

"I see," King Colm said, and though his tone was even, he looked dangerous. "And does Rethneryl wish to dictate those terms to us? Or to discuss them with us?"

"Well," Gwen said, "that very much depends on your majesty's willingness to work with us in this regard. He is in the best position to enforce terms on Varondam. And if he is willing to enforce any terms we agree to here today, then Rethneryl would be happy to make reasonable accommodations to his views on the subject."

Those two words seemed to drop a chill on the room. *Reasonable accommodations.* The moment those words were out of Gwen's mouth, the king's aspect darkened and the queen raised one eyebrow as though about to pronounce a sentence of death.

Even the harpist stopped playing.

Those two words, spoken by Gwen, hung in the air, while all else around was still.

Reasonable accommodations.

Aefric tried not to breath. She'd basically issued an ultimatum to the crown, hadn't she?

Elbar's Blood, they'd just finished one war...

The eldrani harpist began another tune on his great cherry wood harp then, which felt entirely wrong to Aefric. This was *not* a situation that should have been scored by soft, gentle music.

Gwen, to Aefric's left, looked as tense as he felt. But Ashling, to his right, looked completely at ease.

It was Queen Eppida who was first to speak.

"And if Armyr is unwilling to enforce terms in which it was given no say?"

"Your majesty misunderstands me if she believes Armyr would be given no say," Gwen said.

"Rethneryl offers us nothing more than 'reasonable accommodation' to terms that have already been decided," King Colm said. "I find that difficult to accept, and see in it little motivation to use my superior position to Rethneryl's benefit. Let alone that of Hatay and Shachan."

"If Armyr forces us to proceed without them in this matter, we will," Gwen said. "But we would remind your majesty that when he called upon Rethneryl to aid him against Caiperas, we did not hesitate. Even though, when the call came, we had no pressing need to pursue action against Caiperas ourselves."

"Perhaps we should hear the conclusions our neighbors came to," Ashling said, "before we decide whether or not we like them?"

"Before we do," King Colm said, "I would hear Rethneryl acknowledge that without the aid of Armyr, their princesses would yet remain the captives of King Dalius."

"Rethneryl acknowledges this without hesitation or limitation," Gwen said. "And we are most grateful for Armyr's role in this matter."

"I am told that Rethneryl speaks for Hatay and Shachan as well?" King Colm said.

"Then please allow Rethneryl to express also the acknowledgment and gratitude of Hatay and Shachan."

"One more point," the king said, raising an index finger. "I wish it also formally acknowledged that, without Armyr's aid, *not one* of your kingdoms would even know who *captured* your princesses. Let alone who *held* them."

"Hatay and Shachan, after all," Queen Eppida added, "had not even admitted that theirs had been seized."

Aefric fidgeted uncomfortably in his seat. Beornric placed a calming hand high on his shoulder.

Gwen steadied herself through a breath. In that moment of silence, the harpist began a positively jaunty tune.

"Wait," Queen Eppida said, raising one hand. "Harpist! We thank you for your music, but have no further need for your services at this time. You may leave your instrument here in safety as you leave."

The harpist looked as though he'd rather be parted from his right arm than his harp, but he bowed to the queen and left.

"Rethneryl, Hatay and Shachan all acknowledge that it was Armyr who discovered and tracked the kidnappings, and Armyr who led the subsequent rescue," Gwen said. "Further, all three express their deepest gratitude to Armyr for its hard work and swift aid in these matters, most especially to his grace of Deepwater, without whom Varondam would yet hold advantage over us all."

Aefric seriously considered turning himself invisible.

"Excellent," King Colm said. "Now. With those points in mind, we look forward to hearing what Rethneryl has to say."

Gwen drew another deep breath.

"It is the opinion of Rethneryl, Hatay and Shachan, that Varondam should face the following penalties. First, that they pay us reparations, with two shares of these reparations going to Rethneryl, who was twice harmed in this matter."

"I see," King Colm said. "And would Rethneryl's two shares constitute half of the total? Or two-fifths, with the remaining share going to Armyr?"

"Two-fifths," Gwen said, "for though Princess Maev Stronghand demonstrably rescued herself, we in no way wish to belittle the fact that she had, indeed, been taken captive by Varondam and held against her will."

"One share hardly seems equitable," Queen Eppida said, "given the other harms caused us by Varondam."

"A point, if I may?" Ashling said, and waited for both King Colm and Gwen to nod before she continued. "These reparations are *specifically* being paid for the kidnapping and holding of the princesses?"

"That's correct," Gwen said.

"Ah," King Colm said. "I believe what my peer of Merrek is pointing out is that these reparations would not cover the betrayal we suffered for Varondam's falseness regarding marriage and alliance."

"I can assure your majesty that we would take no issue with Armyr seeking separate restitution for those harms," Gwen said.

"Then if I might suggest," Ashling said, "the reparation terms at issue need only a slight modification. Perhaps a half-share more to Armyr, to cover the costs of their enforcement."

"We would be amenable to that," Gwen said, "if Armyr were also willing to transport our shares as far as Hatay's shores. After all, Armyr certainly has enough ships in the area."

"Done," King Colm said. "What's next?"

"Second," Gwen said, "that the four most prominent families in Varondam be required to foster their two eldest children in Hatay, Shachan and Rethneryl for the next three generations."

"Amend that to include Armyr," the king said, "and you have a deal."

"Done," Gwen said. "This brings us to the last, and perhaps most important point. That apart from the preceding fosterage agreement, Varondam be isolated. That their trade no longer be welcomed, their goods no longer purchased, their ships and travelers turned back at every port. That none answer the call to aid, should they be attacked at land or at sea, whether by pirates, monsters, or another kingdom. That from this day forward, Varondam stands alone."

"No," Aefric said, though in truth it came out little more than a whisper. His heart started hammering in his chest.

"I've no doubt Malimfar would join us in that," King Colm said thoughtfully. "The Free Baronies might balk—"

"Would they balk if trading with Varondam meant no more trading with any of the rest of us?" Gwen asked.

"No," Aefric said again, but he was still too shocked by what they were saying to get the word out properly.

"We can't stop their trade entirely," Ashling said. "Kefthal, of course, will trade with anyone. And we'd never be able to enforce our ban on the other side of the Risen Sea..."

"No!"

Hey. Aefric finally got the word out. Of course, now everyone was looking at him, surprised.

"This is a mistake," he said. "It's going too far."

"How do you mean?" Ashling asked, drawing an irritated look from the king, who likely had the same question.

"It isn't *Varondam* that harmed any of us," Aefric said. "It's King Dalius." He saw objections rise on several lips, so he quickly added, "Please. Let me finish."

Nods all around.

"His court had no idea," he said. "I know this, because when I revealed it to them, well, I may be the least experienced noble here, but I know a shocked crowd when I see one. So Dalius was acting alone. Or at least with nothing more than the aid of a handful of advisers."

"That's more than enough," King Colm said.

"But I have a point beyond that, your majesty," Aefric said. "Right now, our enemy is King Dalius. And he *must* be punished for his crimes. But if we isolate *Varondam*, we'll make an enemy of their *people*. Their nobles might hate us for their lost income, but their *people* will *starve* and *die*. And the hatred of the survivors will grow *deeper* and *stronger* than anything those nobles could hope to conjure against us. In punishing one enemy, we'll create *multitudes*."

"I believe you're overstating the case," Queen Eppida said.

"But there is merit to his point," Ashling said. "If Dalius acted alone, there's no reason to alienate Varondam's peers. Especially as, if I know Princess Maev, she's been building goodwill toward us ever since her arrival at Vaaran Tir this past spring."

"True..." King Colm said.

"Thus," Ashling continued, "rather than isolating *Varondam*, we should visit our punishment primarily on their *king*."

"You cannot expect us to forgo relief," Gwen said.

"Of course not," Ashling said. "Nor will Varondam's peers, if they are reasonable. But we send a stronger message if we require — in addition to that relief — that King Dalius Swiftblade the Third abdicate his throne and be banished, penniless. Not only from Varondam, but across the Risen Sea, not to return on pain of death. After this is done, the Varondami peers must select a new king or queen from among themselves. Perhaps even one our four kingdoms must approve."

King Colm raised an eyebrow at Gwen, and Aefric could practically *hear* his intended question.

"I can tentatively agree to that," Gwen said, "with the understanding that I'll need to consult my king. This constitutes a large change to something I understand they were rather insistent on."

"I think they'll see reason," King Colm said. "Because our duke's point is well-made, if perhaps a trifle exaggerated. And the compromise proposed by our duchess is certainly suitable."

"Then I must return to my rooms at once and contact his majesty," Gwen said.

"Excellent," King Colm said, standing. "Then for the moment, we stand adjourned. Pages will see you all back to your apartments."

BACK IN THE ROYAL PALACE'S LUXURIOUS DEEPWATER APARTMENTS, Aefric sighed deeply as he sank down into a couch, with the Brightstaff standing just behind him. Beornric took a seat on the couch across the burnished calinwood coffee table from him.

Karbin and Jenbarjen came over, each taking one of the armchairs at the ends of the couches. Karbin to his right and Jenbarjen to his left.

At Aefric's nod, the other knights joined them. Arras sitting beside Aefric on his couch, Micham beside Beornric, and Deirdre perching on the arm of Aefric's couch, just to his right.

From the look Beornric gave her — which she pretended not to notice — that was inappropriately close.

Karbin made a point of looking over Aefric's slumped posture. "How did it go?"

"I went to a conversation and a negotiation broke out."

"Sounds awful," Deirdre said with a grimace.

"The ambassador from Rethneryl surprised his majesty with something?" Arras asked.

"A couple of things," Beornric said. "Largest was that King Edan had already discussed reparations with Hatay and Shachan, and was bringing those terms to his majesty. Which went ... about as well as one might expect."

"Never good to talk to a king," Deirdre said, shaking her head. "And *dictating* to one, that's just *asking* to have your neck stretched."

"For you, certainly," Micham said. "But for an ambassador, it's expected from time to time."

"Expected does not mean well-received," Jenbarjen said.

"No, it does not," Aefric said, then shook his head. "They were going to *isolate* Varondam."

"That's hardly a surprise," Arras said. "Varondam can't expect to kidnap princesses from four kingdoms and not pay a price."

"But it wasn't *Varondam* doing that," Aefric said. "It was their king."

"Hold, please, all of you," Beornric said, clearly *not* addressing Aefric. "Let's not ask his grace to rehash a stressful meeting. I'll bring you all up to speed on the relevant points later."

"Right now," Aefric said, "Gwen — that is, the ambassador from Rethneryl — is checking with her king. While the rest of us wait."

"Perhaps your lordship should take a nap?" Jenbarjen said. "I find naps to be a great reliever of stress, myself."

"I just slept for two days," Aefric said, chuckling. "I doubt I'll be able to sleep anytime soon."

"Then perhaps a nap without sleeping?" Deirdre asked with a smirk.

"Demon scars, Deirdre," Arras said. "He hasn't been cleared yet."

"Those scars don't start until partway up his chest," Deirdre said. "That does leave open a few intriguing possibilities."

"I appreciate the thought," Aefric said, "but I might be called back at any time. Wouldn't do to keep their majesties waiting while I chase a bliss moment."

"Oh, that won't be a problem, your grace," Deirdre said. "I know how to shortcut the chase when I want to."

"Deirdre," Beornric said, in a tone of voice that brooked no debate.

She sighed. "You've been hanging out with Yrsa too much, Beornric. You're becoming a killjoy."

"There are more important matters before us than bliss moments." He turned to Aefric. "This was a major step for you today, as a noble. You acquitted yourself well in there."

"Did you know this was going to turn into a negotiation?" Aefric asked.

"Not until I saw that we were meeting in a throne room," Beornric said. "Still, it's a possibility anytime you gather several high-ranking nobles, let alone royalty. You should watch for that at parties, feasts and balls, as well."

"Lovely."

"But not only were you quiet when you needed to be — which is a step many have trouble taking — you also fell into the patter and rhythm of formal speech well, when you spoke."

"I was just following their examples," Aefric said. "I only barely remembered in time that Gwen's title was Duchess of Neastall. I almost referred to her as the Duchess of Rethneryl."

"That would have been acceptable," Arras said, "because she's the Rethneryl ambassador. Referencing her specific duchy was definitely better, though."

"Thank you," Aefric said. "But why was his majesty willing to begin before Ashling arrived?"

"Because while inviting the both of you to that meeting was a privilege, it was also your due as peers. Arriving after things began would have been a mark against her grace."

"That reminds me..." Aefric said.

"The lunchtime conversation, yes," Beornric said. "That ... was complex."

"How so?"

"Forgive me," Beornric said, "but this conversation now requires fewer ears."

"Then it's likely to get boring," Deirdre said, standing up. "Arras? Micham? Up for some sparring in the courtyard? The rain's stopped, but the stone will still be slippery..."

"It's like asking for a beating," Micham said, standing. "But I can't resist the challenge. I'm in. Arras?"

"Always," she answered, smiling as she stood. Together the three headed for a door at the far end of the room.

"I *have* to see if she's as good as they say," Jenbarjen said, hopping down from her chair.

"Then I'll come along as well," Karbin said. "I've seen enough of her fighting to give you a decent commentary."

"And I suppose Arras and I are just quintains, are we?" Micham asked in mock outrage.

"Only compared to me," Deirdre said with a grin.

Once they were through the door, and it was closed, Beornric let out an easy breath.

"One thing you have yet to learn," Beornric said. "Trust and friendship are not enough. Some conversations, some *information*, can be dangerous. And should be handled with care."

"We are talking about the kneeling question, yes?" Aefric said. "Ashling's crack about not kneeling to the king, because her sister did enough for both of them?"

"That wasn't quite what she said," Beornric said. "And the difference is important. She said, 'I'm sure my sister kneels for him often enough. He doesn't need me doing it too.'"

"So she *was* talking about oral sex?"

"She was talking about two things. One, a courtesy, the other, a rumor."

"I don't understand."

"I know," Beornric said. "But that's all right. Now, the courtesy is simple. When you arrive at Armityr and are brought before the king, what do you do?"

"I take a knee, as I'm supposed to. He's the king."

"He is. And you are his vassal. And therefore his due is to have you kneel to him, as others bow to you. Yes?"

"Yes," Aefric said, but hesitantly.

"Except that you are also a *duke*. Which means you are not only his vassal, but his *peer*. Do you kneel to Ashling?"

"No. I shake her hand."

"And this is where it gets tricky. See, as duke, you are both peer and vassal. When you kneel before the king, you are telling him that you consider the liege-vassal part of your relationship to be the controlling factor. You are honoring him with a show of devotion."

"And if I shook his hand, I'd be saying I'm his peer?"

"More than that," Beornric said. "You'd be saying you're his *equal*. That not only do you consider the peer part of your relationship to be the controlling factor, but that you don't consider the vassalage portion important."

"I'd be overstepping my bounds," Aefric said.

"Arguably," Beornric said. "But at the very least, you'd be making a public statement about your dissatisfaction with his majesty as king. It could even be seen as the first step before rebellion."

"And Ashling doesn't kneel."

"No, she does not. Except perhaps at the most formal of occasions, where his majesty not only represents himself as king, but the very crown of Armyr. If you understand the distinction."

"When he represents not only himself as current monarch," Aefric said, "but all the kings and queens ever to rule Armyr."

"Just so," Beornric said with approval. "Outside of those situations, she refuses to kneel, emphasizing that she is a peer of the realm. But you'll notice she *does* offer her hand to kiss. Which means she acknowledges that, even as she is his peer, she is still his vassal."

"Stopping short of insult, or anything that could be construed as an act of rebellion."

"Precisely. It is generally acknowledged that she behaves this way to remind everyone that her family is older, and ruled land here long before Armyr was formed."

"The principality of Fyr," Aefric said, nodding. "But there's no *harm* in my kneeling to the king, is there?"

"None. Though his majesty is so well-disposed toward you at this point that you could forgo it and I doubt he'd bat an eye."

"So that's the courtesy," Aefric said. "What's the rumor?"

"You must remember that she's the oldest of the Fyrenn sisters in her generation. Which means that she was the first of them to grow into her beauty. At the time, Byrhta Ol'Caran was still a little girl. And so it was Duchess Ashling, in her youth, who was widely considered the most beautiful woman in Armyr."

"And the king desired her," Aefric said.

"A great many desired her," Beornric said. "Her preference for women became clear at an early age. So while the similarly inclined noblewomen of Armyr rejoiced in this, the noblemen gave her beauty little attention beyond the occasional appreciative glance."

"Until she began to experiment with men," Aefric said.

"Just so," Beornric said with a nod. "This was right around her majority, and when word got out that the beauty of the realm was showing interest in men, well, I'm sure you can imagine the response."

"The stampede, you mean?" Aefric said, chuckling.

"Everyone by then had a sense of her taste in women," Beornric said. "But no one knew what her taste in men might be. So a great many assumed she would favor *them*. Which made Fyrcloch a very popular destination for the better part of a summer."

"And she had a royal visitor?"

"His majesty had some other official excuse to visit Fyrcloch, but he wasn't fooling anyone. Everyone knew why he went there."

"And she rebuffed him?"

"That ... is an interesting question." Beornric's brow furrowed, as though he'd been there at Fyrcloch himself. Which, to be fair, he might've been. He was still in service to the king at that time.

Aefric didn't rush him.

"He dined with her. He danced with her. They went riding and hunting together. And finally one night when he came to her rooms, she didn't turn him away."

"So she *didn't* rebuff him."

"That part is known only to her grace and his majesty," Beornric said. "It is known that he left her rooms later that night and returned to his own. His body servants told me that when they saw him returning he did not look ... satisfied. And that he did not sleep well that night. But that part is not widely known. What *is* widely known is that he left Fyrcloch the following morning. Even though he was not due to leave for an aett."

"What is known about his majesty's ... habits, in that regard?"

"Where he finds pleasure, he tends to seek it several times before moving on." Beornric shook himself, as though shaking away a memory. "Some claim that she was too inexperienced with men to please him. Some claim she never bedded him at all, and he left in frustration. But only the two of them really know."

"And after the death of his wife, he married Ashling's sister."

"Which resurrected the rumors for a time," Beornric said. "And some say that—"

There was a knock on the door.

———

THE KNOCK TURNED OUT TO BE NESTA, RETURNING TO BRING AEFRIC back to the royal presence. He was again allowed to bring Beornric, and while he didn't hesitate to do so, he did notice that he'd been the only one with an adviser at that last meeting.

Were the others declining the option? Or was the option only presented to Aefric, as a nod to his inexperience? And why *didn't* the others have advisers present? Wouldn't they normally for that kind of meeting?

Unfortunately, his instinct here was to ask Beornric, which might've been all the answer he needed.

Nesta led Aefric and Beornric back to the same room, where once more Rashien escorted them through those two sets of dark oak doors with their gold-leaf engravings, and into the throne room, where she announced him.

No harpist on the small stage this time, though the middle-aged serving man still stood his post near his cabinets. No one on the couches. And of the black oak thrones, only one was occupied.

The king's.

"Ah, good," his majesty said, standing. "I knew I could count on you to answer the call swiftly, Aefric. Come. Have a seat, and tell me everything about your Reyvenue adventure. And feel free to forgo finer details in the cause of speed."

Aefric reclaimed his seat on the burgundy backless couch, with both Beornric and the Brightstaff standing behind him, and began to recount his trip to Reyvenue.

He left out the teak box, but otherwise told how he'd found a way through into the mirror in Ashling's closet. How he'd been ready to steal away with Ashling and her three companions, but that she'd had a better idea.

He told of how she planned their capture of King Makarios and Reyvenue, and how, together, they and his knights, soldiers, and wizard had accomplished it.

When he finished, King Colm shook his head in disbelief.

"You managed all that without a single casualty?"

"Your majesty, there were twelve," Aefric said. "Though it is true that all were soldiers of Caiperas."

"Yes, yes," King Colm waved that away. "Those you incinerated to prove a point. But considering that you captured a *royal palace*, that's practically bloodless."

Before Aefric could object to that characterization, the king looked past him to Beornric.

"And you, Beornric, did not only the job of general during the siege, but personally captured Crown Prince Acastos?"

"Your majesty, with only a hundred and a half soldiers under me," Beornric said, "I believe the technical term would be commander, not general, but otherwise—"

"It was not an oversight," King Colm said, raising an imperious eyebrow. "The numbers might've implied a commander, but you were clearly acting as my duke's general, while he undertook an even more dangerous mission."

"Your majesty," Beornric said with a bow, "I meant no offense."

"I doubt you *could* offend me, Beorn," his majesty said with a smile. "I've known you too long. But I won't stand for being contradicted when I'm offering accolades."

"Accolades accepted with the highest gratitude, your majesty," Beornric said with another bow.

"And you, Aefric," King Colm said, smiling wider still and shaking his head. "I swear. The word 'impossible' has no meaning to you. If Deepwater were invaded tomorrow, you'd find some way to animate that tremendous dragon skeleton in that great chasm of yours and make it slaughter your enemies."

"Your majesty is too kind," Aefric said. "And I hope I will be forgiven for reminding him that it was *Duchess Ashling's* plans I and mine were executing at Reyvenue."

King Colm chuckled. "Precisely why I made sure my pages called you here first. Beornric. What is the old saying about plans and battles?"

"Plans are the first—"

"No, Beornric," King Colm said with a wicked smile. "The *real* saying the knights use when they think their leaders aren't listening."

"Once the enemy is sighted, plans hold their shape the way green recruits hold their water."

The king laughed.

"Delightfully vulgar," he said, "but accurate enough. Plans are wonderful things, Aefric. But the real skill in war is in improvising the areas where the plan collapses."

"But her plan *did* succeed," Aefric said.

"Beornric?" King Colm asked.

"There were ... times where we had to improvise a bit. Changes to guard rotations, activity in certain hallways. But overall, it held together quite well."

"That shouldn't surprise me," King Colm said with a sigh. "That woman's mind scares even me sometimes. But, Aefric, even you yourself must admit that all did not go according to plan in Makarios' presence. Or you wouldn't have had to kill those soldiers."

"We always knew there was a possibility that some would die," Aefric said. "And while the surface details of her plans might've changed, its bones held together."

"They did," King Colm said. "And she absolutely deserves to be rewarded for her quick thinking, her skillful planning, and her excellent use of resources. And especially for her negotiating skills, when the time came. But does she deserve *equal* credit with the man who actually made it all happen? No, she does not."

"But your majesty," Aefric started, but King Colm stilled him with a raised hand.

"And let us not forget that it was *you* who provided the means of *safely leaving* both Reyvenue and Caiperas, bringing with you not only the agreement, but the reparations." He smiled. "*And* King Makarios' family sword. I have to hand that one to Ashling. Making him surrender it to me was a brilliant move on her part."

"Which is part of the reason—"

"No, Aefric. Believe me when I say that I have no intention of belittling her work. She shall be well-rewarded, once certain other factors are taken into account. But the dragon's share of the credit for our victory over Caiperas goes to *you.*"

"But your majesty—"

"I have spoken."

Aefric gritted his teeth, but swallowed his words and nodded. Realizing that might not be enough, he forced himself to say, "Yes, your majesty."

Rashien knocked at the door then.

King Colm smiled. "Ah. Excellent. We've finished just in time. Come in, Rashien. Let us hear what our cousin from Rethneryl has to say."

IT FELT AS THOUGH *SEASONS* PASSED BEFORE AEFRIC FINALLY GOT TO leave that meeting and return to the Deepwater apartments.

Rethneryl, speaking for Hatay and Shachan as well, did agree to the abdication and banishment of King Dalius. So long as Armyr stipulated to the isolation of Varondam if its peers refused to abandon their king.

So many factors there. Pride. Economy. History. Which would prove to be the deciding factor for those Varondami nobles?

Or would the answer be as simple as power? Surely one of their major families would *love* to replace the Swiftblades as Varondam's royal line. In fact, wasn't it likely that more than one peer would lust for the crown?

Which meant it might come down to whether or not they could agree *which* of them would wear the crown. And if King Dalius was a good manipulator, or even simply remained the lesser evil in the eyes of rival nobles, the isolation might go ahead...

No way to know. Not here and now.

But that seemed to be a larger concern for Aefric than the others. Because the abdication-isolation discussion was the *easy* part of the meeting. Once resolved, there was a far more detailed and difficult question to address.

The reparations Varondam would pay.

That. Took. *Forever.*

Gwen and the king going back and forth and back and forth. With Ashling and the queen pitching in here and there.

Who would get how much money now? Who would get how much over the next five years? Should the reparations extend to ten years? Or was five enough to drive their point home? And shouldn't there be *land* involved in all this? And if so, how much? And if not, shouldn't they be asking for more money?

Oh, how they went round and round and round.

Worse, the more they talked about it, the less it felt like a punishment for Varondam. As the numbers climbed — then jumped, to leave "wiggle room" for when Varondam pushed back on the total — it just felt more and more like greed.

Less about how much Varondam *should* pay, and more about how much everyone else *wanted.*

Aefric tried to tell himself that it wasn't actually greed. That they were offended by what Dalius had done, both personally and as monarchs. That they were trying to send a message that anyone foolish enough to strike out at their royal families this way would *suffer* and *regret.*

But the way they talked about the numbers still sounded like greed.

And then there was the question of what constituted a "reasonable share" for enforcing, collecting, and transporting the first payment.

That was an even longer debate.

They went back and forth over the difference between percentage points and an absolute number, and which was more appropriate and why, and what the value offered truly constituted.

Aefric himself managed to stay quiet through most of the meeting. In fact, he'd only spoken up the one time.

"Don't you think making them give us money sounds less like a punishment for kidnapping our princesses and more like a fee for taking them without our permission?"

Oh, that had been a mistake. He realized it the moment he saw their faces. The king, the queen, Gwen, Ashling — they all looked as though he'd said something foul. Offensive. And they took up the conversation again a moment later as though he hadn't spoken at all.

Well. No. That wasn't entirely true. As one they seemed to agree to drive the price up. As though to ensure the reparations could *only* be interpreted as punitive, and not transactive.

Still seemed greedy to Aefric. Enough so that by the time the meeting ended, he felt the need for a good, long bath. And not because of stress.

His knights and wizards were missing when he returned to his rooms. In fact, the only people he saw were his Armityr valet — Tashen — and a pair of young servants.

Tashen was old enough to be well-wrinkled and gray, and spoke with a quaver in his voice, but none of these things diminished the sharpness of his posture or the crispness of his movements.

"Where is everyone, Tashen?"

"At dinner, your grace."

"I'm surprised it wasn't held for their majesties."

"Oh, the court is having no formal dinner tonight, your grace. Your grace's knights were invited to join the Knights of the Crown for their dinner, and your grace's wizards have gone to join the royal wizard for hers."

"Nayoria is back?" Aefric asked.

"Yes, your grace," Tashen said with a bow. "I believe she returned two days ago."

"Good," Aefric said, smiling for the first time in ages. Malimfar released her. Which meant they knew he'd told them the truth. "Hungry, Beornric?"

"Ravenous, your grace."

"Would you send for dinner for us, Tashen? I think I'd just as soon eat in here tonight."

"I'll have it sent to your grace's dining room at once," Tashen said, then turned and nodded at one of the servants, who left. "And if I might suggest, I believe your grace looks as though he could use a glass of ishka."

"He could indeed," Aefric said with a sigh, heading for the couches. "Please. And one for Beornric, of course, if he wants one."

"He wants two," Beornric said. "But he'll settle for taking them one at a time."

"Then, good ser knight, I shall make sure not to stint your portion."

"You're a good man, Tashen," Beornric said, as he and Aefric reclaimed their seats from earlier.

Tashen returned with two small, cut-crystal glasses. The ishka they carried was a dark caramel color, and indeed it looked as though more had been added to Beornric's glass than Aefric's.

Which was as it should have been.

"To surviving that meeting," Aefric said, lifting his glass.

Beornric raised his glass in confirmation, and they each sipped.

It was good, strong ishka. Its flavor made Aefric think of a storm in the mountains, as seen from the safety of a castle tower. When the lightning illuminates the wet stone, and for a heartbeat the unforgiving rocks are beautiful.

They sat in silence for a moment, but only a short one. For Beornric broke their silence.

"I don't suppose I need mention that the 'fee' comparison was ill-chosen?"

"No, I figured that out all on my own. I was surprised they didn't remove me from the room. Or at least tell me to be quiet and let the adults talk."

"Had you been anyone else, they might've." Beornric chuckled. "Right now you get more leeway."

"I want to go home."

"I know. I do too."

"He's going to send us to Varondam, isn't he?"

"I'm not sure," Beornric said. "It wouldn't surprise me. But on the other hand, his majesty mentioned earlier that he'd sent Princess Maev on some kind of mission. He never did say what it was."

"I noticed that," Aefric said. "But after the 'fee' mistake, I didn't want to ask."

"That would've been a safe question. His majesty, after all, had mentioned it earlier. Even said something about coming back to the subject."

Someone knocked on the door. Tashen answered.

"Your grace," he said, "the duchess of Merrek is at the door, seeking admittance."

"By all means, admit her," Aefric said, dragging himself to his feet while Beornric did the same.

As she entered, Aefric decided that the demon scars had to be fading. Because he couldn't help noticing how well she wore that aggressively cut crimson gown. And from the smile in her eyes, she'd caught him noticing.

"Please, come sit with us, Ash," he said with a smile. "We're having ishka. Would you like some?"

"Thank you, Aefric, I would," she said, then turned to Tashen. "Is it the Mountain Home?"

"Your grace, it is the Silverlake," Tashen said with a bow. "From Duke Wylyn's own distillery."

"Really," she said, taking a seat beside Aefric on the couch. "I didn't know Wylyn had a distillery."

"As I understand it," Tashen said, pouring a measure into another cut-crystal glass, "his grace ordered the project begun when he returned from the wars. The bottles here at Armityr are from the first batch he considered worthy."

Ashling took hers from Tashen. Raised it in toast.

"To the team of Merrek and Deepwater," she said. "Where *would* the crown be without us?"

"I'll drink to that," Aefric said, raising his glass, "so long as I don't have to answer the question."

She laughed as Beornric, too, raised his glass, and they drank.

"Oh, that *is* good," she said. "I'll have to have Wylyn send me some."

"I was thinking the same thing," Aefric said.

"A word of advice, Aefric," Ashling said. "Never use the word 'fee' to a noble, and *especially* not to royalty. Fees are things paid by common folk."

"Don't our ships pay to dock in foreign ports?"

"*Our* ships? Never."

"Seriously."

"Perhaps your grace has overlooked this at Ajenmoor and Kivash," Beornric said. "But he has never once paid a docking fee. And if he sails the *Duke's Hand* into any civilized port, no one would dream of asking him to do so."

"We *are* money, Aefric," Ashling said. "Money follows everywhere we go. Even the most *obnoxious* of the Free Baronies wouldn't ask us to pay a docking fee, for fear they'd offend us. That we'd simply leave and take our custom, our entourage, and all our future business, with us."

"It's true," Beornric said. "Nobles are simply too valuable. The benefits of your presence vastly outweigh the loss of small fees here and there."

"If you'd been anyone else," Ashling said, "you'd've offended all of us by comparing the reparations to fees. But we all know you're new to nobility. We all know you learn quickly. And strangely enough, I think we all like you."

She smiled and reached to pat his shoulder.

Aefric caught her hand. "I'm not sure the demon scars are fully healed."

"You do pay a price for your heroics, don't you?"

"But apparently not a fee."

"No," she said, raising her ishka. "Not a fee."

Aefric confirmed the toast, but he had mixed feelings about it.

AEFRIC, ASHLING AND BEORNRIC SAT FOR A TIME ON THOSE COUCHES, drinking ishka and talking of small matters. For long enough, in fact, that Aefric began to wonder where his dinner was.

He didn't want to ask, though. The discussion about fees had him feeling guilty. After all, nobles were the ones who could best afford to pay any fees, and they were the only ones not asked to?

Didn't sound fair.

"Oh, by the way, Aefric," Ashling said with a smile. "I did notice that you were already present in the black oak throne room when Eppi and I arrived."

"Um, yes," Aefric said, unsure he was supposed to talk about what he'd told the king.

She chuckled softly. "Don't worry. I won't ask."

"Thank you."

"I don't need to, anyway. Colm undoubtedly wanted to take your report about Reyvenue without any other witnesses."

"How do you do that?" he asked, which made him decide he'd had enough ishka. He hadn't actually *intended* to ask that aloud. But then, he'd never been as heavy a drinker as many of his adventuring fellows.

"I *should* claim feminine mystery," Ashling said with a smile. "Or perhaps a lifetime of training. But in truth, it doesn't take long. You need only pay attention to the way people talk, and the way they act. Even the subtle ones still tell you who they are. They can't help it."

"Very much like what I tell knights in training," Beornric said. "Only I'm talking about reading movements on the battlefield."

"As am I," Ashling said, shrugging one shoulder. "In a manner of speaking."

"Fair enough," Beornric said with a nod. His face had gotten a little red, and his eyes lingered now and then on Ashling. Which suggested that perhaps he was done drinking as well.

"The most important thing," Ashling said, leaning a little closer to Aefric and lowering her voice, "is not to forget what they teach you this way. Keep it in mind every time you deal with someone."

She put her hand on his thigh and gave it a squeeze. "Do that, and you'll find people much easier to read and predict."

Her hand lingered. Aefric narrowed his eyes at her.

"You're not even tipsy, are you?" he made it an accusation.

Ashling laughed as she sat back and set down her glass.

"See?" she said. "You're learning already."

"But how?" Aefric held up his empty glass. "This is strong stuff."

"That, my dear duke of Deepwater, is a secret I shall carry alone."

Someone knocked at the door. A moment later, Tashen called back.

"Her majesty the queen."

He didn't ask for permission to admit her, merely did so. Queen Eppida came in smiling while everyone stood. Ashling, the only one of them to take her time doing so.

"Not interrupting, I hope," the queen said.

"Not at all, Eppi," Ashling said. "I have a feeling our dear peer will be leaving with the dawn, and I wanted a little more of his time before he left."

"Then we are of similar minds," Queen Eppida said. "I was hoping to hear the tale of Reyvenue from Aefric's own lips this evening."

"Oh, you're going want to save that for another time," Ashling said softly.

"Why?"

"Because his grace is still recovering from that demon attack. Chest, shoulders and back, all scarred and healing."

"But that means—"

"It does," Ashling said. "And I doubt you want him to tell you how heroic he's been until he's ... fully healed."

Queen Eppida frowned as she considered that.

"Trust me, Eppi," Ashling said in a low tone. "It's a *thrilling* tale."

Queen Eppida sighed. "Well, then, I suppose that shall have to wait. And I may save offering my personal thanks for your saving my sister until I get to *hear* that tale."

"Then I shall look forward to the telling, your majesty," Aefric said.

"And I, for now, shall leave you to your ishka," the queen said. "But before I do, I can at least do this much. Come closer and give me your hand."

Puzzlement wrinkled Aefric's brow, but he did as he was bid.

Queen Eppida kissed his hand, but gave her head a small shake when he went to press his forehead to her knuckles.

"Aefric, from this day forward, whenever the occasion is not formal you may call me Eppida."

"Thank you, your—" He cleared his throat. "Thank you, Eppida."

"It is my pleasure, Aefric." She stroked his cheek then, and left.

Once she was gone, Ashling chuckled as they all sat again.

"Poor Eppi," she said. "Her tastes are specific, but they are *strong*. You may need to have a healer standing by when the time comes for that telling."

Beornric cleared his throat and visibly looked away.

"Ah, good Ser Beornric," Ashling said. "You always were able to tell what you should hear from what you should not."

"Alas, a skill I'm having trouble imparting to certain others," Beornric said.

"Doubtless the fault lies in them, not in you," she said, then stood and smiled at Aefric. "Would that I could stay longer, but unfortunately there are details I must see to tonight. Come kiss me, in case I don't get to see you again before you leave."

Aefric stood, and they each kissed the other on both cheeks.

"And do you also know where I'm going?" he asked.

"That depends," she said, shrugging one shoulder. "I don't *expect* Colm to send you to Varondam, but he might. If not, he'll likely give you leave to go. Which doubtless means that by midday tomorrow you'll be as far away as that ship of yours can carry you."

Aefric chuckled. "Yes, but mostly because I want to go home."

"Of course you do," she said. "But don't deny you've had your fill of upper-tier politicking for the time being."

"And then some. Good night, Ash."

"Good night, Aefric. And wherever you go in the morning, may Ulna bless your travel."

"And yours, when you finally get to return to Merrek."

She left then, and just as Aefric and Beornric reclaimed their seats, a servant entered and spoke quietly to Tashen.

"Your grace," Tashen said, "dinner is served."

"And bless all involved for that," Aefric said, standing again.

Someone knocked at the door.

Aefric tried to fight down his groan, but he was pretty sure part of it escaped.

THAT KNOCK WAS SOMETHING BAD. HAD TO BE. THE EVENING HAD BEEN going well. Aefric'd enjoyed a casual conversation with both Ashling and Beornric. He'd drunk his share of ishka, and maybe a trifle more.

He was tired. He was hungry. And he really wanted to finally have his dinner.

"Steady," Beornric said softly. "This is what life's like at the capital."

"Your grace," Tashen called from the door, "the ambassador from Rethneryl seeks admittance."

Aefric sighed relief so profound he could almost hear the silvery, tinkling sound of Kalinda laughing at him.

"By all means," he said, smiling as she entered. "Welcome, Gwen. Beornric and I were about to sit down to dinner. Would you care to join us?"

"Or just join his grace," Beornric said quickly. "I would be more than happy to take my dinner elsewhere, should you so desire."

"Thank you, Beornric," Gwen said. "In most circumstances, I would be more than happy to have your presence at the dinner table.

But at the moment, if I am invited to do so, I would prefer to dine alone with Aefric."

"You would be most welcome," Aefric said, puzzled. "Your company is a pleasure. Beornric, I will speak with you later."

"Of course, your grace," Beornric said with a bow.

Tashen then escorted Aefric and Gwen into the dining room. Which, compared to most of his dining rooms, was an intimate affair. The table sat only eight, and no other tables surrounded it.

Table and chairs both were burnished calinwood, and artfully tooled along their edging. The light was provided by actual candles, both in sconces around the small room and on the table in silver candlesticks.

Aefric took the head of the table, and Gwen sat at his right hand. They both drank their palate wine, which did an admirable job of clearing the taste of the ishka.

The first course brought in by servants wasn't a salad, but a savory bisque that featured fresh river trout.

Gwen raised her crystal glass of white wine. "To the alliance between Rethneryl and Armyr. May it last a thousand thousand years."

Aefric raised his glass in confirmation of the toast, and they both drank. The wine had a touch of citrus that would pair well with the bisque.

"I wanted to thank you, Aefric," she said, while they ate. "For your point about the people of Varondam. The common folk are so often forgotten when kings argue."

"I'm a little surprised to hear you say so," Aefric said, between spoonfuls. "You seemed set on the isolation."

"I'm an ambassador," she said. "I must represent the interests and views of my king ahead of my own, when there is conflict." She sighed. "And I knew persuading Edan to go along with this would be difficult."

"Nevertheless, you managed it," Aefric said.

"I suspect I had support from his advisers while he was 'thinking about it.'" She quirked a half-smile. "And he certainly can't argue with the reparations we'll be getting him. Even if he'll gripe that land was not included."

"What would he do with land that far away anyway?" Aefric asked.

"Collect a new title and rents," Gwen said with a small shrug. "And perhaps more to the point, deny those things to someone else."

"Would've hurt the cause of keeping their peers on our side, though."

"That it would," she said. "But enough of business. Let's just talk. You tell me more about Deepwater, and I'll tell you more about Neastall."

"Now *that*," Aefric said with a smile, "sounds like fun."

They took their time over a dinner with roast pheasant stuffed with a variety of mixed vegetables. Laughing and telling stories and describing all the locations in their homes that they'd most come to love.

That dinner with Gwen proved to be the most pleasant he'd enjoyed in, well, days at the least. Beyond that, to be honest, he had trouble being certain.

He'd traveled too far too fast. Done too many things in too short a time. And the moments of fun in between seemed few and fleeting.

And so it was almost a shame to reach the point where they both realized that they'd lingered over their dessert as long as they reasonably could. Their dishes of chocolate with whipped cream had been long since scraped clean.

Aefric was tempted to invite her to stay for a drink and prolong the conversation, but he knew where that would lead. Especially the way her gaze wandered down his chest and arms from time to time. The way she occasionally toyed with her ruby pendant, as though to draw his eyes to her gown's low neckline, and the way the dark blue silk contrasted with her lovely, pale flesh.

The temptation was just too strong.

So he found a graceful way to end the conversation, and escorted Gwen to the door of his apartments. Along the way they passed couches filled once more with his knights and wizards, all of whom stood as the two of them entered the sitting room.

A servant opened the door for him.

"Good night, Gwen," Aefric said with a smile. "Thank you for your company. It's been a pleasure."

"It has indeed, Aefric," she said. "Promise you'll come visit us in Neastall sometime."

"A promise I make happily," Aefric said with a smile. "And I certainly hope you'll come to Deepwater for a full visit, and not just to stow away on my ship again."

"I promise," she said with a laugh, then surprised him by kissing him on both cheeks. She looked nervous after having done so, but relaxed visibly when Aefric returned the gesture of friendship.

"Good night," she said with a smile, and left.

"Your grace does make friends well," Arras observed, and something in her posture and tone suggested that they'd gotten into the ishka. "But charm he has in abundance."

"Of course he does," Micham said, almost complaining. "What isn't he good at?"

"Magic theory," Karbin said, and he and Jenbarjen both laughed. Though Jenbarjen quickly stopped, looking aghast at herself.

She set down her glass of ishka.

"Forgive me, your lordship," she started, but Aefric waved her to a stop.

"That's quite all right," Aefric said with a smile. "I hope the day never comes when I can't laugh at myself." He cocked an eyebrow. "And the truth is that Karbin only likes to *say* that because he knows, in some ways, I'm better at magic theory than *he* is."

"Oh, you're not," Karbin said. "You just *cheat*."

Aefric laughed, and the others joined in, Deirdre loudest of all.

"Please forgive the intrusion, your grace," Tashen said, stepping up. "But his majesty wishes your grace's presence."

Aefric stopped laughing. "Please tell me I haven't kept him waiting."

"Not in the least," Tashen said smoothly. "I was told to wait until your grace had finished his dinner to inform him."

"Thank the gods for that, at least," he said. "Send for a page, will you?"

"Your grace, one already awaits," Tashen said. He snapped his fingers at a servant, who went into another room and returned with Nesta.

"Your grace is ready then?" she asked brightly.

"Nesta," Aefric said with a smile. "Don't they ever let you off duty?"

"My last task of the day is to escort your grace both to and from the royal presence," she said with a bow.

"Then, for your sake, I hope it won't be a long conversation."

Nesta escorted Aefric down the hall the same direction she had earlier, but this time they went up those sweeping marble stairs, not down.

Two floors later, they departed the stairs for a hallway even finer than the one surrounding the Deepwater apartments.

Here the white marble of the ceiling, walls and floor was veined with gold and silver. And some of those gold veins in the ceiling glowed with gold-tinged white light, providing ample illumination.

A rich red carpet ran down the center of the hall, so fine it must've been cleaned twice a day.

Crystal vases here and there held fragrant floral arrangements, featuring daffodils, rhododendrons, roses, violets and more.

Every three steps, on alternating sides, was a slightly recessed arch featuring a full portrait — head to toe — of some member of the Stronghand family, dressed for either a ball or a battlefield.

Occasionally, one of those arches held an arched white door instead of a painting.

Nesta led Aefric to an arch that had neither a painting nor a door. It was a direct opening into a martial gallery. Armor and weapons everywhere. Mounted on walls and pedestals. Some of it polished and beautiful. Some of it broken or damaged. And every display featured at least one card, telling something of the item's history.

Aefric could see his majesty, toward the back of the room, talking with two noblemen Aefric hadn't met.

Nesta announced him, and by the time she finished the naming off his titles and honors, the two unknown nobles had left the room by some other door.

"You know," Aefric said softly to Nesta. "You can probably stop the recitation after Netar and I don't think anyone would object."

"That's all right, your grace," she said with a wink. "I rather enjoy getting to say it all."

"Aefric," King Colm said, with laughter in his voice, "stop flirting with my pages and come here."

Nesta bowed herself back into the hall, and Aefric made his way between displays to join his majesty at the back wall, near the center.

The king had changed into a simple red silk shirt, over purple hose. His belt and shoes were both a dark leather that looked soft. He wore a rapier at his side, and Aefric noticed that it was enchanted. Perhaps as much as the protective bracer his majesty wore under his left sleeve.

"Look at it," King Colm said, admiring the broadsword that hung, point down, on the wall before him. Hilt of gold, featuring a large ruby at the guard. Its blade, blued steel, with a coating of gold along the fuller.

"Is it not magnificent?" the king said with a smile. "Kaerdwan. The Zaredes family sword for some ... two hundred twenty years. And it's now *mine*."

"It is a beautiful weapon, your majesty."

The king's face wrinkled in distaste. "Enough of that. Call me Colm outside of formal occasions. You've more than earned the right."

"Thank you, Colm," Aefric said, only just checking himself from using the courtesy anyway.

"And you can save the kneeling for formal occasions, too."

"I'll try to remember," Aefric said with a self-deprecating smile.

"I'll make sure Beornric reminds you," Colm said, turning back to the sword. "A *masterstroke* on Ashling's part. Throwing the sword in with the surrender."

"Well, we *did* have them at something of a disadvantage."

"Yes," Colm said, shaking his head. "But this ... this is not something I can credit to *you*. Getting me that sword was *pure* Ashling."

"I'm ... not sure I understand," Aefric said, only just managing not to add *your majesty* to the end.

"That woman plays politics as though she's Elysant reborn." Colm sighed and shook his head in admiration. "She knew my natural inclination would be to attribute our victory entirely to you. Or at least, the largest share of it."

"But—"

"It's a reasonable conclusion, after all," Colm said, not letting Aefric get a word in. "Hardly half a year you've been my duke, and you've won me two wars — three, really, if I were to include Varondam."

"Well—"

"And that's not all. You've saved your king and queen from *assassins*. Uncovered foreign plots. Resolved a *logjam* of a problem in an important mine, and gotten Netar's forges working *full speed* again when I needed them. Not to mention that you hunted down and destroyed *Nelazzi*, who's not only been plaguing our coastline since before the wars, but been something of a personal monster for *me*."

"Yes, but—"

"And that doesn't *begin* to address the good you've done in Deepwater. Towns and cities rebuilt. Fields restored. Your whole duchy is recovering from the wars much faster than any could have predicted."

"Your majesty ... *Colm* ... I didn't do *any* of this on my own."

"Of course not," Colm said, then laughed. "Oh, I see. You still think as an adventurer first, don't you? That credit for killing the ogre goes to the member of your little band who dealt the death blow."

Aefric paused, jaw slack.

Colm laughed again.

"Oh, if you could see your face, Aefric. You're a *noble* now. *All* the deeds of your people are *your* deeds. Credit them as you like. Reward them as you see fit. But realize that, to the rest of the world, it is *you* who did these things."

"That hardly seems fair."

"Of course it's fair," Colm said. "Let me give you an example. Your agents who tracked down Nelazzi? They only did so because *you* enabled it. Otherwise, they never would have. Would they?"

Aefric frowned, trying to imagine Karbin and Deirdre not only deciding to work together on their own, but choosing to hunt down Nelazzi.

He had to admit, he had trouble seeing how it would have come to pass...

"I believe you're beginning to understand." Colm nodded. "Good. But don't let that change you. Your habit of sharing credit is a sign of your goodness, and one reason your people love you as they do. Just don't expect the rest of the world to care how the sharabi is made. They're only interested in the taste."

"I'll think on that," Aefric said.

"Do," Colm said, turning back to admire the sword. He shook his head. "Which brings us back to the brilliance of Ashling's maneuver. She knew she could count on you to push that she get her share of credit. And by getting me *that sword*, she knows I can't simply ascribe that to your goodness. She's given me a memorable token of how much she contributed."

"To be kept in mind when you divide the spoils?" Aefric asked.

"Exactly," Colm said, and chuckled. "Oh, I'm still giving you the county of Skleros. It's the largest of our new counties, and easily the most valuable. You'll love it."

"Thank you," Aefric said with a bow.

"You're quite welcome, Aefric," Colm said, looking back at the sword. "Gabras will go to Wylyn. I'd say it's more than he deserves in this, except that his ships have been a big help in Varondam."

"I'm sure he'll appreciate it."

"He will," Colm said confidently. "And he'll understand the choice. Good, practical mind, Wylyn Stormsent."

"And the other two counties?"

"I'd been *planning* to keep Balsamun for myself, and give Ashling Dalassenos, which is less valuable." He sighed and looked at Aefric. "But no. She deserves Balsamun. I'll give it to her."

"If I may say so, I think that's the right call."

"I know you do. I hope she doesn't make me regret it."

"How so?"

"Politics is a war that never ends, Aefric. You'll understand that soon enough."

Aefric nodded, and they both looked at the sword again. On closer inspection, there were small runes in the gold of the fuller. Perhaps the key to its enchantments...

"You'll leave in the morning," Colm said.

"Am I going to Varondam?"

"Varondam?" Colm said, with a quirked smile. "No. Believe it or not, we *can* do some things without you. Maev and Killian will handle Varondam just fine, once Nayoria brings them their instructions."

"I didn't mean to imply—"

"Of course you didn't," Colm said, with a dismissive wave. "No. I'm sending you back to Deepwater. Right now four princesses are waiting to woo you."

"Oh, that's right," Aefric said, with a sinking feeling in his stomach.

"So you'll leave in the morning, just as soon as your share of Caiperas' reparations are loaded on that *magnificent* ship of yours."

"Of course, your—" he cleared his throat. "Of course, Colm. Though I'll have to go to Netar first."

"You won't," Colm said, not looking away from the sword. "Your baronial wizard and soldiers can find their way home just fine. Consider this a royal command."

"Yes, your majesty."

14

———————

Loading the *Baron's Will* took longer than Aefric expected that next morning. The treasure chests had to be carried up to the parapets, then loaded onto the longboats. And once aboard the ship, the chests had to be carried down to the hold.

It took long enough for Aefric to not only enjoy a traditional Armyrian breakfast with Beornric, but also have one more round of goodbyes with Colm, Eppida, Gwen and Ashling.

"You know about Balsamun?" Ashling asked quietly while they waited for Aefric's longboat to return for him.

He nodded, smiling.

"Would that I could give you a hug," she said. "But for now, at least, consider that I owe you."

"You don't," Aefric said. "You earned that county."

"I did," she said with a nod. "But I'd be a liar if I said I would've gotten it without your aid. So still that humble voice inside you for a moment and accept my thanks."

"You're quite welcome, Ash."

"Have fun with the princesses," she said as they parted at last.

And the ship proved that it was, indeed, a wonder. Perhaps a full hour followed the dawn before they left the skies above Armityr, and yet they were in the air above Lake Deepwater before the sun reached its zenith. A trip that had once taken an aett, now not half a day's travel.

Jenbarjen had truly outdone herself. He'd need to come up with some good way to reward her.

Clear skies that day, as Aefric looked down over the rail at traffic on the lake and in the city. All was good and busy.

"Business is picking up," Karbin said from beside him. "Doubtless word is getting around about Nelazzi."

"That'll be part of it," Beornric said from Aefric's other side. "But the rest will be the beginning of a last push for cargo before winter, when the seas will be rougher. And voyages less profitable, compared to their risk."

Aefric left them to their trade talk and wandered over to the helm, where the captain was giving instructions to his pilot.

"Captain Karsten," Aefric said, getting a wave of acknowledgment from the captain while he finished what he was doing. He walked over a moment later.

"Yes, your lordship?"

"Is this vessel watertight?"

"Yes, your lordship. It was tested in the Maiden's Blood."

"Can you put her down at my dock at Water's End?"

The captain hesitated a moment, but nodded.

"Aye, your lordship. If I set her down myself."

"Then do so. No reason to leave us drawing attention in the skies day and night."

"Of course, your lordship."

"And another thing. While we're in Water's End, I'll provide you a local crew and captain for training."

"Your lordship?" Captain Karsten asked, slightly aghast. "Have we done something to offend?"

"Not in the least," Aefric said. "You and your crew have been exemplary. But if I have only the one crew, you'll all be away from your families for the long stretches of time I'll spend here in Deepwater or elsewhere."

"We're sailors, your lordship. We expect to spend long stretches away on voyages. And what families we have know and expect that as well."

"So you're saying…"

"Your lordship, captaining this ship is the finest job I could ask for. And I'm confident my crew feels the same way. If it's all the same to your lordship, we'd rather not share either the duty or the honor with another captain and crew."

"Oh," Aefric said, not hiding his surprise. "Well, I guess there's no need for you to do so then."

"I can assure your lordship that every man and woman of us appreciates the thought. And I'll pass word to the crew that any who want more time at home are authorized to train such local replacements as your lordship sends us."

"Have the list sent to my Water's End seneschal, Kentigern Ol'Klimath. He'll provide the sailors for training."

"Yes, your lordship."

"Then I guess that's all for now. Set us down when you can."

"Would your lordship object to my setting us down out here in the lake?"

"In the lake?"

"Yes. The last part of the trip will be a bit slower, but I'll be able to guarantee to avoid any who, well, aren't smart enough to get out of the way of a descending ship."

Aefric chuckled. "That'll do just fine."

As the captain brought them down out of the sky, Karbin asked for permission and took off, flying to the castle by his own magic.

"I don't think he cares much for sailing," Beornric said. "Never seems to spend a moment longer aboard a ship than he has to."

"Probably eager to get started researching something he discussed with Sirondfar and Jenbarjen."

"While you were stuck socializing with nobles," Beornric said with a wolfish smile. "Does it kill you not to know what they discussed?"

"*Kill* is an exaggeration," Aefric said, but Beornric started laughing.

"Who are we killing?" Deirdre asked brightly as she joined them at the rail.

"No one at the moment," Aefric said. "I was just admitting that I'd've loved to know what magics Karbin discussed with Sirondfar and Jenbarjen."

"Oh, that was boring," Deirdre said. "All they wanted to talk about was this ship."

"I can understand that," Aefric said. "Quite an achievement, after all."

"Yes, but an achievement that can't be duplicated," Deirdre said, shaking her head. "So what's the point?"

"Doesn't mean there's nothing to learn from it," Aefric said.

"Theory, theory, theory," Deirdre said, shaking her head. "You and I *both* know that what matters most is *practice*."

"Theory still has its place, Deirdre," Beornric said. "Without theory — in any field — we'd have no progress."

Deirdre actually had a counterargument for that, and it made for a lively discussion to fill the remainder of their voyage.

THERE WERE A GREAT MANY THINGS AEFRIC WANTED TO DO WHEN HE got back to Water's End.

He wanted to retire to his apartments. Rest a bit. Do some more research into the magic of the teak box. Really take some time to feel at home.

And then there were the responsibilities he wanted to tend to. He wanted to call a meeting of his advisers. Find out what all had been going on in Water's End — indeed, throughout Deepwater — while he'd been away. Find out how the winter preparations were going. How the coastline towns were coming along.

All of those things, and so much more.

But he couldn't do any of it. Not until he dealt with the first item on his agenda.

Those four foreign princesses.

So Aefric paused only long enough to dispatch a messenger with an invitation before he returned to his rooms and changed into something more fitting for what he had in mind.

A soft gray silk shirt over midnight blue hose. Belt and shoes of pale calfskin. No hat, despite Ocheda's pushing, but he did accept the soft, gray woolen cloak she forced on him.

And then he went all the way back downstairs to his ducal flower gardens, where he awaited his guests in the section devoted to roses.

The flower gardens were a beautifully designed area on the castle's north side.

And the roses formed a rainbow arch some thirty bushes deep, shifting slowly along the walking paths through the arch, from the darkest shades of violet here inside the heart of the curve, all the way through the brightest red along the outermost part of the arch.

Aefric waited among the green soapstone benches under the center of the arch. His nearest guards were Vria and Temat — near the edges of the rose rainbow — who had been more than happy to relieve Arras and Micham.

The day was slightly chilly, so he was glad of the cloak. And despite the clear skies, under the pungent smell of roses, he thought he could detect some oncoming rain.

But the winds were still gentle. And the thick grass a lovely, dark shade of green. So his wait was pleasant enough, and perhaps more peaceful than anything else he'd done recently.

The princesses chose to come to him unannounced, which left poor Aefric scrambling to his feet as they approached around a corner of violet roses.

They were all dressed more casually than when he'd last seen them.

Princess Brigit Haltallan, tall and willowy, wore her black curls down again today, and chose a modest gown of dark yellow, slashed with burgundy to wear under her burgundy cloak.

Princess Adsaluta Haltallan wore her auburn locks down as well. The dark blue gown she chose to go with her own burgundy cloak wasn't quite as modest, but Aefric doubted anyone would call it daring. More likely just a way to avoid letting Brigit's height make her look too young.

Princess Jodis Ol'Nariss wore her reddish-brown hair in a complicated arrangement that showed off its naturally orange highlights. She wore a dress of bright orange, to emphasize those highlights, and with them, perhaps, her eldrani heritage. Unlike the others, she wore no cloak.

Princess Raedrun Al'Trener's waves of dark blonde hair cascaded down her shoulders, acting as a second cloak beneath her rose pink wool. Her gown was a honey brown color.

He gave them each the formal greeting of taking one hand, kissing the princess on one cheek, and letting her kiss him on one cheek in return.

Once that was done, he welcomed them to take seats on the soapstone benches, while he stood facing them.

"Your highnesses, I cannot thank you all enough for being here," he said. "And for being so good as to wait for my return, while my king called me away to war."

"A war, I understand, *you* won for him," Princess Jodis said.

"True," Princess Adsaluta said.

"And where else *should* we be?" Princess Brigit asked. "After all, we would all still be captives of that vile King Dalius and his pirates, were it not for your grace."

A general round of agreement followed, before Princess Raedrun spoke up.

"Beside all of that," she said, "your grace knows why we are here. And I daresay our purpose has only firmed, through experiencing firsthand the wonders your grace works."

Aefric had to speak over the agreement that followed that.

"And I take it as the highest honor that your kingdoms judge me fit to consider in marriage to their beloved princesses."

"Why do I suspect I know where this is going?" Princess Raedrun asked, but not as though she expected an answer.

"Because a great deal has happened since your four royal persons were sent to me. I have looked my own death in the face. And dealt with forces and choices that required me to reevaluate who I am as both a person, and a peer of the realm."

"Ah," Princess Brigit said. "Of course."

"Forgive my cousin," Princess Adsaluta said. "Do continue, your grace."

"And one thing I have realized. I do indeed know to whom my heart belongs. And I would wrong both her, and all of you, if I pretended otherwise any longer."

"You know who you want to marry," Princess Jodis said. "And there's no point in us courting you. Is that it?"

"More direct than I would have put it, but yes," Aefric said with a small bow. "I admit I have yet to ask her, but I confess I do feel confident about how she'll reply."

"As well you should," Princess Adsaluta said, standing up. "She's crazy about you. Any fool can see that."

"I did hope you didn't share her feelings," Princess Brigit said, standing up as well. "But I cannot claim to be surprised. Not after seeing the two of you together at Vaaran Tir."

"Yes," Princess Jodis said, standing now as well, though she looked more irritated than resigned. "We might've known that Maev would steal your heart before any of us had a chance to win it. There's nothing that girl can hunt that she can't bag."

"I, for one, do not take this as a defeat," Princess Raedrun said, standing in a smooth movement. "One cannot lose a match one hasn't entered. And I certainly don't feel I had the opportunity to enter this particular match. Wouldn't you agree, your grace?"

"I would," he said. "Please understand I had every intention of—"

"Yes, yes," Princess Jodis said. "We all know that."

"My point is this," Princess Raedrun said. "As I have not courted your grace, I have not been rejected. Thus, I wish your grace to know that, should he find he receives an answer other than the one he expects, I would be more than happy to return and see if I might win his heart."

"Your highness honors me," Aefric said with a bow.

"That may be," Princess Jodis said, "but I do not feel the same way. It may be Varondam's fault, not that of your grace, but I still feel as though I've been through the hazard to no good effect. And I have no wish to repeat the experience."

"I understand completely, your highness," Aefric said, offering her a bow.

The two princesses from Rethneryl whispered to each other for a moment, then turned to face Aefric again.

"As for we of Rethneryl," Princess Brigit said, "we agree with our cousin from Hatay. Should your grace's proposal receive an unwelcome answer, *we* would welcome an invitation to return."

"It would be my honor," Aefric said with a bow.

"You can invite us anyway," Princess Adsaluta stage whispered, then winked.

Princess Brigit's cheeks colored at that, which made her cousin smirk.

***

Under the circumstances, Aefric's royal guests wanted to be on their way as soon as possible.

And so he helped Kentigern with the arrangements, and saw all four princesses onto their own personal ships and away by midafternoon.

Aefric had been a little surprised to learn that the princesses *had* ships in his port, but when he thought about it, he decided he shouldn't have been. Of course their monarchs had sent ships, just as soon as word reached their courts that their kidnapped princesses had been safely recovered to Water's End. This way, they would have their own transportation, their own guards, their own attendants, their own luggage, and any other comforts they missed.

He stood on his dock in the midafternoon sun, waving his final goodbyes, accompanied by Kentigern, Garnotin and Beornric, as well as Vria and Temat. Beornric was finally out of his armor and in tunic and hose again — dark orange over brown — while both Kentigern and Garnotin had dressed up to say goodbye to the princesses. The former in his black velvet, the latter in purple silk over dark blue hose.

"It's a good thing your grace saved them from King Dalius," Garnotin said, shaking his head.

"Just Dalius now," Beornric said. "Or if not now, soon enough."

"Good thing he saved them from Dalius then," Garnotin said.

"Is that supposed to be a surprising observation?" Kentigern asked.

Garnotin chuckled. "No. I just mean their three monarchs can only get so mad at his grace for rejecting their princesses—"

"Please," Aefric said, feeling a touch of nerves. "No more marriage talk for now. There are too many other important issues to cover today."

And with that, they returned to his black oak meeting room — which after so much time away felt as comfortable as a favorite cloak. Aefric called in Karbin and Elkari and held a full, formal meeting of his advisers.

This took the rest of the day, but Aefric was glad he did it.

His armies had all returned, and were dispersed to their normal barracks and assignments. Some of which, through this winter, would be out at the coast, helping to protect his newly rebuilt towns.

In addition to his regular troops, of course, were the levies required by his majesty. These were now all back with their families, and at their farms and trades and the normal business of their lives.

Of all Aefric's lands and vassals, the county of Goldenfall was still the worst off following the wars. Even with the help of those Green Lord clerics from Havenford, Goldenfall's full recovery was about two years away.

However, under Kentigern's guidance and with loans and grants from Aefric, they'd been able to move enough food and seed where it was needed, to ensure that no one would starve during the coming winter.

From the coast to Kerrik Forest, everyone in Deepwater would have shelter. Everyone would have clothing and heat. And everyone would have enough to eat.

There was still a good deal more to do, but that would suffice for now.

He didn't have to worry about Netar in that regard. The wars had passed them by. One of the few places that could say so.

"The lost Iers project is going well," Kentigern said, continuing down the list.

"That isn't an accurate name for it," Elkari said casually, while noting something on her parchment. "They've recovered ... three times as many common folk as nobles, so far."

"I only have to verify the names and lineage of the nobles," Kentigern said. "So forgive me if I focus on them."

"Focus where you like," she said, without looking up. "I'm just telling you that the name is inaccurate."

"Elkari," Aefric said, interrupting their back and forth. "Is there some sort of martial significance to black oak in Armyr?"

"Of course, your grace," she said, looking astonished that he didn't know this already. "It goes back to the founding of Armyr, and the first—"

"Elkari," he said, interrupting her. "I don't mean to disrupt the meeting with this. Could you either write up a report for me, or, if it's covered in a book, tell me the title?"

"It's in *The Founding of Armyr* of course," she said. "I mean, your grace. Every noble household has a copy. I'll see to it that ours is sent to your grace's rooms later."

"Thank you," he said, and got them back on topic.

Which meant more discussions of trade and business. Of travel and tourism. And of course, the influence on all these things of the fall of Nelazzi, both in what effects they were seeing now, and what more they could expect in the coming year.

Aefric was amused to realize that he enjoyed the details covered in these meetings far more than he expected to. Likely he owed some of that to the computer games that he played as Keifer, back on Earth. Those resource management simulations. He could lose a weekend at a time, playing them. At least, when he wasn't playing roleplaying games with his friends.

He wondered what they'd say, if they could see him now. Keifer's old gaming friends, from Portland. Zan, his old game master. Zan would've been talking about all the things Aefric had done wrong, and how *he* could have done them better. And then there was Deon. Deon was such an aggressive gamer, he'd never have had the patience for ruling a duchy.

Yeah, Deon would've grabbed Deirdre and split across the Risen Sea *seasons* ago.

And Nikki. Oh, poor Nikki. If anyone on Earth was more into the *Torn Kingdoms* than Keifer had been, it was Nikki. If she really knew what became of Keifer, she might never have gotten as far as talking about what he'd done right and wrong. She'd've been too steeped in her own jealousy that *he* got to do this and she didn't.

So Aefric continued through his meeting until he felt good and caught up about everything that had been going on in his duchy while he was gone.

By then, of course, it was time for dinner.

"You *will* dine with the court tonight, yes?"

"Why, Kentigern," Aefric said with a smile. "That sounded rather aggressive."

"Then I must beg—"

"You don't need my pardon," Aefric said. "I'm teasing. I'll have dinner with the court."

"*Thank* you, your grace," he said, and Garnotin nodded support. "After Nelazzi and Caiperas, I think your nobles would riot if they didn't get a chance to hear your grace tell his own stories. And perhaps bend his ear about this or that."

"Speaking of your nobles," Beornric said. "You should probably see Bebara before dinner. Arras tells me she didn't catch so much as a *hint* of a flinch when you tested your scars this morning. But I know you want your healer's clearance before resuming the noble privilege."

"And I can *guarantee* some will be seeking it tonight," Garnotin said. "Feels like *aetts* have passed since I had a day without one of your grace's noblewomen asking after him."

"He defeated both a pirate queen and a kingdom," Elkari said, without looking up. "Such things do tend to heat the blood of most noblewomen."

"Then they can bank their fires for now," Aefric said. "I'll see Bebara *after* dinner, and I don't want company tonight."

"Your grace is waiting until she gets here?" Kentigern said with a smile. "How romantic."

"Until who…" Garnotin said, then smiled at Aefric. "You've decided, haven't you?"

Aefric nodded, but he knew nerves had weakened his smile.

"And you're not telling?" Garnotin asked, aghast. "Beornric, do you know?"

"His grace hasn't told me, but I believe I do."

"I've known for seasons now," Karbin said. "I've been waiting for *him* to figure it out."

Aefric gave Karbin a look, then started laughing. "Of course you know."

Karbin gave Aefric his most roguish smile. The one he saved for special occasions.

"Am I the *only* one who doesn't know?" Garnotin asked, frustrated.

"I don't know," Elkari said. "But honestly, until the proposal is accepted or rejected, it's all conjecture."

"Which is why," Aefric said, standing and taking the Brightstaff in hand, "This meeting is now adjourned."

DINNER WITH AEFRIC'S COURT THAT NIGHT WAS BOTH GOOD AND BAD. It was good, in the sense that none of the nobles were of a mind to push for this advantage or that one. A circumstance unusual enough to be remarkable.

The reason was clear enough even before the soup was served. There was a general sort of awe among them right now. As far as they were concerned — it seemed — Aefric had accomplished at least two impossible tasks since they last really saw him, and topped them off by sending away the princesses who wanted to marry him.

Or perhaps it was finally dawning on them just what it *meant* that their duke was an accomplished adventurer. And they weren't quite sure what to do with that information. How it needed to adjust the way they interacted with him.

In that sense, some of the noblewomen might've been glad to hear that he had demon scars curtailing certain of his activities. Or if not, at least those who'd asked about coming to his rooms later certainly seemed to understand why he refused them, without taking it as a personal rejection.

So everyone was friendly, and polite. And everyone wanted to hear stories.

And stories, he could give them. Swapping tales of adventure had always been part of his life, so he made sure to tell it true, but pace the details to thrill his listeners all the same.

Yes, all of that was the good part of dinner.

The bad part, though, was that deep down, Aefric was a bundle of nerves. Seasons, it had taken him to decide whom he wanted to marry. And now that he knew, he had to wait for the chance.

And with the waiting came the uncertainty.

What would her answer be?

Yes, it certainly *seemed* to be the case that his question would be met with enthusiastic acceptance and no small amount of personal celebration, before making the general announcement.

But what if he was wrong?

What if he'd misread something? Some tell? Or what if his delay had soured everything? Or what if another had stolen her deeper affections, while Aefric had been busy dithering?

His fluttering nerves didn't restrict themselves to his stomach.

They covered the entire region from his knees to his shoulders to his elbows, occasionally coming up high enough to whisper what-ifs into his ears.

And through it all, he had to play host.

So while his court was on its best behavior, and he spent a good portion of the evening telling stories, nerves stole enough of his attention that he hardly remembered any of it. By the time he was seeking out Bebara, he'd already forgotten who all he'd been talking to, and about what.

Despite the hour, he found Bebara in her formal offices.

Well, he was used to *thinking* of them as her formal offices. In truth, her little part of the castle involved a temple to Nilasah, where she conducted various rites and services only some of which involved healing. Her own office, another office for her apprentices — or did she call them novices? Neophytes, maybe?

And then there was the hospital section, including Aefric's own ducal hospital room.

He found her in the temple.

The temple was a large room, easily forty feet on a side, and done in colors of soft blue and yellow, right down to the stained-glass windows behind the altar.

The altar itself was made from peach wood, and featured seventeen yellow candles, all lit. In the air, the comforting scent of hazel root and ginseng.

Bebara knelt before the altar, arms up and outstretched, her steely gray hair bound in a long ponytail down her back. She prayed aloud in a sibilant language that sounded familiar to Aefric, but was not one he spoke.

He waited while she finished, not minding that the wait took a while. While he waited, he offered a few silent prayers of thanks to Nilasah, for all the healing he'd received over the years.

When Bebara finally did finish, she stood easily and turned.

"Your grace is kind to wait," she said, beginning to speak before she even saw him, and showing not the least surprise that he was there.

"Far be it for me to interrupt a cleric at her devotions," he said. "How did you know I was here?"

"No one enters or leaves my temple without my knowing." She put her fists on her hips and frowned as she looked him up and down. "What has your grace done to himself this time?"

"Nothing new, I promise," he said, smiling as he took the jar of ointment out of his black velvet belt pouch. He tossed it to her and she caught it easily.

"Scars all better then?" she asked, sounding a little mollified, at least.

"I think so, but..." He shook his head and sighed. "I don't want to be wrong about this. And I don't want to put anyone else at risk only to find out I was kidding myself. I was hoping you could confirm their status."

She nodded appreciatively. "Very thoughtful, your grace. And have the applications been consistent then, and timely?"

"To the best of my knowledge."

She tilted her head and frowned in curiosity.

"I ... pushed myself too hard and slept for two days. I'm told that while I slept, my knights made sure to apply the ointment morning and night."

"Your grace has good knights."

"I'm quite fortunate that way."

"And two days you slept, you say?"

"That's right."

She nodded. Gestured to his shirt.

He stood the Brightstaff beside him, undid the buttons of his shirt, and opened it.

Bebara drew a deep breath, and her eyes unfocused. She looked back and forth at him a couple of times, then nodded to herself. She reached out one hand, and felt the air just short of the three deepest demon scars, which happened to be on his chest. Though even those scars had faded somewhat, from their initial damage. She nodded again.

Without warning she jabbed a scar with her finger.

"Ow," he objected, but out of surprise, not pain.

She looked at her fingertip. Smelled it.

"While your grace was pushing himself too hard, he saw the tendrils, yes?"

"I did," he admitted. "And they thickened—"

"Into branches, but no further, yes?"

"That's right."

"Not trunks?"

"Not trunks."

Bebara nodded. "Then I'm reading it right. The corruption is entirely gone. And because the treatment was both timely and complete, the scars themselves will fade to white lines within ... perhaps a season. Your grace is fortunate that his knights continued to apply the ointment while he slept."

She made a point of looking into his eyes as she added, "Had they *not*, the demon's corruption would have settled in your dreams, and I'd need Astryma's own luck to get rid of it."

"Astryma fell. Kalinda is goddess of magic now," Aefric said automatically as he began to rebutton his shirt.

She jabbed his chest again. This time his yelp was from pain. He wouldn't be surprised if she'd left a bruise.

"Do I tell you about magic?" Bebara asked sharply. "No? Then don't tell me about gods. I understand the gods better than you ever *hope* to."

"I only meant—"

"Kalinda rules over magic, and that's to be sure. But *Astryma* used to watch over luck as well. And no one's picked that up for her." She shook her head. "Luck's all cattywampus these days. Watch the gamblers in a tavern some night."

Aefric chuckled. "I haven't set foot in a tavern in..."

"Might do your grace some good. Might do his people some good too. Remind 'em that you're a mortal like the rest of us, not some remnant from the Godswalk Wars."

"No one's saying that, are they?" he asked as a chill raced through him.

"Not yet. But if you keep making miracles, they'll start."

Aefric considered that as he buttoned up his shirt.

"Anyway," Bebara continued, as though she hadn't just thrown verbal cold water in his face, "my money's on Ulna, if your grace will pardon the pun. Always thought luck and travelers went together."

"Makes sense," Aefric said, but he wasn't really listening.

"Off you go, then, your grace. I'm sure there's a passel of noble-women waiting to share your bed."

Aefric gave her a distracted nod and left.

A LONG, HOT BATH IN HIS RIDICULOUSLY LARGE AND COMFORTABLE TUB helped, but Aefric didn't sleep well that night. Between nerves over his coming proposal and now worries that people were coming to see him as connected to the gods...

He couldn't even discount that as possible exaggeration by Bebara. Not after the touch of awe that seemed to underlay the behavior of his nobles at dinner.

These were people who'd come to know him — to lesser and greater extents — since he'd taken up the duchy last spring. How much stronger a reaction would he get from the common folk, who knew him almost entirely by reputation alone?

He knew what Ashling would tell him. Or thought he did, at least. She seemed likely to say that he should enjoy it while it lasted and *use* it to push his own goals for Deepwater before it faded.

But was that *right*?

Questions that plagued him through the night, and through his breakfast, and through his morning meeting.

He skipped lunch then, and some of the appointments that had been made for him, and went to his personal meditation chamber on the second floor of his apartments.

There, he lit the room with a single candle, placed in a silver candlestick in the middle of the white oak floor. He skipped the desk and padded couch for the couch carved from teak.

There, he sat. Regarding the light gray walls in the dimness, and going through all his old exercises to clear his mind of everything that was not important.

And at the moment, only one thing mattered. His next breath.

Inhale slowly through the nose. Filling the lungs and diaphragm. Exhale through the mouth, just as slowly. Lips barely parted. Pushing the air from the base of the diaphragm up through the very upper chambers of the lungs and out.

One breath, and then the next. Paying no attention to any cares and concerns and questions that passed through his head. They could all wait for later.

Right now, there was only breathing. One slow breath at a time.

It took a lot longer than usual for thoughts to stop intruding, but eventually they did. Then, it was just him and the cycle of breathing. Aware of the comfortable sensation of air on his skin, of the silk of his clothes, of the teak couch beneath him, the fit of his shoes, and the floorboards and stone beneath.

Aware of the dim light of the candle, and the vague smell of its beeswax. Aware of the pale gray of his walls. Of the more comfortable couch along one wall. Of his desk, with its waiting parchment and ink and more.

Aware of the wards at the outer walls of the castle, and from his nearby laboratory. Of the magic of the Brightstaff standing beside him, and of the bracer on his left arm, and of the pouch at his belt.

Aware of all of it. But giving none of it any more attention than his cares.

Breathing in. Breathing out.

At some point, there was a knock on his door. Two short raps. Ocheda's knock.

He opened the door with a gesture.

Ocheda stood in the doorway, apparently unsurprised that he'd opened the door for her, even though he'd never done it before.

"Yes?" he asked.

She smiled, and it was the first soft thing he'd ever seen from his so-severe chief daytime valet.

"Your grace," she said, "she's here."

Aefric's heart jumped from a slow, steady pound to a rapid jog. "Where?"

"I asked her to wait in your grace's private solarium. I hope this was the right choice."

"So do I," he breathed as he stood and took up the Brightstaff. "I'm sure it is. How do I look?"

"Positively regal, your grace," she said.

Aefric crossed the room to her. Hesitated.

"Should I have food brought? Drink? How long has she been at Water's End?"

"Your grace's seneschal made sure to give her time to rest and refresh herself after her voyage. I am told she has declined food and drink for the time being."

"This is it, then," he said.

"Relax, your grace," she said, reaching out to straighten his clothes, and dust him a bit. "You're about to make her the most envied woman in Armyr."

He raised an eyebrow at her.

"Of course Dajen and I know, your grace," she said with a bow. "Nothing happens in this castle without the two of us finding out."

He'd heard that from them before, of course. And Bebara had said something similar about her temple just last night. But then, in Bebara's case, it was probably part of that strange magic that clerics wielded.

As for Dajen and Ocheda, though ... well, he'd speculated at times that his valets practiced a kind of service magic that he did not recognize or understand.

But this was not the time to enquire. He had a far more important question to ask first.

THE DOOR TO AEFRIC'S PRIVATE SOLARIUM USUALLY PLEASED HIM TO SEE it. The door itself was ornately carved teak, and featured a stained glass sunset that took up most of the top half.

At the moment, it was just a door between him and where he was going.

Aefric reached for the latch, then stopped himself.

He wouldn't knock. He was a duke, and this was *his* solarium. Knocking would be going too far. However…

Aefric stood the Brightstaff beside the door and mentally told it to remain there until called.

Then he steadied himself through a breath and opened the door.

People occasionally asked Aefric how he could live two seasons as master of Water's End without visiting the top of the Spike. Some even went so far as to jokingly ask if it was just too many steps for him to climb. As though he couldn't simply fly to the top anytime he wanted, if he didn't feel like taking the stairs.

But no. This room was the reason.

His private floor solarium was an entirely interior room. Technically. He knew full well that the walls and ceiling around him were there, and of solid stone.

But long ago — perhaps even when Water's End was first built — some enterprising magic-user had enchanted those walls and ceiling, so that standing on the floor of this room was like standing on a stone disc, thirty feet wide, perfectly balanced atop the Spike.

Absolutely breathtaking sights to see in every direction.

Sunset approached, and the view to the west was glorious. The city below. The countryside beyond. Even hints of the Risen Sea in the distance.

The first guests Aefric had brought to this room had hardly wanted to stray from the twin, soft gray couches in the center. Standing too close to the edge gave them vertigo, even though they could reach out and touch solid wall anytime they wanted.

But not her. She stood at the western wall right now, admiring the setting sun and the colors of the sky while Aefric admired her.

Even more beautiful than any sunset. The sight of Byrhta

Ol'Caran in a gown of canary yellow chiffon. Her long, dark forest green hair wound in a loose weave down her back.

"Do you know I've never been in here?" Byrhta said, still looking at the sunset, while Aefric approached.

"The only room here or at Behal I'd never been in," she continued. "Apart from Arinda's own laboratories and meditation chambers, of course. She never invited any guests into her private solarium though. Not even me."

Byrhta turned to face Aefric. His heart and breath caught, and his mouth dried.

"Thank you for sharing this with me, Aefric."

He had to force a swallow before he could say. "I should have before now. There are so many rooms—"

"What's the matter?" she asked, touching his arm. Noting the missing Brightstaff. "Does it have to do with why you've called me here from Riverbreak?"

He managed to nod. Tried to get the words out, but they kept getting tangled up on their way to his tongue.

Byrhta's eyes widened. But then she blinked and nodded.

"I suspected," she said, turning back to face the sunset. "From the moment I heard about Vaaran Tir. The two of you fighting side-by-side. I can't compete with that."

No. This was all wrong. Aefric's heart jumped to double-speed and the world started getting a red sheen.

"Thank you, though, Aefric," she said, looking further away from him. "For bringing me here. Telling me in person. It means a lot to me that you give me that consideration."

Aefric shook himself, and whipped through a quick series of focusing exercises.

Suddenly the red sheen was gone and his tongue worked again.

"Byrhta," he said, reaching out to take her hand.

She let him, but wouldn't look at him. "Please, Aefric. I need a moment to compose myself."

"Byrhta," he said, "please look at me."

She turned. Tears made her eyes shine, and traced tracks down her cheeks.

He wanted to reach out and wipe them away, but he couldn't. Not yet.

He got down on one knee.

Her brow furrowed. She didn't understand what he was doing. Was that not how things were done in Armyr? Should he have asked someone first?

He expelled those worries with a breath. Focused.

"Byrhta," he said, taking her hand in both of his now. "Words alone cannot express what a wonderful woman you are. All Qorunn lauds your beauty, but I have been fortunate enough to come to know the woman *behind* the beauty. To see her fire and her brilliance. To laugh with her. Sing with her."

The tears stilled. Something between hope and fear in those wide amber eyes now.

"And as I have come to know you," he said, "you have come to know me. The man behind the titles and adventures. I know I have shared more of myself with you than I have with anyone else in this world. And I'd like to think ... you could say the same of me."

"I could," she whispered.

He switched to High Eldrani.

"Byy yrh taah, my heart came to love you before my head was ever wise enough to see the truth."

"Oh, Aefric," she whispered.

"There is no one in all Qorunn I would rather see last before I sleep and first when I wake. Whom I would rather share joys and sorrows with. Whom I would rather have by my side, from this day until the end of all days."

She seemed to stop breathing. While his own heart was pounding harder than ever as he switched back to the common tongue.

"Would you marry me, and make me the happiest man on Qorunn?"

She stared at him for an eternal moment.

"You're being foolish," she whispered. "You must know that. My family—"

"I don't care."

"All those princesses—"

"Will find other husbands just fine without me."

"But ... you are a *duke*. A peer of the realm. You're supposed to marry an *equal*. To marry for *advantage*. I have *nothing* to bring you. Nothing but..."

"You bring yourself," he said, standing now and looking deeply into her eyes. "And there is nothing more I want or need."

"But—"

"Everyone tells me to choose, Byrhta. Well I choose *you*. The only question now is will *you* choose *me*?"

"Of course, Aefric," she said, smiling at last, even if it was through a fresh round of tears. "The answer has always been yes."

They kissed then, and that kiss lasted long past the sunset.

Aefric and Byrhta's personal celebration lasted through dinner and late into the night. Dajen even managed to produce for them a bottle of that rare eldrani beverage, *flisnaath*. They drank it properly, of course — speaking the right words as the corks were removed, and sharing its sweet, dry taste slowly. And in this case, interspersed with not only good conversation, but a good deal more kissing.

And the way the *flisnaath* shifted its range of temperatures and characters — from a cinnamon so warm it might've been a variety of cocoa to a spearmint so cool it might've been iced — only made many of those kisses more enticing and adventurous. And led them naturally to the bedroom.

It was later that night. The *flisnaath* had been drunk, the servants dismissed, and the two were naked and entwined together, smiling and resting by firelight between bouts of celebration.

Suddenly Byrhta started laughing.

"What?" Aefric asked, rising up on one elbow among the mess of silk sheets.

"Oh, it just occurred to me." she said, smiling. "All the noble-women of your court are going to be so *frustrated*."

"I seriously doubt anyone currently at Water's End believes herself to be a bridal candidate."

"Oh, not because of that," she said, then tilted her head. "Though some of them have doubtless enjoyed the occasional fantasy that direction."

"What then?"

"Their handsome, dashing duke has been away, slaughtering pirates and winning wars, and generally making himself even *more* exciting than usual. And now that he's back, and they're all hoping to chase bliss with him ... *I'll* be the one in his bed every night."

"Yes, you will," Aefric said, leaning down and nibbling at her shoulder. Oh, her spicy, exotic scent was enticing.

"And not just for bliss. Oh, no." She tapped him on the forehead, so he looked her in the eye. "It will be our duty to the duchy for you to put an heir in me as soon as possible."

"True," Aefric said, smiling at the thought.

Huh. Odd. It wasn't all that long ago that the thought of having children with anyone here in Qorunn made the Keifer part of him feel disloyal to Andi.

He really *was* moving on...

"In fact," Byrhta continued, "perhaps tonight should be the last time we drink nysta tea together."

"Seems a bit soon, doesn't it?" Aefric said, pulling back and settling on the mattress beside her. "Don't you think we should wait until we're actually *married*? I mean, we haven't even discussed this with your father yet."

"Father has already given me permission to marry you, if I got the chance." She winced, and added slowly, "It's ... part of the reason he sent me to you last spring."

"And here I thought you came to Behal to petition the new duke for aid in recovering from the wars. That the rest was just ... us."

"Petitioning for aid was the major reason," she said. "But Father ... has made no secret of his frustration that I refused those kings. When he heard that our new duke was about my age—"

"He told you to marry me if you could?"

"Essentially," she said.

"I see," Aefric said, raising an eyebrow. "And now you're worried that part of me will always wonder if you're only marrying me to be a dutiful daughter? To make up to your father for the rejection of those kings?"

"I swear that's not—"

Aefric put two fingers to her lips to still her.

"I don't know if you recall all of our conversations at Behal this past spring," Aefric said, taking back his fingers. "But you told me once that I *shouldn't* marry you. I'd be a fool to."

"I remember that," she said softly.

"You repeated the same idea only hours ago."

"I'm not the smart choice," she said. "There's no political advantage in marrying me. I'd be lying if I said otherwise."

"And I know you don't lie to me," Aefric said. "As I don't lie to you."

Byrhta let out a slow, relieved breath.

"I know you're not marrying me to please your father." He quirked a half-smile at her. "And if making your father happy happens to be a side-effect of our marriage, then so much the better."

She chuckled breathlessly.

"And by the way," he added casually. "It's not true that there's *no* political advantage to marrying you."

"Oh?" she asked.

"I think you'll make a *magnificent* duchess." He stroked her cheek. "Smart and charming is a devastating combination."

"Smart and charming you can get from—"

Aefric leaned in and kissed her, stretching the kiss out until it was a languorous bliss unto itself.

When he pulled back, he said, "I've made my choice, thank you."

"Thank *you*," she said, and her hands began playing with his new scars.

"Before we get distracted again..." he said.

"Yes?" she asked, but she sounded distracted, and her eyes were roving over his body.

"I still think we should keep up with the nysta tea until we're married."

"Why? The sooner I produce you an heir, the better."

"Won't people think—"

"Remember, Aefric," she said gently. "There's no stigma to bastardy here in Armyr. I could bear you a child before the wedding, and that child would still be your lawful heir. No one would even bat an eye."

"Well," he said, "I suppose, then. I guess I'm still adjusting to certain truths here. I've seen lands where bastardy is a curse word, and an unforgivable crime."

"But not Armyr."

"As Ashling has pointed out about her son, Dives." He snorted amusement at himself. "And anyway, since your father's permission isn't an issue, we can announce our plans as soon as we've notified him—"

"And Maev," Byrhta said suddenly. "Or have you told her already?"

"I haven't told anyone. Oh, some have guessed, I think. And Kentigern and some of the castle staff appear to have figured it out. But—"

"You must tell Maev," she insisted. "And before we announce it. She needs to hear this from *you*. And not by spell or letter. Face to face. She deserves that."

"She does," he said, then caught again that she'd been calling Maev *by name*. "You've been corresponding with her?"

"Of course," she said. "Ever since we had our famous talk about you."

"I never did find out what the two of you had to say to each other."

"She should be the one to tell you," Byrhta said. "You'll understand why later."

"I guess I should go to Varondam tomorrow then," Aefric said.

"No, don't," she said. "Let Maev finish her work there without distraction. She'll stop here on her way back to Armityr anyway, to see you."

"That may take a few aetts," Aefric warned. "Depending on how negotiations go."

"Then it takes a few aetts," Byrhta said. "The announcement can wait." She smiled. "In the meantime, I think we have enough to keep us busy."

"For the duchy?"

"For the duchy begins tomorrow night," she said. "Tonight is just for us."

"Good," Aefric said, and kissed her again. And this time, the kiss was a beginning of its own.

ACCORDING TO THE REGULAR REPORTS COMING IN, PROGRESS IN Varondam was going slowly. Removing Dalius from the throne and banishing him had been accomplished easily enough. But the Varondami peers were having a good deal of difficulty selecting their new monarch. And both Maev and Prince Killian were working hard to bring them to a compromise.

In the meantime, Aefric kept as busy as possible.

His first order of business was Vercy Ol'Karmak. She was due to reach her majority not far into the new year, but Byrhta swore the girl's training was more than complete. That for the past half-season she herself had been doing little more as baroness regent than watching over Vercy's decisions, suggesting no more than a change or two, and approving them.

And over the last few aetts, the number of suggested changes kept getting smaller and smaller.

So Aefric invited Vercy to Water's End, so she could finally take her formal oaths and be installed as Baroness of Riverbreak. And even Aefric had to admit, she seemed more a woman than he remembered her. More confident and poised. She conducted herself well through those long oaths and the small celebration that followed.

As a gift for taking up her barony, Aefric gave her a fine young black stallion that she named Ceridwyn, after the queen who first created Riverbreak.

Once that was dealt with, Aefric delved right into working with his Deepwater vassals to make sure they were prepared for winter. But then word came from Armityr.

By order of the king, Aefric had to bring his entourage to the capital for a formal celebration of the victory over Caiperas. And given that the *Baron's Will* could make the trip in less than half a day, Aefric knew he could hardly refuse.

That celebration lasted four days. Four days of cheers and dancing and speeches. Four days without Byrhta — bringing her would have started enough rumors to render an announcement moot — which meant indulging in the noble privilege, if only to keep up appearances.

Four days of gifts. Jewelry and artwork, rare alcohols, ceremonial swords and daggers and even a staff — this one was the more common, orange variety of thunderwood, studded with gems and capped and butted with silver and gold. Even small trinkets of magic. Little rings and bracelets and necklaces that did little, but served as status symbols among certain nobles and merchants.

In truth, the celebration at Armityr probably continued past that fourth day. But it was late that day that his majesty *finally* gave Aefric permission to take his people to Netar. The excuse that secured that permission, of course, was that Aefric needed to hold the formal launch and celebration of that wonderful airship. Which meant more speeches and dancing and feasting and dallying, but it couldn't be helped.

Going to Netar also gave him a chance to reward Jenbarjen personally for her incredible work on the *Baron's Will*. He gave her a portion of the baronial vineyards as her own lerdom, to be passed down to her children and her children's children.

She actually wept with gratitude.

More practically, during the two days that Aefric was in Netar, he managed to ensure that all was running well in his little barony.

After Netar, he spent three days in his new county of Skleros, to formally take possession of those lands and title.

And there were *his* new lands and title. Aefric had hoped that the old count, Algallon Kalmanos, would stay on. But the old count was just that. Old. And he had no heir. Or, at least, no *legitimate* heir so far as Caiperas was concerned. So rather than change allegiance to a new crown, Count Algallon opted to abandon his ancestral home to live out his remaining days in new lands provided by the crown his family had served for generations.

Aefric was grateful to Count Algallon, though, for the man had run his lands his no small amount of skill, in terms of domestic management. Their rebuilding following the Godswalk Wars was doing quite well, and they used an irrigation system that Aefric wondered if his own farmers would benefit from.

That was a spring question though. Not something to worry about with winter coming.

So Aefric rushed a bit as he checked out the state of things in Skleros. And when it came to assessing his castle staff, he cheated.

He brought along the *Sinflissacta*. A pair of dark skinned eldrani named Li'nasachal and Li'sheneesha, both with vibrantly purple hair, and eyes the yellow of candle flame.

They'd been refugees this past spring when he took them in, and then learned that they practiced an obscure type of eldrani magic they called "soul reading."

While he didn't truly understand how their form of magic worked — it was closer to cleric magic than anything else he could think of — he did know that they would tell him true as Taesark who among his new aides, servants and vassal could be trusted and who could not.

That led to only half a dozen dismissals, but it did mean that his

Skleros castle needed a new castellan. On Beornric's advice, Aefric gave the post to a trustworthy knight from Water's End. Ser Surta Ol'Faricai. She'd been a solid, reliable knight in service to Deepwater for four decades, and was more than eager for the new challenges Skleros presented.

On his way back to Water's End, Aefric stopped by Storbakki for three days, doing much the same thing. Storbakki was a much smaller territory — Armyr would have called it a barony — but the wars had missed it. So it was in good shape. And to his surprise, the *Sinflissacta* found no one there who meant him harm.

Apparently Princess Astrid had told the truth, when she said that many in Malimfar held him in high esteem, for his prowess in battle. And since their last arl had turned out to be a traitor, the people of Storbakki welcomed Aefric with open arms.

While Aefric was busy with those celebrations and visiting his various lands, Byrhta returned to her father's castle at Vabarett. Both for her first visit home in quite some time, and to carry the news to her father and brother — privately — about her engagement.

She was still away when Aefric returned to Water's End.

Finally, a breakthrough in negotiations came, and Varondam selected their new monarch: Queen Atosa Haakenii.

The Armyrian fleets all sailed home triumphant. And Yrsa returned to Water's End a hero, bringing with her the prince and princess of Armyr.

The *Swift Wave* docked at Water's End at close to midday, to be greeted by cheering crowds, and trumpeters playing the royal and ducal fanfares.

Aefric led the formal greeting, of course, with a speech that probably focused on Yrsa and her naval brilliance more than it should have. But he made sure to heap praise on Maev and Prince Killian for their adroit politicking, and on all the captains and crews for their hard work and steel under fire.

Once that was done, Aefric wanted to talk to Maev right away, of course. But that was not to be. The moment his speech finished, even while the crowd cheered, Prince Killian shouted to him, "You and I must talk. At once."

Aefric could only nod agreement, and have the two of them escorted to his auxilliary office on the first floor of the castle, the closest private room he had to the docks.

This office had never been deemed important enough — or saw enough use — to merit light enchantments. Slits high in the wall didn't provide enough light to see comfortably, so Aefric lit up the yellow diamond of the Brightstaff, rather than the candelabra on the desk.

No rug on the red maple flooring. Only three cabinets and the one desk, with two chairs for visitors, but at least all these things were of burnished red calinwood. The smell in the air wasn't floral, but at least it was the pleasant smell of the lake.

The soft, gray walls featured a recent portrait of Aefric, as well as the flags of both Armyr and Deepwater.

The moment they were alone, with the door was closed behind them, Killian said, "Let's not sit. I've been sitting too much lately."

"Would your highness rather talk somewhere we could walk? The gardens—"

"No," he said, looking about. "This is good. Appropriate."

Prince Killian took another moment looking around. Aefric, hesitant, gave him that time.

Finally, the prince turned back to face him.

"What I have to say is for your ears alone, Aefric. This is between the two of us, and needs to *stay* between the two of us."

"Of course, your highness," Aefric said carefully.

Prince Killian frowned. Inhaled sharply through his nose. On him, even that expression probably appealed to women. He had a good face for brooding.

"I need to know," he said. "What did you tell my father?"

"About what happened on the hunt for Nelazzi?"

The prince nodded abruptly.

"I didn't," Aefric said. "Your highness will recall that I sent Deirdre—"

"You sent a *messenger*," the prince said. "Her words were your words."

Aefric raised an eyebrow. "Your highness *has* met Deirdre."

"I have," Prince Killian said. "And I know she'd do anything for you."

"Then your highness has learned the wrong lesson about her," Aefric said. "Deirdre Ol'Miri would kill for me without hesitation. Indeed, she often seems eager to do so. She would die for me, as well, if she felt she had to. And she would do a great many other things besides. But she wouldn't lie for me, which your highness seems to be implying she did. And I wouldn't ask her to."

"There's lying and there's *lying*," the prince said. "One is telling falsehoods. The other is a game of politics—"

"And if your highness believes Deirdre has *any* patience for politics, he has learned *nothing* about her at all."

That actually stopped him. The prince rolled in his lips as he thought about that. Looked away at the flags through a breath. Brought his eyes over to the portrait.

"That's actually a good point," he said finally.

"As for what I wrote in the *letter* she carried for me without having read," Aefric said, "I told the truth about everything. And I asked his majesty to question Deirdre as he wished. Even under the guidance of a justiciar, if he chose."

"Father's justiciar was away at the time," the prince said, then furrowed his brow as he looked at Aefric. "You're going to make me ask directly, aren't you?"

"Apparently I must," Aefric said, "because I fear your highness has held part of this conversation without me."

"All right then," Prince Killian said, meeting Aefric's eyes now. And Aefric could see some of King Colm's force of personality developing behind those eyes. "Tell me the truth, Aefric. Father's story about Nelazzi wearing a Necklace of Fire. Was that your idea?"

"No," Aefric said. "All I wrote in that letter was the truth about the voyage. And I sent it to his majesty to ensure that my people got the credit they were due." He shook his head. "The story about the Necklace of Fire is entirely your father's idea."

Prince Killian looked a little closer at Aefric. Nodded a little.

"And what do you think of that story?" he asked.

Aefric sighed. "I think it's the *official* story. And as a loyal vassal to your father, I will, of course, support it."

"No arguments?"

"Not even in private."

"But you don't wear the necklace."

"Have you *seen* that necklace?"

Prince Killian laughed, and tension leaked out of the room. "It *is* gaudy, isn't it?"

"I swear," Aefric said, "some magic-users have no taste."

"I've wronged you," Prince Killian said. "You invited me on your voyage. Protected me while still giving me the chance to blood myself in battle. And I thanked you by acting the child."

"You acted without thought," Aefric said. "Nothing more."

"It's not easy, you know," Prince Killian said. "Growing up a crown prince, I mean. All around you, people act as though you're cleverer than everyone else. *Better* than everyone else. And there's so much praise. Just learning to walk or speak some new language, to swing a sword or hold up a shield, to ride a horse without falling off. When I do these things I hear ten, perhaps a *hundred* times the adulation that anyone else gets for doing the *exact same thing*."

He scoffed. "I know. It sounds wonderful. But in truth, it's hard not to let it all sink in. To start *believing* the praise. To start thinking you're better than everyone else. That even bad things you do can be good, just because it's *you* doing them."

Prince Killian shook his head and wandered over to the flag of Armyr. Reached up and touched it.

"You fight it. Remind yourself that, ultimately, you're a servant." He turned and looked at Aefric. "Father is brilliant that way, you know. Never lets me forget that I owe everything I have ... everything I *am* ... to my vassals and my people."

He looked back at the flag.

"But then, sometimes, when you least expect it, the old habits creep in. You do something that turns out wrong. Or someone defies you. Maybe both. And instead of stopping for a moment to wonder who is in the right, what your own mistake might've been. Instead you amplify one mistake with another. And maybe another still..."

He sighed and hung his head for a moment. Drew another breath and straightened. Turned back to face Aefric.

"When the bout of foolishness passes," the prince said, "there are two things you must do. The first, of course, is apologize. The second is to make up for what you've done."

"That sounds wise."

"I've apologized to Father for Nelazzi," Prince Killian continued. "Because my rash deed prevented Father from trying her publicly, and all the good that would have come from that. I see that now."

Prince Killian reached out and clasped Aefric's shoulder.

"Now, I must apologize to you. Aefric, I am deeply sorry. For her death. For the credit I tried to steal, from you and from yours. And for the way I behaved later. I deeply regret it all, and hope you can find it in your heart to forgive me."

"Your highness—"

"Please say nothing about it now," the prince said. "Take time and really think it over. Do not tell me you forgive me because of who I am and will be. Tell me only if your truly mean it."

Aefric nodded.

"Now, there is only so much I can do to make up for her murder," the prince continued, "save for learn from it. But about the credit, *that* I can help."

"What does your highness have in mind?"

"Simple. I'll take a lesson from my peer." Prince Killian gave Aefric's shoulder a squeeze. "When I tell the story, I'll include the part Father wants me to tell. But I'll also tell of the brilliance of Duke Aefric, his wizard, Karbin, and our several great knights. Especially Sers Beornric, Vria and Deirdre."

"Tell it well enough," Aefric said with a smile, "and Deirdre may even consider chasing the bliss moment with you sometime."

"You think?" Prince Killian said with a smile that he quickly banished. "Well, if so, that will be a most welcome side benefit. But it's not my purpose. I'll tell the whole story as true as I can — with Father's amendments of course — and I'll highlight the true deeds most of all. Beornric's command of the skirmish. Karbin's battle with the *Squid's Revenge*. Vria's desperate leap to save you. Deirdre's brilliant capture of Nelazzi. And, of course, your own magnificent airborne battle with the pirate queen."

Aefric smiled. "I look forward to the telling. Kentigern has the formal feast prepared for tomorrow, so your highness should have plenty of opportunity."

"Perfect," the prince said, then gave a relaxed sigh. "Oh, and Aefric?"

"Yes?"

"I'd appreciate it if you'd call me Killian again."

"I'd like that, Killian."

Killian offered his hand, and Aefric shook it.

AEFRIC RETURNED TO HIS APARTMENTS, INTENDING TO SEND MAEV AN invitation to join him in his public floor solarium.

To his surprise, she was already waiting for him. Lounging among the couches of his public floor sitting area, clad in ... doeskin this time, if he wasn't mistaken. The material of her tunic and breeches looked softer than her usual. She wore her jet black hair loose and wild as her smile.

Sylkanis lay beside her on the forest green couch they shared, head in Maev's lap. Being scratched between the ears like a housecat, not a great forest lynx. The air smelled lightly of salmon, which Aefric suspected meant that Ocheda had brought Sylkanis a snack.

"You're already here," Aefric said.

"Where did you expect me to be?" Maev asked, arching an eyebrow. "Settling into my rooms?"

"I *had* thought you might want to refresh yourself," he said, standing the Brightstaff and sitting on the matching chair just outside arm's reach. "Not a short sea voyage from Varondam."

"Bet it's a lot faster in that new airship I've been hearing so much about."

"I'll have to take you and Killian flying in it." Aefric smiled and shook his head. "It's amazing."

"Are you going to forgive him?" Maev's smile quirked. "He's been fretting about talking to you *at least* since we left Varondam."

"It's the first time he's done something like this that I know of," Aefric said. "So yes, I'll forgive him."

"I thought you would," she said with a nod. "And to answer your implied question, I haven't. So we'll just have to take a bath before things really get going." She gave him a wicked smile. "I hope your court will forgive me, but you and I won't make it to dinner tonight."

"There's something we need to talk about first," he said.

"Oh?" Her smile turned sly. "There is, is there?"

"There is," he said. "Ocheda? Her highness and I need privacy for a time."

"At once, your grace," Ocheda said, and cleared the area of any lurking servants and pages.

"A *private* matter is this?" Maev asked, still with that smile that Aefric was too busy lamenting to enjoy.

"It is," he said, then drew a deep breath and tore the bandaging right off. "I've asked Byrhta to marry me, and she's accepted."

Maev blinked and her smile faded. "I see."

"We haven't announced it yet. We both felt I should tell you myself first."

"Thank you for that," she said, looking away. "I'm glad I didn't have to hear this from anyone else."

She gathered herself through a breath. When she looked back at him, she was smiling, but Aefric could see pain in her eyes.

"I wish I could say I'm surprised," she said. "But ever since Father sent me to Varondam, I knew this was a possibility. Me being off negotiating for an alliance while she was the one back here, winning your heart."

Aefric wasn't sure what to say to that, but Maev kept talking.

"Some alliance." She shook her head. "It was all for nothing." She frowned. "Well, not *nothing*. We certainly made political gains in Varondam. That new queen seems quite open to further talks with us *and* Hatay. And the reparations are far from insignificant."

She looked back at Aefric. "Tell me this much. Had it been a fair fight. Both of us here. Do you think..." She shook her head. "No. Don't answer that. Either way, I don't think I want to know."

"I still wish you'd been here," he said softly. "That we'd had our chance. All our talk of hunting—"

"Oh, the hunt isn't over," she said with a wistful smile. "The hunt doesn't end until one of us is, well, mounted."

Aefric gave a soft chuckle.

"But that won't be today," she said with a sigh. She stood, disturbing Sylkanis, who rumbled a protest. "The pain is too fresh." The smile Maev gave him then was steadier. "I think I'll wait until she's given you a child. Or at *least* has a belly swollen enough to be near her time."

She nodded. "Yes. I like that idea. Then I could be here for the birth, and still have some fun. I've waited this long. I can wait a little longer."

"You won't be the only one looking forward to it," he said, standing.

"I know." She reached out and stroked his cheek. For a moment, she looked as though she might kiss him, but the moment passed. She withdrew her hand.

Sylkanis leapt down to the floor, as though given some signal Aefric didn't catch.

"I'm not going to be at dinner tonight," Maev said. "I'll send my apologies—"

"No need," Aefric said. "Ocheda will see it's taken care of."

"Thank you." She shook her head. "I haven't even gotten to hear about Caiperas yet."

"If you'd like to—"

"Not yet," she said. "I'll be here a few days. I'll want to talk with Byrhta before I leave, and Ocheda tells me she isn't due back until the day after tomorrow."

"That reminds me," he said. "I understand that the two of you have kept in touch, going back to your first conversation about me. But she said I needed to ask you about it."

"Well," Maev said with a small smile. "We keep in touch because we've become friends. We have a lot to talk about that isn't you. But I'm pretty sure you're asking about the conversation I said she and I needed to have, if she was serious about you."

"That's the one."

"I wanted to know what kind of woman she was," Maev said thoughtfully. "And I think I saw in her some of what you must see. Behind the beauty, I mean. Because I told her that if I didn't get to marry you, she damn well better do it. Because otherwise you might marry some foreign princess, who'd *gloat* every time she saw me."

"Those four *were* the type to gloat, weren't they?"

"You have *no* idea," Maev said with a snort. "But Byrhta ... if it's not going to be me, I'm glad it's her. You'll be good for each other."

"Thank you."

"And Aefric?"

"Yes?"

"I hope you'll still contact me by spell once in a while. I mean, we're still friends, aren't we?"

"Of course we are," he said. "And the only thing that would have stopped me was fear you wouldn't welcome the contact."

"Are you kidding?" she asked. "I'll *miss* it if I don't hear from you that way from time to time."

"Then rest assured. You shall."

"Good."

"And Maev?"

"Yes?" she asked, a little wary this time.

"You're still the best forester I've ever met. Can I still call on you if I need a hand?"

"You *better*," she said. "I find out you didn't, you're in trouble."

"Well we wouldn't want that," he said with a small smile.

"In the meantime," she said, "I'll see you ... when I'm ready."

"You'll always be welcome."

She flashed him a quick half-smile then, and left.

Aefric sagged down onto the cushions of his chair.

Without asking, Ocheda brought him a cut-crystal glass of ishka.

He nodded his thanks to her, and drank it slowly.

To Aefric's amusement, Killian didn't wait for the feast to start telling stories about the hunt for Nelazzi. He began that very night, at dinner. And Aefric had to admit, the prince was a good storyteller.

Killian hadn't even witnessed Karbin's victory over the *Squid's Revenge*, but he still supplied enough tension and detail to make a skald proud. He drew so much attention that Aefric was finally able to slip away unaccompanied, to exchange a private word with Byrhta by spell before bed.

"Maev seemed to take the news well. She wants to see you. Killian actually apologized and wants to make things right. I miss you."

"Almost done helping Taeric prepare for winter. Glad to hear about Killian. I want to see Maev, too, but I want to see you more."

With the next dawn came the feast. With jousting and a melee, games and acrobats and singers and musicians and more, all while the sun was still shining.

Aefric couldn't formally thank Yrsa on Armyr's behalf — that would have to wait for *another* celebration at Armityr the following aett — but he was, at least, allowed to celebrate her. So he did.

On the stage, after his and Killian's speeches before the throngs of celebrants, Aefric formally presented Yrsa with a shield made of solid gold and etched with the image of Lake Deepwater. A symbol of how she stood between the duchy and all harm.

That shield was so freaking heavy Aefric needed both arms to hand it to her. But she slipped it on as though she'd wear it into battle, and raised her arm in triumph as though the shield weighed nothing at all.

And from what Aefric could tell, even solid, practical Yrsa enjoyed her moment of adulation from the crowd.

He didn't let it end there, though. She was the guest of honor that night, sitting at his right hand at dinner. And she opened the dancing with no less a partner than the crown prince himself.

Yrsa being Yrsa, though, she still opted for tunic and hose instead of a gown for the dancing. But at least she wore silk for the occasion.

It was an excellent feast. Made all the better, because this time Aefric wasn't the focus. He felt more at ease to sit back and enjoy the festivities properly. Though he would've enjoyed them even more, had Byrhta been with him.

As it was, he found himself spending that night with Karaleca Ol'Nara — the noble wife of Lachedran's mayor, and woman in charge of the so-called "lost lers" project — who had come down for the celebration.

Byrhta finally did return that next day, after the feast was over. And she and Maev held a private conversation that lasted the better part of that day. Aefric never asked what they talked about.

That night, for the first time, Aefric and Byrhta finally lay together without drinking nysta tea first. And the following morning, they announced their plans to wed.

From there, life became a whirlwind.

Aefric had thought that nothing could be more complicated than ruling a duchy as large as Deepwater.

He was wrong. Planning a marriage for the duke was much more complicated.

They would *have* to get married at Midwinter, because that was the most auspicious date possible. Despite the fact that it would be in the middle of freaking *winter*, and there would likely be *snow*. Which meant preparing under the assumption that pavilions would not be a reasonable option.

Which meant putting together not only the *extensive* guest list, but setting that list in order of *priority*. Someone had to decide who got to stay at the castle, and who would be hosted by the nearest lers.

The castle at Water's End could house a great many guests. So many that Aefric found it hard to believe that there would be spillover into the nearby lerdoms.

But there would. Because the Water's End group were only the beginning. Preparations had to be made for the *first* overflow group, who would be staying at Behal. And then for the *second* overflow group staying somewhere around Lachedran.

Simply *unbelievable*. Had Aefric gotten married the year before, he could have counted his guests on both hands. Now so very many people would attend his wedding that some would be expected to lodge more than fifty miles away and *sail in* each morning for the festivities.

Because, oh yes, for a peer of the realm, a wedding was an aett-long affair.

Lodgings had to be arranged for more than *two thousand* people. And that only included the ones expected to attend. Aefric's counts and barons. The Armyrian royal family, peers and important nobles. The royal families, peers and prominent nobles from *nearby* king-doms — Rethneryl, Hatay and Shachan, of course, but also Malimfar and Varondam, now that Armyr was on better terms with both.

Given the many ways Aefric had made his name resonate since he took up his duchy, they would *all* come to his wedding. Either to thank him for something, or just to meet him. And while they might not bring full, formal entourages for every noble, there would be family and attendants and a certain number of knights and guards.

Then there were the common folk to consider. The merchants and guild masters and mayors, as well as the farmers and smiths and others who wouldn't receive formal invitations, but who would come to celebrate their duke's marriage all the same. More than enough to fill the inns and hostels around Water's End to capacity.

Aefric's predecessor, Duchess Arinda Soulfist, had died unmarried, so this would be the first ducal wedding Deepwater had seen in close to forty years. No one wanted to miss it.

And while Aefric wasn't required to lodge the common folk, he still had to find enough food and entertainment for all who came, common folk and nobles alike.

So on top of all the performers and dancers and musicians and singers and actors and fireworks and spectacle, the wedding would have to have a *full* tournament. With days of jousting and melee and archery and other competitions. Each of which, of course, required a prize of some value.

Planning and coordinating it all was a monster of a feat involving dozens and dozens of people, all working under the supervision of Kentigern and Garnotin, but ultimately answering to not only Aefric and Byrhta, but to *Eppida*.

Because as soon as the wedding announcement was made, Queen Eppida came to Water's End to oversee the wedding, and make sure it was all done *just right* to represent not only Deepwater, but Armyr.

Which meant that Aefric was forced to negotiate fine details between Eppida and Byrhta from time to time, though in the end they always reached agreement.

Aefric didn't want to *think* about what the expense involved in this wedding would be. Fortunately, between his share of the reparations from Caiperas and Varondam — plus the rather significant dowry Colm graciously provided Byrhta, keeping a promise that Aefric himself had forgotten — Aefric was confident he could afford it.

All the same, when Eppida insisted that that the crown would pay a portion of the costs as well, he didn't object.

Part of the wedding preparations had included renovations for the gargantuan great hall of Water's End. The floor was tiled now, instead of hardwood. And the tiles were of a type of stone called *reshikol*. Noted for both its deep, navy blue color and for its natural sparkle, which might look red, gold, silver or purple, depending on the lighting and angle.

The plastered walls had been freshly repainted their soft, Deepwater gray. And for the wedding, they were hung with banners for every kingdom in attendance. Armyr being the most prominent of course.

On the wall above the dais, where the ceremony would take place, hung the sigil and battle flags of Deepwater. The one being the image of a sword emerging from a lake hilt first, and the other being ascending chevrons of navy blue and gray.

Underneath those flags hung the personal sigils of Aefric and Byrhta. His, the image of a golden staff with two bolts of lighting coming up from it, one to the sinister and one to the dexter, on a royal blue background. Hers, a golden harp on a red background.

No flag for Goldenfall, of course. For though Count Cyneric was Byrhta's father, he was also Aefric's vassal.

Up above, the immense stained-glass dome had been freshly cleaned — Aefric hadn't asked how — so its many interesting patterns and colors would shine brightly once daylight hit them.

That wouldn't be until after the ceremony though. Nobles in Armyr were expected to wed at the most auspicious time of day, sunrise, and the great hall was at the western side of the castle.

Sunrise, unfortunately, was also the *chilliest* time of what everyone expected to be a very cold day. Fortunately, the great hall's two massive hearths — along facing sides of the long northern and southern walls — would be kindled to a decent blaze. And between them, and the gathered crowd, Aefric had been told to expect the hall to be plenty warm. Perhaps even too warm.

Those fires wouldn't shed *nearly* enough light though. So Karbin was to provide gently glowing balls of pale luminescence, floating here and there around the hall at about thrice the height of the tallest man.

And then, of course, there was the matter of clothing for the bride and groom.

Armyr didn't have any traditions about when and where the groom could see the bride's wedding dress, but that didn't matter. Byrhta didn't want to show it to him in advance, because she wanted him to see it for the first time at their wedding.

Aefric's wardrobe for the big day was designed for him by a battery of tailors following the specifications of the queen. He would not wear the Deepwater colors. Those would be prominent enough.

Instead, he would wear a woolen tunic of sky blue, to bring out his eyes, and a dark red doublet with gold brocade. After a great deal of debate on the subject with Dajen, Ocheda and Byrhta — notably without input from Aefric — Eppida had decided that instead of hose or breeches, he should wear dark riding leathers as a nod to his past as an adventurer.

He would wear soft, calf-high leather boots of the same color though, like his belt, they would be buckled with gold.

He was not to carry the Brightstaff for his wedding. But Eppida allowed that it could follow him about like an attendant.

Which was a good thing. Nervous as Aefric knew he would be, the Brightstaff would likely have shown up anyway.

Caught up in the whirlwind of planning, Aefric felt as though he'd stepped outside of time. He lost all sense of days and aetts. There was only the next thing he had to do, followed by another, followed by another.

But the morning of his wedding came at last. And he only knew what day it was because, for the first time in nearly a season, he awoke without Byrhta beside him.

She'd laughed during one of their planning sessions, when Aefric told her he'd been raised to believe it was bad luck for the bride and groom to see each other before the service. But he was following all Armyr's traditions so she'd humored him, and gone to her family's rooms that night.

Strange, to awaken without her though.

Aefric was grateful that morning for the focusing exercises magic required of him. Because though everything about the *event* of his wedding made him nervous and scattered, he could throw himself into the *rite* of his wedding from the moment he awoke.

He didn't *have* to do that. Technically his part of the ritual didn't begin until he got to the great hall. But treating every step of his morning as part of a crucial magic ritual — from getting out of bed to bathing to dressing and making ready — would help him.

Dajen seemed to understand that without being told. When he woke Aefric in the predawn gloom, he did so with Aefric's wedding candle in his hand.

Dajen immediately lit the candle with a taper from the hearth, and handed it to Aefric as he rose from his bed.

The candle was gold as summer sun, and made of a beeswax that smelled of horses and leather and ... was that a hint of dragon's blood incense?

His wedding candle represented his life. And though it was merely metaphoric, Aefric treated the candle with the solemnity and focus it would have merited had spells actually bound his life to its flame.

He wasn't expected to eat before the ceremony. Which was a good thing. He doubted he could digest anything, the way his stomach kept bouncing around.

But he breathed. And he honored his candle. Housed it in an old, iron sconce as he bathed with slow, certain efficiency. And when he was clean and dry, he took up his candle again and went into his closets.

His body servants were waiting for him with a tall, iron candle-stick. Aefric housed his candle there, but he didn't let his attendants dress him. Instead, he allowed them to hand him his clothes, item by item, which he donned with slow deliberation.

He considered how each item had been designed just for him. Cut and tailored just for him. He honored each tailor and tailor's assistant as he dressed.

He did allow a body servant to comb out his hair, and with each stroke of the silver comb, Aefric honored the many servants and attendants who worked for him. Not only here at Water's End, but at Behal, Kivash, Netarritan ... at all of his castles and more.

Once that was finished, he took up his candle again. He called the

Brightstaff to his hand, then allowed it to follow him as he began the journey down to the great hall.

Aefric had expected to make his way down alone, but no. Beornric stood waiting just outside the door to the ducal apartments. His full plate armor freshly polished and gleaming. His graying black hair freshly washed and combed. His bushy mustache freshly trimmed.

Even his longsword's scabbard looked to have been oiled that very morning.

They didn't speak. Merely exchanged nods before Beornric led the way by the light of Aefric's candle.

There were a great many steps to take from Aefric's apartments all the way down to the great hall. And with each step, Aefric honored the many, many people who owed their allegiance to him.

His advisers. His vassals, from the counts down to the least of his lers. His many knights. His soldiers. The mayors of his towns and cities. And all the countless servants and workers and others he employed in some capacity.

From there he honored the rest of his common folk. The thousands upon thousands of farmers and sailors and crafters and traders and more.

All of these people, bound to him in one way or another. All of these people lived within the light of his candle. And every one of them helped keep it burning.

Beornric escorted Aefric to the foot of the great hall. The second entry chamber from the outside, where all that stood between Aefric and the great hall were those two tall, arched doors that formed its main entrance.

The chamber had been emptied on his approach. Not even any guards around him. Only Aefric and Beornric, in the light of Aefric's candle.

Beornric looked the question at Aefric. Aefric nodded.

Beornric opened both doors wide.

Karbin's globes of light were all lit, of course. But they'd been moved to the edges of the hall, casting the standing crowd largely in shadow, around the white runner carpet that formed Aefric's path to the dais.

He stood within the glow of only his own candle.

The rumble of conversation died to a murmur.

One slow step at a time, Aefric made his way down the runner carpet. Thinking of the steps he'd taken in life that brought him to this point.

From Keifer's youth in Minnesota to his life in Oregon. How he'd met and fallen in love with Andi. Married her. Lived happily. Lost her to the accident. How he'd spiraled downward, until his only joys in life were pickup games of basketball and roleplaying in the *Torn Kingdoms*.

He thought of that day the rain had poured down and ended his pickup game. And the poor, soaked orange cat he'd found, lost in the park, and the happy family who'd reclaimed him. Especially that little girl.

What was her name?

Marcy. She'd drawn Keifer a picture, and insisted that she and her mother bake Keifer cookies, all as a thank-you.

He thought of the Jumpstart campaign for the sixth edition of the *Torn Kingdoms*. The Duke of Deepwater reward level that apparently only he had seen.

How Kainemorton showed up on his doorstep. Brought him to Qorunn.

How Keifer had become a street rat in Sartis named Aefric, and started life again. The years and adventures that followed. The Godswalk Wars.

That day in Kainemorton's tower, when Aefric remembered his life as Keifer and the two lives melded into one.

And all the things that had happened since then. All of them, steps in the journey of his life, as he took those steps again along that white runner carpet.

Kentigern had been right. With both fires blazing and that huge crowd around Aefric, the hall *did* feel too warm. And there were so many different smells and perfumes, his nose couldn't sort them all out. He focused on the scent of his candle: horses, leather and drag-on's blood.

He ascended the dais. His ducal throne had been removed for the day, and in its place, a small, simple altar. It was made from white hawthorn, sanded smooth, but without any lacquer or varnish.

A white linen cloth was spread in the center, hanging down in front to show the stylized Watchful Eye of Vera, done in sunflower yellow.

A black-handled steel dagger sat on the cloth, as well as a large, sunflower yellow pillar candle, set into an equally large golden candlestick.

At the ends of the altar, two small, bronze censers smoldered, issuing thin trails of white smoke that smelled of sweet, blessed cunitas.

The cleric of Vera was a tall, thin man. Taller than Aefric by a good handspan. He had large, owlish eyes that never seemed to blink, and a narrow face whose expression seemed to say he could look right through Aefric and see everything he'd ever done, and every-where he'd ever been.

His robes were the dark purple of predawn, for that was said to be the time that most needed watching. Around his neck he wore a thin gold chain that ended in a large rendition of Vera's Eye, carved out of pure citrine.

He spoke quietly without seeming to move his lips. "Stand just to my left, if you would, your grace."

Aefric said nothing, but did as he was bid, with the Brightstaff following to stand behind him as though on guard.

The cleric raised his left hand, holding it over Aefric's head.

"I see this man before me," he called, in a high, clear voice that would have been excellent for singing. "But he is cloven. Twain. Half of him is missing. So where is his other half?"

A murmur went through the crowd, as though they were looking about for Aefric's missing half while the cleric swept his owlish eyes left and right. Scanning the crowd as though to find her.

"His other half is not among us," the cleric said. "I see it not. And so we must beg great Vera to bless us with Her sight. To show us the way. To help us find this man's missing half."

The cleric raised both his hands then, and though he closed his eyes and lowered his head, he continued to project his voice so well that they must've heard him in the corners of the hall.

"Blessed Vera. Holy Vera. Watcher by night and by day. Protectress unfailing. Guardian of us all. We beg You now, hear our prayer."

"Vera, hear our prayer," the crowd echoed.

"Blessed Vera. Holy Vera. Watcher by night and by day. We beseech You to look into this being who stands before me. To gaze into the light of his life. To see how it flickers, lonely, aching for want of its other half."

"Vera, hear our prayer," the crowd chorused.

"Blessed Vera. Holy Vera. Watcher by night and by day. We beseech You. Turn Your Watchful Eye upon us. Look among us for the missing half of this man. Be it born into man or woman, we pray You, Holy Vera, find his missing half."

"Vera, hear our prayer."

"Blessed Vera. Holy Vera. Watcher by night and by day. We beseech You to find this man's missing half. To call his missing half here, that the twain might be reunited, and together their flame might burn all the stronger. We pray You, Vera, bring us his missing half."

"Vera, hear our prayer."

"*There!*" The cleric called, eyes open wide again as he pointed to the double doors.

They opened.

Byrhta stood in the doorway, illumined only by the light of her own candle, which was the silver of midwinter moonlight.

Her dark, forest green hair had been twisted into an elegant arrangement that highlighted her face and neck. Her gown was the same color as her candleflame. And part of Aefric wanted to look over every stitch and contour of it. To see the detailing and appreciate what he knew to be some tailor's masterwork, done to best present her astounding beauty.

But deep down, all he really wanted to do was meet her eyes. So that was what he did. Together they shared a private smile among a gathering of more than a thousand people in this one room alone.

And nothing else mattered.

She approached in silence, as he had. Likely following the ritual steps as he'd done, thinking with every step how every action and decision in her life had led her to where she was now and what she was doing.

Finally, though, she mounted the steps to the dais and took her place, facing him, at the cleric's right hand.

They weren't to speak to each other. Not yet. But with his eyes, Aefric tried to convey to her all the emotions he was feeling. Love and joy and excitement and anticipation and more.

The cleric addressed his next words to Byrhta.

"Great Vera has searched the world for this man's missing half, and it is you who come to answer Her summons. Look deeply into this man's eyes. Under the blessing of Vera, see him for all his strengths and flaws. All the good that is in him, and all the evil. See him laid bare before you, in Vera's name."

"In Vera's name," the crowd chorused.

Byrhta's already large eyes widened as she looked at Aefric, and he found himself wondering if there was cleric magic in this that he hadn't been told about.

Her lips parted in surprise, and Aefric felt sure of it then. She wasn't just looking at him. She was seeing something more.

She couldn't have gazed at him that way for more than a dozen rapid heartbeats, but the moment felt eternal.

Suddenly she started blinking rapidly, and when the blinking stopped, the cleric spoke.

"Vera has shown you this man in a way no other has seen him. Praise be to Vera."

"Praise be to Vera," the crowd said. Aefric almost joined them, but remembered he was supposed to hold his silence.

"Now that you have seen what you have seen, I ask. Is this man your missing half?"

"He is," Byrhta said in a loud, clear voice.

The crowd cheered. The cleric gave the cheer a moment to die down, then addressed Aefric.

"Aefric Brightstaff, you have called on Vera to find your missing half, and, in Her glory, She has sought for you and found this woman, Byrhta Ol'Caran. Praise be to Vera."

"Praise be to Vera," the crowd said.

"Byrhta Ol'Caran has consented to look into you with Vera's blessing. To see into your very heart and soul as no other has or could. And she has said that she is indeed your missing half. Do you agree?"

"I do," Aefric said.

The cleric turned to the altar and picked up the sunflower yellow pillar candle in his left hand and the black-handled dagger in his right.

He turned back to face them. Held the pillar candle between them.

"It is with this candle that great Vera will bring your souls together in marriage. Entwine your right hands above the candle, palms down."

They did, and the cleric, in a single, deft movement, nicked their middle fingers with his dagger. Each dripped three small drops of blood onto the pillar candle.

"Light the candle together," the cleric said, "and become one."

Moving slowly, Aefric brought the wick of his golden candle to the wick of the pillar. Moving at the same speed, so they'd arrive together, Byrhta did the same with her silver candle.

The sunflower yellow pillar candle flared to life, bright as a torch, while both smaller candles extinguished.

"As Vera has reunited the two bodies of this soul, so does She promise to safeguard them from this day until the end of days. Praise be to Vera."

As the cleric said those words, the gold candle vanished in a flare of light, and both their cuts were healed.

"Praise be to Vera!" The crowd cried out. And this time Aefric and Byrhta got to say it too.

EPILOGUE

The spectacle of Aefric's wedding was finally over. The guests were all on their way home. And he and Byrhta had sworn they were going to sleep until midday.

Like so many things in Aefric's life, it hadn't quite worked out that way. Dawn came, and he found himself awake. Restless, for some reason he couldn't explain.

So, rather than toss and turn and risk waking his pregnant wife, he slipped out of bed. Donned a dressing gown, a thick pair of winter slippers, and a heavy woolen robe. He wandered out onto his private floor balcony to watch the sun rise against the gray clouds.

The stone crunched underfoot with a sheen of fresh ice, but yesterday's snow had been cleared away, and no fresh had fallen overnight.

The morning was so cold he could see his breath, but he didn't mind. He'd faced worse, wearing less. And anyway, the brisk air felt good. Woke up his skin.

Down below, life was already underway on the Deepwater. Fishing vessels were about their day's work. Even some enterprising merchants had caught the first tide of the day.

"Far cry from that ruined Zhenderran inn where we took shelter while hunting those foul Ankterrien, wouldn't you say?"

Aefric chuckled as he turned to face his old friend and mentor, Kainemorton.

The Mage of Marrisford was dressed the way he had been that day on Keifer's doorstep. An orange robe with red trim, with golden symbols stitched along the trim. Those old, worn leather boots that he must've had for centuries, but kept wearing all the same. Belt just as old and worn, with its dozens of pouches in various sizes.

He covered his bald head today with a floppy, wide-brimmed brown traveling hat, and he'd organized his long, snow white beard with a leather thong near its end.

No oaken staff this time, but his periwinkle blue eyes still seemed to twinkle nonstop. And, of course, the man positively *radiated* magic.

"Hey," Aefric said, smiling, "you're the one who knew the countryside, but you made *me* find us a place to sleep. That was the best I could do."

"Aye, and it was the best to be had for miles," Kainemorton said with a grin. "Not that I'd've admitted it then." He looked Aefric up and down. "More of a morning person now than when we first met, I see."

"Was that when we first met?" Aefric asked. "I'm not entirely sure how time works when it comes to there and here."

"In an absolute sense it's when we first met. But I might've had some help juggling timelines a bit."

"Help from Del Baker?"

"That would be telling," he said with a wink. "See you still carry that everywhere."

Aefric realized he was holding the Brightstaff. Must've picked it up automatically as he left the bedroom.

"I'm fairly certain that, by now, it's an extension of me."

"More right than you know, I suspect. Speaking of which," — he nodded to the platinum wedding ring on the middle finger of Aefric's right hand — "I thought the hero was supposed to marry the princess."

"I didn't think you'd made it for the wedding."

"Oh, I was there. I just know my presence can be a distraction, so I wore a disguise."

"Fair enough," Aefric said, then leaned back against the rail, feeling its cold seep in even through his thick robe. "I could give you the logical reasons I recited for my advisers, if you want to hear them. But the truth…"

Aefric looked away north for a moment, then back at his old friend.

"I know everyone was expecting me to marry Maev. But in some ways, she reminds me too much of Andi. The daring forester-princess, shunning convention while still managing to shine in diplomatic situations? *Exactly* the kind of character Andi loved to play."

"Is that so," Kainemorton said with a small, mysterious smile.

"And I think … part of me would always *want* her to be Andi. Which wouldn't be fair to her. Or to Andi. While with Byrhta…"

Aefric shook his head as he tried to explain something he understood better with his heart than his head.

"It was while I was in Byrhta's arms that I dreamed my final goodbye to Andi. And after that big eruption with Killian down on the docks. I thought I wanted to be alone. To deal with it the way I'd dealt with so many things in my life.

"But Byrhta was already in my rooms when I got there," he continued. "And I realized then that I didn't have to face it alone. I didn't *want* to face it alone. There *was* someone I wanted to share that pain with, and it was Byrhta."

Aefric shook his head and looked up at Kainemorton.

"This was the first time I'd felt that way since Andi died." He chuckled softly. "If I'd been smart, I'd've proposed that night. But I was too caught up in a million different things."

"Aye, the price of ruling is an uneasy mind," Kainemorton said.

"Took me getting two solid days of sleep to wake up with enough clarity to see what part of me already knew. I was in love with Byrhta. Not infatuated or charmed or any lesser term. It was love. After that, there was no more competition. Not inside."

Kainemorton nodded sagely, as though he'd known this all along. But then, he always had that knowing look about him. And he was right often enough to be irritating.

"At the wedding, she looked at you with Vera's eyes—"

"Yes," Aefric said, cutting in. "Shouldn't I have gotten to look at her the same way?"

"I'm not the one to ask, lad," Kainemorton said, chuckling. "I've been many things in my long life, but a priest has never been one of them. My point *is*, I imagine she had a few questions that night?"

"I don't lie to her."

"Good policy for a marriage, if you can keep to it."

"I told her about Earth, and my life as Keifer, if that's what you're asking."

"Have you told anyone else?"

"No one."

"Good," Kainemorton said. "Best if you keep it that way."

Aefric nodded.

"And now, lad, I think you're ready to ask a question that I *know* has itched at you for a long time."

"Why me?" Aefric said. "Why not someone like Nikki? She was a bigger *Torn Kingdoms* fan than I ever was."

"Would you like me to tell you you had a destiny?" Kainemorton said with a smile. "That you were born to be a great hero, and I'd come up with a way to test for that?"

"I'd like you to tell me the truth."

"Then I think you already know the answer."

Aefric pondered that a moment.

"Nikki had a life. A career she loved as a tattoo artist. A girl-friend she loved even more. She had her activism, too. People would've missed her. Hardly anybody would've missed Keifer McShane."

"Close, but not quite," Kainemorton said. "Nikki was *living*." He jabbed a gnarled finger at Aefric. "*You* were marking time until death. After the accident, you gave up. But you still had a lot of life in you. And so you were one of the ... roughly one-hundred-seven people who might've seen the Duke of Deepwater reward level on that Jumpstart."

"And I got to it first?"

"Perhaps," Kainemorton said with a smile. "I think the rest of it should stay a mystery."

"You and your mysteries."

"Helped you with that teak box, didn't it?"

Aefric scoffed. Twice. "You've *got* to be kidding me."

"What?"

"You *knew* about that teak box?" Aefric turned away to get hold of himself, and when he turned back...

Kainemorton was gone.

Because *of course* he was. It was just like him to drop a tidbit like that and vanish without explanation.

"One of these days," Aefric said, shaking a finger at the sky, "I'll do this to *you*. And *you* can see what it's like."

"Do what to who?"

The voice came from behind him, but it wasn't one he recognized.

Aefric whirled around, white fire already playing along the Brightstaff's length.

Before him sat an orange tomcat.

A *familiar* looking orange tomcat.

"Tommy?" Aefric asked in disbelief, extinguishing the Brightstaff.

"I'd rather you continue calling me Zeus," the cat said. "Sounds better coming from you. Tommy is Marcy's name for me."

Aefric laughed as he crouched and scritched the tom between the ears. "How did you get here? Is Marcy okay?"

"She's fine," Zeus said. "Or do you know differently?"

"What?" Aefric asked, confused. "I mean, she's your person, isn't she?"

"In that world, yes. But I'm a cat. And in the manner of all cats, while I sleep, I wander the worlds freely." He flattened his ears for a moment. "I must say, I had a devil of time finding you. Might never have, if not for that moment on the ship, with the mirror."

"I'm surprised you recognized me. I've changed more than a little."

"To physical eyes, yes," Zeus said, looking him over. "But it's still you inside, which is what I see. What were you doing with that mirror, anyway?"

"Learning to travel through mirrors."

"Handy trick, if you can pull it off." He twitched his tail impatiently. "Can we go inside? It's a might nippy out here."

"Of course," Aefric said, scooping up the cat in both hands, and letting the Brightstaff follow him. "And there's someone I want you to meet."

Zeus immediately began to purr and, together, they went inside where it was warm.

SIGN UP FOR STEFON'S NEWSLETTER

Stefon loves to keep in touch with his readers, and loves to keep you reading. The best way for him to do both is for you to sign up for his newsletter.

Sign up at http://www.stefonmears.com/join

If you sign up for Stefon's newsletter, you get...

- Monthly updates about his publishing and travel schedules
- His latest news, in brief, and answers to reader questions
- A free short story for signing up
- List-only offers and occasional specials
- Plus a free short story every month!

ABOUT THE AUTHOR

Stefon Mears hopes Aefric made the right decision. Stefon has more than thirty books to his credit, and he never stops writing. He earned his M.F.A. in Creative Writing from N.I.L.A., and his B.A. in Religious Studies (double emphasis in Ritual and Mythology) from U.C. Berkeley. He's a lifelong gamer and fantasy fan. Stefon lives in Portland, Oregon, with his wife and three cats.

Look for Stefon online:
www.stefonmears.com
himself@stefonmears.com